A REGENCY TRIO

Cecily
Georgina
Lydia

by Clare Darcy

WALKER AND COMPANY
NEW YORK

Cecily
or A Young Lady of Quality

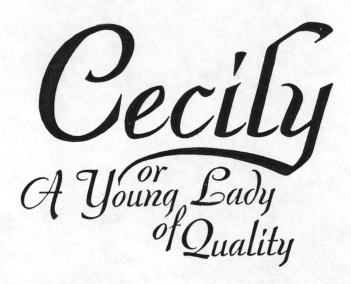

Cecily
or A Young Lady of Quality

by Clare Darcy

WALKER AND COMPANY
New York

To Lois Dwight Cole

1 The curtain was about to fall on the second act when Mr. Ranleigh arrived at the theatre—a piece of indifference which Lady Comerford, who had invited him to make one of the party in her box that evening, was inclined to regard not so much with indignation as with despair. She should have known what to expect, she told herself bitterly, for she had more than once been warned by Mr. Ranleigh's outspoken mother, Lady Frederick Ranleigh, that not even a young lady so much sought after as Miss Comerford would be likely to induce her son to alter the habits that had for years defeated the efforts of the wiliest of matchmaking mamas.

"Not," Lady Frederick had added, "that I should not be excessively happy to see him settle at last, but when a man has reached the age of two-and-thirty without falling into any of the *dozens* of traps that have been laid for him, it is of no use to expect him to marry until he has made up his own mind in cold blood to take the step."

All of which meant, Lady Comerford thought with doleful candour, surveying Mr. Ranleigh's tall, impeccably attired figure as he bowed over her hand, that Robert Ranleigh was handsome, immensely wealthy, agreeable—if one were prepared to overlook a certain autocratic brusqueness in his manner, and a sometimes uncomfortably ironical expression in his grey eyes—and related to half the best families in England, in addition to being the acknowledged Nonpareil in those sporting pursuits on which gentlemen seemed to set such store. It was obvious that he might have his pick of the young ladies on the Matrimonial Mart; all she could allege, in justification of her own hopes, was the fact that he had seemed to seek her Gussie's company somewhat more frequently since Gussie had let him see, with a freedom of conduct which her mama deplored, that she was very fond of *his*.

But he had recently declined a week's shooting at Comerford, though he must have known that Gussie would be present, and had pledged himself merely to "look in" on them at the theatre this evening—a vague promise which he apparently considered committed him to no more than that, for he remained in the Comerford box only until the end of the ensuing act, and then went off to engage in conversation with his cousin, Lord Portandrew, and a group of the latter's friends.

He was greeted by these gentlemen with a great deal of enthusiasm, and, after having been complimented by one on a new hunter which had performed to advantage with the Quorn the week preceding, was invited by his cousin to give his opinion of a young actress appearing in a minor role in the play.

"Miss Daingerfield-Nelson," Lord Portandrew pronounced reverently. "Tell me, Robert—*have* you ever seen such a deuced enchanting creature? I mean to say, those eyes—!"

Mr. Ranleigh, after considering for a moment, inquired if the young woman who had taken his cousin's fancy was the one who resembled a startled fawn, and who had very nearly driven the leading lady into an apoplexy, at a dramatic crisis in the latter's affairs during the act just past, by forgetting her lines completely.

"No, really!" Lord Portandrew protested. "I don't mean to say she can *act!* Wouldn't expect her to—not a girl with a face like that! Dash it, she don't look like she ought to be out of the schoolroom!"

Mr. Ranleigh said that perhaps it would be as well if she were not. He was regarding his cousin's longtailed coat, with its extravagantly padded shoulders and nipped-in waist, with an expression of frank revulsion, which prompted his lordship to inquire with asperity why the deuce he was looking at him like that.

"Just because you don't care to cut a dash yourself," said his lordship, "there's no need for you to look down your nose at someone who does. If you want *my* opinion, Robert, that rig of yours is too sober by half."

As Mr. Ranleigh's exquisitely cut coat of blue superfine, worn with a plain white waistcoat from which no more than one fob descended, and with a single pearl set in the folds of his snowy neckcloth, was known to have excited the admiration even of such a connoisseur of fashion as the Prince Regent, Lord Portandrew was interrupted at this point by several voices, all reminding him rudely that if he were endowed with the Nonpareil's fine figure and broad shoulders there would be no need for his tailor to seek to give him consequence by the use of buckram wadding and buttons as large as crown-pieces. Lord Portandrew, who was not egotistically inclined, accepted this set-down in good part, remarking equably that he had no intention of entering the lists with his cousin sartorially or in any other way.

"Wouldn't do me any good if I did," he said simply. "Look at Gussie Comerford now—hasn't taken her eyes off him since he left their box. Do you know I tried all last season to fix my interest with that girl? Fact! Came dashed close to offering for her, but I knew it wouldn't answer. Deuced embarrassing if every time one's cousin walked into the room one's wife forgot one was alive."

Sir Harry Brackenridge, a tall gentleman with hair of an odd brassy-yellow colour, whose air and style of dress proclaimed him to be a buck of the first head, remarked languidly that he rather fancied Miss Comerford's predilection for Mr. Ranleigh was not a fair test of the matter.

"The fact is," he said, "the fair Gussie and her mama have an eye out for a great fortune, dear boy. I'm afraid Robert would be no more favoured than the rest of us if he weren't so disgustingly rich."

"Well, I don't know *that*," Lord Portandrew said obstinately. "All I *do* know is that he has only to raise a finger and females come running." He nodded toward the stage, where the curtain was about to rise. "Take Miss Daingerfield-Nelson," he said. "Here the lot of us have been trying all week, one after the other, to get her to take supper with us after the play. But ten to one, if Robert sent round *his* card with a word of invitation scrawled on it, he'd be able to walk off with her on his arm this very evening."

Sir Harry's brows rose. "Care to venture money on that, Tony?" he inquired. "Lay you a monkey he couldn't bring it off."

"Done!" said Lord Portandrew, with a happy disregard for the fact that it was scarcely in his power to carry out the terms of the wager, since this must depend entirely upon his cousin's willingness to oblige him by making the test.

The rising of the curtain at that point put an end to any further discussion of the matter, for Lord Portandrew settled down at once to a careful scrutiny of the stage, anxious to miss no single moment during which its boards might be graced with the presence of Miss Daingerfield-Nelson.

These moments, unfortunately for his lordship, were few, for the young lady's part was a very brief one, involving in this act no more than her appearance on stage in a group of relatives of the heroine to whom a will was to be read. She spoke the few lines allotted to her quite creditably, however, in a clear, though slightly hurried, voice, and—what was more important to her admirers—afforded them meanwhile an excellent view of a pair of enormous eyes under the fashionable coiffure *à la Tite* in which her dark locks had been dressed, and of a slender figure set off to admiration by a high-waisted tamboured muslin gown.

Mr. Ranleigh, raising his quizzing-glass to observe more closely the young woman who had roused such interest among his friends, was not inclined, however, to revise his earlier opinion of her. He found her lamentably lacking in presence, and, while acknowledging the effect of those great eyes, still felt that one might as well fall into raptures over an engaging colt. Obviously the chit *did* belong in the schoolroom, and what she was doing on a London stage—bidding fair, by her very novelty, to become the newest rage among a set of bored young Tulips of the *Ton*—he could not well imagine. His lips twisted in a wry smile. Plainly the girl was gently bred, but it would be wonderful if, after a few months or years of finding half the bucks in London at her feet, she did not end as little better than Haymarket-ware. She had neither experience nor—as her very presence on that stage betokened—protectors, and, without talent to make her way in the theatre, her fall must be as rapid as her rise.

Perhaps he half-expected that the hasty wager concluded between his cousin and Sir Harry Brackenridge at the rising of the curtain might be forgotten by its fall at the end of the act; but such was not the case. Sir Harry, whose long-nourished envy of the position occupied by the Nonpareil in Corinthian circles had recently been intensified—almost, his friends considered, to the point of obsession—by the twin humiliations of a resounding defeat in a London-to-Newmarket curricle race and Mr. Ranleigh's easy success with one of the most brilliant of the West-End comets, whose favours Sir Harry himself was known to have coveted, reverted to the matter at once. He said provocatively that if Ranleigh did not care to venture his prestige on the trial he would consider Lord Portandrew's stake forfeit.

This was enough for Lord Portandrew, who promptly asserted that of course his cousin would stand buff.

"Give me one of your cards, Robert," he demanded. "I'll write the message——"

"Under *my* eyes, I hope," Brackenridge intervened. "A simple invitation to supper it must be—no mysteries to intrigue her with the idea that there is any more than that in it for her."

"Oh, very well!" Lord Portandrew said. He held out his hand. "Now, Robert, don't throw a rub in the way!" he adjured him. "Let me have your card-case."

Mr. Ranleigh did not move to oblige him. "You'll be gapped, you know, Tony," he remarked calmly. "The girl is obviously not town-bred. If she was not to be moved by an invitation from an Earl, she will certainly not be tempted by one from a mere 'Honourable.'"

"Gammon!" his cousin replied. "Wherever she comes from, she'll have heard of *you*. Be a good fellow now, Robert, and give me one of your cards!"

Mr. Ranleigh, who was not known as a persuadable man, might have resisted this entreaty also had not several gentlemen in the company shown a tendency to fall into warm contention over the matter. This appeared to decide him, and, taking out his card-case, he handed one of the cards it contained to his cousin, at the same time rising and remarking that he really must return to the Comerfords' box.

"But if she accepts——?" Lord Portandrew expostulated, attempting to detain him.

"My dear boy, she won't!" Mr. Ranleigh said lazily, and strolled off.

He remained in the Comerford box for the remainder of the evening, dismissing the matter of Miss Daingerfield-Nelson from his mind—not quite successfully, however, for it did perforce occur to him once more when that young lady appeared again on the stage and immediately began to subject the Comerford box to an artless scrutiny. She showed no interest in the several ladies there, and gave the merest glance to Lord Comerford and to Gussie's latest flirt, a dashing captain in Life Guardsman's uniform who sat just behind her. Obviously it was Mr. Ranleigh who was the object of her attention, and if he had any notion that it was curiosity alone that was prompting the examination it was dispelled when an attendant's discreet tap on the door of the box at the end of the evening heralded the arrival of a missive bearing his name.

Mr. Ranleigh, unfolding the tiny slip of paper, read the following simple message, penned in a schoolgirl's round, careful hand: "Miss Daingerfield-Nelson accepts with pleasure Mr. Ranleigh's kind invitation to supper this evening."

Mr. Ranleigh's plans for the evening had assuredly not included a tête-à-tête supper with a young lady half his age, his taste notoriously running to females of riper years and experience. But there was nothing to do but to resign himself to fulfilling the engagement that had been made in his name, and accordingly, after saying good night to the Comerfords, he strolled round to the Greenroom, where he found Lord Portandrew, Sir Harry Brackenridge, and several other of the gentlemen who had been privy to the wager already gathered, some of them in conversation with the players who had been entertaining them a short while before. These gentlemen, indeed, although they were never heard to enter into knowledgeable discussions on the decline of the theatre since the days of Garrick and Siddons, or on the comparative merits of the Hamlets of Kemble and Kean, were connoisseurs of the theatre in their own way, their attention being chiefly directed toward the younger female members of the various companies. They were at home not only in the Greenrooms of Drury

Lane and Covent Garden, but also in those of the less fashionable London theatres, and were to be found with equal frequency in the narrow pink room behind the stage at the Opera House, where they might observe the dancers practicing their steps before the long pier-glass mirror and choose a new *chère-amie* with the same careful attention they displayed in the selection of an enamelled snuff-box or other expensive article of *virtu*.

Mr. Ranleigh, glancing about the Greenroom as he entered, observed at once that Miss Daingerfield-Nelson was not among the brightly gowned, berouged young women whose trilling laughter and quick, flirtatious movements gave colour and brilliance to the predominantly male scene. Brackenridge noted his questing glance and said, with a malicious smile, "So she didn't come up to scratch and you have decided to see what personal persuasion can do. Is that it, Robert?"

Mr. Ranleigh put up his brows. "Not at all," he said. "Owing to your curst busy tongue, Harry, I find myself under the necessity of escorting a schoolroom chit to supper—something to which I assure you I am not looking forward." He added, beckoning an attendant to him, "By the bye, you had best pay Tony that five hundred you owe him."

Lord Portandrew uttered a triumphant: "Aha! Told you so, dear boy! Never pays to lay your blunt against Robert; he comes through every time!"

"Indeed!" Brackenridge said, dispassionately. "May I see the evidence, Robert?"

"I daresay it—or should I say *she?*—will put in an appearance presently," Mr. Ranleigh remarked, as the attendant, to whom he had uttered a brief sentence or two, hurried off. He frowned slightly at his cousin, who was showing an unsportsmanlike tendency to crow over his vanquished opponent. "Do try to contain your raptures, Tony," he said. "You are far too mature to be flying into alt over a chit's blue eyes!"

"They ain't blue," Lord Portandrew corrected him. "Grey. Nearly black in certain lights. See if I'm not right." He added hopefully, "You'll introduce me, of course? Might put in a good word for me during supper, as well—tell her what a good fellow I am, generous as Midas, charming manners——"

Mr. Ranleigh sighed. "You're sure you wouldn't like to take her off my hands tonight?" he asked, and then broke off as a tall, dapper individual, who had figured in the playbill as *Lord Hetherton—Mr. Jillson*, came into the room and purposefully approached him.

"Mr. Ranleigh?" Mr. Jillson, who appeared, as far as one could tell under the disguise of his make-up, to be about forty years of age, exuded a jaunty assurance that showed not the slightest embarrassment at the necessity of addressing himself to what he would undoubtedly have characterised as a group of bang-up swells. He was, in point of fact, already a familiar figure to most of them, for he and his wife, a buxom Titian-haired Irish actress some five years his junior, had appeared over the past dozen years in any number of productions at various London houses, the gentleman having assumed with equal success such diverse roles as those of Aspic, the parasite, in *Education*; the would-be seducer, Sir Charles Cropland, in *The Poor Gentleman*; and Lord Belmour, the dull gallant in *The School for Friends*. "Jillson is the name, sir—as you see, a humble member of the troupe that has just had the honour of entertaining you. I have a matter of some delicacy to discuss with you; if you would care to step aside with me for a moment——"

"What's this?" Brackenridge interposed. "If it's about Miss Daingerfield-Nelson, there's no need to draw him off; we all know about that supper engagement. Or do we?" he added, looking at Mr. Jillson's thoughtful face. "*Is* there such an engagement, or is there not? Speak up, man! There's a matter of five hundred pounds riding on this!"

Mr. Jillson looked shrewdly from Sir Harry to Mr. Ranleigh, as if he were endeavouring to decide which of several possible answers it would be most to his advantage to return. Temporising, he said at last, "In a manner of speaking, my dear sir, there *is* an engagement—and in a manner of speaking, there is not."

Lord Portandrew frowned. "What does that mean?" he demanded. "Damme, if Robert says there *is* an engagement——"

"Let us say there *was* one," Mr. Jillson emended his statement, his hesitation apparently overcome by the wrathful expression in his lordship's eyes. "No need to fly up into the boughs, my dear sir; naturally I have no intention of impugning Mr. Ranleigh's word! However, the fact of the matter is that the young lady is not her own mistress. She is unfortunately under the care of a Female Dragon—if I may use such an unflattering term to describe a lady of the first respectability—who accompanies her to the theatre each evening, and who is highly opposed to Miss Daingerfield-Nelson's accepting invitations from gentlemen personally unknown to her." He withdrew a folded slip of paper from his pocket and handed it to Mr. Ranleigh. "Miss Daingerfield-Nelson," he said, "has already left the theatre, I regret to say, but before she did so she directed me to see that this note reached your hands."

Mr. Ranleigh, receiving the paper, unfolded it and scanned its contents. "I am *desperately* sorry," the same round schoolgirl hand informed him—this time, however, with marked signs of haste, "but it is quite impossible for me to meet you tonight. Would you be so kind as to come to the Running Boar at eleven tomorrow morning? I am *most* anxious to speak with you." Squeezed into a corner there was added, handsomely: "If convenient."

Mr. Ranleigh, whose impassivity in the face of extraordinary social situations was famous, betrayed no signs of perturbation to his audience, but he was conscious of the inward stirring of an emotion halfway between exasperation and amusement. He was not accustomed to being cavalierly commanded by schoolroom misses to appear at unfashionable inns at an hour at which he had customarily not left his bedchamber, and his first impulse was to request Mr. Jillson to inform Miss Daingerfield-Nelson that he would not be able to keep the rendezvous she had appointed.

But no more than a moment's thought was required to make him decide against this course. He had not the slightest interest in the girl, but it did not suit him to see Brackenridge triumph. He therefore said calmly to Mr. Jillson, as he pocketed the note, "You may tell Miss Daingerfield-Nelson that I shall keep the appointment."

"*What* appointment?" Lord Portandrew demanded, his countenance lightening. "Do you mean she didn't simply cry off, after all?"

"Not at all," Mr. Ranleigh replied. "I have it on her own authority that she is extremely anxious to see me at another time. If convenient," he added scrupulously.

"Let me see the note, Robert," Brackenridge suggested, with a rather mocking grin.

Mr. Ranleigh's eyes narrowed slightly. "Oh, no," he said softly. "I have no notion what *your* ideas are on the proper treatment of a lady's private correspondence, but my own assuredly do not include passing it about among my acquaintance."

"Damme," Lord Portandrew put in warmly once more, "if Robert says it's so——"

"It *is* so, naturally," Mr. Ranleigh concluded it for him, resignedly. "Yes, we know, Tony—but you really must allow Harry to keep his stake until he is quite convinced that he has lost it. Supper, you said, I believe, Tony, so supper it assuredly shall be, even though the Female Dragon must be included in the invitation."

He nodded to the company and strolled from the room, leaving Mr. Jillson, who had been attending closely to the conversation, to prognosticate comfortingly to Sir Harry that, if the wager lay as it appeared to him, he would certainly come out the winner.

"Not a doubt of it," he declared. "I need scarcely tell you gentlemen that in Miss Daingerfield-Nelson you see a young lady of quality, who has been educated in the most genteel style, and who, I may inform you, has hitherto resided in the strictest retirement in the country. She is, if I may take the liberty of phrasing it so, a protégée of mine, and I have great expectations of her success on the boards. But I do *not* think," he went on, with a smile which Lord Portandrew described later as "dashed self-satisfied," "that she will accept Mr. Ranleigh's invitation. In fact, if I did not consider it unfair to take advantage of my superior knowledge of the situation, I should lay a little wager on that myself!"

2 The hour lacked some minutes of noon on the following day when Mr. Ranleigh's curricle, drawn by a pair of match-bays that were, as Lord Portandrew had enviously phrased it, "complete to a shade," turned into the yard of the Running Boar in a raw November drizzle. It had required some ingenuity of inquiry for him to find out its whereabouts, for it was not among the hostelries usually frequented by the members of the more important London theatrical companies. He had eventually discovered it in the vicinity of Seven Dials, in a neighbourhood so unremittingly squalid that he was pleasantly surprised to see that the Boar itself appeared to be a reasonably respectable house. It even boasted an ostler who, appearing at the sound of carriage wheels, stood gazing with an incredulity amounting almost to awe at the high-couraged pair and elegant sporting vehicle which Sivil, Mr. Ranleigh's groom, was now jealously guarding from any attempt on his part to take into his charge.

Obviously neither the ostler, standing scratching his head behind Mr. Ranleigh as the latter walked leisurely into the taproom of the inn, nor the assorted jarveys, labourers, and watermen who witnessed his entrance into their snuggery could conceive what business a Corinthian of his cut might have at the Running Boar. But Miss Daingerfield-Nelson's name, when he inquired for her of the tapster, appeared to bring enlightenment to that worthy, at least.

He said doubtfully, however, that he was not sure whether the young lady would care to receive a caller—a statement that was immediately endorsed by a female voice, speaking in refined but decidedly waspish accents and apparently emanating from the passage outside. Mr. Ranleigh, turning, saw a small, erect, elderly lady, in a serviceable pelisse and a flat-crowned bonnet that might have been in the mode a dozen years before, standing just outside the taproom door, regarding him from a pair of remarkably spirited blue eyes.

"May I request that you step out into the passage, sir?" she addressed him acidly, her gaze sweeping over him in a comprehensive glance that seemed to sum up his entire appearance, from his gleaming top-boots to the Bedford crop that severely restrained a tendency of his crisp fair hair to curl, and cast it into the outer darkness of her disapproval. "It may suit *your* notions of propriety to bandy my niece's name about in a common taproom, but I can assure you that it does not suit mine!"

Mr. Ranleigh, who could not remember the last time he had been taxed with faulty manners—an occurrence probably dating back to schoolroom days—began to perceive that his pursuit of the elusive Miss Daingerfield-Nelson was to prove the source of more than one new experience for him. However, he stepped out into the passage with an unmoved countenance, and assured the lady—in whom he had no difficulty in recognising Mr. Jillson's "Female Dragon"—that it was at Miss Daingerfield-Nelson's own request that he was inquiring for her here.

"I don't believe it!" the lady said flatly, and, placing both hands inside the small muff she was carrying, stood confronting him as if she dared him to prove her wrong.

Mr. Ranleigh, aware that any efforts along this line would lay him open to an accusation of having the bad manners to contradict a lady, gave her the faint smile with which he had charmed dozens of far more experienced females into exchanging indignation for complaisance. It appeared to melt her for a moment, but she immediately jerked herself back into antipathy.

"And don't think you can cozen me into letting you see my niece with one of your smiles!" she said. "Let me tell you, sir, that that child is *not* a light female, though she *is* at the moment obliged to appear upon the stage!"

"Madam, I assure you that I have not the slightest notion that she is," Mr. Ranleigh said, with perfect truthfulness.

But at this point he was interrupted by a feminine voice that struck with some familiarity on his ear, proceeding from somewhere over his head.

"Mr. Ranleigh!" He glanced up to see Miss Daingerfield-Nelson herself peering at him over the bannisters at the top of the staircase. "Oh, do come up!" she exclaimed cordially. "It is so *very* good of you to come—though indeed I wish you might have arrived sooner!"

"Cecily!" the elderly lady interposed, looking up at her with an incredulous expression on her face. "What in the *world* has come over you? You will go back to your room immediately! *I* shall deal with this gentleman!"

Miss Daingerfield-Nelson sighed. "Oh dear, Aunt, I was *sure* you would not understand," she said. "That is why I didn't wish you to know until after—— But there is no use talking of that now. Do please bring Mr. Ranleigh up, for I *must* speak with him, and I don't suppose you had rather I did it in the passage."

The elderly lady gasped, and looked at Mr. Ranleigh to see what effect this forward speech had had upon him. As he seemed not at all shocked, however, she gathered the remnants of her own composure and remarked with dignity, "I am afraid, sir, that my niece has quite taken leave of her senses. However, she is right about one thing, at least: it will not do to continue this conversation here!"

She thereupon turned about and marched up the stairs, giving Mr. Ranleigh tacit permission to follow her if he chose.

He was not at all certain that he was wise to do so, but by this time his curiosity was thoroughly aroused, and follow her he did. At the top of the staircase he came face to face with Miss Daingerfield-Nelson. She wore a shabby round gown of blue kerseymere, made up high to the throat, with neither frills nor lace, and, with her dark locks ruthlessly confined by a ribbon, looked even more disarmingly youthful than the elegantly attired young lady he had seen the night before at the theatre. She gave him her hand with a mixture of shyness and enthusiasm and said in a rush, "How do you do? I am so very glad to meet you at last, for I've known about you forever, though I should never have dared to call myself to your notice if you had not expressed the wish to make *my* acquaintance. You see, my name isn't *really* Daingerfield-Nelson; it's Hadley, and—that is, we're related, you know!"

Mr. Ranleigh, finding a situation at last that refused to submit to being encountered with an air of polite boredom, frowned and said, "Oh, my God!" rather bitterly.

Miss Hadley looked taken aback. "I—I beg your pardon!" she faltered. A vivid flush suddenly overspread her face. "Oh! I see! You aren't pleased —of course you're not! But *pray* don't be angry until you've heard me out. I don't intend to ask you for financial assistance; truly I don't! It's only— you see, we have always lived in the country and we don't know *anyone*," she floundered on desperately, "and you must know so many people, all of them of the *first* respectability——"

Mr. Ranleigh, whose sense of humour had betrayed him into abandoning a proper indignation on more than one occasion, found that it was doing so again.

"Oh, not *all* of the first respectability, I'm afraid," he murmured, a gleam of amusement entering his eyes.

Miss Hadley checked, looked at him doubtfully, and was encouraged to give a small chuckle herself.

"No, I expect they are not," she conceded, "for Corinthians *do* go to such places as Cribb's Parlour—do they not?—and to watch pugilistic exhi-

bitions and cock-fights and things of that sort, where the company is probably not at all *comme il faut*—"

"Cecily," her aunt interrupted, scandalised, "you will oblige me by dis-
continuing this extremely improper conversation immediately! If Mr. Ranleigh is indeed related to you, he will certainly take a very odd notion of
your upbringing if you speak to him in such a fashion!" She looked up at
Mr. Ranleigh pertinaciously. "*Are* you connected with the Hadleys, sir?"
she demanded. "If you are not, you had much better go about your business at once."

It occurred to Mr. Ranleigh that this was an excellent piece of advice,
but, somewhat to his own surprise, he found that he was not about to take
it. It might have been reluctance to see Lord Portandrew lose his stake
that decided him, or, again, it might have been the imploring look in Miss
Hadley's eyes. He merely remarked, therefore, that he believed he could
satisfy her on that point—a statement which impelled Miss Hadley to say
triumphantly that she had known it was so from the start.

She promptly led the way into a small and excessively ill-furnished
parlour and, having made her aunt known to him as Miss Dowie, invited
him to sit down. She and Miss Dowie then placed themselves opposite,
the latter perched stiffly on the very edge of her chair, as if she were
prepared to bounce up at the slightest hint of impropriety and sweep Mr.
Ranleigh from the room.

Miss Hadley, however, at once began the conversation on a subject of
which even the highest stickler would have found it difficult to disapprove. She said, with a rapidity which showed how familiar she was with
her facts, "Your grandmother was born Mary Hadley—was she not? She
married Lord Henry Ranleigh, the second son of the Third Duke of Belfour, who later became the *Fifth* Duke when his brother Alfred, the
Fourth Duke, died without issue. And *my* grandfather was Robert Hadley, whose father and Mary Hadley's father were brothers, so that Robert
and Mary were cousins, you see." She looked at him anxiously. "Of course
it is a very distant relationship," she said conscientiously, "but I am sure
you will find Robert—my grandfather—if you look on your grandmother's
family tree. He married very much against the wishes of his family, I am
afraid, so that they quite cut him off—but that doesn't alter the relationship, does it?"

"Not if it exists," Mr. Ranleigh agreed. He was rapidly reviewing Miss
Hadley's genealogical history in his mind; it was accurate enough as far as
his own family was concerned, but, beyond the vaguest of memories of

some errant relative of his paternal grandmother who was said to have married the daughter of a City merchant and drunk himself into an early grave, he had no recollection of ever having heard of a Robert Hadley. He regarded Miss Hadley coolly. "Even supposing that you are correct in assuming that it *does* exist," he said, "I do not quite gather what it is that you wish me to do?"

Miss Hadley, quelled by this unencouraging inquiry, swallowed visibly and said in a small voice, "Only—if you would be kind enough to recommend me to some—some respectable family of your acquaintance that is in need of a governess? You see, it is necessary for me to earn my own living, and it is excessively uncomfortable for me to do so on the stage."

"*Is* it?" Mr. Ranleigh asked, raising his brows—a piece of cold-blooded scepticism that brought Miss Dowie, bristling, into the fray.

"I should think, sir," she said with asperity, "that any gentleman worthy of the name could perceive at a glance that this child does not belong in the theatre!"

"Then I wonder that you should allow her to appear there," Mr. Ranleigh remarked calmly.

To his surprise, tears sprang into Miss Dowie's blue eyes, but she blinked them away swiftly, saying to him with a fierceness which quite belied her diminutive form, "Do you think I should do so, sir, if there were any other way to keep a roof over her head? Yes, it has come to that with us—but there is no reason, of course, why that should interest *you*. *You* have come merely to amuse yourself by tempting this child into a life that she is as far above as your own sister is, if you have one. But let me give you my word, sir, that *that* you will not succeed in doing, as long as there is breath left in my body!"

Mr. Ranleigh, finding himself cast in the role of heartless seducer by one lady, and of charitable patron by the other, found it expedient to clarify the situation. He therefore explained that his presence at the Running Boar was due merely to an imprudent wager made by a young kinsman of his, and assured Miss Dowie that his interest in her niece did not extend beyond escorting her to supper on a single occasion. This explanation did not mollify Miss Dowie, but, somewhat to his surprise, Miss Hadley herself greeted it with every appearance of relief.

"Oh, I am so glad!" she said. "It makes it so very much more comfortable, you see, if you are not interested in me in *that* way. Not," she added frankly, "that I ever really believed you were, for my neck is too long and my mouth far too wide, and you are, of course, accustomed to the company of the most beautiful ladies of the *haut ton*——" She noted Mr. Ranleigh's rather startled look and added kindly, "It says so constantly in the society journals, you know. Naturally we did not subscribe to them ourselves, but Mrs. Ackling was *very* fond of them and took them all, and she let me borrow them regularly."

"And who," he inquired, fascinated by this disclosure, "is Mrs. Ackling?"

"Was," she corrected him regretfully. "She died last spring, you see, just before Papa did. Well, she was a neighbour of ours in Hampshire—in fact, the *only* neighbour who ever called on us, for, in spite of being a *very* high stickler herself, she did not seem to mind Papa's Unfortunate Habits as much as the others did."

Miss Dowie sniffed, and said that, in *her* opinion, the only reason Mrs. Ackling had called at the Grange had been to poke her nose into business that was no affair of hers.

"Telling me that I ought to remove the child from Hadley's influence and take her to my brother Timothy's!" she said. "*That* would be moving from the skillet into the fire, indeed!"

Mr. Ranleigh was strongly aware that, by remaining where he was, he was being irresistibly drawn into the personal affairs of a pair of females of whose very existence he had been happily ignorant four-and-twenty hours previously; yet he made no move to depart.

"That may well be, ma'am," he said to Miss Dowie, "but it still appears to me that it would be more suitable for you to place your niece under your brother's protection than to allow her to appear in the theatre."

Miss Dowie received this speech with a slight compression of the lips and a distinctly militant expression.

"Your reasoning, sir," she remarked witheringly, "is quite correct, except for one circumstance. You are not, I take it, acquainted with my brother, Sir Timothy Dowie?"

"I have not that honour," Mr. Ranleigh acknowledged.

"Then pray do not be making foolish suggestions about my placing my niece under his care," Miss Dowie snapped. "The man is a Monster, sir! He has made it quite plain that he will do nothing for the child—and even if he would," she added, with dark inconsistency, "her reputation and morals would certainly be in greater danger under *his* roof than they are under this."

Mr. Ranleigh looked inquiringly at Miss Hadley, who shrugged her shoulders slightly and said that she had met her uncle only twice, so that she could not say that she knew him well.

"But I daresay it would do no good if we were to appeal to him," she said, "for he wrote Aunt an excessively disagreeable letter when Papa died, and said he expected Papa had been able to leave us enough to live on, and if he had not, she need not think *he* was able to do anything for us. And that is the last we have heard from him."

"But, my good child, if he is your uncle and nearest of kin," Mr. Ranleigh said reasonably, "surely he will not leave you to face the world without a penny when he is made aware of the true state of your affairs. I should certainly advise you to write to him at once, or to visit him if he is in town."

Miss Dowie shuddered. "Nothing," she said, "would induce me to enter That Man's door," and then utterly destroyed the high drama of this pronouncement by adding prosaically, "Besides, he wouldn't let me in. We quarrelled on the occasion of Cecily's mama's death, when I left Dowie House to go to live under my brother-in-law's roof and undertake the child's rearing, and we have not been upon terms since. In fact, his conduct—morally speaking—has been such in recent years that I have found it necessary to sever the connexion altogether."

Mr. Ranleigh, in his unaccustomed role of family adviser, was about to utter a pithy homily on the absurdity of maintaining a personal feud when one's bread-and-butter was at stake, when there was a jaunty tattoo upon the door and Mr. Jillson walked into the room.

"Ah! Mr. Ranleigh!" he remarked, observing that gentleman with a benign air. "Our genial host told me I should find you here. Ladies—your obedient servant!"

Seen in the muddy daylight filtering through the unwashed windows, and in a costume consisting of a very short blue jacket and a pair of yellow pantaloons that bagged visibly at the knees, it was apparent that the elegance that had invested Mr. Jillson the evening before had been exclusively theatrical in nature. His air of assurance, however, was unimpaired. Finding himself regarded by Miss Hadley with frank dislike, and by her aunt with a disapproval so marked that it would have made a more sensitive man quail, he looked with bland equanimity at Mr. Ranleigh and remarked, "I scarcely expected to find you honouring this humble roof with your presence, sir. But I perceive that you are a gentleman of more than usual persistence of character, and that once you have made up your mind to something, you are not easily baulked of your purpose. May I inquire how you have succeeded in your errand?"

"You may not," Mr. Ranleigh replied, with equal equanimity. "May I, however, inquire of *you,* sir, whether it is your practice to intrude uninvited upon a private conversation in a lady's parlour?"

"Not at all," Mr. Jillson protested affably. "You mistake the situation, my dear sir. I stand—if I may say so—in the role of protector to these two friendless females, and as such——"

Miss Dowie, interrupting indignantly at this point, requested to know what reason he had to believe that the loan of the paltry sum of fifteen pounds gave him any such pretensions.

"You are an impudent coxcomb, sir!" she said. "Have the goodness to leave this room at once!"

Mr. Jillson bowed. "Your wish, dear lady, is my command. May I remind you, however, that *my* interest in Miss—er—Daingerfield-Nelson is quite without ulterior motives, beyond the praiseworthy one of earning an honest livelihood for us both?—an advantage I believe I have over Mr. Ranleigh and the other gentlemen moving in the exalted circles customarily favoured with his presence."

Miss Dowie gave him a glance of loathing. "Oh, go away and stop your blathering, man!" she said unceremoniously. "And *do* give over calling my niece by that ridiculous name! Daingerfield-Nelson! Of all the shabby-genteel monstrosities to foist upon her!"

Mr. Jillson, who had apparently become inured to Miss Dowie's frankness in the course of his dealings with her, bowed and implied that he would be very happy to take himself off if he might have the privilege of a word in private with Mr. Ranleigh. This brought Miss Hadley into the argument.

"Oh, no!" she protested. "Mr. Ranleigh is not going yet!" She cast him a hopeful glance. "You *won't* go—will you?" she begged. "Not before I am able to put before you how *easily* you could assist us——"

Mr. Ranleigh rose. "I fear I must," he said.

"Oh, no!" Miss Hadley exclaimed again, in dismay. "Indeed, I have told you the truth, sir; we do not at all wish to hang on your sleeve, but a mere recommendation could mean *so* much——"

"I shall look into the matter," Mr. Ranleigh said noncommittally. "May I bid you good morning, Miss Hadley—Miss Dowie? Mr.—Jillson, is it? If you are quite ready——"

Mr. Jillson, impelled out of the room by no more than the flicker of a glance from Mr. Ranleigh's cool eyes, found himself, in the space of five seconds, standing in the passage outside with the door closed behind him. Mr. Ranleigh faced him, waiting.

"Yes?" he said unencouragingly.

Mr. Jillson's air of assurance faltered slightly under that cold, steady gaze. He recovered himself and said, "My dear sir, surely there is no need to be in such a hurry! Perhaps over a glass of ale——"

"If you have something to say to me, you had best say it at once," Mr. Ranleigh said curtly. "What is it?"

"Why, I——" Mr. Jillson came aground again, then plucked up and said impudently, "You're in a tearing hurry, ain't you? Well, I'll put it to you straight, then. The fact is, you're looking for no more than a bit of fun, but it's bread-and-butter to *me*, you see! The chit will be worth a fortune, once she's learned her way about a bit—but *not* if she has her head turned by such as you. You know as well as I do what will become of her if she's taken up by *your* lot before she's had the chance to make a name for herself."

"And what," Mr. Ranleigh asked directly, "will become of her under *your* protection, Jillson?"

Mr. Jillson described an airy gesture which appeared to encompass infinite space. "The world, my dear sir," he said, "will be at her feet! Even now I am coaching her in the leading female role in *The Beaux' Stratagem,* a part ideally suited to her talents, with which I expect to establish her firmly upon the London stage. Then, let us say, a dozen years on that stage under my aegis—for I shall, of course, in due time form my own company as a setting for her talents. During this period she will reign as the toast of the metropolis—after which I shall retire to a life of well-earned ease, while she marries whichever of her noble suitors has the plumpest purse and the least dislike to bringing an actress into the family."

"A pretty picture," Mr. Ranleigh said dryly, beginning to descend the stairs. "You surprise me, Jillson. I had not suspected you of such romantic dreams."

"Not in the least, sir!" Mr. Jillson said, following him. "I assure you it all lies in the realm of sober reality. You have seen the young lady herself, and you will admit that there is something about her—something surpassing beauty; I might almost say surpassing charm—which instantly appeals to the male heart. She cannot fail, if properly managed—a matter to which I intend to devote the considerable store of experience I have gained in twenty years upon the boards."

He was following close behind Mr. Ranleigh, and was slightly disconcerted, as he reached the foot of the stairs, when that gentleman suddenly halted and turned about, facing him.

"Tell me, Jillson—exactly where did you come upon her?" he demanded.

Mr. Jillson, having no time to reflect, was surprised into speaking the truth.

"As a matter of fact, in Southampton," he said, "where the theatrical company which was at the moment enjoying the benefit of my own and Mrs. Jillson's talents was playing at the New Theatre in French Street. I made her acquaintance at the hostelry in which she and Miss Dowie had been obliged to seek refuge after having been turned out of their lamentably highly mortgaged home following the death of the young lady's father, and was able to be of some slight assistance to them in certain financial embarrassments having to do with paying their shot at the inn." He added cautiously, "Why do you want to know?"

"The merest curiosity," Mr. Ranleigh said briefly and, without lingering for any further conversation, walked out the front door and summoned his curricle.

3

Mr. Ranleigh drove immediately to his house in Mount Street, where he found his mother, Lady Frederick, entertaining Lady Comerford and Miss Augusta Comerford in the Crimson Saloon. When he entered this apartment he found the two elder ladies seated together on a handsome satinwood sofa, enjoying a confidential gossip on the recent marriages of the three Royal Dukes of Kent, Cambridge, and Clarence. Miss Comerford, a dark and opulent beauty whose oval green eyes were reputed to have broken a score of hearts during her two London seasons, was seated opposite.

Lady Frederick, an imposing dowager of sixty, wore a purple-beribboned cap and a rather remarkable yellow gown with a point lace ruff, for she had a dislike, she was accustomed to saying, of the niminy-piminy colours of the modern vogue. She regarded her son with an air of hauteur that successfully concealed her fondness for him, and remarked to him, in her richly regal voice, "So you've come in—have you? To what am I to attribute this honour, pray?" She turned to Lady Comerford. "You do not know, Letitia," she informed her acidly, "how fortunate you are to have only daughters. At least you may keep *them* about when you have need of them. Now it does *me* no more good to come to town than if I was to remain at Hillcourt, for if Robert is not in Leicestershire when I am here he is at Newmarket, and if he's not there he's on the Continent. As for Hillcourt, it might fall into ruin if it weren't for me, for he never goes near the place when he can help it."

Mr. Ranleigh, exchanging greetings with Lady Comerford and Gussie, strolled up to his mother, possessed himself of her hand, and kissed it lightly.

"What has happened to put you in such a bad skin, ma'am?" he inquired, smiling down at her. "More royal marriages? I thought I caught Clarence's name as I came in the door."

"Nothing of the sort," Lady Frederick said roundly. "If that parcel of middle-aged fools want to make cakes of themselves with their German brides—and I am sure Kent's, at least, was chosen for him because her previous marriage had already proven her a good breeder—that is entirely their affair." She gave a short bark of laughter. "Lord! There is Clarence with ten bastards already," she said, "but I daresay he is played out by this time. What a pity it is that he couldn't have married his actress! *That* would have put an end to all this scurrying about for an heir to the throne!"

"Louisa! Really! Before Gussie——!" Lady Comerford protested feebly. "Pooh!" said Lady Frederick. "Gussie's not one to put on Bath-miss airs. *She* knows the time of day a great deal better than you do, Letitia."

Gussie indeed seemed quite unperturbed by her hostess's frank speech. She was giving her attention to Mr. Ranleigh, who came over to sit beside her; there was a note of half-teasing pleasure in her voice as she spoke to him.

"Indeed, I told Mama that we ought not to call in Mount Street today," she said. "I was afraid we had already put your civility to too great a test last evening at the theatre, when you would no doubt much rather have been paying court to Miss Daingerfield-Nelson than sitting tamely in our box."

"Good God, has that tale made the rounds already?" he asked without discomposure. "I daresay you had the whole of it, then—that I was pitch-forked into the business trying to save Tony's groats?"

Lady Frederick demanded at this point to be told what it was they were talking of, and was given a highly coloured version of the previous night's events by Miss Comerford—a piece of frankness that was greeted by her mama with a scandalised request to know where she had heard such an extremely improper story.

"From Brackenridge, of course," Gussie said. She turned again to Mr. Ranleigh. "You must know," she said, "that he, of all people, will lose no opportunity to spread the tale of your discomfiture. Your only recourse will be in parading the Daingerfield-Nelson chit on your arm before the eyes of the town. I daresay that is not *quite* beyond your powers of persuasion?"

Mr. Ranleigh gave her a light answer and turned the conversation to another topic; but when Lady Comerford and her daughter had departed some few minutes later and he was left alone with his mother, he returned to the subject of Miss Daingerfield-Nelson at once.

"There is a matter on which you can be of considerable assistance to me," he remarked. "*Was* there a Robert Hadley who was cousin to my father's mother, and who made a rather unfortunate marriage?"

Lady Frederick stared at him. "Lord, how should I know?" she replied brusquely. "I never paid the least heed to your father's family. Fools or rascals, every one of 'em, except Frederick—and he may have been one, too, only he was such a handsome rogue no one ever found him out! Why do you wish to know?"

Mr. Ranleigh shrugged. "Because I seem to have discovered his granddaughter. I saw Miss Daingerfield-Nelson this morning, and she informs me that her name is not Daingerfield-Nelson, but Hadley, and that her grandfather was a cousin to my grandmother."

Lady Frederick snorted. "A pretty tale! And she took *you* in with it? She *must* be a beauty—and a sharp one, to boot."

Mr. Ranleigh disposed his long limbs comfortably in a chair, crossing one leg over the other and allowing his abstracted gaze to rest on the highly polished boot that adorned it.

"No, she is not a beauty," he said critically. "Neither has she taken me in. Nevertheless, I am much inclined to believe that she was speaking the truth."

Lady Frederick's dark eyes took on a scornful expression. "Speaking the truth!" she repeated. "A common creature from the theatre connected with a Duchess of Belfour? Lord, Robert, you are talking like a flat, and *that* is something I never thought to hear! You, with all *your* experience——"

He smiled slightly. "My experience, my dear, is something which you are presumed to know nothing about!" he said. "Are you trying to scandalise me, as you did poor Lady Comerford?"

"Oh—Letitia!" she said impatiently. "Of course I know all about your petticoat affairs——or as much as I want to, at any rate. But it's time you were thinking of settling down, all the same. If you'll take my advice, you'll offer for Gussie Comerford. The family's a good one, she's handsome enough, and I daresay she'd lead you a lively enough dance that you wouldn't have time for your bits of muslin. Not," she added tartly, "that *my* opinion will carry any weight with you. Who is this hussy you're dangling after now?—besides being related to Mary Hadley, of course."

Mr. Ranleigh said, a slight smile gleaming in his grey eyes, "You are wrong on all points, ma'am. I do value your opinion: it is precisely what I am seeking now. And the girl is far from being a hussy; on the contrary, she is extremely young and innocent, and quite out of her depth in the company in which she finds herself at present. Neither am I 'dangling after her'; schoolroom chits are hardly in my line. But if she is indeed a Hadley——"

"What makes you think she is?" Lady Frederick demanded. "Good heavens, Robert, anyone could make such a claim!"

"Exactly," he agreed. "However, her aunt, who is obviously a lady, in spite of being a Tartar of the first order, supports her claim, and gives herself out as being the sister of one Sir Timothy Dowie. You would not, I expect, happen to be acquainted with him?"

Lady Frederick's brows came together in a slight frown. "Dowie?" she said. "No, I am not, but I've heard the name. My brother Albion knew him in his salad days, I fancy. A shocking loose-screw, if I remember correctly—the sort of person Albion *would* know. But that was years and years ago—thirty at least, I should think. If this is the same man, he should be almost sixty now."

"As Miss Dowie seems to be near that age herself, that would be very probable," Mr. Ranleigh agreed. "At any rate, from what I can gather, he seems to have turned a very cold shoulder to his niece when her father died some months ago—so cold that Miss Dowie was impelled to accept the assistance of a chance-met actor named Jillson in placing the girl on the stage."

Lady Frederick, who, in spite of the harshness of her tongue, was well known for her autocratic and eccentric charities, began to find the conversation of interest. However, she only said severely, "Nonsense! It sounds to me very much as if you had been dipping into lending-library novels— an occupation which I find particularly revolting in a man. I daresay *you* have been cast in the role of Lord Bountiful in this sentimental drama?"

"If you mean that the girl is hoping to obtain financial assistance from me, she assures me that she is not," Mr. Ranleigh said. "She *has* given me to understand, however, that she would appreciate a recommendation to a family of the—er—first respectability which finds itself in need of a governess."

Lady Frederick surveyed him grimly. "Coming it much too strong, my boy!" she said pungently. "Hire a governess off the London stage! You cannot suppose I shall believe that she actually proposed *that* to you!"

"I assure you, she did, however," Mr. Ranleigh reiterated, smiling slightly. "I told you she was very young and very, very green."

"If that is so, it appears to me that it is that aunt of hers who should be seeking employment, not this child!"

"Yes, that has occurred to me, too," Mr. Ranleigh admitted. "But if I am any judge, Miss Dowie is past the age to be readily employed to look after young children. She might hope to become some elderly lady's *dame de compagnie*, but I doubt that she would be able to hold such a position long. She lacks," he explained, a reminiscent gleam in his eye, "a certain tact."

Lady Frederick said unsympathetically that at least that might be more tolerable than Henrietta Wixom's behaviour, which was so extremely tactful that you might tell her the moon was made of green cheese without her making bold to differ with you; but apparently her mind at that moment was on neither Miss Dowie nor the distant kinswoman who served as her own companion. There was a faraway expression in her eyes, and after a few moments she announced firmly that Sir Timothy—if the peculiar tale she had just attended to were true—should certainly be induced to do something for his relations.

"Exactly what I have been thinking, ma'am," Mr. Ranleigh agreed, a muscle quivering at the corner of his mouth.

His mother looked at him suspiciously. "I daresay you have been leading up to this all along," she said. "Now, tell me—why should you interest yourself in this chit? You say she ain't a beauty and you ain't dangling after her, but I've yet to see you stirring a step out of your way for girls who are far more closely connected with you than *this* one claims to be— that brood of Belfour's, for example."

"Ah, but my cousin Belfour's daughters are not in the hands of a seedy rascal who considers them in the light of salable merchandise," Mr. Ranleigh remarked. "I find I have a certain dislike to seeing anyone of my blood in that position. She has, by the bye, an odd look of that Reynolds portrait of my grandmother in the Ivory Saloon at Hillcourt—the same slender neck and enormous eyes——"

Lady Frederick said, "Humph!" and then, grudgingly, "I expect something must be done. Of course the Hadleys were merely County people, and I doubt that the old Duke—your great-grandfather—would have countenanced your grandfather's marriage into that family if there had been any expectation at the time that he would inherit the title. Still there's good blood there—some of the oldest in England. It won't do to have it dragged in the mud. You had best go to see Albion. He may be able to tell you where Sir Timothy Dowie is to be found."

As a matter of fact, Mr. Albion Wymberly, when Mr. Ranleigh ran him to earth at White's a short time later, was quite willing and able to be helpful along this line. Mr. Wymberly, a gentleman of an extreme rotundity which had been agreeably nourished over some fifty-odd years on the delicacies prepared by his own and his carefully chosen friends' French cooks, was somewhat surprised to find himself the object of his nephew's attention, and took advantage of the opportunity to inquire whether it would be convenient for him to make him a small loan.

Mr. Ranleigh took out his pocketbook. "How much?" he asked resignedly.

Mr. Wymberly looked injured. "Only a miserable pony. *You'll* never miss it. I'll tell you what, my boy, if you're going to be as damned tactless as this when a man makes a civil request of you, you'll soon find yourself looking for friends."

Mr. Ranleigh gave him a rather twisted smile. "Oh, no, I think not—so long as I contrive not to wake up a pauper some morning," he said. "Having now satisfied *your* request, Albion, I'll ask you to satisfy mine. Are you acquainted with a Sir Timothy Dowie?"

"Dowie?" Mr. Wymberly repeated. "Why, yes. Ran into him only yesterday—and a more repulsive sight I must say I never laid eyes on. His cravat, dear boy! Greasy—positively greasy! And he was used to be rather dapper-dog thirty years ago."

"What's his family?" Mr. Ranleigh asked. "Or don't you know that?"

"Of course I know," said Mr. Wymberly, affronted once more, for he was something of an amateur of genealogy. "Hampshire people—never distinguished, though the baronetcy dates back to Elizabeth."

"Money?"

"Oh, no—a competence merely. He was a great gamester in the old days, and ran through the better part of his estate. Still has the place in Hampshire, though, I believe." Mr. Wymberly regarded his nephew with suddenly suspicious eyes. "If you're running some sort of rig that involves Tim Dowie, let me tell you, you're better out of it," he said. "The way I understand it, he's turned into a damned squeeze-farthing these days, with a taste for taking a man to law for damages if he so much as sends him a crooked look. Best keep out of his path, my boy!"

"Oh, he'd find me an ill bird for plucking," Mr. Ranleigh said indifferently. "You can tell me one thing more about him if you are able, though. Had he a sister who married a man named Hadley?"

"Hadley? No, I don't know that—though he did have sisters, if I remember rightly. But Hadley was your grandmother's name——"

"Exactly," Mr. Ranleigh said. "And she had, if I am correctly informed, a cousin named Robert, who seems to have contracted an ill-advised marriage."

"Daughter of a Cit," Mr. Wymberly corroborated promptly. "Before my time, of course, but I remember my father mentioning it. Dashed silly thing to do—the girl wasn't even plump in the pocket. Why do you want to know?"

Ranleigh rose. "I doubt that my reasons would be of interest to you," he said. "Might I trouble you for Sir Timothy's direction, if you know it?"

"Always used to put up at Limmer's but look here, Robert, I'm serious!" Mr. Wymberly said urgently. "Take my advice and stay clear of him. Good God, if there *is* a connexion, you'll get nothing from acknowledging it but the pleasure of finding yourself with a set of dirty dishes on your hands."

"Yes, I rather fear you are right," Mr. Ranleigh agreed imperturbably, and took his departure, leaving Mr. Wymberly—who was well acquainted with his nephew's notorious lack of interest in family ramifications—with his mouth acock behind him.

4

Inquiry at Limmer's Hotel brought the information that Sir Timothy Dowie was not at present among its guests. A knowledgeable clerk, however, was able to tell Mr. Ranleigh that he had been seen there within the past day or two, and had been heard to let fall a statement to the effect that he was staying at a house in Upper Wimpole Street that had been lent him by its owner. Mr. Ranleigh, who had several engagements for the day, none of them in the vicinity of Upper Wimpole Street, looked less than pleased on hearing this, but he was not in the mood to be diverted from his purpose. Driving back to Mount Street and remaining there only long enough to dispatch several messages, he proceeded on at once to beard Sir Timothy Dowie in his borrowed den.

He ran his quarry to earth in a respectable but melancholy-looking house, seated at a table in a small back room with a miserable fire guttering in the grate. As the remainder of the house, its furniture muffled in holland covers, was as chill as a tomb, Mr. Ranleigh was not surprised to find his host wrapped in a greatcoat, and began to wish he had not surrendered his own to the bleary-looking individual who had opened the front door to him.

Sir Timothy, whose old-fashioned garrick allowed only a half-bald head, a grizzled red face, and a somewhat stooped figure to be discerned in the half-light coming through the heavily draped windows, gave him an unwelcoming glance as he walked into the room.

"Ranleigh," he said, without rising. "I don't know any Ranleighs. One of the Belfour connexion, I expect. Above *my* touch. What the devil d'ye want with me?"

Mr. Ranleigh, finding that he was not invited to seat himself—an omission which might have been explained by the fact that all the chairs in the room, other than that occupied by Sir Timothy himself, were encumbered by piles of papers and ledgers—unhurriedly removed an untidy heap of documents from one and sat down.

"No, we have not had the pleasure of a previous meeting, I believe," he said, in an unruffled tone. "If my information is correct, however, we have a mutual connexion, and it is on this subject that I came to speak to you. You have, I believe, a niece named Cecily Hadley?"

Sir Timothy's brows shot up. "Hadley? Ay, my sister Grisell's brat—but what the devil has that to do with you?" He checked suddenly. "Wait now!" he commanded. "Wait! There was some.Ranleigh connexion there, after all; I remember the silly wench's boasting of it when she married Hadley. But what's it to do with you? If ye're the man I take ye to be, ye've better things to do than to be wasting your time over me *or* my niece."

"You are quite correct. I have," Mr. Ranleigh assured him. "It has been brought to my attention, however, that your niece—owing to her reduced circumstances since her father's death—has been obliged to support herself by appearing upon the London stage. I daresay the matter has *not* been brought to *your* attention, which would account for your not having come forward to offer her your assistance."

Sir Timothy stared at him for a moment, and then broke into a crack of laughter.

"The stage?" he repeated. "Not *my* niece. You must be raving, man! Why, she's naught but a half-grown chit with her hair in a tangle and her finger stuck in her mouth; nobody'ud pay a farthing to look at her!"

"You have not, I take it," Mr. Ranleigh remarked, "seen her lately. Let me assure you that the picture you have drawn is at present a quite inaccurate one."

"It is, is it?" A look of comprehension crept into Sir Timothy's eyes. "Ah, so that's the way of it—is it?" he said, giving Mr. Ranleigh a leer and a wink. "Growed to be a woman—has she?—and now the dogs are after her. Well, what's that to you, my buck? Don't want to marry her—do ye? Because I gi'e ye fair warning—not a penny of *my* coin will ye see settled on her."

"Thank you, that is a matter that is not of the slightest interest to me," Mr. Ranleigh said. "I met Miss Hadley for the first time only this morning, and my one concern is to see her removed from her present entirely unsuitable situation to the protection of some relative."

Sir Timothy looked at him doubtfully. "Ah, well—if that's so——" he said, and then continued grudgingly, "Well, I daresay there's no reason she shouldn't go down to Hampshire—though, mind you, I shan't stand the nonsense for any new gowns and kickshaws! If she wants to lead a plain country life and make herself useful, I'll not close my door on her, for poor Grisell's sake. I expect Hadley had something to leave her—eh? They say the Grange was mortgaged, but there must have been a bit left."

"As I understand it—nothing," Mr. Ranleigh said bluntly.

Sir Timothy's face flushed with annoyance. "Ay, that 'ud be Rob Hadley!" he said bitterly. "Drink and game every groat of it away, and then leave *me* with his brat to feed and house."

He would have gone on, but he was interrupted at this point by the opening of the door and the unceremonious appearance upon the scene of a buxom middle-aged female in a pelisse of magenta velvet and a bonnet to match, its high poke lined with a pink silk which contrasted boldly with the carroty curls beneath it. Advancing into the room with hand outstretched, she said briskly to Sir Timothy, "Well, I'm off now, ducky. You must give me some brass for my shopping, as you promised." She broke off to gaze in some surprise at Mr. Ranleigh and, obviously impressed by the sporting neckcloth, gleaming top-boots, and exquisitely fitted coat that proclaimed the out-and-out Corinthian, to exclaim, "Eh now, who's this?"

"None of your affair, my dear," Sir Timothy said, not mincing words. He opened a drawer in the table at which he sat and extracted a number of coins, counted them out carefully, reflected, replaced one in the drawer, and closed the drawer again. Before the intruder could take the coins from him, however, he had once more changed his mind and drawn back again. "Nay," he said hastily, "ye won't need so much as *that*," and, reopening the drawer, dropped in another of the coins and handed the remainder to her.

"A-ah, ye're a clutch-fisted old rascal!" she remarked disparagingly. "Ye said I was to have new clothes when we came up to town, but it's as much as I've been able to do to set a joint on the table and keep coals enough in the house to save us from freezing to death, on the ready I've had from you. But I'll gi'e ye fair warning, Sir Timothy—*this* lot goes on my back, if we go supperless to bed!"

Sir Timothy, who seemed not in the least embarrassed either by her appearance or by her conversation, made her a spirited rejoinder, to which she replied in kind, and she thereupon flounced out of the room.

"My housekeeper, Mrs. Cassaday," Sir Timothy pronounced imperturbably, as soon as the door had closed behind her. "A greedy bitch—but they're all alike, ain't they? I'll send her packing one of these days: see if I don't!"

"I should rather hope you might," Mr. Ranleigh said dryly, "if it is your intention to take your niece and your sister under your roof. I am persuaded that she and Miss Dowie would not deal in the least."

"What's that? My sister?" Sir Timothy looked up sharply, with a sudden frown. "Who the devil said anything about my sister? Damme, I wouldn't let that meddlesome old brimstone inside my door if it was to save her from perdition!"

Mr. Ranleigh's brows went up. "You must pardon my ignorance, sir," he said. "I was not aware that Miss Dowie had independent means."

"Means? She hasn't a groat. But that's none of *my* affair," Sir Timothy said callously. "Hadley was the one should ha' provided for her; she saved him the expense of a housekeeper a matter o' fifteen years. And now she means to come begging to me, does she? Well, you may tell her she'll get nothing out of *my* pocket."

Mr. Ranleigh, who had not taken Miss Dowie's fierce account of the terms on which she stood with her brother quite at face value, began to perceive that that lady might not, after all, have been indulging in exaggeration. He was not ordinarily accounted a persuasive man, having been fortunate enough to stand all his life on terms with the world where his will was bowed to without argument; but he now swallowed down an inclination to tell Sir Timothy exactly what he thought of his lack of proper family feeling and made an attempt instead to bring him to reason by more diplomatic means.

His efforts were in vain. As a matter of fact, Sir Timothy, instead of abandoning his opposition, showed alarming signs of being about to fly into a towering rage, and at last told his visitor rudely that if he had such a deal of sympathy for Miss Dowie he had best open his own purse to assist her.

"I'll ha' the girl but I won't ha' her, and that's flat!" he said, fulminatingly.

"That is well said, sir," Mr. Ranleigh retorted blightingly, controlling his own temper with an effort. "But surely you must be aware that Miss Hadley will not consider abandoning her aunt without some provision's being made for her. Even *my* brief acquaintance with her has made me quite certain of that."

"Then let the two of 'em starve together and be damned to 'em," Sir Timothy said, "for I won't ha' Mab Dowie under my roof! It's a hard thing, at any rate, that a man who's never married must be saddled with another man's brat! I'm not a rich man, Mr. Ranleigh, and I've had to learn not to waste my substance. Ye say the girl's on the stage—well, it ain't what I'd choose for her, but I'll wager she'll not need to stay there long." He cast a shrewd glance at Mr. Ranleigh from under his brows. "Eh, my lad? When a buck of your cut goes out of his way to look after a chit he's only just met, I fancy she must ha' turned out a handsomer piece of goods than I'd ha' bargained for, so ten to one there'll be some young sprig wanting to put a ring on her finger before she's many months older."

Mr. Ranleigh, hearing his host fall into these complacent reflections, realised that he had indeed been wasting his time in attempting to persuade him of his family obligations, and rose abruptly.

"Allow me to tell you, sir, that I consider your attitude unfeeling to the highest degree," he said scathingly, "but I see that you will not be moved by my opinion, so I shall take my leave of you."

"Ay, do that!" Sir Timothy said cordially. "I'm a busy man, with no time to waste; why, I've an action coming up against my neighbour Kirkstall, ye see, and I mustn't stay on in town too long, neither, or there'll be the devil to pay in Hampshire, for they'll go on down there like I was rich as Golden Ball if I ain't there to put a stop to it. You wouldn't believe what my bill for candles was last quarter, and as for coals——!"

Mr. Ranleigh cut short these observations by striding from the room and letting himself out the front door. Sivil, who had been walking the bays up and down before the house, saw from a single glance at his master's hard grey eyes that his mood was an unpropitious one, and hastened to take his place beside him as he sprang into the curricle and took the reins. Sivil was a small, spare man who had been in the late Lord Frederick's employ when his present master was still a boy, and there was puzzlement now in his mind: whatever it was that had had Mr. Robert chasing about town all day in the unlikeliest neighbourhoods, it did not seem to him that it was something that had given him any degree of satisfaction.

He was quite right: his master was in a state of wrathful frustration that was decidedly rare in his experience. There was nothing that he could do to compel Sir Timothy to act as he should in regard to his niece, which meant, it appeared, that the girl must continue to remain under Jillson's aegis.

But at the remembrance of that gentleman's impudently smiling face Mr. Ranleigh's mouth tightened. He had no interest in Miss Hadley beyond the brief compassion he might have felt for any gently bred girl hustled into the rough world of the theatre without suitable protection, but, as he had informed Lady Frederick earlier in the day, it did not suit him to see anyone of his blood in such a position.

He repeated this observation to her a short time later, when, having driven back to Mount Street, he found her again in the Crimson Saloon, about to go upstairs to place herself in the hands of her dresser. Yielding, however, to her son's request for five minutes' private conversation with her, she sent the meek Mrs. Wixom, her *dame de compagnie*, from the room, and listened in surprise and disapproval to the brief account he gave her of Sir Timothy's obduracy.

"This is monstrous! *Quite* unheard-of!" she pronounced, when he had concluded. "But I do not at all see why you have come to *me* with the story. There is nothing that can be done for the girl, now that she has ruined herself by appearing publicly upon the stage. Do you know I have had Anthony here twice since you went out, *demanding* to see you about that ridiculous wager? He seems quite taken with the girl, which will be most disturbing to poor Almeria, for she has been trying to interest him in Woodstone's eldest, and you know there is no earthly use in talking to him of marriage when he has one of his fancies on the brain."

Mr. Ranleigh said uncompromisingly, "I am not interested in Tony's fancies, ma'am. What I am interested in is in getting the chit out of Jill-son's hands. He does not intend ill to her, I believe, but, if I am any judge of character, he is one of those talented, improvident rogues who never quite attain success in their profession, and he will have no scruples in making use of her in any way that will help him to feather his own nest. I have been considering the matter, and it seems to me that the girl's own idea may serve her best. If she could be placed in some respectable family as a governess——"

"A governess!" Lady Frederick regarded her son incredulously. "When she has been exhibiting herself on the London stage!"

"She has been exhibiting herself there only for the space of a week or so, and under an assumed name," Mr. Ranleigh said impatiently. "That will stop immediately, of course. You will take her and Miss Dowie down to Hillcourt when you go there on Friday, and I have no doubt that in a short time, if you will make inquiries among your friends, you will be able to find respectable employment for her in a quiet country household where her London exploits will not come into question. Possibly also for Miss Dowie——"

He checked, observing that Lady Frederick was regarding him with a look of astonishment, not unmixed with asperity.

"I perceive," she uttered, with awful calm, "that you have worked the matter out to your entire satisfaction, Robert. You have miscalculated in only one respect—and that is that I have no desire whatsoever to invite this young woman to stay at Hillcourt."

For a moment two pairs of very autocratic eyes—one a hard grey, the other dark and brilliant—challenged each other. Then Mr. Ranleigh gave a sudden laugh.

"Very well!" he acknowledged. "I should have consulted you before laying my plans, ma'am. Let us say that all I shall ask you to do now is to see the girl, and to judge whether you wish her to remain in her present situation. If she does, I believe I can guarantee that within a year she will have been ruined in good earnest, whether she remains with Jillson or is taken up by any one of half a dozen who have the fancy to make her the latest craze—Brackenridge, or Lovett, or Tony——"

"Anthony!" Lady Frederick snorted. "He is more of an old woman than I am. If *he* is all she has to fear, her virtue is as safe as mine. And what, pray—if I *do* invite her to Hillcourt—am I to say to anyone who meets her there and recognises her as a young woman whom they have seen upon the stage? It is all very well for you to tell me that she is appearing under an assumed name; people are not blind! And I suppose we can hardly shave her head to change her appearance——"

"Of course not," Mr. Ranleigh said, with renewed impatience. "It won't be necessary. She will probably not be at Hillcourt longer than a few weeks, and she need not go into company at all while she is there. And if she should happen to be seen by someone who believes he recognises her as Miss Daingerfield-Nelson, you do not require *me* to tell you that you are quite capable of freezing any impertinent comments with a few well-chosen words on the unaccountability of chance resemblances."

Lady Frederick's face relaxed in a frosty smile. "No, you abominable boy, I do not!" she said. "I wish it were as easy to give *you* a set-down, for you are sadly in want of one. You are growing as highhanded as a Turk—quite insufferable!" She rose from the winged armchair in which she had been sitting. "I must go up now," she said. "I dine at the Comerfords', and then go on to Carlton House—a most boring affair, I fear it will be, for Prinny is in one of his melancholy moods, which is the reason for my being asked, I daresay. He says I remind him of the old days, when Frederick was alive."

"But you will do as I ask in the matter of Miss Hadley, ma'am?" Mr. Ranleigh said, refusing to be put off by this change of subject.

Lady Frederick looked at him with some acerbity. "Is that a question or a command?" she demanded. "No, never mind answering me; I'm quite aware that you are capable of turning a graceful phrase when you like, but you will still expect to have your own way." Mr. Ranleigh, smiling, took her hand and pressed it lightly to his lips. "Oh, go along with you!" Lady Frederick said tartly. "Very well, then—I shall see the girl. You may tell her that she may call here tomorrow."

Mr. Ranleigh, recalling his interview with Miss Dowie, shook his head, a glint of amusement in his eyes.

"I believe, my dear, that we shall do better to call upon her, instead," he said. "I may, you see, have prevailed upon you to see *her*, but I am not at all certain that—highhanded as you may think me—I should be able to prevail upon Miss Dowie to allow her niece to come here to see you!"

5 Early on the following afternoon the ostler at the Running Boar had, for the second time in two days, the privilege of beholding a fashionable turnout— this one an elegant barouche with a pair of spanking chestnuts between the shafts—draw up before the door of the inn which employed his services. The lady who was handed down from it by the Corinthian the ostler had seen the morning before wore a lilac velvet pelisse and a fashionably high-crowned bonnet, and favoured her surroundings with a glance of such comprehensive disapproval before she swept inside that Ben Ostler, as he later confessed, was "fair knocked into horsenails," giving it as his opinion that the old Queen herself could not have held herself any higher.

Lady Frederick, whose opinion of the entire House of Hanover was extremely low, would scarcely have been flattered by this comparison; nor was she propitiated by the obsequious courtesies rendered her by the Running Boar's landlady when she perceived her entering her door.

"My good woman," she informed her in her piercing voice, "you would occupy yourself far more fittingly in sweeping the dirt from your floors than in bowing and scraping to me in this ridiculous manner!" She turned to her son. "If I *must* go up those horridly steep—and, I am certain, quite unsafe—stairs, you must give me your arm, Robert!" she declared. "Really, it is reprehensible for people to live under such conditions, when a little energy is all that is required!"

Mr. Ranleigh, perceiving that she was rapidly attracting an audience consisting of every employee on the premises, to say nothing of the inmates of the taproom, escorted her up the stairs with a smile of some amusement, which still lingered on his lips when he knocked at the door of the room in which he had had his conversation with Miss Hadley and Miss Dowie the previous morning. It was opened by Miss Dowie, who gazed in some surprise at the imperious dame confronting her.

"You will be Miss Dowie, I expect?" Lady Frederick said, without ceremony. "May we come in? My son tells me that he met you yesterday and that your niece has some tale of being connected with my late husband's family."

Mr. Ranleigh, endeavouring to counter the effect of this unpropitious beginning, accomplished a more orthodox introduction once he and Lady Frederick had been admitted into the little parlour, but he was too late: Miss Dowie's hackles had already risen. She said stiffly, when she had invited her two visitors to seat themselves, "I hope you have not come here under the misapprehension that *I* wished to see you, my lady. It was not with *my* approval that my niece agreed to have any communication with Mr. Ranleigh."

"Hoity-toity!" Lady Frederick said. "You need not get up on your high ropes with me, Miss Dowie. It appears to me that you are sadly in need of assistance from someone who has your niece's best interests in view, and *that* I have come prepared to offer you. Where is the girl?" she inquired.

"She is resting," Miss Dowie said defiantly. "The theatre, my lady, requires late hours, and I do not intend to see her health undermined by constant keeping of them at her age."

Lady Frederick nodded her approval. "Very commendable," she said. "May I inquire how old your niece is, Miss Dowie?"

"She is turned eighteen."

"That is indeed too young for a constant indulgence in late hours. However, the fact of the matter is that, if she is who she claims to be, she has no business being on the stage at all. Perhaps you would favour me with a history of her parentage, Miss Dowie? Or you may be able to produce some family documents that would confirm her story?"

"I could, but I shan't!" Miss Dowie snapped, her eyes sparkling dangerously. "Not unless *you*, ma'am, are willing to produce *your* credentials to prove to me that you are what you say *you* are!" She rose from her chair. "I believe this has gone quite far enough," she said. "I did not seek your help, ma'am, and I have no idea of being insulted by you under my own roof, poor as that roof may be! May I bid you good day?"

"No, you may not," Lady Frederick said imperturbably. "You are quite right to be angry; so should I be if I were in your place. But I will tell you to your head that you are a fool if you allow that to weigh with you. If your situation is indeed as desperate as my son informs me it is, you should be grateful for any attempt, no matter how ungraciously offered, to assist you."

Miss Dowie seemed slightly mollified by her guest's frank characterisation of her own conduct, and appeared to be on the point of making some milder rejoinder when the door leading into the adjoining chamber was opened and Cecily herself came into the room. At sight of the visitors she checked.

"Mr. Ranleigh!" she exclaimed. "Oh, I did not know that it was you!"

"I have brought my mother to see you," Mr. Ranleigh explained, rising. He turned to Lady Frederick. "May I present Miss Hadley to you, ma'am?" he said.

Lady Frederick surveyed Miss Hadley in a single eagle glance that took in her outmoded frock, her beautifully erect figure, and the entire lack of anything resembling artifice in her appearance. The result seemed to satisfy her, for she said, "Come here, child," and indicated to her son that he should place a chair for Cecily beside her. Upon his complying, Cecily obediently sat down, looking at her ladyship rather wonderingly. Lady Frederick, in her customary imperious manner, tilted up her chin the better to survey her face, and, having completed her inspection, remarked decisively, "You are quite right, Robert; she has certainly the look of your grandmother Hadley. A disgraceful business, this! How came you to be in such straits, my dear? Did your father make *no* provision for you?"

"I am afraid, ma'am, he was very—very deeply in debt during the last years of his life," Cecily stammered.

Miss Dowie, who had also sat down again, interpolated at this point, "If you must know, ma'am, he had a pair of Nasty Habits—gaming and drinking. Well, they have been the ruin of wealthier men than he was! The long and short of it is that when he died everything went—house, land, furniture, the very jewellery that should have come to my pet. We were left with the clothes on our backs and little more. But *that*," she added, "is no concern of yours, my lady. I have told Cecily plainly that she has no claim on Mr. Ranleigh, nor has she any more on you." She sent a glance of marked disfavour at Mr. Ranleigh, who had been content to watch the proceedings thus far with an air of detached but somewhat unholy amusement. "Not," she said tartly, "that he hasn't brought it on himself. If he had not tried to lure her into pursuits which no virtuous young lady——"

"Nonsense!" said Lady Frederick. "I expect he has explained to you that the whole affair was simply the result of a foolish wager. My son has a great many faults, Miss Dowie, but I can assure you that seducing schoolroom misses is not one of them."

"Thank you!" Mr. Ranleigh said sardonically.

Cecily, regarding him with interest, caught the gleam in his eyes and was encouraged to inquire whether he would lose a great deal of money by her flight from his invitation.

"Not at all," he said. "It is my cousin who laid the wager—not I."

"And a pretty wager it was!" Miss Dowie said. "Your friends may think very highly of you, Mr. Ranleigh, to expect that you would succeed where the lot of them had failed, but let me tell you that in *my* day a gentleman who would lend himself to such a game would be thought no better than an impudent coxcomb."

Lady Frederick, who unexpectedly appeared to find this sally to her liking, said with satisfaction, "Ha! You have caught it this time, Robert—and quite rightly, too. However," she went on, to Miss Dowie, "that has nothing whatever to say to your predicament. I will tell you flatly that I believe my son is quite right in his opinion that your niece must instantly be removed from the situation in which she now finds herself. Indeed, I wonder that you should ever have permitted her to enter it!"

"I assure you, ma'am," Miss Dowie said, "that it is not my wish to see her in it! I had hoped that she might be able to find employment as an instructress of the young in some respectable household on her father's death, in which case I should have gone into lodgings near her and taken up whatever occupation might have come to my hand, whether it was giving lessons or trimming hats. But our inquiries in Hampshire were quite unsuccessful, and we soon found ourselves in such straits that we were obliged to accept Mr. Jillson's offer to bring us to London."

"Well, I do think," Lady Frederick said candidly, "that you might have considered that you were likely to fall into some such predicament before you quarrelled with your brother—not that it appears to me, from what my son tells me, that his roof would be one under which a modest young female might properly be placed."

Miss Dowie sat up straighter, looking at Mr. Ranleigh. "I thought you told me you was not acquainted with my brother!" she accused him.

"At the time, that was quite correct," he informed her, gravely. "However, on yesterday I had the pleasure of making not only his acquaintance, but also—Mrs. Cassaday's, I believe it is?"

"Aha!" Miss Dowie said, nodding martially. "So he has carried that creature up to town with him, has he? As much as I should deplore such a connexion, I have told him to his head that if he won't get rid of the woman he ought to marry her—but it would be too much, I daresay, to expect him to do either."

"Yes, I believe so," Mr. Ranleigh acknowledged. "I will do him the justice to say that he *did* offer your niece a home, ma'am—rather reluctantly, and most pointedly excluding any possibility that he would do the same for you. But that arrangement appeared to me, in view of Mrs. Cassaday's situation and—may I say?—your brother's own character, scarcely a satisfactory one."

"You may say what you please," Miss Dowie handsomely allowed. "The man is a Monster, as I have told you before."

"In that case," Lady Frederick said briskly, "you must, I believe, place yourself in our hands, Miss Dowie," and she thereupon proceeded to lay before her the scheme her son had unfolded to her the day before.

Miss Dowie and Cecily heard the plans that had been made for them with equal astonishment, but with widely differing sentiments. Miss Dowie appeared to be dealing darkly with the notion that a lady as obviously unconventional as Lady Frederick, and as indisputably a member of those tonnish circles whose moral principles she held in high suspicion, might be lending herself to the furtherance of some deep-laid design of her son's on Cecily's virtue. On the other hand, Cecily was gazing at Mr. Ranleigh with a flush of gratitude on her face—an emotion which prompted her to exclaim to him impulsively, "Oh, I *don't* know how I am to thank you—and when I had been thinking such horrid things about you, too, after you went away yesterday without a word! It all goes to prove, I daresay, that Aunt is right when she says one should *never* judge by appearances!"

Mr. Ranleigh, though unaccustomed to the idea that his appearance might be such as to prejudice any young lady against him, accepted this rather backhanded compliment without visible perturbation, merely remarking that he hoped they might consider the matter settled then. He added that, if the two ladies would be in readiness to leave London on the following morning, his travelling-chaise would call for them at nine.

But this statement again brought Miss Dowie's suspicions to the fore.

"Travel to Sussex in *your* company, sir?" she inquired, her face plainly betraying her mistrust.

"By no means," Mr. Ranleigh said. "I do not go down to Hillcourt at present. However, as my mother is travelling with her companion and her maid, it will be a more comfortable arrangement, I believe, if you and your niece make use of my chaise."

Miss Dowie could find no fault with this, but she had one more rub to throw in the way—the matter, she confessed, with a rather truculent lift of the chin that showed how much against the grain it went with her to mention it, of the fifteen pounds Mr. Jillson had lent them.

"It has been impossible for us to repay the whole of it as yet," she said, "and I do not see how we can go off while we are still in his debt——"

Mr. Ranleigh, in a matter-of-fact tone, assured her that nothing could be simpler than for him to advance her a sufficient sum to allow her to satisfy Mr. Jillson's claim before she left London, advising her, by the way, to place the money in trustworthy hands for delivery to him *after* her departure, so that that gentleman's active curiosity would not be aroused as to the source of her sudden affluence. His failure to suggest anything so repugnant to her independent nature as the notion that this new debt need not be repaid did much to raise her opinion of him, but she kept her expressions of gratitude meagre until, upon his opening the door as he and Lady Frederick rose to take their leave, Jillson was discovered lounging outside in the passage. This transparent piece of surveillance cast her at once on Mr. Ranleigh's side as he undertook, with a few pithy words that quickly erased the genial smile from Jillson's face, to send the interloper about his business.

"I vow I shall be so glad to be rid of that creeping rascal that I would almost put myself under the devil's protection to do so!" she declared—and thereupon informed Mr. Ranleigh with the greatest cordiality that she and Cecily would certainly be ready to leave at the time appointed.

Mr. Ranleigh, having escorted his mother back to Mount Street—a journey enlivened by her handsome acknowledgement that he had acted quite properly, for once in his life, by undertaking to remove a gently bred child from the influence of such a rogue as Jillson—repaired, with some relief at having disposed of the matter of Miss Cecily Hadley, to White's. Here he was at once accosted by Lord Portandrew.

"The very man I wanted to see!" his lordship declared, dragging him upstairs to the card-room. "Made a regular nuisance of myself yesterday, calling at Mount Street—but, deuce take it, I want to know what you've done about my wager!"

"Done?" Mr. Ranleigh said calmly. "Nothing at all. You will have to pay, Tony. I warned you not to lay your blunt on me."

"Yes, but—but——!" his lordship sputtered indignantly. "You said she'd appointed you a meeting! Didn't you go?"

"Oh yes, I went," Mr. Ranleigh replied. "But that fellow Jillson was quite right, you know. The girl is very well guarded. If I were you, I should give the whole thing up."

"Give—it—up!" His lordship sent him an incredulous stare. "Dash it all, Robert, I can't do that! I'm in love with her!"

Mr. Ranleigh grinned slightly. "Coming it a bit too strong, Tony!" he said. "You've said the same thing at least half a dozen times before."

"Yes, but this is *different!*" Lord Portandrew said, revolted by his cousin's lack of perception. "I *must* manage to meet her, one way or the other!" He looked darkly at Mr. Ranleigh. "It's *my* opinion you're hiding something from me," he said. "*I* know that smug look of yours. You've probably come to an understanding with her yourself and now you want *me* to step out of the picture. Well, I won't do it, Robert, and that's flat! She may have been dazzled by your reputation, but when she comes to know us both she's bound to realise that *I'm* the one with the sincere, generous, and affectionate nature——"

Mr. Ranleigh grinned again. "Will you *stop* making a cake of yourself, Tony?" he begged. "I have come to no 'understanding' with Miss Daingerfield-Nelson, nor have I the slightest desire to do so."

"Well, you might make the attempt, at any rate!" Lord Portandrew argued inconsistently. "Deuce take it, we shall have Brackenridge crowing over us this month to come. Pretty figures we shall cut! I expect you know he's spread the story all over town already?"

"Oh, yes. Gussie Comerford told me," Mr. Ranleigh said, quite unmoved.

"Well, I must say I never thought you would be so poor-spirited as to let it be said that Brackenridge had cut you out!" his lordship said. "Because he will, you know! He'd do anything to get the better of you, and he'll be more than ever determined to if you admit you've failed. What's more, he'll succeed. See if he don't!"

"Oh, I rather doubt that," Mr. Ranleigh said carelessly.

But his volatile kinsman, his mind already diverted into new channels, interrupted any further reassurances by remarking abruptly, "By the bye, if you won't make a push to help me win *that* wager, you might with another. *Are* you going to offer for Gussie Comerford? I can get two to one here that you ain't."

Mr. Ranleigh looked a trifle startled. "Good God, are they laying bets on *that?*" he asked.

"Why, yes! I thought you knew. Your mother's been puffing the match, and I must say I thought myself you were going to come up to scratch this time." His lordship looked at Mr. Ranleigh somewhat severely. "You've been more than a little particular in your attentions to her, you know!"

Mr. Ranleigh, conscious that the matter was a sore point with his cousin, whose unsuccessful pursuit of Miss Comerford during the season just past had been notorious, returned a soothing answer and turned the subject—a ruse that served very well, as the topic he chose was the possibility of his agreeing to sell his lordship a pair of chestnuts much coveted by him.

But it was not so easy for him to dismiss the matter from his own mind. There was a slight, thoughtful frown between his brows as he left the club a few minutes later. He had no great wish to marry, but he was conscious that he had reached a period in his life at which it would be natural for him to do so. The debutantes of a dozen seasons having failed to do more than bore him with their compliant manners and eager smiles, he supposed he might do worse than to offer for Gussie Comerford, who—in addition to possessing birth and beauty—had a lack of conventionality which made her company less insipid than that of most of her contemporaries.

And since, he concluded the argument in her favour ironically, he was past the age at which a man is green enough to look for romance, what odds did it make that he was not in love with her nor she with him? Gussie's affections, he had reason to believe, would never be deeply engaged; her disposition was both restless and shallow, but this was a matter of no great moment to him. She would be admirably suited to take her place in society as the wife of a man who was one of its leaders, and he did not doubt his ability to keep her in hand if she were to do him the honour of becoming his wife.

The only thing necessary, therefore, to the settling of his future was the speaking of some half dozen words by him, but it was odd how little satisfaction this comfortable reflection appeared to give to him. On the contrary, his mother, when he returned to Mount Street, considered that he looked unwontedly unapproachable, and, attributing his mood to the disagreeable business in regard to Miss Hadley that had been occupying him for the past two days, thought it was as well that he was not escorting her to Hillcourt. She promised herself to settle Miss Hadley and her aunt in some suitable situation quickly; if she did not, she told herself, with a sardonic lift of the brows that made her look momentarily very like her son, it might be some time before Robert decided that he would favour Hillcourt with his presence.

6 Miss Hadley, arriving at Mr. Ranleigh's country seat in Sussex on the following day, had, for her part, an exhilarating feeling that she was living in a dream, from which she was not at all anxious to awaken. From the moment when, stepping into Mr. Ranleigh's elegant travelling-chaise, she had leaned her head against its blue-velvet squabs to the moment when, as the chaise rounded a turn in the road that led from the lodge-gates to the house, she saw the rose-pink brick walls of Hillcourt for the first time, she had felt that she had been pitchforked into the very lap of luxury. Lady Frederick, riding before her in her own carriage, impressively flanked by outriders, might, she reflected, have been a fairy godmother, so magical had been the transformation she had wrought from the dirt and discomfort of the Running Boar to her present situation.

Her sense of living in a fairy tale did not diminish when, upon entering the house, she was conducted up an imposing staircase to the west wing, where, in a bedchamber furnished in the first style of elegance, she found a comfortable fire sending the light of its flames flickering over the rose silk curtains that shut out the November dusk outside.

She was not aware that Hillcourt—built during the Restoration by a peer who had been obliged to see it pass into the hands of an immensely wealthy Northumberland family—was held in rather low esteem by the Ranleighs, who considered it one of the less interesting of their seats. It had come into the family on the marriage of Mr. Ranleigh's father to the heiress into whose possession it had passed—a damsel who had obligingly died without issue within two years, leaving Lord Frederick free to offer for his first love, Louisa Wymberly, who had unfortunately not possessed the fortune considered necessary for the wife of the fourth son of the Duke of Belfour. Hillcourt, the Ranleighs were used to say, was elegant and convenient, but it had no history; but Cecily, relaxing in an armchair with hot tea and macaroons before her, while an abigail deftly unpacked her few belongings, was in no mood to pine for Tudor glories. She thought the room she was in the most beautiful she had ever seen in her life, and the entire house of a magnificence that was almost breathtaking.

A knock shortly sounded on the door, and, thinking it was her aunt come to compare notes with her on the journey, she called, "Come in." To her surprise, a slender boy of about fourteen, with a thin, mischievous countenance, walked into the room.

"Hello!" he said cheerfully. "Are you Miss Hadley? I'm Neagle—that is,

you may call me Charlie if you like. Everyone else does. Don't they,
Alice?"

The abigail, who had finished the unpacking, gave him a giggle and
then, recollecting herself, a disapproving look.

"Now, my lord," she said, "you'd best run along. I'll warrant her la'ship
and Mr. Tibble don't know you're here!"

"You're right. They don't," Lord Neagle agreed, coming across the room
and selecting a macaroon from the dish before Cecily. "Nor are they
likely to miss me, I might say, because Mrs. Wixom is having hysterics in
the Small Saloon. I knew she would," he went on, disinterestedly biting
into the macaroon. "As a matter of fact, I tried to lay a wager on it with
Tibble, but he wouldn't take it."

Cecily, regarding the young gentleman with mingled astonishment and
amusement, delved into her memory for a reference Lady Frederick had
made to the effect that her young grandson, Lord Neagle, and his tutor
were at present staying at Hillcourt, during the Dowager Lady Neagle's
absence in Jamaica for reasons of health. Cecily had understood that
young Lord Neagle had not been sent to Eton as yet, also for reasons of
health—but, surveying the boy before her, she was inclined to concur with
Lady Frederick's opinion that there was nothing wrong with his lordship's
health, but something amiss with his mother's judgement.

"Ever since she lost Neagle—an accident on the hunting field, which
had nothing at all to do with the state of his health—she has been quack-
ing herself and fussing over the boy," Lady Frederick had said. "I see that
I shall have to interfere in the matter myself, for he needs to be sent to
school; Tibble has no control over him whatever. If it were not for Robert's coming down now and then and taking him in hand, he would be
quite insupportable! For the worst of it is that he is so engaging, you
know, that one cannot be severe with him!"

Cecily, as she looked at Lord Neagle, could well believe this statement
to be true. Within the space of five minutes he had routed Alice from the
room, devoured half the macaroons on the plate before him, and given her
an account of the scene that had just taken place in the Small Saloon,
where Mrs. Wixom, put in possession of an urgent message that had arrived for her that morning, to the effect that her niece had come down
with influenza and three of the children with the chicken pox, had instantly succumbed to a fit of hysterics.

She would soon, Lord Neagle gave it as his opinion, be on her way to
Derbyshire, which would be good riddance, as there was nothing he liked

less than being asked regularly how he did, in a tone of voice implying that she rather expected him to announce his imminent demise.

He then asked Cecily directly if she were indeed his cousin, and, if so, why a "suitable position" must be found for her.

"I should think you had rather marry someone instead," he remarked. "You're not at all bad-looking, you know."

"Oh, I should!" she admitted candidly. "But in the meantime I am dreadfully poor, you know, so I must find some way to support myself."

"That's what Tibble says," Lord Neagle said, nodding wisely. "He's my tutor—a curst rum touch, but he *does* manage to get on to most of what happens around here. It's my belief he gossips with the servants. Of course it's devilish hard to get anything out of him, but I have my methods, you see."

Cecily laughed. "I should rather think you had!" she said.

He grinned engagingly. "Well, you know, it's deuced dull down here when Robert's not around," he said. "How is Robert, by the way? I haven't clapped eyes on him this month. I rather *thought* he might have come down with Grandmama."

Cecily said that she believed Mr. Ranleigh was very well, and, conscious of an unaccountable desire to continue the conversation on this subject, unscrupulously encouraged Lord Neagle to go on talking of his uncle.

It was, she found, a topic on which he was most willing to expatiate. In a short space of time she had gathered that Mr. Ranleigh was quite by way of being the idol of his nephew, who considered him not only a prime gun, a nonesuch among whips, and a pattern of all those manly accomplishments which such milksops as Mr. Tibble were wont to frown on, but also a friend in need to a boy surrounded by the cautions of a pack of females.

With this opinion Cecily was quite willing to concur. Though she had told Mr. Ranleigh truthfully, on the occasion of his first visit to the Running Boar, that she was relieved to find that his interest in her was not of the kind that might have been expected of a gentleman who had issued an invitation to supper to an actress whom he had never met, she was not on that account immune to the attractions he presented. Moreover, having been reared in the seclusion of a country household, she had had ample time, before she had ever met him, to idealise the distant cousin whose exploits she had had no difficulty in becoming familiar with even in rural Hampshire.

And now that he had stepped into her life to rescue her so unexpectedly from her difficulties—quite in the best style of the heroes of romances—it was scarcely to be wondered at that she should agree even with the most extravagant of young Lord Neagle's encomiums.

He ended his panegyrics, however, on a gloomier note.

"The thing is, though," he informed her, "that I shall probably see a good deal less of him soon than I do even now. My mother is bound to come home from Jamaica before long and carry me off to Neagle House, and even if she don't, I expect Robert will be marrying Miss Comerford soon."

Cecily felt a sudden rather empty sensation in the pit of her stomach. "Oh?" she said, endeavouring to assume an appearance of impersonal interest. "Who is Miss Comerford?"

His lordship shrugged. "Well, they call her *L'Étoile*—that's French for *The Star*, you know," he said. "Tall girl, loads of black hair, green eyes—Lord Comerford's eldest daughter. All the Bloods are mad over her, but Tibble says it's Robert who is first oars with her."

Cecily remarked hollowly that she understood statuesque young ladies were the high kick of fashion just now, and inquired whether Mr. Ranleigh too was mad about *L'Étoile*.

"Oh, I shouldn't think so," his lordship said frankly. "But he's expected to marry, you know, so I daresay he will offer for her. I think it's a great nuisance myself; females always spoil things."

He then asked if Cecily rode, and, on being informed that she had done so since she had learned to walk, fell into a conversation with her on the subject of hunting that lasted until a scratching on the door heralded Miss Dowie's appearance.

Miss Dowie, attired in a black bombazine gown of ancient cut, received with some suspicion an introduction to Lord Neagle, and promptly gave it as her opinion that well-bred young gentlemen did not visit young ladies in the latter's bedchambers.

"Oh, well!" his lordship said, undaunted. "I'm her cousin—ain't I?"

"I doubt very much that your grandmother would care to hear you claim the relationship," Miss Dowie said tartly.

His lordship looked intrigued. "Wouldn't she?" he demanded. "Why? Ain't you respectable? You look deuced respectable to me!"

Miss Dowie regarded him austerely. "I daresay," she snapped, "if the truth were known, we are a great deal more respectable than a good few of your relations, my lord. We are *not*, however, affluent."

"Well, that makes no difference to *me*," Lord Neagle said equably, "and I shouldn't think it would to Grandmama, either—though," he added thoughtfully, "Tibble *did* drop a hint that I needn't go about on the high gab about your being here, because you weren't going into company."

Perceiving that he was scenting a mystery, Cecily promptly said, "We are in mourning, you see," and got up, saying she must not keep her aunt waiting.

The two ladies then went downstairs together, where they were shortly afterward served a dinner of two full courses, including, in addition to a number of side-dishes, semelles of carp removed with a few larded sweetbreads and a raised pie, a dressed lobster, a broiled fowl with mushrooms, and several jellies and creams. Cecily, dazzled by the array of silver dishes, the elegant footmen, and the imposing dimensions of the room, was glad that the company consisted only of Lady Frederick, Mrs. Wixom, and Mr. Tibble, a rather wispy-looking young man whose pale blue eyes wore a permanently disapproving expression, and that the conversation dealt almost exclusively with Mrs. Wixom's projected journey into Derbyshire.

After dinner the four ladies repaired to the Ivory Saloon. This was a double-cube room done in ivory and dull gold, the doorways and ceiling coves being decorated with gilded wood of such gossamer delicacy that Cecily could not refrain from an expression of delight on entering it.

She had little opportunity to examine it further, however, for Lady Frederick, seating herself on a sofa, indicated that she was to place herself beside her and at once began the conversation on a somewhat intimidating note.

"If I am to recommend you to my friends as a governess, child," she said, "it may be as well for you to tell me of your accomplishments. You play the harp or the pianoforte tolerably well, I collect?"

Cecily said doubtfully, "N-no, ma'am. Not very well, that is. You see, I had no instrument at home, though Mrs. Ackling *did* sometimes allow me to practise upon hers."

Lady Frederick shrugged. "Well, I daresay you will contrive," she said. "You paint in water colours, of course?"

"No, ma'am."

Her ladyship's brows rose. "Not?" she said. "Nor sketch?"

Cecily shook her head, casting an anguished glance of appeal at Miss Dowie.

"Well, upon my word!" her ladyship said, her colour rising slightly. "I must say I do not know what you can have been thinking of, my dear, to lead me on to believe you were qualified to become a governess! If I had had the slightest notion of your ignorance——"

But she got no farther, for at that moment Miss Dowie entered the lists.

"Ignorance!" she repeated. "I'll have you know, ma'am, that I consider my niece to have received as thorough an education as any young woman of her age in England—which is not surprising, since I instructed her myself. She has a considerable knowledge of ancient and modern history, is conversant with the most improving works of our English authors and those of antiquity——"

But this time it was her turn to be interrupted. "A blue-stocking!" Lady Frederick exclaimed, in accents of horror. "But, my dear Miss Dowie, such information is *quite* useless for the purposes for which your niece is to be employed. She will be expected to teach the accomplishments—music, sketching, a little French——"

"My niece's mind, let me assure you, has not been cluttered with such insipidities, ma'am," Miss Dowie said grandly. "It is my opinion that the shocking state of morality today is due solely to the faulty system on which our young females have been educated, and I should have considered myself derelict in my duty if I had not endeavoured to form Cecily's mind on quite other principles."

Cecily, perceiving that her aunt was launched on one of her favourite subjects, desperately put a question to Mrs. Wixom on the state of the roads she expected to find on her journey, but to no avail. That docile lady merely gave her a nervous stare, quite unwilling to put herself forward to interrupt her patroness's conversation, and the result was that for the ensuing quarter hour a battle-royal was waged over Cecily's hapless head.

As neither of the two ladies was in the least inclined to give ground, hostilities were abated only on the entrance of Mr. Tibble into the room after his enjoyment of a single abstemious glass of brandy in the dining-room. Lady Frederick, perceiving the inadvisability of continuing the subject before him, allowed it to drop, but not before she had promised roundly to write to her son that very evening to request his advice on what she was to do about recommending to her friends as governess a young woman who obviously had not the least qualification for the post.

7 She was as good as her word, and the letter that she penned duly arrived in Mount Street, just as Mr. Ranleigh was sitting down to breakfast on a chill grey morning. He had time, however, to do no more than break the seal and unfold the single sheet of which the letter consisted before the butler entered to announce the arrival of Lord Portandrew, and the next moment his lordship himself burst impetuously into the room.

"So I've caught you in!" he said, in a wrathful tone that set Mr. Ranleigh's brows instantly on the rise. "Well, I'm deuced glad of that, or I should have had to go chasing all over the town for you!" He waited until the butler had retreated and closed the door behind him, and then demanded, "I want to know—and don't try to fob me off, Robert!—exactly what you've done with that girl!"

Mr. Ranleigh carved a slice of ham in a leisurely manner. "Girl? What girl?" he inquired. "Care for breakfast, Tony?"

His lordship glanced, revolted, at his cousin's well-filled plate. "No, I do not care for breakfast!" he said. "And don't try to flummery me, Robert! You know very well what girl I mean. Miss Daingerfield-Nelson!"

"What about Miss Daingerfield-Nelson?" Mr. Ranleigh asked, still quite unmoved. "Really, Tony, you might have more tact than to come barging in at this hour posing conundrums. I spent last evening at the Daffy Club, and I don't seem to be quite at my best this morning."

"Well, I spent it at the theatre," Lord Portandrew declared, "and I'll have you know—only you probably know it already—that Miss Daingerfield-Nelson wasn't there!"

"Really? A trifle down pin, perhaps?" Mr. Ranleigh suggested. "Not feeling quite the thing?"

"She wasn't there," his lordship said, in a tone which implied that he was keeping his temper only by a heroic exercise of patience, "because she has disappeared! And what's more, I have a strong suspicion that *you* know where she has gone!"

Mr. Ranleigh's brows again went up. "What has led you to this rather startling conclusion?" he asked, imperturbably continuing his repast. "Can it be—let me guess—that you have been consulting the admirable Jillson?"

"Yes, I have!" his lordship said. "Well, what else was I to do? I go out of town for a few days and, dash it, the girl disappears—nobody knows where she's gone to—vanished into thin air. But that ain't the point," he continued severely. "The point is that fellow Jillson says *you* called to see her twice last week at her lodgings, and that on Friday she went off in a travelling-chaise that sounds to me curst like it might have been yours. Now what I want to know is just what kind of rig you're trying to run, Robert!"

"Did he also tell you, I wonder," Mr. Ranleigh asked, calmly buttering a slice of bread, "that on the second occasion I called on Miss—er— Daingerfield-Nelson I brought my mother to see her as well? Really, Tony, even you cannot be such a gudgeon as to believe that I should have done that if I had intended to run off with the girl!"

"Yes, but——" His lordship looked nonplussed. "He *did* tell me that," he confessed, "and I'll tell *you* that neither of us knew what to make of it. Deuce take it, even Aunt Louisa ain't broad-minded enough to help you make your way with the girl, though I daresay she knows well enough what games you are up to in the petticoat line!"

"Yes, I believe you are right," Mr. Ranleigh agreed, with a faint smile. "Mama seems to have an uncanny knack of knowing everything that is going on in town, even when she is buried in Sussex. In the present case, though, there is nothing for her to know. As I told you, I am not interested in Miss Daingerfield-Nelson. She is a very innocent and inexperienced young girl whom Mama has now removed from an excessively uncomfortable situation and placed in one more suitable to her years and education." He paused, regarding his cousin, whose face was rapidly taking on a beet-red hue, with a solicitous eye. "Feeling a trifle out of curl, Tony? You don't look at all well," he remarked.

"Don't look well!" his lordship exploded. "No, I should think I didn't! Look here, Robert, if you think I'm such a flat that I'll swallow *that* story, you're dicked in the nob! Aunt Louisa wouldn't concern herself over a girl like that, and even if she would—it would have to have been you who put her up to it, and if you think I'll believe *you*'ve turned philanthropist——"

"I haven't," Mr. Ranleigh assured him. "And I'm not asking you to believe anything except that the girl is now out of your reach—as well as out of Brackenridge's, Lovett's, and the rest of that set's. If I were you, I should forget her."

"I'm hanged if I will!" his lordship vowed, his ordinarily good-humoured face still alarmingly wrathful. "Oh, I know what it is: you've crept into her confidence and lured her out of town—though how you brought Aunt Louisa into it I'm dashed if I can think! And what do you intend to do with her when you've tired of your game, you—you Bluebeard! That girl ain't one of your birds of paradise that you can send to the right-about with a king's ransom in diamonds around her neck and no hard feelings on either side! Deuce take it, she's hardly out of the schoolroom!"

"Just so," Mr. Ranleigh said coolly. "Which makes me wonder—since you realise that—what your own plans were concerning her. You did not contemplate marrying her, I believe?" Lord Portandrew opened his mouth, shut it again, and contented himself with glaring at his cousin. "Exactly," Mr. Ranleigh said. "And now, if you don't mind—the subject is beginning to bore me. You won't object if I go on reading my letters?"

His lordship did object, but nothing he said seemed to affect Mr. Ranleigh to the extent of distracting his attention from his correspondence. He was, in fact, perusing Lady Frederick's epistle with a frown of irritation, seeing his plans for driving to Epsom that day—where a meeting between a promising young pugilist and a famous veteran of the Ring was to take place—going glimmering in the face of his mother's imperatives. For Lady Frederick had stated in no uncertain terms that she expected him to come down to Hillcourt at once and resolve the question of what was to be done with his protégée, now that finding employment for her as a governess was clearly out of the question.

Lord Portandrew, coming out of an indignant harangue to note his cousin's expression of displeased abstraction, momentarily forgot his injuries and inquired with curiosity, "Bad news? Ain't that my aunt's hand? Can't mistake it—as stiff-backed as if she used a ramrod instead of a pen! Nothing wrong at Hillcourt, I hope?"

"No—nothing of any consequence. But it is a curst nuisance: I expect I shall have to go down there for a few days." Mr. Ranleigh glanced up, saw a suspicious look cross his lordship's face, and added carelessly, "It appears that Mrs. Wixum has been obliged to go off suddenly to succour her niece's family, and Mama is at a stand without her. She is not as young as she once was, you know," he said shamelessly, "and these things upset her more than they were used to."

It was fortunate that Lady Frederick did not hear this allusion to her failing powers fall from her son's lips, for she was in poor enough charity with him as it was, when he arrived at Hillcourt later that day. He found her in the Small Saloon, writing letters, and was greeted with an even brusquer coolness than that with which her fondness for him was customarily expressed.

"So you are come!" she said. "And high time, I must say!"

Mr. Ranleigh laughed, kissing the cheek that was austerely offered to him, and then sitting down in an armchair opposite his mother and stretching his long legs, clad in buckskins and top-boots, comfortably out before him.

"Nonsense!" he said. "I set out the moment I had your letter, and driving my own curricle, in this weather, so that I should arrive before you had had the opportunity to grow out of reason cross. But I see my best efforts have been in vain."

"I am *not* cross!" Lady Frederick corrected him starchily. "I *am*, however, highly perturbed. Tell me at once, if you have the faintest idea— *what* am I to do with that tiresome girl?"

"*Is* she tiresome, ma'am?" Mr. Ranleigh asked. "I am sorry to hear that; I should not have imagined——"

"No, no, of course not!" Lady Frederick made a gesture of compunction. "I ought not to have used such a term. Miss Dowie, indeed, is one of the most opinionated females I have ever met, so that I am compelled— yes, compelled!—to quarrel with her half a dozen times a day; but the child has been nothing if not obliging. Still, you *must* see what a position you have put me into by cozening me into bringing her down here, Robert! I do not know what I am to do with her, for naturally I cannot send her back to the theatre and that horrid Jillson."

Mr. Ranleigh, looking at his mother's face, realised, without a great deal of surprise, that what was disturbing her was not the vexation of having an unwanted guest on her hands, but rather a genuine concern for Miss Hadley's future. Lady Frederick's sharp tongue, he knew, concealed a generous heart, and it would have been odd if Miss Hadley, with her engaging ways, had not been able to arouse the same sympathy in it that various categories of philanthropic objects, from mistreated sweeps to unwed mothers, had previously done.

He was wise enough not to put his perceptions into words, however, but merely inquired calmly, "Where is the girl now?"

"In the billiard-room, with Charlie. He is teaching her the game; the two of them, I should tell you, deal extremely together. She is quite as daring as he in the saddle, it seems, and they have been roaming all over the countryside together—to Damer's dismay. He vows they would be in less danger of breaking their necks if they were hunting with the hardest goers in Leicestershire. What Maria would say if she were to hear of it, I do *not* know!"

Mr. Ranleigh shrugged. "Well, there is no need to coddle the boy up to

Maria's notions," he said. "If it is her scheme to confine him to the pace of an elderly groom mounted on a slug——"

"Yes, I know!" Lady Frederick agreed, thawing somewhat toward her son in her agreement with his criticism of his elder sister. "Really, I can't think how I ever came to have such an odiously *sober* daughter as Maria, and I am sure it is even worse for Charlie to have her as a mother." She then recollected herself and said more severely, "But *that* has nothing to say to the problem. What *are* we to do with that child, Robert? She is *quite* unfit, it seems, to be a governess, for her aunt has stuffed her mind with Latin and history, to the entire neglect of any feminine accomplishments——"

"What accomplishments?" Mr. Ranleigh asked impatiently. "The ability to strum a little upon the pianoforte and to produce abominable water colours? Good God, Mama, if the girl is intelligent enough to learn Latin, she can certainly be crammed with enough of that nonsense in a month or two to permit her to pass herself off with sufficient credit to instruct schoolgirls!"

Lady Frederick stared at him, throwing back her head with an expression of surprise and reluctant approval upon her face.

"Sometimes, Robert, you quite astonish me!" she said. "That is an excellent plan—I wonder that it did not occur to *me!* I shall send to Binkie at once. Nothing will delight her more than to return to Hillcourt for a time —and though she may be superannuated, she is still perfectly competent, I am sure."

With her customary impetuosity, she immediately returned to her writing-table to compose an urgent message to Miss Tabitha Binkley, the lady who had instructed her own daughters many years ago and who now lived in retirement in Bognor Regis; and Mr. Ranleigh, seeing that he was *de trop,* strolled off down the hall to the billiard-room.

Here he was at once pounced upon by his young nephew.

"Robert!" Lord Neagle exclaimed, in jubilant tones. "How long have you been here? You might have told a fellow! *I* didn't know you were coming!"

"Didn't know it myself until this morning," Mr. Ranleigh said, allowing his gaze to wander idly from his nephew to Miss Hadley, who was standing at the other side of the room, a billiard cue in her hand and a look of rather shy inquiry on her face. "Well, Miss Hadley," he said, "I am glad to see you have made friends with Charlie." He glanced down again at his nephew, who had not ceased to pour out importunate quer tions. "Take a damper, Charlie!" he commanded. "I don't know myself how long I'm staying. A day or two, I expect—until I can arrange Miss Hadley's affairs to your grandmother's satifaction."

"Is that all?" his lordship said indignantly. "Come all the way down here and then go straight back to London again!" He looked out the window at a few flakes of snow blowing by in the wintry dusk and declared, "I hope it comes on to snow for a week! Then you won't be able to leave. And I call it dashed unhandsome of you, too, to come for Cecily when you wouldn't for me!"

"Ah," Mr. Ranleigh said, with a faint smile which Cecily, watching him, could only characterise as perfectly indifferent, "but Miss Hadley is a responsibility, you see, Charlie, and you are not."

Miss Hadley, who had spent some few of her waking hours since she had come to Hillcourt in picturing the circumstances of her next meeting with Mr. Ranleigh, in all of which shy dreams she had been distinguished by that gentleman's interested attentions to her, began to experience a sense of strong ill-usage. If, she thought indignantly, Mr. Ranleigh considered her only as a burdensome charge, why had he taken her up in the first place? Obviously his only interest at the present moment was in his nephew, for, though it was clear that it was her dilemma that had drawn him down to Hillcourt, he did not so much as mention that subject to her, but only went on chatting with Lord Neagle about hunting and other such mundane matters.

It did not make her feel any more kindly toward him to learn from Miss Dowie, when she went upstairs to dress for dinner shortly afterward, that he had already settled on a plan for her future. She was, her aunt informed her, to be instructed in the female accomplishments by the lady who had been charged with the education of his sisters, after which her original scheme of becoming a governess might be carried out. Cecily, finding her difficulties thus summarily disposed of, characterised his behaviour roundly as highhanded, only to find, to her surprise, that her aunt quite failed to agree with her.

"Decision," Miss Dowie said approvingly. "I like that. No dithering or pondering or beating about the bush. Walked into the house and in ten minutes, Lady Frederick tells me, had the matter in hand."

"But he did not say a word to *me* about it!" Cecily said, quite unmollified. A recalcitrant expression appeared upon her face, and she said, "Perhaps I do not choose to be instructed by Miss Binkley!"

"That has nothing to say to the matter!" Miss Dowie said tartly. "You will do as you are told and apply yourself diligently—*and* express your gratitude properly to Mr. Ranleigh for the considerable trouble and expense you are putting him to. I confess I scarcely expected, when I first met him, to find him a man of sense and proper feeling, but he is acting in this matter just as he ought, and so I have told him. Give the devil his due!" she added, nodding briskly as she went off to her own room to prepare for dinner.

Cecily was left to stare dissatisfiedly at her reflection in the mirror—a quite absurdly youthful one, she considered, for her years—and to wish that, only for this one evening, she might be able to wear any of the fashionable gowns which she had displayed in the theatre, and which would make it quite clear to anyone that she was *not* a child to be ordered off to the schoolroom.

As it was, she was obliged to content herself with dressing her hair modishly high on her head, and she did not even succeed in exhibiting this piece of sophistication in the dining-room, for Miss Dowie, coming back into her bedchamber when it was time to go below, took one look at her coiffure and, declaring it highly improper for a girl who aspired to be a governess, obliged her to arrange her dark locks in the plainest style.

It appeared, indeed, that Miss Dowie, in spite of her commendation of Mr. Ranleigh's conduct, did not entirely trust that gentleman to keep the line, and was anxious for her niece to attract as little of his attention as possible. But her care was found to be quite unnecessary. Mr. Ranleigh addressed scarcely half a dozen words to Cecily at dinner, and if his eyes rested on her in any but the most casual way it was more than Miss Dowie's sharpest inspection could discover.

Since he behaved toward Miss Dowie herself, however, with the greatest civility, she found herself more than ever of the opinion that she had wronged him in her first summing up at the Running Boar.

"I am quite certain now that it was only that excessively ill-advised wager of his cousin's that made him seek you out," she said, "for there was nothing in the least particular in his manner toward you this evening. But that is not surprising, for it would be very odd indeed if a man of his stamp were to look twice at a mere child like you." She went on, with the air of one making a large concession, "I have been thinking that it might be proper for you to work a pair of slippers to present to him at Christmas——"

But she got no farther, for Cecily, rising impetuously to her feet, declared that she had no intention of spending a moment of her time in preparing gifts for a person who looked upon her in the light of a probably undeserving object of charity.

"I am sure Papa would not have liked it in the least for us to be beholden to someone who cares nothing for us except that anyone connected with *his* family should not be an embarrassment to him!" she said, rather incoherently. "No, and *I* do not like it——"

"Your papa," Miss Dowie interrupted scathingly, "was never in his life averse to being beholden to anyone! You are behaving like a ninny-hammer, Cecily! Sit down!"

Cecily, after a rebellious moment, did so, and was then treated to a pungent lecture on the sin of ingratitude, and an ultimatum to behave properly toward a gentleman who had nothing but her best interests at heart or risk her aunt's serious displeasure.

"Well, I do not care!" Cecily said unrepentantly, as Miss Dowie wound to a close. "Everyone else in this house toadeats him abominably, exactly as if he were the Emperor of China; but I do not care how rich and fashionable he is, and how *condescending!* I do not wish to be condescended to! And I shall *not* toadeat him, no matter what *you* choose to do!"

Having relieved her feelings by this outburst, she felt a great deal better, and, as she had quite as much spirit as her aunt, determined to put aside the agreeable dreams in which she had been indulging and think no more about them. This was not the easiest thing to do, with Mr. Ranleigh actually under the same roof, where she would be obliged to see him several times each day. But she consoled herself with the reflection that he would remain at Hillcourt only for a day or two, and that by the time she saw him again—if, indeed, she saw him at all—she would have quite got over her foolishness in regard to him.

8

As it happened, however, the following day brought a pair of events which made a considerable alteration in Mr. Ranleigh's plans.

The first of these was the fulfillment of Lord Neagle's wish in regard to the weather. Long before noon the leaden skies from which a few snowflakes had occasionally fallen during the night had darkened ominously, and his lordship, who had been induced to leave the house for his customary morning ride with Cecily only by his reluctant realisation that his uncle would undoubtedly feel no overwhelming desire for his company at such an early hour, was obliged to agree with Damer that the thickening snowfall made it advisable for them to return to the house.

The second event was the arrival at Hillcourt, at a moment approximately coinciding with this decision, of a curricle-and-four driven by Lord Portandrew. He was looking extremely cold and uncomfortable—in spite of the splendour of an elegant driving-coat sporting no fewer than sixteen shoulder-capes—as he tossed the reins to his groom and walked up the steps to the front door; and the evident surprise of Welbore, the elderly butler, on seeing him appeared to do nothing to dispel the rather defiant anxiety his mien proclaimed.

"I beg your pardon, my lord—was her ladyship expecting you?" Welbore inquired, as he received the driving-coat, his lordship's curly-brimmed beaver, and his York tan driving gloves and passed them into the care of a footman.

"Well, no, she ain't," his lordship confessed. "Matter of fact, I didn't expect to be here myself, but—long drive—deuced uncomfortable weather, you know——"

Welbore, who had been acquainted with his lordship since he had been a schoolboy at Eton, reflected tolerantly that this was another of Master Tony's starts, and said soothingly that he believed her ladyship was in the breakfast-parlour with Mr. Ranleigh. But the mention of his cousin's name, far from soothing his lordship, appeared to have exactly the opposite effect.

"Oh—he's here, is he?" he said, nervously. "Wondered about that. Anyone else, Welbore? I mean to say—any guests staying in the house?"

Welbore, who was quite aware that there was some mystery connected with the two ladies her ladyship had brought back with her from London, coughed and said cautiously that there were.

"Oh?" His lordship appeared struck. "A young lady?"

"A young lady *and* an older lady," Welbore replied, still discreet. "Perhaps you would like me to announce you, my lord?"

"No, I—— Well I'd as lief announce myself!" his lordship said hastily. "Deuced awkward business, coming in like this—— Might be as well——"

He did not complete this muddled speech, but walked down the hall in the direction of the breakfast-parlour. The door to this apartment was standing open, and as he approached it he appeared to reconnoitre, for the purpose—it seemed to the puzzled Welbore—of seeing who was inside it.

His behaviour was equally puzzling to Lady Frederick, who was sitting facing the door and thus had the advantage of observing her nephew's peculiarly indirect approach.

"Anthony?" she exclaimed in astonishment. "Is that you? What in the world are you doing here?"

His lordship, even in his confusion at being thus addressed by the lady who—as he had once confessed to his cousin—always had the ability to make him feel himself nine years old again, with his fingers in a jam jar, was able to observe that there was a none-too-pleased expression in his cousin's eyes as he turned in his chair to survey him. His lordship coughed, and plunged into speech.

"Hello, Robert!" he said, in a propitiatory voice. "Rather thought I'd find you here. Aunt Louisa——" He bent over her hand.

"Why shouldn't you find me here?" Mr. Ranleigh asked, not very cordially. "I told you I was coming—didn't I? But what the devil are *you* doing here? That's what *I* want to know."

"Yes," Lady Frederick concurred, "for I haven't invited you, Anthony; I am quite sure of *that*. Are you absolutely certain you've come to the right house, my dear boy? You *know* what a wretched memory you have!"

Lord Portandrew made a disclamatory sound in his throat. "Don't mean to stay," he managed to articulate. "Took a fancy yesterday afternoon to drive down and see Great-aunt Ethelreda—racked up last night at the King's Head at Cuckfield—thought I'd just pop in on you this morning on the way——"

He paused, seeing that both his aunt and his cousin were regarding him with patent disbelief.

"Great-aunt Ethelreda!" Lady Frederick exclaimed. "Why should you wish to visit her? I am sure you haven't been near her since you were out of short-coats!"

"Exactly the point!" His lordship seized on the idea. "Deuced long time, you see—old lady growing devilish feeble, I've no doubt——"

"And she has *no* fortune at all to dispose of, if you *are* run off your legs —which I don't for a moment believe, with *your* income," Lady Frederick said, fixing severely penetrating eyes upon him. "Anthony, tell me this instant—are you *foxed,* at this hour of the morning?"

Mr. Ranleigh smiled a trifle sardonically, as his cousin attempted a horrified denial. "No, he's not foxed," he said. "Nor, may I add, has he any intention of visiting Great-aunt Ethelreda. You came to spy—didn't you, Tony? Have you pumped Welbore yet? What did you discover?"

His lordship reddened indignantly. "Well, I must say, that's a deuced disagreeable way to put it!" he declared. "I have half a mind to walk straight out of here and go on with my journey—though," he added, looking doubtfully at the snow now swirling down thickly outside the window, "it's come on dashed unpleasant out there in the past half hour. Never would have left the King's Head if I'd known——"

"Oh, sit down, Tony!" Mr. Ranleigh said, with an impatient shrug. "Now you are here, I suppose you will have to be told—but I hope to God you will have sense enough to keep a discreet tongue in your head!" He explained to Lady Frederick, "The fact is, ma'am, that Tony has come in search of Miss Daingerfield-Nelson, whom he is persuaded I have brought down from London for—er—purposes too indelicate to mention before a lady."

Lord Portandrew's face had by this time become beet-red, but he stood his ground doggedly.

"Well, dash it, it's true—ain't it?" he demanded. "The girl *is* here— though how you have persuaded Aunt Louisa——"

He paused, intimidated by the affronted stare his aunt now turned upon him.

"Am I to understand, Anthony," she said awfully, "that you believe that I—*I!*—am lending countenance to an immoral exploit of my son's?"

Lord Portandrew hastily assured her that such an idea had never crossed his mind.

"Good God, no!" he said. "Merely occurred to me—plausible fellow, Robert—might have taken you in——"

He cast a glance of desperate appeal at Mr. Ranleigh, which his cousin callously ignored.

"No, don't look to *me* to bail you out," he said unsympathetically. "You got yourself into this, and you would be properly served now if Mama took it in snuff and showed you the door."

Her ladyship, as a matter of fact, appeared to be experiencing such

strong disapprobation of her nephew's conduct that it did not seem unlikely that she would do just that. But at that moment an interruption occurred in the form of young Lord Neagle, who came prancing into the
room with Cecily following rather shyly in his wake.

"Oh, I say, they told me you were having breakfast, Robert!" he began,
catching sight first of his uncle. Then, seeing Lord Portandrew, he broke
off, staring. "Tony! What are *you* doing here?" he exclaimed in surprise.

But Lord Portandrew had no eyes for him. He was gazing at Cecily
with an expression so comically compounded of incredulity, indignation,
and admiration on his face that Lord Neagle was moved to inquire of his
grandmother, "What's the *matter* with him? He looks moonstruck."

"He *is* moonstruck," Lady Frederick snapped. "Close your mouth, Anthony, and *do* try to look less like a perfect knock-in-the-cradle!" She said
to Cecily, "My dear, I think you had best go to your room. I am sure you
will find it much more agreeable there until I have got rid of this idiotic
nephew of mine!"

Cecily, who was looking quite at a loss over the powerful effect her appearance had had upon the unknown young dandy in her hostess's
breakfast-parlour, nodded in bewilderment, and was about to withdraw
when Lord Portandrew uttered a resounding negative.

"Not until I've got to the bottom of this!" he said violently. "Dash it,
Aunt Louisa, you *can't* expect to fob me off like this! I want to know what
Miss Daingerfield-Nelson is doing here!"

The sound of her stage name brought a modicum of enlightenment to
Cecily, and caused Mr. Ranleigh to say, with a flicker of amusement,
"You had as well tell him the whole, Mama, or you'll have him babbling
the affair all over London. Miss Hadley, may I make Lord Portandrew
known to you? He is the graceless cousin whose wager brought me to the
Running Boar. Tony, this is Miss Hadley, a young relative of mine who is
staying here at present, and will hopefully soon be employed as a governess in some respectable family. You will oblige her—and me as well—if you
will quite erase from your mind the fact that you ever saw her gracing the
boards as Miss Daingerfield-Nelson."

He paused, seeing that Lord Portandrew seemed to be incapable of as-
similating more information than had already been given him; but Lord
Neagle, quicker of apprehension, said, looking at Cecily with new respect,
"Jupiter! An actress! I always thought there was something smoky about
your coming here! But why do you want to be a governess if you can be
on the stage?"

"She wishes to become a governess," Lady Frederick said severely, "because she values the advantages of respectability—which is more, you scamp, than I can say of you!" She threw up her hands in despair. "Robert, what in the world are we to do now? Even if Anthony can be trusted to keep a quiet tongue in his head about all this, here is Charlie——"

"Charlie will say exactly nothing to anyone," Mr. Ranleigh said. "Do you understand that, Charlie? Under threat of my *severest* displeasure!"

Lord Neagle, awed, declared that wild horses would not succeed in dragging information from him, but Lord Portandrew was not so easily brought round. Recovering his tongue, he demanded fuller information, looking at his cousin meanwhile with an expression that appeared to warn him that he was dealing with a man who would see through any attempt to deceive him. Cecily, who was beginning to find the situation diverting, in spite of Mr. Ranleigh's obvious, if rather bored, irritation with his cousin, sat down beside Lady Frederick and listened with attention to the brief account that gentleman gave of her situation, now and then interrupting to clarify some point with a remark of her own. This at length had the effect of turning Mr. Ranleigh's exasperation upon her.

"We shall do very well without your help, Miss Hadley," he said. "My mother, I believe, has advised you to go to your room. May I suggest that you do so?"

She stood up, flushing, only to find Lord Portandrew at once springing to her defence.

"No, dash it all, Robert!" he said wrathfully. "You wouldn't speak to her so if she weren't alone in the world! What right have *you*——?"

"Will you *stop* trying to enact a Cheltenham tragedy over my breakfast-table, Tony?" Mr. Ranleigh begged. "I am beginning to find your addiction to high drama more than a little tiresome! Miss Hadley's affairs are no concern of yours; in fact, now that you have succeeded in prying out the information you came for, I strongly suggest that you take your leave of us and go on with your journey."

Lord Portandrew pointed out the window. "Can't do that," he said, in simple triumph. "Look at the weather. Couldn't send a dog out in a snowstorm like that. I shall have to stay."

A small chuckle escaped Cecily. Mr. Ranleigh said resignedly, "Oh, my God!" and then announced, to the unrepentant Miss Hadley, "In that case, you shall have your meals upstairs until my cousin leaves. I have no idea how much reliance can be placed on *your* good sense, but I have a fair idea of the amount Tony possesses, and—whatever he may think—I did *not* send you down here to have you subjected to improper solicitations."

"I wouldn't!" Lord Portandrew asseverated indignantly. "Dash it, Robert, you can't believe I'm such a loose-screw as that! I have the greatest respect for Miss Hadley! And if you think you are going to shut her up, like a dashed Turk with his what-do-you-call-it——"

"Harem," Cecily supplied helpfully.

"That's it!" his lordship said. "Well, if you think that, you're fair and far out! If you don't trust me to keep the line, I'll have *my* meals in my room!"

"To the best of my knowledge, you have no room," Mr. Ranleigh reminded him, repressively. "I don't recall anyone's asking you to stay."

"Yes, but we shall have to, my dear," Lady Frederick said, surveying the snow tumbling down outside the window. "I simply could not face Almeria if I were to turn Anthony out in such weather. You *know* what a hubble-bubble creature she is, and if he were to take a chill she would be certain to lay it at my door! I shall ring for Welbore and have your things taken up, Anthony," she went on severely, "but I warn you that if you cast so much as a glance at Miss Hadley that might be construed as particular, or disclose to anyone that she is Miss Daingerfield-Nelson, I shall be obliged to take steps. Very strong steps, in fact!"

What measures his aunt might take that would materially cut up his peace Lord Portandrew knew no more than any other person in the room, but her warning had the desired effect, and he promised fervently to give her no cause for disapproval if he were allowed to remain at Hillcourt. He was then led away by Welbore, and Cecily, having no desire to face Mr. Ranleigh's displeasure over the part she had played in the scene just past, swiftly took her leave as well and went off to change her riding dress.

9 Miss Dowie, whom she found in the little sitting-room next her bedchamber that had been set aside for the visitors' use, received with some suspicion the news that the gentleman who had instigated the infamous wager that had brought Mr. Ranleigh to the Running Boar had arrived at Hillcourt. He was presented to her when the household gathered for nuncheon some time later, and was favoured with such a curt acknowledgement of his civilities that he was quite abashed, and scarcely dared open his mouth throughout the repast.

His situation—between two formidable elderly ladies and his disapproving cousin—was indeed so lamentable that Cecily felt obliged to take pity upon him. Mr. Ranleigh's agent having arrived at the house just as they were rising from the table, Mr. Ranleigh went off to closet himself with him in the estate-room, and Cecily, aware that Lady Frederick and Miss Dowie would now enjoy a digestive hour in the Small Saloon, suggested to Lord Neagle that the three younger members of the company might retire to the billiard-room.

Her stratagem was unsuccessful. Miss Dowie, overhearing, said severely that she was to come along with her and Lady Frederick to the Small Saloon. She was obliged to obey, and as a consequence was treated to the unusual spectacle of her aunt and Lady Frederick in amicable conversation together, the two ladies joining in an attack on Lord Portandrew's many faults of character and the excessively bad *ton* of his having forced himself, with the aid of the weather, upon their company.

So engrossed did they become in this agreeable occupation that she was presently able to slip away and join Lord Neagle and Lord Portandrew in the billiard-room, where, in the course of a friendly game, she soon dropped into the same unceremonious terms with the latter gentleman as those on which she stood with young Lord Neagle. As a matter of fact, when Mr. Ranleigh strolled into the room an hour later, all three of its inmates were laughing immoderately together over the success of one of Cecily's highly unorthodox shots—a circumstance that set that gentleman's brows on the rise. He looked into Cecily's triumphant face and Lord Portandrew's blissfully merry one and said lazily, "I am glad to see that you are amusing yourselves, children. Miss Hadley, if I am not mistaken, your aunt wishes to see you upstairs."

Cecily put up her chin. "I can scarcely believe that you are my aunt's messenger, sir," she said, with an outspokenness that would have won her that lady's severest censure, "but I daresay you wish me to leave, so I shall go."

She then bestowed a dazzling smile upon Lord Portandrew and walked out of the room, having the satisfaction of hearing the beginning of his lordship's expostulation as she departed: "No, really, Robert! This is the outside of enough! You can't shut Miss Hadley into her room merely because I'm in the house!"

"If she had her deserts, it would be on bread and water," Mr. Ranleigh said, subduing the amused twitch of the lips that Cecily's defiance had aroused. "I should be on my guard if I were you, Tony. That abominable brat means to display her independence by flirting with you, unless I very much miss my guess."

"Flirt with me! Miss Hadley! She's the most innocent creature I've ever clapped eyes on!" Lord Portandrew said indignantly. "Ask Charlie. Not a word she said to me she wouldn't have said to him as well!"

Mr. Ranleigh, surveying his nephew, said he rather believed he was not a proper judge, and was then tactless enough to inquire whether that young gentleman expected life to be a perpetual holiday simply because his uncle and his cousin had come down from London. Lord Neagle, recalled to a sense of duty, reluctantly left the room, and Mr. Ranleigh then favoured Lord Portandrew with a short but pungent lecture on the conditions of behaviour under which he would not be dismissed from Hillcourt to rack up at the nearest inn—conditions so stringent, as far as Miss Hadley was concerned, as to wring a protest from his lordship.

"I'm dashed if I can see why you are acting this way!" he said. "If she goes for a governess, she'll have to meet men now and then—won't she? I mean to say, governesses don't dine with the family, but they must run across a fellow or two when they're out walking with the brats. And there are always curates underfoot in the kind of devilish dull sort of place my aunt will look out for——"

Mr. Ranleigh, interrupting, observed rather pointedly that Miss Hadley might meet as many men as she liked, with his good will, provided that the object of their attentions to her was matrimony.

"No, dash it—not a curate!" Lord Portandrew said feelingly. "A girl like that buried in some scrubby country parsonage! I tell you, Robert, she was like to have set the whole town by the ears. never saw a girl so much admired! It ain't so much *what* she looks like, you know; it's the way she has of—of smiling at you as if you was the only person in the world she cared to see——"

Mr. Ranleigh, who had himself observed this enchanting effect of Miss Hadley's smile, did not appear pleased to have it called to his attention, but merely remarked that the projecting of it to a theatre full of people must inevitably cause some confusion, to which his cousin seemed to have fallen victim. This his lordship took as an aspersion upon Miss Hadley, and an interchange resulted from which Lord Portandrew, speedily worsted, retired in a miff.

He had recovered his good humour by the dinner hour, however, when he appeared in all the splendour of a corbeau-coloured coat of superfine, much padded at the shoulders and nipped in at the waist, and a neckcloth arranged in the intricacies of the Mathematical style. To his satisfaction, he found that his cousin had repented of his resolution to banish Miss Hadley to her room during his stay in the house, for she was already in the Ivory Saloon with Miss Dowie and Lady Fredcrick when he entered. He went over to sit beside her, and she inquired at once, with a demure glance, whether he had observed that it was snowing still.

"I should think I have!" he said enthusiastically. "Devilish disagreeable weather. Shouldn't think I'd be able to go a mile without coming to grief."

Lady Frederick, overhearing, said dampingly that it was a great pity, since she had depended on his leaving in the morning.

"And I expect it will delay Miss Binkley's arrival as well," she said, "since she cannot be expected to travel in such weather. However, at least Robert will not be able to leave, either—which is my *one* consolation in this entire affair."

Mr. Ranleigh, entering the room on this remark, immediately observed that she was quite right, and said that he had no intention of leaving Hillcourt as long as his cousin remained there.

It began to appear shortly thereafter, however, that even his presence in the house would not be sufficient to dampen the romantic flame in Lord Portandrew's breast. His lordship, never famed for successful subterfuge, had made it plain to everyone in the household by the close of the evening that he was smitten to the point of idiocy with Miss Hadley, and even Cecily herself had began to grow somewhat uneasy over the matter by the time she carried her candle up to her bedchamber. She refused, however, to confess this to her aunt, who came to her room while she was undressing to lecture her on her conduct.

"I don't know what you are talking of!" she said mendaciously, when Miss Dowie accused her of leading his lordship on. "I behaved toward him exactly as I did toward Charlie."

"It might be more to the point if you were to behave toward him as you do toward Mr. Ranleigh," Miss Dowie said. "Your conduct toward *him* is enough to make him think you the most ungrateful chit alive— while you *lavish* smiles upon Lord Portandrew!"

Cecily was about to begin a heated rejoinder, but reconsidered, and after a moment fair-mindedly acknowledged that perhaps she *had* been at fault.

"But I did it only to set Mr. Ranleigh's back up," she said, in self-defence. "He is so odiously condescending—as if I were twelve years old and no man in his senses would waste a glance on me!"

Miss Dowie looked at her forebodingly. "Cecily," she said, "are you developing a *tendre* for that man?"

Cecily blushed, but said airily, "For Lord Portandrew? Good heavens, no!"

"You know very well I do not mean Lord Portandrew," Miss Dowie said. "I mean Mr. Ranleigh, miss!"

A deeper colour appeared in Cecily's face. "Of course not!" she denied quickly. "I have told you before that I think him quite abominably top-lofty—and even Lady Frederick says that he is shockingly highhanded——"

"Fiddle!" Miss Dowie snapped. "He is shockingly attractive—as you very well know. But let me tell you that if you allow yourself to develop a partiality for him you will be the greatest widgeon in England! I have it from Lady Frederick that he is on the point of offering for a young lady who is at all points a highly suitable bride for him—Miss Augusta Comerford. He and Lady Frederick are to spend Christmas in her company at her uncle's seat in Somerset, and Lady Frederick has no doubt that, on the head of it, an announcement will be forthcoming."

"I am very glad to hear it!" Cecily said, endeavouring to pay no heed to the disturbingly hollow feeling that this piece of intelligence evoked in her. "Charlie has already described Miss Comerford to me, and, indeed, I believe I have seen her myself, in the box with Mr. Ranleigh the evening he came to the theatre. She is very handsome, but seems a dreadful flirt. I daresay they will be very well matched."

"Well matched or not, it is no affair of yours," Miss Dowie retorted, "and so I will thank you to remember!" She added, on a fidgeting note, "I wish that the roads would improve, so that Miss Binkley might arrive. Once *she* is here, your time must be fully occupied, and then I daresay Lord Portandrew will go away, and Mr. Ranleigh as well."

10   But Miss Binkley, a prudent maiden lady on the shady side of sixty, was quite unwilling to entrust herself to roads that progressed, during the following week, from snow-covered thoroughfares to treacherous quagmires as a quick thaw set in. As a result, Cecily was free to enjoy the company not only of Lord Portandrew, but also of Mr. Ranleigh, whose determination to allow his cousin no opportunity for private conversation with her caused him to assume the unlikely role of chaperon when neither Miss Dowie nor Lady Frederick was able to do so.

These occasions consisted chiefly of outdoor excursions. Cecily, country-bred, had no notion of allowing the dismal condition of roads and lanes from deterring her from her favourite diversion, and was to be found hacking a high-couraged chestnut about the countryside each morning that she could prevail on someone to agree with her that the weather was not too bad for such expeditions. Lord Neagle, who had been used to accompany her, would have discontinued his attendance on her to seek his uncle's company if obliged to make a choice betweeen them; but he was not. Lord Portandrew *would* accompany Miss Hadley, and Mr. Ranleigh *would* be of the party if his cousin was. So Lord Neagle made one of Cecily's entourage as well.

She would have been less than human if she had not derived a certain satisfaction from this arrangement. It was certainly agreeable to find herself escorted daily by no fewer than three gentlemen, and if only she could have believed that she owed the pleasure of Mr. Ranleigh's company to inclination, rather than to duty, her cup of enjoyment would have been quite full.

As it was, it frequently had a rather acrid taste. Mr. Ranleigh did not scruple to let her see his cool displeasure at being obliged to guard her from his cousin's ardour, nor was he averse to putting this displeasure into words. Indeed, the frankness of his speech on several occasions drove Lord Portandrew, who had all his life looked up to his Top-of-the-Trees cousin with something like awe, to forget his deference in the heat of his remonstrance, and once even to go so far as to offer to call him out.

"Don't be a gudgeon!" Mr. Ranleigh merely advised him briefly. They had turned their horses homeward after an excursion that had left the gentlemen's top-boots splashed with mud and Cecily's shabby riding habit in an even more disreputable state than it had been in when she had left the house; and Lord Neagle, tiring of the sedate pace at which they were progressing, had already cantered on ahead to the stables. "In the first place," Mr. Ranleigh continued, "it is the height of impropriety for you to say such a thing before Miss Hadley, and in the second, you are such a devilish poor shot that it is folly for you to think of calling anyone out."

"We'll see that!" his lordship said wrathfully. "Dash it, Robert, I know I'm no match for you with pistols, but if there's any justice in this world——"

"There isn't," Mr. Ranleigh assured him. "You'd be cold meat, Tony, so do come down from the boughs and try to behave as if you had *some* modicum of sense left in your head."

Cecily said to him, taking up the cudgels in Lord Portandrew's defence, *"He* was not the one who began it, you know; *you* were. So I think *you* must be the one to offer apologies—though even if you do not, I warn you that I shan't let him go out with you. Papa fought a duel once, and was brought home on a hurdle, as he well deserved to be, for it was all quite irregular and they were *both* foxed, and a more disagreeable month than Aunt and I spent nursing him you cannot imagine! I made up my mind then that I should not allow anyone *ever* to fight a duel over me."

"My good child," Mr. Ranleigh said wearily, "I wish you will disabuse yourself of the notion that I have the slightest intention of letting Tony's blood. If you would have the propriety not to encourage his remarkably absurd predilection for you, there would be no need for heroics on your part—or on his, either."

"No, dash it, Robert!" Lord Portandrew interrupted. "You won't say such things of her in *my* presence!"

Unfortunately for the remainder of the speech which his lordship intended to make, his vehemence at this point led him to clap his heels into his horse's sides, and that spirited animal at once bolted off down the lane, leaving Cecily dissolved in helpless laughter behind him.

Mr. Ranleigh, controlling a telltale twitch of his own lips, said to her, "Yes, it's very well for you to laugh, you incorrigible brat—but you are causing the devil of an amount of trouble, you know! Do you realise how shockingly you imposed on me the first time we met, with that schoolroom demureness of yours?"

"Oh, I didn't! That is, I didn't mean——" Cecily suddenly ceased laughing and looked at him with some anxiety. "You don't *really* believe I set out to deceive you?" she asked. "Pray do not, because it is not at all true! It's only that—I *do* try to behave with propriety, but Aunt says all the Hadleys are sadly unsteady, and I *am* a Hadley—well, I can't help that!" she ended, smiling at him again, a little shyly and ruefully.

"No, you cannot," Mr. Ranleigh agreed, with slight acerbity. "But you *can* refrain from encouraging my cousin to make a cake of himself over you. He will not marry you, you know, and I can't believe you are bird-witted enough to wish to lead him on to offer you a *carte blanche*."

The smile died out suddenly from Cecily's eyes. She turned pale, and jerked out, in a voice of anger quite different from her youthful indignation of a few moments before, "You would not say such things to me if I were not—if I were Miss Comerford!"

She put her horse into a gallop on the instant; before he could reply she was flying—heedless of mud and snow—toward the house. A startled frown creased Mr. Ranleigh's brow; he uttered a vexed exclamation and followed her.

He was not vouchsafed an opportunity to make his apologies to her, however, if that were his intention, for she reached the house before he did and, consigning her mount to a groom, ran indoors at once. She went immediately to her bedchamber and did not reappear until it was time for nuncheon, when she came downstairs in Miss Dowie's company, looking pale and a little subdued. Miss Dowie said that she had the headache, and recommended that she drink a glass of camphorated spirits of lavender and lie down upon her bed. Whether she followed this excellent advice or not Mr. Ranleigh had no way of knowing, for she disappeared into the west wing of the house at the end of the brief repast and was seen no more that afternoon.

Lord Portandrew, meanwhile, having received unmistakable hints from his aunt and his cousin that the state of the roads need no longer prevent his departure, found himself in a quandary. A period of solitary reflection in the library, and the consumption of an amount of his cousin's excellent brandy that might be considered reasonable in a man screwing his courage to the sticking-point, sent him, at about four o'clock, in search of Miss Dowie, whom he found in her small sitting-room. What passed there between them was to remain unknown, but it had the effect of sending Miss Dowie, after a considerable period of time, into Cecily's bedchamber with a very odd expression on her face.

She found her niece seated by the window with the handkerchief she had taken up to hem dropped upon her lap, and said to her at once, "My dear, I have come on a very delicate errand. It is not at all what I like, but his lordship is quite determined, and indeed I scarcely know what to do in the matter. He contends that neither Lady Frederick nor Mr. Ranleigh has the authority to control your actions, and that if he has *my* permission to pay his addresses to you it is everything that is needful. *My* feeling is that if you do not wish to receive them there is no need for me to embarrass him by drawing Lady Frederick into the matter. On the other hand, if you wish to give him an affirmative answer, I should not consider it at all proper to allow him to address you without her knowledge. You know, my dear, it is a very serious matter to marry a man whose entire family is set against you——"

Cecily, who had been listening with eyes growing wide with surprise, at this point could contain herself no longer.

"Marry?" she exclaimed. "Lord Portandrew? Is *that* what you are talking of, Aunt?"

Miss Dowie sat down. "Well, of course!" she said testily. "What else have I been saying these five minutes past? He has asked my permission to pay his addresses to you, exactly as I have told you——"

"But is he serious?" Cecily interrupted, her head in a whirl, but uppermost in her thoughts the rather bitter triumph of knowing that Mr. Ranleigh had been mistaken when he had informed her that his cousin would not offer her marriage. "He truly wishes to *marry* me?"

Miss Dowie adjusted her spectacles upon her nose. "You are not ordinarily slow of comprehension, Cecily," she said severely. "Have I not told you that, as plainly as it is in my power to do? However," she went on, relenting, "I daresay it may come as something of a surprise to you, and it is possible, I am aware, to be somewhat bewildered by the headache. How *is* your headache?"

"My headache?" Cecily passed one hand mechanically over her brow. "Oh, it has quite left me, Aunt! But—but Lord Portandrew——"

"A very amiable young man," Miss Dowie conceded, "although not, I fear, possessed of the highest powers of intellect. However, his manners are excellent and his birth unexceptionable, and he assures me that his affairs stand in such a case that he has no need to look for fortune in choosing a wife. There is also the advantage of the title: as little store as I set on such matters personally, I expect you would find it agreeable to be a Countess."

Cecily, who did not appear to be attending to her, but had pressed her hands to her temples as if she were endeavouring to quiet the whirling thoughts within them, said at this point, in a stifled voice, "But I do not love him, Aunt! Indeed, I never thought—I never expected——"

Miss Dowie looked affronted. "Love!" she said roundly. "Romantic fancies! Pray, what has that to say to the matter? A rational regard on both sides is what must be looked for in such affairs. Of course, if you have taken Lord Portandrew in dislike——"

"But I have not!" Cecily said. "I mean, I do not *dislike* him—but—but I am sure I could never feel for him the regard which—I should like to feel for the man I marry——" She sprang up, and began to pace the room. "Oh dear, Aunt, indeed I *do* see that this might be the end of all our difficulties!" she said miserably. "I expect I am perfectly birdwitted even to think of refusing such an offer, for I should be Lady Portandrew, and never have to return to that odious Jillson, or go for a governess, or do anything disagreeable so that we may not find ourselves without a roof over our heads——"

Miss Dowie, who, for all her lack of sentimentality, was not wanting in feeling, saw the distress in her niece's eyes and said brusquely, "Now, my dear, there is no need for you to put yourself into a taking! It would be in the highest degree repugnant to me to think of your entering into marriage only for an establishment. I assure you that I have always believed it to be a much lesser evil to be obliged to earn one's own bread."

Cecily came across the room and dropped impetuously on her knees beside her aunt's chair.

"Dear Aunt," she said gratefully, "it is exactly like you to say that, when I am sure anyone else in your place would be telling me that I *must* accept this offer or be cast off by them forever! And I *do* feel a perfect monster not to wish to do so, for I quite see how splendid it would be for both of us."

Miss Dowie nodded, shrugging her shoulders with the air of one casting away some agreeable dream, and gave Cecily's hand a bracing pat.

"Tiddle!" she said. "If you don't wish to marry the man, you don't. I need not scruple to tell you, at any rate, that I had hoped for something better for you—for though he may be an Earl, and wealthy into the bargain, he does *not* appear to me to be a man of sense. Now *don't* go off into any high flights!" she concluded, regarding with disapproval the tears welling up in Cecily's eyes. She rose and shook out the voluminous folds of her old-fashioned gown. "I shall give him his answer," she said briskly. "No need for this to go any further."

Cecily jumped up. "Oh, no—if you please, Aunt, I had much rather tell him myself," she said.

Her feelings might oblige her to reject Lord Portandrew's offer, but she was aware that Miss Dowie's outspoken tongue might make the manner of that refusal doubly unpalatable to him, and she was unwilling to wound him further than was necessary.

Miss Dowie was not at once prepared to accede to this idea, but she eventually allowed her scruples to be overcome and Cecily went off to the sitting-room. Here she found his lordship nervously pacing up and down. His face lighted when he saw her, but she dashed his hopes by saying quickly, "Oh, my lord, my aunt has told me what an honour you have done me, but indeed it will not do! I am quite sure that we should not suit, and—and that you would be far better advised to offer for some young lady whose circumstances are more similar to your own."

His lordship's face fell. "No, dash it!" he objected, looking revolted by this prospect. "Never met a girl before I saw you I'd care to offer for— well, perhaps one or two," he added hastily, recalling certain events having to do with what his long-suffering mama customarily referred to as "Anthony's fatal propensity to fancy himself in love with the *most* ineligible young females." "But that don't signify: I never knew *true* love before I met *you*, Miss Hadley. And as for your circumstances, I don't care a rush about them, so *that* has nothing to say to the matter." He looked at her with a slight appearance of hope dawning on his face. "Perhaps I've been too quick for you," he said. "The thing is, I haven't had time to fix my interest with you, what with Robert and my aunt taking the deuced gothic position they have. You wouldn't like to take time to think it over?"

"No, I am afraid not," Cecily said gently. "You see, I am *quite* certain of my own mind."

"Yes, I can see that," his lordship said, in the dismals again. "Thought you was—but it never does any harm to try one's luck." He reflected for a moment. "I shall have to leave here tomorrow, you know," he said gloomily. "No telling when I shall see you again."

"I think that will be all for the best," Cecily said encouragingly. "I am sure you will soon forget me under those circumstances."

"Will I? No, dash it, I won't!" his lordship said feelingly. "I expect I shall wear the willow for the deuce of a time."

Obviously he was not in the mood to be comforted by such philosophic reflections as Cecily was able to call to mind from her aunt's many improving lectures on the subject of young persons who fancied their lives blighted by unrequited affection; and when she was at last able to induce him to leave her she felt that she could congratulate herself upon only one point—that at least he would be spared the mortification of having the fact of his rejection known to anyone but himself.

11

But here she was reckoning without Lord Port-andrew. It was quite out of his character to keep such an event to himself, and the result was that the first words she heard addressed to her by Lady Frederick, when she came downstairs with her aunt at the dinner hour, were: "Well, my dear, so you have had the good sense to refuse my nephew! I was most gratified to hear it—quite as much as I was mortified by his having had the bad taste to pursue you with his attentions under my roof."

Cecily blushed and, at a loss for words, looked to her aunt. That lady, appearing to take Lady Frederick's words as an affront, informed her at once in a starchy tone that, except for her lack of fortune, she considered Cecily in no way an unsuitable match for Lord Portandrew.

"Not," she conceded, "that I should have allowed him to address him-self to her if she had not assured me that she had no intention of accept-ing his offer, for I do not consider—in view of the obligation under which we stand to you—that she is free to act as she chooses in a matter that touches your family so nearly."

This speech, which implied a certain criticism of Lady Frederick's atti-tude in taking it for granted that it was out of the question for Cecily to think of becoming Lady Portandrew, led to a spirited dialogue between the two elder ladies, which was interrupted only by the appearance of Mr. Ranleigh, who, taking the situation in at a glance, turned the conversation into more unexciting conversational channels. His manner, as he did so, seemed quite as usual, and he did not allude to his cousin's offer, but Cecily guessed that it could not be unknown to him. She rather wished that he *would* speak of it, if only to give her the satisfaction of seeing that he was aware how unfounded his assertion had been that Lord Port-andrew had no thought of offering her marriage; but, as he continued to engage her aunt and Lady Frederick in civil chitchat, the lowering reflec-tion was gradually forced upon her that the whole affair was one of indifference to him.

In this conclusion, however, she was not correct, for the news that his cousin had thrown caution to the winds and made an offer for Cecily's hand had had an odd and highly disagreeable effect on Mr. Ranleigh. He was, in fact, startled to find that the absurd child in whose concerns he had so negligently involved himself had the power to move him out of his boredom into positive anger—anger with Tony for having placed a girl who might be considered as being, at the moment, under his protection in the awkward position of being obliged to reject his addresses, and anger with Cecily herself for having led his cousin on to make those addresses.

Lady Frederick, in discussing the matter with him, had been much inclined to praise Cecily for her good sense in rejecting a match which—however repugnant it must have been to his lordship's family—would certainly have been to the highest degree advantageous to herself. But with this encomium her son was far from agreeing.

"Good sense!" he repeated impatiently. "The two of them together have not exhibited as much of that commodity as one might reasonably expect from Charlie! Tony cannot marry that chit; he knows that as well as you and I do. The moment Aunt Almeria got wind of such a scheme she would be down on him with every argument and entreaty known to female ingenuity, and he is no more capable of withstanding her than he is of flying to the moon. There would be a scandal, and the engagement would be broken off at once. That, let me assure you, ma'am, would effectively put an end to any hopes you may have of establishing the girl respectably, for her career in the theatre could not possibly escape notice under such circumstances!"

Lady Frederick, though obliged to acknowledge the justice of these observations, was still, however, inclined to credit Cecily with having behaved very properly in the circumstances.

"For it was quite to be expected, you know," she remarked, "that a girl in her situation would be so dazzled by the idea of marrying an Earl—even such a nodcock as Anthony—that she would spend not a moment's thought on the unsuitability of the match."

Mr. Ranleigh gave a short laugh. "The unsuitability of the match!" he said. "Do you believe for a moment, ma'am, that *that* was what decided her against accepting Tony? If you have been in her company this many days without learning that she has no more worldly wisdom than an infant, you must suddenly have become strangely lacking in perception. Depend upon it, she has acted from impulse and nothing more—an impulse I can scarcely wonder at, for poor Tony is far from being a romantic figure in the eyes of a schoolroom miss."

Lady Frederick, who could not remember the time when her son had been sufficiently exercised by the conduct of any young lady to be moved by it out of his usual satirical calm, gave him a sharp glance. It had occurred to her once or twice during the days just past that his irritation over his cousin's pursuit of Cecily was somewhat excessive, but she had not previously imagined that it might be due to any interest of his own in that direction. She still did not believe that this was likely—it was more than probable that his exasperation arose from his dislike of the sort of scandal into which his befriending of the girl had threatened to plunge them—but she kept a watchful eye on him during dinner.

Nothing, however, could have been more indifferent than Mr. Ranleigh's manner toward Miss Hadley. His conversation was addressed almost exclusively to Miss Dowie and to Mr. Tibble, the latter of whom, in happy ignorance of the emotions under which the remainder of the company were labouring, was flattered to receive so much of his attention and fervently agreed with every word that fell from his lips. Lord Portandrew, who sat throughout the meal in depressed silence, was vouchsafed no more than the curtest of civilities from his cousin. As for Cecily herself, she appeared quite subdued, scarcely lifting her eyes from her plate throughout the meal.

Lady Frederick would have had her doubts concerning her son set even more to rest had she been privileged to be present during the conversation that took place between him and Miss Hadley just before that young lady retired to her bedchamber. Cecily had pleaded a recurrence of her headache to escape the prospect of an evening spent under the surveillance of the all too many persons who knew what had occurred that day, and had just set her foot on the lowest step of the staircase, when Mr. Ranleigh strolled into the hall from the library.

"Going up so early, Miss Hadley?" he inquired, with a rather sardonic inflexion that at once set her hackles on the rise.

"Yes," she said shortly. "I have the headache."

He did not appear to receive this news with sympathy; as a matter of fact, he did not appear even to believe it.

"You are wise," he said coolly. "May I suggest, however, that if you had displayed this delicacy a little earlier you might have spared both yourself and my cousin an excessively disagreeable interview?"

Her colour heightened. She said warmly, "It was not my fault; I never imagined——"

"Then you cannot have attended very carefully to the several warnings I dropped on the subject," Mr. Ranleigh said bluntly. She tried to speak again, but he went on ruthlessly. "I realise, of course, that you are very young, but you appear to have been brought up with *some* notions of propriety, and if you are not to fall into a far worse scrape than this in the very near future, I should recommend that you adhere to them."

Cecily said, her eyes positively flashing now, "I have fallen into no 'scrape,' as you put it, Mr. Ranleigh! I have received an offer of marriage—which *you* predicted I should not be honoured with—and I have refused it. That is no more than hundreds of other perfectly respectable young women might say—and I am sure you would not think of casting aspersions upon *them!*"

"Should I not? But I rather believe I should, Miss Hadley, if they were in your position. If you intend to conduct yourself on these principles, you had as well go back to the theatre, for it is quite as simple a matter for a giddy chit to be taken in by a callow youth who makes up, with a promise of marriage that he will never keep, to the pretty governess hired to instruct his sisters as it is for her to be ruined in *that* profession!"

She stared at him, startled. "Oh!" she said, after a moment, moved out of her anger by a sudden sense of mortification. "Do you mean—Lord Portandrew would not *really* have married me, even if I had accepted his offer?"

"No, my girl, he would not. I do not say he might not *wish* to, as the young fools you will meet as a governess may do as well—for a time. But if *you* are persuadable, you would do well to remember that so are they, and that there will always be weeping mamas and adamant fathers to do the persuading."

Cecily felt her sense of importance over having received her first offer rapidly diminishing. Under Mr. Ranleigh's cool summing up of the situation, she was made to perceive herself as she no doubt appeared in *his* eyes —a silly chit who had been playing with fire, and who had embroiled a peaceful household in a tiresome brouhaha. The colour flamed up into her face; she said hotly, "I think you are the most disagreeable person I have ever met—and I don't wish to be obliged to you—and I shall leave this house tomorrow!"

"You will do nothing of the sort," Mr. Ranleigh said calmly. "Tomorrow Miss Binkley will be here, and you will then devote your energies to learning as rapidly as possible all those abominable female 'accomplishments' that you will be expected to impart to your future charges."

She gave him a smouldering look, which had the unexpected effect of making him laugh.

"Don't look at me as if you were contemplating murder, you absurd brat!" he said. "You will thank me for this some day"—a statement which, however, as he turned away from her to go back into the library, seemed to him to ring with a somewhat hollow optimism.

Would she thank him for helping her to a life of respectable drudgery?

It was a bleak prospect—certainly one unworthy of a creature as vital and glowing as this one. He frowned over the selection of a book from the shelves, took one down, and riffled through its pages.

"Damn Tony!" was the rather unusual reflection engendered by this inspection.

He replaced the book on the shelf and left the library forthwith to return to the Ivory Saloon. It was not often that Mr. Ranleigh was driven to seek company to save himself from the necessity of encountering his own thoughts; but it was certain that that was what he was doing at this moment.

12 On the following morning Cecily, coming down to breakfast, found both Lord Portandrew and Mr. Ranleigh on the point of departing for London. When they had gone, the house rapidly appeared to sink into a quiet gloom, which could scarcely be said to have been enlivened by the arrival, at an hour somewhat past noon, of Miss Tabitha Binkley.

Miss Binkley, a tall, silent female in a hair-brown pelisse and bonnet, lost no time in coming down to business with her new pupil. Not an hour after her arrival, Cecily was summoned to the schoolroom on the third floor where she had formerly held sway, and found herself set down at once with a sketchbook before her, being inaugurated into the mysteries of depicting in water colours the trees, shrubbery, and similar innocuous objects Miss Binkley considered suitable subjects for a young lady's brush.

From this she escaped only to one of the back drawing-rooms below, where a pianoforte awaited her attention, and where she spent an arduous pair of hours in practising five-finger exercises and stumbling perseveringly through a Haydn sonata.

This regimen was repeated on the following morning, much to Lord Neagle's disgust. His lordship had looked forward to enjoying an early ride with Cecily, and expressed himself in terms of strong disapprobation when he learned that henceforth she would be too much occupied with her studies to have the leisure for such diversions.

Cecily herself was privately only too ready to agree with his sentiments. The prospect of an unremitting schedule of schoolroom drudgery was certainly bleak when one had been enjoying the pleasures of life at a country seat of the first elegance, complete with the attentions of a peer and the company of the Nonpareil; but she had some of her aunt's good sense, in spite of her inexperience, and was prepared to realise that *that* interlude had been in the nature of a blissful dream.

The dream became even more remote when Lady Frederick and Lord Neagle shortly afterward departed from Hillcourt on holiday visits—the first to spend the Christmas season at the Somerset estate of Lady Comerford's brother, Lord Langworthy, whose wife was a connexion of hers, and the second to go to the Lincolnshire home of his aunt, Lady Furzebrook. Cecily, aware that Mr. Ranleigh and Miss Augusta Comerford were both to be of the Somerset party, found that she was rapidly descending into a case of the dismals as the month of December drew on, for the contrast between her own days and the pleasures being enjoyed by the beautiful

Miss Comerford was a severe trial to her. No doubt, she thought bitterly, *that* young lady was now being assiduously courted by Mr. Ranleigh, who would probably consider this a suitable occasion for making her an offer in form.

Sometimes it seemed to Cecily that she would have done a great deal better to have accepted Lord Portandrew's offer and married him in the teeth of his family's opposition, if only to prove to his odious cousin that she *could* enter his world and Miss Comerford's as an equal—for that, it seemed to her, was all she was longing to do. If she were Lady Portandrew it was quite certain that Mr. Ranleigh could not lecture her as if she had been a tiresome child!

So she spent an agreeable hour picturing herself, clad in an elegant satin-and-gauze gown, seated in her own box at the opera and receiving the compliments of a great many gentlemen of the *ton,* while Mr. Ranleigh stood by in an attitude of dark and brooding jealousy, looking somewhat as one might imagine Lord Byron to do. However, the fact that Mr. Ranleigh had not the slightest tinge of romantic melancholy in his nature presently caused this agreeable tableau to fade, and she was left to face the unalterable fact that in order to give him the opportunity to develop these sentiments she would be obliged first to marry Lord Portandrew—something which she did not at all desire to do.

Neither Lady Frederick nor Lord Neagle returned to Hillcourt until almost a fortnight after the New Year, by which time Cecily had made such excellent progress in her studies that Miss Binkley reported to her patroness that she believed she might soon be capable of undertaking the education at least of young ladies of tender years.

"Good!" Lady Frederick said approvingly. She had sent for Miss Binkley to her dressing-room, where she was undergoing the ministrations of her dresser in preparation for dinner. The whole household was in a bustle, for Mr. Ranleigh had escorted his mother back to Hillcourt from Somerset, and Lord Neagle, too, had arrived only an hour before under the charge of Mr. Tibble. "In that case," Lady Frederick went on, "I have found just the situation for her. Lady Langworthy was most kind in inquiring whether anyone in the neighbourhood might require the services of a governess, and learned of a Lady Bonshawe who is in need of someone to undertake the education of her two little girls, aged, I believe, eight and eleven. I made it my business to call upon Lady Bonshawe—*not,* I may say, a woman of the slightest distinction, for her father was in trade, and her husband as well, before he was knighted—but a very comfortable, good-hearted creature."

Miss Binkley, who would not have dreamed of disputing any of her patroness's pronouncements, at once agreed that such a situation must suit Miss Hadley exactly; but Miss Dowie, when the same information was imparted to her, said she wondered that Lady Frederick should snatch at the first situation that offered, for she believed Lady Bonshawe might well be one of those noisy, vulgar creatures whose household would not be at all the sort of place for Cecily.

Lady Frederick eyed her quellingly. "My dear Miss Dowie," she said, "I am *not*, as you phrase it, snatching at the first thing that offers. In fact, I have already rejected two other situations for which I might have recommended your niece—both in households of considerable rank and fashion."

Miss Dowie bristled. "Then perhaps, ma'am, you do not believe that my niece belongs in such *elevated* surroundings?" she inquired.

"To put it to you roundly—no, I do not!" said Lady Frederick. Then, observing that Miss Dowie was preparing to fire a broadside of her own, she went on with some acerbity, "Don't be a ninnyhammer, woman! Have you not sense enough to see what must be the outcome of it if Cecily is placed in a household where there are gentlemen of fashion who may recognise her as a young woman they have seen upon the London stage? Even if she were not recognised, with her charm she would be fair game for any young man of rakish tendencies who was familiar in the household."

Miss Dowie, holding her fire to consider this statement, was obliged to acknowledge its merit.

"Exactly!" Lady Frederick said. "The Bonshawes, on the other hand, are worthy people of no fashion whatever, and have as well, I believe, that mania for respectability that one so often finds among people who are desirous of forgetting their origins. And, as their family consists only of the two little girls whose education Cecily will be called upon to superintend, I believe I may assure you that their house will *not* be frequented by young men of fashion. Lady Bonshawe and Sir William live quite retired, as a matter of fact, on his very respectable estate not far from Bath. I have not met him, but have been assured that he is some years older than his wife, and addicted to nothing more dangerous than whist."

Miss Dowie, considering this information, was moved to the unusual concession of granting that Lady Frederick's remarks showed a good deal of sense. Her ladyship shrugged.

"Naturally!" she said. "I have grown very fond of Cecily, and have expended a great deal of thought over the matter of her future. She must marry some day, of course, but she is very young still, and until the proper young man has been found for her I believe she will do very well with Lady Bonshawe. In the meantime," she added, "I have a matter to propose to *you*, Miss Dowie. I am aware that you have had it in mind, when Cecily should be settled, to seek some employment as well. What should you say to remaining here? That foolish creature, Maria Wixom, has been persuaded to stay on in Derbyshire indefinitely and devote herself to her niece's family, and so it happens that I am left in need of a companion."

If she had expected to astonish Miss Dowie with this statement, she was disappointed. Miss Dowie sat primly in her chair, with her hands folded calmly in her lap, and gave the matter her consideration. After some moments, she nodded briskly.

"Very well," she said. "No doubt you will regret it, but so, I daresay, shall I. On the other hand, mistaken as I consider your opinions frequently to be, I find your conversation quite stimulating."

Lady Frederick gave an appreciative crack of laughter. "And I yours," she said. "There is nothing so boring as living with someone who merely echoes one's own opinions, and quakes like a blancmange at the very hint of a set-down. Now *you*, my dear Miss Dowie, are quite incapable, I should think, of quaking."

"Oh, yes!" Miss Dowie said simply. "You see, I have lived with my brother, and, compared to the disagreements I have had with *him*, ours have been merely bagatelles."

"Indeed!" said Lady Frederick—and was spared further comment by the entrance of Lord Neagle into the room.

Dinner that evening was a lively meal, with the two elder ladies both in excellent spirits and Mr. Ranleigh his usual urbane self. Only Cecily seemed subdued. She had been acquainted by her aunt with the plans that had been made for her, and for that lady herself, but she had displayed a surprising lack of interest in them, seeming more concerned with endeavouring to discover whether Lady Frederick had had any news involving her son to impart to Miss Dowie.

Miss Dowie, however, had shown herself impervious to hints, and Cecily had eventually been obliged to ask her directly if Mr. Ranleigh had returned to Hillcourt betrothed to Miss Comerford.

"And what business is it of yours if he has?" Miss Dowie inquired dampingly.

Cecily's heart went down. "Oh!" she said, rather faintly. "Do you mean —he has?"

"I know nothing whatever of the matter," Miss Dowie said. "Lady Frederick did not confide in me, nor did I feel it proper to make any inquiries on the subject."

She looked so unencouraging that Cecily did not pursue the matter further, but she scanned Mr. Ranleigh's countenance rather anxiously when she saw him a little later, as the household gathered for dinner that evening. It told her nothing at all, however, and, as the conversation during the meal did not touch on Miss Comerford, she was left as much in the dark at its conclusion as she had been at its outset.

Nor was she more fortunate when the gentlemen joined the ladies in the Ivory Saloon after dinner. Lady Frederick, her energies not at all diminished by her journey, was all for making up a table for whist before retiring, and Mr. Ranleigh, Mr. Tibble, and Miss Dowie accordingly sat down with her, while Cecily was encouraged by her patroness to demonstrate her new proficiency on the pianoforte that stood in the room.

She was obliged to comply, though with considerable misgiving over the quality of the performance she was about to give. At the conclusion of her efforts she received a kind commendation from Lady Frederick, who was quite unmusical, but, encountering Mr. Ranleigh's quizzical glance, she excused herself in some dudgeon from any further exhibition of her skill— or lack of it—and went immediately to her room.

She was too young for her problems to interfere greatly with her slumbers, but she awoke early in the morning and, finding that sleep had deserted her, rose and dressed, intending to go for a walk before breakfast. The sun had just risen on a fine midwinter morning when she came down the stairs, expecting to find no one stirring but the servants. As she reached the last step, however, she was surprised to hear a quick, firm tread in the hall, and a moment later Mr. Ranleigh himself came into view. He wore top-boots and a long, many-caped driving-coat, and was apparently on the point of leaving the house.

He checked on seeing her, surveying her cloaked figure in slight surprise.

"Miss Hadley? Where are you off to?"

She was annoyed to feel that her colour was heightening at this sudden encounter with the person who had been occupying her thoughts so disturbingly, and replied rather more coolly than was necessary, "For a walk."

"Alone? At this hour?"

"Yes, alone!" Her colour rose still further at the disapproval implied in his tone, and she went on rashly, "I am not a governess *yet*, Mr. Ranleigh! I suppose I may do as I please for a few days more, and I please to go for a walk, and I *shall* go!"

Somewhat to her surprise, he did not take umbrage at this speech, but smiled—a most disturbing smile, as a number of ladies of his acquaintance could attest, for it at once erased the coolly ironic expression his face habitually wore and made one realise what a warm and humorous light could appear in those glinting grey eyes.

"Spoken like a true Hadley!" he remarked. "I expect you were not acquainted with my grandmother, but my own rather imperfect memories of her all seem to have to do with the fact that the merest hint of opposition was enough to bring out the Tartar in her."

Cecily laughed, her brow clearing. "Yes—isn't it abominable!" she said penitently. "I should not have said it, I am quite aware! It makes me sound dreadfully ungrateful."

He shrugged. "Oh, as for gratitude——!" he said. "You may be wishing you had never clapped eyes on either me or my mother, once you are immured at the Bonshawes'. Taking charge of a pair of brats who have not the slightest claim upon you except for the wages that are paid you is scarcely a matter for congratulation, it would appear to me."

As these were exactly her own sentiments, she could not dispute them with any degree of conviction, but she did manage to summon up enough civility to say, "Yes, but it *was* very kind of you and Lady Frederick to give me such an excellent opportunity, and Aunt is forever saying that I do not show my appreciation properly." She blushed furiously all at once and went on, "In fact, I daresay she is right and you think me quite ragmannered—but now that I am going away and may never see you again, I should like you to know that I—that I shall never forget——"

She paused, seeing a suddenly arrested look in his eyes that confused her. For a moment she took the full light of a very penetrating gaze: then the cooler, more familiar look returned and he said lightly, "Oh, I don't believe we need be quite so final as that. I have no doubt you have not seen the last of my mother. She has grown very fond of you, you know."

"Oh, yes!" Cecily said, with unsuitable mournfulness. "But that is different. I expect she will not be living *here* after—when you are married."

As for the look he had surprised in those great candid eyes—a look that should certainly not have astonished him, for young girls were notoriously liable to romantic fancies—*that*, if anything, should only have put him more on his guard. But the odd fact was that it had taken him *off* his guard, for he had not until that moment imagined that his protégée had come to regard him with anything but a rather smouldering dislike.

Gathering his reins and nodding to Sivil to let go the leaders' heads, he found a sudden question as to why he had not, after all, offered for Gussie Comerford flickering through his mind. Certainly it could have nothing to do with that abominable child! His interest in her was simply a desire to see her respectably established, out of the reach of that rascal, Jillson: only the night before, as a matter of fact, he had approved his mother's plan of taking her again under her own roof in a year or two, when the notoriety attaching to her appearance on the London stage should have been forgotten, so that she might find a suitable husband for her.

Yet it was strange that the thought of her being given in marriage to some red-faced country squire or earnest young man with an eye to a minor post in the diplomatic service seemed so unsatisfactory to him now. Mr. Ranleigh, turning out of the lodge gates on to the road, found himself thinking somewhat sardonically that it might be as well that he had remained only one night at Hillcourt on this occasion. It would have been too much indeed if little Miss Hadley, having driven Lord Portandrew into a most unbecoming state of confusion on the occasion of *his* last visit to Hillcourt, should have succeeded this time in doing the same for his cousin.

"When I am *what?*"

"Married—to Miss Comerford," Cecily said perseveringly. "Should I not speak of that, either? Charlie—I mean, Lord Neagle said——"

"I see that I shall have to have a word with Charlie," Mr. Ranleigh said. "No, you should *not* speak of it, Miss Hadley; in fact, if you will heed a word of advice from me, you will wait until you read an announcement in the *Gazette* before you run to conclusions on any of your acquaintances' matrimonial plans."

She looked a little daunted, but was unable to prevent the improved state of her spirits from appearing as she said defensively, "Well, I did not know. And I expect *I* am not to blame if you lead people on to think you are going to offer for them and then do not!" A thought occurred to her and she said seriously, "It must have been *very* depressing for poor Miss Comerford."

He flung back his head and laughed. "When last I saw Miss Comerford, she was enjoying a dashing flirtation with a handsome captain in the Guards," he assured her, and then, collecting himself, went on with a severer air, "Good God, how came we to be talking of such matters? If you feel that you genuinely wish to express your gratitude to me, you will oblige me by curbing your wish to discuss my affairs with anyone—including myself!"

Again the smile in his eyes belied the sternness of his words. Cecily, hesitating on the stairs, said rather shyly, "Well, I shan't do so again, if you do not like it."

"See that you don't," he recommended. Unexpectedly, he took one of her hands in his, lifted it to his lips, and imprinted a light kiss upon it. "Good-bye! I am going into Leicestershire and shan't see you before you leave, so you must take my good wishes now," he said. "You will let us know—will you not?—if you find the tyranny of those two brats more than you can endure."

He was gone, leaving Cecily staring rather dazedly at the hand he had kissed. Of course, she was obliged to tell herself, he had meant nothing by it; he had merely intended to be kind and civil. But it was a great deal, at any rate, to know that he had not offered for Miss Comerford!

Had she but realised it, Mr. Ranleigh, getting into the curricle awaiting him before the front door, was not feeling at all kind and civil; he was asking himself, in rueful wrath, what the devil he had meant by behaving toward that chit as if she were not merely an engaging child for whom he had enlisted his mother's good offices. Certainly it was no excuse that she had looked so absurdly young and vulnerable, standing there on the stairs in her shabby cloak, that it had suddenly seemed a wickedly cruel thing to send her into the world alone to earn her bread.

13

Not quite a fortnight after Mr. Ranleigh's departure from Hillcourt, on a dark winter morning near the end of January, Cecily too set out from it on her journey into Somerset.

Lady Frederick, who quite agreed with Miss Dowie's notions that it would not do for her to travel alone, had also not been amenable to the idea of her making the journey on the stage, and as a result she enjoyed the luxury of Lady Frederick's own travelling-chaise and the company of one of her ladyship's abigails. Lady Frederick, who had taken Lady Bonshawe's measure most accurately during her brief meeting with her, had shrewdly calculated that nothing would be more likely to ensure that lady's kindest behaviour toward the new governess than the latter's arriving in an elegant private chaise, accompanied by an abigail.

Lady Frederick was quite correct. Lady Bonshawe was so impressed by these unmistakable tokens that Lady Frederick considered Miss Hadley rather in the light of a relation than as a dependant that she made a hasty rearrangement of her domestic plans, which resulted in Cecily's being shown up to a pleasant guest-bedchamber instead of to the bleak little room on the third storey that had been intended for her.

She was also honoured with an invitation to dine with the family that evening—"for we shall not be seeing company, you know," Lady Bonshawe said, in defence of her own condescension. "Not that I expect you mightn't sit down with us even if we was, for—lord!—I daresay the Arberrys and the Casewits would like nothing better than to meet a young lady who is connected with the Ranleighs and has been staying at Hillcourt! I am sure I shall be only too glad to hear all about it from you myself!"

Cecily had been forewarned by Lady Frederick what she was to expect of her new employer, but she found Lady Bonshawe's fluctuations between patronising condescension and respectful curiosity too much for her lively sense of humour, and surprised that good lady on at least two occasions by what appeared to her to be a quite inappropriate ripple of laughter, immediately repressed.

"But, there! You are not much more than a slip of a girl yourself," Lady Bonshawe said good-naturedly. "And I am glad to see that you are not one of the prim sort, for that would never do for my Millie and Clemmie. As lively as grigs they are, the pair of them. But here they are now!" she added, as a pair of schoolgirls, both of them fair and plump like their mama, peeped into the room. "Amelia! Clementina! Come in, my dears! This is Miss Hadley, your new governess."

Cecily, who had been brooding with some foreboding during her journey over her shortcomings in the field of the female accomplishments, was relieved to see that neither Amelia nor Clementina appeared to be of a studious nature. A visit to the schoolroom, where the two young ladies were commanded by their mama to display their skill on the pianoforte that had been installed there for their use, did even more to erase the doubts of her competence to instruct them that had been assailing Cecily. Her pupils were evidently a pair of romps, and the most arduous of their governess's duties would be that of attempting to imbue in them some notion of the proper conduct expected of well-bred young ladies, rather than that of burdening their heads with any more esoteric knowledge.

When Cecily was left alone in her bedchamber to change her dress for dinner she took stock of her situation, and acknowledged that it might have been a great deal worse. Inglesant itself, which had been purchased by Sir William Bonshawe some few years before, was a handsome Tudor manor, and it had received every modern improvement at its new owner's hands. Her own bedchamber was furnished elegantly, though without a great deal of taste, in green damask and mahogany, and the rest of the house had been done in the same expensive fashion. She had not the least doubt that she would live there exceedingly comfortably; it also appeared to her that she need anticipate few difficulties in dealing with Lady Bonshawe. Amelia and Clementina were not ideal pupils, perhaps, but, though they appeared to have been indulged by their mama, they were not spoiled beyond reason.

All in all, she told herself, resolutely putting from her mind the remembrance of a tall, broad-shouldered gentleman whom she had last seen at the foot of the staircase at Hillcourt, she had much for which to be grateful. And what, after all, had so elegant a figure as Mr. Ranleigh to do with a governess in the establishment of what he would unhesitatingly have characterised as a mushroom squire? She might, in fact, never see him again, and it assuredly behooved her to think no more about him, but to devote her energies instead to satisfying her new employers.

She was privileged to meet Sir William Bonshawe at dinner that evening, and was favoured by him during the meal with several items of conversation, most of which dealt with the prices he had paid for the dinner service from which they ate, the ornate epergne that graced the table, and the crystal chandelier that glittered above it.

"Everything in the first style," he said complacently. "No expense spared, and no trumpery, either, for I meant to make Inglesant—and so I told 'em!—the equal of any gentleman's seat in the county. Well! What d'ye think of it, Miss Hadley? Have I succeeded, or haven't I?"

Cecily said civilly that she was quite sure he had, and was rewarded by an approving nod of her employer's bald head.

"Ay! I thought you must say so! And Lady Bonshawe tells me *you'd* be the first to know, because of your being connected with all the nobs. Hill-court, eh? I looked it up in the guidebooks but it ain't as old as Inglesant. Still I daresay it's a fine place in its way. Well kept up, I expect?"

Cecily said demurely that it was.

"Well, I don't doubt it," Sir William handsomely allowed, "for they say Ranleigh is nearly as rich as Golden Ball. But no handle to his name, Lady Bonshawe says! Hanged if I see why he'd settle for an 'Honourable' when he has that much brass! And a Duke for a cousin! Now if *I* stood in his shoes——"

The picture was too much for Miss Hadley; she choked, hastily drank a sip of water, and thought with unholy anticipation of the probable look on Mr. Ranleigh's face when she told him of this conversation. She then reminded herself that it was not at all likely that she would ever have the opportunity of doing so—a damping thought which made it possible for her to attend to the remainder of Sir William's remarks without the slightest desire to give way again to laughter.

On the following morning she took up her duties in the schoolroom. However, in the midst of a persevering attempt to instruct her pupils in the use of the globes, a message arrived summoning her downstairs: one of Lady Bonshawe's neighbours, Mrs. Casewit, was below, and Lady Bonshawe was desirous of introducing the new governess to her. Cecily was obliged to sit for a quarter of an hour answering the inquiries of the two ladies about her noble connexions—for it appeared that Mrs. Casewit, a native of Sussex and well-acquainted with the exalted position occupied by the Ranleighs, was willing to display her curiosity concerning them even more undisguisedly than was Lady Bonshawe.

"A very pretty, well-behaved young woman, I am sure," she pronounced Miss Hadley to be in a quite audible voice as Cecily was leaving the room. "But, I declare, Amelia, she is wearing a positively plain gown! Ay, they are very great people, the Ranleighs, I don't doubt, but I'd take shame to myself to see *my* connexions looking no more elegant than that!"

Fortunately for Cecily, Mrs. Casewit's stout figure, encased in a purple-bloom silk gown and surmounted by a dazzling hat with a huge poke-front lined with Sardinian-blue silk, had already engaged her risibilities, and she was therefore able to smile at the bluntness of the lady's remarks instead of taking offence at them. In point of fact, it had been Lady Frederick's wish to equip her young protégée for her post with an entire new wardrobe; but, as neither Miss Dowie nor Cecily could be prevailed on to accept so lavish a gift, she had been obliged to confine her generosity to adding to Cecily's own modest wardrobe two new gowns—a long-sleeved walking-dress of French cambric and a pretty jaconet muslin.

Cecily had occasion to wear both of these frequently as the days progressed, for her duties, she found, were not confined to the schoolroom. Lady Bonshawe might have complied with her spouse's wish to live in the country, but she was herself city-bred, and liked nothing better than to drive in to Bath for an agreeable hour or two of shopping in Milsom Street. On such occasions she frequently yielded to the importunities of Amelia and Clementina to be allowed to accompany her, and Cecily too then made one of the party, for Lady Bonshawe, once set down in a silk warehouse amid the distractions of satins and gauzes, could not be expected to concern herself with looking after her lively offspring.

Cecily was not at all averse to these interruptions in a daily routine which, while it could not be said to be dull, with such damsels as Amelia and Clementina in her charge, was scarcely an agreeable one to her. It never occurred to her that she might meet anyone on these excursions who would recognise her as Miss Daingerfield-Nelson, for, even were someone who had seen her on the London stage to come across her in Bath, they would scarcely connect that dashing young lady with the demurely attired governess shepherding two schoolgirls through the Milsom Street shops.

But her feeling of security in this respect was quite shattered one afternoon in late February when, as the carriage proceeded along George Street, she suddenly perceived Mr. Jillson in the throng passing on the flagway. She uttered a startled exclamation and shrank back against the squabs.

"What is it, my dear?" Lady Bonshawe asked, with her ready curiosity.

"Nothing at all!" Cecily said hastily. "That is—I thought for a moment that I had seen someone I knew, but it is no such thing."

Lady Bonshawe gave her hearty laugh. "Well, it is someone you don't much care to see, I'll be bound," she said, "for you have turned quite as pale as a sheet, my dear."

Cecily, who was wondering anxiously whether Mr. Jillson had seen her through the window of the chaise, tried to smile and return a negligent answer, but she was conscious that she succeeded ill in this endeavour.

The sight of Mr. Jillson had, in fact, given her the severest cause for apprehension. She had been long enough in Lady Bonshawe's household to realise that propriety was the goddess before whom that worthy dame worshipped, for it was the highest ambition of both her and Sir William to advance themselves in the world which Sir William's wealth had enabled them to enter. Therefore, if Mr. Jillson were to betray her to them, it was quite impossible that they would wish to continue to employ her. Even the aura cast about her by her highborn connexions would not then be sufficient, she feared, to cause them to accept the gossip that must arise when it became known that they were employing as governess a young woman who had appeared upon the London stage. She would be sent back to Hillcourt without ceremony, and, what was worse, Lady Frederick must be exposed to the censure of Lady Bonshawe and Mrs. Casewit and their set, which would certainly spread beyond it and perhaps eventually reach even those more elevated circles in which Lady Frederick and Mr. Ranleigh themselves moved.

When the chaise stopped in Milsom Street and she was obliged to step down from it, she cast a glance of trepidation along the street, but to her relief Mr. Jillson was nowhere in sight. She hurried Amelia and Clementina into the shop—much to the discontent of Clementina, who had spied a street-crier selling hot spiced gingerbread—and was able to breathe more easily once the door had closed behind them.

It was not to be supposed, however, that one of Lady Bonshawe's shopping expeditions would be confined to her entering a single warehouse, and, once she had settled upon the purchase of a spotted ermine muff, she led the way down the street in search of a set of silver filigree head ornaments. Again Cecily's eyes anxiously scanned the passing pedestrians, and again she found herself safely inside a jeweller's shop without having had a sight of Mr. Jillson.

A half hour had now passed since she had seen him in George Street, and she was beginning to feel that she might relax when Lady Bonshawe, recollecting that she had brought along a book to change at Duffield's Library, requested her to undertake that errand for her while she decided among the several sets of ornaments that had been brought out for her approval. Cecily was obliged to comply, and set out alone from the shop.

She had not gone ten paces from it, however, when she saw, to her dismay, that Mr. Jillson was crossing the street toward her, nimbly dodging between the wheels of a gentleman's tilbury and those of a lumbering wagon. She averted her eyes and hurried on, hoping that he had not as yet seen her and that she would be able to make her escape before he had done so; but her hope was in vain. In the space of thirty seconds he was beside her, raising his hat and falling into step with her as she continued to hurry along the flagway.

"Miss Hadley!" he said. "I thought I could not be mistaken! What an agreeable surprise!"

For a moment she thought of refusing to recognise him, but it would not do: she knew him well enough to be sure that she could not be rid of him by any means so simple as a quelling stare and icy silence.

She tried a direct attack instead. Halting on the flagway, she said to him determinedly, "What do you want of me, Mr. Jillson?"

He looked at her reproachfully. "Why, my dear, what an unhandsome greeting to an old friend!" he said. "One might almost imagine you were not pleased to see me."

"Well, I am not pleased," Cecily said downrightly. "I wish to have no more to do with you, Mr. Jillson—and if it is that money you lent us, you know very well that Aunt left all that was still owing of it for you at the Running Boar before we set out from London."

"But, my dear young lady, of course she did! And even if she had not— can you think I should have been guilty of such a solecism as to approach you with a dun in mind?"

She looked him up and down, noting that his raiment, though decidedly fashionable, displayed a telltale shabbiness.

"Well, you certainly look as if you might be in need of money," she said frankly, "so I should not be at all surprised if you had."

"A merely temporary embarrassment," he assured her, waving the observation away with an airy hand. "Owing to an unfortunate concatenation of circumstances, my spouse and I find ourselves at the present moment between engagements, but we shall be returning next week to London, where the managers of the Surrey Theatre have assured me that a prominent place awaits us in their company, so that we shall soon be living as high as coach-horses. Which I have reason to think, my dear, *you* are not doing at the present moment, any more than I am. If my eyes have not deceived me, you are wasting your considerable talents in the capacity of governess to those two female imps in whose company I saw you a half hour back."

"So you *did* see me!" Cecily said accusingly. "And have been hanging about ever since, I daresay, hoping for the chance to speak to me!"

"Exactly," said Mr. Jillson, unabashed. "Not," he added, "that I was unprepared, if need be, to approach you in the company of the estimable, if somewhat overdressed, female who appears to be your present employer——"

"You wouldn't!" Cecily interrupted, indignantly.

Mr. Jillson regarded her with an expression of some interest. "Ah!" he said. "So the good lady is *not* informed of your career as Miss Daingerfield-Nelson? I rather fancied that she might not be."

Cecily, her eyes flashing, gave him back look for look. "No, she is not!" she said. "And if you are thinking of telling her, you are the shabbiest creature alive! What is more," she added, "if you believe I shall go back to the theatre if she dismisses me, you are *quite* mistaken. I—I am by no means as friendless as you think me, Mr. Jillson!"

"No?" he said, interested. "And who *are* these obliging friends of yours, Miss Hadley? Do they still include in their number, for instance, the famous Mr. Ranleigh? That appears to me highly doubtful, I must confess, considering your present situation——"

He paused, observing that Cecily's brows had drawn together in a distinctly menacing frown.

"That is none of your affair," she said, beginning to walk on down the street.

"Well, well, at any rate, it need not concern us now," he agreed. "The point of the matter is that I am prepared to offer you a handsome future—infinitely more appealing than the grubby drudgery into which you have at present fallen—if you will agree to throw in your lot with me once more."

Cecily halted again. "Well, I shan't!" she said bluntly. "You are wasting your time, Mr. Jillson. I am *quite* content where I am!"

"My dear," he said, frankly surveying her, "if you could but see your face when you say that, you would not make such a ridiculous statement! Content to bury yourself here in Bath—or is it in the country, which is even worse?—looking after another woman's brats, when you might be the reigning toast of London? I do not believe it."

Cecily, about to make a heated denial that she found anything in the least repellent in the notion of spending the remainder of her days as a governess, checked, conscious that she would be quite unable to make such a statement at all convincing. After a pause, she said instead, "Well, it does not signify whether you believe it or not, because, whatever happens, I am *not* going back to the theatre."

"Another rash statement," Mr. Jillson said, shaking his head. "I see that it is matrimony you have in mind, dear child—but let me point out to you that to achieve that happy end is not a simple matter for a penniless young lady. On the other hand, were you to gain the plaudits and the fortune which I am offering you, you might look to establishing yourself eventually in the first style. Why, my dear, there are any of half a dozen you might have if you played your cards properly—Brackenridge, Lovett, young Portandrew—They were all cast into flat despair when you disappeared; in fact, they made devilish nuisances of themselves, trying to find out where you were gone to!"

"I do not care about that!" she said obstinately. "And I beg you will stop following me, for I do not at all wish to talk to you any longer, and I must get back to Lady—to my employer."

He shook his head again, with a more melancholy air. "If you wish, my dear," he said. "But you are making a great mistake, you know." He viewed her unyielding profile and sighed. "Very well," he said. "I shall importune you no further. But if you should change your mind, pray remember that a message conveyed to the Running Boar will reach me promptly, and that news of my whereabouts can always be obtained there."

He then raised his hat politely and walked off, leaving her free to pursue her errand alone.

The encounter had been an unnerving one, but by the time she rejoined Lady Bonshawe and her charges she had succeeded in shaking off the greater part of her agitation, and was able to present a tolerably cheerful countenance to her employer. She was excessively relieved, however, to find that she saw no more of Mr. Jillson that afternoon, and she returned to Inglesant with far less than her usual regret at leaving the bustle of Bath for the quiet of the country once more.

14
But her relief at having escaped having her career as Miss Daingerfield-Nelson called to Lady Bonshawe's attention was short-lived. Not a fortnight later, on an afternoon early in March, Lady Bonshawe arrived home from a drive with her friend, Mrs. Casewit, in a flutter of pleasurable agitation.

"Only think, my dear, whom I have met today!" she exclaimed, unbosoming herself, for want of a better confidante, to Cecily, whom she found supervising Clementina's practice upon the pianoforte. "Do leave the girls for a moment and come into my dressing-room, for I must tell someone about it or I shall burst!"

Cecily, surveying the bronze-green carriage dress into which her ladyship had squeezed her ample form, was of the opinion that such a fate was not improbable, whether she succeeded in unburdening herself of her news or not. But she was too happy to escape from Amelia and Clementina to waste more than a moment on considering the appropriateness of Lady Bonshawe's words, and followed her thankfully down the stairs to her dressing-room.

Here Lady Bonshawe discarded her high-crowned Pamela bonnet without ceremony and, plumping herself down in an easy chair, immediately inquired of Cecily if she had ever heard of Sir Harry Brackenridge.

"But I daresay you have not," she went on, too unobservant to note the start which the name had drawn from Cecily, "living retired in the country as you have done. I assure you, though, that he is quite as well-known as Mr. Ranleigh—a very Pink of the Ton. Well! Would you believe it?—it turns out that he is a nephew to Lady Kerwin and has come down on a visit to her, and Maria Casewit is to get up a party for next Saturday, which he means to come to, and, depend upon it, will come to Inglesant as well if I can but prevail on Sir William to allow me to send out cards for a dinner party. For he is all condescension, my dear, not in the least what one would expect, for he moves in the very *highest* circles, and, while Lady Kerwin *did* call when Sir William and I came into the neighbourhood, we are not at all intimate with her, and I have always considered her odiously toplofty."

Cecily, sitting in stunned silence before this conversational avalanche, paid very little heed to it; she had, in fact, heard nothing after Lady Bonshawe's announcement that Sir Harry Brackenridge had come into the neighbourhood. She would not recognise Sir Harry if she walked straight into him at high noon, but it was certain that he would recognise *her*, for his name had been signed to one of the invitations to supper that she had received during her brief theatrical career. What was more, Mr. Jillson had mentioned him, not a fortnight since, as being one of the gentlemen who had made strenuous efforts to discover her whereabouts, and it was to be gathered, therefore, that his interest in her was more than a casual one.

A horrid suspicion that her meeting with Mr. Jillson might have had something to do with Sir Harry's sudden appearance on the scene in Somerset crossed her mind, and the suspicion, far from being allayed, rose to more ominous heights as Lady Bonshawe rambled on, "To be sure, no one could have expected that he would not set himself on as high a form as Lady Kerwin does, so that I thought, when we met him, that he would certainly give us the go-by with no more than a bow, but not at all! He drew up his curricle, just as Maria promised me he would—for he had been introduced to her yesterday at the Allens' and was the *soul* of amiability, so that she had quite decided to ask him for Saturday if she were to see him again. And he accepted without the least hesitation! It quite provokes me with Sir William, that he will not exert himself to go about as Mr. Casewit does, for Maria is always stealing a march on me in this way. But I am determined that he shall give me the chance to ask Sir Harry here to dine, and so I shall tell him as soon as ever he comes in!"

Cecily could only hope that Sir William would find it expedient to veto this plan or that, if he did not, she herself would be permitted to dine upstairs in the schoolroom with Amelia and Clementina; but neither of these wishes was destined to be granted. Sir William, when approached on the matter, was quite as eager as his lady to entertain so notable a social figure as Sir Harry Brackenridge, and Lady Bonshawe, in making up her table for the projected dinner, informed Cecily that she would expect her to be one of the company.

"For of course Sir Harry must be well acquainted with Mr. Ranleigh," she said, "since they move, I understand, in the very same circles, so that I am sure nothing could be more proper than for me to introduce a connexion of his to him. And you need not put yourself into a taking over what you will wear, for I shall have Trimmer take in my sea-green Italian crape for you, for Sir William does not at all care for it and, indeed, the colour is very trying to my complexion."

No argument that Cecily dared advance succeeded in prevailing against her determination. Cecily saw that she intended to make her presence a proof to Sir Harry of her own intimate acquaintance with the Ranleighs, and understood that she would be made to figure rather as a protégée of the Bonshawes than as anything so common as a mere governess. What Brackenridge's response to all this would be, she could not venture the remotest guess. That he must recognise her, she could not doubt; but whether he would betray her or not was something that must be left wholly to the future to reveal.

Tuesday, the day set for the dinner party, arrived all too quickly. No fortuitous illness had smitten her to allow her to absent herself from Lady Bonshawe's table, nor had the happy news arrived at Inglesant that Sir Harry had broken his collarbone in a fall from his horse, or some other such fortunate minor accident. Quite desperate, Cecily ventured to approach Lady Bonshawe at five o'clock with her last forlorn hope, the plea that she felt a dreadful headache coming on.

But Lady Bonshawe, usually the soul of sympathy, merely stared at her in a flustered way.

"A headache!" she said. "Well, I am very sorry, my dear, but it cannot signify, for I can't and won't have my table put out at this hour, not if it was ever so! If you will go and lie down upon your bed for a time, I have no doubt it will soon pass off—though, indeed, I shall be sorry if you feel you must do so, for I have been depending upon you to keep Millie and Clemmie from getting into everyone's way."

In the face of these remarks, Cecily could do nothing but return to her young charges, her problem quite unsolved.

She dressed herself a little later in Lady Bonshawe's sea-green Italian crape with emotions very similar to those of one going to the gallows. Her only hope, it appeared, now lay in Brackenridge's having the good breeding not to betray his surprise at having a young lady whom he had known as an actress named Miss Daingerfield-Nelson introduced to him as Miss Hadley, a governess. If that were the case, she might manage somehow to take him aside during the evening and throw herself upon his generosity. It was a scene which she had the greatest difficulty in imagining herself playing, but at least it would not be so trying as another scene that kept recurring hideously to her mind, in which Sir Harry, already apprised by Mr. Jillson of her deception, exposed her ruthlessly to the company at the moment of their introduction.

That moment soon arrived. She was in the Green Saloon with Sir William and Lady Bonshawe and the early arrivals among their guests when Sir Harry Brackenridge was announced, and her eyes at once flew to the door. She saw a tall man with cold blue eyes and hair of an odd brassy-yellow colour come into the room, his exquisitely fitting coat, intricately tied neckcloth, and air of distinction at once casting every other gentleman in the room into the shade. Cecily gazed at him in despair: nothing in his attitude, as he bowed with what seemed to her rather mocking civility over Lady Bonshawe's hand, appeared to indicate the sort of good nature to which one might readily appeal. She swallowed convulsively as she saw his eyes, languidly surveying the assembled company, come to rest upon her own face for a moment, and when she was finally brought forward to be introduced to him she felt as if she must sink through the floor.

"And this is my young friend, Miss Hadley, who is so kind as to lend me her help in looking after my two darling girls," Lady Bonshawe said, her face beaming with the broad, triumphant smile that had creased it ever since she had beheld Brackenridge step into her saloon. "I daresay you have never met her, but she is a connexion of the Ranleighs, and was recommended most highly to me by Lady Frederick Ranleigh."

Cecily, who had been anxiously watching Brackenridge's face for any sign that he had recognised her, saw the merest flicker of surprise enter his eyes as Lady Bonshawe uttered these last words. But it was gone on the instant, and he said to her with the utmost composure, "Delighted, Miss Hadley! The Ranleighs, you said, Lady Bonshawe? Then I take it that Miss Hadley may be well acquainted with a gentleman with whom I was in company myself not two days before I came into Somerset—Mr. Robert Ranleigh?"

"Oh, indeed she is!" Lady Bonshawe said volubly. "In point of fact, she had been staying at Hillcourt just before she came to us here—such an elegant house, I am sure! I quite long to see it!"

The arrival of new guests claimed her attention at that moment, and, as Brackenridge was seized on by Mrs. Casewit, Cecily was free to move away and to congratulate herself breathlessly on having at least got through that first dreadful moment without discovery.

But by the time the company went in to dinner her self-congratulation had already given way to renewed anxiety. Certainly Brackenridge had not betrayed that he was conscious of having seen her before, but there had been an almost mockingly amused expression on his face as he had looked at her that gave her the uneasy feeling that she might be about to be made the unwilling participant in a game of cat-and-mouse.

In fact, the more she turned the matter over in her mind the clearer it became to her that he must have been aware before he entered the house that evening that he would meet Miss Daingerfield-Nelson there as Miss

Hadley. Jillson! she thought furiously. It would have been a simple enough matter for him to find out Lady Bonshawe's identity in Bath, for she was well-known there, and, once he had realised that his desire to profit by placing Cecily upon the stage under his own aegis could not be fulfilled, he had undoubtedly followed what had appeared to him the next best course by passing his information on to Brackenridge—no doubt at a handsome price, she reflected bitterly.

It was disturbing to her to think that Brackenridge would go to such lengths to pursue her. She was not vain, which gave her the clarity of vison to realise that it might not be infatuation alone that was his motive. Remembrance of the wager that had first brought Mr. Ranleigh to the Running Boar crossed her mind. A rivalry between the two men there well might be: even she was aware that Sir Harry's exploits were almost as famous in the Corinthian set as were those of the Nonpareil himself, nor could she forget the ambiguous flicker of light that had leapt into his eyes when Lady Bonshawe had mentioned her connexion with the Ranleighs.

He was beginning to put the pieces of the puzzle together, she felt; and she felt, too, that if he saw in the situation the opportunity to discomfit Robert Ranleigh he would be willing to use her quite ruthlessly to attain that end.

Fortunately, she was placed at such a distance from him at table that he could neither converse with her nor observe her while the meal lasted. It was a very elaborate one, for Lady Bonshawe had urged her cook to frenzied heights, and as a result the company was treated to two full courses, consisting of half a dozen removes and more than a score of side-dishes. There was a tureen of turtle, removed with fillets of turbot, which in turn were removed with a haunch of venison served with chevreuil sauce; and the second course offered a green goose with French beans and broiled mushrooms, tenderones of veal and truffles, a Gâteau Mellifleur, and a quantity of jellies and creams.

As far as Cecily was concerned, however, she might have dined on cold porridge with equal pleasure, and she was grateful for the cook's efforts only to the extent that the dishes he had prepared were absorbing the attention of the two gentlemen between whom she sat, leaving her free from the necessity of carrying on any extensive conversation with them. This freedom enabled her to gather, from the scraps of talk she overheard from Brackenridge's vicinity, that he was in excellent spirits, and was succeeding in captivating Lady Bonshawe to such an extent that it was probable he might have the entrée at Inglesant whenever he chose during the remainder of his stay in Somerset.

She had a brief respite from his company when the ladies rose from the table to return to the Green Saloon, but not even Sir William's excellent brandy was sufficient to hold the gentlemen long in the dining-room. All too soon Cecily saw Brackenridge's tall figure enter the saloon. He went at once, with graceful address, to Lady Bonshawe, and Cecily took advantage of his preoccupation with her to rise from a seat which she felt placed her in undesirable prominence and retire to one of the pillared alcoves in the corners of the room.

She had reason to regret her choice of retreat, however, when, some quarter hour later, she saw Brackenridge leave Lady Bonshawe and, by amiable degrees, with a word here and a bow there, stroll over to her side of the room. A few moments afterward he was standing beside her, leaning against one of the alcove's fluted pillars and surveying her with a composed smile on his lips.

"So, Miss Hadley," he said, with a slight, satirical emphasis on the name, "you are a connexion of Robert Ranleigh's, it seems. How odd that he has never mentioned it to me!"

She scarcely knew where to look, but pride came to her rescue as she saw how well he was enjoying her discomfiture, and she put up her chin defiantly.

"I do not think it at all odd," she said. "I daresay he does not recite a catalogue of his connexions to all his friends—if you *are* indeed his friend, sir."

"How acute of you to gather that I am not!" Brackenridge murmured, thwarting the efforts of a stout matron in a pomona green turban to catch his eye. "And you, Miss Hadley?" he went on. "Are *you* entirely satisfied with the quality of Robert's friendship? I must own that I find myself somewhat surprised in your case, for he has the reputation of being excessively generous to those who may feel themselves entitled to the reward of his—er—gratitude."

Cecily coloured vividly. "You have quite mistaken the situation, sir!" she said, with as much ice in her voice as she could summon. "I have no such claim upon Mr. Ranleigh."

His brows went up. "No?" he said softly. "Dear me, you modern young females——! No doubt I am sadly old-fashioned to think otherwise."

She was growing more indignant by the moment at his having the audacity to speak to her so, but with the eyes of half the room upon her she was obliged to control herself. She said stiffly, "I should like you to know, sir, that I consider that Mr. Ranleigh and his mother have *both* been excessively kind to me. And if I may suggest it to you—you had much better go and talk to someone else, for I am only the governess here, and it is not at all suitable for you to single me out in this way."

"But I do not wish to talk to anyone else," Brackenridge said, with his teasing smile. "I wish to talk to you, *Miss Daingerfield-Nelson*. As a matter of fact, I came here this evening particularly for that purpose."

She had started visibly at the sound of the name, and could not prevent herself from giving him an imploring glance.

"Oh, that is better! Much better!" he said approvingly. "I infinitely prefer that melting look to your termagant one, my dear!"

Her lips curled angrily. "You are the most detestable man I have ever met!" she said. "Are you going to give me away?"

Brackenridge, raising his quizzing-glass to his eye, became absorbed in the details of a portrait across the room. "That, my dear," he said, "depends entirely upon you."

"Upon *me*? How can I prevent you——?"

He allowed the quizzing-glass to fall and looked down at her again. "Oh, quite easily!" he said. "You have only to ask it of me with the proper complaisance."

Cecily's eyes flashed. "Well, I shan't! I shan't ask anything of you—ever!"

"What a singularly rash statement to make!" Brackenridge said, smiling once more. "Are you fond of wagers, Miss Hadley? I should like to lay one with you that you will very soon find you are *quite* mistaken."

Cecily said grittily, maintaining an appearance of decorous calm only with the greatest of efforts, "If you do not go away at once, sir, I shall get up from this chair and walk away from *you*."

"Oh, no, you will not," Brackenridge assured her silkily. "That is, of course, unless you have a fancy to hear me entertaining this worthy company with an exact description of the circumstances under which Robert Ranleigh first became acquainted with you."

"Oh!" she gasped. "You would not! You could not be so odious!"

"That," he agreed, "is entirely possible. Let us say, at any rate, that I am open to persuasion. However, this scarcely seems the proper place to allow you to put forth your best efforts in that regard. Shall I look forward to a more private conversation with you tomorrow?"

"But I can't! You must know I can't!"

"Nonsense!" he said encouragingly. "I am sure, if you consider the alternative——"

"Oh, very well!" she said, casting a despairing glance at him. "I—I shall come down early tomorrow morning and—go for a walk in the shrubbery—alone."

"Excellent! Shall we say eight o'clock?"

She nodded miserably, and had the inestimable relief of seeing him bow and walk off, just in time to prevent their being joined by Sir William, who evidently considered it his duty as host to see to it that Brackenridge spent his time with more exalted personages than a governess. He bore Sir Harry off, and Cecily was left to calm her agitated feelings as best she might.

Brackenridge did not approach her again during the evening, which was of some assistance to her in this endeavour. But she could not think without the greatest foreboding about the assignation that she had appointed with him for the following morning, for unless she could succeed in persuading him then not to reveal to the Bonshawes the facts of her career as "Miss Daingerfield-Nelson," her employment at Inglesant, she was convinced, must come to an end.

She went to bed that night in flat despair, and could only hope that the morrow might bring new counsel to enable her to extricate herself from her dilemma.

15 But the morrow—a cloudy March morning, threatening rain—offered no new ideas to her troubled mind. She arose early and, dressing quickly and throwing a cloak around her shoulders, stole downstairs and out to the shrubbery. It was shortly before the appointed hour of eight and the household was hardly stirring yet, after the festivities of the previous evening. She paced up and down anxiously for several minutes in the bare shrubbery, so immersed in her own reflections that she quite failed to hear the tall gentleman in the coat of dandy russet and the exquisitely fitting buckskins strolling up behind her until he was almost upon her. Then she gave a little jump of surprise and whirled around.

"Sir Harry!" she exclaimed. "Oh! You startled me!"

"But you were expecting me, surely?" Brackenridge said, smiling at her in the tantalizing way she had already come to detest. He reached out and calmly possessed himself of both her hands. "Come, my dear, don't let us play games with each other," he said. "We have both of us come here this morning with a very definite purpose in mind. Yours, I imagine, is to persuade me not to reveal to the worthy, but exceedingly uninteresting, Sir William and his wife the details of your past career——"

"Yes, yes!" she interrupted him eagerly. "That is it, exactly! And you will not do so, will you? Surely you were only teasing me last night! You can have nothing to gain——"

"On the contrary," he said, still maintaining his hold on her cold, ungloved hands and pausing to raise first one and then the other to his lips, "I have everything to gain, my dear. In other words, your compliance."

"My—my compliance?" Cecily stammered, endeavouring to wrest her hands from the hold which he kept on them and observing with increasing alarm the intent smile on his face as he prevented her from doing so. "I don't understand——"

"But you understand perfectly," Brackenridge contradicted her with the utmost tranquillity. "I should like to take you back to London with me. Failing that—if you still wish to persist in your peculiar determination to remain in this dull, but undoubtedly respectable, position in life—I intend to make it the principal end of my existence to persuade you to be at least as kind to me as you have been to Robert."

"But I—I haven't been k-kind to *him* at all!" Cecily said desperately. "Indeed, you have quite mistaken the matter, sir!"

"Have I?" Sir Harry surveyed her through suddenly narrowed eyes. "Almost, my pet, you persuade me to believe you! But in that case I am doubly determined not to fail as he has done."

"But he didn't fail!" Cecily said urgently. "I mean—he—he didn't *want* to——Oh, you don't understand! He doesn't even *like* me! The only reason he asked his mother to invite me to Hillcourt was that I am *truly* connected with his family." She dashed into a breathless explanation: "You see, my grandfather and his grandmother——"

Brackenridge, releasing her hands, held up one of his own in protest. "Spare me the details!" he said. "I am quite willing to accept your word that you are connected with the Ranleighs. But, my dear girl, what has that to say to *our* affair? You surely cannot believe that the fact that you are related to Robert makes it any the less piquant for me?"

She looked him full in the face, the earnest flush dying out of her cheeks and an expression of warm contempt suddenly appearing on her countenance.

"I see," she said. "I *was* right, then. You are doing this merely to spite Mr. Ranleigh."

He met her accusing gaze, his own quite unmoved. "What an excessively crude way to put it!" he remarked composedly. "I assure you, I was quite smitten with your charms before Robert had ever appeared upon the scene. You know, my dear, you really are something quite out of the common way. That rogue Jillson is entirely correct in thinking that you might make your fortune upon the stage, if only you could be brought to drop your foolish prejudice against it."

"Well, I shan't drop it," Cecily said bluntly. "But I had a good deal rather do so than do what *you* would like me to do."

Brackenridge laughed, not entirely pleasantly. "That is plain enough!" he said. "But it is the privilege of your sex to change your mind, and we must see if I cannot persuade you to do so. I might tell you that I am thought not to be an ungenerous fellow; in fact, knowing that I should meet you when I came into Somerset, I had the forethought to bring with me this small token of my regard." He reached into his pocket and took from it a jeweller's box, which he opened to reveal a pair of diamond eardrops. "For you, my dear," he said.

Cecily looked at the elegant jewels, and then gazed up into his face in astonishment.

"For *me*?" she said. "I think you must be mad, sir! I could not possibly accept such a gift from you!"

"Oh, I think you will find it quite a simple matter to do so," he observed. "You have merely to hold out one of your hands——"

Cecily placed both her hands behind her and backed away a pace or two. "No! I shall do nothing of the kind!"

"But I think you will," Brackenridge said, and, reaching out, drew one of the hidden hands into view and opened its tightly clenched fingers. "You need breaking to bridle, my dear," he said, "but I believe you will find the process not entirely disagreeable, with my hands on the reins." He placed the box in her hand and closed the fingers over it. "No," he said softly, looking into her face, which had flushed with anger and determination, "I should advise you *not* to throw it down upon the ground. Only think what a hue and cry there would be when it was discovered, and explanations can be so difficult—can they not?—when one is dealing with people as hopelessly conventional as Sir William and his lady."

He released her hand and Cecily, forced to concede the truth of what he had said, continued to hold the box in it, regarding him with a smouldering gaze.

"I think you are quite abominable!" she said hotly. "And I shan't wear these—I couldn't!"

"Not here, certainly," he agreed. "But, you see, my dear, I do not think that you will remain at Inglesant forever." He reached out to flick her cheek with a careless finger. "I shall leave you now," he said. "Shall we say tomorrow at the same hour? I shall be seeing you later in the day as well, for I am getting up a little expedition to Wells on which I believe I shall be able to persuade Lady Bonshawe to permit you to go. But that will be meeting in the company of others, and private meetings offer so many more possibilities. Don't you agree?"

He did not wait for an answer, but, slipping one arm about her waist, dropped a kiss upon her averted face as she struggled to free herself and strolled away as he had come, through the shrubbery. Cecily remained standing motionless behind him, seething with fury. This soon gave way, however, to a cold realisation of the almost hopeless position in which he had placed her. If she did not accede to his wishes, he had it in his power to have her dismissed from Inglesant—and what she was to do then she did not know.

But, in any case, she could not remain away from the house any longer. She hurried inside and up to her bedchamber, which she was obliged to leave almost at once, however, on hearing unmistakable intimations that Amelia and Clementina had arisen and required her supervision. She breakfasted with them in the schoolroom, her mind all the while racked with her problem to such an extent that her two young charges misbehaved themselves disgracefully, and were in the act of conducting a battle by flinging lumps of sugar from the bowl on the table at each other when their preceptress finally roused herself sufficiently to part them.

The intrusion of one of the housemaids with a letter that had arrived for her in the post diverted her mind from her problems for a few minutes. It was from her aunt, but, fond as she was of that lady, a letter from her describing a daily routine enlivened by nothing more exciting than young Lord Neagle's latest misdeeds, and containing no reference whatever to Mr. Ranleigh, was quite unable to retain her attention for a longer period of time than was required for her to glance quickly through it.

If it had offered her an excuse for absenting herself for a few weeks from her duties at Inglesant, it might have been otherwise; but both Miss Dowic and Lady Frederick apparently believed that she was content where she was, and neither sent a message that could in any way be construed as an invitation to her to return to Hillcourt.

She set the letter aside disconsolately, only to be seized at once by an idea so breathtakingly brilliant in its simplicity that she could only wonder at her own genius in conceiving it. She could not flee to Hillcourt, ignominiously confessing that she was unable to cope with the situation at Inglesant and throwing herself once again on Lady Frederick's charity: pride forbade that, and the fear that Lady Frederick might simply wash her hands of her and refuse to put herself to any further inconvenience in attempting to obtain another position for her. But her uncle's house lay only a matter of some thirty miles distant, in Hampshire, and she might contrive to make some excuse to go there for a time and thus throw a rub in the way of Sir Harry's schemes. The small matter that no invitation had been offered her did not concern her; Sir Timothy, she felt, could not refuse to receive her when she had stated her dilemma to him, and she had every confidence that, were Brackenridge to go to the length of pursuing her into Hampshire, Sir Timothy would know how to deal with him.

She thought it more probable, however, that Brackenridge, finding her gone—to attend her uncle's deathbed, she improvised further, with a superb disregard for Sir Timothy's notoriously robust health—would have the propriety not to intrude upon her there, and, as he scarcely seemed the man to enjoy kicking his heels in the rural quiet of his aunt's home, she hoped that he would soon return to London.

The more she turned the idea over in her mind, the more satisfactory it appeared to her. She was on tenterhooks to see Lady Bonshawe and obtain her permission to start off for Hampshire, but she was obliged to wait for her interview with her almost until noon, when, on her request, she was admitted to Lady Bonshawe's bedchamber.

She found her sitting up in bed, sipping chocolate, wearing a lace-bedecked wrapper and a cap with lilac ribbons tied under her chin, and at once launched into a hurried and quite mendacious account of the events that required her to go at once into Hampshire.

Lady Bonshawe was astonished. "Your uncle?" she exclaimed. "But, my dear, I'm sure Lady Frederick gave me to understand that you weren't on terms with him?"

"No—yes—that is—you see, it is my aunt, rather, that he has quarrelled with," Cecily explained, somewhat incoherently, "and that is why he wishes to see *me*. People do—do change their minds about their relations sometimes when they are on their deathbeds, ma'am."

"To be sure they do," Lady Bonshawe said feelingly, "and none can know it better than me, for my aunt Kirkmichael left everything she had in the world to her sister Kate, though she had promised me faithfully that I was to have her garnet set and her pearl brooch. But must you go at once, my dear?"

"Oh, yes!" Cecily said fervently. "That is—I do not think I ought to delay, for the letter was quite *gloomy* about the outcome of his illness."

"An apoplexy, you said?" Lady Bonshawe clicked her tongue commiseratingly. "Well, well, it's a wonder it did not carry him off at once, but what a fortunate thing for you that it did not! For if he should have made his will against you, this will give him the chance to alter it, and, though I should be sorry to lose you, for I am sure Millie and Clemmie have taken to you amazingly, of course I should not wish to stand in your way if it is a matter of inheriting your uncle's estate."

She was beginning, Cecily saw, to enter into the spirit of the event with her usual good-humoured extravagance, to the extent that, by the end of a quarter hour, her imagination had magnified Sir Timothy's much encumbered estate into a respectable fortune, and bestowed upon Cecily a future husband—possibly titled—and a country house of some magnificence, where she herself and Sir William would frequently be invited to stay in company with such exalted guests as Lady Frederick and Mr. Ranleigh.

It was not surprising that, in this mood, she should consider it her duty to send Miss Hadley into Hampshire in her own chaise, rather than subject her to the rigours of travelling on the stage. Cecily made some attempt to dissuade her, for she was beginning to feel rather anxiously that the deception she had been obliged to practise upon her to induce her to let her go to her uncle was getting quite out of hand, but to no avail.

"Lord, my dear, what would Lady Frederick say if she was to hear I had sent you jauntering about the countryside on the common stage!" said Lady Bonshawe. "And it is not as though the horses could not easily make the journey within the day, and then Henson may rack up at Romsey and be back here on Friday, which will not discommode me in the least, for we are to go in the Casewits' carriage on the expedition Sir Harry Brackenridge has got up to go to Wells tomorrow."

The mention of Sir Harry's name, with all the disagreeable memories it brought up of their conversation earlier that day, silenced Cecily's objections. She thanked Lady Bonshawe and assured her that she would be ready to start on her journey in the morning, and then returned to her young charges to forestall any further discussion of Sir Timothy's fictitious illness.

No doubt, she told herself remorsefully, she was an unprincipled wretch to deceive the poor lady so grossly; but when she remembered the alternative, and imagined herself obliged either to face Brackenridge in the shrubbery on the following morning or to await his disclosure to Lady Bonshawe of her London career, she could not regret the course that she had taken.

16 So intent had Cecily been on escaping from her meeting with Brackenridge that it was not until she was several miles distant from Inglesant on the following morning that she was able to withdraw her mind from picturing that gentleman's probable wrath when he found she did not intend to appear at their appointed rendezvous and cast it forward to the reception she might receive from her uncle.

She had never visited Sir Timothy's home, her previous meetings with him having been confined to the occasions of the rare visits he had made to her father's house. These had always been brief, and had been discontinued altogether of late years, so that her memories of him were imperfect, consisting chiefly of a picture of a powerfully built but undersized gentleman in an old-fashioned full-skirted snuff-coloured coat and knee-breeches, with a red face and an alarmingly loud voice. He had never betrayed the slightest interest in her, but she had Lady Frederick's word for it that he had expressed his willingness to provide her with a home if she should wish it, and it therefore seemed unlikely that he would be averse to allowing her to remain with him now for the space of a few weeks.

She found herself growing increasingly apprehensive, however, as mile after mile of rolling green Somerset countryside fell behind her, and rehearsed in her mind with some trepidation the speech of explanation with which she would greet her uncle.

But, as it happened, it was not Sir Timothy to whom she was obliged to make this speech, but the redoubtable Mrs. Cassaday. Arriving late in the afternoon at Dowie House, a "black-and-white" half-timbered Elizabethan manor approached by an ancient stone bridge over a dry moat, she found herself facing a buxom middle-aged dame with her carroty curls imperfectly confined under a cap, who demanded to be told what her business was.

"I am Sir Timothy's niece, Miss Hadley," Cecily said, summoning up her dignity under the grinning gaze of the young fellow in greasy corduroys who, though he had opened the door for her, had the look more of an ostler than a footman or a porter. "If you will tell him, please, that I am here——"

"Sir Timothy's gone to Romsey," Mrs. Cassady said uncompromisingly. "You'll have to let *me* know what it is you want."

Cecily's heart sank, but she said, with as much sang-froid as she could muster, "Well, you see—I've come to visit him. I daresay you will not know about it——"

"No more I do, nor he don't, neither, I'll be bound, for he wouldn't have gone off without telling me if he'd been expecting you," Mrs. Cassaday said, her gaze going over Cecily suspiciously. "And I'll tell you something else—I don't know if you're Miss Hadley or Adam's off ox! Nor you needn't be thinking I'll take you in here, when that old nip-farthing as like as not will be in a rare tweak if he comes home and finds I've done it without him telling me to!"

She was interrupted by a look from Miss Hadley that made her realise with some uneasiness that what she had taken for a mere dab of a girl had suddenly become a young lady with an air of decided resolution and a directness of gaze that it was singularly difficult to encounter with impertinence.

"What is your name?" the young lady asked quietly.

Mrs. Cassaday, in spite of herself, found herself dropping a grudging curtsey.

"Mrs. Cassaday, miss."

"Very well, Mrs. Cassaday. I have had a long journey, and I should like to be taken upstairs to a bedchamber immediately. You may send someone out to the chaise to fetch in my portmanteau, and when my uncle arrives you will, of course, inform me at once."

This speech, though delivered, unknown to Mrs. Cassaday, with a good deal of inward trepidation, had the desired effect. The youth in the greasy corduroys was sent outside to fetch in her portmanteau, and she herself was led up the great carved oak staircase to a bedchamber, which, though it had a dusty, unused look, yet held out the comfort of a huge four-post bed.

"You'll be wanting dinner, too, I daresay," Mrs. Cassaday said, tossing her curls with some asperity as she showed her inside. "Well, I hope you ain't too niffy-naffy to have it with me, for that, I can tell you, is what Sir Timothy does!"

She gazed at Cecily, as she spoke, with a bold, meaningful air, and Cecily, her eyes widening, suddenly realised the full significance of the dark hints she had heard her aunt cast out on the subject of Mrs. Cassaday's character. She examined that martially waiting dame with unmaidenly curiosity, wondering rather perplexedly how much she was expected to indicate that she understood from this announcement.

"No," she said at last, cautiously, "I do not *think* I am niffy-naffy, and I am certainly very hungry. Do you dine soon, or do you wait upon my uncle's return?"

Mrs. Cassaday, appearing only slightly mollified by her failure to make any objection to her company, snorted.

"Wait on *him!*" she said scornfully. *"He's* as like as not to stop out all night! *Not,*" she added darkly, "that he won't fly into one of his takings if he *does* come home and finds his dinner ain't on the table on the stroke of five. You'd best see to it that *you* don't keep him waiting, either, or it's a cold welcome you'll get from him!"

And she thereupon flounced out of the room, leaving Cecily alone to assess her rather dismal situation.

She had not much time in which to indulge in reflection, however, if she wished to refresh her appearance after her journey so that she might appear downstairs before her uncle's early dinner hour had arrived. As a matter of fact, she was still putting the finishing touches on her toilette when she heard a door slam violently somewhere below and the sound of a loud masculine voice. She drew a thin shawl over her shoulders against the chill of the old house, gave a last pat to the skirt of her jaconet muslin frock, and, gathering her courage, went downstairs, where she found Sir Timothy already in the dining-room, engaged in refreshing himself from the contents of a large tankard and in conversation with Mrs. Cassaday. She recognised him at once, for he appeared to be wearing the same snuff-coloured coat in which she had last seen him years ago, and, except that the bald head had grown balder and the vinous colour of the face more pronounced, he himself had altered little over the period.

She was aware that the same could not be said in her case, and, indeed, from the blank stare with which he greeted her entrance, she gathered that he did not recognise her at all.

He recovered from his astonishment immediately, however, and, to her intense relief, greeted her with a satisfied chuckle.

"What!" he said to Mrs. Cassaday. "Do ye mean to tell me *that's* Grisell's little wench! Well, she's not got the look of her, and that's the mercy of God, for poor Grisell was muffin-faced, whatever ye may say to her good! Come here, lass!" He set the tankard down and extended both his hands toward her. "Ha' ye a kiss for your old uncle?"

Cecily advanced and found herself seized upon and soundly kissed.

"Ay, that's a good lass!" Sir Timothy exclaimed, holding her off at arm's length and examining her with the eye of a man looking over the points of a new filly. "A trifle short of bone, but a sweet goer, I've not a doubt!"

he decided. "Come to visit me, ha' ye? Well, I won't say ye ain't gi'e me a surprise, but ye're welcome, my dear, as long as ye ain't thinking of staying too long. Not that ye've the look of a strong trencherwoman, so the expense of keeping ye mightn't put me out too much if yc'll be saving on candles."

Cecily, somewhat dazed by this handsome acknowledgement, allowed herself to be led to one of the high-backed oak chairs set around a huge table, over one end of which a none-too-clean cloth had carelessly been cast. Her uncle having sat down beside her, and Mrs. Cassaday opposite, the business of the meal was commenced with the appearance of the youth of the greasy corduroys, which he had now exchanged for an ancient suit of black-and-silver livery, bearing a roast shoulder of mutton and a boiled tongue with turnips. Sir Timothy, once he had doled out frugal portions of these dishes upon Cecily's plate and inquired if she would drink porter or tea, apparently considered that he had fulfilled his obligations as host and applied himself exclusively to his dinner, replying only in grunts to the flow of complaints launched at him by Mrs. Cassaday on the subject of the delinquencies of various members of the household.

When a curd pudding was brought in, Cecily made her own attempt to contribute to the conversation by commenting politely on the antiquity of the house, but Sir Timothy, his mouth full of pudding, only waved her to silence. This was somewhat discouraging, but his mood appeared to mellow a little later, when, having completed his repast, he pushed back his plate, called loudly for Jem to bring him another tankard of porter, and calmly invited Mrs. Cassaday to leave the room.

"I must talk to my niece now, old girl," he said to her simply. "You be off, and see that them gals in the kitchen don't gorge themselves into an apoplexy on what's left of that mutton, or we'll all go home by beggar's bush."

His use of the word "apoplexy" sent a faint blush into Cecily's cheeks, which she was relieved to see that Sir Timothy did not appear to notice. He was, however, regarding her shrewdly, and, when Mrs. Cassaday had gone out, said to her, "Out with it now, my dear! Why did ye come here? The last I heard of ye, from that Blood that came to see me about ye in London, ye'd gone on the stage. Ain't married him and run off from him already, ha' ye?"

"Mr. Ranleigh? Oh, no!" Cecily said, blushing now in good earnest. "He didn't want to—I mean, he was so very kind—and Lady Frederick

Ranleigh, his mother, as well—as to put me in the way of obtaining a position as governess in a—a very respectable family——"

"A governess, eh?" Sir Timothy did not appear best pleased by this intelligence, but, having considered it, acknowledged, "Why, it's board and wages till ye find some young fellow who's willing to leg-shackle himself with ye, at any rate. But why ha' ye come to me, then? Got yourself in some sort of hobble, I'll be bound, or ye'd not ha' done so. Not with Mab Dowie dinning it in your ears night and day that ye'd be better off to go to the devil than to me."

Cecily, finding herself obliged at last to make some explanation for her visit, plunged desperately into words.

"Why, you see, sir, I found that I—that is, there was a gentleman arrived to pay a visit in the neighbourhood who—— In short, he made me the object of such particular attentions that I——"

Sir Timothy banged his tankard down upon the table in some irritation. "Zounds, can ye not gi'e me a plain tale?" he demanded. "Some rogue has been trying to get at ye—is that it? And what of this *respectable family* that ye're working for? Can they not put a stop to such goings-on under their own roof?"

"Truly, sir, the fact is that they know nothing of the matter," Cecily said, "and I dare not tell them, for if I do so the gentleman will certainly inform them that he has seen me performing in the theatre, and then I shall lose my employment. But I thought if I were to come to you for a few weeks he might grow discouraged and leave Somerset——"

"Don't want to offer you marriage—is that it?" Sir Timothy said, wrath kindling upon his face. "A-ah, let him come nosing down here after ye and I'll gi'e him a lesson he won't forget in a month! Damned puppy!" He nodded decisively. "Ye've done the right thing—what's your name?— Cecily?" he informed her. "Damn him, let him come if he likes! I'll send him to the right-about!"

Cecily was much relieved to see her uncle take the matter in this spirit, but her relief turned to dismay when Sir Timothy, after gazing at her ruminatively for several moments, said, with a wise leer, "Ay, but the thing of it is, my dear, ye ought to have a husband, for ye're a well-looking gal, and are bound to ha' the dogs after ye when they zee ye're put out to work with no one to look after ye. And I'm thinking I know just the man for ye—Ned Goodgame it is, for he'd like nothing better than to join his land to mine, and I'd a deal rather zee it go to him than to some dandy

I've never laid eyes on. Marry him, my dear, and ye may ha' everything I own when I go, with my blessing."

But Cecily interrupted him here, between amusement and alarm. "Uncle, how can you say so?" she protested. "The gentleman has never set eyes on me, nor I on him. Surely you cannot propose a marriage between us."

"Can't I? Why can't I?" Sir Timothy demanded. Cecily, whose experience with her father had made her quite cognizant of the signs that a gentleman was, to phrase it politely, a trifle above par, began to perceive that the liberal potations in which Sir Timothy had been indulging were beginning to have their effect upon him. There was a mulish look in his eyes, and his temper, never, it seemed, an equal one, appeared to be showing alarming signs of slipping its leash entirely. "Ye're a well-looking lass, ain't ye?—and Dowie blood in ye, as well, that's been here in the county since kingdom come. And *he's* as right a lad as ye'd zee in a day's journey —a regular good 'un to go, will ride like a streak across the trappiest country, takes his fences in flying style——" He set down his tankard and halloo'd for Jem to come in and fill it again. "I'll send Jem with a message to ha' him to dinner with us tomorrow," he said. "Ay, and he's a warm man, too, for there's a tidy property and old Micah, his father, broke his neck on Michaelmas last, so Ned came into his inheritance only three months after he came of age. Ye needn't be thinking it's an old man I'd be saddling ye with, my dear; nay, it's a lively young un, and a fit match for ye——"

Cecily endeavoured in vain to stem the progress of these optimistic plans. Sir Timothy, growing more and more enamoured of his own device for ensuring the passing of his lands into the hands of a young man who apparently had won his approval by the twin virtues of being a bruising rider to hounds and possessing an unassuming nature, would hear none of her objections. He ended by growing so irritated with her that he said he could see Mab Dowie had had the raising of her, and that for his own part he had no use for a wench who would whistle a fine young fellow like Ned Goodgame down the wind for no more than a set of Bath-miss airs.

"Damme, if I thought ye'd ha' made such a piece of work over it, I'd never ha' opened my door to ye!" he declared. "But ye'll zee him tomorrow or my name's not Tim Dowie, and then, if he likes to offer for ye, ye'd best think twice before ye gi'e him your answer, for *I* won't gi'e houseroom to a stubborn jade—not if she was a dozen times my niece!"

Cecily, managing at last to escape from this tirade, went upstairs to her bedchamber between tears and laughter, for, even in the anxiety into which Sir Timothy's sudden penchant for matchmaking had cast her, she could not but find something comical in this new complication. She thought she might place some reliance, too, on young Mr. Goodgame's not pressing his suit quite so rapidly as Sir Timothy desired, even if he were to fall in with the idea of marrying her, for he seemed, by Sir Timothy's description, to be a bashful young man, who was shy even of those damsels in the neighbourhood with whom he had been acquainted all his life.

It was therefore quite possible, she thought, that she might succeed in remaining for a few weeks under her uncle's roof without finding her situation made too uncomfortable by Mr. Goodgame's importunities. At any rate, she believed that she might prefer them to Sir Harry Brackenridge's, and she was almost certain that she would find them a great deal easier to deal with.

17　The idea had never entered Cecily's head that her flight to her uncle would become known at Hillcourt; but she had reckoned without Lady Bonshawe. That worthy dame, though she could by no means have been called an acute observer, had not failed to notice the manner in which Miss Hadley had been singled out by Brackenridge on the evening of the dinner party at Inglesant, and when Sir Harry, on the expedition to Wells that took place on the day of Cecily's departure, showed a pressing curiosity over all the details of that departure and the reasons that lay behind it, certain agreeable ideas began to stir in her brain.

What a thing it would be, she confided to Sir William, if Miss Hadley and Sir Harry, meeting under her roof, were to make a match of it! Certainly he had displayed the most gratifying interest in the girl, and, since she was so well-connected and Sir Harry's own circumstances were such that he need not look for fortune in a wife, it would not be so strange a match, after all, as might at first appear.

She would write to Lady Frederick at once, she decided, and apprise her of the good fortune that might be in store for her protégée, assuring her at the same time that she herself would do everything in her power to forward so delightful a scheme.

The letter, concluding with proper expressions of sympathy for the unfortunate illness which had called Miss Hadley to her uncle's bedside, arrived at Hillcourt on a windy March morning, four-and-twenty hours before Mr. Ranleigh was to drive down from London to spend a few days there over business matters with his agent. Lady Frederick read it with a puzzled crease between her brows, and then walked upstairs in search of Miss Dowie, whom she found in her sitting-room, her spectacles upon her nose and a weighty-appearing tome in her hands.

"This is very odd," Lady Frederick said, sitting down beside her. "Here is a letter from Lady Bonshawe, saying that Cecily has been sent for to Hampshire to your brother, Sir Timothy, who is on his deathbed with an apoplexy. Do you know anything of this?"

Miss Dowie's spectacles dropped from her nose. "On his deathbed? Timothy!" she said incredulously. "Nonsense! He drinks far too much, but he is as healthy as a horse; he is good for another twenty years, at least. And even if he *were* ill, he would never send for Cecily. He could not, for he has not the least notion that she is at Inglesant."

She took the letter which Lady Frederick held out to her and perused it, uttering a contemptuous—"Humph!"—as she returned it to its owner. "The woman's a fool," she said decidedly. "Who is this fellow, Brackenridge?"

"Sir Harry?" Lady Frederick made a grimace of distaste. "Oh, a man of the town—a dandy in the forefront of fashion—a rather dangerous creature, I suspect. It seems to me in the highest degree unlikely that he can have lost his head over Cecily to the extent of wishing to marry her. That he has made her the object of his gallantry I can well believe—but that is another matter altogether." She frowned slightly. "I cannot recall exactly, but it seems to me he was involved in that ridiculous wager that was responsible for Robert's becoming acquainted with the child. If that is so, it is too vexatious! One cannot in the least rely upon his good will, and if he recognised her when he met her in Lady Bonshawe's house——" She consulted the letter again. "But if he did, he cannot have mentioned it to the Bonshawes," she said, looking increasingly puzzled, "for I am sure that, in that case, Lady Bonshawe would never risk her reputation for respectability by promoting a match between him and Cecily."

Miss Dowie, who seemed more perturbed by the possibility of Cecily's being at the present moment under her uncle's roof than by any speculations concerning Sir Harry Brackenridge, said baldly that, in her opinion, it had been a mistake to send Cecily to the Bonshawes in the first place.

"They do not appear to be at all the sort of people to look after her properly," she said. "If that woman really has allowed her to go gallivanting off to Hampshire, she must be a perfect looby. Who wrote the letter to the child that Lady Bonshawe says she received I do not know, but that it was not Timothy I will take my oath!"

"Naturally he did not write it himself if he is expiring from an apoplexy!" Lady Frederick said impatiently. "But I *must* believe that it came from his household. Only think of the dreadful possibilities if it did not! She may even have been induced to go off to a rendezvous with Sir Harry, giving her uncle's illness as a pretext——"

Miss Dowie sat up straight in her chair. "Do you mean to tell me, my lady," she inquired ominously, "that you believe *my* niece would be guilty of such impropriety?"

Lady Frederick shrugged distractedly. "She is very young, you know. And Sir Harry is attractive and experienced—a rake, if you must have the truth. She would not be the first young female——"

"My niece, ma'am, is *not* 'a young female'! She is a lady—as much a lady as you are, and with notions of propriety that are, I have no doubt, a good deal stricter than those on which *you* were reared!" Miss Dowie got up from her chair and stood confronting Lady Frederick with rigid determination. "There has been quite enough of this," she said. "I shall set off for Dowie House at once, and see for myself if the child is there. If she is not——"

"If she is not, you will have not the least notion where to look for her," Lady Frederick said witheringly. "No, really—we had a great deal better wait until Robert arrives tomorrow. I assure you that I am as upset over the matter as you are, but I am sensible enough to recognise that it is scarcely a matter that we can undertake ourselves. If Brackenridge *is* involved in the affair, you will have no idea how to deal with him, or even how to go about finding him."

Miss Dowie, considering, was obliged to acknowledge the truth of this, but she did so grudgingly, unwilling to give up her plan of going instantly in search of her niece. A little further reflection, however, and Lady Frederick's promise to send her into Hampshire in her own travelling-chaise as soon as Robert arrived, if he had no better plan to propose, reconciled her to the short delay involved in carrying out Lady Frederick's wishes. Obviously she would gain little time by setting out on the earliest stagecoach, and, if she did not find Cecily at Dowie House, she realised that she would be brought quite to a standstill.

She therefore determined to await Mr. Ranleigh's arrival with what patience she could muster, but, as neither her anxiety nor Lady Frederick's abated overnight, frayed nerves caused hostilities to break out between them afresh on the following morning, and it was a pair of highly militant females whom Mr. Ranleigh, arriving at Hillcourt in good time for dinner, found awaiting him in the Small Saloon.

He strolled in, still wearing the top-boots, buckskins, and riding-coat in which he had driven from London, and regarded the two of them with a look of considerable amusement on his face.

"What have I done to merit *this?*" he inquired, crossing the room to his mother's chair and, after bowing over her hand, bestowing a civil greeting upon Miss Dowie. "Do you know, I rather flattered myself, on the way down, that you would be glad to see me?"

"I *am* glad to see you," Lady Frederick said bitterly. "We have been waiting for you, as a matter of fact, since yesterday morning." She held a sheet of elegant hot-pressed notepaper out to him and commanded briefly: "Read this!"

Mr. Ranleigh's brows rose, but he took Lady Bonshawe's letter and perused it. As he did so, the two ladies saw the smile disappear from his face, and, in their relief at having been able to shift the burden of their anxiety on to masculine shoulders, burst simultaneously into speech, demanding to know his opinion of the matter.

His only immediate response was a rather grim frown. He was reading the letter again, more carefully this time, it seemed. When he had done, he looked over at Miss Dowie.

"You knew nothing about this, ma'am?" he asked curtly.

"No, indeed I did not!" she replied. "Nor do I credit a word of it, Mr. Ranleigh. As I have told Lady Frederick, my brother could have had no notion that Cecily was at Inglesant, and even if he were on his deathbed he would not have sent for her."

"I am dreadfully afraid, Robert," Lady Frederick put in, "that it has something to do with that horrid creature, Brackenridge. Was it not he who laid the wager with Anthony over Cecily that brought about your acquaintance with her?"

"It was," Mr. Ranleigh said. Miss Dowie was surprised to see that a slight flush had crept into his lean face and an implacable expression into his grey eyes; she was not a timid woman, but it occurred to her that she would not care to face those eyes if she were the person who had incurred their owner's displeasure. "It is quite possible," he went on deliberately, "that he is involved in this affair in some way." He turned to Miss Dowie. "In what part of Hampshire is your brother's house, ma'am?" he asked. "I believe I had best pay a call on him."

"Oh, will you go yourself, sir? That would be very good of you!" Miss Dowie exclaimed. "It is near Romsey—but of course I shall go with you, and shall be able to direct you."

Lady Frederick, who had been watching her son's face rather anxiously, interrupted at this point to ask him, "But what will you do, Robert, if you find that the girl is *not* with Sir Timothy? Surely, if she *has* been so imprudent as to run off with Brackenridge, it is not your responsibility——"

"On the contrary, ma'am, it is very much my responsibility," Mr. Ranleigh said levelly. "Miss Hadley is under my protection."

"But you would not feel obliged to call Brackenridge out!" Lady Frederick exclaimed, her alarm rising even higher at these words. "No, really, Robert——!"

Miss Dowie, her own cheeks beginning to fly martial colours, said tartly, "I must beg you to refrain from casting aspersions upon my niece's character, my lady! Cecily would never demean herself so as to run off

with a man! You may depend upon it, if she is found to be with Brackenridge, he has abducted her—and in that case, though I have always held
the practice of duelling in the greatest abhorrence, I hope that Mr. Ranleigh *may* shoot him!"

"But *he* may shoot Robert, you idiotish woman!" Lady Frederick cried.
"And I will not have it! Do you understand that, Robert? If that odious
man has indeed succeeded in ruining the child, you will bring her here to
me, and *I* shall see to it that any scandal is scotched—which it most assuredly will *not* be, you must see, if you are foolish enough to call Brackenridge out!"

Mr. Ranleigh, perceiving that the two ladies were quite ready, in their
agitation, to run to the most extreme lengths of conjecture, at this point
deemed it prudent to pour cold water upon their imaginations by remarking that he had no doubt they should find Miss Hadley safe with her
uncle, and thereupon announced that he was going upstairs to change his
dress for dinner.

He then walked out of the room, but in the hall was at once pounced
upon by young Lord Neagle, who greeted him with great cordiality and
inquired hopefully if he would have time on the morrow to take him out
in his curricle and let him handle the reins, so that he might learn how to
point the leaders and turn a corner in style as he himself did.

"No, not tomorrow," Mr. Ranleigh replied, proceeding up the stairs
with his nephew hot on his heels. "I find that I shall have to go into
Hampshire tomorrow."

"Hampshire! But you've only just got here! Are you bamming me?"
Lord Neagle inquired suspiciously. "Grandmama said you were coming
down to see Dyson about estate business."

He followed Mr. Ranleigh into his bedchamber, where Dawe, his valet,
was engaged in laying out his clothes for the evening.

"I say, exactly *what* is going on here?" Lord Neagle persisted. "Hampshire? Has it something to do with Cecily? Grandmama had a letter from
Lady Bonshawe yesterday, and, while she wouldn't tell *me* what it was
about, I could see she and Miss Dowie were both——"

He broke off, under the weight of a resigned stare from his uncle, and
glanced impatiently at Dawe, who, having proceeded to brush an imagi-
nary speck of dust from an exquisitely cut coat of blue superfine, unhurriedly bowed himself out of the room.

When he had gone, Lord Neagle sat down on the bed and said, undaunted, "It *is* about Cecily—ain't it? The two old ladies have been in

high fidgets ever since yesterday morning. Has she run off from that governess place? I rather thought she might, you know. A dashed dull business *I* should think it was for her, after being in the theatre."

Mr. Ranleigh looked down at him, a faint smile appearing on his hitherto frowningly preoccupied face.

"If your grandmother overhears you referring to her as 'the old lady' at any time, I should advise *you* to run off, my lad," he said, "for you won't be able to weather the storm!"

His lordship grinned. "Know what you mean," he said sagely. "But you haven't answered me."

"I didn't intend to."

"Oh! I see. She *is* in some sort of hobble, then. I rather thought she might be. Good sort of girl—I don't mind telling you I'm deuced fond of her—but things seem to happen to her. Like Tony, for instance. Made her an offer—didn't he?"

"That," said Mr. Ranleigh repressively, "is not, to the best of my knowledge, your affair."

"No, I expect not. Still, it would have been if she'd accepted him, wouldn't it? I mean to say—member of the family then." He considered the matter and acknowledged handsomely, "I shouldn't mind making her an offer myself when I come of age; she's not so *very* much older than I am, you know." Advised briefly by his uncle not to be a gudgeon, he went on, with unimpaired frankness, "Well, I know *you* don't like her, but I can't see what you can have against her, except that she does seem to be always getting into some sort of scrape that makes you stir about. What is it this time? She *must* have run off from the Bonshawes if you are going into Hampshire because of her."

Mr. Ranleigh, into whose eyes a rather odd expression had leapt on the allegation of his dislike of Miss Hadley, refrained from commenting on this matter, and, changing the subject rather pointedly, began to inquire into his nephew's recent activities. The device succeeded, and, an agreeable conversation following, in the course of which Mr. Ranleigh promised to make up for the time that would be lost by his going into Hampshire by remaining a few days longer than he had planned at Hillcourt, the topic of Miss Hadley's present whereabouts was allowed to drop.

18 Meanwhile, Miss Hadley herself, having spent nearly a week under Sir Timothy's roof, had been driven to the point of wondering rather desperately if she dared return to Inglesant, on the hopeful chance that Brackenridge would by this time have gone back to London.

There were two reasons for her desire to leave her uncle's house. The first was a very large, very fair, square-jawed young man named Ned Goodgame. The second was Mrs. Cassaday.

Mr. Goodgame, whose acquaintance she had made on the day following her arrival, had fallen in, with what Sir Timothy considered commendable promptness, with that gentleman's plans for his future. He had no sooner set eyes upon Cecily than he succumbed, dazzled, to the future that had been laid out for him. Fortunately, he was too bashful to have—as Sir Timothy impatiently phrased it—"got down to business" yet, but he spent every available hour at Dowie House, feasting his eyes upon Cecily in all the blissful misery of calf-love.

As for Mrs. Cassaday, the second prong of the pitchfork urging Cecily away from Dowie House, her behaviour toward her employer's niece was based upon the purest self-interest. She had hopes, Cecily had discovered, of yet bringing Sir Timothy to the altar, and, as the future Lady Dowie, she had every objection to Sir Timothy's plans to leave his entire property to his niece.

As a result, she sought by every means in her power to discourage Cecily from remaining in Hampshire, and, since these means included a studied lack of attention to her comfort and convenience, it was not surprising that Cecily found the circumstances of her daily life at Dowie House excessively disagreeable.

On the day following Mr. Ranleigh's arrival at Hillcourt Mr. Goodgame had, as had become customary over the past several days, ridden over to Dowie House to dine with Sir Timothy and his young guest. He arrived shortly before five and walked into the Great Parlour to find Cecily seated with a book on the settle beside the fireplace, where a miserable blaze flickered beneath the huge oak mantel. It was a fine afternoon in late March, but with a wintry chill still in the air. Mr. Goodgame, blushing fiery red at the sight of Cecily, walked over to the fire as he greeted her and busied himself quite unnecessarily with a show of warming himself at the dying blaze.

"Squire not about?" he inquired.

Cecily put aside her book with regret, for she could not look forward with any pleasure to the prospect of a tête-à-tête with Mr. Goodgame.

"I believe he has not come in as yet," she said, "but I expect he will not be late. Won't you sit down?"

"Ay. I'll do that, thank ye."

Mr. Goodgame cast his eye about the room, as if debating the choice of several high-backed chairs which offered him their dubious comfort, but abruptly, with an air of casting caution to the winds, took a pair of hasty strides toward her and seated himself beside her on the settle.

Once he had placed himself there, however, he seemed to have no idea how to go on. He twisted his great hands together between his knees, stared down at the tips of his imperfectly blackened boots, and heaved a pair of laboured breaths, which seemed to be a prelude to an announcement of some sort.

"It is—it is *quite* cool for March," Cecily said hastily, in what she hoped was a completely impersonal and discouraging voice. "Don't *you* find it so, Mr. Goodgame?"

Mr. Goodgame, appearing to be somewhat thrown off his stride by this interruption to his mental processes, considered the matter.

"Ay," he agreed at last. "It is." He added ominously, "That ain't what I came to talk to you about."

"No, I—I expect it is not," Cecily said, casting an anguished glance toward the door in the hope of seeing Sir Timothy appear. "But it is very— very odd—don't you agree?—that we are having such a late spring, when everyone expected——"

She shrank back suddenly, for Mr. Goodgame, wisely refusing to clutter his brain with a search for any further preliminaries, at that moment swooped down and enveloped her in a crushing embrace, remarking thickly, "Came to ask you to marry me. Hope you don't dislike it. The old gentleman's agreeable."

"Mr. Goodgame! Please!" Cecily cried, spiritedly fending off his attempts to kiss her by pushing as hard as she could with both hands against his chest. "I *beg* you will not——"

A third voice interrupted her. "Ay, that's it! To her, lad! She'll ha' ye— never doubt it! They're all alike, ye know—she'll hold ye off at the first, but she'll ha' ye, or my name ain't Tim Dowie!"

Mr. Goodgame, almost as embarrassed as Cecily by this gleeful harangue, loosed his hold upon her as abruptly as if cold water had been poured upon him and sprang to his feet, regarding his host, who stood rubbing his hands together in the doorway, with a discomposed air.

"Sir!" he gasped. "I never heerd ye come in!"

"Nay," Sir Timothy said encouragingly, "never mind me, lad! Ye were doing famously!" He turned suddenly as Cecily, recovering herself somewhat on finding herself released from Mr. Goodgame's grasp, also jumped up from the settle and made as if to walk past him out of the room. "Here! Where are ye off to?" he inquired, in the liveliest astonishment. "Ha' ye gi'e him your answer yet? It's time for dinner, ye know, and we must ha' the thing settled now, so we shall be able to dine in peace!"

Cecily, finding her progress arrested by Sir Timothy's determined grasp upon her arm, halted and said, without raising her eyes to his face, in a voice suffocated with embarrassment, "I must beg you to excuse me, Uncle. Indeed, I do not wish for any dinner today! And as for Mr. Goodgame—I have never encouraged him to believe——"

"Why, what miff-maff is this!" Sir Timothy exclaimed, his colour beginning to rise. "Never encouraged him! That's a loud one! Ain't I zeed the two o' ye sitting here together night after night, as thick as inkle-weavers!"

Cecily looked at him imploringly. "Indeed, Uncle, I have never showed him anything but the civility that was due him as your guest!" she said. "You must know——"

"Showed him anything!" Sir Timothy interrupted her wrathfully. "Ay, I should hope ye never showed him anything, and the two o' ye not even betrothed! But what has that to say to the matter? Nay, all that's needed is to clap hands together and strike the bargain, for ye'll ha' him in the end, ye silly jade, and well ye know it!"

"No, Uncle, I know nothing of the kind!" Cecily said resolutely. She turned to Mr. Goodgame, who had been following the conversation with the greatest attention. "Mr. Goodgame," she appealed to him, "I am persuaded that you will not be so ungentlemanly as to press your suit upon me when I tell you that I do not desire it—that indeed I cannot marry you——"

Mr. Goodgame opened his mouth to speak, but was forestalled by Sir Timothy.

"Cannot marry him!" he exclaimed irefully. "And why can ye not, I should like to know! He's a likely lad, ain't he?—none o' your damned caper-merchants, and top-over-tail in love wi' ye into the bargain——"

"Yes, yes, I know, but I cannot wish to marry him, Uncle," Cecily said earnestly. She turned to Mr. Goodgame again. "Please speak to my uncle, sir!" she said. "Tell him that you will not importune me against my wishes——"

But at that moment an interruption occurred that made all three occupants of the room turn hastily and face the door. None of them, in the warmth of the discussion, had heard the sound of carriage wheels upon the drive outside or the vigorous plying of the knocker, and it was only Mrs. Cassaday's announcement now, delivered from the doorway, that first acquainted them with the fact that visitors had arrived at the house.

"Begging your pardon, sir," Mrs. Cassaday said, in a hollow voice which plainly declared that she had already met the enemy and been put to rout, "but here's Miss Dowie come to see you. *And* Mr. Ranleigh!"

Since Miss Dowie herself entered the room hard on the heels of this announcement, Sir Timothy had time to do no more than blink before he found himself confronting the diminutive figure of his sister, still attired in the pelisse and bonnet in which she had journeyed from Sussex.

"Ha!" she exclaimed, her eyes upon Cecily. "So you *do* have the child here, Timothy! And attempting to force her into a marriage with this—this clodpole," she said, turning to regard Mr. Goodgame with no friendly glance, "if my ears are to be believed! You are, as always, quite disgusting, Brother!"

Mr. Ranleigh, who had come quietly into the room behind Miss Dowie, said civilly to Sir Timothy, who appeared quite thunderstruck by the sudden appearance of his sister within his house, "I must ask your pardon for this intrusion, sir, but the fact of the matter is that we have been quite concerned for Miss Hadley's safety."

"But how did you know that I was here?" Cecily cried, the first of the bewildered trio to recover her tongue. "I didn't tell anyone but Lady Bonshawe and Sir William!"

"Lady Bonshawe," said Miss Dowie, "wrote to us, my dear. An excessively stupid letter it was, with Timothy's expiring of an apoplexy all mixed up with Sir Harry Brackenridge's attentions to you. It is no wonder that Lady Frederick and I were quite at a loss to think what could have happened to you."

Cecily's hands flew to her burning cheeks. "Oh, dear!" she said. "I didn't know—I never imagined—I only told her that, you see, because I *had* to get away——"

She got no further, for Sir Timothy, shaking off his astonishment, at this point burst into speech, demanding to know what the devil his sister meant by it to set her foot inside his door.

"Didn't I tell ye, the last time ever I zeed ye, that I wouldn't ha' ye in my house again?" he roared. "Damme, and here ye come a-marching in as bold as brass, looking to tell me my duty, do ye? Well, I won't ha' it, I tell ye! The girl's come to me now, and I'll ha' the settling o' her in life—and a better business I'll make of it than *you* ever did, I'll be bound, that had her first showing herself off on a stage and then sent to live wi' a pack o' boobies that couldn't tell how to look after her so she wouldn't be in the way to be ruined by some damned dandy!"

"Ruined!" Miss Dowie gasped. She turned to Cecily, her cheeks blanching. "Oh, my poor child! Is it true, then?"

"No, no!" Cecily cried hastily. "Pray do not distress yourself, Aunt! My uncle only means that I was obliged to come to him because—because a certain gentleman's attentions——"

"Brackenridge?" Mr. Ranleigh interrupted curtly.

She glanced up in dismay at his cold, thunderous face. "Yes, but—but, truly—it is not at all as you think!" she stammered. "It was only that he said he should inform Lady Bonshawe of my having been on the stage if I would not—if I—— You see, he has *quite* the wrong impression of why you took me away from London—"

She broke off, seeing that her explanations, far from assuaging Mr. Ranleigh's displeasure, seemed merely to be intensifying it. She had no opportunity to mend the matter, however, for Sir Timothy interrupted at this juncture, declaring that he would not have it, to be set upon by a parcel of meddling busyheads just as he was about to sit down to his dinner.

"Ay, and as pretty a rump of beef as ever I zeed dressed and ready in the kitchen," he said, adding pertinaciously, for his sister's ears, "but you needn't ha' it in mind that I'll ask *you* to sit down to it, for I shan't!"

"And *you* need not think," Miss Dowie replied with spirit, "that I would taste a morsel of food in this house, Brother, while you are master in it! I came here for one purpose only—to remove my niece from the contamination of your presence."

"Contamination!" Sir Timothy sputtered. "Zounds, am I *contaminating* the chit to be offering to wed her to as fine a lad as you'll find in the county, with a neat property besides? But I should ha' known," he went on bitterly, "that ye'd turn up to throw a rub in the way, for ye've no sense in your cockloft and never had—coming here blethering about an apoplexy! What apoplexy? Do I look to ye as if I was dying of an apoplexy?" And in his rage he capered about the room in a hornpipe, coming to a halt before his sister and glaring belligerently into her face.

Miss Dowie, unperturbed by the red visage thrust so close to her own, remarked coldly, "Again, *quite* disgusting, Brother! What Mr. Ranleigh must think of such a performance, I blush to imagine!"

"Ranleigh! What do I care for Ranleigh?" Sir Timothy inquired rudely. "*I* never asked him to thrust his nose into my niece's affairs—and if ye're thinking to marry the wench to him, Sister, ye've less brains than even I gave ye credit for, for it ain't an honest country lass like *her* a Blood o' *his* cut would take a liking to wed, but one o' them painted fine ladies mincing about London with their simpering graces and their airs."

"I believe," Mr. Ranleigh observed, stepping forward at this juncture and addressing Sir Timothy with the cool civility that never failed to depress presumption, "that a discussion of *my* affairs is scarcely to the point, sir. Miss Dowie and I came only to assure ourselves of Miss Hadley's safety and to carry her back with us to Sussex." He turned to Cecily. "If you will instruct a servant to pack up the things you have brought with you, I think we need delay no longer," he said.

Cecily, who was ready to sink at her uncle's bald coupling of her name with Mr. Ranleigh's, and the latter's biting reception of this impertinence, murmured an almost inaudible assent and fled from the room. Her uncle gazed after her in amazement.

"And what might she think to be up to, to go off and flout a good lad like Ned Goodgame, that's ready to offer her honest wedlock?" he demanded. "Damme, what more could I do for her than put her in the way of such a match?—for she might set up her own carriage and live as fine as any lady in the parish. I tell ye, there's no understanding wenches; they're all alike, one minute meek as a nun's hen, and the next giving ye the devil's own amount of trouble with their curst contrary ways!"

The honest bewilderment on his face set a telltale muscle to quivering at the corner of Mr. Ranleigh's mouth, and caused him to say in a more cordial tone, "Indeed, I believe you have the right of it, sir. Still, it will not do for you to attempt to force Miss Hadley's inclinations, no matter how contrary to yours and this young man's they run. I am sure that Mr. —Goodgame, is it?—would not himself desire you to do so."

Mr. Goodgame, finding the eyes of the company upon him, coloured beetroot-red and agreed hastily, "Ay! I mean no!" He added hoarsely, "Not that I'd not be glad to wed with her—that is to say, her being willing——"

"But she is not willing, you see," Mr. Ranleigh said remorselessly, "which must alter the matter—must it not?"

Mr. Goodgame nodded glumly, at which point Sir Timothy, who had been momentarily floored by this desertion of his single ally, rattled in once more to the attack.

"Ay, but if she *ain't* to wed him, what will ye do wi' her then?" he demanded. "Send her back to those rubbishing folk in Somerset that couldn't keep her out o' the reach of a damned dandy that meant nothing but her ruin? I tell ye to your head, I'd not gi'e a brass varden for her virtue if ye do—ay, and ye needn't think to be sending her to me to house when she's damaged goods, for I'll ha' none o' such a stubborn toad, that won't ha' an honest gentleman when he's willing to wed her."

"Brother, you are an idiot!" Miss Dowie remarked roundly. "Do you think for a moment that *my* notions of what is a proper situation for my niece are less nice than yours? I assure you that Cecily will *not* return to the Bonshawes——" She broke off, seeing that Cecily, wearing her pelisse and bonnet, had returned to the room and was standing in the doorway. "Oh, are you back already, my love?" she said approvingly. "Where is your portmanteau?"

"Mrs. Cassaday has been kind enough to see to putting up my things and having them brought downstairs," Cecily said faintly, scarcely daring to meet either Mr. Goodgame's or Mr. Ranleigh's eyes.

She went up to Sir Timothy, however, and thanked him earnestly for having given her the shelter of his roof in the time of her need, which caused him to relent toward her somewhat and to remark grudgingly that she was a pretty-behaved gal, after all, if only she would give over her curst airs and wed as he would wish her to.

"I am truly sorry, sir, but I *cannot!*" she said imploringly.

He shot her a darkling glance from under his bushy brows. "Ay, this is what comes o' being in company with lords and ladies and Bond Street fribbles," he said severely, "for it's plain to me that your head has been turned by them so ye can see neither your duty nor your own interest."

Nevertheless, he kissed her and, clapping her upon the shoulder as if she had been a favourite filly, enjoined her to be a good girl and never give cause to her uncle to blush for her.

"For I'd rather see ye dead than ruined," he said frankly, and then, turning to his sister, said to her in a truculent voice, "Do ye hear that? See that ye keep her out o' the way o' dandies, and if *that* one"—sending a challenging glance at Mr. Ranleigh—"gi'es ye trouble with her, ye'll ha' no more than ye deserve."

"Mr. Ranleigh," said Miss Dowie tartly, "has been the soul of chivalry in this matter. And let me tell you, Brother, that it ill becomes *you*, of all people, to speak of virtue, when your own life is a daily scandal, to the point where I consider it to the highest degree improper for Cecily to have spent even a few nights under your roof." She would have gone on, but, seeing that Mr. Ranleigh was regarding with no great appearance of complaisance this introduction of a new subject of contention between herself and her brother, altered her intention and said instead, "But we shall trespass no more upon your *hospitality*" (the last word uttered with a great deal of sarcastic emphasis). "Cecily, come, my love. No doubt your things have been brought down by now."

In truth, Mrs. Cassaday, her efforts spurred by the desire to have both Cecily and Miss Dowie out of the house as quickly as possible, had flung Cecily's few belongings into her portmanteau and already summoned Jem to carry it out to the waiting chaise. A few moments saw it strapped into place; Cecily mounted up beside her aunt, while Mr. Ranleigh took the reins of his own curricle from Sivil. No extended farewells being made, the little cavalcade soon set out on its way, its destination being—as Mr. Ranleigh informed Miss Dowie—a very respectable inn in the neighbourhood, where they might dine and lie overnight before beginning their return journey into Sussex on the following day.

19 It was a very silent party that took the road for Hillcourt the next morning. Mr. Ranleigh, in the experienced eyes of Sivil, looked remarkably like a man with a question of such vexing moment on his mind that he—Sivil—must have resigned himself to being absentmindedly overturned in some unfriendly ditch had it not been for his knowledge of his master's proficiency as a whip. He drove through the chill spring morning mizzle with his eyes fixed frowningly upon the road ahead; and even when the mizzle thickened to a disagreeably cold rain he only turned up the collar of his driving-coat and proceeded on as if he were as impervious to the weather as to any desire for human companionship.

In the chaise ahead, Cecily and Miss Dowie were equally taciturn. Miss Dowie, who on the previous evening had been inclined to be very well pleased with herself after her victorious encounter with Sir Timothy, was beginning to perceive that she had solved only the most pressing of the problems concerning her niece's future. Obviously, it was impossible for her to return to Inglesant, where Brackenridge might turn up at any moment to communicate the damaging information in his possession to the Bonshawes. But, on the other hand, what was to prevent him from seeking Cecily out elsewhere, if he really was determined to pursue her? A chance meeting with someone who had seen her in the theatre had seemed a risk that might reasonably be taken; but to gamble on Brackenridge's abandoning his deliberate attempt to win the girl to his wishes was a more dangerous matter altogether.

Had she but known it, Cecily, whose silence she presumed to be due to the same considerations that were occupying her, had actually spared not two thoughts to Sir Harry that morning. *She* was preoccupied with the recollection of the ice in Mr. Ranleigh's voice when Sir Timothy had committed the impertinence of linking her name with his. Not by a word or a glance, when her uncle had scornfully referred to the unlikelihood of his wishing to marry her, had he given a sign that Sir Timothy had misread his intentions regarding her. Of course he did not wish to marry her! He was a proud man, and the bearer of one of the proudest names in England: was it likely that he would wish to ally himself with a nobody, a young woman who was no longer even respectable, since she had performed as an actress upon the stage?

Cecily, finding that there were tears in her eyes, turned her head away so that her aunt should not see them. As usual, however, Miss Dowie missed nothing. She reached out and patted Cecily's hand.

"I am sure I do not blame you for giving way to your feelings, my love," she said sympathetically. "The events of this past week have been enough quite to overset your nerves. But you must not despair, for Lady Frederick is not at all averse to exerting herself once more on your behalf. Indeed, I believe she will be so overjoyed when she learns that you have come by no harm from that odious Brackenridge that she will do everything in her power to establish you respectably—for you must know, my dear, that she was in mortal dread that Mr. Ranleigh would feel obliged to call Sir Harry to account if you had."

Cecily turned astonished eyes upon her. "But what can you mean, Aunt?" she faltered. "Mr. Ranleigh call Sir Harry to account——? You cannot mean that he would have felt he must fight a duel with him because of me?"

Miss Dowie shook her head disapprovingly. "Well, my dear, you know what gentlemen are!" she said. "There is no telling what maggots they may take into their heads on the subject of honour! And I must confess that there is a certain propriety in Mr. Ranleigh's feeling called upon to do for you what your father or your brother, if you had one, would consider it incumbent upon him to do, had you come by harm at Sir Harry's hands. You are, in a manner of speaking, under his protection."

This was a new and dismaying idea for Cecily. It was no wonder, she thought dismally, that Mr. Ranleigh had appeared so withdrawn that morning at breakfast. If he had disliked being brought into her affairs in the first place, it must be doubly disagreeable for him to feel now that he had been placed in a position in which it might be necessary for him to hazard his own safety for her protection. It would no doubt have been a great deal better, she told herself miserably, if she had never revealed the connexion between them to him, and had remained upon the stage instead.

They arrived at Hillcourt late in the afternoon. Lady Frederick, who had been fidgeting over a game of Patience in the Small Saloon, swept the cards away at the sound of voices in the hall and herself came anxiously out to greet them. The instant she saw that Cecily was of the party her face brightened.

"So you have brought her back! How clever of you, Robert!" she said. "My dear Miss Dowie, how very much relieved you must be!"

She was interrupted by Lord Neagle, who came bounding down the stairs to add his own impetuous greetings to hers.

"Oh, I say, you've brought Cecily with you!" he said. *"Did* you run off from that governess place, Cecily? I told Robert I expected you might. Was it very grim there? Did you dislike it very much?"

"Now *do* give over asking questions, Charlie, and let Robert tell me what has happened!" Lady Frederick said reprovingly. "As a matter of fact, you had much better go upstairs again to Mr. Tibble——"

"Well, I shan't!" his lordship said indignantly. "I am not a child, Grandmama! *I* know there's something smoky going on, and if you think I am going to wait to learn what it is until Tibble has a chance to worm it out of the servants——"

Mr. Ranleigh, allowing Welbore to take his dripping beaver and driving-coat, said wearily, "It is quite all right for him to remain, ma'am. There is nothing to tell except that we found Miss Hadley at her uncle's house, and that he did *not* appear to be suffering from an apoplexy. And now, if you will excuse me, I am going upstairs."

"Oh, in that case, I'll go too!" Lord Neagle said buoyantly.

He followed his uncle up the stairs, while Lady Frederick led Miss Dowie and Cecily into the Small Saloon. Here, steaming cups of tea having been produced to lend assistance to a cheerful fire in dispelling the chill of the journey, Miss Dowie and Lady Frederick at once fell into animated conversation. The nefarious behaviour of Sir Harry Brackenridge was brought up for review; Sir Timothy's rudeness and Lady Bonshawe's stupidity were animadverted upon; and it appeared to Cecily that, for once, the two ladies were about to enjoy a half hour of unremitting agreement in each other's company when Mr. Goodgame's offer was touched upon.

This at once put a different complexion upon the conversation. Lady Frederick, who had been racking her brains quite as busily as Miss Dowie in search of a solution to the new set of difficulties regarding Cecily's future introduced by Brackenridge's pursuit of her, instantly pounced upon what appeared to her to be a gleam of light in the darkness of her dilemma. She instituted an immediate inquiry into the young man's age, appearance, and situation in life, and, upon Miss Dowie's acknowledging that he was twenty-one, not unprepossessing in spite of his unpolished manners, and the owner of a considerable property, unhesitatingly gave it as her opinion that Cecily was a great goose to have whistled him down the wind.

This at once set Miss Dowie's back up. "Indeed, ma'am, I do not at all take your meaning," she said. "Is my niece to be coerced into marriage at my brother's desire?"

"Coerced? Fiddle!" Lady Frederick said. "He sounds a very respectable young man to me."

"A country clodpole!" Miss Dowie said wrathfully.

Lady Frederick shrugged. "My dear, his lack of polish might be mended by his wife, if she chose to take the pains. You refine too much upon the matter."

Miss Dowie's blue eyes sparkled with resolution. "That is very well, ma'am, but if you believe that I shall allow my brother to force a husband for whom she has no liking upon this child—"

"Liking! Pho!" said Lady Frederick downrightly. "You do not appear to understand that neither you nor Cecily is in a position to be picking and choosing, after this unfortunate business with Brackenridge! The rogue will spread the tale all over town; you may be assured of that! It may become quite out of my power to place her in another such position as she was in at the Bonshawes', and yet you will turn up your nose at an opportunity to see her respectably established!"

Cecily, who had been listening to this dialogue in acute discomfort, at this point could remain quiet no longer, and, rising, begged to be excused so that she might go upstairs.

"Ay, and I shall go with you!" Miss Dowie said, getting up in her turn. She added with great sarcasm to Lady Frederick, before she swept out of the room, "It is a pity that you have never become acquainted with my brother, ma'am, for I am persuaded that the two of you would deal extremely!"

Fortunately for Cecily, who had no desire to continue on the subject of Mr. Goodgame, the dinner hour was approaching, so that Miss Dowie was able to give vent only to a few pungent observations on Lady Frederick's interference in Cecily's affairs before she was obliged to retire to her bedchamber to change her dress. Cecily herself, with a heavy heart, donned the pretty jaconet muslin that Lady Frederick had given her. The more she thought of her own affairs, the more tangled they appeared to her to become, and she could almost have wished that she had never set eyes on either Lady Frederick or her son.

At dinner it appeared to her that Mr. Ranleigh had not at all recovered his customary air of imperturbability. He seemed abstracted, and took no part in the conversation except when he was obliged to do so. Once or twice she was conscious that his eyes were resting upon her, but he addressed not a single syllable to her at any time, and she was obliged to believe that he was still out of charity with her over the inconvenience to which she had put him.

Lady Frederick too, it appeared to her, had only severity in her mien when she gazed at her, so that, all in all, she felt the meal to be an ordeal from which she was glad to be released when Lady Frederick at last arose and led the ladies of the party into the Ivory Saloon.

Here Lady Frederick discovered that there was a disagreeable draught, and requested Cecily to run upstairs and fetch a shawl for her. It was not difficult for Cecily to guess that what she actually desired was the opportunity of speaking a few words in private to Miss Dowie before the gentlemen had left sitting over their wine and joined the ladies, and she therefore took her time over the errand. She did not anticipate that her aunt would be won over to take Lady Frederick's view of Mr. Goodgame's suit, but there was still the possibility that Lady Frederick, displeased by her opposition, might wash her hands of any further attempts to find some suitable occupation for Cecily.

With these thoughts disturbingly in her mind, Cecily came slowly down the stairs again, a handsome shawl of Norwich silk over her arm. The door of the Ivory Saloon was open, and she could hear her aunt's voice, delivering some determined statement; then Lady Frederick's, speaking in agitated accents, came to her ears.

"My dear woman, pray do not be such a goosecap! Do you not see what the result of this may be? From something Robert let fall to me just before dinner, I very much fear that he has taken the quixotic notion into his head that the only way out of the muddle is for him to offer for the girl himself! It is quite nonsensical of him, but you must see that she has been placed in such a position by this affair with Brackenridge that marriage with *someone* is now the only practical way out of her difficulties!"

Cecily, her face gone very pale, stood rooted to the spot, the shawl clasped tightly in her arms. She heard her aunt say, with acerbity, "Indeed, my lady, as to that, you need have no fear—my niece does not aspire to the honour of being Mr. Ranleigh's wife. You may believe, too, that I should not countenance such a business for a moment. Cecily is in no way your son's responsibility, and, though I am grateful to him for having so much consideration for her, she has no right to expect such a sacrifice of his own inclinations."

"Exactly!" said Lady Frederick. "But how am I to convince him of that?

Men, my dear, are the most obstinate creatures in the world when it is a question of something they believe touches their honour, and I am sure there will be no moving him if he feels he must really make the child an offer. He will certainly not allow that a mere female can know anything of the matter!"

Cecily, composing herself with a desperate effort, forced a smile to her lips and walked into the saloon.

"Here is your shawl, ma'am," she said to Lady Frederick, in a voice that quivered in spite of herself. "I hope you will not mind if I leave you and Aunt alone now; I find I am quite worn out after my journey, and I believe I should like to retire early this evening."

Both the elder ladies looked at her sharply, but, as she betrayed no consciousness of having overheard what had been said just prior to her entrance, Lady Frederick merely said, "Yes, my dear, of course you must go up if you are tired. I am sure we shall all feel much better after a good night's rest, for this has been an upsetting affair for all of us."

Miss Dowie too said good night to her niece, intimating that she would remain downstairs until the hour at which she usually retired. Cecily was thereupon free to run upstairs. One great sob escaped her as she reached the head of the staircase, but she swallowed it down fiercely and went at once to her own bedchamber. Here she sat down beside the window and for some quarter of an hour remained in the deepest thought, after which she rose and made her way swiftly to the part of the house where Lord Neagle's bedchamber lay.

His lordship was already abed and asleep, as the lack of response to her cautious scratching upon the door informed her. Hearing footsteps approaching down the corridor, she tried the doorknob in desperation and, finding the latch free, whisked herself inside. Lord Neagle's regular breathing announced that he was quite unconscious of her intrusion. She approached the bed.

"Charlie!" she hissed intensely. "Wake up! It's Cecily! I *must* talk to you!"

He merely stirred and yawned. Discerning his sleeping figure dimly in the moonlight that peeped through the drawn curtains, she reached out and shook him vigorously.

His lordship sat bolt upright on the instant. "*What?*" he exclaimed. "Who is it?"

"It's Cecily! *Do* be quiet! Do you want Mr. Tibble to hear you?"

"I don't know. Do I?" his lordship inquired sleepily.

"No! I've come to ask you to help me, and *nobody* must know. Do you understand me?"

Lord Neagle gradually appeared to take a firmer grasp of the situation. "Might tell Robert," he remarked presently. "You in some sort of scrape, Cecily? Dashed good fellow to help a person out of a scrape, Robert."

"*Especially* you are not to tell Mr. Ranleigh!" Cecily insisted fiercely. "Do you understand me, Charlie? If you are going to tell *him*, I won't say another word."

"Oh, very well, in that case——" his lordship conceded. "What is it, then? You must be in the deuce of a pucker, to come to me at this time of night."

"I am!" Cecily said. She was silent for a moment, and then went on in a rush, "The thing is—I overheard your grandmother talking to Aunt Mab just now. She says Mr. Ranleigh feels himself obliged to make me an offer of marriage because—because I am under his protection and that odious Brackenridge will make it impossible for me to obtain another respectable position, now that he knows I am Miss Daingerfield-Nelson. And—and I find that I do not wish to be respectable, after all, and so I am going back to the theatre!"

Having poured this information rather incoherently into Lord Neagle's ears, she halted and waited anxiously for his response. It was not immediately forthcoming, his lordship, it seemed, finding the matter a rather involved one to cope with on being awakened from a sound slumber.

After some time, however, he remarked sapiently, "I take you. You don't want to marry Robert. Cork-brained scheme, at any rate. He don't want to marry you. Don't even like you. Told me so the other day."

"Did—did he?" Cecily faltered, feeling crushed, in spite of her resolution not to allow Mr. Ranleigh to sacrifice himself to his ideas of honourable behaviour. "When did he say that?"

"Well, he didn't actually *say* it," Lord Neagle acknowledged. "We were talking about his being obliged to go into Hampshire after you, and I said it was a pity he had you on his hands because he didn't even like you. Well—he didn't say he *did*——"

"I don't suppose he does," Cecily said, in a small voice. "You see, I have been such a great deal of trouble to him. So I have decided that the best thing for me to do is to go back to the theatre—because Lady Frederick says herself that it will be impossible to establish me respectably now except I am married to someone, and I do not at all wish to be married."

"Well, no one could blame you for *that*," his lordship said. "I mean to say, you'd need to be perfectly birdwitted not to prefer being on the stage. But there'll be a rare dust kicked up when they find out about it, you know."

"They are not going to find out about it until it is too late," Cecily said, resolutely. "Too late for them even to *think* of trying to make me respectable again, that is. And that is why I have come to you, Charlie. *You* must help me to get away from here without anyone's knowing, and lend me some of your clothes, and some money, if you have any—for I am not sure I have enough of my own—and tell me exactly how I am to get to Cuckfield, so that I can take the stage to London."

Lord Neagle appeared to find nothing at all unreasonable in this request, although he did demand to know, after a moment's cogitation, why she had need of his clothes.

"Because I shall go dressed as a boy," Cecily said promptly. "It will not look nearly so odd as if I were to go jauntering about dressed as a young lady, for I shall have to walk to Cuckfield, you know. And then it will throw my aunt and Mr. Ranleigh quite off the scent, for they will not be inquiring after a boy."

"But will you be able to carry it off?" his lordship asked doubtfully. "You'll have to do something about your hair, for one thing."

"Oh, yes," agreed Cecily, quite unperturbed. "Isn't it lucky that the front is already cropped? I shall simply snip the back short too and be quite in the latest mode. And as for carrying it off, there is nothing in the least difficult about it, if one remembers to take long strides and speak in a gruff voice—like this."

And she gave a creditable imitation of his lordship's own boyishly offhand tones.

Lord Neagle nodded. "Well, I daresay you might do it," he said judiciously. "And I must say it's a dashed clever notion, for I don't suppose even Robert would think it was you if he found out about a boy's having been seen on the road to Cuckfield."

"And you won't tell him, Charlie?" Cecily said anxiously. "Will you promise me that? Because it will be worse than anything if he finds me before *I* can find Mr. Jillson and go on the stage again."

His lordship said indignantly, "What do you take me for? Of course I won't split on you! But they'll be in a deuced pucker, you know. May think you've been murdered, or kidnaped, or something of that sort."

"No, for I shall leave a note for Aunt and tell her that I have gone away of my own accord," Cecily said. "And I shall tell her not to search for me, for I am *quite* able to look after myself now, and—and to arrange my own future for myself."

His lordship agreed that this was the thing to do, and a candle was then lighted so that a search might be instituted for the proper clothing for her to wear upon her journey, and for such sums of money as might be found to be in his lordship's possession. The gratifying amount of three half-crowns, together with a guinea bestowed upon him two days before by his uncle, was turned over to her in its entirety, and his lordship's wardrobe was next ransacked for jacket, breeches, hat, and shirt, together with foot-wear more suitable for a youth with a long, muddy walk before him than Cecily herself owned.

"You ought to have a cloak-bag or a portmanteau for your own things, though—oughtn't you?" Lord Neagle inquired, frowning.

"Yes, but that is quite all right, for they haven't taken mine away to the box-room yet," Cecily informed him. "I am glad it is small, since I shall have to carry it all the way."

"*I* think it would be better if I went with you. Couldn't they find something for me to do in the theatre? It would be a good deal more to my taste than staying on here, poring over books with old Tibble."

"Oh, Charlie, do try not to be such a *clunch!*" Cecily said. "Of course you cannot go with me! This isn't a lark; indeed, it is a very serious affair, and I am half out of my mind with worrying that I shan't be able to get away without being discovered, or that Mr. Ranleigh will come after me and find me——"

"Well, he can't *make* you marry him, even if he does," Lord Neagle said reasonably.

"I know that! But I d-don't wish him to m-make me an offer when he doesn't c-care about me in the least——" She broke off, found her handker-chief, and blew her nose defiantly. "And if I do not marry *him,* I shall be plagued to marry Mr. Goodgame, and I had rather die!" she said. "So you see I *must* go back to the theatre, where I can earn my own living and not have to be beholden to *anyone.*"

"Yes, I can see that. Well, I will tell you how you must go about slip-ping out of the house—for I have done it myself once or twice, you know—and then how you must go to get to Cuckfield."

When this information had been satisfactorily memorised by Cecily, she said good-bye to Lord Neagle with many expressions of gratitude and left his bedchamber, fortunately meeting no one while returning to her own room, where she quickly packed up a few necessaries in her portmanteau and then hastily undressed and got into bed.

A short time later she heard her aunt come along the hall on her way to her own room. As Cecily had expected, she looked in to see if she was asleep, and, finding that she was not, came in for a few moments to talk to her. Cecily took advantage of the opportunity to tell her that she was quite worn to a thread, and would probably rise later than usual the next morning, and then, having kissed her aunt—for the last time, as she unhappily reflected—was left alone to perfect her plans.

These were not complicated, involving, as she had told Lord Neagle, merely a flight via stagecoach to London, where she was certain that she would be able to contact the Jillsons at the Running Boar. And then, she told herself, having contrived to place herself beyond the pale of respectability by her reappearance upon the stage, so that Mr. Ranleigh's chivalrous intentions toward her must certainly be abandoned, she would be free to reap all the rewards of fame and fortune offered her by a career in the theatre.

The very thought, paradoxically, was sufficient to induce her to give way to a hearty bout of tears—after which, having resolutely dried her eyes, she rose, attired herself in Lord Neagle's clothing, and prepared to set out on her journey.

20

On the following morning Lord Neagle had the forethought to remind his uncle that he had promised to take him out in his curricle that day for a driving lesson, and successfully managed, by various stratagems, to keep him away from the house until shortly after noon.

They returned to find that Cecily's disappearance had been discovered. In point of fact, Lady Frederick and Miss Dowie were in the Small Saloon, distractedly poring over the note that Cecily had left behind her, when Mr. Ranleigh walked in with his nephew, and both ladies at once pounced upon him with demands for counsel.

"Disappeared?" Mr. Ranleigh said in an incredulous voice, as he endeavoured to sort out the facts of what had occurred from the spate of agitated words hurled at him. "Nonsense! You must be mistaking the matter!"

He stretched out his hand for Cecily's note, which Miss Dowie immediately surrendered to him. It was, he found, quite brief.

"Dearest Aunt," it read, "I am very sorry indeed to give you Pain, but I think it will be much, much Better if I do not cause any more Trouble to Lady Frederick in trying to establish me Respectably, since I am quite old enough to decide my own Future now. Please do not try to find out where I have gone." There were a few splotches on the page which might have been caused by tears, and the note concluded with the signature: "Your loving Niece, Cecily."

Mr. Ranleigh looked up, his face suddenly gone quite white about the mouth. "What in God's name does this mean, ma'am?" he demanded of Miss Dowie. "Have you any notion?"

She shook her head numbly. "No, sir, not the least in the world! The child was out of spirits yesterday and went up early to her bed. And when I looked in on her, she said that she was tired and would sleep late this morning—so that we thought nothing of it when she did not appear at breakfast. But half an hour ago, when I went up to her bedchamber, she was not there, and I found—that."

She nodded toward the sheet of notepaper which he still held in his hand.

Lady Frederick put in, importunately, "Where *can* she have gone, Robert? She cannot have thought of returning to the Bonshawes in this clandestine way—it is too absurd! And *why* should she have taken it into her head that I should not wish to do anything more for her?"

"Well, as to *that*, my lady," Miss Dowie said rather sharply, "I am sure I should not blame her for thinking such a thing, when you pressed it upon her so strongly yesterday that she ought to marry Mr. Goodgame!"

Mr. Ranleigh, who had seemed to be immersed in his own thoughts, interrupted at this point to address a trenchant question to his mother.

"What? Is this true, ma'am?"

"Well, I am sure you need not wonder if it is!" Lady Frederick said. "Certainly it would be the height of absurdity for a girl in her position to think of refusing a respectable offer of marriage, merely because she had not yet had the opportunity of becoming well acquainted with the young man!"

An expression of hard anger that Lady Frederick had not often been called upon to face appeared in her son's grey eyes.

"I see!" he said curtly. "So you too, ma'am, were endeavouring to coerce her into this marriage! Has Mr. Goodgame been accurately described to you, I wonder? If he has, it should not surprise you, I believe, that Miss Hadley preferred to leave this house rather than to be obliged to fear that she would be importuned to wed him!"

"But this is nonsense, Robert!" Lady Frederick said, with some spirit. "Surely the child knew she would not be *forced* into a marriage that was genuinely distasteful to her! What motive could I have for doing anything so cruel?"

Mr. Ranleigh eyed her grimly. "A motive, ma'am," he returned, "which I believe I was singularly foolish to have provided you with last evening when I——" He broke off, becoming conscious that Lord Neagle was still a highly interested spectator of the scene. "Charlie, go to your room," he said, in a voice that brooked no opposition. Lord Neagle reluctantly retired, and Mr. Ranleigh, closing the door behind him, continued to Lady Frederick, "——when I signified to you that it might be my intention to offer for Miss Hadley's hand myself."

A vivid and unaccustomed flush overspread Lady Frederick's face. "But, Robert," she protested, "surely you cannot be surprised that I do not wish you to sacrifice yourself to some overnice notions of propriety! If *that* is my fault——"

But she got no further, for Mr. Ranleigh interrupted her with an odd, harsh laugh.

"Notions of propriety!" he exclaimed. "My dear ma'am, has it never entered your mind that my feelings might be involved in the matter?"

"Your *feelings!*"

Lady Frederick repeated the words incredulously, while Miss Dowie, her own face showing equal amounts of surprise and disapproval, said stiffly, "If this is some jest, sir——"

"A jest?" he said sardonically. "Oh no, it is quite true! Apparently, however, I was as overcome as my mother appears to be by the possibility that I might actually have condescended to conceive a *tendre* for your niece, for certainly I said nothing to her of the matter. But I am wasting time," he added in an altered, but still exceedingly hard, voice. "If she has left this house, she may have been seen on the road, or they may have news of her at the coach-office in Cuckfield."

He left the room as he spoke and walked rapidly into the hall, where they heard him ordering Welbore to send to the stables at once and have the bays put to and his curricle brought round again. Lady Frederick and Miss Dowie sat staring at each other in dismayed conjecture.

"Good heavens!" Lady Frederick said faintly. "I had no idea! To be sure, I *did* think once—but that has been months ago, and I made certain it was only because he was angry with Tony for behaving so badly——"

Miss Dowie, however, was too much taken up with her anxiety over Cecily to spend more than a few moments on thoughts of anything else. She said that it would be time enough when they had found Cecily to think about such matters, and thereupon went back to trying to puzzle out the reason for her niece's departure from Hillcourt.

"She cannot have wished to return to Timothy," she said, "though, indeed, if she *had*, she might well have hesitated to tell me of it, knowing how I should dislike it. But she seemed so greatly relieved to be able to leave there yesterday——"

Lady Frederick shook her head. "It is quite beyond my comprehension," she said. "If it was my urging her to accept Mr. Goodgame's offer that made her run off, as Robert appears to believe, it would not at all have served her purpose to return to your brother's house. Yet it seems equally unlikely that she has gone to the Bonshawes——" She broke off as another thought entered her mind. "Brackenridge!" she exclaimed, in accents of dismay. "Good God, my dear, do you think it is possible——?"

"That she has run off to go to him? No, I do not!" Miss Dowie said roundly. "I shall never believe such a thing of her!"

Lady Frederick, seeing her kindling eyes, refrained from saying any more on the subject; but she could not rid her mind so easily of the idea. As the afternoon hours slipped by and nothing was heard from Mr. Ranleigh, neither she nor Miss Dowie could prevent herself from sinking into blacker and blacker gloom. Miss Dowie at last, feeling that she could no longer endure to sit idly waiting, went upstairs, where she conceived the idea of searching her niece's bedchamber for anything that might give her a clue as to where she had gone.

The results of this endeavour sent her downstairs again to Lady Frederick within ten minutes with a small jeweller's box clasped in her right hand, and with her face almost as white as her tucker.

"My lady," she said, walking into the Small Saloon and interrupting Lady Frederick's game of Patience without ceremony, "do but look at this! I found it at the back of one of Cecily's bureau drawers. Oh, my lady, does it mean—must it mean——?"

She could not go on, but drew out her handkerchief and wiped her eyes, while Lady Frederick, lifting the lid of the box that had been offered her, sat staring at the diamond ear-drops Brackenridge had forced upon Cecily in the shrubbery at Inglesant.

"Bless—my—soul!" she ejaculated. "I should not have believed it! My poor dear friend——"

"There is some explanation! There must be!" Miss Dowie, recovering herself, said fiercely. "She left them behind her—did she not? *Why* should she have done so if she has gone to that man? And why should she have fled to Timothy's house to escape him, if she had already consented to allow him to buy her virtue with such baubles! I will not believe it of her!"

Lady Frederick, who did not know how to reply to her, was spared the necessity of doing so by her housekeeper, Mrs. Keaton, who appeared at the door at that moment, begging the favour of a word with her.

"It's about his lordship, my lady," she said, in a voice that was big with importance. "That is, it's about his clothes, and I *did* think you might wish to know——"

Lady Frederick, who was aware that Cecily's abrupt disappearance could not have escaped the observation of her household, did not fail to gather that the communication Mrs. Keaton desired to make to her had something to do with that event; but she was at a loss to understand the connexion.

"Yes?" she inquired. "What is it, Mrs. Keaton?"

"Why, my lady, I shouldn't think to come worrying you with such a thing, except that it seemed—well, downright queer to me," the housekeeper said, apologetically. "The fact is, Alice tells me one of his lordship's jackets is missing from his wardrobe, and he has no notion how to account for it. *And* it seems there's other things gone as well——"

"What sort of things?" Lady Frederick interrupted. "Speak up, woman! Other articles of clothing?"

"Yes, indeed, my lady—for she says it's a pair of his breeches too, and the half-boots his lordship likes to wear when he goes out shooting—*and* a hat——"

She broke off in dismay at sight of the forbidding expression that had appeared on her mistress's face.

"Would you be so good, Mrs. Keaton," Lady Frederick said, deliberately, "as to send to tell Lord Neagle that I should like to see him at once? *At once*—do you understand?"

The housekeeper dropped a curtsey and hurried off to execute the command, while Lady Frederick, relieved of the necessity of concealing her emotions that had been imposed by her presence, turned a harassed face toward Miss Dowie.

"Is it possible," she demanded, "that that abominable boy can have had anything to do with this? My dear Miss Dowie, my head is in a whirl! Gone off dressed as a boy! Good heavens, I have never heard of anything so improper!"

Miss Dowie, too, looked as if she found this latest possibility too much to support, and could scarcely summon up the spirits even to discuss it during the few minutes that elapsed before Lord Neagle himself appeared in the doorway. He was looking a trifle scared and more than a little defiant, and, on being taxed by his grandmother to tell her immediately what he had done with his missing clothing, set the tone of the ensuing conversation by declaring in a tone of obstinate martyrdom that wild horses would be unable to drag any explanations from his lips.

It appeared, in the course of the half hour that followed, that he had meant exactly what he said. None of the threats, pleas, imprecations, or cajoleries that descended upon him was able in the slightest degree to alter his determination. He drove the two ladies into a state of such frustrated fury that Lady Frederick, hearing at last the sound of carriage wheels on the drive outside, followed by her son's voice in the hall, was goaded to say in accents of grim triumph, "Very well, my lad! We shall see what your uncle has to say to this! I daresay *he* will know how to deal with you! Unless he has succeeded in finding Cecily——"

One glance at her son's set face as he walked into the room, however, was sufficient to tell her that that happy event had not occurred. Mr.

Ranleigh, in answer to the eager inquiries directed to him by Miss Dowie and his mother, said curtly that his efforts had met with no success whatever: not the slightest trace had he been able to find of Cecily.

"Yes, I can well believe it," Lady Frederick said, "for it would appear that you have been led quite off the scent, Robert! *I* have not been able to obtain the truth of the matter from Charlie, but I trust that *you* will. It seems that certain articles of his clothing are missing, and I cannot think there is any other explanation of the matter than that Cecily has gone off dressed as a boy!"

Mr. Ranleigh received this piece of information with no visible manifestation of either surprise or anger, but the light in his grey eyes as he swung round to face his nephew was so menacing that that young gentleman quailed beneath it.

"Well, Charlie?" Mr. Ranleigh asked, ominously.

His lordship swallowed convulsively. "I—I can't tell you, sir," he managed to stammer out, at last. "Honestly I can't! I gave her my word, you see!"

Mr. Ranleigh appeared to consider the matter. "Yes, I see," he said after a moment, in a somewhat less formidable tone. "You do not wish to betray her confidence. But you are old enough to understand, Charlie, that you may be doing her a far greater disservice by keeping silent than by speaking out now. A girl of her age wandering about the world entirely unprotected—even you must be able to see the danger of that!"

"Yes, but she will not be unprotected for long, sir!" Lord Neagle urged, looking relieved by the more reasonable tone in which his uncle had addressed him. "I mean to say—I'm *sure* she knows just what she is doing, and if I was you I should simply stop looking for her, for she don't care to have you marry her, you know, and it will be *much* better if you let her go off and do as she chooses."

To say that this statement produced a sensation among his auditors would scarcely be an exaggeration. Lady Frederick exclaimed, in tones of the utmost astonishment, "Good heavens, how came she to know anything of *that!*" and Miss Dowie, in complete bewilderment, declared that she did not believe a word of it.

"It is quite out of the question that she said any such thing!" she said. "It is Mr. Goodgame whom she does not wish to marry!"

"Well, she don't wish to marry him, either, ma'am," Lord Neagle conceded. "And I do not see why she need do so, after all, for there is another——" He halted abruptly. "I shan't tell you any more," he said, the obstinate look returning to his face. "I promised her I shouldn't—and if you've told me once, sir, you've told me a dozen times: a gentleman never breaks his word!"

Mr. Ranleigh, who had had a very odd expression on his face ever since his nephew had informed him of Cecily's aversion to marrying him, did not appear to have paid a great deal of attention to the remarks that had followed. He said now briefly, to Lord Neagle, "Go to your room, Charlie. I shall come up to you if I wish to speak to you again."

His nephew needed no second invitation to depart. He took himself thankfully out of the room, and Mr. Ranleigh, closing the door behind him, turned to Lady Frederick with a sardonic expression in his eyes.

"Well, ma'am?" he said. "Can you explain to me by what means Miss Hadley could have learned that there was any possibility of her being obliged to receive my—as I must gather—highly unwelcome addresses?"

"Robert, I swear to you that she did not hear of it from me!" Lady Frederick cried, looking upset and indignant at her son's tone. "How can you think I should have done such a thing?—unless," she added suddenly, as a new thought struck her, "unless—oh, my dear Miss Dowie," she exclaimed, turning to her, "is it possible that she could have overheard our conversation last evening? You remember, I had been speaking of it just before she came into the room with my shawl."

Miss Dowie said hollowly that she did indeed remember, but that it did not signify in the least.

"It must be that man, Brackenridge," she said, in a despairing voice. "Oh, Mr. Ranleigh, *pray* do not be angry with the child and give over your efforts to find her now, for I am persuaded that he has come round her—*how*, I cannot tell, for I am sure when she came away from Inglesant she had not the slightest wish to have further dealings with him. But he has contrived somehow to give her *these*"—and she held out the jeweller's box containing the diamond ear-drops to him—"and must, I am persuaded, have offered her marriage as well, or she would never have fled to his protection! But *will* he marry her, knowing of her what he does?"

Mr. Ranleigh, the lines about his mouth and jaw suddenly very marked, was looking at the winking baubles in the box.

"No, he will not marry her," he said levelly. "But if he has harmed her in any way, you have my word that he will answer to me for it, ma'am."

"Fustian!" Lady Frederick cried. "Robert, *do* but consider a moment—if you call him out, you may very well kill him, and what possible good can that do the girl? And then *you* will be obliged to leave the country—— Oh, heavens, was there ever such a muddle! There must be some rational way out of it!"

Mr. Ranleigh, however, did not stay to discuss the matter. He said briefly to his mother that he believed it was probable that he would be leaving Hillcourt within the hour, and that he would be pleased to partake of anything in the way of a cold repast that could be set before him without delay, and thereupon walked upstairs to his nephew's bedchamber.

Lord Neagle looked up apprehensively as his uncle entered.

"Now, Charlie," Mr. Ranleigh said, in a voice that set that young gentleman's heart to thudding uncomfortably against his ribs, "I am going to ask you these questions only once. It is possible that Miss Hadley is in serious trouble, and under the circumstances you need not scruple to tell me the truth. Do you know where she went when she left this house?"

Lord Neagle looked imploringly at him. "Oh, sir, really—*must* I tell you?"

"You must," Mr. Ranleigh said, inexorably. "Cut line, Charlie! To London—was it not?"

His lordship capitulated. "Y-yes, sir."

"By private chaise? Or by stage?"

"By private chaise? Oh no, sir, no one was to take her up. She said she should walk in to Cuckfield and take the stage there."

"Dressed in your clothes?"

"Yes, sir."

"I see. And what did she intend to do when she reached London?"

Lord Neagle, grasping at the last shreds of his code of honour, muttered that he did not know. He consoled himself, under his uncle's hard gaze, with the thought that he really did *not* know what Cecily's movements might be when she reached the city, for she had told him no more than that she meant to find Mr. Jillson, and he had not the least notion of how she intended to go about doing that.

Mr. Ranleigh, however, was not to be led off the subject so easily, and persisted in inquiring if Cecily had mentioned the name of any gentleman in connexion with her flight.

"Well, she mentioned *yours*," Lord Neagle said hopefully.

"Yes, you have already told me that. *And* Mr. Goodgame's. Anyone else?"

Lord Neagle searched his memory desperately. "Brackenridge," he said after a moment, inspirationally.

His uncle's eyes narrowed. "Yes? In what connexion?"

"Oh, lord, sir—I don't know exactly," his lordship said, floundering on. "To tell you the truth, I was devilish sleepy when she explained it to me——" Prompted by the look in his uncle's eyes, he went on hastily, "Well, it had something to do with her not being able to obtain a respectable position any more, and not wishing to marry you, or that fellow she met in Hampshire, either—in fact, she said she would rather die than do *that*——"

He broke off doubtfully, for it occurred to him that his uncle was looking rather formidably grim—a not surprising fact, for Mr. Ranleigh was indeed feeling grim. It now seemed highly possible to him that Cecily, finding insuperable difficulties cast in the way of her career as a governess, and faced with the suits of two gentlemen, neither of whom she wished to marry, had impulsively determined to accept the offer of a man who—however much Mr. Ranleigh might dislike him personally—he admitted knew well how to ingratiate himself with the female sex.

That that offer had meant marriage to *her* mind, he had not the least doubt. That it had meant it to Brackenridge's was another matter altogether. He himself did not for a moment believe that it did, but he was well prepared to believe that Brackenridge, having by some means learned that Cecily had returned to Hillcourt, had managed to convey a message to her that had given her the assurance that she would be safe in throwing herself upon his protection.

If this were so, he had no time to waste. Whether Brackenridge was in London or not he did not know, but Lord Neagle had indicated that that was where Cecily had gone, and it seemed most probable that it was there that he might obtain news of her. He therefore told his nephew briefly that he would deal with him on his return and walked out of the room— leaving that young gentleman to breathe a sigh of immense relief over his having succeeded in preserving at least the core of the secret that Cecily had entrusted to him.

21 Mr. Ranleigh, driving his own curricle, arrived in London shortly before eleven o'clock that night, and went at once, without stopping at his own house, to Sir Harry Brackenridge's in Half Moon Street. A sleepy porter, looking more than a little surprised at the appearance of a caller at this time of night—and one, moreover, whose dress proclaimed that he had but just driven into town—informed him uncommunicatively that Sir Harry was gone out. However, the feel of a handsome gratuity slipped into his hand caused him to recollect that his master had announced his intention of attending an evening party at Lord Comerford's house in Curzon Street— a piece of information which, Mr. Ranleigh felt, must do much to relieve his immediate anxieties. If Cecily had indeed arrived in London that day and put herself under Brackenridge's protection, it seemed highly unlikely that that gentleman would be spending the evening at the Comerfords'.

He had no intention, however, of waiting until the morning to go into the matter further, and accordingly drove at once to his own house in Mount Street, where he changed his travelling dress for the knee breeches, silk stockings, and long-tailed coat suitable for making an appearance at the Comerfords' party. He was aware that he had sent Lady Comerford his regrets on receiving her card of invitation for this event, since he had expected to be at Hillcourt, but she was all cordiality on seeing him enter her saloon at an hour far past that at which she had anticipated the arrival of any further guests, and accepted with complaisance his explanation that, urgent business having brought him back to town, he could not resist looking in on her party.

A quick glance over the crowded rooms, however, failed to give him a sight of Brackenridge. Coming across his uncle, Mr. Albion Wymberly, just emerging from the supper-room, he stopped him and put a question to him as to whether he had seen Sir Harry that evening.

Mr. Wymberly, whose face bore a satisfied smile which could only mean that the lobster patties had been to his liking and the champagne excellent, stared at him.

"Brackenridge?" he repeated. "What the deuce do you want with him? Thought you didn't like the fellow."

"I don't," Mr. Ranleigh said briefly. "Has he been here tonight?"

Mr. Wymberly considered. "Must have been," he decided after a moment, "for he's always at these affairs of the Comerfords' unless he's out of town—which he ain't. Ran into him in Bond Street this afternoon. *Was* out of town," he went on meticulously, seeing the attention with which Mr. Ranleigh had heard this statement, and improving on it with the notion of turning him up sweet, so that he might be in the proper mood when next approached for a small loan. "Daresay you may have heard of it yourself—visiting an aunt in Somerset. Gave out that was what he was doing, at any rate. Shouldn't be surprised if the affair was actually a bit more interesting—after one of those prime little ladybirds he's always coming up with. Heard some rumours to that effect——"

He broke off, dismayed to find that, far from appearing grateful for this news, Mr. Ranleigh was wearing an air of thunderous calm.

"Yes?" he said levelly. "Go on, Albion. You have heard rumours——?"

"Better ask Tony," Mr. Wymberly said hastily, seeing Lord Portandrew bearing down upon them. "He knows Brackenridge better than I do—not in my set, you know——"

He took himself off, and Mr. Ranleigh turned to confront his cousin, who came up, exclaiming in some surprise, "Here, I thought you was going down to Hillcourt! What are you doing in town?"

"As you see, I have come back," Mr. Ranleigh said, grasping his cousin's arm and impelling him toward the door of a small anteroom. "Come along, Tony; I want to talk to you. Have you seen Brackenridge here tonight?"

Lord Portandrew blinked. "Why, yes," he said. "But what's it to do with you?"

"Albion says he's just come back from Somerset, and that there have been rumours concerning a young woman——"

Lord Portandrew's brow darkened. "Oh—that!" he said. "Yes. Meaning to bring that up the next time I saw you. Came back to town yesterday— no, Wednesday, it must have been—and has been hinting we may expect to see him parading *Miss Daingerfield-Nelson* on his arm soon. What do you know about that, Robert? Has he found out where she is?"

"Yes," Mr. Ranleigh said shortly. "And I should like very much at the present moment to find out where *he* is."

"Oh, well, as to that—nothing easier," Lord Portandrew assured him. "Said he was going to look in at that new gaming-hall in Pickering Place— can't have been more than half an hour ago. Ten to one you'll find him still there." He added, as his cousin uttered a brief acknowledgement and turned away, "Here! Wait a minute! I'll go with you. They won't let you in unless you have a card. Devilish discreet sort of place."

"I imagine I shall have no difficulty," Mr. Ranleigh said coolly. "If it is the sort of house that has been described to me, you may be sure they are already well acquainted with the size of my purse and my value as a bird for their plucking."

He did not remain in Curzon Street longer than was required to drink a glass of wine with Lord Comerford, who seized upon him as he was parting from Lord Portandrew, but walked downstairs at once and strolled around to Pickering Place. As he had predicted to his cousin, a brief conversation held with the individual who guarded the door from behind an iron grille quickly secured him the entree to an elegantly furnished hall, from which he was invited to walk upstairs to the gaming saloons.

As he entered the first of these, an apartment given over to French hazard, he was greeted by several gentlemen of his acquaintance and invited to join them. A brief survey of the room informing him that Brackenridge was not among their number, however, he declined the invitation and moved on into the next room, where a faro-bank was in full swing. Here Brackenridge's brassy-yellow head at once caught his eye. Mr. Ranleigh, having exchanged a bill for several twenty-guinea rouleaus, strolled over to take a seat at the table beside his young friend, Lord Heseltine, who greeted him affably and remarked that the play was devilish dull that night. Brackenridge, who was seated across the table, glanced up and favoured Mr. Ranleigh with a look of slightly mocking surprise.

"Isn't this rather out of your line, Robert?" he inquired. "I thought you seldom strayed from Watier's, or White's."

"Oh, I have no objection to being fleeced in a good cause," Mr. Ranleigh said, imperturbably placing his bet. "I came, you see, for a word with you."

Sir Harry's brows went up. "With me? You surprise me!"

"No, I don't think I do," Mr. Ranleigh said, as calmly as before. "I should rather imagine, on the contrary, that you had been expecting something of the sort ever since you returned from Somerset."

Lord Heseltine glanced acutely from Ranleigh to Brackenridge, opened his mouth to say something, thought better of it, and shut it again. Sir Harry laughed softly.

"I see," he said. "So you have not lost interest in that game as yet."

"No, I have not," Mr. Ranleigh said. "May I suggest, however, that we refrain from discussing the matter until you have finished your play here?"

Lord Heseltine, an amiable young man, who stood somewhat in awe of the pair of noted amateurs of the Fancy who, he uneasily felt, were sparring in a considerably more deadly manner than that customarily seen within the confines of Jackson's Boxing Saloon, cleared his throat and ventured a soothing remark to the effect that the room was deuced hot.

"Quite insupportable," Brackenridge agreed blandly. "How very right you are, Heseltine! Do you know, I rather fancy that I should benefit by a little fresh air?" He gathered up his winnings in a leisurely manner and rose from the table. "Are you coming, Robert? It is too bad to draw you away when you have scarcely arrived, but I have the feeling that your heart is not really in the play tonight."

Mr. Ranleigh did not vouchsafe a reply to this remark, but nodded a good night to Lord Heseltine and walked downstairs with Sir Harry. The two, having received hats and cloaks in the hall, left the house together and strolled, on Mr. Ranleigh's invitation, in the direction of his house in Mount Street.

"Not," Brackenridge said, "that I should not appreciate a glass of your excellent Madeira, Robert, but I believe we may very easily conclude this conversation before we arrive in Mount Street. You wish to speak to me on the subject of—er—Miss Hadley, I believe she now calls herself. Do you not?"

Mr. Ranleigh gave him a brief, measuring glance. "Exactly," he said. "How acute of you to guess!"

"Not at all!" Brackenridge demurred. "I must confess, when I first heard that she had descended to the post of governess in some appallingly vulgar household, I was rather of the opinion that you had found that you really did not care to burden yourself any longer with her affairs and had therefore—er—left the coast clear for me. But Miss Hadley herself, when I had the pleasure of renewing our acquaintance in Somerset, rather gave me the impression that the situation was not precisely as I had been fancying it. By the bye, you *did* know that I had seen her in Somerset—did you not?"

"I did," Mr. Ranleigh said evenly. "What I do *not* know is how you can reconcile it with what I can only suppose you call your honour as a gentleman to pursue an obviously innocent girl for purposes that quite evidently have nothing whatever to do with marriage."

The torch of a passing linkboy escorting a belated reveller home lit Brackenridge's face momentarily, and Mr. Ranleigh saw that it had reddened slightly. Sir Harry laughed with a forced hint of derision, however, as he countered, "*Is* she so innocent, then? I find that rather difficult to credit, after she has passed through *your* hands." Mr. Ranleigh halted suddenly, and Brackenridge went on, with an unpleasant smile, "You may force a quarrel upon me if you choose, Robert—but pray consider, before you do, the consequences to the *innocent* Miss Hadley. She seems anxious, for some odd reason, to maintain at least an appearance of respectability—which I daresay must become quite impossible if it is noised about that she has been the object of a brawl between us. Or were you thinking of pistols?"

"If you like," Mr. Ranleigh said, without the least trace of emotion in his voice. "At the present time, however, I should like merely to give you a warning. If I find that you are speaking to others of Miss Hadley in the tone in which you have just spoken of her to me, I shall not send you a cartel; I shall use my whip. Miss Hadley is under my protection—not in the way you imagine, but as a connexion of my family."

"Indeed!" Sir Harry said, angered this time in earnest, it appeared, by Mr. Ranleigh's blunt words. "And what of old Dowie, her uncle—who is at the present moment, I gather, dying of a quite fictitious apoplexy in Hampshire? If the chit, as you claim, looks to *you* for protection, why then has she run off to *him* now?"

He paused, seeing that a very odd expression had suddenly appeared upon Mr. Ranleigh's face. In point of fact, Mr. Ranleigh was feeling very odd: he had the strangest sensation that a crushing weight had all at once been lifted from his heart. For Sir Harry's words could have only one meaning, and that was that he believed Cecily to be still with her uncle in Hampshire. And if this were so, he could have had no hand in her decision to leave Hillcourt, since it must appear that he was not even aware that she had left Dowie House and returned there. It seemed clear, therefore, either that Lord Neagle had been telling a deliberate untruth when he had said that she had set out for London, or that she had had some other scheme in mind in doing so.

Once he had arrived at this conclusion, his chief concern was to rid himself of Brackenridge's company, for if the latter really was ignorant of Cecily's flight it was in the highest degree desirable that he remain so. This he found singularly easy to do; Sir Harry, though evidently puzzled by the sudden alteration in his companion's mood, had no wish to continue a conversation which was not only unprofitable to him, but which seemed in a way to becoming positively dangerous. He was far from being a coward—indeed, he had called his man out on at least two occasions—but he was not fond of entering upon such affairs unless he was certain that his own skill must make it extremely probable that he would come off the victor.

And in Ranleigh's case there was no such probability. He knew him to be a dead shot, and one, moreover, whose coolness could not be expected to desert him when he was facing a loaded pistol aimed at him across a dozen yards of greensward in early morning light.

He therefore made no attempt to prolong the conversation when Mr. Ranleigh showed signs of wishing to conclude it, and soon parted from him, without accompanying him as far as his house in Mount Street.

As for Mr. Ranleigh, on reaching that imposing domicile, he went inside to issue several trenchant orders to his sleepy staff concerning the coming morning, and then repaired to his own bedchamber for a few hours of needed slumber. With Brackenridge eliminated as a factor in Cecily's plans, there appeared to remain only three likely places where she might have gone—to Dowie House, to Inglesant, or, if she had indeed come up to London, to seek out some acquaintance she had made during her brief career in the theatre there.

The last possibility seemed the most remote, but, since he was already in London, he decided to try first to obtain news of the runaway at the Running Boar. If this approach failed, as he feared it would, there would then be nothing for it but to set off for Hampshire and, if need be, for Somerset, to learn if Sir Timothy or the Bonshawes could shed any light on the matter of Cecily's disappearance.

22 These events occurred on a Friday. On Monday Mr. Ranleigh, having obtained no news of Miss Hadley at the Running Boar, and having then pursued his search for that elusive young lady in both Hampshire and Somerset without the least success, arrived back in town to find a note from Lord Portandrew awaiting him at his house in Mount Street. It informed him, in an agitated scrawl, that the newspapers were puffing the forthcoming appearance of *Miss Daingerfield-Nelson* that very evening in a performance of *The Beaux' Stratagem* at the Surrey Theatre, and urgently requested him to use his best efforts to prevent such an occurrence from coming to pass.

On perusing this missive, Mr. Ranleigh, although not addicted to violent language, was overheard by his butler to utter an oath worthy—as that shocked individual later averred—of a jarvey, after which he gave a curt command for his evening dress to be laid out immediately and disappeared into the library. Here he dashed off a pair of lines to Miss Dowie at Hill-court, which he gave orders to be dispatched at once by private messenger, and then ran upstairs and rapidly changed his travel-stained buckskins and riding-coat for correct evening attire.

A glance at his watch had already informed him that he could not possibly reach the theatre until the play was nearing its conclusion, and, in fact, when he arrived there the robbery scene was already in progress, and Miss Daingerfield-Nelson, wearing a nightdress under a diaphanous dressing-gown trimmed with puffs of satin ribbon, with her dark ringlets straying in enchanting disorder from beneath a fetching nightcap of muslin and lace, was being dragged onstage with her mother, Lady Bountiful, by the two rogues, Hounslow and Bagshot. The attendant who showed Mr. Ranleigh to his place heard him utter a heartfelt, "Oh, my God!" and, believing he had misunderstood him, said, "Beg pardon, sir?"

He received no answer. Mr. Ranleigh's eyes were fixed upon the stage, where Miss Daingerfield-Nelson, seeing her lover, Aimwell, burst onstage to her rescue with drawn sword and engage both villains, was exclaiming, "O Madam, had I but a sword to help the brave man!" in tones thrilling enough to evoke a storm of applause from an audience that included half the Bloods in London.

This audience, as Mr. Ranleigh guessed—or the anticipation of it, at any rate—had been responsible for Miss Daingerfield-Nelson's name having been so abruptly inserted in the Surrey's playbill. In point of fact,

Cecily, having arrived in London via the medium of a large green-and-gold Accommodation coach, in which she had played with great success the role of a young gentleman of some sixteen years called from school to attend the bedside of a desperately ill parent in the metropolis, had had not the slightest difficulty in attaining her goal of a rapid appearance upon the London stage. Mr. Jillson, readily located by a visit to the Running Boar, had taken her at once to see the managers of the Surrey Theatre, where he was himself engaged, and these gentlemen, as he had confidently predicted, were found to be not only willing, but eager, to employ the services of a young lady whose disappearance had been one of the *on-dits* of the town a few months before, and whose reappearance upon the Surrey's boards could be guaranteed to draw the male members of the *ton* in droves to their door.

The problem of the choice of a vehicle in which to present Miss Daingerfield-Nelson to this fashionable audience was solved without difficulty. She had been coached by Jillson, during her earlier brief theatrical career, in the leading feminine romantic role of Dorinda in Farquhar's comedy, *The Beaux' Stratagem,* and, although the legal prohibition against legitimate drama's being presented at the minor London theatres was still in force, the recasting of the traditional five acts to three and the addition of a few songs was sufficient to allow any drama to be performed in these houses in almost unaltered form, under the guise of a burletta.

The Beaux' Stratagem, as it happened, was already in the Surrey's repertory, and Cecily was therefore at once put into rehearsal as the lively, innocent Dorinda, who is courted and deceived by the penniless Aimwell only to discover, at the play's end, that her fortune-hunting suitor is not only genuinely in love with her but is actually Viscount Aimwell as well. To give her added assurance in the part, Mrs. Jillson was cast in the role of Dorinda's more sophisticated sister-in-law, Mrs. Sullen, with whom many of Dorinda's scenes were to be played, and Jillson himself as the French officer, Count Bellair.

It was scarcely surprising that Cecily, thus pitchforked into a hectic round of rehearsals and fittings, should have had little opportunity either to consider the results of her decision to leave Hillcourt or to repine over them. In point of fact, she had no wish to do either. If she was to become Miss Daingerfield-Nelson in good earnest, she told herself, Hillcourt and its inhabitants must lapse into the dead past for her, and it therefore behooved her to put them firmly from her mind and immerse herself completely in her new life.

This she proceeded to do, discovering almost at once that the task was made a good deal easier by the novel enjoyments that new life offered her. It was certainly agreeable, for example, to find herself suddenly an object of interest and attention to everyone with whom she came into contact, and she had not become so inured to the glamour of the theatrical world by her previous brief taste of it that the experience of acting one of the principal roles in a gay comedy did not seem a giddily exciting one to her.

She even flirted a little, demurely—perhaps inspired by the character she was impersonating—with the young actor playing opposite her in the role of Aimwell, with the result that he had tumbled half into love with her before they had so much as completed their first rehearsal together. In fact, he and the even younger Thespian who played Archer, his friend, were soon locked in a fierce competition for her attention, and constituted themselves a faithful bodyguard to escort her back and forth from the theatre to the Running Boar, both of them too jealous to be willing to trust the other out of his sight when he was in her company.

This devotion did not escape the observation of the buxom Mrs. Jillson, who advised her, in a feeling aside during a late rehearsal, not to allow herself to become entangled with actors—"for you see what it's led *me* to, love," she said, casting a somewhat jaundiced eye upon her spouse, "and, if I *do* say it myself, I might have caught a baronet on my hook if I had taken the proper advantage of my opportunities. And there's no telling what *you* might achieve, if you was to set your mind to it, for Jillson says he expects the house will be as full of lords as it can hold when we open, and all of them will be come to see you."

These expectations, as Mr. Ranleigh's first glance over the theatre on that Monday evening had informed him, had not been vain, for the Surrey's managers indeed had the satisfaction of beholding quite as many peers as might have made up a respectably full session of the House of Lords enter their doors before the curtain rose on the first act of *The Beaux' Stratagem*. Cecily, to whom this fact was duly reported during the early scenes of the play, received the news with proper gratification; but when, at the conclusion of the robbery scene, Mr. Jillson informed her that Mr. Robert Ranleigh was now said to be a member of the audience as well she turned such an appalled face upon him that Mr. Jillson instinctively said, "Good God!" in the tones usually reserved for his purely professional dramatic moments, and inquired what the matter was.

"N-nothing!" Cecily faltered. "Nothing at all! Are you *quite* sure?"

"Quite sure? About what?"

"About Mr. Ranleigh! Perhaps it is—might it not be someone who resembles him?"

Mr. Jillson began to be conscious of a dubious feeling, somewhat akin to alarm, rising in his own breast. He had had the forethought, upon Cecily's arrival in London, to leave instructions at the Running Boar that on no account were either his own or Cecily's whereabouts to be disclosed to any inquirer—an action which had been responsible for Mr. Ranleigh's failure to obtain any trace of her there.

But the inquirer he had had in mind had been Miss Dowie, whose wrath he had counted on being able to allay more easily once Cecily had actually returned to the stage and it was to be seen how successful her career there now promised to be. He had had no thought whatever of Mr. Ranleigh's still being interested enough in her activities to cast the powerful shadow of his disapproval over them, and, being a prudent man, he found the possibility an alarming one.

An attempt to ascertain from Miss Hadley herself how matters stood between her and the Nonpareil gained him little, however. Cecily, recovering from the first shock of learning that Mr. Ranleigh was actually a member of the audience, merely informed him, in a brief and highly unconvincing statement, that that gentleman's approval or disapproval of her present occupation meant nothing at all to her—an announcement which Mr. Jillson received without noticeable gratification.

"The question is," he persisted, "does it mean anything to *him?*"

"Good gracious, no! Why should it?" Cecily said brightly, wishing that the unaccountable lump in her throat would go away. "If you must know the truth, he is probably very *happy* and—and *relieved* to be rid of me!"

Mr. Jillson eyed her uneasily. "Well, I hope you are right, my dear," he said frankly, "for my own brief acquaintance with him has led me to the unalterable conviction that he is *not* a man I should care to have as an enemy. But I daresay I shall have the chance to see for myself how matters stand, for I have a disagreeable notion that he has not taken the trouble to come to the theatre at this hour without the intention of turning up in the Greenroom after the performance."

"That," said Cecily, tilting up her chin, "is no concern of mine, for *I* shall not be there."

"Oh yes, you will," Mr. Jillson retorted with unaccustomed bluntness, "or we shall risk having the theatre pulled down about our ears! I have been talking to the managers, and they tell me that the only way they have been able to keep the peace here tonight has been by faithfully promising any number of your admirers that you will put in an appearance there as soon as ever the performance has ended."

Nothing that Cecily could say could alter this dictum on the part of her mentors, and she was obliged to bow to the prospect of meeting Mr. Ranleigh face to face within the space of the ensuing hour. It was an event that she could not look forward to with equanimity; in fact, stark panic, which almost sent her fleeing out of the theatre, held her in its grip for several minutes. Fortunately, she was soon obliged to go onstage again, and the concentration required to carry her through her role gave her no further opportunity to dwell upon the dismaying scene to be enacted in the Greenroom upon the play's conclusion.

Mr. Ranleigh, meanwhile, sat through the remainder of the performance with an impassivity which could only be considered as praiseworthy, in view of the severe exercise of self-restraint it involved. At its conclusion he was accosted by Lord Portandrew, who demanded at once, in fulminating tones, to know why he had not put a stop to Cecily's reappearance upon the London theatrical scene.

"My dear fellow, I am not her guardian!" Mr. Ranleigh said brusquely, the ordinary pleasant drawl quite gone from his voice.

"Well, you dashed well acted as if you was when I was at Hillcourt!" his lordship retorted. "And you told me she was gone for a governess! What's she doing here? How did she get here? Has it anything to do with Brackenridge? *He's* here tonight, you know, and looking deuced up in the world over something!"

"So I have observed," said Mr. Ranleigh, who had, in fact, not failed to note Brackenridge's presence in the theatre and the spirits in which that gentleman appeared to be that evening—spirits which had evidently been improved by his having wined and dined very well before the performance. "However, I am hardly in a position to answer your questions," he went on, "for I have just returned from several highly unprofitable days spent searching for Miss Hadley over half of England, my imagination unfortunately boggling at the idea that she would be birdwitted enough to thrust herself into such a situation as this."

"Oh! You have?" said Lord Portandrew, digesting this somewhat bitter statement, but rising at once to Cecily's defence. "Well, she has been driven to it, I expect! Dashed uncomfortable business, being a governess, I daresay!" He added urgently, as Mr. Ranleigh began to move away from him, "What are you going to do now? Can't leave her in *this* fix!"

"If she wishes to remain in it, it is hardly in my power to compel her to do otherwise."

"No, but——"

"I have sent off a message to her aunt at Hillcourt," Mr. Ranleigh said, with admirable but somewhat ominous patience. "Until she arrives in town, neither you nor I can do more than try the effect of persuasion—which, if I know Miss Hadley, means that we shall succeed in making no impression upon her at all!"

And he thereupon walked off toward the Greenroom, leaving his cousin to follow him if he chose.

The Greenroom had already been invaded by more than a score of Miss Daingerfield-Nelson's admirers by the time they entered it, and in a few moments that young lady herself, accompanied by Mr. Jillson, made her appearance. She was still clad in the dashing gown of jonquil crape, cut somewhat indecorously low over the bosom, in which she had just left the stage, and, as she had not had time to wash the rouge from her face, presented the picture of spurious sophistication which she had once so much desired to exhibit before Mr. Ranleigh.

Not entirely to her surprise, however, she found—as her eyes immediately singled out his tall figure in the thronged room—that the picture was not one that met with his approval. As a matter of fact, he looked uncompromisingly *dis*approving—an attitude which, although she could scarcely say she had not expected it, brought a look of distinct challenge into her eyes.

Very well! she thought. If he was determined to despise her, he should have good reason! She turned a warm smile impartially upon the dozen or more gentlemen who immediately flocked to her side, receiving their compliments with an encouraging aplomb that sent Lord Portandrew struggling in dismay through the press to her.

"No, really, Miss Ha—*Daingerfield-Nelson!*" he exclaimed. "Not at all the thing! Shouldn't be here in the first place, you know! Best let me take you home!"

"Oh—Lord Portandrew! Did *you* come to view the performance to-night? How very nice to see you again!" Cecily said, pertinaciously ignoring his protest and extending her hand to him in a friendly manner. "I hope I find you well?"

"Yes, yes—but——"

"And Mr. Ranleigh?" Cecily persisted, feeling herself buoyed up by the excitement of the evening sufficiently to be able to cast a pensively provocative glance in that gentleman's direction. "Dear me, he does not appear so! What can have occurred, I wonder, to make him look so—so very *forbidding* tonight?"

To her considerable chagrin, Mr. Ranleigh did not rise to the bait, but continued to keep his distance from the eager circle about her, regarding her much with the air of a man permitting a troublesome child to go its length in folly before taking steps at the proper moment to remove it unobtrusively from the scene. A flare of stubborn anger rose in her breast, but she continued to flirt her fan with the coquetry well practised for her role in *The Beaux' Stratagem*, attending, with what she hoped was a cool unconsciousness of Mr. Ranleigh's hard gaze, to the various gallant protests directed at her for sparing a moment of her attention to such a fellow as Portandrew.

But her poise was overset completely, within a very few instants, by the sight of Sir Harry Brackenridge strolling into the room and approaching the group around her. *His* presence in the house had not been mentioned to her, and, though she had realised, when she had first conceived the idea of returning to the theatre, that her appearance upon the stage must inevitably bring her once more to his notice, she had consoled herself with the thought that, since she now had no reason to fear his disclosures concerning her theatrical career, he could no longer be a threat to her peace.

But one glance at those cold blue eyes and lazily smiling lips assured her that she had been far too hasty in dismissing him as an important factor in her life. He came up and, bowing over her hand, lifted it gently to his lips.

"My very dear Miss—er—Daingerfield-Nelson!" he said. "So we meet again! I gather that your uncle's health has improved sufficiently for you to leave his bedside?"

Cecily, burningly conscious under his mocking gaze of her rouged face and revealing gown, stammered some disjointed reply, endeavouring at the same time to draw away her hand. He did not immediately release it, however, and was at once challenged rather suspiciously by Lord Portandrew, who demanded to know by what right he claimed such close acquaintance with Miss Daingerfield-Nelson.

"Oh, Miss Daingerfield-Nelson and I are old friends," Brackenridge said, his eyes quizzing her mercilessly. "Are we not, my dear? Let me see: it has been no longer ago than a fortnight—has it?—since we had the pleasure of a most interesting tête-à-tête in Somerset."

Cecily gave him a trapped, imploring look. She saw now that he was quite as capable of making use of his knowledge of her employment at Inglesant, with all its connotations of her relationship with the Ranleighs, to his own advantage as he had been of using his knowledge of her career in the theatre, and endeavoured helplessly to think of a way to still his tongue.

It was unnecessary. She was aware suddenly that Mr. Ranleigh, observing her embarrassment, had moved quietly across the room and was himself now addressing Brackenridge.

"Playing off your tricks, Harry?" he inquired evenly. "Miss Hadley is an unworthy opponent for you, I fear. Had you not rather cross swords with me?"

Cecily, who had grown rather pale on perceiving his approach, gave a gasp at the sound of her true name on his lips, and turned a startled gaze upon him. He was not looking at her, however; his eyes were fixed on Brackenridge. Sir Harry, as surprised as the others—though for a different reason—to hear her addressed as Miss Hadley, laughed rather uncertainly and said, "I wasn't aware that you considered yourself Miss Hadley's champion, Robert! But your solicitude is superfluous, I assure you. Miss Hadley need fear no tricks from *me*."

A dozen voices interrupted to inquire why Miss Daingerfield-Nelson had suddenly acquired a new cognomen, and Cecily was appalled to hear Mr. Ranleigh say, in tones as cool as if he had been uttering the merest commonplace, "Miss Hadley is a young relation of mine who has been foolish enough to enter upon this adventure entirely against the advice of her friends. May I be permitted to escort you home, Miss Hadley? Your aunt will be in London in a day or two, and I believe you will make her much more comfortable if you will put an end to your little performance here at once."

Cecily, gazing up into his eyes, felt as if the blood had quite left her heart. There was nothing to be read in them but a well-controlled anger, but she could not but wonder how much it had cost his pride to make such an acknowledgement before his friends.

That he had had little choice in doing so, she could not doubt. Sir Harry's remarks had plainly shown that he would not scruple to make use of his knowledge of her background to embarrass either her or Mr. Ranleigh; and it must therefore only have been a matter of time until the information contained in Mr. Ranleigh's announcement became public property.

She swallowed a constriction in her throat and said, with determined equanimity, "Thank you, but Mr. Jillson will see me home, Mr. Ranleigh. I should not dream of putting you to so much trouble."

"It would be not the least trouble for *me*, my dear," Sir Harry said. Unlike the rest of the company, who had been so startled by Mr. Ranleigh's announcement that they seemed unable to decide what tone they were now to take with her, he appeared entirely to have recovered his sang-froid, and went on to say to Mr. Ranleigh, in his languid voice, "My dear fellow, you have done your part now: you must see that you have quite frightened off all Miss Hadley's admirers. Really, it is hardly sporting of you; you have had your chance, and should have the good grace to step aside and leave the field to others."

He reached out and audaciously took Cecily's hand in his as he concluded—a gesture which so surprised her that for a moment she did not move, but allowed it to rest there, while her eyes flew to Mr. Ranleigh's, watching her. The expression she saw there made her colour vividly; she gave an exclamation and snatched her hand away, saying vehemently to Brackenridge, "I do not *wish* you to take me home! I do not wish *any* of you to take me home!" She looked around, saw Mr. Jillson hovering nearby, and, feeling that the last vestiges of her self-composure were deserting her, said to him in an unsteady voice, "If you do not take me away this instant, Mr. Jillson, I shall walk home alone, for I mean to leave here at once, whatever *you* do!"

Mr. Jillson, attempting a few hasty apologies, hurried after her as she swept from the room. He was, on the whole, inclined to believe that it was as well for both him and Miss Hadley to retreat from the scene at this point, for he had a well-developed sense of self-preservation and it appeared to him—though he had been unable to overhear the conversation in which she had been engaged—that the atmosphere was beginning to grow ominous. Sir Harry, if his experienced eye was any judge of the matter, had had just enough to drink to make him reckless without making him tipsy, and Mr. Ranleigh bore all the signs of a man who was keeping so hard a rein upon his temper that it would be wonderful if it did not make a bolt for it and escape him entirely.

Such a combination, he felt, was likely to end in an explosion in which innocent—or nearly innocent—bystanders might well be singed, and he therefore made no objection to Cecily's desire to leave the premises at once, following her out of the room with an alacrity that even that overwrought young lady found satisfactory.

23 Mr. Jillson's forebodings turned out to be quite correct. At eleven o'clock on the following morning, while breakfasting at the Running Boar, he received a visit from one of his colleagues at the Surrey Theatre, who had come to tell him of certain events that had taken place the night before. This communication had the effect of sending him upstairs at once to Cecily's little parlour for an interview which he prefaced with the ominous statement that the fat was now fairly in the fire.

"Good gracious, why?" Cecily asked, instantly taking alarm, and putting down the card that had accompanied the third handsome bouquet of flowers that had arrived for her that morning, each bearing the compliments of one of her noble admirers. "Has my aunt arrived in town?"

Mr. Jillson dismissed Miss Dowie with an impatient wave of his hand. "My good child," he said, "I am perfectly capable of dealing with your aunt! Mr. Ranleigh, however, is quite another matter."

"Mr. Ranleigh?" Cecily turned rather pale. "Why, what in the world has *he* done?"

"What he has done," Mr. Jillson said with some asperity, "has been to feel himself obliged to resent certain highly injudicious remarks which I am told were made by Sir Harry Brackenridge at Watier's last evening—resent them, I may say, to the extent of throwing a glass of wine into Sir Harry's face in full view of at least a dozen of his acquaintances!"

"Oh, dear!" Cecily said in a small voice. "Were the—were the remarks about me, Mr. Jillson?"

"As I understand it—though my information, I must admit, comes to me at third hand—they were."

"And—and what happened then?"

"What happened then, my dear young lady, was that Sir Harry called Mr. Ranleigh out!"

"Called him out! You mean—they are to fight a duel?"

"Precisely. And I should like very much to know, if you do not mind telling me—in fact, I should dashed well like to know even if you do mind!—on exactly what footing you stand with Mr. Robert Ranleigh. I thought you gave me to understand last evening that any—er—intimate connexion there might have been between you was at an end."

Cecily's cheeks flew scarlet in a moment. "I never gave you to understand any such thing!" she denied. "That is—I mean—there never *was* any such connexion between us as you appear to think! I am a distant relation of his, and he and his mother were kind enough to interest themselves in finding suitable employment for me. And I should never, never have run away from them," she added feelingly, "if I had had the least notion that anything like *this* would happen, for I quite see now that if he and Sir Harry are to fight a duel and he is hurt, it will be all my fault."

Mr. Jillson, considering the matter fairmindedly, said that he could himself not quite see *that,* but added that he wished she had favoured him with a more exact account of the state of her affairs when she had first arrived in London. It was apparent that his chief concern at the moment was over whether Mr. Ranleigh's interest in his young relation would lead him to resent the part he—Jillson—had played in her return to the theatre as violently as he had taken exception to Brackenridge's remarks, and he could be brought to give little attention to Cecily's anxious questions as to what might be done to halt the projected duel beyond assuring her that such a matter was quite out of the power of either of them to arrange.

Cecily, however, could not agree to this. The shock of Mr. Jillson's announcement had left her feeling little better than a murderess, for her imagination found no difficulty in leaping forward to picture Mr. Ranleigh's lifeless body lying on the greensward, with Brackenridge standing triumphantly over him, a smoking pistol in his hand.

Casting about in her mind, when Mr. Jillson had left her, for steps she might take to avert this appalling tragedy, and rejecting as useless the notion of going at once to Mount Street and imploring Mr. Ranleigh not to meet Sir Harry, she bethought herself of Lord Portandrew. She was not inclined to be hopeful as to the quality of the advice she might receive from him, but it would be better than no advice at all, and she accordingly sat down and scribbled an urgent note to him, begging him to come round to the Running Boar at once. This she dispatched by the hand of the landlady's eldest son, a lad of thirteen, and then sat down hopefully to await Lord Portandrew's arrival.

He was not long in coming. Within the hour he was ushered up to her little parlour, looking torn between gratification at her having sent for him and rather guilty self-consciousness over what he suspected had been her motive in doing so. He made a valiant attempt at first to convince her that he knew nothing about the projected duel, but she cut him short by advising him impatiently not to take her for a perfect ninny.

"Mr. Jillson has heard of it, and if *he* has, I am sure *you* must have, as well," she said. "Why did Mr. Ranleigh quarrel with that odious man?

Was it because of something he said about me? Mr. Jillson says he believes it was."

"Well, as a matter of fact—he's right," his lordship admitted reluctantly. "Harry was a trifle foxed last night, you know—nothing you might have noticed, for he has a devilish hard head—but it made him gudgeon enough to say in Robert's hearing that he believed you was holding out for a wedding ring, but he was willing to lay a monkey he would be able to—— Well, never mind about that!" he concluded hastily. "And that was when Robert dashed the burgundy in his face. Already in the deuce of a temper last night, you know; Harry ought to've known better than to set his back up. Didn't like it above half, your turning up here in the theatre after he'd been chasing about after you for days on end!"

"Oh—d-did he do that?" Cecily faltered, sunk more than ever into a dismal sense of the enormity of the amount of trouble she had caused. "I daresay he *was* dreadfully vexed——"

"Well—stands to reason," Lord Portandrew said judicially. "Very upsetting sort of thing, careering all over England looking for a girl and then coming slap on her in a theatre full of people." He fixed her with a gaze of some severity. "Shouldn't have done that, you know," he said. "Not at all the thing! If you didn't like that governess place, you'd better have married me. Don't say you might have liked that much, either, but, dash it, it'd be better than *this!*"

"No, no! Indeed, I could not!" Cecily interrupted in a stifled voice. "I mean—of course it is very kind of you to offer, but I should not think of d-disgracing you by accepting, for I am a n-notorious woman now—oh, yes! you must know yourself that I am," she reiterated mournfully. "No gentleman of fashion could possibly wish to ally himself with me now!"

"Well, dash it, I don't see *that!*" Lord Portandrew objected. "I don't say you ain't kicked up a pretty row with this notion of yours to go back on the stage, but people ain't so gothic nowadays as to expect you need have as prim a reputation as some governess in a curst dull, respectable household to marry a man of *ton!*"

She shook her head, quite unconvinced. "But *that* does not matter now," she went on, in determinedly steadier tones. "My only concern now is to stop Mr. Ranleigh from meeting Sir Harry."

"Shouldn't think you could do *that,*" his lordship said decidedly. "Deuced stiff-necked, all the Ranleighs; not at all likely Robert will apologise to Brackenridge. Very bad *ton* to try to avoid a challenge, at any rate. Shouldn't think he'd care to show his face in town if he did."

"But Sir Harry?" Cecily inquired anxiously. "Could not he withdraw? If *he* issued the challenge——"

"Daresay there's nothing he'd like better, but he won't," his lordship said promptly. "Thing is, he's mad as fire, and he won't have time to cool down before the whole affair's over and done with. Fixed for tomorrow morning at Paddington Green, you see."

"Tomorrow morning!" Cecily looked at him distractedly. "Oh, I did not know it would be so soon! Do you think, perhaps, if *I* were to ask Sir Harry——?"

"No!" his lordship said, a horrified expression appearing upon his face at the very thought of such an impropriety. "Good God, you ought to know nothing about it! Besides, he's a Bad Man, Harry; likely to take any sort of advantage of you if you so much as went near him with such a cork-brained idea!" He fixed an unwontedly stern eye upon her. "You'd best promise me you'll give *that* notion up," he said. "Wouldn't have a minute's peace if I went away from here thinking you still had it in your head!"

Cecily looked recalcitrant for a moment, but eventually gave in, seeing that Lord Portandrew was alarmed enough to remain indefinitely in argument with her on the subject, and agreed reluctantly that she would not attempt to approach Sir Harry.

As it developed, however, there was no need for her to do so, for Lord Portandrew had scarcely left the house before one of Sir Harry's footmen arrived with a graceful note for her from his master. He was sorry, Sir Harry wrote, that he had had to part from her in such an unsatisfactory manner on the previous evening, having been able to say nothing to her of the matter that was uppermost in his mind and heart, and he hoped she would give him the opportunity of a private conversation with her that day before she went to the theatre. The note ended with a scarcely veiled hint that she had quite mistaken the character of his present intentions, serious reflection over the past few weeks having caused him to recognise the *permanent and sacred* (the words heavily underscored) nature of his attachment to her.

For several minutes after she had perused this missive Cecily was at a loss to understand its meaning. If it had come from any man but Brackenridge, she must have believed that his intention in seeking this interview was to offer her marriage; but she could not credit such a motive in him. Far from expecting that the weeks that had passed since she had seen him at Inglesant would have caused him to form such a plan concerning her, she would rather have expected him to have spent that time in concocting some scheme to pay her out for the disappointment she had visited upon him by running off from him.

Still it was possible, she thought doubtfully, remembering Lord Portandrew's reference to Brackenridge's belief that a wedding ring was her goal, that Sir Harry was by this time so obsessed with the desire to best Mr. Ranleigh by his success with her that he might even be prepared to offer her marriage to attain his end. At any rate, the opportunity his letter held out to her to try to persuade him not to go through with his duel with Mr. Ranleigh seemed much too good to be neglected, and she therefore sat down and dashed off a reply to it, in which she merely stated that she was at home and would be happy to see him at his earliest convenience. This she sent round to him by the footman, and then sat down in considerable agitation to await his arrival.

Her agitation was not decreased by the appearance at the Running Boar, some half hour later, not of Brackenridge but of Mr. Ranleigh. She was gazing out from the parlour window, which overlooked the inn-yard, when his curricle drew up below, and, perceiving his tall figure springing down from it and striding toward the door, she at once shrank back and ran to tell the landlady to deny that she was in. Mr. Jillson, whom she encountered in the passage as she hurried back to her room, halted her to ask what all the bustle was about, and was instantly required in the most distracted of whispers to be silent.

"It is Mr. Ranleigh!" she hissed. "He *must* be got rid of at once, before Sir Harry arrives, for if they meet here they may quarrel again, and then *nothing* can prevent them from fighting that dreadful duel!"

"I should think nothing would prevent them even if they don't meet," Mr. Jillson said candidly. "But what are you up to, my dear? Brackenridge coming here, you say? Why, if I may make bold to inquire, should he come?"

"Oh, hush, *pray!*" Cecily implored, listening tensely to discover if the landlady's representations would satisfy Mr. Ranleigh that she was indeed not in the house. She could not distinguish what was being said below, but a few minutes later the front door closed and she heard the landlady's heavy tread on the stairs.

She was the bearer of a note from Mr. Ranleigh. Cecily, unfolding it, saw at a glance that it was both businesslike and brief. "Miss Hadley," it read: "I am in expectation of Miss Dowie's arrival in Mount Street by tomorrow morning. She will call upon you here immediately, and will hope to find you in. I have just come from seeing the managers of the Surrey Theatre, and may inform you that your engagement there has been terminated. Yours, etc., Ranleigh."

This last sentence drew an indignant gasp from her. "Oh!" she exclaimed, colour flying into her cheeks. "Of all the abominable, high-handed——!"

"What's he done?" Mr. Jillson inquired forebodingly, taking the precaution of dismissing the landlady as he did so.

"He says he has seen the managers of the theatre and I am not to be employed there any longer!" Cecily said, with strong feeling. "It is exactly like him—but he need not think he can order my life as if I were a child, merely because I am related to him! I daresay the Surrey is not the only theatre in London, and even if he is so odious as to make it impossible for me to obtain an engagement here, *you* will be able to inform me how I must go about it to find employment in some theatre outside of London!"

Mr. Jillson, who was beginning to give the impression of a man with an unhappy conviction that he had been drawn unawares into a situation presenting a considerably greater number of dangerous pitfalls than he had ever bargained for, opined tentatively that, if a gentleman as rich and influential as Mr. Ranleigh had a mind to look after her affairs—without, he added obliquely, making those demands upon her which a gentleman might well insist on in such a case—she was a fool not to allow him to do so.

"Demands!" Cecily repeated wrathfully. "But of course he will make demands! He wishes to marry me!"

Mr. Jillson turned a positively thunderstruck countenance upon her. "*Marry* you!" he exclaimed. "Ranleigh wishes to *marry* you? And you're thinking of refusing him? If you will pardon my speaking frankly, my dear, in that case you *are* a fool! Why, you would be rich and important beyond your wildest dreams——"

"He doesn't care for me in the least," Cecily said in a small, gruff voice, her anger cooling as she considered the dismal realities of the situation. "And, besides, it is very likely that I am mistaken about his wishing to marry me *now*, after what happened last night, and all he means to do is to remove me from a position of notoriety and provide for me in some—some retired place where I will not be an embarrassment to him any longer."

She found this such a depressing prospect that for a few moments she failed to realise that voices were again emanating from the hall below, and came to herself with a start only at the sound of tones that were unmistakably Brackenridge's.

"Oh! It is Sir Harry!" she said, in a flurry. "You *will* leave us alone, won't you, Mr. Jillson? For I *may* be able to persuade him——"

"If you believe he'll heed any tears or prayers of *yours*, you are fair and far out!" Mr. Jillson said bluntly. "Take my advice, my dear, and have nothing to do with him."

"Oh, *pray!*" Cecily interrupted, hearing Brackenridge's step upon the stairs. "I *must* speak to him; it's of the greatest importance! Don't you see?"

Mr. Jillson did not seem to see in the least, but, as he appeared to have certain matters upon his own mind that required immediate and serious cogitation, he withdrew in the face of Cecily's pleas, leaving that young lady to whisk herself into her room and the next moment, at the sound of a knock upon the door, turn with a start and utter a rather breathless, "Come in!"

24

Brackenridge entered the room at once. He found Cecily seated primly in the chair into which she had flung herself the moment before, regarding him with a somewhat fluctuating smile.

"Oh! Sir Harry!" she said, allowing him to take her hand and watching rather warily as he smilingly bent to kiss it. "How—how very kind of you to have come so quickly!"

"But what else could I do, when I was so fortunate as to receive an invitation from you?" Brackenridge said lightly, searching her face with a quizzing glance, as if he hoped to read in it the reason for this new complaisance in her manner toward him. She blushed—a sign of confusion that appeared to satisfy him. She saw quite clearly, from the cynical light in his eye, that he believed it was the hint of marriage in his note that had caused her to agree to see him, and had to grit her teeth against the desire to inform him just how mistaken he was in this belief.

She invited him to sit down, however, with as much cordiality as she could command, attempting to conceal her discomposure when he at once drew up a chair quite close to her own and calmly possessed himself of both her hands.

"Now, my dear," he said, "shall we come to an understanding?—for I believe it was for that purpose that you agreed to see me, and it is certainly for that purpose that I have come here. You find yourself—do you not?—in the awkward position of a young woman whose relations do not at all see eye to eye with her as to her future course in life. If it were not so, I should not presume to address you in this sudden manner——"

He broke off as Cecily, showing more than a little discomposure at this very direct approach, drew her hands away and jumped up, retreating to the window.

"Indeed, I do not know what you are talking of, sir!" she said, sparring for time. "My—my relations? Do you mean my aunt?"

"I have not the pleasure of that lady's acquaintance," Brackenridge said, watching her flurried countenance with his usual air of rather mocking composure, "but let us include her in the list, if you like. I was speaking more particularly, however, of Robert Ranleigh."

"Mr. Ranleigh? Oh—yes, of course!" Cecily drew a deep breath and decided, in the absence of the appearance of any inclination on Brackenridge's part to be diverted from his main purpose, to employ an equivalent directness. "That—that is exactly what I should like to speak to you about, sir!" she declared. "That is—what I mean to say is—Sir Harry, *must* you fight that horrid duel with him?"

A somewhat arrested expression suddenly appeared upon Brackenridge's face. "How came you to know of that?" he inquired abruptly.

"I—someone told me. It does not matter." She hurried on, throwing caution and truthfulness alike to the winds, "Of course it was quite odious of him to do what he did, but—but he is said to be a dead shot, and I cannot bear to think that you should expose yourself——"

Sir Harry, digesting with difficulty, it appeared, this evidence of concern for his welfare, gave her another rather hard glance, but could read nothing in her face but the real distress she could not keep from appearing there.

"Why," he said slowly, after a moment, "that is not a matter that need trouble you, my dear."

"Yes, but it does!" Cecily interrupted fervently. "Indeed I shall never be able to forgive myself if anything dreadful comes of it! I am sure Mr. Ranleigh can be the most disagreeable man alive when it pleases him to be, but I daresay it was not entirely his fault that he was out of temper last night, for he had been searching everywhere for me for days, it seems, and—and I expect it was really *me* he would have liked to do something horrid to, only he could not, and so it happened to be you instead."

She paused hopefully, for a sudden laugh had escaped Sir Harry, erasing the wary expression his face had worn.

"Searching for you for days!" he repeated. "So that was it, was it? Let me tell you, my dear, that Robert Ranleigh is not at all accustomed to finding females fleeing from him! I daresay it must have been quite a new experience for him. What had he done to make you run away?"

"N-nothing! Only—I did not at all care to see him——"

"Well, you need trouble yourself over him no further, I assure you! From now on it will be my pleasure to guard you from his importunities."

"But you will not be able to guard me if he shoots you," Cecily pointed out urgently. "Indeed, I think it will be much, much better if you will go to see him and tell him that you understand now that it was quite my fault that he behaved toward you as he did last night, and so he need not fight a duel with you, after all."

"What! Cry craven to him? No, I think not!" Brackenridge said, with a rather ugly little laugh. He approached her and, taking one of her hands in his, imprinted a light kiss upon it. "I am touched, however, by your solicitude!" he said. "May I hope it portends that you will look favourably on what I am about to propose to you? No, don't give me your answer yet!" he said, halting her as she was about to open her lips to utter a hasty demur. "Let me explain. Your situation is such that the usual courses to be followed in such a case as this cannot apply. You are, as I have said, in the hands of your relations, and I fear that, especially after what occurred last evening, Ranleigh at least will never agree to a closer connexion between us. It would be useless for me to speak of my feeling for you to him —and *his* influence, I must believe, will be paramount in any decision that is made concerning your future. That is why I must propose to you that you take your destiny into your own hands and fly with me——"

He paused, seeing that the expression on her face had altered suddenly. She was no longer looking at him with an air of obstinate alarm, but on the contrary appeared quite dazedly happy.

"Fly with you!" she repeated, her air that of a young lady who had suddenly been presented with her dearest wish. "Why, yes! Of course! The very thing!"

"Do you think so?" Sir Harry inquired, looking rather stunned himself at the enthusiasm with which his suggestion had been received.

Cecily turned a dazzling smile upon him. "Oh, yes! I should like it above all things!" she assured him. "Only it must be tonight, you know, for I dare not wait——"

"My dear girl," Sir Harry interrupted her indulgently, "you have made me the happiest of men, but surely there is no need for quite so much haste! You may have forgotten that I have a most urgent appointment tomorrow morning."

"Yes, but there *is* need!" Cecily protested, calling up an expression of histrionic disappointment to her face that would have gladdened Mr. Jillson's heart. "My aunt, you see, is to arrive in town in the morning, and if she finds me here she will take me away and then I shall never see you again! We *must* leave tonight!"

Sir Harry, who had not bargained for such ardour on Miss Hadley's part, looked thoughtful. An experienced man, something warned him against accepting it at face value; a cynical one, his scepticism as to the genuineness of her sudden affection for him merely assured him that it had been caused by the fact that the chit was grasping at the idea of becoming Lady Brackenridge. That he had adroitly contrived to give her the impression that she was to receive that title through lawful matrimony without committing himself to the least promise to that effect he considered one of the minor triumphs of his amatory career, and he was, in fact, so much pleased by his success that his usual cold good judgement was somewhat led astray.

Also, her desire that their elopement be carried out at once had much to recommend it in his eyes. Only the wine-induced recklessness Mr. Jillson had noted on the previous night, coupled with the insulting provocation with which Mr. Ranleigh had countered his remarks concerning Cecily, had been able to overcome his customary prudent rule against entering upon an affair of honour in which his own safety would be in jeopardy. He had issued his challenge to Ranleigh in the white heat of anger, and ever since that anger had had time to cool had been casting about in his mind for some reason he could allege for withdrawing from the affair without becoming an object of opprobrium or ridicule to his acquaintance.

And now Cecily's suggestion of an immediate flight appeared to offer him that reason. Say that, he argued to himself, he carried the girl off to France and installed her as his mistress there: while he sojourned pleasantly in Paris with her, he might be assured that the news of his having boldly snatched her away from under Ranleigh's nose would turn the tide of ridicule so sharply against his rival that the fact that he himself had failed to appear upon the field of honour might be all but overlooked. The whole town knew that their dispute had been over Miss Hadley, and his emerging the victor in this matter must certainly be taken into account in the town's tattle concerning the affair.

And then *this* solution to his problem had the inestimable advantage of offering him both the girl and the safety of his own skin—neither of which he could be sure of if he went through with his engagement on the following morning. If Ranleigh were even to succeed in wounding him, it would be impossible for him to make the least push to carry the girl off for days, perhaps for weeks, and in the meantime she would certainly be removed from London by her aunt and he would have the devil's own time of it to come at her again.

All in all, he decided abruptly, he would be a fool if he did not close with the opportunity that was being offered him. The chit was willing—or she was willing, at any rate, to go posting off to a Gretna Green marriage, which it would be time enough to explain to her was not what he had in mind when it was too late for her to turn back—and all that was needed to change the next twenty-four hours of his life from an appalling nightmare to a highly gratifying amorous adventure was his own resolution to carry the scheme through.

He accordingly informed Cecily in satisfactorily loverlike terms that her wish was his law: the elopement should take place that very night. Rapid plans were made: she could not leave the Running Boar, she told him, until after the Jillsons had left for the theatre that evening, for she did not doubt that they would try to stop her if they knew of her purpose; and Brackenridge agreed that it would be more prudent for them to wait until darkness had fallen before setting out. A hired post-chaise, he added, rather than his own travelling-carriage, would take her up at the appointed time, so that his connexion with her flight would not be evident, and he would accompany the chaise on horseback for the first stage, rather than riding with her in it, as an added precaution against their being seen together in town.

He then took his leave, having possessed himself in parting of a kiss which Cecily, for all her desire to appear properly eager, could bring herself to receive only with excessive reluctance, and left her to face with some misgiving the consequences of the imbroglio into which she had so impulsively flung herself.

She had indeed, on first hearing Sir Harry's proposal that she elope with him, thought of nothing but the fact that here, come miraculously to her hand, was a way for her to get him out of town and so prevent his duel with Mr. Ranleigh on the following morning. Every other consideration had, for the moment, appeared of no consequence beside the paramount one of saving Mr. Ranleigh from injury and perhaps even from death, and it did not fully occur to her in just how awkward a situation she had placed herself until she was able to sit down and consider the matter quietly.

At the least, she realised then, she must engage to spend the better part of the night in apparent acquiescence with Sir Harry's plan to carry her off to Scotland—for she never doubted that Gretna Green was to be their destination—before she could risk telling him that she had no wish to become his wife: otherwise it would be possible for him to retrace his course in time to carry out his engagement to meet Mr. Ranleigh at Paddington Green. That such a deception would strain her histrionic powers to the utmost, she could not doubt. But worse than that was the misgiving she felt as to Sir Harry's reaction when he learned the truth. He would be very angry, of course—but, after all, she told herself, plucking up her courage, he could not force her to accompany him against her will on a lengthy journey, most of it to be accomplished in the full light of day on public roads. She must surely be able to induce him to allow her to return to

London, however enraged he might become at her sudden change of heart.

What she would do when she did reach London again she had no idea, nor had she the leisure to examine that problem at the moment. If her aunt were to seek her out in the morning, as Mr. Ranleigh had informed her that she would, she must, of course, act as she bid her; if, on the other hand, Miss Dowie did not appear, doubtless the Jillsons would assist her in finding some new employment in the theatre.

But at least, she told herself, with a sudden lump rising in her throat, no one would any longer see marriage with Mr. Ranleigh as the solution to her problem, once she had disgraced herself not only by a notorious reappearance on the London stage, but also by spending the better part of a night travelling in company with Sir Harry Brackenridge.

25 Nine o'clock, the hour appointed for her to leave the house, seemed to her to arrive with fatal swiftness. She had half-hoped, half-dreaded that a return visit from Mr. Ranleigh, or perhaps the reappearance of Mr. Jillson with some new plan to propose for the continuance of her theatrical career, might make it impossible for her to go through with the elopement; but neither of these events had occurred. Mr. Jillson, in fact, did not turn up at the Running Boar even when the dinner hour had arrived, and as for Mr. Ranleigh, he had no hope that any interference of his, before Miss Dowie's arrival, would have the slightest effect in diverting Miss Hadley's resolution to engage in any harebrained schemes she might be concocting for the future.

Cecily was therefore quite at liberty at nine o'clock, after having partaken of dinner with Mrs. Jillson, before the latter left for the theatre, and parried as well as she could her curious questions concerning Mr. Ranleigh's interference in her theatrical career, to let herself out the front door, portmanteau in hand, and walk from the inn-yard toward the post-chaise discreetly waiting just beyond.

Her resolution came close to failing, however, when she saw the mounted figure beside it, and only by calling up once more that vivid mental picture of Mr. Ranleigh lying wounded or dying on Paddington Green could she steel herself to continuing on down the street and entering the chaise.

It was of some assistance to her resolution that Brackenridge himself did not dismount to hand her in, but remained at a little distance. But she could not hope that this arrangement would continue beyond their first halt, and for some minutes, as the chaise jolted over the cobblestoned streets, she strove to gather her disordered thoughts and plan what her behaviour toward him would be when he came to ride beside her.

As she was quite unfamiliar with the intricacies of the London streets, she at first paid little heed to the route the chaise took, merely assuming that it was heading in the direction of the Great North Road, which she knew they must traverse on their journey to Scotland. But presently, rousing herself to peer from the window, she was astonished to see the gleam of water beneath and to find that they were crossing a wide bridge. It was the Thames that lay below—there could be no doubt of that—and even in her ignorance of London she was aware that they could not therefore be driving north. In fact, as she continued to gaze out the window in growing bewilderment, she recognised some of the landmarks she had seen when she had journeyed to and from Hillcourt, and she became convinced that they were taking the same road south that she had ridden over on those occasions. For some time indignation superseded alarm in her mind. Even with her imperfect knowledge of the world, she knew that she, a minor, without the consent of her guardian, could not possibly be married in England, and that therefore, if Sir Harry indeed did not intend to take her north to Scotland, he could not have matrimony in mind.

But as the horses galloped on down the road, the chaise jolting and swaying with their speed as the city was left behind, she began to be more frightened. She had counted on Sir Harry's behaving with proper circumspection toward his future bride, which would have meant that she would have nothing to fear but a kiss or an embrace until sufficient time had elapsed for her to be able to tell him that she had changed her mind and wished to return to London. But if he did not intend marriage, her case was infinitely more serious. He might, in fact, she thought, have it in mind to take her to some secluded spot only a short distance from London, in which case not only would she have failed to help Mr. Ranleigh—since Brackenridge would then have ample time to return for his engagement at Paddington Green before morning—but she would herself face a far greater peril than she had ever bargained for.

What was she to do? If she were to jump out from the chaise at the first halt and demand to be taken back to London, she would have gained nothing by all she had risked; if, on the other hand, she remained silent, she might be plunging herself into the greatest danger. She was in a state of miserable indecision, and the result was that when the chaise had rattled into the courtyard of an inn which she recognised as the Greyhound at Croydon, where she and her aunt and Lady Frederick had changed horses on their journey to Hillcourt, she said nothing at all to Sir Harry when he opened the door of the chaise, but only regarded him with a highly unfriendly expression upon her face.

"My dear girl, you look deucedly upset!" Brackenridge said, smiling at her. "What is the matter? Can I procure some refreshment for you? A glass of wine——?"

"No, you cannot!" Cecily said, finding her tongue as she continued to regard him with a smouldering gaze. "And you know very well what the matter is! You are not taking me to Scotland! This road goes south!"

"I am aware," Brackenridge said composedly, getting into the chaise beside her and closing the door. "However, I believe I did not mention Scotland to you, my sweet. I have a dislike to being married over the anvil —such a commonplace and even rather vulgar proceeding, don't you agree? They order—as Mr. Sterne puts it—this matter better in France."

"In France!" Cecily's eyes flew wide. "Is *that* where you are taking me?"

"Yes. Should you dislike it? Most girls would not, I feel sure. My yacht lies at Newhaven; we shall arrive there before morning, and then—a short voyage, a pleasant glimpse of the French countryside, and you will be in Paris, where we shall make it our first business to search the smartest shops for a wardrobe more fitting for your unusual beauty——"

"*I* should think you would make it your first business to find a clergyman who would agree to marry us—*if* there is such a one to be found!" Cecily said, quite unmollified by the alluring picture Sir Harry had drawn of the prospect before her. "I don't believe you ever intended to marry me!"

Sir Harry smiled, but with a somewhat pained expression upon his face. "My dear, pray acquit me——" he began, and possessed himself of one of her slender gloved hands, which she immediately snatched away.

"*Did* you?"

"My dear, really you must not be so blunt," Sir Harry protested, looking amused. "I assure you, it does not become you. Having cast yourself upon my protection, you are hardly in a position to be making peremptory demands, you know."

He spoke lightly, but she saw his eyes through the half-darkness, and the expression in them was not one that gave her comfort. At the same instant the post-boy appeared at the carriage window to inform him that the change had been made and they were ready to start, and Sir Harry at once directed him to drive on. A moment later the chaise was rattling out of the inn-yard, and Cecily was left tête-à-tête with Sir Harry inside.

She turned to him, her eyes flashing indignantly. "I have not said that you may take me any further, Sir Harry!" she said. "I wish you will order the chaise to be stopped at once!"

Brackenridge shrugged. "What? And expose ourselves to the curiosity of every gaping ostler and post-boy in the inn-yard? I think not, my dear. We shall be able to talk far more comfortably here."

"I don't wish to talk to you! And I am *not* going to France with you!"

Mr. Ranleigh's claims on her were by this time quite forgotten; she was seriously alarmed, and if she could have done so without running the risk of breaking a leg, would have jumped from the chaise at that instant. But Brackenridge only laughed at the indignant expression upon her face.

"Oh, come!" he rallied her. "It is not so bad as that, you know. I daresay we shall deal famously together. I am a generous fellow when my heart is touched—which I am sure you will know how to do, my dear—and when you have once lost this foolish fancy for what the world calls respectability, you will see that your position is really not an unenviable one. Marriage would be a very dull ending for such a creature as you——"

"Well, there is one thing you had as well know, and that is that I would rather marry a *toad* than marry *you*," Cecily declared, goaded beyond endurance by his complacent air. "But I never dreamed that was not what you had in mind when you asked me to come away with you—never! —and if you believe now that you can offer me a *carte blanche*——"

"One moment!" Sir Harry's face, which had darkened slightly at her declaration, came closer to hers as he gripped her wrist and bent his head the better to read her countenance. "I think you had best explain yourself, my girl!" he said rather harshly. "You had no idea of marrying me when you came away with me? How is this?"

Cecily, appalled by her indiscretion in having so nearly given away the true reason for her pretended elopement, reconsidered hastily. "Yes—no!" she said disjointedly. "It does not signify! I do not wish to marry you *now*, at any rate!"

"On the contrary, I think it signifies a great deal," Sir Harry said, still scrutinising her averted face, while his grasp tightened even more securely upon her wrist. "What kind of game are you playing with me, my pet? You don't wish to be my wife, you say—or my mistress, either—and yet you have come away with me——"

"I—I have changed my mind!" Cecily said desperately. "Perhaps I *did*—wish to marry you—before——"

Brackenridge gave a short laugh. "And it had to be tonight that we left London—did it not?" he said. "Now I wonder why you found such haste necessary?" He suddenly released her wrist and both his hands came up urgently to grip her shoulders. "Why, you little vixen!" he said, from between clenched teeth. "You thought you would make a laughingstock of me—did you? Lure me out of town so that I shouldn't be able to meet Ranleigh and then run off and leave me standing like a fool——"

"Let me go!" Cecily exclaimed, struggling to free herself from his grasp. "You are—you are *quite* mistaken!"

"Oh, no!" Brackenridge said, with an unpleasant grin. "*You* are the one who is mistaken, my girl, to think you could gull me as easily as that! You have changed your mind, you say. Well, it seems that I have changed mine, too. I shall not take you to France, my sweet. We shall do very well for the night at an inn I know not five miles from here, where they are not fond of asking questions of the Quality, and which is not so far from Paddington Green that I shall not be able to keep my engagement in the morning—— What the *devil*——!"

This last exclamation was caused by the sudden flashing by at break-neck speed outside the window of a curricle-and-four, followed immediately by a confusion of sounds—the swearing of post-boys, the terrified plunging of horses, and the harsh grating of wheels—and by the jolting halt of the vehicle in which they were riding. Cecily and Sir Harry were flung violently back into their seats as the chaise rocked on its protesting springs; before they had had time to recover themselves, the door was wrenched open and Mr. Ranleigh appeared in the aperture.

"I thought no one but you would be so imprudent as to spring hired horses in the dark in this neck-or-nothing fashion, Brackenridge!" he said in a voice of ominous calm. "They told me at the Greyhound that you seemed to be in the devil of a hurry."

"Mr. Ranleigh!" Cecily exclaimed, finding her voice before Brackenridge could recover his, and tumbling out of the chaise into her rescuer's arms without waiting for the steps to be let down. "Oh, how *glad* I am to see you! *Pray* take me back to London with you! You would not *believe* what this horrid man intends——"

"On the contrary, I am quite certain that I *should* believe it," Mr. Ranleigh said, depositing her safely upon the ground, his hands lingering upon her shoulders as he looked her over. She saw in some dismay that, in spite of the coolness of his manner, there was a fine-drawn look on his face and an oddly dangerous light in his eyes that she had never seen there before. "I trust you have suffered no harm, Miss Hadley?" he inquired.

"Oh, no! Only it turns out he never meant in the least to take me to Gretna Green—and he said first that he intended to carry me off to France and then that he would take me to an inn near here——" Cecily explained, incoherently. She added darkly, "Not that I ever intended to marry *him*, for a more odious, *scheming* person——"

"If we are to talk of schemes, my dear," Brackenridge interrupted in a chill voice, as he in turn descended from the chaise, "I believe *you* must carry off the honours. Tell me, was it your own idea to lure me off so that

I should not be able to keep my engagement at Paddington Green in the morning, or were you handsomely paid for playing your little game? You will pardon me, Robert," he went on, turning sardonically to Mr. Ranleigh, "for having the bad taste to imply that it can scarcely have been chance alone that led you here. But has not your arrival come a trifle prematurely? You should have waited until you were quite certain I should not be able to meet you at Paddington before you came so nobly to Miss Hadley's rescue."

He broke off, observing that the two post-boys, having succeeded in quieting the frightened horses, and Mr. Ranleigh's groom, Sivil, standing at the heads of his master's own team, were all three highly interested spectators to the scene going forward in the road. This circumstance, however, appeared to mean nothing to Cecily, for she said at once, indignantly, "Indeed you are quite mistaken! Mr. Ranleigh knew nothing of what I intended to do!" She turned to Mr. Ranleigh, puzzlement in her eyes. "But how *did* you find us here?" she asked.

"Your friend Jillson was good enough to give me a hint of what he suspected was going forward," Mr. Ranleigh said, his eyes never leaving Brackenridge's face. "He seems to have a healthy respect for the influence he believes me capable of exerting against him if any harm were to come to you, to say nothing of an unalterable attachment to what is vulgarly known as hard cash."

"Yes, but I still do not see—— *He* did not know where Sir Harry was taking me."

"No, he did not," Mr. Ranleigh said. "However, after he had left me, I took the precaution of setting Sivil on the watch in Half Moon Street, and when he found Sir Harry hiring a post-chaise-and-four, and learned that the post-boys had been hired as far as Newhaven, he brought me word. Fortunately, I keep my own horses stabled on the Brighton post-road, so I had little doubt I should be able to overtake hired cattle." He added, with such obvious contempt in his voice that Brackenridge stiffened under the words as perceptibly as if he had been struck, "I must say, Harry, that you surprised me. I had not seriously believed that you would run from our engagement or I should have taken more certain precautions against your being able to carry Miss Hadley off."

Sir Harry forced a laugh. "I have not run yet!" he said insultingly. "The jade has her own tale of Gretna Green, but she knew as well as I, when she embarked on this adventure, that what I had in mind was no more than a night's pleasure at an inn very near here——"

He got no further, for Mr. Ranleigh, with a useful right to the jaw, sent him sprawling into the middle of the road, and then proceeded to stand over him with the air of a man having every intention of concluding the business he had begun by the administration of a sound thrashing as soon as Sir Harry should have regained his feet. Cecily jumped and clapped her hands, and the post-boys, setting up a cheer at the prospect of a mill, slid from their horses for a better view of the proceedings.

It was too much for Sir Harry. He had been gulled by a chit of a girl into leaving London on a wild-goose chase that threatened not only to tarnish his reputation but to give him no opportunity of turning the situation into ridicule against his opponent by carrying off the girl who had been the cause of the quarrel between them. He had been knocked down by Mr. Ranleigh in full view of several interested spectators, and it was quite apparent that he would not be allowed to depart now without further punishment being visited upon him. Staring up into his rival's face from his humiliatingly recumbent position on the ground, Sir Harry lost his head completely, and, before anyone had the least idea of what he was about to do, he had struggled to a sitting position, pulled a silver-mounted pistol from his coat, and discharged it pointblank at Mr. Ranleigh.

Fortunately his hasty aim, from such a position, was far from perfect. Cecily, starting violently at the deafening report, closed her eyes for a panic-stricken moment; when she opened them again she saw, with overwhelming relief, that Mr. Ranleigh was still standing on his feet, looking down curiously at his right sleeve.

"Well, I'm damned!" he remarked, softly and reflectively.

Sivil, hastily confiding his team to the care of one of the post-boys, came running up, wrath and concern on his face.

"Mr. Robert, Mr. Robert—are you hurt?" he cried.

"No, no—the ball merely grazed me," Mr. Ranleigh replied. He was looking at Brackenridge, who, his face livid in the pale light of the moon, had picked himself up and was regarding him with an expression of mingled hatred and apprehension in his eyes. "You really are a paltry creature, Harry," Mr. Ranleigh said to him, in a gently contemptuous voice. "Odd—I never knew quite how paltry until this very moment."

The post-boy standing at his horses' heads gave it as his opinion that coves as shot off pistols at other coves ought to be taken up by the constable, and announced his entire willingness to ride back to Croydon for the purpose of procuring the services of one of those useful individuals at once. Mr. Ranleigh, however, did not encourage him in this undertaking. He had drawn a handkerchief from his pocket and, handing it to Sivil, requested him to tie it about his arm.

"Oh, you *are* hurt!" Cecily cried. She turned to Brackenridge, her face kindling. "You are no better than a murderer, to shoot an unarmed man!" she accused him. "The post-boy is quite right! You *should* be brought before a magistrate at once, and all of us here will give evidence against you——"

"I think," Mr. Ranleigh interrupted, addressing Brackenridge in the same cool, dispassionate voice, "yes, I *really* think you had best carry out your plan to go to France, Harry. As you see, you may find England rather uncomfortable for some time to come, for I fear you cannot completely rely on the discretion of all the persons who have witnessed this little affair." Sir Harry attempted to speak, but Mr. Ranleigh, his voice hardening slightly, cut him off. "I am in earnest; you had best go," he said shortly. "You flatter me if you believe that *my* temper may not lead me to commit actions quite as imprudent as yours if you remain in my sight for another thirty seconds. If you can prevail on these fellows to take you up again and to bear still tongues in their heads about what has happened here, you will have done as much as you are able for yourself, I believe."

Cecily, watching him in some awe, saw that, behind the calm with which he had accepted Brackenridge's foolhardy action, the dangerous look that had been upon his face when he had first halted the chaise was rising again. Brackenridge, too, appeared to sense the fact that he had best leave the scene while it was still possible for him to do so with a comparatively whole skin, and, with an oath, turned and mounted into the chaise. At this point the scene achieved an absurd anticlimax when Cecily, suddenly realising that her portmanteau was still in that vehicle, halted his departure by demanding its retrieval. When this had been accomplished, and Sir Harry had convinced the still reluctant post-boys, by dint of flinging a couple of guineas at them, that they should mount their horses once more, the door of the chaise was closed upon him and the horses were finally set in motion.

Meanwhile, Sivil, who had taken the curricle in charge once more, had drawn it to the side of the road and stood waiting at the leaders' heads. Cecily was left standing alone with Mr. Ranleigh. She turned to him remorsefully.

"I am afraid it was quite all my fault," she said, "but indeed I meant it only for the best! I did not want Sir Harry to shoot you—and now he has done it anyway, and without giving you the least chance to defend yourself! Had you not best go to some inn at once, where you can have your wound dressed?"

Mr. Ranleigh, however, assured her that this was not necessary. It seemed to her that there was an unusual constraint in his manner toward her; she felt that her apology had been rebuffed, and was beginning in some mortification to move toward the curricle when he halted her by saying abruptly, "One moment, Miss Hadley. There is something I wish you will oblige me by telling me. You said, I believe, that you had no intention of marrying Brackenridge when you set off with him this evening. What then was your reason for going with him?"

His eyes were searching her face so keenly that she did not know how to answer him. She began to speak, faltered, and was dismayed to see his face harden suddenly as he said rather roughly, "I see. You need not answer me, of course, if it embarrasses you to do so. I should not have believed, though, that even a girl as inexperienced as you are would have been so foolish as to stake her reputation on the promises of a man like Brackenridge——"

"Oh!" Cecily said, finding her tongue and her indignation at the same moment. "As if I should ever, for a single moment, have thought of marrying him! Or of—of going off with him without marrying him! If it had not been for that horrid duel, I should never have agreed even to *see* him again!"

Mr. Ranleigh had turned away, but his eyes, as she spoke, again went quickly to her face. What he saw there appeared suddenly to lift the cloud that had darkened his own countenance, but he said to her in the same hard tone, as if he did not trust himself to abandon it as yet, "You would have me believe, then, that it was as Harry said, and your only intention was to lure him out of town in concern for my safety? Or am I perhaps flattering myself, and it was for *his* safety that you feared?"

Her eyes flashed at him through the darkness. "If you dare to say such a thing to me again, I shall hit you!" she declared. "He is the most odious, abominable——"

"And yet you have accepted expensive gifts from him, it appears."

She gasped. "*What!* Oh—the diamond ear-drops! I do not know how you came to know about *that*, but he forced them upon me at Inglesant—he said that if I did not take them, he would let them fall to the ground for anyone to discover, and that then there must be explanations——" She paused, looking at him ominously. "I *am* going to hit you!" she announced. "You don't believe me!"

A smile suddenly lit his eyes. "Oh yes, I believe you!" he said ruefully. "If it were not true, I am sure you would have concocted a far more plausible tale to tell me—something of the sort that you devised to lead Harry off on this wild-goose chase tonight! Give me leave to tell you, Miss Hadley, that you are an unprincipled, meddlesome brat, and if you had come by your deserts you would even now be reaping the consequences of your harebrained interference in a matter that was no concern of yours. And, to crown it all, I daresay you consider I should be grateful to you, after you have put me through as anxious a pair of hours tonight as any I have yet been obliged to experience!"

"I do not consider that at all," she said stiffly, trying to hold back the rush of tears that his words had unaccountably called up. "I—I am aware that I have been very troublesome to you, but I *could* not wish you to be killed— And now I am tired to death," she ended, on a note of desperation, "and I do not at all care to talk any more about it tonight! *Pray* let us go back to London!"

She saw that he was looking down at her with an expression upon his face which she had never seen there before, and which for some reason made her heart jump in her breast in such a very odd manner that she felt for the moment quite unable to breathe. But, to her immense relief, he only said after a moment, in a much more cheerful voice, "Very well. It will not do for us to remain standing here in the road, at any rate." He added, as he escorted her to the curricle, "I am taking you to Mount Street, by the way. Your aunt arrived there this evening with my mother, shortly before I set out; they will both be anxious to see you."

This information was not calculated to soothe her already much tried nerves, but she felt there was nothing she could say that would have the least effect upon his decision, and therefore allowed herself to be handed up into the curricle in silence. He mounted up beside her and took the reins, his injury apparently being slight enough not to prevent him from driving, and Sivil, letting go the leaders' heads, expertly swung himself up behind as the curricle started forward.

Fortunately, in Sivil's presence Mr. Ranleigh did not seem disposed to enter into any further conversation on the events of the evening, and when they arrived in Croydon shortly afterward his regard for the impropriety of her driving alone in a gentleman's company in an open carriage at that time of night led him to halt at the Greyhound and hire a postchaise there to carry her the remainder of the way to London. Shut up in this vehicle in solitary state, with Mr. Ranleigh driving his curricle behind her, she then had ample opportunity to consider the dismal state of her affairs, with her employment gone, her reputation in shreds, and her aunt and Lady Frederick doubtlessly awaiting her in Mount Street in highly justifiable indignation.

But, strangely enough, it was none of these matters that occupied her thoughts most disturbingly during the remainder of her journey. Rather, it was that disquieting look in Mr. Ranleigh's eyes as he had stood gazing down at her on the dark road.

What that look portended she could only conjecture, but those conjectures were enough to bring the warm blood to her face and the unnerving suspicion to her mind that, in spite of everything she had done to put herself beyond any gentleman's feeling obliged to consider himself the guardian of her reputation, he might still not have relinquished the plans concerning her future that had sent her fleeing from Hillcourt.

This suspicion was strengthened when, on their arriving in Mount Street, he brushed aside all the importunate questions and expressions of concern for his injury with which he was greeted by Miss Dowie and Lady Frederick, and, tarrying only for the briefest of explanations to them, swept her off into the library and closed the door decisively behind him. Cecily found herself, in a highly flushed and discomposed state, confronting a gentleman with a most disturbing glint in his eyes, who stood with his back resting against the door in a manner which suggested that he had no intention of allowing her egress from it until he had said all that he had to say to her.

She put up her chin in a rather forlorn attempt at defiance.

"This is quite—*quite* unnecessary, sir!" she said. "I have nothing at all to say to you—and I beg you will not feel obliged to say anything to me that we shall both regret. I am sure Sir Harry will never trouble me again——" She paused, looking at him hopefully, but he only remained standing with folded arms, his shoulders propped against the door, courteously waiting for her to finish a speech which she felt herself quite unable to go on with. "Oh!" she said indignantly. "You *know* very well what I mean to say! It is quite *odious* of you to stand there looking at me like that!"

"Oh, no—would you say *odious?*" murmured Mr. Ranleigh provocatively, the glint even more pronounced in his grey eyes. "Perhaps *uncooperative*——"

"Yes, that is exactly what I mean! You *know* that it is unnecessary for you to offer for me now, for Sir Harry can do me no further harm, and I assure you I have no wish to be—to be made respectable——"

Somewhat to her surprise, Mr. Ranleigh immediately agreed to this. "Oh, quite unnecessary!" he said affably. "I should not dream of making you an offer upon *that* account. As a matter of fact," he added reflectively, "I never did."

"You—you didn't?" Cecily faltered, taken aback.

"No, you absurd infant, I did not. It did occur to me, however—before you deprived me of the opportunity of laying the matter before you by running away from Hillcourt—that, since I had fallen in love with you, the only course that appeared likely to offer me the slightest degree of future happiness lay in asking you to marry me. Which," he added scrupulously, "I hereby do."

Cecily's hands flew to her burning cheeks. "Oh, no, you cannot mean it!" she exclaimed. "You cannot wish to marry me after I have behaved so *very* improperly!"

"You are mistaken. It is exactly what I wish," said Mr. Ranleigh, unfolding his arms, pushing his shoulders away from the door, and advancing on her in an alarmingly purposeful manner.

Cecily, attempting to preserve the last remnants of rationality, found it next to impossible with Mr. Ranleigh's arms securely about her and her breast pressed tightly against the front of his impeccably tailored coat. She had the oddest sensation that it was beyond her power to prevent herself from flinging her arms about his neck, and succeeded in overcoming this disastrous impulse only by the strongest exertion of will.

"Oh!" she said, in a stifled voice. "It is not at all k-kind of you to take such an advantage of me, Mr. Ranleigh!"

"Do you not think, my darling," Mr. Ranleigh inquired, bending to drop a kiss lightly upon the tip of her nose and then looking down at her with the unmistakable air of a man proposing to repeat this reprehensible action within the space of a few moments, "that, under the circumstances, you might contrive to call me Robert?"

"Under the circumstances—? You cannot mean that you *do* wish to marry me! Oh, no—it is *quite* impossible. That is the reason I ran away from Hillcourt, you know—because I overheard Lady Frederick say that you felt bound in honour to offer for me, even though it was not at all your inclination. And—and Charlie told me that you did not even *l-like* me——"

"You see now what comes of listening to the conversations of persons who know nothing whatever of the subject they are discussing," he said, adding firmly, as she opened her lips to speak again, "I wish you will stop arguing over the matter, for I have not the slightest desire to hear any more objections. Ever since you succeeded in convincing me that you did not really wish to run off with Harry, I have realised that any representations you have made of being indifferent to me were wholly without foundation, for nothing but a most unalterable attachment could have induced even you to embark upon such an outrageous adventure."

"It was *not* outrageous!" she objected, stung into remonstrance. "It might have succeeded very well if Sir Harry had not been so wickedly underhanded as not to intend to carry me to Gretna Green, after all!"

"Damn Sir Harry!" said Mr. Ranleigh. "Let us forget him." He looked with disfavour at her bonnet. "Must you continue to wear this abominable creation on your head?" he demanded. "I cannot contrive to kiss you properly while you do so."

She gazed up at him, still with great misgiving, but docilely permitted him to untie her bonnet-strings and remove the offending article from her head.

"Yes, but—are you *quite* sure?" she inquired anxiously. "Because you know I *might* wish to marry you only because you are very rich——"

"Exactly as you wished to marry Tony," he agreed.

"But I didn't——!"

"Just so," he said. "Have I not told you, my incorrigible little love, that I wish to hear no more objections from you?"

"Yes, you have," she confessed, breathlessly. "Only, Mr. Ran——"

"Robert," he said ruthlessly, taking her into his arms once more.

"Oh, very well!" she said, flinging caution to the winds and making no further attempt to resist the pressing impulse to throw her arms about his neck. "It seems *very* odd of you to wish to marry me, but if you are quite sure—— *Oh!*" It was some moments before she emerged, very much shaken and a little awed, from an embrace that had threatened to crush all the breath from her body. "Oh, I *really* believe you do!" she said radiantly. "It is very unlikely, but I am so happy! Are you going to kiss me again? I wish you will! Oh, Robert—Robert—Robert—*Robert!*"

GEORGINA

Georgina

By

Clare Darcy

WALKER AND COMPANY, New York

1

A hush of expectancy lay over Lady Mercer's house in Great Pulteney Street on this brightest of March mornings in Bath. The entire household, from Finch, Lady Mercer's sedate, elderly butler, to the youngest housemaid, knew that behind the closed door of the Long Drawing-room Miss Georgina was receiving an offer of marriage from Mr. Burford Smallwoods, only son and heir of Sir Anthony Smallwoods, Bart.; and a number of plausible excuses were made by various members of the staff to enable them to linger within sight of that intriguing door.

In what way the news had gotten about it would have been hard to say. Certainly neither Lady Mercer nor her daughter, Mrs. Power, had been heard to mention the possibility of an alliance between Mr. Smallwoods and Miss Georgina, nor had Miss Georgina herself shown any of the signs of a young lady in love. On the other hand, Mr. Smallwoods was known to have been assiduous in his visits to Great Pulteney Street, and his mama, Lady Smallwoods, while drawing on her pelisse preparatory to leaving the house after a call made on Lady Mercer on Wednesday last, had been overheard to say that Miss Georgina was "a pretty creature."

Finch, who was experienced in such matters, gave it as his opinion that it would be a match, which led Mrs. Nudge, the housekeeper, to remark with great feeling that, if Sir John were still alive, there would be no thought of Miss Georgina's being married off to such a pompous little toad.

Their vigilance, on this afternoon, was soon rewarded. Scarcely a quarter of an hour after Mr. Smallwoods had been shown into the Long Drawing-room, the door was abruptly opened and that young gentleman, wearing an exceedingly crestfallen air, came out, ran downstairs, received his curly-brimmed beaver and gloves from Finch, and left the house without a word. Some five seconds later, Miss Georgina herself, looking very fetching in a chintz morning-dress of palest lilac, but with a rather high flush on her face, emerged and marched down the hall to the morning-room, where Lady Mercer and Mrs. Power were sitting over their tambour-frames.

As she closed the door of this apartment with considerable emphasis behind her, what conversation she held there with her mama and her grandmother was to remain unknown. Speculation had it, however, that there would be a rare turn-up when Lady Mercer discovered that Miss

Georgina had whistled Mr. Smallwoods, his prospective title, and his comfortable fortune down the wind.

Speculation in this case was quite correct. Lady Mercer, on receiving the news from her granddaughter that she had refused Mr. Smallwoods, sat bolt upright, declared that of all defects of character ingratitude was the one she most greatly abhorred, and favoured her granddaughter with a glance of such concentrated disapproval that a weaker young lady must have quailed beneath it.

Georgina, however, whose charmingly coiffed head, with its wheat-gold curls cropped in the current mode and clustering in natural ringlets about her face, concealed a buoyant spirit and an excellent understanding, merely remarked, her colour still rather high, "I do not *quite* see how it would be showing gratitude to *you* for me to accept Mr. Smallwoods' offer, Grandmama. To *him*, perhaps—but then what has he done for me but bring me prosy books out of Meyler's Library and escort us all to the Pump Room or Bath Abbey?"

Lady Mercer was a small woman, of a sallow complexion and a general dun-coloured appearance; but any tendency of a person meeting her for the first time to dismiss her as having a character as unimpressive as her appearance was soon dispelled. She said now, with acid emphasis, "I daresay if Mr. Smallwoods were a gentleman of less delicate principles, and had disregarded the fact that, until a fortnight ago, you were in mourning and had escorted you about to frivolous entertainments, you would be more inclined to favour his suit?"

"Not at all," Georgina said decidedly. "I should not like him one whit better if I had stood up at balls with him every day in the week. Do stop crying, Mama!" she said to Mrs. Power, a faded, rather pretty woman who, as usual, had dissolved into tears at the first threat of trouble between her mother and her daughter. "I am persuaded that, whatever Grandmama thinks, *you* cannot have wished me to accept Mr. Smallwoods' offer. He is exactly what Sir John would have called an odious little bounce!"

"Oh, no, my dear!" Mrs. Power faltered, with a terrified glance at Lady Mercer. "A gentleman of the *first* respectability—such an acceptable fortune—everything about him of the most genteel—"

"Mama, that cannot signify when I tell you that I cannot love him!"

Lady Mercer set her tambour-frame carefully aside. "You will oblige me, Georgina," she said quellingly, "by omitting such vulgar expressions from your conversation in future. A young lady of your breeding should indeed *esteem* the gentleman to whom she is betrothed. Any stronger expression of emotion, however, leaves her open to the suspicion of harbouring an unbecoming violence of feeling which is not at all suited to her condition in life."

Georgina looked somewhat inclined to dispute this dictum, but a glance at her mother's agitated face decided her against it. Mrs. Power, she knew, was particularly sensitive on this point, because she herself, at the age of seventeen, had made a runaway match with Owen Power, the improvident younger son of an Irish family of considerable consequence. This was a fact that her mother had never allowed her in the ten years of her impecunious widowhood, to forget. Indeed, Lady Mercer had declared her intention of leaving her own fortune, a very comfortable one, directly to Georgina, as she still, at this late date, found herself quite unable to condone the shocking want of good conduct that her daughter had shown at that crucial period in her life.

It seemed, however, that Georgina, at a similar period in her life, intended to be almost equally disobliging in the matter of fulfilling Lady Mercer's expectations, for she said now, with an obstinate air, "At any rate, I do not at all wish to marry Mr. Smallwoods. And I do not see why I must, for I am only eighteen—not *quite* old-cattish yet, you will admit, Grandmama!"

"Yes, indeed," Mrs. Power said, finding the courage to come, albeit with some timidity, to her daughter's aid. "Recollect, Mama, that she has not had even one Season in London! Perhaps when she has had the opportunity to meet more young gentlemen than she yet has—so retired as we have been living here in Bath since Papa died—and before that, in Herefordshire, she was only a child—"

Lady Mercer cut short this rather disjointed appeal by a single glance cast in her daughter's direction.

"I wonder," she pronounced, "that you should be so ill-advised as to bring up the subject of London, Maria! You must be aware that Lady Smallwoods has been so kind as to offer to allow Georgina to visit her when she and Sir Anthony open their house in Hill Street in May, and to take her about and even present her at Court. Nothing could have been more amiable, or better suited to our own situation, for Dr. Porton does not in the least agree to my exposing myself to the excitements of a London Season. But if the match with Mr. Smallwoods is to go off, of course there the matter must end."

"I do not care about that in the least," Georgina said, unregenerately.

"Sir John always said I should find it a dead bore, going about to balls and fashionable squeezes every night, and being obliged to do the civil to a parcel of people I scarcely knew."

"Sir John," Lady Mercer began, with marked asperity, and then, recollecting that her spouse was dead and that it was therefore scarcely proper for her to cast any of the bitter animadversions on his conduct that had enlivened their married life, checked herself. "Your grandfather's influence on your opinions, my dear Georgina," she said, with austere moderation, "can scarcely be thought to have been a happy one. I blame myself for having allowed your education to have fallen so entirely in his hands."

"Well, you could not help it, of course," Georgina said reasonably, "for once Sir John had made up his mind to something, there was very little even *you* could do to alter it, you know." She gave a tiny sigh. "I miss him very much," she said. "I am sure he would not have liked Mr. Smallwoods any better than I do."

Lady Mercer, though she had shown the strictest nicety in mourning her husband over an entire year, did not appear to share these sentiments. She merely observed her granddaughter with a darkly thoughtful air, and after a few moments said abruptly, "You had best be sent to Ireland, I expect."

"To Ireland?" Georgina looked inquiring, and her mother repeated faintly, "To Ireland, Mama! But how?—where—?"

"To visit your husband's cousin, Arabella Quinlevan," Lady Mercer said, referring to the widowed lady who had been invited by Declan Power, Owen Power's elder brother, following the death of his wife some dozen years before, to make her home, with her son Brandon, on his estate in Kerry so that she might preside over his household and take charge of the rearing of his daughter Nuala. "I had, of course, intended to reply to her letter of invitation, which arrived this morning, with a civil refusal, but under the circumstances it appears to me that it had best be accepted. That, at least, will remove Georgina from the gossip that is certain to arise when it becomes known that she is not to marry Mr. Smallwoods, and relieve Lady Smallwoods of the embarrassment of withdrawing her own very generous invitation to take her to London."

"But—Ireland! The Quinlevans!" Georgina's surprise had begun to merge into interest and pleasurable excitement. "Do you really mean it, Grandmama? Cousin Bella has asked me? But we have scarcely heard from her since she and Brandon visited us in Herefordshire four years ago!"

"On the contrary," Lady Mercer said exactly, "we received, if you will remember, a very proper letter from her on the occasion of the death of your uncle, Declan Power, two years ago, and a second on the equally unexpected demise of his daughter Nuala in Brussels in the following year. I am not, on the whole, an admirer of your cousin Arabella's style, my dear Georgina, but I am obliged to admit that in such matters she is most punctilious. I could wish, however, that in other respects she were less shatterbrained. How, for example, she could have been so careless as to allow vour cousin Nuala to have contracted such a dreadful marriage, I have *never* understood."

"But *she* had nothing to say to that, Grandmama," Georgina reminded her. "Do you not remember that she wrote us that Nuala was visiting in Scotland with friends when she ran off with Mr. Shannon?"

"I should not, I think," Lady Mercer said dampingly, "be likely to forget any of the circumstances of that most regrettable affair—nor do I believe, Georgina, that it is a matter on which a delicately bred young female should allow herself to converse."

"Well, there is no use in my pretending that I know nothing about it," Georgina said candidly, "for Sir John and I discussed the whole matter at the time, and he told me everything—I mean, that Mr. Shannon was a—"

"Georgie!" her mother exclaimed faintly.

"A natural son of the present Lord Cartan's father," Georgina said mildly. "Am I not to admit I know of such things, Mama? Sir John said it was missish for young ladies to pretend they do not."

"If you had the least sense of delicacy, Georgina," Lady Mercer said, with awful emphasis, "it would not be necessary for me to warn you that such sentiments are most improper ones to come from a young lady's lips. It is this sort of behaviour on your part that gives me the gravest misgivings about placing you in Arabella Quinlevan's care, for she has shown herself quite incapable, in your cousin's case, of curbing such reprehensible tendencies. Indeed, I have often reflected on how unfortunate it was that Mrs. Declan Power's early demise obliged your uncle to entrust Nuala's rearing to her. However, I believe she is well served for her carelessness now. She writes me that, as Nuala's fortune has gone entirely to Mr. Shannon, she and her son are now under the necessity of removing from The Place of the Oaks and retiring to her own property at Craythorne—a sad come-down, but one for which I am obliged to confess she has no one to thank but herself."

Georgina considered this. "Well, for my part, I should not think it was at all her fault that Nuala fell in love with Mr. Shannon," she said. "I expect she would much rather that she had not, for it must be dreadfully disagreeable to her now to have to give up living in a great house that she has been used, for years, to thinking of as her home and see it go to a horrid fortune-hunter. Not," she added thoughtfully, "that he is probably *entirely* horrid, or my cousin Nuala would not have fallen so desperately in love with him. In fact, I daresay he may be quite attractive!"

"Georgie!" Mrs. Power again protested, in a failing voice. "*Not* a man of *such* a character!"

Lady Mercer looked grim. "If," she said, "I believed there was the slightest possibility that you would be brought into Mr. Shannon's company in Kerry, Georgina, I should not dream of allowing you to accept Mrs. Quinlevan's invitation. I understand from her letter, however, that he is still travelling abroad and has not yet set foot in Ireland to take up his inheritance. There will therefore be no occasion whatever for you to meet him."

She signified at this point that the interview was at an end by rising, shaking out her skirts, and departing from the room—a circumstance that brought the apprehensive look back into her daughter's eyes.

"Oh, dear!" she said. "She is so very much displeased with you, I daresay, that she cannot trust herself to remain any longer in the room with you!" She looked timidly at her daughter. "You do not think, my dearest love—that is, you would not perhaps care to reconsider—?"

"Marry Mr. Smallwoods? Mama, I could not—even for *your* sake," Georgina said, shaking her curls. "I *know* how agreeable it would be for you if I had an establishment of my own, so that you could live with me, instead of being *immured* here with Grandmama, but indeed I cannot accept Mr. Smallwoods' offer!"

"No, my dear. If you have taken him in dislike, no more must be said of it, of course," Mrs. Power agreed, wistfully. "And perhaps you will meet a young man in Ireland— It would be very pleasant to live in Ireland, I think."

"Miles and *miles* from Grandmama," Georgina said irrepressibly, bringing a faint, but not entirely convincing, sound of reproach from her mother. She jumped up and dropped a kiss on Mrs. Power's head. "Never mind, Mama," she said. "If I am to be sent to Ireland in disgrace, I shall certainly make the most of my opportunities. Perhaps my cousin Brandon will have the house full of young men, and some of them *must* be well-breeched enough to suit even Grandmama's notions!"

"But—he is lame, and very bookish, you recollect, my love," Mrs. Power said, looking up at her doubtfully.

"Oh yes, I know! But still *not* a dead bore—like Mr. Smallwoods!"

She left her mama on this cheerful note, running upstairs to her own bedchamber to begin an inventory of her wardrobe against her departure. Her untroubled demeanour led Mrs. Nudge to spread the opinion below-stairs that it would require more than a rakedown from the old lady to take the curl out of Miss Georgina; but Finch, when he learned of the projected visit to Ireland, made his own gloomy pronouncement to the effect that Miss Georgina, made a Victim of the Gorgon's spite by being sent off into Exile, was merely putting on a brave front to hide a Bruised Heart.

This, however, the youngest housemaid found hard to believe. She was not at all certain what a Gorgon was, but it appeared to her that any young lady who was to have the felicity of escaping, even for a time, from Lady Mercer's iron rule could certainly not be called a Victim. Indeed, she rather thought that, as usual, Miss Georgina had come off the Victor in this encounter.

2

On an April morning some few weeks after these events had occurred, Mrs. Quinlevan was in the estate-room at The Place of the Oaks, going through a jumble of accounts, and having recourse frequently to her vinaigrette to soothe the agitation into which this task always cast her, when her brother, Mr. Jeremy Barnwall, was announced.

"Show him into the book-room, Higgins," she directed the butler, who, as did most of the other servants at The Place since the death of her cousin, Declan Power, seemed to be new, or incompetent, or both. "I'm sure it's the only room in the house that's not in a huggermugger with the moving."

Higgins departed, and she sat gazing disconsolately for a moment at the undulating lawn outside the windows, at the end of which a row of the ancient oaks that gave the estate its name showed the beginning of the Home Wood. Then she sighed and took her round, soft, foolish face, with its French lace cap tied under the chin, and her stout, bustling figure in its dove-coloured morning-dress into the book-room, where she found Jeremy Barnwall's even more ample figure already disposed in the room's most comfortable chair.

"What the deuce are you about, Bella?" he demanded, as soon as she had set foot inside the door. "Never saw such a devilish uproar in my life as you have here! I expected you'd have removed to Craythorne by this time. Drove over there—nobody about—servants raising such a deuced dust it was as much as your life was worth to walk into the place."

Mrs. Quinlevan sank into a chair, requesting Higgins to see if the Madeira had been crated up yet, and, if not, to fetch a bottle for Mr. Barnwall.

"Though I am not sure," she said, "that it will be fit to drink, for you know Papa always warned us that good wine will not bear rough handling, and what they have been doing with it I have *no* way of knowing."

Mr. Barnwall reflected for a moment on this speech. He was a largish gentleman, with a glistening bald head encircled by a crown of stiff black hair. The son of a highly improvident Irish gentleman, cast on the world with neither fortune nor profession, he had early discovered that an excellent baritone voice and a lucky ability at piquet and faro could procure him a very satisfactory existence in London society with the expenditure of scarcely any of the revenues from his modest estate in Kerry. This estate lay within five miles of The Place of the Oaks, and he usually made it a point to drive over and call on his widowed sister on his occasional visits to Ireland.

"The Madeira, eh?" he remarked now, with a slight frown. "Well, I tell you what, Bella, it seems to me you're taking something on yourself there. Doesn't belong to *you*, you know. Declan left everything to Nuala. Shannon would have the right to it now."

Mrs. Quinlevan shook her head, the ribbons on her cap quivering with her exasperation. "Shannon, again!" she said. "I am sure I have learned to detest that name! How it can be lawful—or Christian—or anything at all proper, for him to have *everything*, merely because that foolish girl was weak enough to let him carry her off and marry her—"

"Know how you feel, m'dear," Mr. Barnwall said. "Devilish rum business, having to see it all go out of the family. But the fellow has his rights, you see. Married the girl. Not his fault she died within the year. Might have lived together for forty years, had a dozen children—wouldn't have seemed so queer to you then."

"I daresay it wouldn't, for I shouldn't have been alive to see it," Mrs. Quinlevan said, still with great asperity. "But it puts me out of all patience when I think of a wretch like that coming in and turning us out without a by-your-leave. And now he will be here tomorrow, he writes—tomorrow! It is the most fortunate thing in the world that you have turned up, Jeremy, for I am at my wits' end over what to do! There is Georgina Power arriving this afternoon, and the Huddlestons not being able to remove from Craythorne until two days ago, so that Brandon and I have been obliged to remain here—oh, I am in such a whirl, I have not the least notion where to turn! And then there is that dreadful bailiff, who seems to have made the *worst* possible muddle of the accounts—"

Mr. Barnwall, his jaw dropping slightly at this catalogue of misfortunes, raised his hand at this juncture and said, "Hold up a minute! What's all this? Owen's daughter? Deuce take it, Bella, you don't mean to tell me you invited her here in the midst of *this* rowdy-do!"

Mrs. Quinlevan found her handkerchief, applied it to her eyes, and said defiantly, "Yes, I did!"

"But why, in the name of heaven?"

"Because she is to marry Brandon!"

The arrival of Higgins with the Madeira silenced the startled response that this statement seemed about to elicit from Mr. Barnwall. By the time the butler had departed, however, he had recovered his equanimity sufficiently to be able to say, with some satisfaction, "Well, if that is so, you are a lucky woman, Bella! Never thought you'd be able to make a catch like that for the boy—damme, I mean to say, that affliction of his and all! Not but what he ain't well-looking enough, but I'd never have said you could have settled him so easy, with a tight little fortune like this chit of Owen's will have if her grandmother comes up to scratch."

Mrs. Quinlevan, who had several times endeavoured to interrupt this speech, broke in at this point to desire her brother to stop being such a ninnyhammer.

"Of course it is not settled yet," she said. "Why, she has not seen him since he was fifteen years old! But I think it must be very likely that, if the two of them are together every day, something will come of it—"

This time it was Mr. Barnwall's turn to interrupt. "Tell me the truth, Bella," he said severely. "Is this all a scheme of yours, and nothing more?"

"Naturally it is a scheme now, as you put it," Mrs. Quinlevan said, defensively. "But there is no reason in the world why it should not work out. I am sure she and Brandon dealt extremely well together when we were in Herefordshire—"

"They were children then," Mr. Barnwall said ruthlessly.

"Yes, that is true, but what has that to say to anything?"

Mr. Barnwall shook his head. "Best face facts, Bella. The boy's a cripple, or next to it. Dashed ugly way of putting it, but the truth."

"So," Mrs. Quinlevan retorted, "is Lord Byron! But that doesn't stop half the silly women in England from running after *him*. And Brandon may turn out to be a famous poet, or something of the sort, one day, too, for Mr. Peabody has always said he never had a pupil with more aptitude."

"Come down off your high ropes, Bella," Mr. Barnwall said, with brotherly candour. "*I'm* not saying the boy's not a bright 'un. But if you're bringing that girl over here with the expectation that she'll fall in like a lamb with your idea of her marrying him, you must have windmills in your head. Deuce take it, you know as well as I do that he won't have more than a couple of thousand a year, and you needn't think he'll come into anything handsome from *me* when I die, for I don't mind telling you I'm badly dipped." He added, returning to a consideration of problems more pressingly at hand, "Didn't you tell me you're expecting that husband of Nuala's, too?" He glanced around at the disordered room. "He ain't thinking of taking up residence here *now*, I hope?"

Mrs. Quinlevan gave a distracted shake of the head. "Well, to speak the truth, Jeremy," she said, "I haven't the least idea! You know—or perhaps you *don't* know, for I am sure you paid not the slightest attention to the letters I sent you asking for your advice—that I had heard nothing from that wretched man for months, ever since he wrote me to say that he would continue to travel abroad for a time, as he has done since Nuala's death, and that I could remove from The Place quite at my leisure. And I am sure I had every intention of leaving before now, only, as bad luck would have it, the Huddlestons were unable to vacate Craythorne at Lady Day—" She saw her brother shaking his head disapprovingly, and said with renewed asperity, "Naturally I would have done if I had had the slightest idea this odious Mr. Shannon was to turn up just now. But how could I know that, when I hadn't had a word from him for months, and was almost thinking that he might have caught the fever too, like poor Nuala?" She looked hopefully at Mr. Barnwall. "I suppose it is too much to expect that he is of a sickly constitution, and won't last long?" she inquired.

Mr. Barnwall fetched his snuffbox from his pocket, took a delicate pinch from it, and advised his sister not to place her hopes in that basket.

"From what I hear, he's the image of Cartan—the old earl, of course, not the present one," he said. "Regular out-and-outer old Cartan was in his grasstime, you know—a prime goer after hounds, a top-sawyer with a four-in-hand, devil of a fellow with his fives. *And* lived to be seventy-nine."

"Well, there is no hope in that, certainly," Mrs. Quinlevan said despondently. "I daresay the tiresome creature will be here tomorrow, just as he wrote he would—and what I am to do I have not the least idea, for I cannot possibly go to Craythorne for at least a week."

"Tell him to rack up at the Cock and Stars," Mr. Barnwall suggested. "He may not like it, but you can't have him here. As a matter of fact," he added, "if I was you, I wouldn't have anything to do with the fellow. Give him the keys when you're ready to leave and let him have the place. It's what he was after, and now he's got it, but I'm damned if I'd help him to set himself up in the neighbourhood."

"Indeed I shall not," Mrs. Quinlevan assured him. "I expect he will be excessively uncomfortable here, for nobody intends to take the least notice of him, not even the Malladons, though they have been putting it about that he is not so far beneath one's touch, after all. But that is only because it is *their* doing that Nuala was able to slip off and marry him. I have always believed that Lady Eliza was a widgeon, but, if it had ever remotely crossed my mind that she would be so henwitted as not to see that that man was making up to Nuala, I should *never* have allowed Nuala to travel with her and Colonel Malladon to Scotland!"

Mr. Barnwall said, a trifle uncomfortably, "Well, the way I hear the story, Bella, it didn't exactly happen like that, you know. I mean, about his making up to *her*. Matter of fact, I've had a strong hint or two thrown out to me that it was just the other way round."

"Do you mean to say that Nuala was on the catch for *him?* That I will never believe, Jeremy—never!"

"You can believe what you like, but that don't change matters," Mr. Barnwall said obstinately. "Good Lord, Bella, you knew Nuala as well as I did—better! She never in her life saw something she wanted that she didn't set straight out to get it."

"And you wish to tell me that she wanted this—this Shannon?" Mrs. Quinlevan said, in high dudgeon. "You must be all about in your head, Jeremy!"

Mr. Barnwall pursed his lips. "Fine figure of a man, I understand," he suggested tentatively, after a moment.

"And thirty years old, at least! She would have thought him quite antiquated, I am sure." She added hopefully, as a new thought struck her, "Perhaps he is a very persuadable man? I mean someone that one might easily manage—?"

"No, no!" Mr. Barnwall said. "He's a surly brute, by all accounts— never in his life got on with anyone but Cartan. Not too surprising, for there's wild blood there. The mother, it seems, was some Irish tinker's wench Cartan picked up in Tothill Fields, on one of his roaring nights. She had the brass to take the brat to him when he was eight or nine and set him before him—bid him tell her whether he wasn't his own spit and image. Kind of joke Cartan would have enjoyed. He gave the woman a few guineas, enough to drink herself to death on, I should think, and had the lad scrubbed up and sent to school—"

"I wish you will stop raking up such dreadful stories, Jeremy," Mrs. Quinlevan said fretfully. "After all, Nuala *did* marry him, and though I intend to have no connexion with him it can do our credit no good to have it known that the matter is really as bad as you have been saying. What a pity that Sir John Mercer's estate was entailed on a male heir, for he had the most delightful property in Herefordshire, and I am persuaded that when Brandon and Georgina are married it would be far better for them to set up somewhere quite removed from this odious scandal—"

"Moonshine, Bella!" Mr. Barnwall interrupted her. "You had much better put the whole thing out of your head. By the way, where is Brandon?"

"I sent him this morning to Craythorne, to stir them up there—for there is no depending on the servants in that house since Mrs. Heaton left, you know, and yet she *would* go with the Huddlestons, though I told her I should be very glad to pay her the same wages."

Mr. Barnwall listened for a while longer to her strictures on the servants one was obliged to put up with these days, and presently announced his intention of taking his leave. He was an indolent man, and the prospect of becoming involved in the set of crises his sister was facing now was most disagreeable to him. He accordingly declined an invitation to stay to dinner, pleading pressing business at his own house, and went off, leaving Mrs. Quinlevan in full possession of the problems deriving from the arrival of her two prospective visitors.

The first of these visitors arrived at The Place of the Oaks at dusk. Mrs. Quinlevan had sent Nora Quill, Brandon's old nurse and her own trusted right arm in all affairs of domestic management, to meet Georgina in Kenmare, where the friends with whom she had travelled to Ireland were to part company with her; and the two had made the remainder of the journey to The Place in Mrs. Quinlevan's own travelling chaise. Although Georgina was surprised to learn that she was being taken to The Place instead of to Craythorne—for Mrs. Quinlevan had prudently decided not to jeopardize the plans for her visit by communicating to Lady Mercer the unsettled state of her domestic affairs—she was not in the least disconcerted by the discovery. In fact, when the chaise drove up the carriage sweep before the rambling stone Tudor mansion, she was even able to feel a certain satisfaction in the idea that it was the home of her ancestors that was to receive her, instead of Mrs. Quinlevan's own smaller house at Craythorne.

The front door opened as the steps of the chaise were let down, and Georgina saw a slender youth about a year older than herself, with wheat-gold hair of the same colour as her own, come out to greet her, walking as quickly as an obvious limp would permit.

"Hallo!" he called. "I've been on the watch for you. I must say you made poor time—but then that's to be expected, with these lazy nags my mother keeps."

Georgina gave him her hand with great pleasure.

"Brandon! How you've grown!" she said, looking up at him. "You're a head taller than I am, I am sure—and do you remember, in Herefordshire *I* was the taller by at least an inch!"

"And *you've* turned into a young lady," Brandon retorted, eyeing her fashionable almond-green redingote and shallow-crowned bonnet of the same colour. "Who would have imagined it? For a greater madcap I never saw in those days."

He shepherded her into the great hall, where his mother was waiting to receive their guest.

"My dear love," Mrs. Quinlevan said to Georgina, as she embraced her warmly, "I don't know *what* you will think of us! The house in such a state! Everything at sixes and sevens! But it is all that horrid Shannon's fault, for if he had not taken it into his head to come down on us so suddenly it would not have signified about the Huddlestons' being unable to remove— But I am sure you are tired. Will you go upstairs at once, or shall I send for tea? We keep country hours here, you know, so we usually dine by six, but I have had dinner put back today, knowing you would be late."

Georgina broke in to say that she was not tired at all, but would enjoy a cup of tea. She was thereupon led into the book-room, and, her redingote and bonnet having been borne off by Higgins, while Grady, the coachman, and a stout footman carried her portmanteaux and bandboxes upstairs, she settled down to a cosy chat with Brandon and Mrs. Quinlevan. This was soon interrupted, however, by the appearance of Nora Quill, who came in bearing a tea-tray and giving it as her opinion that no dinner worth the eating would be forthcoming from *that* kitchen unless she returned at once to take charge of it herself.

When Mrs. Quinlevan inquired doubtfully what the matter was, Nora said ominously that the cook, who had not been consulted in the packing up of the kitchen utensils, was unable or unwilling to prepare a meal in the makeshift collection of vessels that had been left to her, and was dropping strong hints of giving her notice on the spot.

Mrs. Quinlevan's response to this news was to demand her vinaigrette immediately. "I do not believe, my love," she said to Georgina, "that I can endure one more such shock today, in the unsettled state of my nerves! You can have no idea what this day has been!"

Georgina could not help but reflect that her own arrival seemed to be lumped in with the other disasters that had overtaken her cousin during the past twenty-four hours. But she was fast coming to the conclusion that Cousin Bella on her home grounds was going to turn out to be an even greater pea-goose than she had seemed four years before in Herefordshire, so she did not allow the reflection to depress her.

When the tea had been drunk, she was shown upstairs to the bedchamber she was to occupy while the family remained at The Place. As did every other room she had seen in the house, it bore signs of having been rifled of all but its heavier furnishings, but there was an ancient-appearing, carved-oak, four-poster bed, a chair that looked as if it, too, had survived from Elizabethan days, and a more modern three-drawer dressing table with a mirror, which she was told had been purchased especially for her cousin Nuala.

Nuala's name again appeared in the conversation when Georgina came downstairs to dinner, having changed her travelling dress to one of French muslin. As she entered the dining-room, the first thing that caught her eye was a magnificent full-length portrait of a young woman on the wall opposite the head of the table. From the recent cut of the high-waisted, sea-green gown, she realised at once that the girl in the portrait must be Nuala, and she scrutinised it with a great deal of interest.

"My cousin Nuala, of course?" she said to Mrs. Quinlevan, as she sat down at the table. "She was *very* beautiful, wasn't she?"

"The belle of the county," Mrs. Quinlevan said with pride. "The young men called her 'The Dark Lily,' for she had black hair, you know, and such a lovely complexion, and great dark-blue eyes with the longest black lashes! Indeed, if she had had a Season in London, there is no telling how high she might not have looked to bestow her hand."

"Well, then," Brandon said, "it is a pity you didn't see she had one, Mama, for I am sure she teased you enough to let her visit the Martin-Burnses in Brook Street two years ago, when she might have made her come-out in style."

"Oh, but she was a mere child then!" Mrs. Quinlevan protested. "And you know how fortunate it was that I did not listen to her, for she would have been out of the country then when her poor father died. I believe, in fact, that I must have had a premonition that that very thing might occur."

"You had a premonition that she'd meet some Bond Street beau who'd offer for her and knock all your hopes that she'd marry *me* into a cocked hat, m'dear," Brandon said, with cheerful frankness. "As if she and I didn't always get on like cats and dogs! She wouldn't have had me if I'd been plated with diamonds—nor I her, for that matter. Curst bad temper, for one thing, that girl had."

Mrs. Quinlevan, ruffling up, said it was no such thing, and he was a wicked boy to speak so. But her indignation faded to distress at the sight of the decidedly unappetising-looking plate of Hessian soup that was being placed before her. It appeared that Nora Quill had been correct in her assessment of the state of the kitchen, and that even her best efforts had been insufficient to inspire the cook to set on the table anything better than what Mrs. Quinlevan despairingly characterised as "a nasty mess."

"I am sure I don't know *what* Lady Mercer and your dear mama would say to my sitting you down to such a dinner!" she said tearfully to Georgina. "I assure you, I should be quite *sunk* in their esteem, and it is no wonder—but how I am to contrive to make anything go right in such a house I do not know! I vow I have never been so plagued in my life as I am with that dreadful man—for we should be quite comfortable if it was not for this moving, and that, as you can see, is all his fault!"

Georgina scarcely thought it could properly be laid at Mr. Shannon's door that Mrs. Quinlevan had engaged what seemed to be a houseful of very unaccommodating servants, or that he could even be considered unreasonable in wishing to take possession of property that had legally been his for the past twelve months, but not wishing to offend her cousin, she kept these thoughts to herself.

It did occur to her, however, that she had placed herself in an oddly uncomfortable situation in coming to Ireland, and if she had not been blessed with an optimistic nature, which required more than a shatterbrained hostess, a muddled household, and a bad dinner to cast her down, she might have been somewhat unhappy at the prospect before her by the time she retired to her bed that night.

3 The next morning, however, she found a fine April day awaiting her, and when she had jumped out of bed and flung open a window she was so pleased with what lay before her that her doubts of the evening before quite vanished. She saw a sky flecked with white clouds over a quiet, lovely park, with hills covered with new boggy grass rising in the distance, and determined to dress quickly and persuade Brandon to take her on a tour of the estate, which, she told herself, she would certainly have no opportunity to see again, once the encroaching Mr. Shannon had settled himself there.

To her satisfaction, she found when she came downstairs that this idea had already occurred to Brandon, and that he was at that very moment in the breakfast-parlour, instructing Nora to see if she could have something more than cheese and ham put together in the kitchen for the luncheon that they would take with them.

"I didn't expect you'd care to stay here and run the chance of meeting Shannon," he explained to Georgina, "though perhaps you're not like other girls, and wouldn't make a kick-up if you were obliged to say half a dozen words to a ramshackle fellow who ain't to be received in respectable society. I must say I'm a bit curious about him myself."

"So am I," confessed Georgina, "but I daresay I shouldn't own it. I expect, though, it *will* be better if we are out of the way when he comes."

"That is what Mama says," Brandon agreed regretfully. "By the way, you are to excuse her this morning; she has Mulqueen, the bailiff, with her in the estate-room, and they are having a tremendous row over the accounts. I expect he has muddled them again, as he always does. And Mama is *not* the one to set him straight."

"No," Georgina said cautiously, as she removed the cover from a dish of decidedly burnt bacon on the side-table and resigned herself to breakfasting on hot chocolate and cold toast, "I can see that she might *not* have a turn for management. Good gracious, Brandon, I hope you will not take it amiss if I say I should think she would be glad to be rid of the responsibility of this place, even if it must go to someone like that wretched Shannon."

"Well, I expect she is, really," Brandon said, "only she has always been fond of the consequence it gives her to be Mrs. Quinlevan of The Place of the Oaks, you know. She had some queer idea for years that Nuala and I would marry one day, and then she'd never have to leave it. I ought to warn you," he added, with an engaging grin, "that she has you set down for her next victim. If she begins on the advantages of *your* marrying me, I wish you will tell her that I personally gave you to understand that I haven't the least notion of marrying anyone."

Georgina laughed. "Well, that is a great relief!" she said. "Not," she added affably, as she sat down at the table, "that I don't believe we should rub on very well, for you are exactly as I remember you, and we dealt wonderfully together in Herefordshire, I recollect. But I have no notion of marrying only to be comfortable."

"And I have no notion of marrying at all," Brandon said cheerfully. "Or not for years and years, at any rate. Why, Dr. Culreavy is of the opinion that, if I continue as I am, I may go up to Oxford later in the year—and I had a good deal rather do that than marry anyone, you know. Though if I *did* have it in mind to marry, I should not at all care if you were the one," he admitted handsomely. "I expect you know you've turned into a devilish pretty girl? And then you're a prime goer on a horse, besides having no nonsense at all about you—"

"Yes, but you had much better not tell that to your mama," she objected. "Say you think well enough of me, but that—that I'm too tall for your taste, perhaps—and a bit obstinate—and fond of my own way—"

"Oh, she wouldn't care a button for that!" Brandon declared. "If I wanted to put her off, I'd be obliged to say Lady Mercer has taken such a dislike to you that she has decided to cut you out of her will."

"Well, you can't tell her that," Georgina said, "for it would be sure to get back to Grandmama and she would not like it at all. Besides, I can't think that Cousin Bella is as mercenary as *that!*"

"Well, our pockets *are* pretty well to let, you know," Brandon said apologetically. "It doesn't bother *me*, for I think it will be much jollier living at Craythorne than in this great, rambling house, but Mama is different. And this is her way of being practical, I expect, inviting you here and then hoping the two of us will make a match of it."

It was somewhat lowering to Georgina's self-esteem to reflect that the welcome that had been extended to her at The Place rested on nothing more personal than the expectation that she would one day inherit a snug fortune, but on the whole she was glad to have had this explanation with Brandon. She had sensed something of what he had just disclosed to her in the complacent manner in which Mrs. Quinlevan had regarded the two of them as they had sat together on the previous evening, and it made her much more comfortable with her cousin when they drove out a little later to tour the estate to know that the same idea was not also in *his* head. Indeed, they were soon on the same brother-and-sister terms with each other that had prevailed during his earlier visit to Herefordshire.

She was enchanted with the beauty of the Kerry landscape as they drove—the leafy woods, the particoloured fields and tiny whitewashed cottages roofed with brownish-grey thatch, and the blue hills from which came the tinkle of bells as sheep and goats browsed in placid flocks. But her eyes, accustomed to the rigorous standards set by her grandfather in the farming of his estate, soon discovered a great deal to find fault with in the management of the land.

"I can't think why you have allowed everything to fall into such neglect!" she said, looking accusingly at Brandon. "I am sure I know nothing at all about farming, except from hearing Sir John's comments when we rode out together, but even I can see that you have let things slide into a shocking state here."

Brandon shrugged. "Well, that is Mulqueen," he said frankly. "Mama *would* hire him as bailiff, though he is known all over the neighbourhood as a great lover of the bottle. She is perfectly bird-witted when it comes to such matters, and is persuaded that because his sister, who was once our housekeeper at The Place, was a very respectable woman, he is cut from the same cloth." He added, "Of course things were not in this state when my cousin Declan was alive. But he has been dead for two years, and since then Mama and Mulqueen have held full sway."

"But surely Cousin Bella was not left in sole charge of The Place!" Georgina said. "Was there no other relative to interest himself—?"

"Yes, there is my uncle Barnwall," Brandon said, "but he is as bad as Mama, besides spending almost all his time in England, so that he has no idea of what is going on." He said ruefully, "I expect you will be saying now that I ought to have looked around myself and prevailed on Mama to use more sense. But to tell the truth, I am not at all interested in farming!"

"Nor I," she said, "but Sir John always said that if one had land, it was one's obligation to see to it that neither it nor the people who lived on it were abused. And he was right, you know!"

Her disapproval shortly vanished in her enjoyment of the excursion, however, and she was obliged to admit, when they stopped at one of the cottages for a draught of new milk to accompany the game pie and Queen cakes that had been packed up in a hamper for their nuncheon, that this "houseen," at least, was in apple-pie order. The broad flagged steps leading to the door were swept and clean, and when they entered, on the invitation of the plain little woman who came to greet them, there was a turf fire on the hearth, with the kettle steaming on the hob, and a great, crusty, new-baked soda-cake on the spotless table.

This was the cottage of Dansel Lynch, who soon appeared himself—a red-faced, good-humoured countryman, whose heavy woollen trousers and hobnailed boots showed the signs of his morning's work in the fields. He made his manners to Miss Power, but it was plain that his chief interest was not in her, but in the second newcomer who was expected at The Place—the new owner.

"I expect there'll be a rare bit of change when he comes," he said unhappily. "Wasn't I saying only this morning now, I've yet to lay eyes on the Scotsman that wasn't clutchfisted? And this one a *claen istock,* to boot. There's never luck in the land when it goes to one of *them.*"

"What is a *claen istock?*" Georgina asked curiously.

"Why, miss," Dansel said, "'tis the man who comes in when there's no son to take up the land—the husband, ye see, of the woman that has the inheritance. And now, with Miss Nuala dead, what should he care about The Place except to wring money out of it?"

"Oh, it may not be as bad as you expect," Brandon said. "After all, you'll be rid of old Mulqueen, and this fellow had the management of Lord Cartan's estates, you know, so at least he's not a greenhead."

But Dansel shook his head forebodingly. "Better a greenhead than a meddler," he said. "No, it's a sad day for us, Master Brandon, seeing the last of the Power blood leave The Place." He looked at Georgina. "Wouldn't it be this young lady's, now, if Miss Nuala had never gone off and married? The old woman and me was saying that only this morning— her being Mr. Owen's one child—"

Brandon grinned and said, "Well, I hadn't thought of it, but you're quite right, of course. It should have gone to her."

Later, as they were driving back to the house, he remarked to Georgina, "So *you* are really the one Shannon is cutting out, and not Mama and me! Do you know, I'm sure that has never occurred to her; she has been too full of *our* wrongs to think of anyone else's. But it's true that you are Nuala's first cousin—her closest relation. Mama and I are more distant cousins."

Georgina looked at the grey, ancient bulk of the house before them.

"Well, I *should* have liked living here," she admitted, "and being quite rich and independent—and then you and Cousin Bella could have lived with me too, just as you did when Nuala was alive. But there is no use in thinking about that now, is there? For I cannot suppose, after all, that Mr.

Shannon should care anything about what my claims might have been if he had never married my cousin."

It was past two o'clock in the afternoon when she and Brandon walked in the front door at The Place, and both were admitting to a certain curiosity as to whether the new owner had yet arrived and perhaps gone off again. He was forgotten the next instant, however, when Nora Quill came hurrying downstairs, her normally ruddy face pale and her manner suggesting that a catastrophe of nature had occurred.

"Oh, Master Brandon, it's only you!" she cried. "I made sure it was the doctor."

"The doctor!" Brandon exclaimed. "Why, what is the matter, Nurse? Why is the doctor needed? Is my mother—?"

"Yes, indeed, it's the mistress," Nora said distressfully. "Oh, Master Brandon, indeed and indeed, you've no idea what a morning this has been! First there was that wicked Mulqueen, taking it into his head to quarrel with the mistress and fling out of here like a lord—"

"Good God, Nurse, you can't have sent for Dr. Culreavy merely because my mother has had words with Mulqueen!" Brandon exclaimed impatiently. "What is the matter with her? Is she really ill?"

"Ill!" Nora said wrathfully. "Why, indeed, she *is* ill, if you'd but give me leave to tell my tale. Fallen down these very stairs she's done—and her so upset with Mulqueen's impudence and that Shannon coming down on us that she didn't rightly know whether she was on her head or her feet. I misdoubt very much that she's broken her leg."

She whipped up the corner of her apron to her eyes, while Brandon and Georgina stood looking at her in alarm. Georgina was the first to recover herself.

"I'll go up to her," she said, but Nora barred her way as she started up the stairs.

"No, indeed, you won't, miss," she said decidedly, "for I've just calmed her down out of a fit of strong hysterics, and there's no saying you might not set her off again. If you please, you and Master Brandon will do much better to stay below and see Mr. Shannon when he comes. Bad cess to him, the divil, to have to turn up on this day of all the ones in the year!"

The arrival of the doctor at that moment put an end to any further conversation, for he hurried upstairs at once to his patient, accompanied by Nora. Brandon and Georgina were left standing in the hall, staring blankly at each other.

"Well, of all the rum starts!" Brandon said unhappily, after a moment. "Fallen downstairs! If she really *has* broken her leg—"

"There's no use in thinking of that until we know it's so," Georgina said firmly. "More than likely it's only a bad sprain. But in the meantime, what are we to do about Mr. Shannon? Of course Cousin Bella can't see him today. Perhaps he could talk to your bailiff?"

Brandon shook his head. "I shouldn't think that was at all likely," he said. "You heard what Nurse said. If he hasn't thrown up the job entirely, he'll be so badly foxed by this time that he won't know his right hand from his left. I can send one of the grooms to fetch my uncle Barnwall, if they haven't done so already, but if he doesn't arrive in time I expect we shall just have to see the fellow ourselves."

"*We?*" Georgina exclaimed.

"Well, you can't expect me to manage the whole business myself," Brandon said, with an asperity that seemed to his cousin to conceal a certain degree of perturbation. "Dash it, Georgie, I should think you'd *want* to stand by me."

"Well, so I do," Georgina said somewhat mendaciously, for she was actually thinking that it was one thing to be an interested onlooker at an affair of this kind, but quite another to be thrust into the position of carrying it off against such a formidable unknown as Mr. Shannon.

She was about to suggest that she should go upstairs and repair her toilette, for she was conscious that the morning's excursion had left her hair in some disarray and that the plain round gown she wore was hardly a dress in which to receive visitors. But at that moment there came a peremptory rap on the knocker. She and Brandon started, and looked at each other.

"It's Shannon, of course!" Brandon said, in a hasty undertone. "We had better not be standing here! Come into the book-room."

He seized her hand and drew her across the hall, and they stood waiting for Higgins to open the door to the caller.

But no Higgins appeared, and the rapping sounded again, this time even more insistently than before.

"Deuce take it!" Brandon muttered, under his breath. "This is really the outside of enough! The whole house at sixes and sevens, my mother laid up, and now there is not even a servant to answer the door! Ten to one they have all been sent off to the garret or the cellar to help in the packing." He tugged furiously at the bell-rope beside the mantel, but there was no response. "I suppose I shall have to go myself," he said despairingly.

"I'll come with you," Georgina said, with dignity. "We shall simply tell him that there has been an accident, and that he must return another time."

"No, good God, we can't do that!" Brandon said. "He owns the curst place, you know. Let me handle it."

He limped across the hall to the door, and Georgina, restraining the curiosity that prompted her to forget her eighteen years and peep from the doorway like a schoolgirl, hastily selected a book at random from the shelves and sat down with it in a chair beside the fireplace. She did not feel called on to carry her pretence of occupation so far as actually to read the page that she opened before her, but instead kept a sharp ear on what was going forward in the hall.

4

The first thing she heard, on the opening of the front door, was a masculine voice inquiring for Mrs. Quinlevan, followed at once by Brandon's rather confused and headlong explanation of the state of affairs in the house that had brought him to the door in place of a servant, and that made it impossible for the visitor to see his mother. Georgina could not overhear a great deal of the colloquy that followed, because the newcomer spoke in a low, calm voice, but she gained the distinct impression that Mr. Shannon was not at all ill at ease in the embarrassing situation into which he had walked. For some reason this raised her hackles. She was quite conscious of being in something of a flurry herself, and of the fact that Brandon was in even a worse one, and their visitor's contrasting self-composure rapidly assumed in her mind the proportions of an intolerable arrogance.

She had no time to form any further impression of him before he walked into the book-room with Brandon. Her concept of arrogance was immediately strengthened by the sight of a tall figure, carried with distinction and set off to careless advantage in a well-fitting drab coat, buckskins, and top boots, and a harsh-featured face with cool grey eyes.

"This is Mr. Shannon, Georgie," Brandon said, his lack of composure showing in the angry punctiliousness of his tone. "My cousin, Miss Power."

Shannon bowed slightly, glancing about the room immediately afterward in a manner that indicated plainly that he considered Miss Power to be hardly his first consideration at the moment.

"I see that I must apologise for coming at such a time, Mr. Quinlevan," he went on at once, rather coolly, to Brandon. "But naturally I had no reason to believe, after a twelvemonth, that my arrival would be entirely unexpected. Nor could I have foreseen your mother's unfortunate accident —which, however, would appear to have nothing to do with the fact that she has not yet removed from this house."

"If you think it is all a hum, to put you off, you are quite mistaken!" Brandon said, reacting hotly to his words. "She really had a fall, you know, not two hours ago! The doctor is with her now."

"Yes, of course," Shannon said, in the same reserved tone. "I assure you, I do not in the least doubt your word. At any rate, there is no need for us to come to cuffs over the matter. Perhaps if I might speak to some older relative of yours— You have an uncle, I believe?"

"He will be sent for, but he is not in the house."

"Then your bailiff—?"

"He—is not available just now, either," Brandon was obliged to admit.

"Indeed? Then perhaps *he* could be sent for?"

"He is—dismissed or drunk, sir!" Brandon replied, flushing up more and more hotly as he was driven into making the confession. "I believe he and my mother had words this morning."

Shannon's brows went up. "In that case," he suggested, "perhaps I might sit down with *you* and have a brief conversation—that is, if you have no more pressing matters to attend to."

"No—of course not," Brandon stammered, suddenly becoming conscious of his woeful deficiencies as a host. "Please sit down, sir! I'll ring for some refreshment."

He pulled the bell-rope, looking imploringly at Georgina as he did so. She came to his assistance and said to Shannon, with an assumption of dignified ease, "You must forgive the disorder in the house, sir. It should hardly surprise you; you can no doubt see that my cousins were almost on the point of removing to Craythorne when Mrs. Quinlevan's accident occurred this morning. Perhaps you might allow me to suggest that, when you have had some refreshment, you would go to the local inn, where I am sure you will be quite comfortable until arrangements are made to receive you here."

She had spoken in her best imitation of her grandmother's most quelling tones, but it infuriated her further that the maddeningly self-composed visitor seemed less than impressed with her dignity.

His reply was even less satisfactory to her. "I beg your pardon," he said, with his rather harsh air of civility, "but that is exactly what I do *not* intend to do, Miss Power, at least until I have satisfied myself that there is someone in this house who is capable of managing its affairs and those of this estate. I had ample opportunity, as I was driving here, to see the shocking state into which the land has been allowed to fall; now it seems that even the house is to be given over to chaos."

Brandon burst out angrily, "That is none of *your* affair"—but caught himself up at once. "Dash it all, yes, it is, of course," he said, flushing up red, "but—but—my uncle—"

He was interrupted by the appearance of Higgins at the door.

"You rang, sir?" he asked helpfully, as Brandon stood staring at him.

And well he might stare, Georgina thought. Higgins, in the helter-skelter state of the house that day, and perhaps in sympathy with the wrongs of his friend Mulqueen, had allowed himself to sample some of

the Madeira that he had been charged with making ready for conveyance
to Craythorne. His gingery hair looked as if he had just come in out of a
high wind, and his manner, far from the modest civility required even of a
passable butler, was confidingly forward.

"Thought you might care to know, Master Brandon," he volunteered, as
Brandon, stunned by his appearance, sought for words. "Mr. Barnwall's
gone back to London. Left this morning. Sent a message to the mistress—
messenger crossed ours on the way."

"That will do, Higgins," Brandon said, in a strangled tone.

Higgins bowed and walked out of the room, adding amiably, as he departed, "Thought you might care to know, Master Brandon."

"This is the outside of enough!" Brandon exploded. "I've told my
mother time and again to get rid of that fellow!"

"An excellent piece of advice, I should say," Shannon remarked dryly.
He rose and said, "If you will allow me, Mr. Quinlevan—I drove my own
horses here, and I scarcely care to leave them standing any longer in this
wind. Would you object if I order my groom to take them around to the
stables?"

"Not at all, sir—if you—if you mean to stay!" Brandon stammered.

"Very well. If you will excuse me, Miss Power—I shan't be a moment."

He strode out of the room, leaving the two cousins almost speechless
behind him. It was Georgina who recovered herself first.

"Of all the—the arrogant presumption!" she said furiously. "He *does*
mean to stay, Brandon; there is no other explanation for it. Oh! No one
but a rag-mannered basket-scrambler would think of forcing his company
on a household at such a time! How *could* my cousin have married him!"

"Hush! He'll hear you," Brandon said uncomfortably. He added, "I
daresay you're right—but all the same, with Mulqueen gone and my uncle
off to London and Mama laid up—well, you know, there really ought to
be someone here to look after The Place."

"We might manage very well ourselves, with Nora and the servants,"
Georgina fumed. "Good God, Brandon, you are not going to be cow-
hearted enough to tell me that you *wish* him to stay? He is an impertinent coxcomb, and it is no affair of *his* if your butler is a trifle bosky. If I
were standing in your shoes, I should tell him straight to his face to go!"

"Then it is a very good thing that you are not standing in them," Shannon's calm voice remarked from the doorway, "since I should certainly pay
no attention to such a piece of impertinence from him." He came into the
room, leisurely stripping off his driving gloves, and went on in the same

matter-of-fact way, to Brandon, "I wonder if it would be possible for you to find *some* servant in this confusion who would have the presence of mind to be able to fetch a bottle of the excellent Madeira my late wife assured me her father had laid down here? I have had rather a long drive, and you were kind enough to speak of offering me some refreshment."

Brandon looked unhappily at Georgina. Apparently he felt that it was his duty to rebuke Shannon for the deliberate rudeness of his remark, but he was far from used to having such responsibilities thrust on him, and finally settled the matter by throwing the idea up and saying, "Oh, Lord, very well, then! There must be *someone*—"

He limped out of the room, while Georgina remained standing by the mantelpiece, regarding Shannon in a decidedly unfriendly manner. Shannon returned the gaze without noticeable expression on his face, and finally remarked, in the tone of quite obviously careless civility that had so offended her previously, "Will you sit down, Miss Power? I can hardly do so myself until you do, and I really believe we might both be more comfortable seated than standing here facing each other as if we were about to engage in a sparring match."

She flushed angrily, conscious of the justness of what he had said even though she disliked intensely the way in which he had said it, and sat down abruptly in the nearest chair. Shannon then deliberately sat down himself and, stretching his long legs out before him in what appeared to her remarkably like the comfortable way of a man making himself at ease in his own house, said to her, "I gather from your name, Miss Power, that we are relations by marriage. Perhaps you will be good enough to tell me in what degree?"

"I am Owen Power's daughter—Nuala's first cousin," she said, with a coldness that matched his own.

He looked thoughtful, as if he were trying to recollect something. "I see," he said. "Then this is not your home? I seem to recollect my wife's speaking of having relations in Shropshire—"

"Herefordshire," Georgina corrected him. "That is, our residence is in Bath now, since Sir John—since my grandfather's death. But I cannot see what possible concern all this is of yours, Mr. Shannon. Your wife is dead, so it may be as well for you to consider that any connexion there has been between us is now at an end."

He bowed slightly, but she had the distinct notion that again he was not impressed by her pretensions of formality and was regarding her with only the rather negligent attention he might have bestowed on a forward schoolgirl.

"In that I shall be happy to oblige you," he said in a level voice. "The fact remains, however, that you are apparently residing in my house, and I have a natural curiosity to know who my guests may be."

She was confounded as to how to reply to this speech, and felt a certain relief when Brandon walked into the room again, carrying a decanter and a single glass.

"Here is your wine, sir," he said stiffly, setting the glass down on a table and filling it.

"You won't join me?" Shannon asked him, with lazy—and, Georgina thought, rather mocking—civility.

"No, thank you!" Brandon said curtly. "Sir, I have been thinking—"

But at that moment there was a slight cough from the direction of the hall, and the eyes of all three of the occupants of the room lifted to behold a small, thin, soberly dressed elderly gentleman standing in the doorway.

"Dr. Culreavy!" Brandon exclaimed. "Come in, sir—pray! How is my mother? Are there any bones broken?"

The doctor looked in some surprise at Shannon's tall figure comfortably reposing in the easy-chair across the room.

"I beg your pardon, Brandon," he said, "I had no idea you had a caller."

"This is Mr. Shannon, the—my cousin Nuala's husband," Brandon stammered. "Dr. Culreavy."

"Your servant, sir," Shannon said, rising with an easy movement. "Will you share a glass of this excellent Madeira with me?"

Georgina gave an indignant gasp on hearing him so coolly assuming the role of host, and Dr. Culreavy, too, looked at him with a certain suspicion and disapproval.

"No, I thank you, sir," he said, with testy formality. "I want only a word with young Quinlevan." He paused, seeming to expect that Shannon would excuse himself and take himself out of the room, but Shannon showed no inclination to do so.

"You have not met my cousin, Miss Power, Dr. Culreavy," Brandon said, turning his back on Shannon with an angry flush.

Dr. Culreavy bowed. "May I say that it is indeed fortunate that you are here, Miss Power?" he said. "Mrs. Quinlevan has had a very nasty shock— very nasty, indeed. There are no bones broken, I believe, but she is experiencing a considerable degree of discomfort from a very bad sprain. I should much dislike leaving her to the care of servants alone, though I have no doubt that Nora Quill will cosset her beyond all need. But *your* presence here must be of the greatest reassurance to her."

Georgina was not certain how much of this speech was to be set down to the doctor's old-fashioned civility and how much to his genuine belief in what her being in the house must mean to her cousin, but she murmured some proper response. Her concern for her cousin Bella was almost swallowed up, however, by her indignation over Shannon's continuing to force his presence on such a conversation.

The next moment that indignation rose even higher when he interrupted Brandon's colloquy with Dr. Culreavy to inquire of the latter, "Am I to understand, then, that it will be some time before Mrs. Quinlevan is able either to remove to Craythorne or to resume any supervision of this house and estate?"

Dr. Culreavy looked at him disapprovingly. "Oh dear, yes!" he said positively. "I won't hear of her leaving her bed for at least a week, and then she must proceed with the greatest of care. A strong irritation of the nerves, you see, my dear sir, coupled with the physical shock and contusions of a nasty fall— And Mrs. Quinlevan is a lady whose nerves are very easily disordered."

Shannon said no more, but as soon as the doctor had departed he set down his glass and remarked to Brandon in a matter-of-fact voice, "That settles it, of course. I shall stay. If one of your admirable servants can be found to fetch my portmanteau upstairs to a bedchamber, I shall employ the time between now and dinner in trying to discover the whereabouts of your bailiff and putting him into a state of sufficient sobriety to be able to give me some sort of account of his stewardship."

He then strode out of the room, as if he had said everything that was necessary to be said. Georgina looked at Brandon, her eyes beginning to sparkle dangerously.

"Cousin," she said, "am I to understand that you are going to allow that *abominable* man to walk into this house and behave in such a way?—as if we were children, as if *we* could have nothing to say—?"

"Well, I don't care for it myself, of course," Brandon said uncomfortably. "But what am I to do? I can't turn him out if he chooses to stay; you must see that."

"I don't see anything of the kind," Georgina retorted. "You might at least show him that you resent his conduct!"

Brandon smiled a little, ruefully. "Lord, you sound as if you would like me to call him out," he said.

"So I would!" Georgina said ruthlessly.

"But he wouldn't pay the slightest heed, if I *were* such a nodcock as to do it," Brandon protested. "He'd only think I was queer in my attic. Dash it, Georgie, *we* are the ones who ought not to be here, if you come right down to it. Mama has had a twelvemonth to vacate and she hasn't done it, and I know for a fact that she has given him promises by the yard, and not lived up to a single one. You can hardly blame him for growing tired of it at last."

The logic of this argument had little effect on Georgina, however, and she incautiously taxed her cousin with being afraid of Shannon, concluding by vowing that if she were a man she would have him out of the house in the space of five minutes. This accusation succeeded in firing Brandon up a great deal more than Shannon's rudeness had done. He declared vehemently that she was making a cake of herself and that for his part he was sorry that she had ever come to Ireland, as they would have got on a great deal better without her, concluding this speech by limping out of the room to go upstairs and see how his mother did.

Georgina swallowed her wrath as best she might, and sat down to consider what she was to do next. After five minutes, however, as no answer presented itself to this problem, she followed Brandon upstairs to inquire after Mrs. Quinlevan. Nora Quill was sitting with her; on seeing Georgina, she rose at once, with her finger to her lips, and went into the hall to meet her, closing the door behind her.

"The doctor's given her a draught and she's gone off at last," she said in a low, rather belligerent voice, "so you needn't be thinking of disturbing her, miss. A sad time she's had of it today, you know, and I'm sure it's a miracle that there's no bones broken."

Georgina expressed her sympathy and inquired if there was anything she could do to aid the sufferer.

Nora, somewhat mollified, shook her head. "Not for the mistress, for I'll see to her myself, miss; I wouldn't have it any other way. But if you could take things in hand a bit belowstairs—for I'm sure Master Brandon is of no more use than a babe-in-arms when it comes to anything that isn't in those wearisome books of his. And now he says that that divil of a Shannon is determined to stop here in the house this very night—as if we weren't in enough of a lather as it is!"

"Yes," Georgina said, "he desires a bedchamber prepared for him." She did not wish to gossip with a servant about the future master of The Place, no matter how angry he had made her, but she had no doubt that

Nora could read her feelings from her looks. "If you could tell me which will be most suitable—" she suggested.

"Suitable!" Nora fired off. "If ye're asking me what's suitable for *him*, I'd tell you the coal-hole!" She shrugged her shoulders at Georgina's disapproving unresponsiveness and said rather sulkily, "Well, then, you might ask Mrs. Hopkins to put him in the green bedchamber at the front of the house. It was Mr. Declan's, and as he's to be master here—"

She returned to her patient, while Georgina went in search of the housekeeper, whom she eventually ran to earth in the kitchen, having words with the cook. The constant turmoil in the house made her wonder how anyone had ever contrived to live comfortably in it, but when she had given directions to Mrs. Hopkins about the green bedchamber and had gone back to the book-room to find Brandon closeted there with a volume of Latin poetry, he enlightened her on the matter by saying that when Declan Power had been alive he had kept all the reins in his own hands.

"Mama has never been worth a button as far as managing *anything* is concerned," he said frankly. "I daresay Cousin Declan never hoped she would be, when he brought her to live here. All he wanted was a respectable female relation to stand behind Nuala; everything else he took care of himself. I mean to say, we had a bang-up housekeeper all those years, Mrs. Curran—but when Cousin Declan died Mama felt it to be her duty to take an interest in household matters, and,—well, the fact of the matter is that Mrs. Curran got up on her high ropes at her interfering, and before we knew it she had packed up and gone back to Cork."

He seemed to have forgotten the note of animosity on which they had parted, and Georgina, glad to find him so forgiving, sat down and asked him what they were to do about dinner. "I suppose Shannon intends to take his meals here," she said.

"I expect he does," Brandon conceded. "I stopped round at the stables just now, and his groom was settling the horses in as if *he* had no idea, at any rate, of going anywhere else today. Pair of match-greys they are, by the way—sixteen-mile-an-hour tits if I ever saw any. Hanger—the groom—says Shannon bought 'em in Cork. Has an eye for good horseflesh: I'll give him that."

"Well, I should not go about it to become familiar with his groom, if I were you," Georgina said severely. "We are obliged to live in the same house with Shannon as long as your mother cannot remove from here, but I, for one, intend to have nothing at all to do with him personally."

Brandon shrugged. "Well, that is your affair," he said. "But there's no use making a kick-up about it, Coz. You said yourself you wanted someone to take hold here, you know. Well, it seems that someone is about to do so, and I must say I am glad of it. It will make it a deuced bit more comfortable while Mama is laid up."

"You are not going to defend him!" Georgina said. "I am sure he is laughing at us, behind that odious civility." She added darkly, "I may be obliged to sit down to dinner with him, but I assure you I shall not give him any more consequence in this house than he has already taken, by addressing so much as a word to him."

This resolution proved singularly easy to carry out, as, when they sat down to the table a little later, Shannon appeared to have no interest whatever in speaking to her. Instead, he carried on a very practical conversation with Brandon on the subject of the estate, endeavouring to learn from him, it seemed, anything that might be of value in his future conduct of affairs there.

Nor did Brandon, who was a little miffed, in spite of his good nature, at the strong words she had spoken to him earlier in the day, make any attempt to draw her into the conversation. As a matter of fact, when the Savoy cake with which the meal ended had been eaten, he seemed quite inclined to remain in the dining-room to sit with Shannon as the latter sampled a glass of Declan Power's excellent brandy, instead of accompanying his cousin from the room. This was too much for Georgina. Finding herself quite provoked by this uncousinly behaviour, she withdrew to her own bedchamber, where she occupied herself for some time in pacing it from end to end, throwing out various indignant and unflattering ejaculations from time to time.

It would have made her even unhappier if she had known that Brandon continued to sit with Shannon for the better part of the hour that followed, and that the conversation flowed amicably all the while. It was, in fact, Shannon, and not her cousin, who put an end to it by declaring his purpose of closeting himself in the estate-room for the remainder of the evening over the accounts.

Brandon then went to seek his cousin, and, on being informed by one of the maids that she had retired to her chamber, went quite contentedly into the book-room to continue his reading.

5

On the following morning Georgina was relieved to find that she was to breakfast, at least, without the benefit of Shannon's company, for she was told, on coming downstairs, that he had already gone out, accompanied by Brandon and the bailiff, Mulqueen. She ate her meal in solitary state, and then went upstairs to inquire of Nora Quill whether her cousin Bella was awake. She was admitted at once to the sick room and found Mrs. Quinlevan sitting up in bed with a breakfast tray, looking much more robust than she had been prepared to see her by Nora's gloomy observations.

When she congratulated her cousin on this, however, she was treated to a long catalogue of the distressing symptoms with which Mrs. Quinlevan had been plagued during the night, so that any hope she might have had of soon being able to leave The Place and Shannon's unwelcome company was immediately laid to rest.

"Of course," Mrs. Quinlevan said, presently making reference herself to the obnoxious presence of the new owner, "*that* has added immeasurably to my anxieties, my love. You have only to imagine my feelings when Nora told me this morning that he had actually spent the night here! So improper! So dreadfully pushing!"

"Yes, indeed, ma'am. So it seems to me, too," Georgina said, "but I beg you won't make yourself uncomfortable over it on *my* account."

"Well, I will not do so, if you are sure it does not trouble you," Mrs. Quinlevan said doubtfully, "but I am not at all certain that Lady Mercer would approve of your even *meeting* Mr. Shannon—far less of your sitting down to dinner with him yesterday, which Brandon tells me you were obliged to do."

Georgina would have been glad to express her own feelings on that subject, but she did not wish to upset her cousin further, and thus merely said that it did not signify.

She left the room soon afterward, on a hint from Nora Quill that her mistress required more repose, and, after returning downstairs, was beginning a letter to her mother in the book-room when Higgins came in to inform her that Lady Mott and her daughter had arrived to inquire after Mrs. Quinlevan. Georgina had no idea who Lady Mott might be, but in Brandon's absence she thought it incumbent on her to act the part of hostess, and she accordingly asked Higgins to show the callers into the book-room.

A few moments later a homely middle-aged lady of imposing bulk, in a pomona-green gown and a high-crowned bonnet decorated with a cluster of curled ostrich plumes, sailed into the room, accompanied by a young girl of about Georgina's own age in a quiet frock of dove-coloured silk.

"My dear child," the elder lady exclaimed, as Georgina rose to greet her, "I came the moment I heard! Now I shan't stand on points with you, for I must tell you that I knew your father when he was still in short coats. Do pray tell me—how is poor Bella?"

"I believe she is much improved this morning," Georgina said. "But you have the advantage of me, I am afraid, ma'am."

"Of course—of course!" the lady interrupted, in her reassuringly frank voice. "Naturally you will not know us. I am Lady Mott, and this is my daughter Betsy. Our land marches with the Powers', you see—or it did, until Nuala Power was wet-goose enough to marry this man Shannon. Pho! I must say it will not suit either me *or* Sir Humphrey to have him as a neighbour, but then I expect Nuala was not considering that when she ran off with the fellow."

Georgina broke in on this flow of conversation long enough to beg the visitors to be seated and to ask Higgins if he would bring some refreshment for them, and then sat down herself to attend further to Lady Mott. She could not help being somewhat amused by her appearance, for indeed the fashionable clothes and bright colours she wore did not at all suit her plain face and stout figure, but at the same time she felt in Lady Mott a kindred spirit—a frankness and a commonsense approach to life that accorded with her own.

Her daughter, who sat silently in her mama's exuberant presence, did not resemble her in the least. She had a rather pretty, good-humoured face, the greatest attraction of which was a pair of blue eyes the colour of cornflowers. As her conversation consisted chiefly of "No, Mama," and "Yes, Mama," Georgina was unable to form much of an opinion of her character or intelligence.

When they had all sat down, Lady Mott had first to hear a full account of Mrs. Quinlevan's accident and Shannon's arrival, and then took matters into her own hands by declaring that in her opinion it would not do at all for Georgina to remain at The Place as Shannon's guest.

"Which is what it comes to, my dear, however one may talk round it," she said. "And with Bella confined to her room, there is no one to chaperon you but Brandon, and that is as good as saying no one at all. No, it won't do. I think it will be much better if you come home with me until Bella is ready to remove to Craythorne. You will be very welcome, you know, and as you and Betsy are of an age, you won't be bored with only the company of old people like Sir Humphrey and myself."

She seemed to believe that the matter was already settled, but Georgina discovered, to her own surprise, that, far from being pleased by this, she was in reality rather put out. Under cover of the pause in the conversation that occurred as Higgins appeared to hand around glasses of ratafia, she made a hasty attempt to examine her own feelings. Certainly it was not because she had taken an instant dislike to Lady Mott that she was disinclined to accept her invitation; on the contrary, she thought she would get on with her very well. Nor was it because she felt that her presence in the house would be of any particular comfort to Mrs. Quinlevan; more probably, she thought, her cousin would be relieved to be rid of the problems of entertaining a guest under such peculiar circumstances.

No, the truth was, she was obliged to confess, that it was Shannon who was making her desire to stay. She had flung down the gauntlet to him, and to run away tamely before the battle between them had fairly been joined was a poor-spirited course of conduct against which all her instincts rebelled. It would be one thing if she were to remove to Craythorne with her cousins in the natural course of events; it was quite another to give him the satisfaction of knowing that his highhanded rudeness had driven her from the house.

Lady Mott, when Higgins had left the room, fortunately gave her added time to formulate some excuse for declining her invitation by charging off into certain rather startling reminiscences of Georgina's father, who had been, it appeared, a childhood playmate of hers, and then by rising and saying that she must go upstairs and look in on poor Bella.

"Not," she added, "that I expect I shall do her a particle of good, for I am never out of frame myself and Sir Humphrey assures me I have no tact whatever with those who are. But of course it won't do for me to go off without looking in on her. And I must see to it that she receives the pork jelly that I brought. Her own cook—as I suppose you have found by this time—is a positive monster of inefficiency, and I doubt can concoct *anything* in the least restorative to an invalid."

She swept out of the room on these words, instructing her daughter to remain behind with Georgina. Georgina then discovered that Miss Mott, relieved of her mama's overpowering presence, could indeed chatter with the best of her sex, for she was treated, in the space of a quarter hour, to a complete description of the amusements the neighbourhood afforded, from assemblies and private balls to picnics and riding excursions, with side glances at the young gentlemen whom she might be expected to meet while attending these events.

"I shall be very jealous of you, I am sure, for you are much prettier than I am," Betsy said candidly, "or that is, I should be, except that I do not believe Robert will be deflected from his devotion to me, no matter to how much disadvantage I appear beside you."

Georgina shook herself out of her own private reflections to a semblance of attention.

"Robert?" she said politely. "Oh—you are betrothed, then?"

Betsy sighed. "Not—betrothed, actually," she said. "Papa believes I am too young."

Georgina stared. "Too young? How old are you? You must be as old as I am!"

"I am turned eighteen."

"So am I," said Georgina, satisfied. "But my problem is exactly the opposite of yours. I have been *plagued* to marry."

"Someone you—could not love?" Betsy inquired, her eyes lighting up at the hint of a romantic story.

"Exactly!" Georgina said curtly. "Someone no one could love—except his mother, who dotes on him."

She caught herself up, feeling that this was no time for exchanging confidences, even if Betsy Mott were the sort of confidante she would have chosen. But Betsy, once on the subject of romance, was not so easily to be led off it.

"How sad!" she said eagerly. "Do you know, I had been trying to picture you, since Mrs. Quinlevan told us you were to visit here, and as you are Nuala's cousin, I always imagined you like her—but I see now that you are much, much different. I mean—how very brave of you to stand out against your family, when they were *determined* that you should marry this—this *man!*"

"Well, as to that," Georgina objected, "one can hardly call him a *man,* for he is only twenty and looks eighteen, and is a perfect looby! And as for my being braver than Nuala, that is nonsense. *I* didn't run off and marry someone like Shannon!"

"Yes, but I expect he married *her,* you know," Betsy said reasonably. "Mama always said she would meet someone some day who would take her at her word—for you must know she was a desperate flirt, and was never satisfied unless she had every man in sight dangling after her. But then everyone here knew she didn't *mean* anything by it—and I expect

Mr. Shannon didn't, or if he did, it didn't signify to him." She leaned a
little closer to Georgina, lowering her voice. "What is he *really* like?" she
asked urgently. "Is he—fatally attractive?"

"He is the rudest, most abominable creature I have ever seen in my
life," Georgina said unequivocally. *"That's* what he's like." She paused at
the sight of Higgins again in the doorway.

"Lady Eliza Malladon," he announced, and, with the words, a lady of
some thirty years, dressed in the first stare of fashion, in a cherry gown
and spencer set off with a pink neck scarf with cherry stripes, swept into
the room. At first sight Georgina scarcely considered that the face, beneath
the tall straight hat trimmed with a tuft of feathers hanging to one side,
was a pretty one, for the nose was a decided pug, the lips were overly full,
and the brown eyes rather prominent. But Lady Eliza had not been in the
room more than five minutes before she had established, by her manner,
that she was accustomed to being the belle of any occasion to which she
lent her presence. She had an exceedingly vivacious manner, which quite
bore down Georgina's attempts to act the hostess, and made the point at
once that, as she was so well acquainted at The Place, she considered *she*
might rather do the honours.

She greeted Miss Mott with condescending amiability, and, after inquiring rather perfunctorily after Mrs. Quinlevan, said to Georgina, "Higgins tells me that you actually have Shannon in the house! What a coil
you must be in! But that is exactly like the creature, you know. He will
never be bound to do as anyone else would." She accepted a glass of
ratafia and sat down comfortably on the sofa. "Tell me, what do you think
of him, my dear? Of course one must admit he is handsome, in his own
abominable way."

"I should not call him so, ma'am," Georgina said bluntly.

Lady Eliza raised her brows. "No? Then I take it he has been behaving
*un*handsomely to you already—for, my dear child, disregarding the face,
which I grant you may be somewhat harsh, that magnificent figure! Cartan—the old earl—was considered quite an Adonis in his day, I believe—
though 'Adonis' may not *quite* convey all that masculinity. And Shannon
is said to be his image. Not that you are not perfectly correct in refusing to
admire such a rogue, my dear. Of course it was your poor cousin's un-
doing!"

Georgina did not at all care for the direction the conversation was taking, considering that Lady Eliza's freedom in abusing the man under
whose roof she was sitting was in at least as bad taste as Shannon's own

rudeness; and she was relieved when Lady Mott again entered the room, having completed her visit to the invalid upstairs.

"Well, Eliza! You here!" she said, regarding Lady Eliza with a glance of some disfavour. "I must say you surprise me. I thought you never rose before noon."

"Nonsense," Lady Eliza said briskly. "Of course I came at once when I heard of poor Bella's accident."

"More than likely you have come to have a look for yourself at what is going on here," Lady Mott said, bluntly demolishing Lady Eliza's charitable pretensions. "I declare I never saw such a muddle as Bella has got herself into now! There she lies, put down on her bed with a sprain and her nerves, while this turkey-cock comes in to rule the roost! If I were in her place, give me leave to tell you, not another night would I spend under this roof, if they carried me out of it to my grave!"

Lady Eliza laughed. "Oh, Lucinda, indeed, you are too severe," she said. "Shannon won't *eat* her, you know! And if you are thinking of Miss Power—I doubt exceedingly that he will try the same game twice in the same family."

"No, indeed he won't," Lady Mott said roundly, "for I intend to carry her home directly with me."

This was too much for Georgina, who did not at all care to be made an object of discussion between the two ladies, as if she were no more than a child.

"As to *that*, Lady Mott," she said with dignity, "as deeply as I appreciate your kind invitation, I really believe I ought not to leave Cousin Bella. I shall remain here as long as she does."

"The deuce you say!" Lady Mott said, in her forthright manner. "Why, I have spoken to Bella and she quite agrees with me that you should be got out of the way."

"I am not a child, Lady Mott!"

Lady Eliza gave her tinkle of laughter again. "No, indeed you are not!" she said. "Which is precisely, my dear, why Lucinda is so anxious to have you out of this." She was seated facing the door, and at this moment her face suddenly lit up with a sparkle of mischief. "But here is Shannon himself!" she said. "Do let us have him in! Shannon! Shannon! Do you not mean to say good morning to your guests?"

Georgina, her eyes snapping across to the door at Lady Eliza's first intimation that Shannon had come into the house, saw him pause in the hall and then come deliberately forward toward the door of the book-room.

He was accompanied by Brandon, who came limping in behind him with a frown that seemed to show that neither Lady Mott nor Lady Eliza was a particular favourite of his.

"Good morning, Lady Eliza," Shannon said, with the same rather indifferent composure that had so nettled Georgina the day before.

She fancied that Lady Eliza did not care a great deal for it either, for there was a note of resentment in her voice as she said, giving him her hand in a negligent gesture, "I see that you are still the same odious creature, Shannon! Have you *no* sympathy for poor Mrs. Quinlevan? Laid down on her bed, and *you* taking over her house—"

"On the contrary, Lady Eliza, it is *my* house." Shannon ignored the slight pat on the sofa beside her with which Lady Eliza had indicated that he was to take his place there, and instead strolled over to the mantelpiece and leaned his shoulders against it, driving his hands into his pockets. "And I have every sympathy for Mrs. Quinlevan," he continued, "which is precisely why I have taken up residence here, rather than see the entire place fall into a state of chaos."

Lady Eliza and Lady Mott, each in her own way, received this speech with an air of complete scepticism, and Lady Mott was moved to utter the comment, "Stuff!"

But Brandon, unexpectedly, came to his host's defence.

"He's right, you know!" he said warmly. "He has spent the entire morning taking things in hand here, and I mean to tell you he has them running more smoothly already!" He grinned appreciatively. "He even has Cook eating out of his hand, if you'll believe it, and as a result I daresay we may have a tolerable sort of dinner here today, instead of the messes we are used to."

At this point Georgina, feeling obliged once more, in this muddled situation, to act as hostess, made Mr. Shannon known to Lady Mott and her daughter in a cool voice which indicated that only a stern sense of the proprieties impelled her to recognise his presence at all. Lady Mott at once added to the effect by rising and saying to him forthrightly, "We are not come to call upon *you*, Mr. Shannon, but to visit Mrs. Quinlevan and Miss Power. Georgina, my dear, if you will direct the servants to send your portmanteaux to Mott House this afternoon, I see no reason why you should not leave with us at once."

Shannon's brows went up, and he looked at Georgina.

"You are leaving us then, Miss Power?" he asked, without—as far as she could determine—the slightest interest in whether she was or was not.

"No!" she said quickly. "That is— Lady Mott, *indeed* I appreciate your kindness, but I cannot feel it is right for me to leave my cousin under these circumstances." She saw Shannon's brows rise again, which infuriated her further. "Not," she said, "but that I should be *most* happy to leave this house—"

"Then do so, by all means," Shannon said. "I imagine that you can be of little real use to Mrs. Quinlevan, and as I understand it may be some time before she may be expected to leave here, I should advise you not to turn down such an excellent offer."

Georgina coloured warmly. "Nonetheless, I shall remain here, Mr. Shannon," she said, adding pointedly, "I cannot see that it concerns *you*. I assure you, my cousin will bear any expense that is incurred."

He laughed unexpectedly, interrupting her. "No, no, I am not so clutchfisted as that!" he said. "You may suit yourself, Miss Power." He pushed his shoulders away from the mantelpiece. "Lady Eliza, my compliments to Colonel Malladon. Lady Mott—Miss Mott—your servant. Brandon, if you are coming with me, come along."

He strode out of the room without further ado, leaving Georgina seething, Lady Eliza looking piqued, and Lady Mott bristling.

"You are right for once, Eliza," the latter declared. "He really is an insufferable man, and has wound Brandon around his little finger already, I see. *And* I expect you, too, miss!" she rounded on Georgina.

Georgina choked. "I! I assure you, ma'am—"

Lady Eliza laughed. "Why, they are at daggers' points, Lucinda; you must be quite paperskulled if you haven't seen that!" she said. She went on, to Georgina, "I believe you intend to stay only to plague him, you wicked girl. But take care! He really can be quite a brute, you know. In fact, I shouldn't scruple to call him dangerous."

A suddenly meaningful note in her bantering voice made Lady Mott look at her sharply, but the next moment she had risen and was saying in a quite different tone, "But do let us go now, Lucinda. I am sure we have stayed quite long enough; I believe I must not inflict another visitor on Bella this morning. Georgina, my love, I have made up my mind that we are to be great friends. As soon as Bella is up and about again and you are removed to Craythorne, I expect you to be constantly at Stokings. I shall be giving a ball in May, you know, and there will be a great deal of company in the house."

Georgina murmured some polite response, feeling that she might indeed find a ball at Stokings enjoyable, but hoping at the same time that she would be fortunate enough to find somewhat more congenial friends in Ireland than Lady Eliza. She did not at all care for her manners, which might do very well in a certain fashionable London set of which she had heard, though she had never met anyone who belonged to it, and she felt, besides, that there was a certain animosity toward herself on Lady Eliza's part, which she was discerning enough to realise came from her dislike of being outshone by a younger, prettier woman.

If Lady Eliza were indeed to have "a great friend" of the female sex, Georgina was quite certain she would be plain and dull and certainly at least as old as the lady herself.

6

As the days went by Georgina found that even Lady Eliza's company would have been a welcome relief to her.

Quite unthinkingly, by her refusal of Lady Mott's invitation, she had placed herself in a highly unenviable situation. Shannon's presence in the house, when it became known in the neighbourhood, was an effective preventive of any further calls, though messages and gifts for the invalid arrived in an almost constant flow. At the same time, her own professed devotion to the task of attending Mrs. Quinlevan's sick bed kept her from receiving any of the invitations that would have been forthcoming had it been known that, in fact, she could be of little use to her cousin.

Nora Quill would not consider leaving her post as nurse to anyone as inexperienced as Miss Power—a decision that was reinforced by her patient's own preference. Indeed, Georgina soon found that her presence in the sick room only agitated her cousin, by putting her in mind of the disagreeable situation in which she had placed her young guest by inviting her to her home at such a time, and thus she fell into the habit of limiting her visits to a brief quarter hour twice a day.

This left her with a great deal of time on her hands. There was Brandon, of course, but his afternoons were occupied with sessions with the elderly clergyman who acted as his tutor, and as he, too, had taken her at her word, that she cared to have nothing to do with Shannon, it seemingly never occurred to him to invite her to accompany them on their morning rides or drives around the estate. Georgina thought rather vengefully that Shannon was properly served by having Brandon tagging about everywhere after him like a friendly puppy, for certainly any use that he might have made of him initially in seeking acquaintance with The Place had soon been exhausted. Brandon knew nothing about either farming or money management, and it was apparent to any unbiassed onlooker that his sole interest in attending Shannon so faithfully was in Shannon's company itself.

It did not occur to her that the boy, who since Declan Power's death had been thrown almost exclusively in the company of women, except for servants and his elderly tutor, was starved for male companionship, particularly that of an older man who might act as a mentor. All she saw in Brandon's predilection for Shannon's company was a direct flouting of her own pronounced dislike of the new owner of The Place, and, as a consequence, the relationship between the two cousins was so lacking in cordiality at this period that it seemed almost to have reached the stage of mutual dislike.

She might have been more content to see her cousin ride out with Shannon every day if she could have had the pleasure of a daily ride herself, with no better company than that of a groom, but unfortunately the reduced stables that Mrs. Quinlevan had kept since Declan Power's death could not provide her with a proper mount. There was no horse suitable for a lady, except the elderly cob that Brandon, to his bitter disappointment, was condemned by his invalid state to ride, and a single dawdling, frustrating excursion on this animal had convinced Georgina that she would rather walk.

So she went for long rambles to pass the time, thinking longingly, on the days when Shannon was driving the gig, of the handsome blood-mare he had bought for himself that was standing idle in the stable. But she would have bitten her tongue off before she would have asked his permission to ride any of his horses.

Soon, as one empty day followed another, she began first to wish that she had never come to Ireland and then to cast about for something to lighten the tedium of her present existence. She found it, about a week after Mrs. Quinlevan's accident, in an escapade she was quite certain her cousin would have disapproved of, had she known of it—but then she had no idea of telling Cousin Bella what she was about.

The idea had come to her when she had broken one of her solitary rambles at the Lynch cottage and had been persuaded by Cilly Lynch, Dansel's eldest daughter, to stop for a cup of tea and a slice of fresh-baked raisin-cake. Cilly was full of the wedding that was to take place the following day at one of the neighbouring cottages on the estate, and in speaking of it to Georgina she described the Kerry custom of "strawing" the newly married pair. A group of boys, she said, were already preparing the straw caps, hats, and skirts in which they would disguise themselves to visit the wedding house. The "strawboys," as they were called, would march in order to the house, where they would join the festivities while still maintaining their disguise, dance and sing with the guests, and then march off again.

What the significance of the straw costumes was Cilly could not say. She knew only that "strawing" was an ancient Kerry custom, and that it was usually impossible, owing to the nature of the costumes, which made their wearers look like walking haystacks, for the disguise of the strawboys to be penetrated.

Georgina, seated in the neat cottage drinking her tea, first thought regretfully of the jollity that would occur so close to The Place, and yet so far removed from her; from this it was only a step, in her bored and restless state of mind, to the idea that it would be perfectly possible for her to disguise herself, with Cilly's connivance, as one of the strawboys, and thus have at least a taste of the excitement of the wedding festivities. It was the sort of prank that Sir John, with his lack of appreciation of the conventions and niceties with which well-brought-up young girls were hobbled, would have had no objection to her planning when she had been half a dozen years younger.

It did not occur to her—or if it did, she put the thought wilfully from her mind—that she was no longer a twelve-year-old schoolgirl engaging in a lark, but a young lady whose dignity would be sadly compromised if she were to be discovered in such a masquerade.

Cilly was by no means an obstacle to her plans. Indeed, she fell in with them with the greatest enthusiasm, promising to procure the proper "strawboy" attire for her and to ensure her acceptance in the company by taking into her confidence her youngest brother, who was to be one of the strawing party.

"He can give out ye're a cousin of ours from Kilgarvan," she said. "He's a shy lad, that niver has two words to say for himself, and sure ye needn't open your mouth at all if ye've no mind to, miss. Oh, it'll be rare fun! I doubt I'll be able to keep from laughing when you walk in with the others!"

"Well, you must not laugh," Georgina warned her sternly, "for if you do everyone will wonder why, and I wouldn't for the world have anyone know of it but you and Tim."

She found that she was growing a little uncomfortable over the escapade already, as Cilly's inventiveness cleared away all the obstacles to it that had seemed to her to exist when she had first broached the matter. But she was too proud to admit this to Cilly, and when she returned to the house she was fully committed to the masquerade.

She had no difficulty, on the following evening, in finding her straw disguise in the spinney where Cilly had promised to leave it, but donning the stiffly pleated cape and skirt so that they perfectly covered her own clothing took some time, and she had only just completed the task to her satisfaction when she heard footsteps in the little wood. It was Cilly's brother Tim, a boy of fifteen, come to fetch her along to the others. He showed her how to pull the tall, pointed straw cap down over her head so that her golden curls and even her face were quite concealed, using a bare minimum of words to convey his instructions, for he seemed to be quite tonguetied at the idea of a young lady's joining in their merrymaking. Georgina was obliged to repeat each question at least twice before she could elicit a response from him, and almost found herself in a fit of giggles at the contrast between the tall, ungainly figure before her, in its stiff straw costume, and the choked adolescent utterances that proceeded from it.

But at last all was arranged to her satisfaction, and the two set off together toward the lane where they were to join the other strawboys.

They soon came in view of them, some fifteen strong. Georgina felt her resolution failing a little as she was confronted with all this exuberant youthful masculinity, even concealed as she was in her straw disguise, but she suffered herself to be introduced as young Master Lynch's cousin and then marched off beside him at the tail of the ranks that were immediately formed. Fortunately the wedding house was around the next turn in the lane. As the whole company was occupied, in the interval before their arrival, in receiving their captain's instructions as to what they were to do when they arrived there, no severe strain was placed on Georgina's anonymity.

The sounds of music and laughter came to her ears as they approached the cottage, and through the open half-door she could see a fiddler leaning against the wall in the kitchen, his bow flying as he played a gay reel for a throng of dancers. The set was broken up, however, as the strawboys entered, and the guests all came crowding up to see the grotesque visitors. Georgina found herself forgetting her apprehensions as she saw that her disguise indeed seemed to be impenetrable, and for the first time began to be glad that she had come. The cheerful cottage, with its newly whitewashed walls, its jovial company, all dressed in their best, and its welcoming aroma of raisin-cakes and succulent roast pig, appeared especially inviting to her after the jumbled disorder and severe isolation she had been enduring at The Place, and she made up her mind to enjoy the evening.

She stood in the ranks of the strawboys as they sang for the entertainment of the company, not venturing to join in herself, but very well pleased to be where she was. She had been relieved, as they had approached the cottage, to learn that only four of the strawing company had been singled out to take part in the dancing, and that her role would be only that of mingling silently with the guests, nodding her head in grave response to their most outrageous guesses as to her identity, and eluding their attempts to make her betray herself by an incautious word. She saw Cilly standing beside the bride, hiding her giggles behind her hand and looking from one to another of the strawboys as she attempted to decide which one of them was Georgina.

Suddenly, however, in the midst of the cheers and the hubbub as the reel came to an end, her heart gave a jump of apprehension. A new guest had entered the house, someone whose presence caused an immediate hum of interest among the company and an abrupt fall in the merriment. From her position beside the dresser she herself had an excellent view of the door, and her first impulse, on seeing Shannon's tall figure entering it, was to flee—but, of course, this was quite impossible. She must remain where she was and only hope with the greatest fervour that the disguise which had thus far protected her from discovery would see her through this further test.

Shrinking back against the wall, she watched with trepidation as Shannon offered his felicitations to the bride and groom. He seemed quite at ease among his new tenants, she noted, and they, too, after their first surprise at his appearing among them, soon overcame their shyness and crowded around him, full of pleasure, it seemed, at the compliment he was paying them. In her own severe disapproval of him, she would not have been astonished to find that he had already been taken in dislike by his tenants, but it appeared that exactly the opposite was the case. He knew almost every one of them by name, and though she found much to reinforce her own opinion of his arrogance in the calm, rather aloof manner with which he dealt with them, apparently they considered this as only proper to his position.

How he had wrought all this approval for himself she was puzzled to know. She did recall, however, Sir John's having remarked to her once that no landlord who knew to a T what he was about and who made it his business to see that his tenants were given every opportunity to make the best of their land would ever run into difficulties with them. She was loth to admit it, but it did seem to her, from the tone of the conversation she heard about her now, that these were the tactics Shannon had used to cause himself to be accepted so promptly by his tenants. No doubt most of them, like Dansel Lynch, had been sorry to see the land go from the Powers, and apprehensive as to the intentions of the new master—but it seemed equally probable that, once they had seen that those intentions were meant for their benefit as well as his own, they were quite willing to be rid of the inexpert regime under which they had laboured ever since Declan Power's death.

Georgina's reflections to this purpose were both hurried and distracted, however, as she was in mortal fear of discovery and occupied in casting about desperately in her mind for some way to escape from Shannon's presence. She thought once, as he accepted the foaming glass of porter that was offered to him in which to drink the newly married pair's health, that his quick grey eyes had singled her out from the strawboy company for a moment's hard inspection, but the next instant he had turned away and she could thankfully breathe again.

All this while she had been keeping her eye on the door, and when the host escorted Shannon into "the room," where the wedding supper had been set out, she saw her opportunity and, under cover of the general move of the company to follow Shannon, edged toward the half-door and slipped through it. Once outside, she breathed a sigh of relief and set off as rapidly as she was able, in her clumsy costume, down the lane. She did not dare remove the straw disguise so close to the cottage, and intended to wait to do so until she had reached the spinney where she had donned it.

She was still some yards short of it, however, when she became aware of the sound of a horse's hooves behind her. The next moment, before she had had time to do more than glance hastily about and see that it was a gig that was bearing down on her, she heard Shannon's voice imperatively calling her name.

"Wait just a moment, Miss Power," he said, drawing up beside her, as she halted in the lane in complete confusion, and speaking in a perfectly matter-of-fact way, as if she had been standing before him clad in the ordinary costume of a well-bred young lady, instead of in her grotesque straw attire. "You have some distance to go to reach the house, and I believe it is coming on to rain. If you will mount up beside me, I shall be happy to drive you home."

His calm certainty that he was correct in his assumption that it was really Miss Power he was addressing for some reason infuriated her to the point that her wrath overcame even her mortification at having been discovered.

"How did you know who I was?" she demanded. "No one else did!"

"I shouldn't be too certain of that, if I were you," he said dryly. "These people have a great deal of tact, Miss Power, and if they were to observe a strawboy wearing footwear of a sort that assuredly is not common among country lads, they would not necessarily take it on themselves to embarrass him—or her—by calling attention to the fact."

She instinctively looked down at the tips of the soft blue slippers peeping from beneath her straw skirt and hastily drew them back into hiding.

"I am afraid it is rather late for that now," Shannon remarked, observing the movement. "As a matter of fact, if I may suggest it, it may be as well for you to remove your entire disguise now, before you attempt to mount up here beside me. My horse, as you can see, seems to have taken it into considerable aversion."

She could only admire the way in which he was controlling, with a seeming lack of effort, the spirited attempts of the young grey he was driving to escape from the vicinity of the startling object she presented. But the admiration did not mollify her wrath, and she replied mulishly, "I have no intention of mounting up beside you, Mr. Shannon. I shall walk home."

"I beg to differ with you, Miss Power. You will do nothing of the kind," he said incisively. "If you have so little sense of the impropriety of a young lady's wandering about alone at night, in or out of disguise, let me assure you that I do not share your lack of concern over the picture you present."

She could not see his face well in the darkness, but she could quite fancy she knew the sort of indifferently arrogant expression it wore. She felt that she was losing her temper completely, in the unfortunate way she had when she had been backed into a corner and knew she was entirely in the wrong, and only with the greatest effort managed to say with reasonable quietness, "How I conduct myself is not in the least your affair, Mr. Shannon. I consider your remarks very intrusive."

"Yes, they are—damned intrusive," he said bluntly. "But there would be no need for me to have made them if you weren't displaying a want of conduct that would make a hoyden blush! As for making it my affair—you are living beneath my roof, Miss Power, and while you are doing so I must demand that you refrain from making yourself the subject of gossip! Once you have removed to Craythorne you may go your length in any folly that pleases you, but while you are in my house you will behave like a lady. Now remove that ridiculous costume and get up here beside me. I have no mind to enter into any more arguments."

She had the satisfaction of gathering, from a sterner note in these last words, that she had succeeded in making him angry as well, but at the same time she also discovered, somewhat to her surprise, that she had no wish to test that anger further. Hastily, with mutinous fingers, she divested herself of her straw costume and, grasping the hand he reached down to her, mounted into the gig.

Once seated beside him, it had been her intention to maintain a frigid silence until they reached The Place, but the urge to justify herself was too strong, and before the gig had proceeded a dozen yards down the lane she found herself saying warmly, "There is no need for you to say such things to me! I had as much right as you to go to the wedding."

"You had a right to go as Miss Power, if you went properly escorted and for the proper reason, not to make a May-game of yourself," he said brusquely. "But you don't need me to teach you manners, my girl."

"No, I don't! And I'll thank you not to try!"

She stifled a sob of pure vexation at having been caught out by Shannon, of all people. Of course she could not defend herself against his merciless logic; she knew as well as he did that she had been entirely in the wrong. She sat rigidly beside him, feeling every moment that passed to be as long as an hour, and wishing fervently that he would put his horse to a faster pace so that they would reach the house sooner.

The only palliative possible for her miserable state was the suspicion that at least she had made him as angry as she was—but even this consolation was snatched from her when he remarked abruptly, after a silence of several minutes, "I expect the trouble is that you've been devilish bored. Young Quinlevan says you ride well. Why don't you work out some of your energy in that way, instead of haring off into a childish prank like this?"

She did not know whether to be more astonished at this revelation that he understood her predicament or offended by his continuing to make her conduct his own affair. Between the two emotions, she managed to say quellingly, "No, thank you! If you had ever had the misfortune to try one of my cousins' horses—!"

"I am not speaking of them. I mean my own. I don't consider Juno suitable for a lady, but there is a very good-looking chestnut hack Hanger brought in this morning from Kenmare that should carry you to perfection."

Her colour rose; taken aback, she could only say, "But I can't—! I couldn't—!"

"Why not?" he asked. "Don't you think you could handle him?"

"Of course that is not it! It is only—I don't care to accept favours from you, Mr. Shannon!"

He laughed shortly. "I'm aware that a few hours' loan of a horse is a very small recompence for having pushed you out of the way of inheriting a fortune, Miss Power," he said. "But still I don't believe you should reject the offer, if it will keep you from entering into any more such crack-brained starts as you have indulged in tonight."

She stared at him in astonishment. It had never crossed her mind that he believed that the incivility with which she had treated him since his arrival at The Place had been the result of her resentment at his having stepped between her and her cousin Nuala's fortune, and the mere idea that he suspected her of such a motive was enough to cause her to flush up hotly with indignation and confusion.

"But that's not—! I never thought—!" she stammered.

"Never thought what, Miss Power?"

"That I— That you— I never expected to inherit The Place; I never gave such an idea a thought!"

She could see him turn his head to look at her incredulously through the darkness.

"Do you expect me to believe that," his caustic voice demanded, "when you've been cutting me up ever since I stepped into the house?"

"But that was only because—" She halted abruptly, feeling quite unable to explain to him that it was his own arrogance, rather than any monetary considerations, that had caused her to take him in such instant dislike. She sent him a quick sidelong glance, almost an appeal to him to smooth the situation over with some innocuous remark, but he showed no disposition to make matters easier for her.

"Because—?" he repeated ruthlessly. "Yes, Miss Power? I am waiting."

Her temper flared again. "Because you were rude, and overbearing, and inclined to consider no one but yourself!" she finished her sentence baldly. "And that is the plain truth, Mr. Shannon! You may believe it or not, but I never had an idea of inheriting The Place, and if you think I am such an odious creature as to take someone in dislike merely because I am covetous of his good fortune—"

Shannon inclined his head rather ironically. "I accept your condemnation of my manners, Miss Power," he said, "but don't you think you are taking something too much for granted when you speak of my wife's death as my 'good fortune'? That is a subject on which I believe you are hardly qualified to speak with authority."

"I didn't mean— That was not what I meant to imply," she began defensively. "I *don't* know about that—and if you are grieved for her death it was very uncharitable of me—" He said nothing to help her out, and she went on finally, rather hotly, "You have put me in the wrong, but that doesn't alter matters. You *have* been detestably rude, and I won't take that back."

"I see no need for you to do so," he said, with his usual maddening composure. "On the other hand, I also see no need for you to decline my offer of the use of one of my horses for a few hours a day merely because you find my manners leave a great deal to be desired. If it will make you more inclined to do so, I will inform you that my motives in making the offer are purely selfish. As I have told you, it doesn't suit me to have you careering about the countryside like a rag-mannered brat while you are living under my roof."

She was silent from sheer vexation. The worst part of the situation was that she was longing to accept his offer, and that he seemed quite aware of this, for after a moment he went on, in an amused tone, "Pride has its drawbacks, has it not, Miss Power? Brandon tells me that you are as clipping a rider as any girl he has ever seen, so I can't think you prefer to go rambling about on foot to being mounted on a prime hack. However, if you really wish to carry your disapproval of me so far as to object to being indebted to me for the smallest favour—"

"I *don't* wish to carry it so far, but I shall," she said darkly. "No doubt it will be good for me, at any rate. Grandmama says one always derives a great deal of moral advantage from putting one's duty before one's inclinations."

"The question is," Shannon said, still with a note of amusement in his voice, "would she consider it your duty to snub me?"

"Yes, she would!" Georgina declared instantly. "Good gracious, if she could see me now—!" She broke off, daunted again by the road into which her imprudent tongue was leading her. "Not that I at all agree with her ideas on *that* point," she said hastily, in a severely judicious tone. "What I mean is—*she* does not know you, or anything about you except that you married Nuala, so she had no grounds on which to judge you."

"You, on the other hand," he said, with perfect gravity, "had the advantage of at least thirty seconds of observation before you made up *your* mind."

"I didn't!" she objected hotly. "It was a great deal longer!"

"On the contrary, I have probably overestimated the time. The expression on your face when I walked into the book-room—"

"I was upset over my cousin's accident! Of course I did not appear cordial!" She broke off, shrugging her shoulders. "Besides, I am sure it did not signify to you how I looked. You had already made up your mind to be disagreeable; you had not been *five* seconds in the room before I knew that."

"We may cry quits then," he said. "But I still do not see why you refuse to try the horse. *That* is mere obstinacy."

As obstinacy was one fault for which not only Lady Mercer, but also Sir John, had frequently rebuked her, she was unable to defend herself with conviction against this charge. At any rate, she found that she did not particularly wish to do so; the more she considered the sacrifice to which her pride was committing her, the more strongly it occurred to her that, in rejecting Shannon's offer, she was, in the old nursery phrase, cutting off her nose to spite her face.

She said cautiously, as the windows of The Place came in sight, "Well, as to that—perhaps you are right. And I daresay the horse *will* want exercising."

"Not a doubt of it," he agreed, in a matter-of-fact voice that won her approbation, as it contained no hint whatever of triumph in it. He brought the gig up the carriage-sweep and halted it before the front door, looking down at her then with a glint of rather sardonic amusement, she thought, again in his eyes. "I won't see you inside," he said. "After all, it would never do to let the servants know that you have been driving with me."

"I was *not* driving with you!" she said, with dignity. "You merely insisted on taking me up, when I would much rather have walked. That is another matter altogether."

"So it is," he said. The amusement disappeared and he said indifferently, "At any rate, it will do your credit no good to be seen in my company, so I shall bid you good night, Miss Power. I'll give instructions to Hanger to have the new chestnut ready for you in the morning."

She thought with still-smouldering indignation, as she mounted the steps to the front door, that he was taking a good deal on himself, as she had not actually agreed to accept the loan of his horse. But she was too much occupied during the next few minutes in coping with the obvious astonishment of Higgins, who opened the door to her, and of Brandon, who came walking out of the book-room, at seeing her come in alone at that hour of the night to have the leisure to think of such matters. Higgins' astonishment was modestly confined to an expression of lively curiosity, but Brandon was not so reticent, and he demanded directly to know where she had been.

"Nowhere! That is—for a walk. It is not your business, Brandon!" she said with some asperity.

She walked directly up the stairs, meaning to go to her bedchamber, but she found that Brandon was following her, and at the head of the stairs she stopped and turned around. He said at once, as he climbed the remaining steps, "Not my business! Well, I should think it was *somebody's* then, if you mean to go wandering about alone at this hour! What is the *matter* with you, Georgie? You've been out of reason cross ever since Shannon arrived here, and now you take to slipping out at night—"

"I didn't *slip!*" Georgina said indignantly. "I walked. And I'm tired now, and I'm going to bed. Much you care what I do, at any rate! As far as you are concerned, I might as well not have existed this past week!"

She walked into her bedchamber and closed the door in his face, feeling some satisfaction at having given him, at least, a heavy set-down. The next instant she had grace enough to regret her action, as she was sufficiently honest to admit to herself that what he had been obliged to receive from her should properly have been Shannon's portion. She was not enough in charity with her cousin either, however, to feel much compunction over what she had done, only promising herself to make matters right with him on the morrow.

7 She rose early in the morning, hoping to see her cousin before he should have gone out with Shannon, but, on inquiring for him when she went downstairs, she was told that both he and Shannon had already gone round to the stables. She felt both disappointed and relieved, as making apologies was not one of her strong suits, and sat down to eat her breakfast with only one pressing matter on her mind—whether or not she would take Shannon at his word and try his new horse that morning.

The view from the breakfast-parlour windows eventually decided that question for her by presenting her with the sight of a perfect spring morning, dew-drenched after a night's gentle rain. The idea of sitting in the house on such a day weighted the scales so decisively in favour of a morning ride that, after a dutiful visit to Mrs. Quinlevan's bedchamber, she went immediately to her own room and donned her riding-habit. She had prudently failed to mention her intentions to her cousin, not so much from the fear that she would disapprove of her accepting Shannon's offer —for it had long been a maxim of Mrs. Quinlevan's never to look either a figurative or a literal gift horse in the mouth—but because of her own embarrassment over being required to explain how he had come to make it.

When she repaired to the stables Shannon's groom, Hanger, at once led out a good-looking chestnut and proceeded to put a lady's saddle on it. This was cool enough, Georgina thought, with mild indignation—as if Shannon had quite taken it for granted that she would wish to ride that morning—but when Hanger brought out one of the greys and saddled it as well before helping her up on her own mount, the indignation turned to resolution.

"You are not thinking of coming with me, surely?" she said. "Where is Grady?"

"Begging your pardon, miss, he's off on an errand for the mistress."

Hanger was a rather slightly built Scotsman, of an age that might have been nearer fifty than forty, as wiry as a whip, and with a dark, pockmarked face which one of the maids had declared in Georgina's hearing to be "enough to fright a babe out of its cradle." He said nothing further now, as if he believed sufficient explanation had been given of his intention to accompany her, but Georgina, when he came round to help her up on her mount, stood looking at him obstinately.

"There is no need for you to go with me," she said. "I am quite accustomed to riding without a groom."

Hanger's dark face remained impassive. "Master's orders, miss," he said briefly.

"Well, he may be *your* master, but he is certainly not *mine*," Georgina said, firing up. "I shall *not* need you, Hanger."

He said nothing, but merely tossed her up on the chestnut. The next moment, however, as she gathered the reins and set the horse into a walk, she heard telltale sounds behind her, and turned to see that Hanger had already swung himself up into his own saddle in preparation to follow her.

There was nothing else for it; she could not engage in a dispute with him under the eyes of gaping stable-boys. With an inward vow to say not a word to him or to indicate by so much as a turn of her head that she was aware of his presence, she set the chestnut into a smart trot and then, as she left the house behind, loosened the reins and cantered off briskly.

She had not been on a horse since she had come to Ireland, with the exception of her single doleful excursion on Brandon's cob, and soon the combination of a high-bred mount and a fine morning did much to improve her humour. Spring was in full blossom now; everywhere she looked great bushes of English furze, the branches of which were much used as firewood by the country people, were showing their rich yellow bloom, and purple violets and bluebells sprang in the coverts beside every hedge. She let the chestnut go into a long, intoxicating gallop, which apparently suited his idea of the proper use of such a morning as well as it did her own, and when she reined him in at last was so much in charity with the world that she could even look around with a smile for Hanger, to see if he was still following her.

He was close behind and, pulling up his grey to walk sedately beside her, said with dour approval, "You handle him to perfection, miss. I told the master he'd make a sweet goer, but I wasn't thinking at the time of him carrying a lady."

"He is a darling," Georgina agreed enthusiastically, reaching out to stroke the chestnut's mane.

"A bit more horse than you need, miss, but that never daunted you."

She laughed at his respectful tone and said, "I expect Mr. Shannon thought I might be 'daunted,' and that was why he insisted you go with me?"

He grinned briefly, but did not deny the charge.

She let her curiosity get the better of her and inquired, "Have you been with him long, Hanger? You're not from these parts, evidently?"

"Oh, no, miss. I was in Lord Cartan's service for twenty years, and I've known the master for that long too. I set him on his first pony, if you'll know the truth."

He spoke with some pride and she realised, with the same surprise she had felt when she had witnessed Shannon's reception by his tenants the night before, that this man, too, held his employer in respect, if not in downright affection. It made her still more uncertain of her own judgment of him, for she had been taught by Sir John to realise that a man who could make himself respected by those who must serve him could not be without valuable qualities of character.

It would have suited her far better to learn that Hanger considered his employer as arrogant and disagreeable as he appeared to her; but she was fair-minded enough to consider it probable that her own judgment of Shannon was biassed, rather than that of someone who had been as intimately acquainted with him as Hanger had been. She rode back to the house in a rather thoughtful mood.

Shannon, as usual, did not appear at luncheon, but Brandon was there, apparently already acquainted with the fact that she had ridden Shannon's horse that morning.

"You were a gudgeon not to have asked him to mount you sooner," he said frankly. "I told him you were quite up even to handling Juno."

"I did *not* ask him for the loan of his horse!" Georgina exclaimed, her cheeks flying scarlet in a moment. "How can you suppose me to have so much brass?—when I sit there evening after evening at the dinner table, never saying a word to him—"

"Oh—that!" Brandon said kindly. "I daresay he only thinks you are rather shy."

"He knows quite well I am not!" Georgina said darkly, attacking the galantine accompanying the game pie and fruit that had been set before them, and acknowledging for the twentieth time how much the meals in the house had improved since Shannon had come into it. "*He* made me the offer."

"Well, it is handsome of him to let a girl handle his cattle; you'll admit that, at any rate," Brandon said. "Not that I hadn't told him you were up to anything, for I don't expect he'd have cared to chance it if I hadn't." He helped himself to the game pie and went on, "He has his eye out for a couple of hunters now, and I told him I'd bring him over to Hauld Hall tomorrow; Sir Landers has a slapping five-year-old there that ain't quite up to his weight. Do you know Sir Landers Hession? I daresay you don't—nor Lady Hession neither, for she and Mama don't deal above half. Devilish high sticklers, both she and Sir Landers, but you can't deny that he knows good horseflesh."

Georgina did not attend very closely to this speech; she was too much occupied with the vexing problem, which had suddenly arisen in her mind, of how she was to behave toward Shannon at dinner that evening. She could not very well snub him as she was used to, after she had accepted the loan of his horse, but the idea of presenting him with an appearance of complaisant gratitude, in the circumstances under which she had accepted his offer, was hardly to be thought of, either.

She carried the problem around with her all afternoon, and the result was that by the time the dinner hour had arrived she had fretted herself into a state of indecision which for some reason required her to don one of her most becoming dresses—a primrose muslin with a narrow skirt and a bodice trimmed with rows of ruching—before she came downstairs.

She found Shannon and her cousin awaiting her appearance to enter the dining-room, and as she passed before the former through the doorway she gave him a tentative, "Good evening." He replied at once in kind, but something in the look in his eyes as he did so gave her an uncomfortable remembrance of the rather sardonic gleam she had caught there the night before, and instantly her hackles went up.

She sat down at the table with an uncompromising gravity of manner, the formal words of thanks that she had been rehearsing all afternoon dying on her lips. She consoled herself with the consideration that it would be more natural to wait until some turn in the conversation afforded her a logical opening before she uttered them, and determined to sink into the background for the time being—a resolution that was immediately thwarted, however, by Brandon's remarking in surprise on her elegant appearance.

"Lord, you are fine enough for a ball!" he said frankly. "I will say it becomes you, but you had better not waste all that on Shannon and me. Wait until we are fixed at Craythorne, and then you'll have plenty of opportunity to parade your duds."

"I am not *parading* anything!" Georgina said, giving him a look of wrathful reproach. "And—I am extremely sorry if you feel my frock is inappropriate."

"Not inappropriate. It's just that we ain't used to seeing you look all the crack like that," Brandon explained, attacking the raised mutton pie which the cook had provided along with a baked carp and a dish of French beans.

Georgina gave him a damping look, which he quite disregarded. She then glanced up to find Shannon's eyes regarding her across the table with a faint, rather disconcerting smile, and her composure deserted her entirely.

"I expect you are waiting for me to thank you for the loan of your horse this morning," she said, blurting the words out, to her own vexation, in the most graceless manner possible.

The look of amusement deepened for a moment on Shannon's face, and then disappeared as he remarked in his usual manner that he trusted she had had an agreeable ride.

"It would have been more agreeable if you had not instructed Hanger that he must come with me," she said. "I wish you will tell him that he needn't do so tomorrow."

"If you will take Grady with you, or one of Mrs. Quinlevan's grooms, he will need no telling," Shannon said.

"Yes, but even if I do not," Georgina persisted, "there is no need for him to go."

"There I beg to differ with you," Shannon said calmly. "Do young ladies in Herefordshire make it a habit to ride about the countryside unattended?"

She was about to say that whether they did or did not was hardly his affair, but, remembering her escapade of the night before and the setdown he had given her then, she swallowed down the retort.

"I expect the thing of it is that you are afraid I cannot manage the chestnut," she said instead, mutinously.

He raised his eyes to her face. "Not at all," he said. "Hanger tells me he has the greatest admiration for your skill. That, however, has nothing to do with the matter of your riding alone."

Brandon intervened at this point to say innocently that, if she found it a bore to ride with only a groom, she might accompany him and Shannon to Hauld Hall in the morning to look at Sir Landers' five-year-old—a remark that elicited only a firm, "No, thank you!" from her. If Brandon was such a nodcock as to believe that her jauntering about the countryside with Shannon, with only himself as chaperon, would not do more to rouse the neighbourhood gabblemongers than her riding alone, she was not.

The subject fell there, but the next morning, when she watched her cousin and Shannon ride off together while she set out alone under Grady's sedate charge, she could not help rather regretting her severe adherence to the proprieties, for it would have suited her much better to go along with them to Hauld Hall to see Sir Landers' horse. The invitation had not been repeated, however, so she cantered off with Grady, and soon recovered her good humour in her pleasure in her favourite exercise.

She returned to The Place some time before the luncheon hour, and was surprised to see Brandon's cob already back in the stables. When she walked into the house Brandon himself came out to meet her, and she saw that he looked flushed and angry, quite unlike himself.

"Oh! I thought it might have been Shannon," he said abruptly, as his eyes fell on her, and without further ado he turned on his heel and limped back into the book-room.

Georgina followed him. "Whatever is the matter?" she demanded. "Have you quarrelled with him? Is that it?"

"No, of course not!" Brandon said. He turned about to face her, his eyes resting on her face with a look almost of animosity in them. "The truth is —and I expect you will be deuced glad to hear it!—that the Hessions were thundering rude to him," he said. "I mean to say—well, there was no bearing it, Georgie! Sir Landers had put it all about the neighbourhood that he was looking for a buyer for that horse, and why he should set himself up now with the idea that dealing with Shannon is beneath his touch—!"

Georgina stared at him, frowning slightly. "Do you mean he wouldn't even let him see the horse?" she asked.

"Oh, he let him see it, right enough!" Brandon replied, the angry colour still high in his face. "He could hardly do otherwise, when I had brought him. But he made it as plain as a pikestaff that he wanted no part of any acquaintance with him—and then, to make it worse, as we were leaving we were obliged to pass that wretched woman's landaulet—"

"*What* wretched woman?"

"Lady Hession, of course! She was driving out with her two eldest girls, and I did not know *what* to do, after the snubbing Sir Landers had given Shannon—whether to introduce him or not, I mean. But I thought it might look as if *I* was ashamed of being seen with him if I did not, so I did. And that harpy cast her chin up in the air, and gave a glance at her daughters as if she dared them so much as to *look* at Shannon, and ordered her coachman to drive on! I could have run her through!" he concluded, his eyes blazing with reminiscent fury.

Georgina sank down into a chair. She was astonished to find that, far from feeling satisfaction at the set-down Shannon had received, something of Brandon's sharply expressed anger was stirring as well in her own breast. It was one thing, it seemed, for her to cross swords with their host, and quite another for her to hear that some odious female had cut him so rudely.

She awakened from her surprise to find Brandon repeating, "I expect *you* will say it was just what he deserved"—and broke in to contradict him warmly.

"I don't say anything of the sort! It was intolerably unkind of her! After all, he has done nothing to offend *her*."

"Well, I don't know that he had done anything to offend *you*, either, before you took to ripping up at him," Brandon said bluntly, "so you needn't give yourself any points over Lady Hession. I don't understand women, I must say—making such a kick-up before they have time to know *what* a fellow is like. Not that Sir Landers wasn't almost as bad."

Georgina said uncomfortably, "I suppose I may have been unjust to him, but you will admit that he has been at least as rude to me as I have been to him! But *this* is another matter altogether. He will have to live among these people, you know, and if this is a sample of the treatment he may expect, it will certainly be excessively uncomfortable for him."

Brandon stared at her. "You are not going to tell me *you* intend to stand on his side now!" he said disbelievingly. "After the things you have said of him—!"

Georgina shrugged, colouring up slightly in her turn. "It is no such thing," she said, with asperity. "Only I can quite see that that stupid woman was shockingly at fault; she might at least have been civil to him. After all, he is not going to eat her precious daughters!"

Brandon, finding his indignation shared, relaxed enough to emit a slight chuckle at this, and owned that Lady Hession might indeed have been thinking of Nuala.

"Yes, that is all very well," Georgina said severely, "but she cannot be so idiotish as to expect that he will be going about the countryside throwing out lures to every stray young woman who happens to come under his eye. If he *did* marry Nuala only for her fortune—which is the worst thing that one can say of him—it is quite clear that he has got it in his hands now and needn't be looking about him for a *second* heiress."

"Deuced little he'd get from any of the Hession girls, at any rate," Brandon said. "There are five of 'em, and, although Peter will come into a very pretty property when he succeeds, Sir Landers is much too fond of good living and good horses to be able to come down handsomely for all those girls when they marry."

"How did Shannon take it?" Georgina demanded. "I expect he did not look cast-down before those people?"

"Oh, Lord, no!" Brandon said. "You know his style—as cool as ice water. If Sir Landers thought *he* was giving the snubbing, he caught one, too, I can tell you! All the same, it's a plaguey awkward business. I don't mean just the Hessions, for they always have been devilish high in the instep, but if people like the Motts and the Malladons mean to act in the same way, I can't think Shannon will have at all a comfortable time of it here. And I *like* him, Georgie; he's a great gun, you know, and it must be a dead bore to him to have me trailing around after him all the time, but he never makes me feel I'm in the way."

Georgina, looking into her cousin's flushed, unhappy face, had a rather guilty realisation of the fact that she had scarcely spent a moment's reflection on Brandon's point of view in all this. It could not be often, she told herself, that he found someone willing to overlook his handicap and give him the time and patience necessary to allow him to participate in the normal activities she herself took so much for granted. Whatever Shannon's motives had been, it had to be admitted that he had done so, and Brandon's distress at the thought that the hostility of the neighbourhood might cause him to lose the company of his new friend became quite understandable to her when viewed in such a light.

She carried her thoughtfulness over the matter upstairs with her later that day, when she went to pay her usual afternoon visit to Mrs. Quinlevan's bedchamber. She found her cousin sitting up in bed in high good humour, inspecting the new French lace cap she was wearing in her glass and making plans for an immediate removal to Craythorne.

"Only think, my love," she said, when Georgina entered the room, "Mrs. Hopkins says the house is quite settled now and ready to receive us! And Dr. Culreavy assured me this afternoon that I shall take no harm at all from the journey if the weather holds fine and Grady is careful to walk the horses. I vow I have never been so pleased at anything in my life, for I have quite fretted myself into the vapours time and again over the idea of our remaining here in this house with that dreadful man."

"Well, as to that, I cannot see that it should have distressed you so very greatly, as you were never obliged yourself so much as to set eyes on him," Georgina said, with more candour than diplomacy. "And I must tell you, Cousin, that he has been excessively kind to Brandon."

"To Brandon!" Mrs. Quinlevan turned a startled glance on her. "Why, my love, whatever can you mean? I am sure, if Brandon has been civil to him, it is more than he deserves, but I cannot see that, except for his being properly grateful for any attention Brandon may have shown him, there is any recompence he can have made the boy."

She went back to a further critical consideration of her cap, but Georgina, finding to her own surprise that she was a trifle indignant over this summary dismissal of Shannon's claims to consideration, went on, "Surely, ma'am, you are aware that we all, to an extent, owe Mr. Shannon our gratitude, for it is only because of his management that the household has not fallen into chaos while you have been laid up. As for Brandon, he has been kindness itself to him, I do assure you."

She broke off, finding her cousin staring at her with perturbation and incredulity written large on her face.

"'Our gratitude'—'kindness itself'!" Mrs. Quinlevan gasped. "My dear child, what *can* you be talking of? Here is this odious creature come to make us all miserable, and you speak as if he had done us a favour by settling himself here! I cannot understand what has come over you, unless"— and at this idea the perturbation on her face deepened to positive horror— "unless he has succeeded in coming round you as he did poor Nuala! But that would be *too* dreadful, indeed! You really cannot mean *that*, my love!"

"Nonsense!" Georgina said, smiling in spite of herself. "Of course he has done no such thing. It is only that I am coming to realise that we may have been overhasty in judging him. Naturally it was quite wrong of him to have married my cousin in that shabby fashion—but people *do* fall in love, you know, ma'am."

"But he was quite thirty years old at the time, my dear!" Mrs. Quinlevan protested, still in high agitation. "People have no right to fall in love at that age, and in my experience they very seldom do. Oh, dear! Where is my hartshorn? I made sure Nurse had left it on the table!"

"There is no need for you to fly into a taking, ma'am, only because I have said a word in Shannon's favour," Georgina said, beginning a search for the hartshorn while not knowing whether to feel more amused or astonished at the idea of her being cast in the role of Shannon's defender.

She found the bottle and handed it to her cousin, who, after fortifying herself with a teaspoon of its contents in a glass of water, declared that it was all very well for her to speak lightly of it, but indeed she could not know, at her age, the wiles with which unscrupulous rakes were accustomed to seduce their young victims. This picture of Shannon as an artful beau was too much for Georgina's gravity, especially when she recalled the rough exchanges that had taken place between them, and she was unable to prevent herself from laughing as she assured her cousin that she was quite certain Shannon had no designs upon her.

"Yes, but you cannot be *sure*, my love," Mrs. Quinlevan protested doubtfully.

On which Georgina remarked, with still greater amusement, "Good God, ma'am, I assure you he has no such thing in mind! If he bothers to waste a thought on me, it is only to consider me as a rag-mannered schoolgirl who wants *all* sense of proper conduct."

"Well, I am sure he has no need to think *that* of you," Mrs. Quinlevan said disapprovingly, "for you are as pretty-behaved a girl as I have ever set eyes on, and *that* I shall not scruple to tell your dear mama when next we meet."

Georgina, relieved to see that she appeared to be satisfied with her explanation, went off presently to her own chamber to change her dress for dinner. She came downstairs a little before the hour, and was just going into the book-room to see if Brandon might be there when the front door opened and Shannon walked into the hall. Looking into his face, she saw that it bore an expression of more than ordinary grimness upon it, which she at once attributed to his encounter with Sir Landers and Lady Hession that morning.

But she was surprised to read something else there as well, in the unguarded moment before he glanced up and saw her standing at the book-room door—a weariness that seemed quite out of keeping with the picture of total self-sufficiency his powerful figure always presented. With something of a shock she realised what the past few weeks must have been for him—the whole burden of a neglected estate suddenly thrust on him, days spent in the saddle or striding over rough fields, long conciliatory hours with obstinate or hostile tenants, with additional long hours spent at work over muddled accounts when the rest of the household was in bed. And all this without benefit of a comfortable house, or even a pleasant hour of relaxation with friends or family to look forward to.

She was conscious of feeling somewhat ashamed of herself: however disagreeable her own relations with him had been, she was fair enough to admit that the blame for this could be laid as much at her door as at his. A moment's uncomfortable realisation of what Sir John would have said of her behaviour came to her: the prudish scruples she had heard Lady Mercer express over the misfortune of Shannon's birth would have carried no weight whatever with him, and he would have considered her eagerness to take offence at her host's blunt manners intolerably missish.

All in all, it was in a chastened mood that she walked into the dining-room a little later. She even went so far as to attempt to begin a civil conversation on the good points of the new chestnut hack, but she was rewarded by no equally civil response from Shannon. He answered her curtly and went back to his dinner. The snub did nothing to increase Georgina's budding feelings of charity toward him, and she subsided into silence.

Brandon overbore the awkwardness of the moment by bringing up the subject of their removal to Craythorne.

"I expect that will be the last of my riding out with you," he said to Shannon, unhappily, "unless"—he went on, as inspiration struck him—"I were to give instructions to be roused early enough each morning so I could ride over here before you are ready to leave—"

Shannon glanced up at him briefly. "I shouldn't think that would serve," he said discouragingly. "In the first place, a five-mile ride back and forth, added to what you'd do with me, might be rather too much for you. To say nothing of the fact," he added, with the hint of a contemptuous downcurve of his lips, "that I doubt your mother will care to have you pursue my acquaintance, now that she is able to remove to her own house."

"My mother has nothing to say to it!" Brandon declared hotly.

The rather ugly look vanished from Shannon's face. "Oh, yes, she has," he said more mildly. "You are under age, you know, and she is your guardian. She does quite right to be concerned over the company you keep."

"I shan't come to any harm in *your* company," Brandon said mutinously, "and so I shall tell her."

Shannon shrugged. Georgina found herself growing angry with him once more for his cavalier dismissal of Brandon's suggestions, and then reflected that she might again be doing him an injustice. It was quite possible that, having been made to realise that morning the depth of the animosity in which he was held in the neighbourhood, he was taking this means of disengaging Brandon from the onus of his friendship.

At any rate, she thought, as she retired that night to her chamber, it would soon be no concern of hers. She would be at Craythorne on the morrow, and her forced association with Shannon at an end. It was odd, she thought, that this event, to which she had looked forward so eagerly, did not inspire her with any particular feeling of joy, now that it had actually come upon her.

8 Craythorne was a rather small, rosy-brick house built in the Wren style, with a hipped roof and dormer windows and a charming fanlighted doorway. Mrs. Quinlevan, Georgina knew, considered it a sad come-down from The Place, but for her own part she found its comfortable, low-pitched, chintz-hung rooms a great deal more cheerful than the grander but half-empty apartments in The Place, and was well pleased with the change.

Her approval extended as well to the alteration in their mode of living that set in immediately on their arrival at Craythorne. She had scarcely time to see her portmanteaux and bandboxes unpacked before a steady flow of company began to arrive at the house, and she had had half a dozen invitations tendered to her before twenty-four hours had gone by.

The first of these was from Lady Mott, who insisted on her joining a party of young people that had been got up for the assembly ball the very next evening. Georgina, though her upbringing had been of a sort to make her fonder of riding to hounds than of dancing, had no aversion to attiring herself in the lilac jaconet muslin, with its row on row of frills round the ankles, which her cousin Bella assured her would be suitable for the occasion. With the assistance of her cousin's maid, her wheat-gold hair was dressed high, with a single curl escaping to fall negligently over one shoulder; she wore blue sandals and long French kid gloves, and when Mrs. Quinlevan had seen her complete at all points, with a shawl of Albany gauze caught up over her elbows, she declared with pride that she was sure she would be quite the belle of the evening.

Georgina's expectations, tempered by the far more modest success she had had at Bath under the quelling aegis of one of Lady Mercer's friends, did not run so high, and she was agreeably surprised, on arriving at the assembly rooms, to find her hand solicited eagerly by the succession of gentlemen whom Lady Mott introduced to her. She made the acquaintance as well of several young ladies living in the neighbourhood—among them two of the five daughters of Sir Landers Hession, who were being chaperoned by their mama, a tall, Roman-nosed matron, in puce satin and a turban, who seemed so much aware of her condescension in gracing a provincial ball with her presence, when she was accustomed to spending the Season each year in London, that Georgina could well believe in the veracity of the scene Brandon had described of her meeting with Shannon at Hauld Hall.

In Lady Mott's barouche, on the way to the assembly rooms, Betsy Mott

had begged her assistance, in a hasty whisper, in a matter of vital importance, so that Georgina was not surprised when Betsy drew her into a
corner in an interval between dances and breathlessly requested her to accept the invitation of one Mr. Robert Darlington to lead her in to supper.

"He does not dare ask *me,* you see," she explained, "because Mama
would be sure to disapprove, but if he is with *you* she will have nothing to
say, and we can all be together quite comfortably."

Georgina was somewhat surprised to hear this, as she had already met
Mr. Darlington—a rather large, cherub-faced young gentleman who was
the heir, as Lady Mott had let fall to her, of a considerable property in the
neighbourhood. As a matter of fact, Lady Mott had even begged her, with
a chuckle, not to set her cap at him, of all the young men in the room, as
he had quite a *tendre* for her Betsy and she rather thought the two of
them would make a match of it in the end.

"Of course she is young still," she said comfortably, "and Sir
Humphrey doubts she knows her own mind well enough to fix her affections yet. But if the two of them continue to rub on together until the
New Year, I believe we may well see a wedding at Mott House next
spring."

Georgina had assured her, with a smile, that she would make every
effort not to disturb so promising an arrangement, even if—which she
greatly doubted—it were in her power to do so. The situation standing
thus, she could not help being astonished by the earnest application for
her assistance that Betsy made to her later, until she reflected that Miss
Mott, having received her notions of romance from lending-library novels,
was probably merely attempting to invest her own placid love affair with
the tribulations always encountered by their heroines.

At any rate, she herself had as yet seen no young man that evening to
make her regret the necessity of going to supper with Mr. Darlington, and
she accordingly accepted his rather blushing application to her with great
complaisance.

"I expect Betsy—Miss Mott—has been talking to you," he confided to
her, as he escorted her into the supper-room. "I think it's gammon, but
she's persuaded that Lady Mott don't like it above half if I act any way
particular toward her. It won't do for her saying the same about Sir
Humphrey, though, for he told me himself, the last time we hunted together, that I was well up to anything, and I don't think he would have
said that if he didn't like me—do you?"

Georgina said gravely that she was sure he would not, and contrived with no difficulty to hand him over to Betsy as soon as they had sat down, contenting herself with the conversation of the handsome young man, a few years older than herself, who had led Betsy into the supper-room. She found him agreeable enough company at first, until she learned that he was none other than Peter Hession, Sir Landers' son and heir. *Then* she suddenly discovered that his manner, which seemed to show a great deal more of town-bronze than that of most of his contemporaries at the ball, was self-consequential rather than easy, and that his very long-tailed blue coat, amazingly striped waistcoat of watered silk, and neckcloth arranged in all the intricacies of the *Trône d'Amour,* betrayed not the gentleman of fashion, but the dandy.

It was therefore a relief to her when Lady Eliza Malladon, coming into the supper-room presently, sat down beside her and engaged her in conversation, after sending the young man who had escorted her into the room off to fill a plate for her from the array of creams and Chantillies that had been set out for the guests. Lady Eliza was very smart for a country ball in a gown of celestial blue crape cut low over the bosom, and a headdress supporting a plume of curled feathers. After inquiring for Mrs. Quinlevan, she at once declared that Georgina must come to drink tea with her at Stokings before the week was out.

"We shall have a comfortable coze and get to know each other much, much better," she said, her bold eyes roving over the room with a lack of attention to the person she was addressing that made the rather excessive cordiality of her manner seem somewhat less than convincing. "That is, we shall if I am able to take you away from the gentlemen," she said, "for you should know that Giles has an eye still for a well-favoured female, and tomorrow we are expecting a pair of his friends who, I am afraid, have the same sad failing. But you need not be discomposed by them, my love, for they are all far beyond the age of attracting a child of your years. Major Rothe and Sir Manning Hartily are bachelors, indeed, but I believe they are both past praying for."

Colonel Giles Malladon came up at this point and was presented to Georgina. She was astonished, in view of the character his wife had just given him, to find him a tall, ruddy gentleman who, she immediately guessed, would be a clipping rider to hounds and a man with few interests beyond his horses and his profession. She had met many such under her grandfather's roof, and could scarcely conceive how he and Lady Eliza went on together, Lady Eliza's interests appearing to lie exclusively in the world of fashion.

She soon discovered, however, that on Lady Eliza's side this difficulty was overcome by her completely ignoring her husband's wishes and pursuing her own way to the farthest extent possible without creating an absolute scandal, while Colonel Malladon, for his part, gave her her head for the sake of a peaceful life and built his own existence around quite different friends and occupations.

When he had gone off, Lady Eliza resumed her conversation with Georgina.

"So you are at last free of that abominable Shannon," she said to her. "Poor Bella! I declare I was never so sorry for anyone in my life as I was for her when I heard he had settled himself at The Place. I expect she is excessively glad to be at Craythorne now?"

Georgina said in an unencouraging voice that she believed she was, but the brevity of her reply did not lay the subject to rest, for Lady Eliza seemed determined to pursue it.

"I must say it surprised even *me*—and I know the creature's audacity," she said, with a tinkling laugh, "to learn that he had actually determined to stay at The Place while Bella was still occupying it. I wonder what his purpose was? Perhaps he thought if he forced the acquaintance Bella would be obliged to recognise him, which she had told me beforehand she had no intention whatever of doing."

Lady Mott gave it as her opinion, uncompromisingly, that the man was an adventurer, whose queer starts no person of breeding could be expected to predict. This brought an appreciative smile from Mr. Hession.

"Oh, indeed, ma'am, very well spoken!" he said. "But you have not heard his latest, perhaps? He had the audacity to present himself at Hauld Hall a few days ago, on the pretext of wishing to buy a horse from my father. You may believe that Sir Landers gave him a thundering set-down! It's my regret that I wasn't there to see it!"

Georgina said steadily, feeling the colour rise slightly in her face, "I fear you have the matter somewhat amiss, Mr. Hession. My cousin Brandon persuaded Mr. Shannon to accompany him to Hauld Hall in the belief that your father wished to sell a horse that Mr. Shannon might be interested in buying."

She checked, conscious that the entire company was staring at her, and that Mr. Hession, in particular, was regarding her with a rather superior smile.

"Oh, my dear Miss Power," he said, "I must say I think you are fair and far out there! I mean to say—it seems to me, a fellow with no acquaintance in the neighbourhood, and likely to have none, would be ready enough to pick up any pretext to fob himself off on people of substance."

"I am sorry to disagree with you," Georgina said, her flush mounting still higher under Lady Mott's disapproving frown, "but I believe I am in more of a position to know the true facts than you, Mr. Hession, and I am *quite* persuaded that Mr. Shannon would have visited a farmer's barn as readily as he went to Hauld Hall if he had believed he might find a horse suitable for his stables there."

Lady Mott said, "Really, my dear!" and Lady Eliza laughed and said it was quite apparent that Shannon had found a champion. This had the effect of taking the conversational ball away from Mr. Hession, which was as well, for the shock of hearing Hauld Hall compared to a barn seemed to have quite deprived him of speech for the moment.

"So he has come round you, too, you silly girl!" Lady Eliza said, shaking a finger smilingly at Georgina. "I always wondered how he managed it with Nuala, for we scarcely saw him save by the merest accident, and then he was *quite* uncivil to the lot of us, as if he considered us in the way of his precious sheep, or rye, or whatever it is they raise in Scotland. Lord Cartan was used to apologise for his manners whenever he showed his face—and then one fine evening there the girl was off with him! How does he manage these conquests? Indeed, I am most curious to learn!"

Georgina said in vexation, "He has made no conquest of me, ma'am. I beg you will not say such a thing, even in jest."

Lady Eliza laughed indulgently. "Well, it is likely to be no jest to you if you take him seriously," she said. "Giles and I saw a good deal of Nuala in Brussels before her death, you know, and I must tell you that a more sadly unhappy girl I never clapped eyes on. Indeed, I have seldom seen anyone so altered. She was soon disillusioned of her romantic folly, it seems!"

Lady Mott said firmly that she did not doubt this, but that she was sure Georgina was not so giddy a miss as her cousin had been, so they might as well give over the subject. Georgina, grateful for her intervention, yet felt her thankfulness slightly diminished when Mr. Hession took advantage of the turn in the conversation to request her hand for the set of country dances that was about to form. She was obliged to stand up with him, but her air, as she did so, was not such as to encourage him to believe that she was doing so from any reason other than that of the merest civility.

She could not help modifying her distant air to some degree, however, when he confessed to her, with more ingenuousness than her original opinion of him would have allowed, that he had consented to lead Betsy Mott into the supper-room only when he had learned of the scheme she had been hatching with young Darlington.

"Fact of the matter is, I had it in my head to ask *you,*" he said, "as soon as I could find the chance to be properly introduced to you. Spotted you straight off as the prettiest girl in the room. Are you staying long at Craythorne, Miss Power, or will you be going to London for the Season?"

Even their previous crossing of swords over Shannon could not entirely remove the pleasure of receiving so outright a tender of admiration—and from a young man who, as she could see from the envious glances being cast in her direction, was Top-of-the-Trees in the minds of most of the other young ladies in the room.

She only replied, however, in the most demure fashion, "Oh, I believe it may be some time before I return to England. Do *you* go to London, Mr. Hession?"

"Yes, dooce take it—much too soon for me, if you are staying here!" he said frankly. "My father has a house in Portland Place, you see, and one of my sisters is making her come-out this year, so I'm expected to put in an appearance. Not that I'll feel called on to fix myself there for the entire Season, you know! I daresay, if you are still in Kerry then, I might find myself back here by the middle of May."

Georgina laughed, and said she was sure he would not allow such a consideration to govern his movements—a statement that was immediately and vigorously contradicted by Mr. Hession. It was evident that she had made a conquest, and it was also evident that he was not averse to advertising this to the company by soliciting her to stand up with him again later in the evening.

On her part, she could not like the cavalier fashion in which he had dismissed Shannon as quite beneath the touch of anyone of consequence in the neighbourhood, but she found him lively and amusing company, and his attentions flattering, in view of his obvious attractions for the other young ladies in the room. She concluded by accepting his invitation —an incautious action which, during the homeward drive, exposed her to certain congratulatory comments from Lady Mott and Betsy that seemed to her to be taking entirely too much for granted.

"I wish you will not refine so much on my having stood up with him twice!" she felt obliged to say at last. "You will not tell me, I am sure, that every time a girl does such a thing in Kerry she must be suspected of falling in love with the young man!"

"Oh, no! But how could you help it, with Peter?" Betsy said, naïvely. "I imagine you cannot have met many young men, even in Bath, to equal him in appearance and address. Of course he has had the advantage of being much in London, which Robert—Mr. Darlington—says is responsible for his always knowing what is the latest crack in fashion."

"Oh, I am sure he is a very Pink of the Ton," Georgina said, with some irony. "But I can assure you that, in spite of his being knowing enough to have his coats made by Weston and his boots by Hoby, I should not have stood up with him the second time if I had known I should be suspected of losing my heart to him on that account!"

To this Lady Mott responded bluntly, "Well, my dear, that is all very well, but you will admit he is a handsome young man, in spite of his being a bit too dandified for *my* taste, and I assure you he is quite the beau ideal of most of the girls in the neighbourhood. And, as it is always a spur to other young men when they see one of their number endeavouring to fix his interest with a young lady, I can't think you should be quite so niffy-naffy about being obliged to dance with him twice."

Georgina shrugged. Miss Mott, however, with her romantic turn of mind, continued to find the situation of great interest, and confided to Georgina in an undertone, as she saw Lady Mott nodding under the influence of the late hour and the soporific motion of her well-sprung carriage, that if it were not for her eternal devotion to Mr. Darlington she would be much in danger of losing her own heart to Mr. Hession, in spite of the fact that she had been acquainted with him since he had worn nankeens and a frilled shirt.

"He was used to tease me half to death when I went to Hauld Hall to play with his sisters," she said reminiscently, adding in a more soulful tone that the Darlingtons were comparative newcomers in the neighbourhood, so that she had never had the pleasure of seeing her dear Robert so attired.

She then inquired thoughtfully whether Georgina had considered how Mr. Shannon would have appeared at that era in *his* life—an idea which made her more literal-minded companion choke as she attempted to stifle a spirit of laughter.

"No, really I have not," she said.

"Nor I," Betsy said. "But it is very affecting to think of it. I mean— Mama, of course, has not told me all the details," she went on, sinking her voice to a whisper as she kept a wary eye on her dozing parent, "but I do believe his history to be a very sad one, don't you? And I consider it quite *noble* of you to have taken his part tonight against the others."

"Goodness! Don't be such a goosecap!" Georgina interrupted her downrightly. "There was nothing 'noble' about it. It was merely that I could not sit by and listen to that ridiculous boy putting a face on the matter that it did not at all deserve."

"All the same," Miss Mott persisted, "I think it was exceedingly romantic, your being obliged to live in the same house with him all the while, with Mrs. Quinlevan confined to her bed and no one but Brandon to chaperon you. Even Papa said it was highly improper. Did he—were you—was it at all—?"

"No, it was not," Georgina said rather crossly, catching the drift of the question Betsy was trying to get out. "And I wish you will stop putting such ideas into anyone's head! It is bad enough to have Lady Eliza dropping her odious hints, without your behaving as if there was anything havey-cavey about Shannon's staying at The Place. We scarcely exchanged two words with each other the whole time, if you must know."

Miss Mott seemed somewhat disappointed at having this damper put on her romantic imaginings, but did not pursue the subject further, in view of Georgina's obvious displeasure.

By what means Mrs. Quinlevan learned the details of what had occurred at the assembly ball Georgina did not know, as she herself gave her cousin only a brief account of the proceedings the next morning, which included no mention of Mr. Hession's name. As early as that afternoon, however, when Georgina returned from a country ride with Betsy Mott and some of the other young people in the neighbourhood, in which she had had the pleasure of being mounted on a fine roan hack from Sir Humphrey's stables, she found her cousin Bella awaiting her return with every indication of a pressing anxiety in her manner. She was reclining on a sofa in her dressing-room, but exerted herself to sit up when Georgina, obeying the summons that had been delivered to her by Higgins, walked into the room, still wearing her riding-habit.

"I hope you are no worse, ma'am?" Georgina inquired solicitously. "I would not have left you if I had believed—"

"No, no, it is nothing of the sort!" Mrs. Quinlevan replied. "In fact, Dr. Culreavy has only just gone, and he finds me so much improved that he says he has no objection whatever to my driving out— But that is not at all the thing I wished to speak to you about!" she exclaimed, catching herself up in vexation. "Sit down, my love. I *do* feel I should have a serious conversation with you."

"About what, ma'am?" Georgina asked, seating herself obediently in a chair, but showing her puzzlement in her manner.

"About—about gentlemen, my dear! And about Peter Hession in particular!"

Georgina's brows came together in a sudden frown. "Why, what of him, ma'am?" she asked, not very encouragingly.

Mrs. Quinlevan clasped her hands together imploringly. "Oh, indeed, if you take that tone, my dear, it must have gone farther than I had imagined!" she said. "But you must believe me—you must *credit* me with having only your best interests at heart, when I tell you that it will not do! You cannot know him yet—you cannot know *any* of those odious Hessions—"

"Indeed, I am quite at a loss!" Georgina said, rising and looking sternly down at her cousin. "What have the Hessions to do with me, pray?"

Mrs. Quinlevan looked somewhat struck by her young cousin's uncompromising and wholly unself-conscious attitude. She faltered: "You are not—not particularly *taken* with him, then?"

"Taken with him!" Georgina repeated. "Good gracious, I met him for the first time only last evening!"

"But did you not stand up with him twice then? And ride out with him today?"

"He was of the party today, certainly," Georgina said, "but I assure you that there was nothing at all particular between us." She felt a slight qualm of conscience as she made this statement, for Mr. Peter Hession had, in fact, distinguished her by granting her his almost undivided attention during the entire course of the ride. She then continued, on firmer ground now, "I cannot think who may have been putting such ideas in your head, but you have my word for it that they are quite mistaken if they believe I regard Mr. Hession as anything more than the merest acquaintance."

Mrs. Quinlevan showed her a countenance of doubtful relief. "You are quite sure?" she persisted. Then, as Georgina opened her lips for a more vigorous affirmation, she went on, without waiting for her words, "I know I ought not to have thought it of you, my dear, and indeed, as for old Mrs. Scanlan, who told me of it, she has not been near an assembly ball for years, and only repeats whatever her grandnieces bring home to her, which she often does not have *quite* right, so I should have known better from the start. I am sure it was only the wretched state of my nerves that made me give credit even for a single moment to what she said. But you know, my love, that I am to stand in your dear mama's place, now that you are with me, and in Lady Mercer's as well, which I feel to be an even more solemn obligation—as strict as *her* notions are!—so you must not be vexed with me if I wish to know these things."

"I assure you, ma'am, if I feel I am in danger of losing my heart, I shall tell you," Georgina said. "But as for Peter Hession, our acquaintance is so slight that I am sure you may safely disregard any gossip you may hear about my having a partiality for *him*."

Mrs. Quinlevan's face had brightened as this speech progressed, and she now said, with a confiding smile, "Well, I am happy to hear it, my love, for *indeed* that young man is quite unsuitable for you, to say nothing of the misery any girl must look forward to who has the misfortune to find herself daughter-in-law to Miranda Hession. I do not say that Peter is *fast*, but the Hessions spend much of their time in London, you know, and it seems, by what my brother Jeremy tells me, that he has got into some very strange company this past year—*most* unsuitable for a young man of his age. I wonder at Lucinda Mott, that she did not tell you of this before you were obliged to stand up with him twice! I daresay it is something of a trial to you to be dragged about to country balls, at any rate, for I am sure you are the kind of girl who does not care to be flaunting herself before young men in the very *daring*—I shall always say!—gowns young ladies are obliged to wear these days to be all the crack, and would much prefer to spend a quiet hour strolling with your cousin in the shrubbery, or sitting in agreeable conversation with him. We have a very pretty shrubbery here at Craythorne, you know! It was a great concern of my late husband's, and I am sure the Huddlestons saw that it received the most constant attention, for it was always in the neatest order when we visited here while we were living at The Place."

At this point Georgina, perceiving that her cousin was craftily steering the conversation toward a subject which she herself did not at all care to discuss—her relationship with her cousin Brandon—with an eye to discovering how well her matrimonial plans in that direction were progressing, made an excuse and fled the room. It occurred to her, as she walked down the stairs, that she had seen little of Brandon since they had removed to Craythorne, and she wondered whether he was carrying out the plan he had formed of riding over to The Place in the morning to join Shannon on his rounds of the estate. If he was, he was being very sly about it, but that was not surprising, for his mother, if she heard of it, would be certain to do her best to put an end to it.

She found him now in the small yellow morning-room at the back of the house which he and the Reverend Mr. Peabody used when they were reading together; he was alone, and looked up in slight surprise as she put her head round the corner of the door and asked if she might come in.

"I thought you were gone for the afternoon with your *inamorato*," he said.

"My *what!*" She saw the grin on his face and went on threateningly, as she walked into the room, "If you ever say such a thing to me again—! I've just come from your mother, so I must suppose you are speaking of Peter Hession?"

He closed his book. "Who else?" he asked, serenely disregarding her minatory air. "She has been in such a taking this afternoon that I made sure I was to wish you joy the very next time I clapped eyes on you."

She gasped, dropping into a chair. "Oh, dear!" she said ruefully. "Was there ever such a piece of work made over nothing! I stood up with him twice last evening—that was all there was in it, and now some busyhead, it seems, has been spreading insinuations—"

"Oh, no! There you are fair and far out," Brandon assured her. "There were no insinuations, only a plain fact or two dropped; from that time on Mama took the bit in her teeth and was off and running. She has been so busy with her own matters, you see, that she had been taking it comfortably for granted that you and I were going on according to her wishes. But the news of your flirtation with Peter has now caused her to see the error of her ways."

"Brandon, I warn you!" Georgina said irefully. "I am *not* setting my cap at him—which your mother all but accused me of doing just now. He is too full of his own consequence, and far too much of a dandy for me."

"Oh, you mustn't be taken in by the neckcloths and waistcoats," Brandon persisted, grinning again. "A very hard goer, Peter—you should see him after hounds." He held up a hand as she opened her mouth to speak again. "Very well! Don't eat me! I cry quits! I take it you've smoothed Mama's feathers, then?"

"Yes, I *think* so. But Heaven forfend I meet a man I really could hope to like while I am here!" She went on, accusingly, "I thought you were going to tell her you would not marry me on any account."

"So I have, m'dear—at least half a dozen times. It won't do. She says I'm too young to know my own mind."

"And so I should think you were! Nineteen is entirely too soon for a man to think of marrying."

"I agree with you entirely. Still, we could be betrothed, you know," Brandon said, a look of unholy innocence appearing on his face.

"Brandon!"

"Save you a good deal of trouble," he suggested. "Save us both a good deal of trouble, when you come right down to it. Then when you leave we could break it off."

"It wouldn't save *me* a good deal of trouble," Georgina declared. "Why, at the merest hint of such a thing, Grandmama would have me back in Bath before the cat could lick her ear! You aren't by any means rich enough for her, and you haven't a title—not even a baronetcy—"

"I expect she *would* be better satisfied with Peter Hession," Brandon said helpfully. "*He* will be Sir Peter some day, and then you might be Lady Hession."

His cousin peremptorily desired him to stop making a cake of himself, and turned the subject by asking him what he had been doing since they had removed to Craythorne.

"I've been so busy racketing about that I've scarcely laid eyes on you," she said. "Have you been to The Place?"

"I went yesterday." A rueful look came over Brandon's face. "It wouldn't do, though," he said. "Shannon sent me home. Said he wasn't going to see me making trouble for myself by being known as a friend of his. He can be dashed autocratic when he wants to be, you know!"

"Yes, I *do* know," Georgina said, in feeling remembrance. She frowned thoughtfully. "It is those odious Hessions," she went on, after a moment. "I expect they brought it home to him that he isn't to hope to be received in the neighbourhood. It puts me out of all patience to see people setting themselves up in that way! I wish there were something we could do about it."

"*We?*" Brandon said sceptically. "You don't even like him. Why should *you* want to do anything for him?"

"I do not at all see what that has to do with it," Georgina said, with some heat. "If it is unjust, it is unjust, regardless of what my personal feelings may be."

Brandon shrugged. "At any rate, it will do you no good to think of interfering," he said. "If he won't hear of *my* even coming to The Place, he certainly won't take kindly to the idea of *your* poking into his affairs."

This aspersion brought a somewhat spirited rejoinder from Georgina, and a discussion ensued in which Brandon assured her that Shannon was *his* friend and therefore *his* affair, while Georgina maintained that, as she had been the more uncharitable toward him, she had the greater amends to make, and therefore ought to take it on herself to see to it that the entire neighbourhood did not repeat her mistake.

What either of them was to do about the matter, however, was something that for the moment quite eluded their ingenuity, as Shannon himself had forbidden Brandon to come to The Place, and Georgina felt that her own situation, especially in view of Lady Eliza's hints and Miss Mott's eager curiosity, was one of such delicacy that even a word spoken by her in his defence might be misconstrued.

Both young people, however, concluded hopefully that something would eventually turn up that would enable them to set Shannon on a secure basis in the neighbourhood, and on this amicable agreement they came to terms with each other, and, indeed, appeared in such charity with each other at dinner that evening that Mrs. Quinlevan quite took heart, and made sure that her own plans for the two of them were in a prosperous way to be fulfilled.

9

Lady Eliza was true to her word: two days after the assembly ball she came to Craythorne to carry Georgina back to Stokings with her for the afternoon. She was driving a smart sporting phaeton, drawn by a pair of showy match-bays, with a groom riding behind her on a neat bay hack, and made such a dashing appearance in a severely cut bronze-green cloth habit and a tall-crowned hat of the same colour, with a peak over the eyes, like a shako, that Georgina was at once filled with the desire to emulate her. Sir John had never raised objections to her mounting any horse in his stables, or to her riding neck-or-nothing to hounds in a way that had made her the envy of many a young gentleman in Herefordshire; but a lady handling the reins of a sporting vehicle drawn by a pair of sweet-goers was "fast," in his opinion, and he had never permitted his granddaughter to do more than tool a sedate one-horse gig down country lanes.

She noted now, as they set off, that Lady Eliza handled the ribbons with careless ease; and the manner in which she brought her pair up to a brisk trot with a flick of the whip, and then caught the thong with a dexterous turn of the wrist, at once showed that she was expert in the use of that article. She seemed aware of her passenger's interest, for they had gone only a short distance when she pulled up the bays and invited Georgina to take the reins herself for a time.

"I can see that you are quite longing to," she said, "and I am sure I shall be taking no risk in entrusting them to you. Your fame as a horsewoman has already reached us, you see."

Georgina rather ruefully shook her head. "Oh, I should dearly love to," she said, "but I am afraid you are mistaken about my skill. I have never driven a pair, you see, and I am the rankest amateur at handling the ribbons."

"Nonsense!" Lady Eliza said, laughing. "I am sure you are being far too modest."

She would not hear of a refusal, in spite of Georgina's continued protestations, which she evidently set down to a missish reluctance to put herself forward, and Georgina soon found herself, the reins in her hands, driving down the road at as sedate a pace as her inexperience and the rather restive spirit of the bays allowed.

"There! You see how simple it is," Lady Eliza said. "I knew you would be very well up to it."

Georgina herself was not so satisfied with her performance, for the bays, in spite of their showy appearance, seemed hard-mouthed and of uneven temper. But Lady Eliza, quite unaware of this unflattering opinion, sat comfortably looking out over the green spring countryside, leaving Georgina to go her own way without the least thought of attending to any problems she might encounter.

"Giles, you know, was quite cross when I insisted on his buying this pair for me," she rattled on, blithely. "He would have it that they were not at all suited to a lady's management, which is perfect nonsense, as you can see for yourself. I have not had the least trouble with them in the fortnight that I have had them. He and Major Rothe were unkind enough to say last night that I should not be so fortunate in the long run, and that I should end by being overturned, but they are both such slow-tops that they are sure to look on the gloomy side of any matter. I vow they would quite send me into a fit of the vapours if it were not for Sir Manning Hartily's being in the house as well. I positively insisted that Giles ask him, for there is no one so agreeable to have about in a country house—always so obliging and full of spirits! You will meet both him and Rothe today, my love, but I daresay you will not find that a very exciting matter, for of course your interest will lie with the younger beaux—though there is a sad lack of *them* in these parts. Still you need not be in despair, for I shall have the house quite full of company for my ball next month, and then I think I can promise you gentlemen of the first stare of fashion."

Georgina gave only a limited amount of her attention to Lady Eliza as she chattered on, finding that she had more than enough to do in handling the pair of restive young horses. If she had been obliged to give her opinion of them, she would have stated without hesitation that Colonel Malladon had been correct in his appraisal, and she was on the point of saying frankly to Lady Eliza that she did not at all believe they were a pair to be given into the hands of an amateur when a sudden combination of circumstances put an end to every thought in her mind but that of holding the bays under control.

The first of these was the abrupt appearance on the road of an urchin of five or six years, who bolted out of a hedgerow, with two or three of his peers in hot pursuit. The second was the violent objection taken by the bays to this eruption of small boys in their path, the visible signs of which were their vigorous attempts to rear up simultaneously in the shafts. The third was the approach, around a bend in the road, of a curricle and pair, which came bearing down on the scene of confusion at such a rapid pace that Lady Eliza shrieked and the groom behind her tumbled off his horse into the road in his zeal to get to the horses' heads.

For a moment it seemed to Georgina that either the phaeton or one of the children in the road must certainly be run down, as she grimly fought to hold her team. All her strength and skill would not be sufficient, she feared, and she was conscious of a surge of relief that was almost painful when she became aware that the driver of the curricle, who had wrenched his own greys to a halt, at the same time turning them dexterously across the road, had flung his reins to the groom beside him and leapt down to go to the bays' heads. The whole thing was over in a matter of seconds, and she found herself, pale and shaken, looking down into Shannon's face as he quieted the plunging horses, while simultaneously bestowing some choice epithets on the frightened urchins who were now huddling together at the side of the road.

"None of you scratched? That's more than you deserve!" he said sharply. "You've been taught better than to run into a road under carriage wheels. Now be off with you, you idiotic brats, and don't let me see such manners from you again!"

They scampered off in dismay, while Lady Eliza, who had been clinging to the seat with her eyes tightly shut, popped them open at the sound of a familiar voice and exclaimed, "Shannon! Oh, it is you! I might have known—sweeping down on us like the devil around that turn in the road!"

Georgina rounded on her indignantly. "Indeed, Lady Eliza, that is very unjust of you!" she said. "If it had not been for Mr. Shannon we must certainly have been overturned, for I am sure I could not have held this pair of yours. Colonel Malladon was quite right; they are not fit to be driven by a woman."

"Then I wonder you should have attempted it, Miss Power, if you were already acquainted with Colonel Malladon's opinion of them," Shannon said ungratefully. Abandoning the bays to Lady Eliza's groom, who had by this time picked himself up from the road, he jumped up into the driving-seat of the phaeton, rudely crowding Georgina against Lady Eliza. "Unless you prefer to walk to your destination," he said, in cool explanation, "I believe you will have to make shift with my driving you there; your cattle are in no frame to be handled by a woman, Lady Eliza, and your groom seems almost as shatterbrained as yourself."

Without waiting for her assent, he called to Hanger to take the curricle on and complete the errand on which he himself had been engaged, and immediately set the bays at a safe trot down the road.

"You were going to Stokings, I take it?" he inquired with ironic civility, of Lady Eliza.

She, recovering quickly from her fright, had already set straight the bronze-green hat that had been flung askew during the near-accident, and now peeped at him across Georgina with a laughing and—Georgina thought—rather self-conscious countenance.

"Yes, but—what an abominable autocrat you are, Shannon! As if I should not be able to handle my own horses!"

"If I were genuinely abominable, I'd let you try," Shannon retorted. "It is lucky for you that I have sufficient charity not to care to see you and Miss Power overturned in the nearest ditch."

"I am sure he is right," Georgina said, with conviction. Then, seeing Shannon glance momentarily down at her with the glint of sardonic amusement on his face that always set her back up, she went on, addressing him in some asperity, "You need not look at me like that! I have no pretensions to be a nonpareil; I told Lady Eliza before I took the reins that I had never driven a pair before in my life."

"The more fool you were, then, to try it for the first time with a pair like this," Shannon said, with unfeeling candour.

Georgina relapsed into mortified silence. She was quite aware that she had come off the worse in this exchange, but she would not excuse herself by laying the blame on Lady Eliza's insistence that she drive the phaeton.

Lady Eliza, however, at once stepped into the conversational breach and, after requesting Shannon not to make such a to-do over nothing, inquired of him in a careless way how he was going on at The Place.

"Very well," he answered, briefly and unencouragingly.

Lady Eliza allowed herself a small pertinacious giggle. "Oh, indeed? That is not at all the tale we hear!" she said. "I understand that you are quite in Coventry out there. Lady Hession has been running all about the neighbourhood telling everyone what a famous set-down she and Sir Landers gave you when you tried to foist yourself upon their acquaintance. Indeed, Shannon, I fear you have not a friend in the county!"

Georgina gasped. Inexperienced as she was in the ways of flirtation in the fashionable world, she was yet dimly aware that this audacious sally of Lady Eliza's had some significance beyond mere rudeness; it might have been an attempt, she thought, to gain and fix Shannon's attention by the very outrageousness of the remarks she had made.

If so, however, the attempt appeared to be a signal failure. Georgina, looking into Shannon's face, saw it harden slightly, but he did not turn his eyes from the road and only remarked, in an even voice, "That is a state to which I am not unaccustomed, Lady Eliza." He then dismissed the subject by addressing Georgina and inquiring how Brandon was getting on at Craythorne.

"Very well," she replied, thankful to be able to do her part in dispelling the effect of Lady Eliza's remarks. "But you have disappointed him, I fear, by telling him that he must not come to The Place."

He shrugged, indifferently, it seemed, and remarked that such disappointments were soon got over.

"I do not think so," Georgina said warmly. "My cousin is not like other boys of his age, you know. He has few diversions, and when he makes a friend it is a matter of importance to him."

Lady Eliza, who was not easily snubbed, broke in at this point to say with a slight laugh that it appeared she had been mistaken. "You have at least *two* friends in the neighbourhood, it seems," she said, "young Quinlevan and Miss Power. Is there some fatal quality in that family, Shannon, that makes you able to captivate its members so easily?"

At this Georgina lost her temper entirely and, speaking with a frankness of which Sir John would have approved, but which would have sent Lady Mercer into an access of horror, requested Lady Eliza to refrain from making a goose of herself.

"I can't think what is the matter with you, to be twisting the merest civility so," she said.

To which Shannon added dryly, "You are certainly on a false scent there, Lady Eliza. Miss Power holds me in even greater dislike than Lady Hession appears to do, though apparently she has the good manners not to run about the neighbourhood boasting of it."

This was a speech that set Georgina between mortification and pleasure —mortification at the idea that her own previous conduct had fully warranted the implication of the same sort of prejudice of which Lady Hession was guilty, and pleasure at the left-handed compliment to her that had ended Shannon's speech. Indeed, the pleasure seemed quite inordinate for the very cool quality of the compliment she had received, and for a startled moment, as the phaeton proceeded steadily along the road, she asked herself what the meaning of this might be. She was not so foolish, surely, as to be developing an interest in a man like Shannon, a gazetted fortune-hunter, more than a dozen years older than herself, who certainly considered her as little more than a tiresome schoolgirl!

She could feel the scarlet colour beginning to rise in her face, and she was grateful that Lady Eliza only said to Shannon, "Oh, very well, if you will have it so! But have you never thought of applying to Giles and me to stand your friends? We might do so, you know, if properly approached. Giles is the best-natured creature alive, and can never be made to think ill of anyone, and I—well, I am of a forgiving nature, I must own! I might even be prevailed on to send you a card for my ball, if I were certain you would conduct yourself properly."

Shannon cut her short. "I am looking for no invitations, Lady Eliza," he said curtly. "I find my time well occupied."

"With horses and sheep, and crops, and stupid tenants!" she said. "That was all very well when you were Cartan's agent, but you are Shannon of The Place of the Oaks now, and if you had the slightest ambition you would make a push to be accepted in that position! I vow I had no notion you could be so meek-spirited as to let people like the Hessions make you look nohow and then do nothing about it!"

This time she had not even the satisfaction of seeing the slightest appearance of resentment in his manner, for he only said indifferently, with a glance at Georgina, "This is a subject that can hardly interest Miss Power. Since I am here only in the capacity of your driver, may I suggest that you turn your attention to entertaining *her?*"

Lady Eliza laughed, but Georgina caught the annoyance in the sound. "You really are an ungrateful creature, Shannon!" she said. "I shall be surprised, though, if the day does not come when you will be glad enough to accept my assistance—undeserving of it as you may be."

She then directed herself to pointing out to Georgina the objects of interest along the way, opening a conversation that Georgina was glad to let fall when the gates of Stokings came into sight. Lady Eliza then turned again to Shannon.

"You will come in and take some refreshment with us, as a reward for your *gallant* gesture in rescuing us?" she asked him, in a teasing voice.

"No, I have business to attend to."

She sighed. "Not even, 'No, I thank you,'" she said. "Really, Shannon, you will never get on if you insist on behaving so ferociously!" She added, "But if you are in such a great hurry to be gone, you must certainly take the phaeton for your own use when you have set us down at the front door. Your groom can return it later—or perhaps you had rather do so yourself, when you are less pressed for time."

"I shall do neither, thank you," Shannon said. "I prefer to walk."

"To walk! Oh, you are funning now! It is five miles to The Place, at least!"

"Nevertheless, I prefer to walk."

She shrugged her shoulders with a petulant look, and, when he had halted the phaeton before the door, alighted in haste and swept into the house, drawing Georgina, who was attempting a more civil leavetaking, along with her.

"I vow," she declared, as she stripped off her gloves and handed them, with her hat, to a footman, "there was never a more vexatious creature than that man! There is no doing anything for him—not that I should even wish to attempt it, for he has a shocking character, but I dislike seeing *anyone* set on as he has been. Giles! Giles! What do you think?" she went on, leading Georgina into a red saloon elaborately decorated in the Chinese taste, where three gentlemen sat together. "We were nearly overturned in the phaeton by the most shocking mischance, and Shannon felt obliged to drive us home—as if I could not manage my own horses! If I had been driving myself, of course, it need not have occurred, as Miss Power tells me that, in spite of her being such a notable horsewoman, she is quite an amateur at handling the ribbons."

Having flung all this information pellmell at the gentlemen, she demanded a glass of ratafia for Miss Power and herself and sank into an easy-chair, indicating to Georgina with a wave of her hand Major Rothe and Sir Manning Hartily. The latter, a florid, extremely stout gentleman in the palest of pantaloons, the most gleaming of Hessians, and a neckcloth arranged in all the intricacies of the Oriental style, at once demanded explanations of the ladies, creaking ponderously across the room to settle himself beside them and raising his quizzing-glass to his eye to have a more appreciative stare at Georgina, while Colonel Malladon occupied himself with seeing that she was comfortable and had what refreshment she desired—a task Lady Eliza seemed quite content to relegate to him.

Major Rothe, meanwhile—a sensible-looking man of about eight-and-thirty, with none of the dandified airs of his fellow guest—also turned his attention to the less highly coloured account of the events Lady Eliza had sketched which Sir Manning was drawing from Georgina, and said with a faint smile, when she had done, "Yes, I am afraid that is quite in Mark's style. He has a horror of being beholden to anyone for the slightest favour."

Georgina looked at him in surprise. "Mark?" she said. "Oh—you mean Mr. Shannon? Are you acquainted with him, then?"

"Very well acquainted," Major Rothe answered. "I had an uncle who was a neighbour of Lord Cartan's in Scotland, and until his death a few years ago I was used to stay with him often. Mark is some years my junior, of course, but I have seen a good deal of him from the time we were both lads."

Lady Eliza broke in at this point to say, "Really? I did not know you had been so well acquainted with him. Now that I recollect, though, when we visited Nuala in Brussels, it seemed you were forever one of the company. Tell me—has he always been so disagreeable? Or is that merely something he has acquired over the years?"

Major Rothe answered her with a seriousness which he seemed conscious the flippancy of her question did not quite merit.

"Why, as to that, Lady Eliza," he said, "yes, he has always been a solitary person, with few social graces. But then you must remember that he has had scant opportunity to develop them."

He glanced at Georgina, as if unwilling to proceed further without knowledge of how much of Shannon's history was current in the neighbourhood. But Lady Eliza overrode his scruples by declaring at once, "Oh, you need not have the slightest concern about telling tales out of school, Major! Everyone knows that Shannon is a by-blow of Lord Cartan's; you cannot imagine that *that* would not have become common gossip here as soon as his marriage to Miss Power was found out."

Major Rothe, however, still appeared reluctant to discuss the matter, and turned the conversation to another topic, in spite of Lady Eliza's obvious desire to continue on the subject of Shannon. It occurred to Georgina, as she sat drinking her ratafia, that Lady Eliza's interest in Shannon was so patently displayed that her husband might well have reason to feel jealousy; but apparently he was quite unconcerned. Nor did he seem at all interested in the extravagant compliments that Sir Manning Hartily paid to his wife over the next half hour.

Sir Manning, indeed, had at first seemed inclined to bend the greater part of his attention on Georgina, whom he pronounced in an audible undertone to Colonel Malladon to be "a regular little beauty," adding, "Deuce take me if I've seen a finer pair of eyes these two years in London!" This, she later found, she was to take as a compliment indeed, for in the course of the conversation it developed that Sir Manning was a member of that elegant and sophisticated group known as the Prince Regent's set, and that he was considered, in all matters of taste and beauty, to be a connoisseur of the first rank. For her own part, however, she could well have dispensed with his approval, since it involved a great deal of ogling and a number of compliments so frank as to make her blush, and she was relieved when Lady Eliza, who obviously was not fond of playing second fiddle, imperiously demanded Sir Manning's attention for herself, and she was able to turn to the conversation on the subject of hunting that Colonel Malladon was carrying on with Major Rothe. This eventually ended in Colonel Malladon's declaring that it would not do for such an accomplished horsewoman as Miss Power to depart from Stokings without seeing the two high-bred 'uns he had lately added to his stables, and before Lady Eliza knew what was afoot, he and Major Rothe were leading her young guest outside through one of the long windows opening on the terrace, and strolling with her across the lawn in the direction of the stables.

Georgina was not surprised that it did not suit Lady Eliza to join their company, as she patently was not of a disposition to enjoy tagging along as a belated partaker in a scheme she had had no part in forming; but she was astonished that her pique at her guest's having purloined the attention of two of the gentlemen of her court would lead her, within five minutes of their having reached the stables, to send a footman after Colonel Malladon with the information that she must see him at once to decide on her plans for the remainder of the day. This was a patent excuse, and Colonel Malladon showed, by the tempery manner in which he received it, that he was well aware of this fact.

His displeasure, though it did not extend to his ignoring his wife's summons, did rise to the point of his informing Georgina and Major Rothe that there was no need for *them* to return to the house, and of his requesting Major Rothe to act as his deputy in showing Georgina around until his return. He then strode off purposefully toward the house, leaving his two guests to discover, when they turned their eyes on the other's face, that a mutual smile was lurking behind a proper air of gravity on each. Georgina was the first to laugh, and Major Rothe then joined her in a quiet chuckle.

"Oh, no! There won't be wigs on the green," he assured her. "Malladon is really a very mild-tempered fellow, you know."

Georgina said a little tartly, "Perhaps it would be better for everyone if he were not," and then caught herself up, looking ruefully at her companion. "Oh, dear! My wretched tongue!" she said. "Grandmama has always warned me that a young lady should have *no* personal opinions to express except those that are of a complimentary nature."

"I am afraid we should have a dull world of it if *all* young ladies adhered strictly to that rule," Major Rothe said, with a slight, amused smile. He added, after a moment, "I take it that you are not well acquainted with the Malladons, Miss Power?"

"No. I have been in Kerry only a matter of a few weeks, and for the greater part of that time my cousin, Mrs. Quinlevan, has been out of frame, so that I have not gone about much until very recently. You know my cousins, the Quinlevans, I expect, if you have often visited here?"

"As a matter of fact, I have not; this is my first visit to Kerry also," Major Rothe explained. "But I have heard Malladon and Lady Eliza mention them. They are the family Mark Shannon has dispossessed from The Place of the Oaks by marrying—your cousin, was it, Miss Power?"

"Yes." She looked at him curiously. "I was surprised to hear that you were Shannon's friend," she said then, frankly. "I had not supposed him to have any, as uninterested as he seems to be in making himself agreeable to other people. But perhaps you merely meant that you have been *acquainted* with him over a long period of time?"

"On the contrary, I consider him to be one of my closest friends," Major Rothe said.

"Oh! Do you?" She asked naïvely, "Then he is not always so—so disagreeable as he seems here?"

Major Rothe smiled. "Since I arrived only yesterday and haven't yet seen how he performs here, I can't speak for that," he said. "As I remarked to Lady Eliza, he has few social graces, yet I do not recall that his manner, when he is among people who are willing to accept him for what he is, is such that it would repel a man of sense."

Georgina nodded thoughtfully. "Well, I rather thought as much," she confessed. "I daresay he came here expecting to be set down, and that is why he has had his hackles up from the start. But it was the very worst thing that he could have done, you know. I am sure that people like Sir Humphrey and Lady Mott are not so high in the instep that they would not have been willing to accept him in the neighbourhood, once they had seen that he was not the odious sort of adventurer they had been led to expect. But he has done nothing to conciliate them or anyone else, and the result is that he is in a fair way to being quite ostracized."

"I am sorry to hear that," Major Rothe said, looking grave. "But it is early days for him here still. Perhaps when he is better known—"

"He will not be known at all if something is not done soon," Georgina said bluntly. She added, "Of course it is his own fault. I will own that I felt much the same about him, except then I saw his kindness to my cousin Brandon, who is lame and often slighted on that account, and that he has already won the good opinion of his tenants—"

"I am glad to hear that," Major Rothe said. "It could scarcely have been otherwise. He has more knowledge of the land than any man I have ever met; in the old earl's day it was always said that the Cartan land was in better heart than any other in the neighbourhood, and he had the full management of it then."

"I wonder Lord Cartan did not make some provision for him when he died, since he had been so useful to him," Georgina said, her curiosity getting the better of her again. "I gather that he did not?"

"No," Major Rothe replied. "I must admit that has puzzled me, too, but then the relationship between them was an odd one, you know. They were very much alike, in many ways—both hard men, who neither gave nor received easily. Mark, when he was a lad, had to earn every privilege, every word of approbation, he ever had from the old earl. I suppose Cartan was probing to find if the resemblance to himself that was so marked physically was there within the boy, as well. And then," he added, drawn on to speak further, apparently, by the obvious interest with which she was attending to him, "Lady Cartan never liked him, you see. She was an excellent woman, and a very fair one, I believe, but she could not care to have Mark brought up in the house with her own children, almost on terms of equality, and she had great influence with her husband. They had a numerous family, and I daresay she might have persuaded Cartan that any provision he made for Mark must have been taken out of the pockets of their children."

Georgina, her underlip caught in her teeth, had been following this speech while absently stroking the mane of a beautiful little mare that had come inquisitively to look at the intruders. She remarked thoughtfully, when Major Rothe had concluded, "And I suppose, when the old earl died, the present Lord Cartan felt the same?"

"Yes. The two of them had never dealt together, you see. Mark was the older and stronger, so he escaped the petty persecution one boy can visit on another when he is in a position of superiority, but I daresay his bread was made bitter for him more than once by the taunts that he was obliged to bear." He added quickly, "I should not like you to think that he complained of this to me. Any knowledge I have of it comes from one of the younger boys, Edmund, who was rather well disposed toward Mark and used to tell me tales occasionally that might perhaps better have remained in the family."

"And so, when the old earl died, the present Lord Cartan gave Shannon his *congé?*" Georgina asked.

"No, not immediately. I must admit I was surprised that Mark did not make a move then himself, but he was much attached to the place, I believe, and perhaps thought he and the new earl might rub on tolerably well together if each would agree to keep out of the other's way. The fault in that arrangement was that Cartan had a fancy to take the reins into his own hands, and within a year matters had come to such a pass between them that Mark was on notice to find some new post for himself. I didn't learn of this until some time later, after his marriage, as a matter of fact, for he is stiff-necked enough not to wish to seek assistance from a friend, even though it would be gladly given. The first I knew of it, he had married your cousin and was travelling on the Continent."

Georgina, who was finding the conversation of considerable interest, was somewhat vexed at this point to see Colonel Malladon coming toward them, as his arrival must inevitably mean that the subject would be dropped. So, in fact, it was. Colonel Malladon, his good humour apparently restored by the explanation he had had with his wife, at once reverted to the good points of the mare Georgina had been stroking, suggesting that they must certainly get up an excursion on which she should be Georgina's mount, and in the conversation that followed the subject of Shannon was quite forgotten.

There was no opportunity for Georgina to speak further about him to Major Rothe before the carriage was ordered to take her back to Craythorne. But this did not at all mean that he did not occupy her thoughts almost to the exclusion of any other topic during her homeward journey. She had been made to feel more and more acutely, as her conversation with Major Rothe had progressed, how improbable it was that her first opinion of Shannon had been a just one. Major Rothe was a sensible, well-bred man, with agreeable manners and an intelligence that she had realised to be superior. If he, after an acquaintance with Shannon that had covered many years, was able to describe him as one of his closest friends, it seemed that the uneasiness she had been feeling over her own instant dislike of him must be only too well founded.

Then, too, the account that the Major had given of Shannon's early years had done much to explain to her the harshness of Shannon's manner. Brought up in a household in which the stigma of his illegitimacy was constantly held before him, able to form none of the ordinary attachments of youth except for his father, whose nature had apparently been as reserved as his own, it was small wonder, she thought, that he had failed to develop the social ease that would have smoothed his way in the situation in which he now found himself. He had come expecting to be rejected, and rejected he assuredly would be, unless something was soon done to set matters to rights. Major Rothe's presence at Stokings might help, she thought, but, as a guest there, he was in no position to instigate any positive action in his friend's favour.

An idea began to take shape in Georgina's mind, and she determined to discuss it with Brandon at the earliest opportunity.

10 The opportunity offered itself that very evening, when Mrs. Quinlevan had gone upstairs for her after-dinner nap. Georgina followed Brandon into the yellow morning-room, whither he had retired with a book, and said directly, "Brandon, I want to speak to you. About Shannon."

"About Shannon? What about him?"

"I intend to make a push to have him accepted in the neighbourhood. Do you think your mother would be willing to give a small informal party here next week if I dropped a few hints to her?"

Brandon closed his book and looked at her suspiciously. "Now what the deuce are you up to?" he demanded. "You must be dicked in the nob if you think Mama would invite Shannon here, to an informal party or any other kind!"

"Yes, I know that," Georgina acknowledged. "But if *I* were to offer to send out the cards of invitation—"

She did not feel it necessary to conclude the sentence, looking at him with a serene expectation of his understanding her drift that drew a sudden shout of laughter from him.

"You mean *you* would invite him? Well, you are a Trojan! But what do you think Mama would have to say when he came walking in the front door?—that is, if she didn't take one of her spasms and collapse on the spot!"

"I should warn her beforehand, of course," Georgina assured him, seriously. "Not too *far* beforehand, for that wouldn't do, but enough so that the shock would be taken off. Do you think it a good idea, Brandon? Once he is here, she can hardly send him packing, and if it is seen that he is invited to *this* house—"

Brandon was still chuckling. "Of all the corkbrained schemes!" he said. "He won't come, in the first place, and even if he did— Lord, I'd give a monkey to see the stir it 'ud make! But it won't fadge, Coz."

She sat down beside him. "Why won't it?" she asked, obstinately. "Brandon, I have been talking to Major Rothe at Stokings. He says he has known Shannon since he was a boy, and the account he gives of him makes me feel quite certain that I have misjudged him dreadfully, and *must* do something to make up for the shabby way I have treated him. *You* will not care for it yourself, you must own, if he is not to be received by anyone in the neighbourhood. But if we can once show people that he is not the ramshackle sort of man they believe him to be, there will be no difficulty in *your* continuing your friendship with him."

This argument, she perceived, had some effect on her cousin. She knew how galling he felt it to be obliged to give up an association in which he had taken the liveliest pleasure, and, in fact, in spite of the misgivings which he continued to voice, his eagerness to stand on easier terms with Shannon finally led him to admit that there might be some merit in her scheme, after all, and to consult with her seriously on the subject of how they were to go about inducing Mrs. Quinlevan to give a small party at Craythorne within the coming week.

As it developed, the matter presented fewer difficulties than either of them had anticipated. The initiation of the idea had been left to Brandon, who—as it was well known that he did not care for parties himself— broached it merely by saying in a joking way to his mother that it surprised him, in view of the many invitations Georgina had received since they had come to Craythorne, that she had not started any plans to return all this hospitality by some entertainment of her own. Georgina was then about to take up her part in the conversation, but to her surprise and satisfaction she found herself interrupted before she could well begin.

"It is odd that you should mention that," Mrs. Quinlevan said seriously to Brandon, "because that is exactly what I have been thinking myself. Of course it is out of the question for me to be considering anything elaborate in my state of health, but I do believe I could manage a small evening party, with dancing for the young people. A formal ball would not be expected, and indeed the house is quite unsuited for such a thing, for it is not at all to be compared to The Place, where we had some charming balls, you remember, when poor Nuala was alive."

Georgina, anxious to see that she did not lose the thread of her thought by wandering off into reminiscences of the past, here interrupted in her turn, and declared that of all things she would enjoy a party given at Craythorne.

"And, indeed, ma'am, it need be very little trouble to *you*, at all events," she said, "for I am sure I could relieve you of many of the tasks that go along with such an undertaking. If you will give me your list, for example, I shall be only too happy to send out the cards of invitation."

"Would you, my dear? That would be very kind of you!"

"And I might deal with Mrs. Hopkins about the refreshments as well, if you would permit me, and—oh, I am sure there are any number of details I might take off your hands, if you will only let me know what you would like me to do."

Mrs. Quinlevan found all this helpfulness greatly to her taste, and, as she was a gregarious soul, who liked nothing better than to be giving or attending entertainments of almost any sort, she soon found herself, under Georgina's guidance, making definite plans for an event that until a few minutes before had been only a vague notion in her head.

A list was soon being discussed, which included the names of all the more prominent families in the neighbourhood. The Motts, of course, were to be invited, as were the Hessions, and the Malladons and their house guests, Major Rothe and Sir Manning Hartily. The latter, Mrs. Quinlevan informed Georgina, must be a notable addition to the party, if only he would consent to honour it with his presence.

"For he is a man of the first stare of fashion, you know, my love," she said, "and for him to have consented to make a stay at Stokings is a high compliment to Lady Eliza, I do assure you. I daresay he felt a quiet week or two in the country before the Season begins would be quite the thing for him, for he is somewhat troubled with gout, I believe."

Georgina sat listening to her cousin's rambling monologue, as each new name was set down on the list, in the greatest of good humour, secure in the knowledge that she herself was to be entrusted with the supply of elegant gilt-edged cards on which the invitations were to be inscribed; and the very next day penned them carefully and sent them out, with, shuffled among the rest, one addressed to Mark Shannon, Esquire, at The Place of the Oaks.

She wondered, during the next few days, what his emotions would be on receiving it. Astonishment, certainly, he would feel, for he could never have anticipated that her cousin would so far overcome her antipathy for him as to invite him to her home on any occasion. He might, she hoped, take the idea that Brandon had prevailed on his mother to include him.

But no matter how great his puzzlement was, she did not believe that he would decline the invitation. Even a man as careless as he was of the world's opinion could scarcely fail to see the advantages that recognition by his dead wife's family would bring to him. To reject such an olive branch would be to cut himself off indeed from any hope of future acceptance by them, and she could not believe that he was either vengeful or stupid enough to wish to salve his pride by the paltry gesture of returning a refusal.

As it developed, she was quite correct in her assessment of the situation.

Instructions had been given that all messages and correspondence should be in her domain during the week, so that when Shannon's reply came in she was the one who opened and perused it. "Mr. Shannon accepts with pleasure, etc., etc."—she read the formally correct missive through and, repressing a crow of triumph, bore it off to show to Brandon.

To her surprise, he did not appear to share her satisfaction. Instead, he viewed the sheet of paper with some appearance of misgiving, and said at last, "Well, I never thought he'd come up to scratch, and now that he has —dash it, Georgie, I don't like it at all!"

"Why?" she demanded. "Because your mother will fly up into the boughs? I wish you will not worry yourself over *that*, for you know that she never bears a grudge from one moment to the next, and I am quite sure I shall be able to turn her up sweet by the very next day."

Brandon shook his head. "It ain't my mother. It's Shannon," he said bluntly. "If he should find out she never meant to invite him—"

"How could he find out? You won't tell him, nor will I, and Cousin Bella wouldn't! Well, you *know* what a high stickler she is; she simply would not insult a guest so in her own house!"

"She'll let it out somehow," Brandon said gloomily. "You wait and see. You don't know how jingle-brained she can be when she's really in a pelter over something." He added, "I wish you hadn't done it," which made Georgina demand of him why he had not said this to her when she had first broached the subject to him.

"I did. The thing is, you wouldn't listen," he said, firing up in his turn.

"Well, we can't cry off now. That's certain," Georgina said, with decision. "We shall have to go through with it. But I am quite sure we shall be able to carry it off."

"Are you? I ain't!" Brandon said, unencouragingly. "I have half a mind to ride over to The Place tomorrow and tell him the truth."

"Brandon! You wouldn't!" The scarlet colour flew into Georgina's cheeks. "He'll think— I don't know *what* he would think of me! Promise me you will do no such thing!"

But, as it happened, the promise she exacted from him was quite unnecessary, because by the next day he was in no condition to ride to The Place or anywhere else. A wetting he had received that afternoon when out riding brought on a troublesome sore throat and a chill that evening, and Dr. Culreavy, summoned the next morning by Mrs. Quinlevan, gave it as his opinion that his young patient would do well to spend the next several days in bed.

The news, conveyed to Georgina, cast her into double gloom: not only was she sorry for Brandon, who must spend an uncomfortable and boring time confined to his bed, the recipient of the cosseting he detested from Nora Quill and his mother, but she was also cast into some perturbation by the knowledge that she would now be without his support on the evening of the party. Her cousin's indisposition was not so serious that this must be cancelled—though Mrs. Quinlevan, in the pucker she had been thrown into by the doctor's pronouncement, did consider it for a time—and she would thus find the burden of calming her cousin Bella's justifiable indignation on that occasion thrown entirely upon her own shoulders.

In addition, she had greatly counted on Brandon to see to it that Shannon was not neglected during the evening, for her hovering about him herself, she considered, was quite out of the question. But now this task, too, would be her responsibility, and she found her resolution tested to the utmost by the idea.

Her one consolation lay in the assurance that Major Rothe was to be present at the gathering. Certainly she would be able to rely upon *his* support, and, with it, she believed she might squeak through. Lady Mott and Sir Humphrey, too, though both were outspoken in the extreme, were fair-minded enough, she believed, to be able to meet Shannon without feeling the necessity of turning a cold shoulder to him before he showed he deserved it, while Miss Betsy Mott seemed so kindly disposed toward him, as a figure—in her mind, at least—of romance, that Georgina was sure Shannon would meet with no rebuff from that direction.

The evening of the party arrived. The Motts and the Malladons and their house guests had been asked for dinner at eight, and at seven-thirty Georgina, attired in the gown of rose-pink sarcenet with tiny puff sleeves and a narrow skirt trimmed with a double pleating of ribbon that she had chosen for the occasion, scratched with some trepidation on the door of Mrs. Quinlevan's dressing-room. Bidden to enter, she stepped inside to find her cousin already arrayed in a gown of puce satin, with her maid engaged in arranging on her coiffure a headdress of the same colour, supporting a plume of curled feathers.

"Oh, my love, I was just about to send Anson to you," Mrs. Quinlevan exclaimed, as Georgina came into the room. "You cannot have managed with only that silly creature Mrs. Hopkins engaged last week!"

"On the contrary, ma'am, I managed very well," Georgina said, smiling, but feeling her heart thudding uncomfortably under the knowledge of the announcement that she must soon make.

Mrs. Quinlevan was surveying her critically, and seemed satisfied at all points, from the expression of approval that gradually came over her plump face.

"Why, yes, my love, I must admit you *do* look quite the thing this evening!" she said. "But then with hair like yours, one need never fret oneself over the arrangement of it, for it falls naturally into the most enchanting ringlets!" She frowned at her own reflection in the glass before her, sighed, and told her maid that she might go. "Oh, but do send Mrs. Hopkins to me at once!" she said, adding to Georgina, as Anson left the room, "I have the most *lowering* presentiment that ices and wafer-biscuits are not at all the thing to be serving tonight, as the weather has turned so cool and damp."

Georgina, foreseeing a monologue on the deficiencies of the dinner and the refreshments to be served later that would endure until Mrs. Hopkins made her appearance, hurriedly interposed, "Cousin Bella! Indeed I do not wish to interrupt, but there is something of most particular importance that I must say to you."

Mrs. Quinlevan checked in some surprise. "Why, very well," she said. "But what can it be?" A sudden look of alarm crossed her face. "The lobsters!" she said. "Oh, *do* not tell me it is about the lobsters!"

"No, no! Indeed, ma'am, it is nothing of the sort," Georgina said, her own trepidation subsiding momentarily in a smile of amusement at the instant apprehension of high tragedy that had crossed her cousin's face. "I assure you it is nothing so paltry."

"Paltry!" Mrs. Quinlevan gasped, in indignant amazement. "How can you speak so, when I have Sir Manning Hartily about to sit down to dinner in this house, and everyone knows he is used to the first style of elegance in everything, particularly in cookery—"

"I am sure it is so," Georgina agreed hastily, anxious to head off another monologue, this one on the subject of Sir Manning. "But, indeed, to my knowledge there is nothing amiss with the lobsters, and I beg you will listen to what I must tell you!" Seeing from her cousin's face that she was still obstinately intent on the inner contemplation of some culinary disaster of her own imagining, she plunged desperately into the subject. "The fact is, ma'am," she said, "that I have taken the liberty of inviting Mr. Shannon to your party this evening."

If she had informed Mrs. Quinlevan that an aroused peasantry was even now at the gates of Craythorne, bent on massacring all its inmates and exhibiting their heads upon pikes, in reprehensible imitation of what had occurred in France in the days of her youth, it was impossible that an expression of greater horror could have appeared on that lady's face. However, the very next moment it had disappeared under a look of slight annoyance—such a ludicrous come-down from the tragic to the commonplace that Georgina, as nervous as she was, had difficulty in repressing a giggle.

"I wish you will not be funning now, of all times, my love!" Mrs. Quinlevan said reprovingly. "It puts me in mind of your poor father, who was somewhat addicted, I fear, to practical joking."

"But I am not funning, Cousin Bella, I do assure you!" Georgina protested. "It is true; I *have* invited him! I know it was shockingly forward of me, but—"

She got no further, for Mrs. Quinlevan, closing her eyes, with one hand clasping her ample puce satin bosom in the general direction of her heart, had sunk down alarmingly in her chair and was distractedly murmuring something about her vinaigrette. Georgina flew to procure that useful article for her, and was relieved in a few moments to see her cousin rouse herself and look up at her with piteous blue eyes.

"My dear love," Mrs. Quinlevan implored her, "*tell* me that you did not mean it! That *man*—no, you *could* not—a girl brought up so *very* carefully—"

"I am dreadfully sorry, Cousin Bella, but indeed I *do* mean it," Georgina said remorsefully. "I had no idea it would upset you so greatly! You see, I had been talking to Major Rothe—and he has known Shannon forever, and is *quite* persuaded he is undeserving of the treatment he has received here—indeed, he considers him one of his closest friends—"

She broke off, conscious that the explanation she was offering was a very lame and disjointed one, but she had the satisfaction of seeing that it had at least produced the effect of returning a slight look of hope to her cousin's face.

"Major Rothe?" Mrs. Quinlevan repeated feebly. "Do you mean that *he*—? But, indeed, it was very wrong of him to encourage you to do such a thing!"

"No, no, Major Rothe knows nothing about the matter," Georgina said hastily, aghast at the thought of drawing that gentleman into the imbroglio. "It was my own idea entirely—and Brandon's, a little—for you must know that Brandon has always liked Shannon—"

"Brandon," Mrs. Quinlevan said with severity, "is a child! Surely, Georgina, you have not allowed yourself to be persuaded by his most unsuitable partiality—"

"I have been persuaded by no one," Georgina said. "It was entirely my own idea—and I must say, ma'am, that I wonder that you will set yourself so against Mr. Shannon, for the very credit of the family! Surely it must be better to have it thought that my cousin Nuala married a man who, except for the misfortune of his birth, is quite respectable than to persist in making it appear that he is the sort of person no one can receive!"

Mrs. Quinlevan, with doubt of the wisdom of her own conduct now added to horror over her young cousin's, could only clasp her vinaigrette for comfort.

"But—but Jeremy *said* I was to have nothing to do with him!" she wailed. "And it is quite settled in the neighbourhood: even Lady Mott, who is the *soul* of good nature, says that Sir Humphrey will not call upon him, and that it is quite right of him—"

"Lady Mott is following *your* lead, ma'am," Georgina said, pressing the momentary advantage that she saw herself to have obtained. "Of course she does not wish to put herself in your bad graces by making overtures to a man with whom you are determined not to be friendly. But I am persuaded that she would also follow your lead in recognising him, if you were to do so."

"Would she? I don't know," Mrs. Quinlevan said dubiously. "It *may* be true—but still I cannot help feeling that we should all be *far* more comfortable if only you had not asked him here tonight, and we could go on exactly as we have been doing. I cannot *think* what possessed you to do such a thing—though Louisa Middlethorpe warned me before I ever brought you here that you had had a very strange upbringing with Sir John, and that Lady Mercer was often at her wits' end— But I should not have said that!" she broke off, conscience-stricken. "I am sure you have always behaved very prettily under *my* roof, and if it were not for that *odious* man, who seems to take pleasure in setting us all in a bustle—"

"No, really, ma'am! You shall not lay this at Mr. Shannon's door," Georgina said, half-laughing at her cousin's peculiar logic. "Mr. Shannon knows nothing of what I have done; as far as he can tell, he has received an invitation from you to attend an evening party at Craythorne, and I am sure you are too well-bred to snub him when he presents himself at your door. If you are to be angry with anyone, it must be with me."

"Yes, but—to receive him *here*, my dear, as if there were nothing odd about his being asked, when everyone *knows* I have said a dozen times that no one in the family intended to recognise him—! Oh, dear! Oh, dear! I *wish* I knew what I must do!"

Mrs. Quinlevan's face puckered up. She appeared to be on the verge of tears, and Georgina could only be grateful when the housekeeper's appearance at the door put an end to this highly unsatisfactory colloquy. She fled to her own room, reflecting in some dismay on her inability to obtain a pledge of cooperation from Mrs. Quinlevan, and looking forward with increasing dread to the remainder of the evening.

Only a firm conviction that her cousin, as caper-witted as she might be, would not wish to make a scandal by turning a cold shoulder to a guest in her own home sustained her, and even that reflection was tempered by the fear that Mrs. Quinlevan's nerves would get the better of her sense of propriety, and that the company might consequently be treated to a display that would make both Georgina and Shannon excessively sorry that she had ever conceived her well-meant plan.

11

When she went downstairs a few minutes later she found the Motts, who had arrived with unfashionable punctuality, already in the hall, divesting themselves of their wraps. Fortunately for both her and Mrs. Quinlevan, who Georgina perceived was still in a flutter of agitation, Lady Mott was in a talkative mood, and carried the conversation until the arrival of the Malladons some quarter of an hour later.

But Georgina was then cast into an even greater apprehension than that which was already enveloping her, for she saw that Colonel Malladon and Lady Eliza were accompanied only by Sir Manning Hartily: Major Rothe was nowhere to be seen. Lady Eliza explained this at once by saying to Mrs. Quinlevan, in a careless voice, "My dear Bella, positively you must not eat me, for I know it will upset your table shockingly, but we were unable to bring Rothe! He has had an urgent summons to England; it appears that his only brother is at death's door, and he was obliged to go scrambling off at once, with no regard whatever for the proprieties. I promised to convey his deepest regrets to you—but what good do regrets do, I should like to know, when one's table has been set awry?"

Georgina, looking at her cousin, saw from the expression on her face that she considered this latest blow of fate so minor, in comparison with the ordeal before her, that she could accept Lady Eliza's offhand apology without a blink of dismay; but, for her own part, she was cast into flat despair. If Major Rothe was not to appear that evening she had lost her last ally, and would be obliged to carry the situation off alone—a quelling prospect, even for one of her optimistic nature.

Casting about desperately for expedients, she saw Miss Betsy Mott, who, in a demure, pale-blue muslin gown trimmed with knots of white ribbon, appeared to be agreeably contemplating an evening spent in the company of Mr. Robert Darlington. An idea suddenly occurred to Georgina. Betsy was not the ideal person to whom she would have chosen to confide the straits in which she stood, but at least she was well disposed toward Shannon, and it might be that she would be willing to aid her in her attempt to see to it that his appearance at Craythorne did not lead only to his receiving an unmerciful snubbing.

She sat through a dinner that seemed interminable—for Mrs. Quinlevan, anxious to satisfy the culinary expectations of Sir Manning Hartily, had inspired her cook to set before them two full courses, with half a dozen removes, and side-dishes ranging from a matelot of eels to broiled mushrooms and a Rhenish cream. It was not, in spite of its pretensions, a particularly successful meal, for Sir Manning was seen to look dubiously at some of the dishes, and subsequently sought consolation in a spirited but somewhat one-sided flirtation with Georgina, who was seated beside him. This did not at all suit Lady Eliza, who wished it to be well understood that Sir Manning was her own property, but neither Mrs. Quinlevan nor Georgina was inclined to be disturbed by the thinly veiled conversational barbs her pique led her to direct toward them. Each was already too much occupied by the far weightier difficulties on her mind.

When the ladies rose from the table, Georgina, instead of following her cousin and the older ladies into the Green Saloon, caught Betsy's arm and drew her aside in the hall.

"I must speak to you in private for a few moments," she said urgently. "Will you come upstairs with me? You can tell your mama one of your ribbons came unfastened and you were obliged to have it tacked on."

Betsy, her blue eyes opening wide with interest at this hint of a mystery, obediently followed her up the broad staircase to her bedchamber. Once they were inside, Georgina closed the door carefully and, standing with her back to it, said rapidly, "I scarcely know how to begin; there is not time to explain it all to you, but I am persuaded you will help me if you can. The truth is that I am in the most abominable fix! Brandon and I invited Shannon here this evening without Cousin Bella's knowledge, and now Brandon is ill and cannot appear, Cousin Bella is in a pelter, and even Major Rothe, who is an old friend of Shannon's and whom I was depending on to smooth matters over, will not be present. Will you stand by me and help me see to it that Shannon does not have a most disagreeable evening?"

She halted, waiting for an answer from Betsy, who was staring at her with a look of fascinated interest on her face.

"*You* invited Mr. Shannon?" she repeated. "But why—?"

"Because I am persuaded he does not deserve the shabby treatment he has been receiving," Georgina said impatiently, feeling her colour rising slightly under her companion's candid stare. "It is too long a matter to go into now, but, according to Major Rothe's account of him, he is quite— quite respectable, and—and worthy of our notice—"

"Oh, I *do* believe you," Miss Mott said, so fervently that Georgina began to feel some slight qualms at having confided her secret to her. "And I shall do my very best, only—what exactly am I to do?"

"Do?" Georgina had not had time to consider this herself, and said after a moment, rather lamely, "Well, you can dance with him, of course, if he asks you to stand up with him—"

"Oh, I should dearly love to waltz with him!" Betsy said earnestly. "Only I should be quite petrified with fright: he has such a shocking reputation, you know! However, as you say it is not deserved, I think I may venture it." Another thought struck her at this moment, and she said doubtfully, "But if he does not ask me—?"

"If he does not ask you, of course you cannot stand up with him!" Georgina said, despairingly characterising her new ally as a hubble-bubble creature, whose support seemed likely to be of little value to her. "But you can at least speak pleasantly to him, and say to anyone who is interested that you think it is unfair to condemn him before he has had an opportunity to show what he is."

"I shall say *that* to Robert," Miss Mott decided. "He said only the other day, after we had passed Shannon on the road driving a very neat pair of chestnuts"—she wrinkled her brow—"or were they greys?—that he could not imagine that anyone who owned such bang-up horses could be so ramshackle a fellow as he is said to be. So you see he is well disposed toward him, to begin with." She added, much less brightly, "But I do not think I should dare say such a thing to Mama or Papa. I quite wonder at you, dear Miss Power, being so brave as to invite Mr. Shannon without Mrs. Quinlevan's knowledge! I am sure I should never have had the courage to do such a thing!"

Georgina, in her present desperate mood, felt that foolhardiness, rather than courage, would have been a more accurate word to describe her conduct; but there was no shabbing off now. She accordingly gave Betsy a few additional instructions, with little hope of their being efficacious, and led her downstairs again into the Green Saloon.

Within half an hour of this time most of the other guests had arrived and dancing had begun. When another half hour had passed without Shannon's appearance, Georgina for the first time that evening permitted herself to nourish a faint glimmer of hope. Perhaps, she thought, he had changed his mind and drawn back at the last moment, either from pride or from embarrassment, and she could at last discard the worry that had been dogging her dismally all day.

Apparently a similar glimmer had penetrated Mrs. Quinlevan's agitated mind, for she took the occasion of an interval between country dances to draw Georgina aside and whisper to her in a hopeful voice, "My love, you *were* hoaxing me, weren't you, when you said you had asked that dreadful man here? If you were, it was not at all kind of you, you know, for I have been in such a state all evening that I do not know if I am on my head or my heels."

"But I was *not* funning!" Georgina replied. "I have already told you so! Only—only perhaps he will not come, after all—"

The words died on her lips. She was looking at a tall, broad-shouldered man, dressed quite in the most approved fashion for evening—long-tailed coat, frilled shirt, knee-breeches, and silk stockings—who was just being ushered into the room, and though there were several people between them and she had been accustomed to seeing him only in a shooting-jacket and buckskins, she could not be mistaken. It was Shannon.

Beside her, she heard Mrs. Quinlevan give a gasp of dismay. "Oh, my love! Here he comes! Oh, what in the *world* am I to do? Before all these people—! I feel ready to sink!"

Georgina put an end to these agitated exclamations by seizing her cousin's elbow and propelling her ruthlessly across the room in Shannon's direction. The music was about to begin again, and she knew she was engaged for this set to Peter Hession, but she cast Mr. Hession's claims to the winds and approached Shannon with a smile on her face that she hoped conveyed the impression that she was delighted to see him.

"Mr. Shannon! How good of you to come!" She gave Mrs. Quinlevan's elbow a little shake. "Cousin Bella, do say good evening to Mr. Shannon and tell him how sorry we are that Brandon isn't able to be of the party this evening."

From the comprehensive glance that Shannon's grey eyes cast over her and her totally discomposed cousin, Georgina, with a sinking heart, saw that he was aware that something was decidedly amiss. Chatter as she might, she could not hide the aghast, helpless expression on Mrs. Quinlevan's face, or the surprised glances that were being directed at him from every part of the room. As he bowed over Mrs. Quinlevan's hand, uttering a few brief civilities, she had an overwhelming impulse to confess the whole truth to him; but instead she heard herself talking chattily on, in a way she would have despised in any other girl, deploring the dampness of the night and the closeness of the crowded rooms. Her one excuse was that Mrs. Quinlevan had managed no more than the faintest "Good evening" in response to all her promptings, so that obviously someone had to cover the awkwardness of the moment.

Her hand was in his then, as she automatically offered it to him and he bowed over it, and for one wretched moment she thought, to her own as tonishment, that she was about to burst into tears. She had made a mull of it; she knew that now, as Mrs. Quinlevan stood fluttering in distracted silence beside her. Cousin Bella was not going to be able to carry it off; already it must be apparent both to Shannon and to the other guests that the situation was not one of her own making, but one into which she had been thrust entirely against her will.

Georgina saw the expression on Shannon's face as his eyes met hers—an expression which, in spite of the control that had often vexed her, held surprise in it, and some mortification. It was gone in a moment, as the mask of indifference descended once more, but she responded to it immediately, saying, with a slight laugh which, in her confusion, she could not save from artificiality, "I hope you will not think me too forward if I claim the honour of being the first young lady to dance with you this evening. I believe you are not very well acquainted here as yet, but I shall do my best to remedy that a little later."

He could not, she thought, fail to respond to this bold invitation, and she saw, in fact, that she had caught him by surprise. To her great annoyance, however, as he was about to lead her into the set, they were accosted by Peter Hession, who informed her directly that he believed she was engaged to him for this set.

"Thought you might have forgotten," he said blandly, looking straight through Shannon in a way that made her long to shake him. "Asked you three days ago, if you'll recollect."

"Indeed, I do not recollect!" Georgina said mendaciously. "I am sure you said the quadrille, Mr. Hession."

He put up his brows at her slightly. "Did I? I don't think I could have done that, Miss Power," he said, still ignoring Shannon's presence. "Fact of the matter is, I'd had the bad luck to be trapped into asking Lizzie Flournoy for the quadrille before I ever spoke to you. Her mother and mine are bosom-bows, you know."

At this point Shannon put an end to the matter by saying in a coolly civil voice that he had no desire to stand in the way of such a long-standing arrangement and at once moved off. Georgina, in great vexation, was obliged to surrender her hand to Mr. Hession, and had the additional vexation of being asked by him, as soon as Shannon was out of earshot, what had got into her cousin to have invited such a curst rum touch to Craythorne. She fired up at once, and told Mr. Hession that she could not see what possible affair it was of his.

"I daresay it ain't any," he agreed, with a maddening imperviousness to the set-down she had meant to convey. "All the same, it looks bad for the neighbourhood, you know—that sort of thing. I mean to say—none of us has called on the fellow, nor means to."

"That," said Georgina emphatically, "is entirely *your* affair, Mr. Hession. Who is asked to this house, however, is, I believe, my cousin's."

"Well, that's true enough," he admitted. "But it ain't at all her style, you know. Devilish timid little woman, Mrs. Quinlevan. Not like her to set the neighbourhood by the ears." He continued reflectively, as Georgina maintained a somewhat guilty silence, "Still, you never know what dashed queer starts you'll find a woman taking. Look at my mother: there ain't a higher stickler in all of Ireland, but she has a dótty old cousin she'll trot out before the company at every blessed party she gives. Believe the fact of the matter is, some female she has on her black books once gave the old lady a snub. That would be enough for my mother. Never forgets a thing like that."

Georgina could not help smiling. In spite of his dandified ways, which had expressed themselves this evening in higher shirt-points and a more intricately arranged neckcloth than could be boasted by any other gentleman in the room, to say nothing of a stunning array of fobs, seals, and pins and an elaborately chased quizzing-glass hung on a ribbon about his neck, he was really very much of an ingenuous boy still, with a good humour that made even his toploftiness lack offence. She could guess that, removed from the supercilious coldness of Sir Landers and the formidable self-consequence of Lady Hession, he might develop into an agreeable and amusing companion, but such an event seemed little likely to occur. The only boy in a family of girls, he had been courted and petted from birth by both his parents and his sisters, and his situation at home was made so agreeable for him that Georgina believed it improbable that these ties would be relaxed even on his marriage.

She had little leisure at the present moment, however, to indulge in thoughts concerning the character and prospects of her companion; she was too much occupied in endeavouring to discover how Shannon was getting on. She saw that Mrs. Quinlevan, coming at last to some recollection of her duties as hostess, was making a feeble attempt to present him to a pair of impecunious middle-aged ladies who had been invited only because they were distant connexions of her husband's family, but the conversation did not flourish, and when next she was able to find him in the crowded room he was making his way toward the alcove that led into the dining-room, which was now serving as a supper-room for the dancers.

Immediately the set was over, she rid herself of Mr. Hession by requesting him to bring her to her cousin, and then, before Mrs. Quinlevan had had time to utter more than two words of an almost tearful complaint to her, flew off into the supper-room herself. To her relief she found that Lady Eliza, at least, was not above entering into conversation with Shannon, for she was standing beside him, looking up at him with a wicked sparkle of laughter in her eyes as she spoke to him, and tapping his arm with her fan.

But her relief vanished in utter confusion as Lady Eliza, catching sight of her, called out to her, "Oh, my dear, you are exactly the person I was most wishing to see! You must come and settle a wager for me: I have staked a guinea against Shannon that Bella knew nothing of his having been asked here until the moment he walked into the house! Was this your doing, you naughty creature? I expect you know you have set the whole company by the ears!"

Georgina, feeling that she could quite willingly have strangled the impudently smiling Lady Eliza, did not know where to look. She managed, however, to say with a tolerable assumption of composure, "Of course you are funning, Lady Eliza. Have you tried the lobster patties? I wish you will; I am assured that they are particularly fine tonight."

But Lady Eliza was not so easily to be led from her subject. She said, with another little laugh, "Well, my dear, that is all very well, but you shall not hoax me; I know you are 'running a rig,' as the gentlemen say. But I must bid you adieu, Shannon: Miss Power's reputation may be good enough for her to be able to play games with you in public, but I am persuaded that mine is not!" She bestowed another tap of her fan on his arm and said to him, the sparkle very pronounced now in her prominent brown eyes, "Come and see me in private at Stokings, when you are tired of romping with the nursery set."

She then moved out of the room, flirting her fan on its ivory sticks and leaving Georgina in a state of such fury that she had much ado to maintain an air of decorum.

"Oh! What an abominable woman!" she exclaimed. "Mr. Shannon, you *cannot* believe—"

She could not go on; as she saw his grey eyes fix themselves steadily on her face the consciousness of guilt overwhelmed her, and her words faltered into silence.

Fortunately, it was that moment that Betsy Mott chose to inaugurate the action to which she had pledged herself earlier in Georgina's bedchamber. She had come into the supper-room with Robert Darlington; seeing Shannon, she gave a visible start, coloured, and then, with an appearance of equal hesitation and resolution, approached him.

"Mr. Shannon," she said rather breathlessly, holding out her hand to him, "you may not remember me, perhaps, but we met at The Place—when Mrs. Quinlevan was ill? Mama and I had come to inquire for her—"

"I remember you very well, Miss Mott," Shannon said.

He spoke civilly, but there was a slight frown between his brows as he glanced from Betsy to young Darlington, who was looking none too pleased at the spectacle of the young lady he considered almost as his affianced bride publicly soliciting the notice of a man like Shannon. Georgina, stepping quickly into the breach, said at once, "Mr. Shannon, I believe you have not yet met Mr. Darlington?"

Bows were exchanged, a very stiff one on Mr. Darlington's part and a very slight one on Shannon's. Apparently Mr. Darlington's admiration of Shannon's horses, which Miss Mott had signified earlier that evening to Georgina, did not extend to the point of his wishing to make their owner's acquaintance, at least under a dozen pairs of censoriously watching eyes.

Miss Mott, however, with a total disregard for her escort's uneasiness, had embarked on a rather disjointed monologue, directed toward Shannon, in which, having first informed him that she considered the party a delightful one and the house charmingly decorated for the occasion, she went on to inquire into his taste in dancing.

"Mama, of course, thinks the waltz shockingly *fast*," she prattled on. "But they say it is being danced even at Almack's now, and though we *are* very much cut off from London here, in the very *depth* of the countryside, you might say, still one does not like to think one is *entirely* out of the mode. Do you waltz, Mr. Shannon?"

This transparent dangling for an invitation had the effect of deepening the look of uneasiness on young Darlington's face to one of positive alarm.

"Well, I'd like to say—coming it a bit too strong, ain't you, Betsy!" he protested. He said to Shannon rather defensively, by way of explanation, "She don't waltz, sir, I'd have you know—not except at morning-parties, with only a few couples. Lady Mott don't approve of it."

Betsy turned on him, her blue eyes indignant. "Why, what a thing to say!" she exclaimed. "Really, I do not know what affair it is of *yours*,

Robert! If Mr. Shannon chooses to waltz with me, I can't think what *you* should have to say to it!"

Shannon, who had been observing the altercation with a rather sardonic expression on his face, put an end to it at this point by saying bluntly, "But I do *not* choose to waltz with you, Miss Mott." She gave a gasp, and turned from Darlington to him with a high flush mounting in her good-humoured face. He went on at once, "Don't put yourself about. I have no wish to be rude, but I seem to have caused such a scandal already merely by walking into this house that I think I should do ill indeed to add to it by dancing with a young lady of such high respectability as yourself." He then turned to Georgina, said, "My compliments to you, Miss Power, on having succeeded in enlivening what must otherwise have been a rather tame evening for one of your tastes," bowed slightly, and walked out of the room.

Miss Mott was the first to recover from the stunned silence into which the three remaining participants of this scene had been cast.

"Oh, I think it is too bad!" she said, casting a reproachful glance at young Mr. Darlington. "Need you have been so *very* rude to him, Robert? Of course you have offended him."

"Well, deuce take it, I wouldn't have done if you hadn't put yourself forward like a brass-faced monkey!" Mr. Darlington defended himself. "Making a dashed cake of yourself before everybody! What's come over you, Bet? Just because Mrs. Quinlevan chose to ask the fellow here—" He broke off, looking uncomfortably at Georgina. "I beg your pardon, Miss Power. Of course it is none of my affair," he said.

"I should think it was not!" Georgina replied.

She was looking flushed and angry, trying to make up her mind whether to go after Shannon at once and have it out with him, or to forbear for the sake of causing no more public to-do than she had already created. She decided on the latter course, and as a result young Darlington received the benefit of the pent-up emotions she was unsuccessfully attempting to bridle. She told him in no uncertain terms that she considered his behaviour toward Shannon unpardonable, and compared it bitterly to that of the Hessions.

"I thought you had both more good nature and more good sense than they have, but it seems I was mistaken," she said. "Anything to puff up your own consequence at the expense of someone you do not know and have no reason to dislike!"

She then walked out of the room into the Green Saloon, where she was at once seized on by her cousin Bella.

"Oh, my love, he has gone!" Mrs. Quinlevan said, in a tone of devout thankfulness. "You cannot think how relieved I am! I shall say it was all a misunderstanding, and that as soon as he saw that he wasn't expected—"

"Cousin Bella, if you say such a thing, I shall never speak to you again!" Georgina said fiercely.

Mrs. Quinlevan fell back before her in slight alarm. "But, really, my dear," she expostulated, "you cannot wish people to go on saying that *you* asked him to Craythorne only for a lark, which is what they are all thinking now!"

"I am quite sure it is what they are thinking, with Lady Eliza to put the idea into their minds!" Georgina said, with no signs of mitigating her opposition. "She is *bent* on making mischief, and I will not have it! If you will not say you invited him yourself, I shall tell anyone who mentions the matter to me that I did indeed ask him here without your knowledge, but *not* as a lark—that I believe the neighbourhood is using him abominably, for no good reason—"

"No, no, my love, you must not say *that!*" Mrs. Quinlevan protested, quite horrified by the thought. "They will think you are setting your cap at him, or some such vulgar thing, and indeed it will not do, not after poor Nuala— Oh, dear! Oh, dear! I do wish Lady Mercer were here, or your mama! I am sure I do not know at all what to do. Nuala was such a pretty-behaved girl, though she *did* flirt a little, I must admit, but no one can take exception to *that* in a girl as beautiful and as lively as she was, and then she kept the greatest sense of propriety with it all—"

Georgina said ruthlessly, "It is no use your holding Nuala up to me, ma'am. If you find my conduct offensive you must send me away, but I will *not* have people saying I was unfeeling enough to ask Mr. Shannon here so that he could be humiliated for my amusement. Either I tell them the truth or you will say you invited him yourself; there is no other course I will agree to."

Faced with this ultimatum, Mrs. Quinlevan could do nothing but capitulate. She said weakly that perhaps no one would mention the matter, after all—a piece of optimism that was immediately laid low by Lady Hession's sailing up to her, looking more Roman than ever in imperial purple, to commiserate with her on Shannon's having had the effrontery to show his face in her house.

"I *have* heard it said that Miss Power was playing a May-game with us," she said, in a tone that showed how majestic her disapproval of such conduct would be, "but I cannot believe—"

"No, indeed!" Mrs. Quinlevan interrupted hastily, with a helpless glance at Georgina. "That is *quite* untrue—and, in fact, if you will but consider, my dear Lady Hession," she floundered on, "that we are all Christians—and that it was only last Sunday that the Vicar was speaking of our duty—though, indeed, I cannot but think that it is sometimes very difficult to know just *what* one's duty is—"

"My dear Mrs. Quinlevan, this is all very well," Lady Hession said. "But still I cannot believe that *you*, of all persons, who have already suffered so much at this man's hands, should feel it incumbent on you—"

"No, no, indeed I do not feel it so!" Mrs. Quinlevan said earnestly, and then, seeing Georgina's stern eyes on her, faltered, checked, and went on in a rush. "That is—of course I *do* feel—but you must believe—I mean, you cannot believe— Oh, dear! There is poor Lizzie Flournoy without a partner, and I daresay Mr. Cartwright might— If you will excuse me, *dear* Lady Hession!"

She hurried off in an ample flutter of draperies, leaving Lady Hession confronting Georgina with an expression of some surprise, which gradually melted into one of majestic approval as she surveyed Georgina's gown of rose-pink sarcenet and her golden curls.

"You are in quite exceptional looks tonight, my dear Miss Power," she said complimentarily, evoking a rather startled acknowledgement from Georgina, who had not thought to find herself at that moment in the good graces of the formidable matron before her. "Pink becomes you very well —though I must tell you that I am not myself in favour, on the whole, of seeing young girls dressed in colours for an evening party until they have had their first Season in London. I gather, from what my son tells me, that you have not yet made your come-out, Miss Power?"

"No. You see—my grandfather's death—" Georgina began.

But she discovered at once—as persons with whom Lady Hession conversed customarily did—that that lady's questions were usually meant merely as rhetorical ones, requiring the briefest of responses or none at all, for she went on at once, "It is a great pity that you are not to spend at least a fortnight in London this spring, my dear child, for my own Amelia, you must know, is making her come-out this year, and I should have been only too happy to have presented you as well. Perhaps you are not aware that my late mother, Lady Larkin, was one of your grandmama's dearest friends? Their parents' estates marched together in Lincolnshire. I had almost forgotten the matter until Peter chanced to mention to me that you were Lady Mercer's granddaughter, and that, of course, immediately brought it back to me."

Georgina had a puzzled feeling, as she murmured some appropriate response, that she was being summed up and her good and bad points catalogued for future reference, with the balance, it seemed, coming out in her favour. Was it possible, she was obliged to ask herself, that Lady Hession was considering her in the light of a future daughter-in-law? It was true that she had been seeing Peter Hession almost daily, at one or another of the rides or excursions or impromptu parties that seemed to abound among the young people of the neighbourhood, and that he always appeared to find the opportunity to spend much of his time at her side. But it had never crossed her mind that he was already entertaining serious thoughts concerning her.

Perhaps, she told herself, Lady Hession was the sort of woman who could not see her son stand up twice with the same young lady at a ball without making it her business to meddle in the matter by encouraging or discouraging his attentions to her. The rejected Mr. Smallwoods' mama had been just such a managing female, and, whatever Mr. Hession's personal advantages might be over that unprepossessing young man, Georgina could not but feel that they must be dimmed by his close relationship with such a gorgon.

Her perturbation was not decreased when Peter himself, encouraged by finding her attended only by his mother while a set of country-dances was forming, came up to request her hand. She could not refuse him, and, indeed, she was given no opportunity by Lady Hession to do so.

"I am sure," that fond mama said, bestowing a tap of her fan on her son's arm, "you will be quite the handsomest couple in the room! You must forgive a mother's partiality, Miss Power—though I daresay, when you consider the matter, you may wish to tell me that it is not partiality in the least, but a mere recognition of an indubitable fact."

Georgina, catching the wicked light of amusement in Peter's eyes, said demurely that modesty prevented her from making any such remark, as she herself had been involved in the compliment, and was thereupon led off to the set, carrying in her ears Lady Hession's parting remark that she really must induce Mrs. Quinlevan to bring her to Hauld Hall very soon, so that they might become better acquainted with each other.

"She's right, you know," Peter said, grinning as he walked down the room with her. "You really should know my mother better, Miss Power.

Dooced efficient woman. Nothing you can think of she can't accomplish if once she sets her mind to it."

She could only guess that he was making oblique reference to the stamp of her approval that Lady Hession had just given his attentions to her, and she felt a sudden blush mounting to her cheeks. She was determined, however, not to let him see her discomposure, and only said with a smile, "Oh, I am afraid we should not deal at all. I am persuaded she is inclined toward young ladies of irreproachable conduct, and I have often been given to understand that I do not fit that description in the least."

"Well, I daresay you may not," Mr. Hession agreed imperturbably, "especially if you are generally fond of such kick-ups as inviting that fellow Shannon here tonight to see what a dust you could raise."

He was about to go on, but she cut him short, demanding, "*Who* says I did such a thing?"

He looked surprised. "Why, everyone is saying it. Ain't it true?"

"Of course it is not!" she said angrily. "This is Lady Eliza's doing. I cannot think why she has such malice against Mr. Shannon."

"I expect it's because she knows him better than the rest of us do," Mr. Hession remarked frankly, drawing an exasperated look from his partner that only made him grin at her again. "Don't try to tell me you ain't cutting some sort of wheedle," he said. "I ain't exactly a flat, you know!"

Nothing that she could say could move him from this opinion, and it was almost a relief to her when, at the end of the set, her hand was claimed by Sir Manning Hartily, who was of no mind to concern himself with anything so unrelated to his own interests as speculation on the reasons why Shannon had been invited to Craythorne.

Relief, however, soon gave way to discomposure when it became evident that she was to be obliged to endure a ponderous flirtation as long as the set lasted. Sir Manning even took the opportunity of remarking soulfully to her that he was devilish close to letting London go hang, Season or no Season, so that he could bask a while longer in the light of her blue eyes.

"I beg you will do nothing of the sort, Sir Manning," she said, in some slight alarm that he really meant what he said. "I am quite sure your friends would be sadly disappointed."

His corpulent frame shook in a satisfied chuckle. "Mind you, I don't say they wouldn't be," he acknowledged. "If I must say it myself, Manning Hartily is generally considered to be the life and soul of any gathering to which he lends his presence. But one word from you, my dear little puss, and they shall be obliged to do without me."

She gave him an immediate assurance that that word would not be spoken by her, to the blighting of the expectations of so many of his noble friends, and presently succeeded in making her escape from him, only to fall into the hands of another partner bent on eliciting from her the whole tale of Shannon's presence there that night. She was obliged to improvise explanations for the remainder of the evening, and then, when the last guest had gone, to bear with her cousin Bella's lamentations and reproaches for a good half hour before she was permitted to go upstairs to her bedchamber.

All in all, she decided bitterly, it had been a dreadfully unsuccessful evening. The only thing she had accomplished was to make Shannon— and probably at least half the guests whom her cousin had assembled— believe that she was an unfeeling romp, who would go to any lengths to perpetrate a hoax. Decidedly, this would not do, and before she went to sleep that night she had made up her mind that the first thing she must do in the morning was to go about setting matters straight.

12 How this was to be accomplished, however, presented her with something of a problem. Obviously, she could not simply request Mrs. Quinlevan to order out the carriage to take her to The Place, so that she might see Shannon and explain matters to him; her cousin would be horrified at the very thought.

She carried her dilemma to Brandon's room that morning and found him sitting up in bed, feeling a good deal better and eager to hear all that had happened the night before. His disgusted—"I told you so!"—at the conclusion of her recital did nothing to raise her spirits, which were so low by this time that she did not even resent his censure, but only asked him despairingly, "But what am I to *do?*"

"I should think you had done enough already," Brandon said, unhelpfully. "You've made a mull of it, and as far as I can see there's nothing you *can* do now that will set matters straight."

"But I *can't* have him thinking that I asked him here only to make game of him!" Georgina expostulated. "I must put him right on that score, at least. Only I haven't the least idea how to go about it."

"Write him a note," Brandon suggested, adding pessimistically, "I daresay he won't believe you, at any rate. It was a dashed harebrained thing to do, you know, and after the way you've always behaved toward him, you can hardly expect him to think you were only trying to help him."

As such was the conclusion that Georgina had already arrived at in her own mind, she could not controvert it with any real conviction. She accordingly left her cousin's room in even lower spirits than she had been in when she had entered it, and somewhat hopelessly went downstairs to the morning-room to try to compose a letter to Shannon that would, however inadequately, convey an explanation and an apology to him.

After several fruitless attempts she was about to throw her pen down in despair when Miss Mott was announced. Georgina was scarcely in a mood to welcome being obliged to rehearse once more with Betsy the disagreeable events of the previous evening, but she asked resignedly that the visitor be shown into the Green Saloon, where she herself presently joined her.

She found Betsy, becomingly attired in a simple high-necked gown of jaconet muslin and a *bergère* hat, in a state of the dismals that quite equalled her own. She embarked at once on a tearful account of the quarrel with Mr. Darlington that her imprudent championing of Shannon had provoked, looking at Georgina, at its conclusion, as if she felt she must be the one to advise her on how to mend it, since it had been her plea for aid that had landed her in the suds in the first place.

Georgina's response to this was a rather impatient suggestion that, since Mr. Darlington was obviously head over ears in love with her, she had only to wait a few days and his pique would wear itself out.

"But if it does not—?" Betsy protested.

"Don't be a pea-goose!" Georgina replied. "Of course it will." She added darkly, "If you think *that* is a problem, I could wish you had mine. I am quite certain that Shannon thinks I asked him here only to roast him, and he will go on thinking it unless I can somehow manage to see him and explain—" A sudden inspiration flashed into her mind; she broke off and said rapidly to Miss Mott, "I cannot go to The Place alone, you see, but if you were to go with me— Yes, I am persuaded that would be quite the thing to do!"

"If I were to go with you?" Betsy faltered. She looked at Georgina with a wariness born of the unhappy results that had followed on her earlier attempt to be of assistance to her. "But I couldn't possibly—" she protested. "I mean, Mama would never permit me—"

"Your mama need know nothing at all about it," Georgina said. "We shall simply make an engagement to go for a ride tomorrow morning. I suppose you have a groom you can trust? Or we might make some excuse to rid ourselves of him for half an hour—" She checked, seeing Betsy staring at her in dismay, and said, "Good God, what harm would you be doing? I cannot visit Shannon alone, and how I am to contrive to tell him I meant only to help him by asking him here last night is something that has had me at my wits' end all the morning."

It did no good for Betsy to suggest, as Brandon had done, that Georgina set her explanation down in a letter; Georgina demolished that argument at once by stating that that was exactly what she had been attempting to do for the past hour, with absolutely no success.

"One can always *say* things so much better than one can write them," she said incontrovertibly. "And then the person one is talking to is obliged to answer, and one gets into a discussion or even a quarrel, when one can say all kinds of things one would feel exceedingly silly trying to write in a letter."

Miss Mott obviously did not see how quarrelling with Mr. Shannon would mend matters, but she was a biddable girl, with a strong romantic tendency that made her look on a visit to The Place as a desirable, though

GEORGINA

perilous, adventure. In the end she agreed to go with Georgina, and forthwith engaged herself to ride over to Craythorne the following morning, bringing Sir Humphrey's roan hack as a mount for her friend.

As no objections were entered either by Lady Mott or by Mrs. Quinlevan to the unexceptionable plan of two young ladies to take a morning ride together, accompanied by one of Sir Humphrey's grooms, Georgina and Miss Mott set out at an early hour on the following day. It was Georgina's plan to attempt to forestall Shannon before he rode out over the estate; they need not then even go into the house, she assured Betsy, for she could say all she desired to while she remained on her horse and Shannon on his.

"You had best ride out of the way a little with Hussey while I talk to him," she said, "for I shall have to tell him, of course, that it was I, and not Cousin Bella, who sent him the invitation, and if *that* is spread about the neighbourhood I had as well spare all my trouble."

Instead of engaging to do this, however, Betsy unexpectedly spent the following half hour in urging Georgina to abandon her scheme entirely. It appeared that she had made up her quarrel with Mr. Darlington the previous evening, and that he had lectured her so strongly on the inadvisability of having anything to do with so ramshackle a fellow as Shannon that she had ended by meekly promising to heed his advice.

Her conscience was therefore troubling her severely this morning, and she did her utmost to convince Georgina that her plan of seeing Shannon in secret was not only reprehensibly unbecoming, but must, in addition, very probably become known in the neighbourhood, leading to dire consequences not only for Georgina but for herself.

"For Robert will be so dreadfully angry if he hears of it," she pleaded, "and indeed I cannot blame him, for I promised him faithfully—"

"Well, *I* have promised nothing at all," Georgina said mulishly, "and it makes no difference to me what your precious Robert says— *I* am going to see Shannon!" She added, "If you don't care to go with me, of course you need not. I shall go alone, and bring your father's horse back to Mott House when I have finished my errand."

But to this Betsy, knowing full well what her mother would say if she allowed Georgina to go jauntering about the countryside alone, could not agree. After a good deal of rather heated discussion a compromise was finally reached: Betsy would ride with her friend toward The Place until it could be seen if Georgina's plan of meeting Shannon outside the house could be carried out, but at the first sight of the master of The Place she and Hussey would make off, leaving Georgina to have her conversation with Shannon alone and then rejoin them later at a prearranged spot.

What would happen if they were not fortunate enough to meet Shannon was not decided, Betsy no doubt hoping that in that case she would be able to persuade her friend to abandon her plan, and Georgina quite determined to do nothing of the sort.

Luckily for both, the first thing they saw when they came in sight of The Place was Shannon just leaving the stable area on his mare Juno. He did not immediately perceive them, and was turning the mare's head in another direction when Georgina called to him, spurring the roan toward him while Betsy ordered Hussey in an agitated tone to follow her and rode off in the way they had come. Shannon, raising his eyes at Georgina's hail, checked the mare and brought her around. In another few moments Georgina was beside him and, reining her horse in, said to him eagerly, "Mr. Shannon! How fortunate that I have met you! I have something of particular importance to say to you—"

She had progressed so far when it occurred to her that the cool grey eyes she was looking into were regarding her with something less than cordiality, and she faltered, breaking off.

"Yes?" Shannon prompted her, ironically. "Something of particular importance, Miss Power? May I be permitted to guess that it has to do with the prank you played the other evening? An apology, perhaps? I assure you it is quite unnecessary. I was no doubt somewhat credulous to have been gulled into thinking that such an action was quite beneath a young lady of your breeding, but in these cases the butt of the joke has only his own lack of wit to blame, I believe."

For a moment, finding the ground cut from under her feet in this way, she could only regard him in dumbfounded protest. Then the colour flew into her face and she said with dignity, "I was *not* about to apologise to you! I have nothing to apologise for! I merely wished to offer you an explanation."

"I imagine that it makes very little difference whether we call it an explanation or an apology," he said indifferently. "Consider it made, Miss Power. And now, if there is nothing else to detain you here—"

"But there *is* something! You do not understand in the least, and now you will not even listen to me! Oh," she continued, her fury rising as she looked into his unmoved face, "you make me sorry that I even *tried* to help you!"

"To help me?" He gave her a swift glance; then the sardonic expression returned again to his face. "No, that won't fadge, Miss Power," he said dryly. "You must think of some better tale than that."

"But it's true! I thought I should be doing you a good turn, and that if people saw you were invited to Craythorne they would stop behaving toward you in such an abominable manner—which I am *quite* sure now that you thoroughly deserve!"

To her surprise, she saw a rather ironical smile suddenly light his face. "Good God, I believe you are telling the truth!" he said. "You addlebrained child, did you really think you could play such a May-game as that off on people and bring it to any good end?"

"Yes, I did!" she said. "And I might have carried it off, too, if Brandon had not become ill and Major Rothe been obliged to go to England."

He looked at her incredulously. "Did Rothe know of this, then?"

"No, of course not! I met him only once, at Stokings; it is not very likely that I should make any plans with *him*. But he let fall a few words about you—that he considered you one of his closest friends, and—and certain other things that made me even more sure that an injustice was being done you—"

"Which you thereupon took it upon yourself to right," he said.

She saw that he was looking amused again, and her anger returned.

"I see nothing to smile about!" she said crossly. "You will be excessively uncomfortable, living here, if no one will recognise you."

"Oh, I believe not," he said carelessly. "I am not a very sociable creature, Miss Power—as you have probably discovered for yourself. But I suppose I must thank you for your good intentions, at any rate."

"Pray don't put yourself to the trouble," she said stiffly. "Sir John—my grandfather—was used to say that pretended gratitude is worse than none at all."

He knit his brows, surveying her oddly. "Was it your grandfather, I wonder, who gave you your peculiar notions of propriety and your severe sense of justice, Miss Power?" he asked. "As I recall, young Quinlevan told me you were in the care of two female relatives who were the highest of sticklers, which has given me something to puzzle over from the start."

She blushed, interrupting him. "Grandmama and Mama," she said. "But that is only since Sir John died. Before that, I was almost entirely in *his* care. And I am sure his ideas were all very good ones," she added, firing up again, "except that I am not a boy, which is what he would have liked, Grandmama always said. Only I cannot see that that signifies, for if it is just and honourable for a boy to do certain things, it cannot be less so for a girl."

He smiled again, this time, it appeared to her, without irony. "Now you are putting *me* to the blush, Miss Power," he said. "I am beginning to believe that, if apologies are in order, it is I who owe you one, instead of the other way around. But how was I to guess that you were not like other well-looking girls of your age?—thinking only of your own amusement, and the devil take anyone who is burned in the process—"

He broke off, seeing the rather startled look on her face. The remembrance had suddenly entered her head that Nuala had been much of her own years when he had married her, and certainly one might have thought that, with her memory so fresh in his mind, he would scarcely have voiced such a sweeping stricture.

He seemed to read what was passing through her head, for after a moment he said, rather shortly, "Are you thinking of Nuala? You should know as well as I whether that description fits *her*."

She shook her head; the renewed harshness of his tone, which seemed to her to have softened somewhat in the course of their conversation, made her uncomfortable.

"No, I *don't* know," she said. "You see, I never met her." She ventured tentatively, "She was very beautiful, I'm told."

"She was," he said, so briefly and coldly that she was made quite aware that he did not wish to continue the subject. She was left to wonder whether the sudden alteration in his manner was due to the fact that his loss was still too painfully recent for him to be able to discuss it, or to indifference toward—or, indeed, positive dislike of—his dead wife. He did not give her the leisure to resolve the question in her mind, but went on almost at once, in much the same tone, "Speaking of the proprieties—you are not left to wander about the countryside alone by that pair I saw shabbing off just now, are you?"

"Oh, no," she assured him. "I am to meet them later: that was part of the plan. You see, Betsy was afraid to come this far with me because she had promised Mr. Darlington—"

She broke off in vexation at having almost been betrayed into uttering what could only sound to him like another slight.

But he finished it for her quite coolly: "—Because she had promised Mr. Darlington that she would have nothing to do with me. Do you imagine that surprises me? I assure you it does not. The only thing that *does* surprise me is how you prevailed on her to come this far with you—and to be so obliging to me the other evening at Craythorne, for I am sure that must have been your doing as well."

"Well—yes," she admitted, adding demurely, with just the hint of an upturn of the corners of her lips, "but I must confess that it wasn't difficult. You see, she considers you a romantic figure."

He stared at her wrathfully for a moment. "Getting your own back, Miss Power?" he demanded.

"No, no! I assure you, it's quite true."

His rather harsh smile erased the frown. "You'll not deny that you're roasting me *now*," he said, "whatever you may have intended the other evening." Somewhat more grimly, he added, "I only hope you do not share Miss Mott's bird-witted delusion. There is not a grain of truth in it, as you may discover some day to your cost."

"Oh, I am quite aware of *that!*" she said at once. "Sir John always told me that men who were long on length and brawn, like yourself, were hardly ever poetically inclined, and usually turned out to be much more prosaic than some little dyspeptic creature a girl reared on lending-library novels would never trouble to turn her head after. But I am not romantically inclined, you see, like Betsy—Miss Mott. Indeed, Grandmama often says that I have a *loweringly* practical mind, which she considers quite unsuitable in a well-bred young female."

She looked hopefully at him and saw that, in spite of his continued dourness, there was the glint of a smile in his grey eyes.

"If your ideas of practicality include inviting unwanted guests to your unsuspecting relatives' homes, I can see that your grandmother's opinion may be justified," he said.

"Do you? I do not at all! I still think it would have been a splendid idea, if only I had had a little help in carrying it off. Even as it is, no one knows for certain that Cousin Bella did not ask you to Craythorne herself, for I persuaded her not to give me away."

"Persuaded her or coerced her?"

"Oh, very well—if you wish to cavil!" she said. "But she really is a very good-hearted creature, you know; it is only that she is frightened half to death of you, and of what people will think—" A thoughtful expression came over her face. "As a matter of fact," she went on, "I wonder if it would not be a good idea for you to call at Craythorne to apologise for having come in upon her without her knowledge? If you did, I am quite persuaded she would take it in good part, and if you were civil to her she might even begin to like you a little, and to see that there really can be no objection to your being friendly with Brandon—"

"How is Brandon keeping these days?" he cut in, ignoring this hopeful suggestion.

"Well, he is not in very good frame just now," she admitted. "He came down with a putrid sore throat the other day, and Dr. Culreavy has insisted on his keeping his bed—which he finds excessively boring, poor boy. I am sure *he* would be very grateful for a visit from you," she added perseveringly.

She saw his lips twitch, the coldness again gone from his face. "I see that you are still determined to rehabilitate me," he said. "Do you never admit defeat, Miss Power?"

"Hardly ever. Sir John always said—"

He flung up a hand, halting her. "Thank you, I can guess what Sir John's sentiments were on the subject. I doubt, though, that he would have considered your present project an entirely admirable one."

"Well, I do not know that, either," she disagreed, "but we will not argue over it. The main thing is—you *will* come, will you not?"

"I shall do nothing of the kind. Mrs. Quinlevan was shockingly upset by my arrival the other evening, and I have no intention of repeating my blunder." He added, after a moment, "You may tell Brandon that I am sorry he is laid up, and that if he cares to ride over some morning, when he is feeling more the thing, I shall be happy to see him."

"Thank you!" she said. "He will be pleased, you know, for he *does* consider it hard that he is not to be allowed to see you merely because of people's stupid prejudices." She gathered up her reins, saying, with a look of mischief on her face, "Will you drop your ban against the rest of us at Craythorne as well if I prevail on Cousin Bella to ask you to tea some afternoon?"

"I should take such an invitation for exactly what it is worth, Miss Power—as another of your well-meant hoaxes."

"Oh, no—that is too bad! Depend on it, I shall send no more invitations without Cousin Bella's knowledge; I have been burnt too badly already at that game! But it really *would* be much better if the two of you cried friends, you know. Family quarrels are always a cause for gossip, and if she wishes whatever scandal there may have been in your marrying Nuala to be forgotten, she would do far better to go on terms of ordinary civility with you than to keep up this stupid quarrel." She saw that he was regarding her oddly, and asked involuntarily, *"Now* what have I said to make you look so—so queer?"

"I was only wondering—has it never occurred to *you* to resent my having carried off your cousin's fortune, when you might have been mistress of The Place now yourself? You told me once that you did not, but—"

"But you were out of patience with me at the time and did not believe me," she finished it for him. "Well, I *don't* resent it. I daresay I might if I were to have nothing, but Grandmama is very well to pass, you see, and unless she becomes out of reason angry with me, she is certain to provide very well for me." She gave him a straight look and added, "So you see, not having my cousin's fortune merely means that *I* shall run less risk of having people say when I marry that the offer was made only because I was an heiress."

The expression in his eyes as she concluded this speech disconcerted her: under that direct, penetrating gaze she felt all the artificialities of their relationship suddenly stripped away, leaving her defenceless, almost breathless, in the presence of an emotion she had scarcely dreamed of only instants before.

But he merely said to her curtly, after a moment, "I hardly think they will be able to say such a thing of *you,* in any event," and then turned his horse's head in the direction in which Betsy had disappeared, remarking, "I'll ride with you until you are in sight of your friend. Come along!"

He set his mare into a brisk trot, taking it for granted, apparently, that she would follow him. Nothing was said until they came in view of Betsy, who had halted her horse at the top of a slight rise and seemed to be anxiously awaiting her friend's reappearance. Shannon then checked his mare and, turning in the saddle, said to Georgina in a harsh tone that seemed quite altered from any he had used to her previously, "I'll leave you now. May I give you one piece of advice? I am a poor subject for altruism, Miss Power. You had best lay no more plans concerning me."

Their eyes met; hers were the first to fall, as she felt perturbed colour flooding her face. The next instant he had wheeled his horse and galloped away, leaving her to pursue her way more slowly up the rise toward Betsy.

Miss Mott's face, as Georgina approached her, wore an expression of mingled relief and curiosity.

"What did he say to you? Was he very angry?" she whispered, as they turned their horses' heads toward Mott House.

The groom was at a discreet distance behind, out of hearing of a low-voiced conversation, but Georgina was not communicative.

"No," she said briefly. "Not—angry."

"He *looked* angry—or at least very odd," Miss Mott persisted. "I should think—"

"Well, it is of no use for you to think anything at all! You didn't have the spirit to come along with me, so you have no right to ask questions now," Georgina said, in a voice which, in spite of herself, was not quite steady.

She saw Betsy's startled gaze on her, and took herself sharply in hand. It would be quite like Miss Mott to whisper the tale of her discomposure to everyone who would listen, if she were to allow her to see it, but the task of appearing her ordinary self was a severe strain on her powers of dissimulation. She did not feel at all like her ordinary self; she had become aware of something, in those few moments when her eyes had met Shannon's, that had set her brain in a whirl and her pulses racing.

She wished now, fervently, that she had never been so unwary as to involve herself with him. At one time she had thought, with some incredulity, that she might be conceiving an interest in him; it occurred to her now, to her shaken amazement, that she was already far gone in love for him, and that—unless she had quite mistaken the look in his eyes that had so perturbed her on their parting—it was highly probable that her feelings were returned.

13
She gave only a brief report of her encounter with Shannon to Brandon—merely enough to convey to him the message about Shannon's willingness to see him at The Place—and none at all to Mrs. Quinlevan. She had thought it would be as well if her cousin knew nothing of the purpose of the expedition on which she had set out that morning, and had accordingly pledged Betsy to secrecy, without a great deal of hope, however, that Miss Mott would abide by her promise.

Her mistrust was not unjustified. Two days later Mrs. Quinlevan came home from a gossip with Lady Mott to inquire of her, in the utmost dismay, whether she had indeed gone off to meet Shannon at The Place.

"Lucinda said Betsy could not be perfectly sure it was an *assignation*," she said agitatedly, "or, rather, the fact is that she could not manage to get a straight story out of her after Betsy had let slip a word about the matter. But she was certain you had seen Shannon—"

"It was *not* an assignation!" Georgina said warmly. "Betsy Mott is a goose-cap! If she *must* let her tongue fly about matters that are no concern of hers, she might at least see that she tells the truth! Shannon knew nothing about my intending to see him. I wanted to apologise to him for the bumblebath I led him into here the other night, and I did, and that is the whole of the affair!"

Mrs. Quinlevan plumped down in the nearest chair, turning a distracted countenance on her young cousin.

"But, surely, my love, you *must* know how improper it is for you to be putting yourself in a position where such things can be said of you!" she protested faintly. "I vow I was ready to sink when Lucinda confided the matter to me—not that I believe she is ill-natured enough to repeat it to anyone else, but you know yourself how Betsy allows her tongue to run away with her. I have no doubt it is all over the neighbourhood by this time."

"I hope it is!" Georgina said unrepentantly, bringing a moan of horror from Mrs. Quinlevan, who was vainly attempting, with fluttering fingers, to untie her bonnetstrings. "Yes, I do!" she repeated. "I should like them to know that there is one person, at least, who feels properly about the disgraceful rudeness to which he was treated here the other evening. And if they wish to gossip about me because I have done what I am sure Sir John would have considered the right thing for me to do, I don't care! In fact, I am glad of it!" she declared, throwing caution to the winds.

"Yes, but Sir John is dead, my dear," her cousin reminded her piteously, finally succeeding in disentangling the strings of her bonnet and flinging that elegant article of *gros de Naples* and purple ribbon down with a disregard that betrayed her perturbation. "We must think of your grandmama now, and I am *sure* Lady Mercer would never approve— Not but what I *will* admit that he acted very properly here the other evening, for I will give the devil his due, and I am sure he was got up as elegantly as any gentleman present, which was a compliment to me, I have no doubt, as Lucinda says no one ever sees him except in a shooting-jacket and muddy boots, with one of those horrid Belcher neckerchiefs instead of a proper cravat—" She broke off, waving a plump hand distractedly. "Oh, where was I? That is not at all what I meant to say!"

"I know exactly what you mean to say, ma'am, so I beg you will give yourself no more trouble over it," Georgina said, smiling in spite of herself. "You will put yourself quite out of frame if you allow yourself to be so upset by a word of gossip. And, at any rate, I can assure you that I plan no further meetings with Mr. Shannon."

"Yes, but, my love, you *will* meet him, you know," Mrs. Quinlevan objected, "for Lady Eliza has sent him a card for her ball and he has accepted." Georgina looked startled, but her cousin nodded her head in agitated confirmation of her words. "Yes, indeed she has," she said, "for she told Lucinda so herself, and though she vows it was out of consideration for Major Rothe, who is a great friend of his, Lucinda says *she* is persuaded that what she really wishes is to set us all in a bustle."

"Is Major Rothe at Stokings again, then?" Georgina interrupted, wrinkling her brows in an attempt to unravel all the significance of her cousin's disjointed account. "I thought he had not meant to return."

"Yes, so did we all, but it seems his brother is much recovered, and Lucinda says Lady Eliza tells her he came back on Mr. Shannon's account, because he had scarcely had an opportunity to see him when he was here previously. But if that is true I do not see why he does not stay at The Place, so that Lady Eliza will not be obliged to invite Mr. Shannon to Stokings."

"She is not obliged in the least to invite him," Georgina said, in a cool little voice. "She did it, I am sure, only because she wished to."

Mrs. Quinlevan stared at her. "My dear child, you do not know what you are saying!" she protested. "I know she flirts with every man she takes a fancy to, in that shocking London fashion of hers, but Mr. Shannon is quite beneath her touch!"

"Oh, yes!" Georgina agreed. "I am sure she thinks so, too. But she is determined to bring him round her thumb, all the same." She became aware that she was speaking with a bitter emphasis that was causing Mrs. Quinlevan to regard her in astonishment, and hastily added, "Not that it is any concern of mine, of course. Lady Eliza may do as she pleases, but I should think that Colonel Malladon—"

"Oh no, my dear, Colonel Malladon will have nothing to say to it," Mrs. Quinlevan assured her. "He has never been able to control her, and, indeed, I believe he has ceased to try to do so. But one would think, after what happened to poor Nuala while she was under her protection, that she, of all people, would take care not to put herself into a position where she will be open to scandalous gossip on Mr. Shannon's account! I am *persuaded* that she must be asking him only from good nature."

Georgina had little opinion of Lady Eliza's good nature, but she did not choose to debate the matter further with her cousin, and therefore made some excuse to break off the conversation and leave the room.

But the news that Shannon would be at Lady Eliza's ball had furnished her with a great deal of food for thought. She believed she knew very well what Lady Eliza's motives had been in sending him a card of invitation, but what his had been in accepting it, after the embarrassing situation into which he had stepped at Craythorne, she could only conjecture. Her imagination suggested that it might be because he knew he would see her there, and then fell before the practical consideration that he might merely be taking advantage of another opportunity to better his position in the neighbourhood.

But in spite of her lack of assurance on this head, she certainly felt called upon to make every attempt to look her best on the evening of the ball at Stokings a week later. She had accepted Mrs. Quinlevan's offer to have Anson dress her hair, and had gone to considerable pains to procure the exact shade of ribbon that would most becomingly trim her three-quarter dress of white spider gauze, worn over a slip of jonquil satin. Even Mrs. Quinlevan, who was accustomed to speaking of her as a very well-looking girl, though not, of course, to be compared to her poor Nuala, admitted, when she appeared before her in her delicate, high-waisted gown, her golden curls dressed à la Tite, and with a shawl of silver net drapery, Denmark satin slippers, and long French kid gloves completing her costume, that even Nuala would not have been able to cast her in the shade that evening.

But the exceptional looks in which her young cousin appeared merely served to deepen Mrs. Quinlevan's apprehensions over the ball. She had noted with misgiving Peter Hession's attentions to Georgina on the evening of the party at Craythorne and the fact that he seemed to be impelled to call at her house very frequently of late; and the disagreeable idea now occurred to her that perhaps, dazzled by Georgina's appearance that evening, he might be led on to make an outright offer, which it would be her duty to convey in form to Lady Mercer and Mrs. Power. She had little doubt of what the outcome of such a situation must be. The two ladies in Bath, known to be anxious to see Georgina settled in a suitable marriage, would certainly find nothing to object to in young Mr. Hession's fortune, person, or position in life, and their approval of the match must therefore be taken for granted.

Nor had Lady Hession's complaisant manner toward Georgina on the evening of the Craythorne party been lost on Mrs. Quinlevan, and if Lady Hession were to be found forwarding the match, she knew that Sir Landers' consent to it must be assured, for that gentleman seldom moved contrary to his wife's wishes.

Of Georgina's feelings she was less certain, but even in this direction the outlook seemed gloomy. She and Mr. Hession appeared to be on the best of terms, in spite of an occasional disagreement arising from the young man's adherence to the overconsequential ideas of his parents, and, although Georgina had shown no signs of a definite partiality, Mrs. Quinlevan did not doubt that the united influence of Lady Mercer and Mrs. Power would soon overcome any hesitation she might feel over accepting an offer from him.

All in all, it seemed to her that her plans to marry Brandon to his cousin were in a fair way to be completely overset—an apprehension that quite drove her fears regarding Shannon from her head. As a result, during the drive to Stokings she bestowed scarcely a thought on the probability of his appearing there that evening, occupying herself instead with a series of schemes for seeing to it that Mr. Hession had no opportunity to do more than stand up once with Georgina during the evening.

When they arrived at Stokings they found the house lit from attic to cellar, and a steady succession of carriages drawing up at the front door. Alighting from her own landaulet, Mrs. Quinlevan passed with Georgina up the broad steps to the door and entered the house. Like The Place of the Oaks, Stokings had been built in Tudor times, but, unlike it, it had received extensive alterations, and Lady Eliza, since becoming its mistress, had instituted a plan of campaign in regard to its interior decoration that had made it the talk of the neighbourhood. On her previous visit Georgina had seen little beyond the hall and the Red Saloon, which had impressed her, even in daylight, as being somewhat startling apartments, with dragons writhing on crimson silk draperies and Buhl tables bearing porcelain tigers and pagodas.

Now, in the blaze of the hundreds of candles that illumined it, with all its rooms thrown open for the entertainment of the guests, she positively blinked on entering the great hall. Lady Eliza, obviously influenced by her visits to the monstrously ornate Pavilion which the Prince Regent had had constructed in Brighton, had done her best to emulate its Oriental splendour in the unlikely Tudor surroundings of Stokings, and the result was a phantasmagoria of blue and crimson and yellow, blazing with lustres of rubies and brilliants and assaulting the eye with the golden suns, stars, pagodas, water-lilies, and dragons that decorated its walls and sprang from each sofa back and pillar head.

Passing up the stairs to the ballroom, Georgina and her cousin found Lady Eliza receiving in a gown of crimson silk quite in keeping with her surroundings, with a fantastic creation of gleaming brilliants, lace, and ostrich plumes nodding from her head. She greeted them with her usual vivacity, but Georgina felt that there was a certain malice in the glance she cast over her.

"I see you have already learned that I am taking a leaf from *your* book this evening, my dear," she said. "Positively, I have seen you in such looks! But you must not expect too much, you know. It is possible that Shannon will not dare to show his face, after the snubbing he received at Craythorne. You had best content yourself with dazzling young Peter Hession."

Georgina, who had begun to colour vividly as soon as she had caught the intent of Lady Eliza's remarks, was spared the necessity of making any rejoinder by Mrs. Quinlevan, who turned from the civilities she was uttering to Colonel Malladon to say, in a perfect quiver of indignation, "Lady Eliza, I do *beg* you will not make such nonsensical insinuations! What has Mr. Shannon to say to my cousin? He is none of *her* concern, I assure you!"

Lady Eliza laughed. "No?" she asked. "I devoutly hope you are right, Bella dear! But I have been hearing the oddest stories, you see—about excursions on horseback leading to strange meetings, and— But of course I never repeat gossip, you know!"

She turned to the next guest, leaving Georgina and Mrs. Quinlevan to pass on into the ballroom. Here they were at once accosted by Sir Manning Hartily, who begged the honour of standing up with Miss Power for the quadrille.

"Consider myself fortunate to have snatched you up the minute you stepped inside the door!" he beamed. "Daresay you'll have a shocking crowd of young fellows around you all evening. No time then for an old fogey like me!"

"Oh, Sir Manning, how can you say so!" Mrs. Quinlevan cried, making up with her own eager cordiality for a marked lack of enthusiasm in her cousin's demeanour. "I am sure Georgina is always honoured to stand up with you—such an elegant master of the art as you are!"

"Well, I fancy I *am* up to all the latest rigs," Sir Manning said complacently. "Can still keep up with the young fellows, you know, ma'am—dance all night, waltz, quadrille, along with the best of 'em. Do you waltz, Miss Power?"

"No, sir," Georgina was thankfully able to answer, leaving Mrs. Quinlevan to go into voluble explanations of her own feelings concerning such "fast" modern dances, feelings that she was sure even the approval of the august patronesses of Almack's could not alter.

"For what," she inquired of Sir Manning, "can be more distasteful to a well-bred young female than to be twirling about a ballroom floor in the *public* embrace of a young man?"

Here, however, she soon perceived that she had taken the wrong tack, for Sir Manning was very fond of waltzing, to the extent to which his girth permitted him to indulge in it, and considered such old-fashioned notions as Mrs. Quinlevan had expressed to be quite beneath his reputation as a gentleman of the first stare of fashion. Fortunately for her, her brother, Mr. Jeremy Barnwall, who was an old friend of Sir Manning's, walked into the room at that moment, and in the flurry of greetings and demands for the latest London *on-dits* that ensued, Mrs. Quinlevan's solecism was forgotten.

Georgina had not previously met her cousin Jeremy, as he had not returned to Ireland since his precipitous departure from it on the day following her arrival. She greeted him with suitable cordiality, which was somewhat diminished, however, when, after he had surveyed her with the utmost attention for several moments, he remarked frankly to his sister, "You must be touched in your upper works, Bella, to think she'll do for Brandon. Damme, she must have the young fellows buzzing about her like flies!"

"What's this? Brandon? Who is Brandon?" Sir Manning demanded jo-
vially, and, finding himself suddenly jostled by a young gentleman who
had been hovering on the edge of the group, waiting for an opportunity to
enter the conversation, looked around wrathfully into the perturbed face
of Mr. Peter Hession.

"Beg pardon, Sir Manning! Servant, Mrs. Quinlevan—Miss Power—
Mr. Barnwall!" Peter gasped, apparently as overcome by his own rudeness
as was Sir Manning.

All the same, the expression of indignant reproach that had leaped into
his eyes at the moment when he had so far forgotten himself as to intrude
into the circle around Georgina failed to disappear, and it was not difficult
to guess that it had been put there by his overhearing Mr. Barnwall's
blunt reference to his sister's scheme of marrying Georgina to her son.

It had evidently been Mr. Hession's intention to solicit Georgina's hand
for the set of country-dances that was just then forming, but in his embarrassment over having intruded into the conversation in such a peculiar
manner he did not immediately speak, and as a result had the mortification of seeing her led off a few moments later by another young gentleman. This circumstance, though displeasing to him, was highly gratifying
to Mrs. Quinlevan, who confided forebodingly to her brother, as soon as
Peter was out of hearing, that she greatly feared that young man was on
the point of making an offer for Georgina.

Mr. Barnwall, raising his brows, pursed his lips and kindly observed,
"No need to fly into a pucker, Bella. Told you so when you first men-
tioned the scheme to me. If it wasn't him, it 'ud be another young sprig
Pretty as a picture, that girl, you know."

Mrs. Quinlevan uttered an aggrieved and indignant exclamation. "One
would think you cared nothing at all for poor Brandon!" she accused him.
"If you would have made the smallest push to assist me, instead of running off to London in that inconsiderate manner, I daresay we should
have the matter settled by this time. And I must say I take it very ill that
you did not so much as notify me that you were returning to Kerry, and
that I am obliged to run across you here as though we were the merest acquaintances!"

"Dash it all, Bella, you know I'm a bird of passage," Mr. Barnwall objected. "Never know where I'll be from one minute to the next. Popped
over only to buy a horse for a friend of mine. Thought while I was here I
might just look in on Lady Eliza's ball—"

"Well, I hope, now that you *are* here, you will not object to obliging me by doing your possible to see to it that Georgina does not stand up above once with Peter Hession, and that she has no opportunity to speak privately with him." She added, with awful civility, "After all, Brandon *is* your only nephew, and as I, a widowed mother, am left alone in the world to look after my son's interests—"

"Not at a ball, Bella!" Mr. Barnwall said, with a look of injury equalling her own appearing on his face. "Damme if I ever saw such a woman for choosing the wrong time and place to enact a Cheltenham tragedy! No!" he added hastily, seeing her open her lips to speak. "Don't come down on me here! I'll do what I can for you, I promise you, but you're fighting a losing battle—may as well make up your mind to *that!*"

He moved away, greeting Sir Humphrey and Lady Mott, who had just entered the room with their daughter Betsy, with an eagerness that Mrs. Quinlevan darkly considered was due more to his desire to escape from her than to any interest in conversing with them.

A short time later she had established herself on one of the rout chairs that had been set out along the walls of the ballroom for those guests who preferred to watch the dancing rather than to engage in it, joining a group of which Lady Hession was a member. Lady Hession, evidently considering that a country ball which she had postponed her departure to London to attend was worthy of her most elegant finery, was wearing a gown of purple-blue taffeta lavishly ornamented with rouleaux of blue satin, and a turban from which several ostrich plumes rose. Being satisfied that she was putting her companions quite in the shade, she was in an affable mood, and took the first opportunity to congratulate Mrs. Quinlevan on Georgina's being in such high bloom that evening.

"I am sure she and my Peter will be a picture to behold when they stand up together," she said, "as I am persuaded they will, for Peter has confided in me that he will be certain to make every effort to engage her hand not only for a set of country-dances, but for the quadrille as well."

Mrs. Quinlevan tossed her head. "Well, *there* I believe he must be disappointed," she said complacently, noting with approval that Georgina was now safely partnered with Major Rothe, "for we had scarcely set foot inside the door before Sir Manning Hartily was soliciting her hand for the quadrille."

"Indeed!" Lady Hession said, raising her brows. "I am sorry to hear that, for I am persuaded she would have enjoyed herself a great deal more if she had had the pleasure of standing up with Peter. He is accounted an excellent dancer, you know; indeed, I have heard him praised for his skill even at Almack's, where so many gentlemen of the highest dexterity in the art are to be seen. However," she went on, with a majestic attempt at archness, "I daresay if Miss Power is to bestow her hand only on such— shall we say, mature?—gentlemen as Sir Manning and Major Rothe, my Peter will have little to fear in the way of a rival."

Mrs. Quinlevan, rising to the challenge, felt it incumbent on her to plunge in here with a remark which she was well aware Mr. Barnwall would have strongly deprecated her making, had he been present.

"I wonder that you should speak so, Lady Hession," she said, "for I am persuaded you must be aware that, while dear Georgina behaves with per- fect civility toward all the young gentlemen who count themselves among her admirers, she keeps her deepest regard for her cousin Brandon. In- deed, she is not at all one of these light-minded modern young girls who enjoy racketing about constantly to balls and parties, but is perfectly con- tent to spend a quiet day with her cousin as often as may be."

Lady Hession seemed much struck by this speech. "Brandon!" she said, in considerable surprise, which seemed to be strongly intermingled with disapproval as well. "But, my dear Mrs. Quinlevan, this cannot be! I wish to say nothing against the boy, but surely you cannot believe that he is of an age to think of settling himself in life! He cannot be nineteen!"

"He is past nineteen," Mrs. Quinlevan said, her feathers ruffling at this outspoken opposition, "and, indeed, he is very mature for his years—much more mature, I might say, than young men who have their minds fixed on nothing but curricle-racing and dandyism and, for what I know, gaming as well."

Lady Hession turned a repressive stare on her. "Surely," she said, "you do not think to accuse my Peter of being such a young man!" Before her formidable gaze, Mrs. Quinlevan quickly lost her courage and uttered a hasty disclaimer, which drew a satisfied nod from Lady Hession and the amiable concession, "Well, well, we will not talk of it here. I have always felt that, out of regard for one's hostess, one ought at least to attempt to enjoy oneself at a ball, and I am sure Lady Eliza has been at such pains to make this an agreeable occasion that we should be ungrateful indeed if we did not show her pleasant faces." She let her gaze travel around the room and said with satisfaction, observing the steadily increasing throng of guests, "She has done very well for herself this evening, I believe. As I told Sir Landers, since we were postponing our journey to London in order to attend, I made no doubt that there would be many others who would do the same. Even Manning Hartily, as you have observed, is here, and it is most unusual for *him* not to be in London by this date."

One of the younger matrons ventured to repeat a piece of gossip which had lately begun to be discreetly whispered in circles more knowing concerning events across Saint George's Channel, to the effect that Sir Manning was said to be rolled-up, and, finding himself *de trop* amongst his erstwhile noble companions, was hanging out for a rich wife as the only method by which to make some recover for his fortunes.

"At his age! Nonsense! Who would have him?" Lady Hession said loftily, but Mrs. Quinlevan jumped, and looked around anxiously to see if Sir Manning were anywhere in the vicinity of Georgina. It had never entered her head to place *him* on the list of gentlemen to be discouraged from being allowed too free an access to her young cousin, but it occurred to her now that he was always extremely attentive to Georgina when he was in her company, and that, while her cousin's expectations could not be considered brilliant, they were certainly comfortable, perhaps as comfortable as a gentleman of Sir Manning's years and lack of fortune could hope to aspire to.

Her nervousness increased when another piece of gossip—this one referring to the rumour that Lady Eliza had invited Shannon to her ball—was brought into the conversation. She believed she could be certain, from Lady Eliza's words to her and Georgina on their arrival, that their hostess did indeed expect Shannon to be present that evening, and the very thought of what Georgina might feel called upon to do if that abominable man were to walk into the room made her ply her fan distractedly. Looking about for her young cousin, she saw with dismay that she was now standing up with Peter Hession for the boulanger. She endeavoured to compose herself with the thought that it was to be expected that she must dance with him once during the evening, but she could not prevent herself from keeping an anxious watch on them, and several times during the ensuing minutes answered quite at random when a remark was addressed to her.

Had she but been aware of it, her anxiety, at this particular moment at least, was quite misplaced. Far from taking advantage of their proximity in the dance to utter sweet nothings in his partner's ear, Mr. Hession had embarked on a bitter quarrel with her.

"Brandon Quinlevan!" had been his opening gun, uttered in a tone of outraged disbelief. "Do you mean to tell me that you—or anyone else—has taken it seriously in mind that he should marry you! Dashed near floored me to hear your cousin say such a thing, I can tell you! A girl like you, and that—that limping halfling!"

Georgina's colour rose dangerously, and had Mr. Hession been observant—which, unfortunately, even in his calmer moods, he was not—he might have swallowed his disapproval and beat a hasty retreat to a safer subject. As it was, he failed even to catch the menace in the cool tone in which she stated to him, "I cannot see what interest *my* affairs can possibly have for *you*, Mr. Hession!"

"Well, they *do* interest me," he said aggrievedly, "and I should dashed well think you'd know it by this time! I can tell you, too, that I don't like it above half, thinking of your living under the same roof with that young chub day in, day out, and your cousin crying him up in your ears all the while. He may be a bright 'un—I don't say he ain't. But, Lord, he ain't for *you!*"

"I prefer—I *much* prefer not to discuss the subject, Mr. Hession!" Georgina interrupted, this time on a rising note of displeasure that did penetrate into her partner's mind. "You are taking a great deal too much on yourself!"

"Well, I beg your pardon if I have offended you," Peter said, still too perturbed to make more than a perfunctory gesture in the direction of civility. "But there's no bearing such a thing, you know—to hear your name bandied about publicly with young Quinlevan's, as if it was quite an understood thing. I wonder that Mr. Barnwall should show such a want of conduct!"

"Mr. Barnwall," Georgina said, herself incensed beyond civility by this time, "is not the only person I could name who shows a want of conduct! If you do not leave this subject immediately, Mr. Hession, I assure you I shall walk off the floor! *You* may believe it proper to discuss such matters in public, but *I* do not!"

To tell the truth, she was more indignant at his slighting references to Brandon than at his lack of propriety in speaking to her in such a manner in a public place, and there was still a third cause for her perturbation at that moment: she had just seen Shannon enter the room. The evening was by that time so far advanced that Lady Eliza and her husband were no longer stationed at the head of the grand staircase to receive their guests, but had themselves come into the ballroom, and Georgina saw that Lady Eliza, who had apparently perceived Shannon at the very moment that she herself had, was already moving quickly across the room toward him.

Shannon, attired in the same correct evening dress that he had worn on the night of the party at Craythorne, stood for a moment in the doorway with an expression on his face that Georgina could could only characterise as saturnine. He seemed, she thought, to have no idea of having come to make himself agreeable. Knowing that he had certainly not put in an appearance to oblige Lady Eliza, she could not help reverting to the disquieting notion which had previously entered her mind—that if he accepted Lady Eliza's invitation it would be for the sake of seeing *her*.

She found herself paying so little heed to the steps of the dance in which she was engaged that Peter, in astonishment, was compelled to recall her to what she was doing. When the set ended a few minutes later, she saw that Shannon was still engaged in conversation with Lady Eliza, who was looking even bolder than was her wont, laughing and behaving as if it were quite the thing for her to have asked Shannon into her house. However, the matrons ranged along the walls of the ballroom all had their heads together in scandalised comment, and even among the younger set there seemed to be no one willing to brave the disapproval of his elders by coming up to speak to the newcomer. Georgina looked around for Major Rothe, but he was nowhere to be seen, and she guessed that he might have sat down to a game of whist in one of the other rooms.

She made up her mind abruptly, and when Mr. Hession offered her his arm to lead her back to Mrs. Quinlevan said to him decisively, "I wish you will take me to Lady Eliza instead."

"Lady Eliza?" Peter looked around, saw their hostess in conversation with Shannon, and immediately entered a protest. "Oh, no! I think not, Miss Power!" he said. "She's talking with Shannon just now. Dashed rum thing to do, asking him here, in my opinion, but, at any rate, *you* don't want to have anything to do with him. Take you back to your cousin."

"No, indeed, you will not!" Georgina said. "If you will not take me to Lady Eliza, I shall go alone." She looked at him challengingly and inquired, "Are you afraid to meet Mr. Shannon? I can assure you that he does not bite."

Peter reddened slightly. "Not afraid in the least," he said. "But I don't see the sense in having anything to do with the fellow. He ain't received, you know."

"He is received here," Georgina pointed out, incontrovertibly. She put her chin up. "*And* I will remind you that he was received at Craythorne. *I* am going to speak to him!"

Mr. Hession, confronted with this ultimatum, could do nothing but accompany her reluctantly across the room. He noted with disapproval the smile she had for Shannon as she greeted him, and for his own part, when she waved a hand at him and said airily, "You don't know Mr. Hession, I believe? Mr. Shannon!" he scowled and muttered a minimal acknowledgement of the introduction.

Shannon's reply was equally cool, and it was Lady Eliza who, with her tinkling laugh, moved in to cover over the somewhat awkward pause that ensued.

"Oh, dear! I can't have the pair of you glowering at each other like sulky schoolboys!" she said. "Shannon, really—you have already had your innings, you know; you ran off with *one* Miss Power and you shan't be so rag-mannered as to do it again! This time it is Mr. Hession's turn—and, if I am to believe his mama, the matter is already all but settled, at any rate, so you had best take your defeat with a good grace." She turned about, seeing someone come up beside her, and, while Georgina stood staring at her in thunderstruck silence, exclaimed brightly, "Good gracious, Sir Manning! What are you about, stealing upon one like a shadow! May I present Mr. Shannon? Sir Manning Hartily—"

Sir Manning acknowledged the introduction briefly, disclaimed any resemblance to a shadow, and said purposefully that he had come to claim the promised favor of Miss Power's hand for the quadrille. Not being a sensitive man, he did not perceive that he had blundered into a situation so pregnant with ill feeling that, under more propitious circumstances, it might have seemed likely that murder might have been committed. Indeed, Georgina, furious at Lady Eliza's calculated misrepresentation of the relationship between herself and Peter, could cheerfully have strangled her, while Shannon surveyed Mr. Hession's rather startled approval of what had been said in his behalf from narrowed grey eyes that had suddenly taken on an extremely hard, almost implacable expression.

Even Lady Eliza seemed affected by a degree of nervousness under that grim gaze, and her laughter faltered. But Sir Manning, in happy unconsciousness, saw none of this, and merely said to his partner that they had best bestir themselves, as the set was already forming. Georgina mechanically allowed herself to be led off, repressing a strong desire to wrest her hand from Sir Manning's and return to correct the piece of misinformation that Lady Eliza had uttered. But there was no way for her to do so without creating a stir on the ballroom floor, and her sense of propriety, faulty as she had often been assured it was, forbade her to make such a to-do.

Instead, she took her place miserably in the set, looking back over her shoulder as she did so to see that Shannon had disappeared from the place where she had left him and that Lady Eliza, with a high colour in her face and a rather too ready laugh, was now talking to Sir Humphrey Mott.

For the first several minutes of the dance Georgina did not attend to a word that her partner uttered. She was reflecting bitterly that there was not the slightest doubt now that Lady Eliza intended to do everything in her power to prevent the development of any closer relationship between her and Shannon. She was equally certain that Lady Eliza's efforts in this direction were likely to be approximately as efficacious as a straw barrier against a hurricane if Shannon were of a mind to run contrary to them.

That he might very well determine to do so, she could no longer doubt. It had been impossible to mistake the expression that had leapt into his grey eyes when Lady Eliza had given her entirely unjustified interpretation of the situation between Georgina and Peter Hession. Georgina herself had had a strange sensation of being scorched by that sudden blaze, and certainly even Lady Eliza had been taken aback.

An odd, foreboding feeling that the evening was going to turn out to be one of those occasions that one remembers, for good or for ill, all one's life began to take possession of her. She was brought back to her present situation with a start, however, by Sir Manning's aggrieved statement that he had already inquired of her three times when she would be returning to Bath, and gave him a hurried apology for her absent-mindedness.

"Balls are such—such *distracting* occasions!" she said, as she made a rapid attempt to gather her wits. "Don't you find them so, Sir Manning? But I daresay you don't; you are so accustomed to them."

Sir Manning regarded her suspiciously, as if he rather imagined that he was being fobbed off. "Well, if you don't care to tell me—" he said.

"Tell you what? Oh! When I am returning to Bath? Why, I am not at all certain, you see. As long as Mama and Grandmama do not require me there—"

"Thought I might pop down there myself one of these days," Sir Manning said, regarding her with what she could only describe to herself, with a sinking feeling, as a hopeful eye. "Just as you said—deuced bore London can be during the Season, when you've seen as many of 'em as I have. Might look in on you if I do. Great Pulteney Street, is it? Lady Mercer? Don't believe I've had the pleasure of meeting her, but I'll do myself the honour of calling on her. Many mutual friends, I'm sure—including yourself, my dear little girl!" he said, giving her hand a significant squeeze.

The unhappy thought crossed Georgina's mind—as it had her cousin Bella's earlier in the evening—that Sir Manning's attentions might have some more serious purpose than mere flirtation. No doubt it might seem to him that she must be dazzled by the prestige of his long and successful social career, by his intimate knowledge of the world of fashion into which she had scarcely entered, even by the impeccable taste in dress that had earned him the reputation of being a veritable Tulip of the Ton. Certainly, matches were made every day in which the partners were of more disparate years; but she had no desire to be a party to one of them, and told herself in some alarm that the sooner she succeeded in setting down Sir Manning's pretensions—if pretensions they were—the better it would be for everyone concerned.

She accordingly took pains to behave toward him with the coolest civility for the remainder of the dance, and when it came to an end was pleased to be able to walk off at once with Betsy Mott, who had had the misfortune to tear one of the lace flounces of her gown the moment before, and now applied to her to accompany her into an anteroom and help her pin it up.

"I daren't take the time to run upstairs and ask Lady Eliza's maid to do it," she confided breathlessly, "for I am to stand up with Robert for the next set, and I would not disappoint him for the world." As she and Georgina walked into a small room at the back of the house which, like the others, was furnished in the Oriental style and was lit by a single lamp in the shape of a water-lily that shed a rather murky light over the assembled dragons and mandarins, she chattered on: "Mr. Shannon is here! Have you seen him? Of course I shall not dare to speak to him; I could not, after the dreadful quarrel I had with Robert over him! I do hope he does not ask me to stand up with him! Do you think he will?"

Georgina said curtly that she was very sure he would not, attempting to discourage the subject as she knelt beside Betsy, repairing the damage to the flounce with the pins which her friend provided from her reticule. She had almost finished her task when she heard the sound of hasty footsteps approaching, and the next moment Mr. Hession burst into the room.

"Miss Power! I must speak to you!" he exclaimed at once, disregarding Betsy, who gave him a startled stare and asked him frankly, "Good gracious, Peter, whatever is the matter with you? One would think the house was on fire!"

Mr. Hession looked at her imperatively. "Go away, Betsy!" he commanded. "I want to speak to Miss Power."

Betsy's stare widened. "Indeed, I shall do nothing of the sort!" she said downrightly. "It would be *quite* improper to leave you here alone with Georgina. Mama would make me very sorry indeed if I were to do such a thing."

"You will be even sorrier in a brace of seconds if you do not go away at once!" Mr. Hession declared, advancing a few steps threateningly toward her. "Don't make a nuisance of yourself now, Bet. Be off! What I have to say to Miss Power," he added more grandly, "is not for your ears."

Georgina, who had by this time risen from her knees, had a moment's apprehension that pink champagne was responsible for Mr. Hession's peculiar behaviour. But a second glance at him made it necessary for her to discard this theory in favour of one involving the mingled effects of ardour and jealousy working together in a young man's impetuous brain. She was not alarmed—indeed, she was rather amused by her young friend's lofty manner—but Miss Mott seemed inclined to take her old playmate's words at their face value. Before Georgina could detain her she had scurried out of the room, uttering some obscure threat as she did so about informing his mother of what he was up to.

Georgina, who could not help smiling at this warning, attempted to follow her, but she was astonished to find her way barred by Mr. Hession, who informed her in no uncertain terms that he had come to have it out with her then and there.

"Can't go around all evening thinking you're angry with me!" he said. "I know I shouldn't have said that about Brandon—very fond of Brandon—always was! But dooce take it, you can't marry him! Your cousin must have windmills in her head even to think of such a thing."

Georgina's colour rose. "I have told you before, Mr. Hession, I won't discuss the matter with you," she said. "Now if you will please to stand aside—"

"But I don't please!" Mr. Hession said desperately. "Dash it, Miss Power—Georgina—can't you see I'm all to pieces over you? There's no bearing it—first this talk about you and Brandon, and then that fellow Shannon— I should think, after the way he behaved toward Nuala, you wouldn't care even to be in the same room with him, yet there you were—"

"I *cannot* see that Mr. Shannon is any more your affair than my cousin Brandon is!" Georgina said. "You are being extremely tiresome, Mr. Hession!"

She again attempted to move past him, but this time he seized her arm and the next moment, before she could realise what he was about, he had thrown prudence to the winds and was attempting rather wildly to sweep her into his embrace. She was a tall, well-built girl, but her struggles were somewhat hampered by the knowledge that if she tore her gown or ruined her coiffure it must be observed by the other guests at the ball, and she might have ended by being kissed had not aid abruptly reached her in the shape of a heavy hand laid on Mr. Hession's shoulder, which flung him reeling across the room. Georgina, regaining her own balance, looked up, startled, to see Shannon standing before her, sardonically regarding Mr. Hession, who was picking himself up from the sofa on which he had landed and was showing every evidence of rushing to attack the intruder.

His martial instincts were quickly dampened, however, by Shannon's voice advising him rather brutally, "I don't recommend it. I know a little about that game, and can give you four inches and two stone, besides."

Peter, halting, regarded him doubtfully, as the justice of these words was borne in on him. He was no coward, but the sight of Shannon's formidable figure looming before him was enough to give any young man of his moderate inches pause, and he was conscious, as well, of a certain weakness in his own moral position. Certainly it would be easier for Shannon to defend his action in rescuing a young lady from attentions that must have appeared forced upon her than it would be for him to uphold his own in doing the forcing.

He swallowed down his wrath and said stiffly, "If you think I am such a shagrag as to start a mill here, you are mistaken, sir! All the same, it was no business of *yours* to come barging in on a private conversation."

"I suppose that might be one term for it, but it is not the one that *I* would choose," said Shannon, with a cool expression of scorn on his face. "And if you have any ideas of continuing such behaviour on another occasion, I shall warn you that you had best forget them, for nothing would give me greater pleasure than to toss you into the nearest horse-pond, my lad!" He turned then to Georgina, the harsh expression on his face not altering. "I might add, Miss Power," he said, "that you might not find yourself in hot water quite so frequently if you would not agree to remain alone with young men in dimly lit apartments—"

"I didn't!" she interrupted, indignantly. "That is—it was not in the least my fault! Betsy *would* leave, and when I tried to follow her—" She felt her cheeks flaming scarlet and broke off, exclaiming, "I might have known you would try to put me in the wrong! But if you had not been spying after me, you would not have known I was here, and *that*, let me tell you, I do not consider to be at all gentlemanly behaviour!"

Mr. Hession, plucking up his courage as he heard her launch into this spirited attack on her rescuer, intervened here to say vehemently, "She's right, you know. What the devil business was it of *yours?*"

"Oh, Peter, *do* be quiet!" Georgina interrupted, rounding on him heatedly. "I wish you will go away and leave me in peace; you have caused quite enough botheration for one evening!"

"And leave you here alone with *him?*" Mr. Hession exclaimed, outraged. "I most certainly will not! If *that* wouldn't be the outside of enough!"

Georgina paid no heed to him; she was looking at Shannon, who met her gaze with an ironical glint in his own eyes that did not long remain there. She had the oddest feeling, as those hard grey eyes, strangely softening now, met hers, that her heart was trying to jump into her throat, and for a moment she quite forgot her surroundings—the Oriental splendour of the room in which she stood, Lady Eliza's ball, even the indignant Mr. Hession—and might have answered, rather dazedly, if she had been questioned on the matter, that she was standing in a wide empty space of some sort, far removed from any place she knew, and quite alone with Shannon.

14 Only a moment elapsed, however, before she was abruptly recalled to her true circumstances. The matter that brought this about was Lady Eliza's brisk entrance into the room. She checked just over the threshold, and, looking from Mr. Hession's thunderstruck face to Georgina's bemused one, turned her own maliciously sparkling eyes on Shannon, who was favouring her with no very friendly regard.

"Oh, it's true, then!" she said. "I thought the Mott child was quite out of her reckoning, but it seems she really was speaking the truth. And you, Shannon—no, let me guess!—*you*, of all men, have taken up the unlikely role of knight-errant, galloping in to rescue the maiden in distress! Oh, dear! I shall fall into whoops, and that won't do in the least, for I can see you are all three of you determined to play your scene out in deadly earnest."

She broke off suddenly, even *her* assurance failing before the contempt she read in Shannon's eyes. Georgina, quite confounded by this new turn of events, could for the moment think of nothing at all to say, and it was Mr. Hession who came to Lady Eliza's aid by beginning a very stiff and sheepish exculpation of his conduct, which allowed his hostess to regain her own composure by playfully attacking him.

"Oh, you need say no more to me, you odious boy!" she said. "I quite know how it is with you young men when you have taken it into your head to become nutty upon someone—but, indeed, you must not play your little games under *my* roof. If you have the slightest regard for my reputation as a respectable hostess, you will go back instantly into the ballroom—and you as well, Shannon," she said, turning to him. "And I beg that when the two of you have arrived there you will behave properly, and give the lie to the story Miss Betsy seems only too anxious to spread about. Peter, you are the younger—do you go first."

Mr. Hession, pokering up at the suggestion that he leave the field to his rival, looked obdurate, but he was not, in the end, obliged to put his valour to the test, for Shannon suddenly and without a word turned and walked out of the room. Mr. Hession, who by this time was beginning to feel the full embarrassment of the wide publicity his ill-timed amorousness was receiving, was only too glad to stammer an excuse and follow Shannon's example, and in a matter of moments Georgina and Lady Eliza were left alone.

Georgina was still too disturbed by the events of the past few minutes, and in particular by the implications of what she had read in Shannon's eyes, to speak. She would have given a great deal, in fact, to be able to be alone for a few minutes, and had to struggle for sufficient control to face Lady Eliza without betraying her emotions.

That she was not entirely successful in her efforts was evident from the shrewd expression on Lady Eliza's own face as she stood regarding her, slowly tapping her ivory-handled fan against the palm of her left hand.

"My dear," she said abruptly, in a smooth voice, "you will not mind if I speak frankly to you? I am some few years older than you are, and have had a great deal more experience in the world, and I should feel the shabbiest creature alive if I did not put at least a word of warning in your ear. Will you sit down for a moment?"

She gestured toward a sofa covered in yellow-and-white satin, with tigers' heads carved on the ends of the arms, moving toward it as she spoke, but Georgina did not follow her lead. Instead, she gathered her disordered thoughts and said, with as much civility as she could muster, "Indeed, I had rather not, Lady Eliza. I am engaged for this set—"

"My dear child, if you are afraid to hear what I have to say to you, you must be in a worse case than I had imagined," Lady Eliza said. She sat down and patted the sofa beside her. "I promise that I shan't keep you more than a pair of minutes," she went on, "and that I have no intention of scolding you. Indeed, I am quite sure, from Betsy's tale, that you are not in the least at fault in what has happened. Young men who fancy themselves in love are quite unaccountable creatures—as I know only too well! Now *do* sit down here beside me and listen to what I have to say!"

Georgina had an uneasy feeling, as she looked into Lady Eliza's smiling face, that she would do much better *not* to sit down beside her. But she could not walk out of the room at this point without being guilty of the grossest incivility, so she reluctantly moved to the sofa and took the place that Lady Eliza had indicated to her.

"That is much better," Lady Eliza said approvingly. "Of course I have put you in a flurry by being so grave about all this—but, really, it is a very serious affair when one sees a young girl about to jeopardise her whole future happiness by her imprudence! In your cousin Nuala's case, I did not know what I now know concerning Shannon, nor did I believe that she would be so foolish as to be cozened into an elopement—"

Georgina, who had stiffened at the mention of Shannon's name, broke in here to say, as coolly as she could manage it, "Indeed, I cannot imagine why you should take it into your head that this can have anything to do with me, ma'am. I am sure you know that what Mr. Shannon did these few minutes past was only what any other gentleman would have done who found me in the same predicament."

Lady Eliza shook her head disbelievingly. "My dear, I am not a pea-goose!" she said. "Anyone with eyes must have seen that there was something more to it than that, from the very expression on your face, and on Shannon's, when I walked in here. Now you may flirt with young Peter Hession as much as you choose, and nothing worse will come of it than a stolen kiss—and, if I am not sadly mistaken, an abject apology accompanied by a formal offer the next time he manages to come into your presence. But *do* believe me when I tell you that the same behaviour directed toward a man like Shannon is not only dangerous, but absolutely fool-hardy. You do not know him—"

"I do not know him well, but I believe I may say that I know him better than you do if you think I stand in any danger from him," Georgina said, her anger mounting, though she strove to preserve a calm demeanour.

She would have gone on, but Lady Eliza interrupted her, her sparkling eyes for once excessively grave.

"My dear child, I am sure that is precisely what your cousin Nuala thought," she said. "She could have had no idea, when she agreed to marry him, of his true character; indeed, she told me herself that she had not, in Brussels, shortly before her death. She was a most unhappy creature at that time, you must know—sadly changed from the bright, happy girl her friends had been acquainted with."

"That may well be, ma'am," Georgina said, still endeavouring to keep her indignation under rein. "But I am not so green—and certainly *you* are not—as to be unaware that there are many couples who find, after marriage, that they do not suit, through neither's fault."

Lady Eliza again shook her head, and shrugged up her shoulders slightly with a fatalistic air. "Oh, if you are of a mind to make yourself his champion, I see that there is nothing for it but for me to speak plainly," she said. She laid one hand on Georgina's, which were clasped tightly together in her lap, and went on, in a lowered voice, "You must believe me when I say that it is excessively painful for me to spread such a story as this, but I feel, under the circumstances, that it is my duty to tell it to you. It was said quite openly in Brussels at the time, my dear, that Shannon was not guiltless in the matter of his wife's death."

For a moment Georgina could scarcely credit her ears. She said in a stunned voice, "Not guiltless! But what are you trying to say, ma'am? That he—"

"Murdered her?" Lady Eliza supplied the words Georgina had not been able to bring herself to utter. "No, I do not say that in so many words. I only say that the suspicion is there. She died very oddly, you see—of an internal disorder associated with a fever, it was given out, yet no medical man ever professed to have found the cause of that fever. I must tell you that the rumour of poison was rife in Brussels after Shannon buried her so quickly and then disappeared from the city that same night—to go to Greece, it was said, or some such out-of-the-world place. If Brussels had not been in such an uproar at the time—it was just before the battle at Waterloo, you know—I am quite certain that inquiries must have been set on foot." She looked into Georgina's dazed face and patted her hand sympathetically. "Of course this must come as a dreadful shock to you," she said. "Shannon's manners are harsh, but there is nothing in them to suggest that he might be capable of such a horrid crime. But when one considers what he stood to gain—"

Georgina wrenched her hands from Lady Eliza's grasp and jumped up. "I don't believe you!" she said hotly. "It could not be! Pray, ma'am, do you mean to warn me, by repeating such a piece of gossip to me, that Shannon has it in mind to murder *me?*"

"Not at all," Lady Eliza said. She looked up at Georgina with the pitying expression still on her face. "It may be that he is genuinely attached to you, as he never was to Nuala—for I am bound to say that, as often as I saw them together, I never saw him look at her as he was looking at you when I walked into the room just now. But, my poor child, what has that to say to anything? It cannot be that, no matter how strong an attachment he may feel for you, *you* would be able to think of uniting yourself with a man who is capable of murder—and murder of the vilest sort, of a young girl whom he had sworn to cherish as his wife—"

Georgina stood staring blindly at a lacquer screen on which a bowing mandarin in a flaming crimson robe was portrayed. She felt physically sick; in spite of her resolution to place no credence in Lady Eliza's words, she could not help recalling that Shannon had never mentioned his wife to her in a manner that had implied the least affection, and that, in fact, it had more than once occurred to her that he was anxious to avoid the subject of Nuala, not out of grief, but—she broke off an anguished thought that suggested to her that the emotion he had felt might well have been guilt. Clinging to straws, she rounded on Lady Eliza accusingly.

"This is all very fine, ma'am," she said, "and yet you would have me believe that, even though you are convinced that this wicked gossip is true, you have invited such a man into your own home—"

Lady Eliza shrugged again, a more familiar expression of malicious recklessness appearing in her eyes. "Oh, as to that," she said, "I own to being sadly wicked, my dear, but I did think it might be amusing to tame such a brute of a man! Have I shocked you very much? You do not know London ways, my love; there are too many of us who will do anything to stave off boredom, and you must confess that such an adventure might keep one entertained for months. But *I* should be risking very little, you see—only my reputation, which I shall take care is not damaged beyond repair—but you— My dear child, it is your whole future that is at stake! I should blame myself bitterly if I had not spoken out to warn you, and, believe me, I shall speak to your cousin Bella too, if need be, repugnant as it would be to me to add to the burden of her grief over Nuala's loss by repeating such an unsavoury tale to her."

Georgina felt that she could listen to no more. She managed to say, in a far firmer tone than she would have believed herself capable of, "Indeed, there is no reason for you to do that, Lady Eliza. I have no interest in Mr. Shannon, and I beg you will not repeat this story to my cousin on any account."

She then turned and walked out of the room, hurrying back at once to the ballroom for fear Lady Eliza would persist in continuing the conversation if she were able to be alone with her.

The last thing in the world she desired to do at that moment was to engage in inconsequential chitchat, but there was no escaping it. Before half a dozen moments had passed she had been seized on by the eager young gentleman—one of the London Tulips Lady Eliza had boasted she would bring to Stokings for her ball—with whom she had promised to stand up for this dance, and for the next half hour she had to endure the misery of smiling and responding to her partner's polite gallantry when every thought in her mind was still agonizingly on the conversation she had just had with Lady Eliza. At one moment she was inclined to put her hostess's revelations down to sheer malice; at another, she felt obliged to acknowledge that it seemed improbable that even so reckless a woman as Lady Eliza would have invented such a story out of the whole cloth.

That there was some unsavouriness about Shannon's marriage she had always sensed, yet everything she knew and felt about him gave the lie to the idea that he might have done away with his wife. Harsh-mannered and uncompromisingly abrupt he assuredly was, and that a young girl who had been petted all her life by her adoring family and admirers might have found him an uncomfortable sort of husband she could well imagine. But that he could cunningly and cold-bloodedly have contrived her death she could not believe.

When the set was over, she was seized on at once by her cousin Bella, who demanded in the greatest agitation to be told the truth of the story that was being whispered about, she informed her, on all sides.

"That silly little Mott girl has been saying that Peter Hession insisted on making you an offer here, this very evening!" she said, almost tearfully. "Oh, my love, *do* tell me that it is not true! I was quite of the opinion, when I saw you leave the room with the chit—who I am persuaded was in a plot with the Hession boy to lure you off alone—that I ought to hurry after you, but that prosy Lady Kilmarnan seized on me and I *could* not manage to escape!"

Georgina said dampingly, "I wish you will not put yourself in a taking, ma'am. You are making a great piece of work about nothing. No offer has been made to me—"

She was looking around the ballroom as she spoke, observing that, though Shannon was nowhere in sight, Mr. Hession was standing across the room regarding her uncertainly, as if he were endeavouring to make up his mind whether or not to approach her. She felt at that moment, with the knowledge of what Lady Eliza had told her still fresh in her mind, that she could not possibly face another scene with Peter, and turned impulsively to her agitated cousin.

"The thing is, ma'am," she admitted, "that I did have a somewhat disagreeable time persuading Mr. Hession that this was *not* the place to speak of such matters, and I find that it has brought on a shocking headache. Would you object very much if we were to leave now? I believe I am too much discomposed to dance any more this evening."

Mrs. Quinlevan's face brightened visibly at these words. Evidently she had noticed Mr. Hession's brooding gaze turned in her young cousin's direction, and she was only too happy to be given the opportunity of sweeping her away from the young man's obviously ill-restrained ardour.

"Of course we shall not stay if you are not feeling the thing," she said, with eager sympathy. "It is the most disagreeable thing in the world to be obliged to stand up in a hot room and smile and make insipid conversation, when one wants nothing so much as to be laid down on one's bed. I am sure Lady Eliza will understand."

Georgina felt that Lady Eliza would understand a great deal more than Mrs. Quinlevan had any notion of, but at that moment she was too over-set to care. She felt for the first time in her life that if she could not manage to be alone soon she might burst into tears in spite of everything she might do to attempt to restrain them.

As it was, she had to endure the slow journey back to Craythorne behind her cousin's fat, lazy horses, and Mrs. Quinlevan's lengthy animadversions concerning young men who showed such a shocking want of conduct as to indulge in making scenes at a ball. It seemed an eternity to her before she could close the door of her bedchamber at Craythorne and indulge in a hearty cry.

She then felt better, told herself stoutly that she did not believe a word of what Lady Eliza had disclosed to her, and fell asleep at last in the rather frightening happiness of her remembrance of the expression in Shannon's eyes as he had looked at her that evening, just before Lady Eliza had come into the room.

Why that expression should give her so much satisfaction she was at a loss to understand, for it was obvious that, even if Lady Eliza's words had been wholly false, the fact that Shannon might be in love with her could not rationally be supposed to bring about any results that might be counted on to lead to her future tranquillity. In a state between waking and sleeping, however, reason has little command over the mind, and for that brief space of time, at any rate, she was free to indulge in delicious fantasy, in which the hard facts of her present circumstances need play only the smallest part.

15

She was brought back to a drear daylight review of those facts, however, when, at a rather late hour the next morning, she descended the stairs to the breakfast-parlour to find a letter directed to her in her grandmother's hand lying beside her plate. If she had had any idea that morning must bring some solution to the problems that had beset her the previous evening, it was demolished at once by the first line of Lady Mercer's brief and exceedingly trenchant missive.

Her grandmother wrote that it had been brought to her attention, by a person who had her granddaughter's interests at heart, that Georgina had succeeded, during her stay in Kerry, in embroiling herself to a most unseemly degree with the *gentleman* (the word was heavily underscored, as if for sarcastic emphasis) who had married her unfortunate cousin, Nuala. Lady Mercer felt that she need not point out to her granddaughter that she had anticipated no such shocking want of conduct in her when she had agreed to her visiting her cousins, and she was now of the opinion that it was imperative that Georgina return to Bath at once.

"I have been informed," the letter went on, "that Sir Landers and Lady Hession—the latter of whom I find is the daughter of one of my dearest friends, now unhappily long deceased—are about to make their annual visit to London. I am sure that Lady Hession, to whom I am writing at the same time that I send this off to you, will be agreeable to your accompanying her party, and I shall make all the necessary arrangements for your conveyance to Bath once you have arrived in England under her protection. Be so good as to hold yourself in readiness to attend her convenience.

"Naturally I shall write to inform Mrs. Quinlevan of the termination of your visit. I may add that I have been *most sadly disappointed* (again the heavy underscoring) in the quality of the chaperonage she has given you."

It required only a single glance, when Georgina raised her eyes from her perusal of this missive to look across the breakfast table at her cousin, for her to gather that the letter Mrs. Quinlevan was at that moment engaged in reading also came from Lady Mercer's pen. Her cousin's plump face had grown quite pale under its lilac-beribboned lace cap, and expostulations began to pour from her lips even before she had looked up and found Georgina's eyes upon her.

"Oh, no! What a shocking thing to say! As if I would— As if *you* would— Oh, my love, I have had the most *dreadful* letter from your grandmama!" she cried. "She writes that you must return to Bath at once, and that I— Oh, dear! Where *did* I put my vinaigrette? I am quite sure I feel one of my spasms coming on!"

The fact that Georgina was required to spend the next few minutes in ministering to her cousin's agitation gave her a welcome opportunity to master her own, and she was thus able to discuss the matter with tolerable composure when Mrs. Quinlevan had become sufficiently calm to pour out a great many tearful questions.

"*Who* could have been so spiteful as to write such nasty gossip to Lady Mercer?" she demanded. "I cannot believe it was Lucinda Mott, for though she *did* tell me that story of Betsy's about your having ridden over to The Place to see Mr. Shannon, she swore to me most solemnly that she would not repeat it to anyone else, and I have always found her to be the most trustworthy creature alive. And it cannot be that Betsy would have dared address your grandmother, who is *totally* unknown to her, with such a tale—"

"No, indeed. I am sure it was not Betsy," Georgina agreed. After the first shock of reading Lady Mercer's letter, her mind had begun to work with an odd, cool clarity, and she went on to say to her cousin, with a calmness that surprised even herself, "It must have been Lady Eliza, of course. No one else of our acquaintance could have thought of doing such a thing."

"Lady Eliza!" Mrs. Quinlevan turned an astonished face on her. "But why should *she*—? Oh, my dear, I hesitate to say such a thing to you, but I assure you that she is entirely lacking in the feminine delicacy that would lead her to be so nice as to censure you for your imprudent behaviour in regard to Mr. Shannon!"

"Yes," Georgina admitted, "with that I must agree, ma'am. But her reasons for addressing Grandmama with such a tale, I am persuaded, had nothing to do with a tender regard for my reputation." She saw that her cousin was regarding her with an expression of doubtful inquiry on her face, and, unwilling to enter into explanations that would necessarily involve a revelation of the scene that had taken place between her and Lady Eliza on the previous evening, said quickly, "But it does not matter a great deal *who* the talebearer was, I am afraid. The question is—what am I to do?"

Mrs. Quinlevan had found her handkerchief and was applying it to overflowing eyes.

"Oh, my love, you must return to Bath, of course!" she said. "You cannot disregard your grandmama's wishes—though perhaps if I were to write to tell her that she is *quite* mistaken—" The momentary ray of hope that had kindled in her face faded. "But there will never be time for that," she said dejectedly. "Lady Hession remarked to me last evening that she and Sir Landers are intending to set out no later than Thursday, which is but two days from now."

Georgina's own mind, while her cousin spoke, was rapidly surveying the alternatives that were open to her, and it appeared to her that Mrs. Quinlevan's gloomy evaluation of the situation must be set down as the correct one. Even if her cousin were willing to abet her in flouting Lady Mercer's wishes by continuing to make her welcome at Craythorne, there was nothing that she could hope to gain by such an act of defiance. She certainly did not wish to be pushed into a marriage with Brandon, and as for Shannon—

She broke off the thought abruptly. Try as she might, she could not put the words that Lady Eliza had spoken to her the night before out of her mind: *It was said quite openly in Brussels at the time that Shannon was not guiltless in the matter of his wife's death.* She did not for a moment believe that Lady Eliza had spoken from anything but the same selfish malice that had prompted her to send Lady Mercer such a highly coloured account of Georgina's relations with Shannon, but still she felt an imperative need to hear from his own lips a retraction of her monstrous insinuation.

And if she received it? This was a question that she could not answer. That he loved her she could scarcely doubt, after the look she had surprised in his eyes the evening before. But that he would offer marriage to her if she were to remain in Kerry was another matter altogether. She could not believe that he would. Nothing that he had ever said to her had given her the least impression that he intended again to disregard the universal disapproval that must attach to his marrying a well-brought-up young girl against the wishes of her family. He had been burnt once—or, if one chose to accept the vulgar view, he had already obtained the fortune that he had desired—and it seemed unlikely that he would venture into such a marriage a second time.

Tormented by these doubts, she was obliged at the same time to bear with Mrs. Quinlevan's agitated attempts to discover if there were any hopes to be placed on her arriving at an understanding with Brandon before she returned to England, and the afternoon brought still further complications with the arrival of Lady Hession at Craythorne.

That formidable matron, ushered into the saloon where Mrs. Quinlevan and Georgina were sitting, presented herself to them in a pomona-green carriage dress and a hat of the same colour with a full-poke front, trimmed with drapings of thread-net and puffs of ribbon, and disclosed at once that she, too, had been the recipient of a letter from Lady Mercer.

"I need not tell you, dear child," she said to Georgina, with what she evidently felt must be the most gratifying condescension, "that Sir Landers and I will be only too happy to have the pleasure of your company on our journey. Indeed, I discussed the matter with Sir Landers this morning, after I had received Lady Mercer's letter, and he agreed with me that it would be quite the thing for us to convey you to Bath ourselves. It will not signify if we arrive in London a little later than we had planned, and both Sir Landers and I are most anxious to make the acquaintance of Lady Mercer and your dear mama. I fancy you can guess why!" she said, casting a glance of majestic archness in Georgina's direction.

Georgina, with a sinking heart, felt that she could indeed make such a guess, but she schooled herself to return the visitor's glance calmly and to say quietly that she would be very sorry to put Lady Hession to so much trouble.

Lady Hession gave her affected laugh. "Oh, my love, we will not talk of trouble, if you please!" she said. "I have become quite attached to you, you know! But, really, I see what it is—you are still somewhat put out over last evening, and so I told Peter it would be. 'Depend upon it,' I said to him, 'Miss Power has very pretty notions of propriety, and you have done yourself no service with her by allowing your feeling for her to display itself before you have addressed her guardians in form.' But so it will be with these ardent young men, my dear!"

Georgina, trapped by civility into listening to these broad hints of what lay in store for her, could only cast a glance of mute appeal to her cousin. But she was rewarded merely by having now to attend while Mrs. Quinlevan pertinaciously brought Brandon's name into the conversation, the two matrons renewing their contest of the evening before over the relative merits of their respective sons, while Georgina sat by in miserable embarrassment. She had never in her life been more relieved than when Lady Hession at last rose to bring her visit to a close, stating that she would have the carriage sent round to Craythorne at nine o'clock on Thursday morning to pick Georgina up for the journey.

When she had gone, Mrs. Quinlevan seemed disposed to continue her arguments on Brandon's behalf, and Georgina, in despair, fled to Brandon himself, who was enjoying the spring sunshine and his release from his sick room in an easy-chair in the yellow morning-room. By this time she was so full of the various problems that were besetting her that she could not help pouring the whole of them into his ears, reserving only any mention of her feelings concerning Shannon or his for her.

She was rewarded by seeing an indignant frown gather on her cousin's brow as she told him of Lady Eliza's insinuations, and by his quick, angry remark, when she had concluded, of: "Gammon! She must be touched in her upper works to put such stuff as that about! Why, it would mean he must have poisoned her— Shannon! Of all men in the world, I would not believe it of *him*. He may be rough, but a scheming scoundrel he is *not!*"

"That is exactly what *I* thought," she agreed, her spirits rising a little at this confirmation of her own opinion. "It is completely out of his character to do such a thing."

She checked, seeing the suddenly suspicious look that had appeared in Brandon's eyes.

"But why should she have told such a tale to *you*, of all people—and at a ball—after she had kept mum about it all this time?" he demanded. "Is she caper-witted enough to have taken it into her head that you and Shannon—?" The vivid flush that he saw instantly appear on his cousin's face as he uttered this question brought him to a blank halt. "Good God, Georgie," he burst out, when he had recovered his powers of speech, "you can't mean to tell me you've fallen in love with him!"

She attempted a confused denial, but was so unsuccessful that he flung up a hand almost at once to halt her.

"No, stop trying to bam me!" he said. "It won't fadge; why, it's written all over you, girl!"

She put up her chin. "Very well, then, perhaps I do—care for him— somewhat," she conceded. "And what affair, pray, is that of yours?"

"Now don't get up on your high ropes," he recommended, with cousinly frankness. "It *ain't* my affair, naturally—except that I like him, and I like you, and so if I see you about to stick your head in a hornets' nest I ought to try to stop you, hadn't I? Lord, a rare dust my mother'd kick up if she heard what you just said! To say nothing of your own mother, and Lady Mercer—"

"They are not likely to hear it," Georgina said bitterly, torn between confusion at having betrayed herself and the strong impulse, once she had done so, to confide her difficulties to a sympathetic listener. "The Hessions are to leave on Thursday, and I am to go with them, so the whole matter is at an end—or," she added, as a new thought struck her, "it will be unless I can contrive to see Shannon before that time. Brandon, I *must* hear from his own lips whether there is any truth or not in that dreadful story Lady Eliza told me last evening."

"What good will that do?" Brandon objected. "He ain't likely to give himself away to you if it *is* true—not that I think for a moment that it *is*."

"Nor do I," Georgina averred. "But at least he will know then what is being said of him, and *I* will know—"

She broke off under her cousin's understanding and censorious gaze. "You will know whether he has tumbled as head-over-ears in love with you as you have with him, is that it?" he asked. "Well, if you want *my* opinion, he hasn't—because, though you are a well-enough-looking girl, you've been coming to cuffs with him ever since you first laid eyes on him, and, from as much as *I* know about it, that is *not* the way to fix a fellow's interest. Here, what are you about?" he demanded in some surprise, as Georgina, sitting down abruptly in the nearest chair, suddenly appeared to him to show an alarming tendency to burst into tears. "You ain't going to cry, are you?"

"No, I am not," Georgina said, incensed, blinking the suspicious moisture from her eyes. "But it doesn't matter what you think, Brandon—I *must* see Shannon before I go! May I borrow your cob tomorrow morning, early? I can ride over to The Place then and perhaps catch him before he goes out."

"Alone?" Brandon demanded. "*I* can't go with you, you know; Culreavy has me chained to this curst house for at least a few more days. And to tell the truth, even if he hadn't, I doubt that I'd be able to make such a jaunt. You'd best give *that* idea over."

"No, I won't," Georgina said obstinately. "There is no reason why I shouldn't go alone. I shan't stay above ten minutes, and you may tell Cousin Bella, if she asks for me, that I have gone out for a last ride about the countryside."

Nothing that Brandon could allege against this plan had the least effect upon her determination; and the next morning, long before Mrs. Quinlevan had left her bedchamber, found her at the stables, where she discovered to her satisfaction that Brandon had indeed given instructions for the cob to be made ready for her use. She gave a decided negative to Grady's plans to accompany her, to his considerable disapproval, and in a few minutes was trotting sedately off in the direction of The Place through the early morning mist.

It would be a fine day, and even the cob's mild disposition seemed to be enlivened by the fresh May morning, with the skylarks singing over his head and the blooms of the whitethorn bushes shining like stars through the thin lifting mist. Georgina felt her own spirits rising, and hopefully envisioned any number of improbable scenes with Shannon, all of which ended in her being assured that he returned her feelings and that the tale Lady Eliza had confided to her on the night of the ball had not an iota of truth in it.

As she neared The Place, however, these optimistic imaginings began to fade before the necessity of considering what she was actually to say to him. The closer she came to the house, the more forcibly it was borne in upon her that what she was doing was quite beyond the acceptable pattern of behaviour for any properly reared young female. Certain bluntly descriptive phrases Shannon had used in the past in reference to her conduct began to recur blightingly to her mind, and she had all but reached the point of turning her horse's head and riding cravenly back to Craythorne when the sight of Shannon himself, cantering toward her on his chestnut hack, made her draw rein abruptly. He was beside her in a few moments, and accosted her with a greeting that she could scarcely regard as a cordial one.

"What are you doing here?" he demanded.

"I came to see you," she replied, feeling again that strange racing of the blood, almost like anger, that his presence invariably provoked in her.

"Then you had better turn round and go back to Craythorne again," he retorted as uncompromisingly as before, "for I have no wish to see *you*, my girl!"

She flushed up slightly, this time in genuine indignation. "You might have the civility to wait until I have told you why I have come before you send me to the devil!" she exclaimed.

A faint, twisted smile touched his lips, but it faded at once before a harsher expression, one more bitter than any she remembered ever having seen there before.

"I am not sending you to the devil, Miss Power," he said. "On the contrary, I am doing my best to keep you out of those regions—with very little cooperation from yourself, I might add."

She said decidedly, "Well, if you are speaking of avoiding gossip, that is a very stuffy way to look at it, *I* think. I am sure you have not ruled your whole life by consideration of what people may say of you, and I have no intention of doing so, either." The chestnut, who was taking exception to standing tamely at a halt after having had every expectation, on being taken out of the stables, of stretching his legs in a satisfactory gallop, required Shannon's attention at that moment, and Georgina said impulsively, "Oh, *do* let us dismount and walk a little way! We can't talk properly like this."

He looked at her directly for a moment, and then gave rather odd, sardonic agreement to her request.

"Very well!" he said. "I see you still have that rather dramatic little scene that took place at Stokings tickling your brain. It may be as well to put an end to *that* business at once."

He swung himself from his saddle and, tethering the impatient chestnut to the great crooked sally tree beside which they had halted, assisted Georgina to dismount. For a moment, as she felt his hands grasping her in their strong clasp, she had a very odd impression that she was about to be swept into his arms, but the next instant he had released her and was busying himself with the cob.

When he had tethered it securely, he said to her in the same curt voice in which he had spoken before, "We will walk for five minutes, and then you will return to Craythorne, Miss Power. Are you under the impression that there was any significance in that singularly foolish little scene I enacted for you at Stokings the other night? I assure you that there was not. I am not usually accounted a chivalrous man, to be sure, but it has become a habit with me, it seems, to happen along to pull you out of your more embarrassing difficulties. It was no more than that—believe me."

She had caught up the tail of her dark-blue riding-habit over one arm, and was endeavouring to match her own steps to his long strides. A little out of breath, she said, "You are in a great hurry, are you not?" He halted and looked down at her, and as she saw the look of compunction in his eyes her spirits rose and she went on rather mischievously, "Oh, I was really not speaking of your stride, though I must confess that in another few moments, if we kept on at that pace, I should be too much out of breath to say anything at all—which I daresay is exactly what you would wish! But what I actually meant by it was that you are in a great hurry to explain away something for which I have asked no explanations. How do you know that I came to talk to you of what happened the other evening at Stokings?"

His brows snapped together in a frown. "Did you not?"

"Not at all—though if *you* would like to discuss the matter," she added obligingly, "I might tell you that I think you have just taken some shocking liberties with the truth. For example, you did not *happen* to find me with Peter Hession, I believe. Would it not be more accurate to say that you followed him when you saw him following *me?*"

She looked up into his face suddenly, surprising a look there that made the dawning smile fade quickly from her own. He did not wear his heart upon his sleeve, and she had never thought to see a look of such bleak unhappiness in those grey eyes. It was gone in an instant, and he said in an almost jeering voice, "You may believe so if it pleases you. Are you thinking to add me to the list of your conquests, Miss Power?"

A frown touched her own clear eyes. "I wish you will stop calling me 'Miss Power,' " she said. "I always have the strangest feeling, when you do so, that you are reminding yourself of Nuala."

"I have no need to remind myself of her."

She regarded him puzzledly, her heart sinking as she saw the grimness of his expression and remembered the hideous insinuation that Lady Eliza had dropped into her ears on the night of the ball.

"You did not—love her?" she found herself asking, in a very gruff little voice that she could scarcely recognise as her own.

"No, I did not."

She felt a shiver creep down her spine as she heard the uncompromising coldness of the words. After a moment she raised her eyes rather blindly to his face.

"Lady Eliza says—" she whispered, rather than said.

The bitter, mocking expression was there again in his eyes. "Oh, I can well conceive what Lady Eliza says!" he said. "You may spare yourself the recounting of it!"

"Is it—true, then?"

She felt that her heart had stopped, waiting for his answer, and when it came she took it like a blow.

"Yes."

"All of it?"

"Oh, yes! The worst of what she can find to say! By God, you *are* an innocent if you did not believe her! What sort of schoolgirl nonsense have you been fool enough to nourish in that green head of yours, not to see at a glance what I am capable of?"

She walked on mechanically. There were blue Kerry skies above her, with wisps of fleecy cloud making patterns on the grass, and violets springing in the shadow of the fresh green ferns that grew among the rough stones of the old wall beside which they walked, but she saw none of this. She felt only that a numbing hand had been laid on her hopes for future happiness, pressing the life from them with its cold weight. If what Lady Eliza had told her was true—and that it was, she had just heard confirmed from Shannon's own lips—she must forget him, forget every feeling she had ever had for him except one of revulsion.

She could no longer bear to walk there beside him in the blue Kerry morning. Abruptly she came to a halt and said to him in a voice that sounded queer and strained even to her own ears, "I must go now."

"Yes," he said, his own voice grim. "I have been telling you that. Come along!"

He took her arm and turned her about. As she came face to face with him suddenly she raised her eyes to his and before she knew what she was about the wretched words came tumbling out: "But you should not lie to me, at all events! It wasn't chance the other evening; I couldn't have been mistaken! I saw it in your eyes—"

He gave his bitter laugh again. "Oh, yes—if that is any comfort to you! You may add me to your list, my love—though I know you too well to believe that that will afford you any satisfaction." He seized her wrists for a moment, as if in spite of everything he would have drawn her to him—but then, flinging them away, said almost roughly, "It is too late for that, however! If things had been different— But they were not!"

He strode back to where the horses were tethered; when she came up beside him he had loosed the cob and was waiting to toss her up into the saddle. Mounted again, she gathered her reins and looked down at him standing there beside her.

"I am going away tomorrow morning," she said, in a voice that she was obliged to struggle to keep from shaking. "Back to England—to Bath—"

His own face grew stony as he heard the words. "Good-bye, then, and Godspeed. I doubt we'll meet again."

She tried to smile. "Oh, yes! I shall come back again to visit some day— and you will have The Place running just as you like, and everything will be—"

Everything will be different! her heart cried. *He will be married, or you will have grown tired of living with Grandmama's reproaches and will be the wife of some acceptable young man, like Mr. Smallwoods or Peter Hession—*

She choked back a sob and, turning her horse's head, gave him the office to start back to Craythorne. Only once she looked back: Shannon had already swung himself into the saddle and was riding off—slowly, under rigid control, it seemed—in the opposite direction.

She did not return immediately to Craythorne. Some time must elapse, she felt, before she could face her cousin Bella's questions. So she turned into side lanes, dallying beside sleepy little streams or walking the cob slowly through lonely glens. It was long past the luncheon hour when she left her horse at the stables and walked up to the house, and the first person she met as she stepped through the doorway was Brandon, who came limping out of the yellow morning-room to warn her that his mother was in the deuce of a pucker over her long absence.

"What's more, she has Peter Hession on her hands now as well," he said. "Came to see *you,* he says, and ain't about to leave until he does." He glanced keenly into her white face and asked abruptly, "Did you see Shannon?"

"Yes."

She bit her lip. Watching her, he ejaculated suddenly, "Good God, you don't mean to tell me that that story is true!"

She nodded numbly, turning toward the stairs to forestall any further conversation. But at that moment Mrs. Quinlevan sailed out of the Green Saloon, exclaiming, "Georgina! My love! Where have you *been?* Oh, what a dreadful pelter we have been in over you! Brandon assured me you had only gone for a ride, but at such a time, and quite alone! And here is that odious Hession boy absolutely *rooted* in my house, and refusing to leave except I give him my permission to go searching for you—for we were *both* persuaded, as you can well conceive, that some accident had befallen you!" She waved a distracted hand, which was clutching, Georgina saw, her vinaigrette. "Do come in with me at once and let him speak to you, so that he will agree to leave us in peace," she implored. "He wishes to apologise to you, he says—but why he must do so in *my* house, when I am sure Lady Hession will give him every opportunity he desires to converse with you while you are travelling to Bath with them, I *cannot* conceive!"

Georgina, whose first sensation was one of relief that Mrs. Quinlevan's preoccupation with young Mr. Hession prevented her from inquiring more closely into her own activities that morning, took the opportunity of a pause in her cousin's breathless recital to indicate her willingness to see the visitor, and walked into the Green Saloon, with Mrs. Quinlevan at her heels. Here she found Peter, alerted by the conversation in the hall, standing in expectation of her entrance. He had got himself up for what he had apparently conceived of as an important, if somewhat embarrassing, situation in an impeccably fitting coat of corbeau-coloured superfine, panta-

loons of a dashing yellow, and a neckcloth arranged in the elaborate folds
of the Osbaldestone, but the face that emerged from between his extremely high shirt-points bore the expression more of a guilty and rather
sulky stripling than that of the supercilious Pink of the Ton he aspired to
be.

"Miss Power!" he exclaimed, starting forward on Georgina's entrance.
"Dooced glad you've come! Began to fear all manner of accidents had happened to you!" He sent a rather glowering glance in Mrs. Quinlevan's direction. "Your cousin didn't like it above half, my staying here," he went
on, "but what could I do when no one could tell what had become of
you? Dash it all, I might have been *needed!*"

Georgina did not sit down, nor did either she or Mrs. Quinlevan invite
Mr. Hession to do so.

"I am much obliged to you for your concern, but indeed it was quite
unnecessary," she said, surprised to find how commonplace a tone she
could give to her words as she spoke. "I merely went for a last ride about
the countryside and forgot the time." Casting a glance at Mrs. Quinlevan,
who was standing beside her, she saw, with the rigid erectness of one who
perceived her duty to remain in the room and would in no wise be fobbed
off from doing it, she added, "I am excessively sorry to have kept you waiting, but, as you see, I am hardly dressed to receive callers just now."

Mr. Hession, however, was not disposed to take the broad hint that was
conveyed to him in these words.

"Yes, but—dooce take it, I came to offer you my apologies!" he expostulated. "Can't go away until I've done that! Would have come yesterday,
but m'mother persuaded me I ought to let her see you first and smooth you
down—not that I think she *did*," he added, eyeing her set face doubtfully.
"I *told* her I'd best come myself!"

"If you mean to imply that I am angry with you, I am not," Georgina
said, her civility strained to the utmost by the necessity of dealing with
Mr. Hession's volatile feelings when her own were crying out for solitude
in which to recover from the shock they had received. "It is only that we
are in a bit of a scramble here, you see, over my sudden departure, and—
and, do believe me, I should much prefer simply to forget the whole incident!"

To this Mrs. Quinlevan, judging it to be time to take a hand in the proceedings herself, added in a severely virtuous tone that if Mr. Hession
believed for a moment that she did not know her duty better than to allow
him the opportunity of discussing any *particular* matters in private with

her cousin before he had received the permission of her mama and Lady Mercer to do so, he had *quite* mistaken her.

"Not," she said, with a bitterness that betrayed the extremity of her agitation at the unfair advantage over her own son that Mr. Hession was being allowed in making the journey to Bath in Georgina's company, "that I daresay they won't jump to give it, but while you are in *my* house, the proprieties will be observed!"

Mr. Hession, somewhat abashed, remarked that it was not at all his intention to flout anyone's notions of propriety, and, finding himself confronted by a pair of entirely unencouraging faces, appeared to judge that the time had come to beat a strategic retreat. He accordingly took his leave, promising to ride over beside the travelling-chaise when it came to take Miss Power up the following morning.

As soon as he had departed, Georgina, cutting short Mrs. Quinlevan's agitated attempts to bring her to a sense of the extreme unwisdom of accepting an offer from a young man of Mr. Hession's known Corinthian tendencies—"as ridiculous as he makes himself, my love, in trying to ape such gentlemen, who care for nothing but curricle-racing and pugilism and such vulgar sports, and I am sure make the worst husbands in the world"—excused herself and went to her bedchamber, where she had rather expected to unburden herself with a hearty cry.

But no tears came. She could only pace the room, revolving again and again in her mind Shannon's bitterly jeering words: "By God, you *are* an innocent if you did not believe her! What sort of schoolgirl nonsense have you been fool enough to nourish in that green head of yours, not to see at a glance what I am capable of?" She had heard it from his own lips, that he was guilty of the dreadful deed of which Lady Eliza had accused him, and the fact that he had, almost in the same breath, admitted his love for her only added to her anguish over the revelation.

She might have borne it better, she told herself, if she could have believed that he was indifferent to her. Then pride might have come to her rescue; but now there was only the aching sense of what might have been, if only—

"If only he were not a scoundrel!" she told herself fiercely. "A man utterly without principle or heart, a man I should despise—and I do despise him—I do!"

With this determined asseveration she turned her attention to the many matters requiring her attention that her projected departure had brought up, resolving to banish Shannon from that moment from her mind. This was accomplished the more easily for her having presently to deal once again with her cousin Bella, and with the maids who were engaged in packing her portmanteaux for her journey. But it was long before she slept that night, and she awoke with the first birdsong, remembering how lightheartedly she had come to Kerry so short a while before, never dreaming of the misery that lay in store for her there.

What she would do when she returned to Bath she could not imagine, nor did she wish to speculate on the future now. She must live from day to day for a time, it seemed; and as she viewed the dreary succession of them that stretched before her, her spirits dulled and her heart dropped like lead.

16

The Hessions' travelling-chaise arrived to take her up promptly at nine o'clock. She said her farewells to Brandon and to Mrs. Quinlevan, the latter assuring her tearfully that she would write immediately to Lady Mercer, informing her of the gross misrepresentation of Georgina's conduct that had been made to her, in the hope that Georgina might soon be permitted to return to Craythorne.

Georgina herself had no such hope, or even desire. It seemed to her that, no matter how disagreeable her situation might be in Bath, anything was preferable to remaining in Kerry, where she might chance to meet Shannon at any time and everything must remind her of him. Better to make a clean break, she thought. Whatever her problems might be in Bath, they would, she told herself, most certainly not include her falling in love with a man who was wholly unworthy of her regard.

She had not been looking forward with any pleasure to the journey that must precede her return to Bath, and, in the event, her premonitions turned out to have been quite correct. Nothing could have exceeded the discomfort of the situation in which she found herself, bound to the company of a family with whom she had nothing in common and who seemed to follow Lady Hession's lead in taking it for granted that she would soon be one of them. Sir Landers, though a singularly undemonstrative man, put himself out to give her this impression, and even Miss Amelia several times forgot her absorption in the subject of her approaching come-out sufficiently to drop a giggling hint of her approval of having Georgina as a sister.

As for young Mr. Hession, it was perfectly clear, from the restrained ardour of his manner, that he was waiting only until he was afforded the opportunity of requesting the permission of Lady Mercer and Mrs. Power to make her an offer in form. She could not dislike him—he was in every way so anxious to please her, and so ingenuous in his belief that she must accept his offer, when it was made—and at times, in despondency, she almost felt that she *would* accept it. At least, she thought, if she were married she would be mistress of her own household, instead of an unwanted dependant in her grandmother's. And certainly it was not to be expected that she would ever fall in love again.

A very rough crossing, somewhat delayed by a spring storm, did nothing to add to her pleasure in this vexatious journey, and by the time the post-chaise in which she arrived in Bath had turned into Great Pulteney Street her dread of facing her grandmother's wrath had quite succumbed to her relief at finding herself at the end of her enforced intimacy with the Hessions. Her travelling companions had engaged rooms at the York House, and, as it was quite late when they arrived in Bath, went on to their hotel at once as soon as they had deposited her at Lady Mercer's door, promising themselves, as Lady Hession majestically put it, the pleasure of calling there in the morning.

Lady Mercer had already retired to her bedchamber by the time Georgina entered the house, but she found her mother in the Long Drawing-room when she had greeted Finch and run upstairs, and from her face she read at once the fact that she was in deep disgrace. It was not that Mrs. Power was not happy to see her, or that she was at all inclined to give her a quelling scold; but she had lived for so many years in dread of Lady Mercer that she was entirely unable to set herself against her mother's opinion, and what that opinion now was Georgina could very well see in the tearful eyes that greeted her.

"Your grandmother is *extremely* vexed," Mrs. Power confided to her, dismally. "Indeed, I am persuaded that she retired to her bedchamber so early only because she could not bear to see you this evening, my love! Of course I do not wish to reproach you, for I am *sure* those odious stories about you must be grossly exaggerated, but—oh, dear!—I *do* wish you might have conducted yourself with a *little* more circumspection, so that your grandmama would not have been cast into such a taking!" She looked anxiously into Georgina's set face and went on, "My dear, it is *not* true, is it? You have not conceived a—a *tendre* for that dreadful man?"

"No, I have not," Georgina said roundly. "In fact, I should much prefer never to set eyes on him again!"

Mrs. Power's face brightened. "Oh, my dearest love, indeed you do not know how happy I am to hear you say that!" she exclaimed. "I *told* your grandmama that I was sure the whole story was nothing but a Canterbury tale—not that I would wish to say anything against Lady Eliza Malladon, for I am persuaded that she must have believed it her duty to write to your grandmama, or she would never have addressed herself to a lady who was quite unknown to her—"

Such a dangerous sparkle appeared in Georgina's eyes at this confirmation of her suspicions concerning Lady Eliza's meddling that Mrs. Power, seeing it, paused doubtfully. But Georgina, who had no desire to become embroiled in a discussion of the reasons for Lady Eliza's interference in her affairs, said nothing, merely letting her mother's expressions of relief over the news that she had, after all, no interest whatever in Mr. Shannon run their course and then, admitting her weariness after her journey, allowing herself to be led off to her bedchamber.

By the time she made her appearance the next morning she was happy to see that her mother had already informed Lady Mercer of the main points of their conversation of the previous evening. Lady Mercer, however, was not quite so complaisant toward her as might have been anticipated from this fact, for she had had the wind taken out of her sails, and that was an experience that she did not at all relish.

It was fortunate for her that the occurrences of that very day gave her a new stock of ammunition against her granddaughter. She had been obliged, at breakfast, to fall back upon Georgina's rejection of Mr. Smallwoods' suit to justify her general dissatisfaction with her; but the arrival of Lady Hession and Mr. Peter Hession in Great Pulteney Street, and the events that followed it, immediately drove that rankling occurrence out of her mind.

As chance had it, Georgina was in her bedchamber when the guests were announced, and Mr. Hession, with his mother's strong support, at once seized the opportunity of laying his hopes of obtaining their permission to address Georgina before the two elder ladies of the household.

It could not be said that Lady Mercer was favourably impressed by a young gentleman who, as she afterwards expressed it to Mrs. Power, seemed to her to be somewhat addicted to dandyism and who made use, in her presence, of several cant phrases which she felt were quite unsuitable for a lady's drawing-room. But any personal objections that she had to Mr. Hession were quite outweighed in her mind by the fact that he was a highly eligible *parti*, the only son of a baronet whose estate was respectable and whose affairs stood in excellent order, and that he was the grandson of one of her oldest friends. Lady Hession's mother, as Lady Hession had informed Georgina in Kerry, had been an intimate of Lady Mercer's in earlier days, and though Amelia Court had now been dead for many years and the connexion between the families had been allowed to lapse, Lady Mercer was much inclined to believe that any young man who bore the blood of Amelia Court in his veins could not, in the long run, turn out to be a disappointment to her.

To add to her inclination to approve the match, she and Lady Hession almost immediately discovered in each other a kindred spirit, who, on every topic that was broached between them, could be counted upon to take the proper attitude. Mrs. Power, indeed, who found herself reduced to the merest cipher in the presence of the two older ladies, had an unhappy presentiment that it might not be very comfortable for Georgina to have such a woman as Lady Hession as her mother-in-law, but, when she was applied to for her own consent to Peter's addressing her daughter, she did not venture to utter a word of disagreement.

So Georgina was sent for to come downstairs, and Lady Hession, secure in the belief that she and Lady Mercer had arrived at a most satisfactory agreement, took her leave.

Georgina, when she was informed that she was to come down to the Long Drawing-room, had a fairly accurate notion of what was in store for her there. As a matter of fact, she had lain awake for several hours during the night, trying to decide what answer she would return to Mr. Hession. Every point in his favour—his excellent birth, his respectable fortune, his personable appearance, his easy temper, his manifest partiality for her— was brought up and reviewed, and she came several times to the conclusion that she would be perfectly henwitted not to accept his offer, only to have all her certainty whirled away in an instant by the memory of a harsh-featured face and a pair of cool grey eyes that she had seen grow so unexpectedly warm when they had fallen upon her.

This weakness on her own part infuriated and distressed her, and as she descended the stairs to the Long Drawing-room she adjured herself sternly not to be gooseish, and to accept with suitable gratitude the answer to all her difficulties that was to be offered to her.

But no sooner had her eyes alighted on young Mr. Hession's resplendent form as he started up to greet her than doubts began to mount in her mind. How, she asked herself, was she to marry a man whose taste in waistcoats would come near to sending her into whoops each time she looked at him, and whose shirt-points were of such a monstrous height that it would be impossible for him to turn his head to attend to what she was saying? It was in vain that she hurried through a hasty mental catalogue of all the points in his favour as they exchanged civilities; all she could feel was a mounting vexation at the assurance with which he plunged into his declaration to her.

"Wouldn't have held off this long," he confided, "except m'mother said you'd prefer it if I did it all in form. But I must say *your* mother and Lady Mercer have both been dooced kind, so I shouldn't think there need be any rub now." He looked into her face and, apparently somewhat surprised at the suddenly mulish expression he saw there, added hastily, "You *know* how I feel about you, don't you? Made a dashed cake of myself that night at the Malladons' ball—should think you couldn't help realising I'm nutty on you."

Georgina, obliged to say something at this juncture, agreed reluctantly, "Yes—yes, I *do* know, but—"

"No point in going all over it again, then," Mr. Hession said, relieved to find himself so well understood. "I should think we might have the wedding in a couple of months—give you time to get your bride-clothes and all that flummery—"

"Mr. Hession, you are taking a great deal for granted!" Georgina said, an astonished and not too cordial light appearing in her eyes. "I have not said that I will marry you!"

Astonishment made its way into Mr. Hession's face as well. "Well, you ain't said you won't," he reminded her, reasonably. "Matter of fact, what have we been talking about all this time?"

"*You* have been talking about your feelings for me. I don't believe you have yet inquired about *mine* for *you!*"

The astonishment on Mr. Hession's face turned to something like dismay. "But—but, dash it all, you oughtn't to have any— I mean to say, not like mine for you!" he objected. "Young females don't, m'mother says—at least if they've been brought up properly! It ain't at all the thing—not until you've received an offer, you know. I daresay you'll grow fond enough of me after we're married."

Georgina, struggling with a strong desire to laugh at this extremely proper concept of how her emotions were expected to bloom, once they had received official authorisation to do so, managed to smile instead, and to remark in a somewhat unsteady voice, "That might very well be true, if I were to wish to put the matter to the test. As I do not, I expect we shall never know whether it is or not."

He stared at her. "'As I do not—'" he repeated, in amazement. "But—what do you mean by that—?"

She shrugged her shoulders, the smile fading into a contrite expression. "Oh, Peter, believe me, I do not wish to offend you!" she said, with a frankness that took the sting from her words. "But we are *quite* unsuited; you *must* see that, if you will only consider the matter coolly."

"Coolly!" Mr. Hession interrupted, with a violently aggrieved air. "How can I consider it coolly? I'm in love with you—head over ears—told you that at the start, didn't I? And your mother's agreeable— Lady Mercer too—"

"Unfortunately, you do not wish to marry either my grandmama or my mama," Georgina pointed out, suppressing an unsuitable impulse to smile at the picture of outrage Mr. Hession was presenting.

"Of course I don't!" he sputtered. "What a cork-brained thing to say! Years and years older than I am—both of 'em! I shouldn't think of making such a cake of myself!"

"No, of course you wouldn't," she said soothingly. "But, really, you must see—if they objected to you, I should be obliged to take their objections very seriously, but I cannot—I really *cannot* be expected to marry simply to please them!"

The aggrieved expression did not leave Mr. Hession's face. "Never thought you would," he said. "Dash it, I ain't *that* gothic—but when you say we shouldn't suit, you're bamming me! You know as well as I do that we've always got on famously. Never stood up with a girl in my life I enjoyed dancing with more, and you've the best seat and hands of any female I ever saw—be a pleasure to hunt with you!"

"Thank you," Georgina said. "But I *do* think—don't you?—that there is more to marriage than dancing and hunting. Indeed, I am *very* sorry to disoblige you, but I can't believe, really, that we should suit."

To her surprise and considerable discomposure, Mr. Hession, instead of showing dejection at this rebuff, which was uttered in as decided a voice as she could command, seemed cast down by it only for a moment. He then brightened and said, "Oh, well—no need to tie it down fast and firm today, of course. M'mother warned me—girls like to flutter about a bit before they settle down to give you a tight answer. I'll be popping down from London any time this next month, and we can settle it then. Know how you feel! Took me the better part of a fortnight last year to make up my mind to buy Jack Worthing's chestnuts. Knew I'd do it in the end, of course. Never saw such a well-matched pair in my life!"

Nothing that Georgina could say could bring him to the realisation that she was not, in fact, merely coquetting with him, and he went off at last in quite an amiable mood, leaving her to explain to her mother and Lady Mercer what the situation was between them.

This she was entirely unable to do to those ladies' satisfaction. Lady Mercer said acidly that she was a pea-goose, and demanded to know what sort of paragon she was expecting to snare that she had refused two such eligible offers as Mr. Smallwoods' and Mr. Hession's. Mrs. Power, as usual on the occasion of any disagreement between her daughter and her mother, burst into tears and declared herself in sinking tones to be the most unhappy creature in the world.

"Depend upon it," Lady Mercer said to Mrs. Power severely, when Georgina had fled to the sanctuary of her own bedchamber, "she is thinking of that abominable man who cozened your niece into marrying him. She may pull the wool over *your* eyes, Maria, but she cannot flummery me! What else would lead her to refuse such an offer?"

As Mrs. Power had no answer to this question, she returned none. Her own view of the matter was that her incomprehensible daughter was determined, for her own reasons, to end up on the shelf—a matter of considerable concern to her, as she had frequently thought that, when Georgina was married and presiding over a home of her own, she might contrive to visit her rather frequently and so escape, at least for a time, from her mother's domineering ways. The years of her widowhood had not been easy for the poor lady, and it was hard for her to give up such a dream as this for the harsh realities of the sort of household in which it seemed she was henceforth doomed to live, with brangling and disagreement around her all through the day. She wondered naïvely how Georgina could bring herself to reject an offer—and so eligible a one, too!—that would remove her permanently from such a situation.

"I am sure I should jump at the chance, if it were presented to *me!*" she told herself, in the privacy of her own bedchamber that night—and then, looking at her face in the mirror (she was not yet forty, but the beauty that had led Owen Power to run off with her had long since faded, and there were threads of grey in her fair hair), admonished herself mentally, in Lady Mercer's own forbidding tones, not to be such a widgeon as to imagine any such chance would ever again be offered to *her.*

17

As it happened, the brangling that Mrs. Power had foreseen over Georgina's rejection of Mr. Hession's offer did not rise quite to the heights that she had dreaded.

The fortunate circumstance that brought this about was the appearance in Bath, only a few days after Georgina herself had arrived there, of Sir Manning Hartily. Sir Manning lost no time in calling on the ladies in Great Pulteney Street, as he had promised Georgina that he would do, and it was obvious from the start that his purpose in doing so—and, indeed, in coming to Bath at all at this season of the year—was to seek her hand in marriage.

This fact, in Lady Mercer's eyes, at once put a new complexion on the whole affair of her granddaughter's future. As it happened, Lady Mercer, though herself in no way addicted to fashionable frivolities, had long been an avid follower of the activities of the Court, and in particular those of the Prince Regent, who in his youth—roughly coinciding with her own— had epitomised for her the glamour and courtly romance which her own life had sadly lacked.

Marriage with a blunt-mannered country squire and her subsequent years of retirement in Herefordshire had afforded little opportunity for this veneer of romantic-imagining to be rubbed off by reality. The Prince— now an extremely stout, florid-faced libertine to those who were well acquainted with him—was to her still the handsome Florizel of her youth, and the appearance in her drawing-room of Sir Manning Hartily, who, she was well aware, had long been privileged to be one of the Regent's "set," cast her into a highly agreeable flutter.

Her perception of the fact that that gentleman's purpose in presenting himself was to attempt to fix his interest with her granddaughter at once drove Mr. Hession's pretensions out of her mind. It did not signify to her in the least that Sir Manning was more than twenty years older than Georgina. She was even impervious to the insinuations cast out by envious Bath acquaintances to the effect that Sir Manning, finding himself, after years of improvident living, in Dun territory, was now hanging out for an heiress. Georgina's expectations, to Lady Mercer's mind, were far from brilliant enough to attract such a man as Sir Manning, for she never doubted—quite overlooking his years, his rather scandalous reputation, and his imposing bulk, which he made manful efforts to confine in a Cumberland corset—that he might marry any number of young ladies with far greater fortunes than Georgina's any time he chose to throw his handker-chief.

Sir Manning himself could have disillusioned her on this point, for he had made several attempts during the twelve months just past to "snabble a warm 'un," as he frankly put it to his friends, without encountering the least success. The ladies he met in his usual haunts were either too well acquainted with his situation or too well guarded by equally knowl-edgeable parents to succumb to the lures he had cast out to them, and not until he had gone to Ireland had he found, in Georgina, what he believed might be a modestly satisfactory solution to his problems.

To be sure, it might be some years before she would come into posses-sion of Lady Mercer's considerable fortune, but his expectations, on marry-ing her, would be sufficiently improved to quiet the most importunate of his creditors. He also rather fancied that, in dealing with females of the age of Lady Mercer, he was adept enough to make certain that she came down handsomely in the marriage settlements.

Sacrificing the amusements of the London Season, therefore—for, in truth, in his impecunious state, it had become more than a little em-barrassing to him to remain in town—he had driven himself to Bath in his curricle and installed himself at the York House. Introducing himself at once to the ladies in Great Pulteney Street, he became, within a week, an indispensable member of their little circle, squiring them to the Pump Room or to such concerts and other amusements as this unfashionable sea-son of the year provided. He had little fear of meeting any of his own par-ticular set in Bath at this time, who might throw a spoke in his wheel by giving Lady Mercer an uncomfortably accurate picture of his current financial situation, and, as he was of a sanguine disposition, he did not at all despair, with Lady Mercer's good will, of soon obtaining her grand-daughter's hand in marriage.

Georgina herself made every effort in her power to discourage these pre-tensions, but found herself sadly at a disadvantage in her attempts because of the decided partiality of both Lady Mercer and Mrs. Power for her ad-mirer. She was finally reduced to the stratagem of pleading a headache or a similar indisposition whenever she was invited to accompany her mother and Lady Mercer on an excursion in Sir Manning's company—a fact that was responsible for her being alone in the Long Drawing-room on a fine morning, some two weeks after his departure for London, when Mr. Peter Hession called in Great Pulteney Street.

So plagued had she been by Sir Manning's ebullient courtship that she

almost welcomed the arrival of her younger suitor, and she greeted him
with a cordiality that caused him to exclaim, "Well, that proves it! Knew
you only wanted a little time to come about! How have you been keeping
yourself? Looking a little down pin, ain't you?"

"I should think I might!" Georgina said, trying not to blink at the
splendour of Mr. Hession's elegant attire, which included a coat of blue
superfine with very long tails and very large buttons, a pair of exquisitely
fitting pantaloons of the palest primrose colour, and a number of fobs and
seals depending from a rather startlingly striped waistcoat. "Do sit down,
Peter," she invited him, "and *try,* if you can, not to plague me into marrying you, at least for today! I have had *quite* enough of that this past
week."

"Why, what the dooce do you mean?" Mr. Hession demanded, in some
surprise. "I ain't been near you, or even sent you a letter— Oh! You mean
some other fellow's been at you!" he suddenly took her meaning, his
hackles rising. "Who is it?"

"Sir Manning Hartily," she said, between despair and amusement.
Peter gave a shout of laughter and she said, in some asperity, "Yes, you
may well laugh, but it is very disagreeable for *me,* I can tell you. Mama
and Grandmama have been completely taken in by him."

"What! That old court-card!" he said incredulously. "You're bamming
me! They can't think that a girl like you— I mean to say, it would be
different, of course, if you were some fubsy-faced old maid at her last
prayers! But what would a regular out-and-outer like you want with that
bag-pudding? Why, he's as fat as a flawn, and more than twice your age,
into the bargain."

"Yes, I know," Georgina said, sighing. "But I assure you, Grandmama
thinks him an elegant figure."

"Rats in her upper works!" Mr. Hession said, decidedly. "I don't say,
mind you, that he ain't of the first stare when it comes to *what* he wears,
but, good God, even Weston can't do anything about *how* he looks in the
coats he makes for him. Enough to send any first-rate tailor into the dismals, having to cut a coat for that tub of lard!"

He cast an approving glance over his own figure as he uttered this stricture, an action that drew a slight gurgle of mirth from Georgina. Mr. Hession reddened slightly, and demanded to know if she found anything
amiss with the way he looked.

"Nothing at all!" she assured him. "You are *bang up to the nines,* as Sir
Manning would say. You must forgive me. I have been used to live in the

country, you know, where gentlemen are not quite so—so *particular* in their dress."

"Now *there* you are mistaken," Mr. Hession said seriously, and went on to describe to her in full detail the boots he had just ordered from Hoby for country wear—"white hunting-tops, you know, with very long tops, the latest crack"—a description that was presently interrupted by the entrance of Lady Mercer and Mrs. Power. They had just returned from Meyler's Library, where they had had the pleasure of a conversation with Sir Manning, and the sight of Georgina entertaining Mr. Hession alone in the drawing-room, when she was presumed to be laid down on her bed with the headache, sent Lady Mercer's lips to pursing in instant disapproval.

Mr. Hession, who had left Bath a fortnight before in the happy belief that the two elder ladies of the household favoured his suit, heart and soul, was then treated to a quarter of an hour of coolly civil conversation, containing several hints of his want of conduct in encouraging Georgina's ramshackle behaviour in receiving him alone. It ended in Georgina's feeling obliged to come to his defence, which she did so warmly that, when he had taken his departure, Mrs. Power was moved to say to her mother that she believed Georgina would accept him after all, if only she were left to herself for a time.

"And Sir Manning, you know, Mama," she ventured to remark, "*is* rather old for her."

To this speech Lady Mercer merely replied that she was a fool, and recommended her to stop casting sheep's eyes at Sir Manning herself.

"You made yourself quite conspicuous this morning," she said blightingly, "hanging on his words with that *gooseish* look on your face. Do try for a little conduct, Maria!"

She added darkly that she was persuaded Georgina was certainly not likely to oblige them by doing anything so proper as accepting Mr. Hession's offer, and gave it as her opinion that she was playing him and Sir Manning off against each other, while still mooning over that odious wretch in Ireland.

For Lady Mercer to accuse Georgina of "mooning" over Shannon was undoubtedly unjust, but still the truth of the matter was that she was far from happy, and the passing days seemed to make it no easier for her to dismiss him from her mind. She had resolved a hundred times that she would forget him, and a hundred times had found herself breaking this resolution when some memory of him intruded without warning into her consciousness. That he had been guilty of the vilest conduct she could not deny, with his own words of admission still ringing in her ears, yet she found herself persisting in believing that there must be some extenuating circumstances. A manifestly absurd belief, she told herself bitterly, and took herself roundly to task for indulging in it.

But, no matter how she scolded herself, she could not dispel the cloud of misery and anxiety that seemed to have been hanging over her since her return from Kerry.

Of her friends in Ireland she heard little news. She had, indeed, had a long letter from Mrs. Quinlevan, but, as it consisted chiefly of lamentations over Lady Eliza's perfidy in having caused Georgina to be spirited away from Craythorne and assurances of Brandon's continued devotion to her, she learned scarcely anything from it that she had not already known. A missive from Betsy Mott was equally unenlightening, for its chief—and, indeed, only—topic was the fact that Sir Humphrey had at last given his consent to her dear Robert's making her an offer in form. She had, of course, accepted it, and the announcement of the engagement, she informed her friend, in a spate of exclamation points, would soon appear in the *Gazette*.

Brandon, who detested writing letters, had not favored her with a line.

One morning in early June, however, when she had been unable to think of an acceptable excuse for not accompanying her mother and Lady Mercer to the Pump Room, an unexpected reminder of her visit to Ireland came upon her notice. The three ladies had scarcely entered the room when Georgina's eyes lit on a large, middle-aged gentleman in a well-cut blue coat and Angola pantaloons, standing in conversation with a retired general well known in the quiet Bath circles frequented by Lady Mercer. Recognising Mr. Jeremy Barnwall, Georgina gave a jump and a gasp, which brought down on her a look of disapproval from Lady Mercer.

"It is Cousin Jeremy," Georgina explained. "Cousin Bella's brother, you know, Grandmama—Mr. Barnwall. I had no notion that he was in Bath!"

Lady Mercer favoured Mr. Barnwall's ample figure with a disapproving stare, and gave it as her opinion that if he were indeed the gentleman whom Georgina had named, it was highly remiss of him not to have called in Great Pulteney Street to present his compliments. As she had never met Mr. Barnwall and had evinced no desire to do so over the years since her daughter had become connected with his family, Georgina could not feel that the omission was one that should cause her any great concern. At any rate, she was determined, for her own part, to speak to her cousin, and therefore made a persevering attempt to catch his eye, once General Tufts had left his company.

She was successful: Mr. Barnwall, perceiving her, came across the room —rather reluctantly, it seemed to her—and greeted her politely. She presented him to her mother and to Lady Mercer, and, these civilities having been accomplished, applied to him at once for news from Ireland.

Mr. Barnwall shook his head. "Haven't any, I'm afraid," he said apologetically. "Never was one to write letters, you know. Had a scrawl from Bella a sennight since, but you know what a curst bad hand she writes—couldn't make out the half of it. The usual story, I expect—Brandon's health, and troubles with the servants. Nothing much ever happens in that corner of the world."

He did not seem inclined to explain his presence in Bath, and made only the vaguest of promises to call in Great Pulteney Street, saying that he was on the point of departing for Kerry, where business demanded his attention. Sir Manning, however, who joined the ladies just as Mr. Barnwall was taking his departure from the Pump Room, was able to enlighten them on the reasons for his reluctance to speak more plainly to them concerning his presence in Bath.

"Rolled up," he said succinctly. "Heard it from Larraby. Ought to have stuck to faro or whist. Always said deep basset would be his ruin. Came here to Bath on a repairing lease—stopping at the Pelican or some such deuced unfashionable place. Attached himself to old Tufts, I hear—travelled down from London in that antiquated chaise of his only to save posting charges. But Tufts ain't going to stand the nonsense here. Poor Jerry'll be obliged to go back to Ireland soon."

"Yes, he said as much," Lady Mercer agreed.

She eyed Mr. Barnwall's departing form in disapprobation, and delivered it as her opinion that gaming was the curse of modern society—an animadversion with which Sir Manning, hoping devoutly that his own losses did not reach her ears before he had succeeded in coming to the point of a public announcement of his betrothal to her granddaughter, promptly agreed.

No more was said concerning Mr. Barnwall, but Georgina, returning to Great Pulteney Street, was for the rest of the day in as low spirits as she ever fell into, for her cousin's unexpected appearance in Bath had vividly recalled to her mind the last occasion on which she had met him—at Lady Eliza's ball at Stokings. She slept but little that night, and at the breakfast table in the morning, when Lady Mercer proposed that she accompany her and Mrs. Power to do some shopping in Milsom Street, she was truthfully able to plead that she felt not at all disposed to leave the house.

She was inclined to consider this circumstance a fortunate one when, just as the meal was coming to an end, Finch brought the post into the room. Among the letters there was one, which appeared to be of several sheets, for her from Brandon, and when she broke the wafer with which it was sealed the first thing that met her eye was Shannon's name. Knowing full well that she could not hope to read such a letter without betraying herself by a change in colour that would bring inquiries down on her from Lady Mercer, she hastily refolded it and said, with an assumed air of lightness, that it appeared Brandon had written such a volume that she would put it by and read it later.

Lady Mercer remarked that she could not conceive what her cousin could find to write of to her at such length—a sentiment with which Georgina, for once, heartily agreed. She was on tenterhooks to know the meaning of Brandon's sudden epistolary enthusiasm, and scarcely waited until the front door had closed behind Lady Mercer and her mother before she fled into the Long Drawing-room with her letter.

It began without the least attempt at the usual civilities.

"Dear Cousin," Brandon had written, "I thought I must write to tell you what I have found out concerning Shannon. There is likely to be the devil of a dust kicked up when it all comes out, which it is bound to do as soon as he begins to take the necessary legal steps, though at present no one knows of it but Rothe and me. You see, he intends to give up The Place to you and go to America. It is the most dashed addlebrained thing in the world for him to do, I am persuaded, for you will not know in the least how to go on there, besides having expectations of your own from Lady Mercer, while he has not a farthing besides; but I had as lief talk to a brick wall as try to argue with him about it. He says that The Place would have been yours if he had not married Nuala, and that he does not wish to benefit by that step."

Georgina, by the time she had read so far, had been cast into such perturbation that her hands shook as she held the paper, and she could scarcely comprehend the meaning of what she read. At one moment it seemed to her that this determination of Shannon's must have its root in his regard for her; at another, she thought with sick apprehension that his resolution not to benefit by his marriage to her cousin could only be a confirmation of his guilt in regard to her death.

She read on, hastily: "I am making a great muddle of this, I expect, for

I should have told you first that it is as I suspected, and that that maggot you have taken into your head about Shannon and Nuala is nothing but moonshine. You have met Rothe, so you will know that his word can be depended on. He is staying at present at The Place with Shannon, and, as I ride over there almost every day now, I have had several opportunities to talk with him alone, while Shannon is engaged on estate matters.

"The other day I put it to him direct about that bouncer Lady Eliza told you when you were at Stokings. I have never seen a man more shocked in my life. He said he was in Brussels himself at the time of Nuala's death, and that nothing could have been farther from the truth than that Shannon had any hand in causing it. On the contrary, he said, he was excessively disturbed, called in no less than three physicians to attend her, and these the very first in their profession. Rothe says, furthermore, that if there was any gossip it must have been set about by Lady E. herself, for he never heard it, and indeed there was no reason for it. Lady E.—how I am to put this delicately enough for your ears I don't know—but the fact of the matter is that she took a great fancy to Shannon from the start, and, as he has always set her down in that cool way of his, I daresay she was bound to have her revenge—especially when she saw in what quarter the wind sat as far as you and he were concerned. It is like a woman to cut a man up behind his back!

"As for your saying he told you himself that the story is true—I fancy that, ten to one, if you will look back on what was said, you will find that you jumped to conclusions in your usual harebrained way. I must say it seemed dashed unlikely to me from the start that any man who had committed murder would admit it to the first person who put a question to him about it. I expect he *does* feel it wasn't the thing for him to have married Nuala, for Rothe is persuaded that it wasn't a love match on his side. But he was in a curst bad situation at the time, with Cartan throwing him on the world without a groat to his name, and I daresay thought he could do worse than to marry Nuala, who had set her heart on marrying *him*. You never knew her, of course, but she was a devilish good-looking girl, and up to all the rigs when it came to getting her own way. I should think a man would have to have been a saint to resist the chance to have her *and* The Place without lifting a finger, and Shannon ain't a saint, as you well know.

"I asked Rothe what should be done about Lady Eliza's spreading that story, and he was at *Point Non-Plus* about it, just as I was. Said he thought the best thing to be done was to say nothing at all to Shannon, but to put a flea in Colonel Malladon's ear when the opportunity arose. I expect he thinks it may all have been done for your benefit and that she won't repeat it, now you are gone, for I imagine he knows how the land lies as far as you and Shannon are concerned. He could scarcely fail to, with this scheme of Shannon's of giving The Place up to you—besides which, Shannon has been going about looking as blue-devilled as if he had lost his last friend ever since you left Kerry. I'm dashed if I ever saw him in this mood—or Rothe either, so he says.

"It's my opinion that you had best come back here and have the whole thing out with him, one way or the other. I daresay there would be a rare dust kicked up if you decided to marry him, and of course I am only guessing that that is what *he* wants, for he's never so much as mentioned your name to me, except for this business about The Place, and wouldn't have then if Rothe hadn't brought the matter up. I must say it don't seem to me that the two of you would suit in the least, but that is your affair, and I should be devilish glad to see the thing settled, for I can tell you that I shan't like it above half if he holds to his word and goes to America. . . ."

Georgina could read no further. She started up, crumpling the letter in her hand, tears of frustration springing into her eyes. How like Brandon it was, she thought bitterly, to advise her calmly to return to Ireland! There was not the least possibility that her mother and Lady Mercer would consent to such a scheme, and without that consent she could not move.

In a fever of agitation she began to walk up and down the room, pausing now and again to unfold the crumpled letter in her hand and hastily reread one of Brandon's blunt sentences. *Ten to one, if you will look back on what was said, you will find that you jumped to conclusions in your usual harebrained way,* he had written. She searched her memory. Could it be true indeed, as Brandon had surmised, that she had misinterpreted Shannon's words, and that the guilt which he had affirmed to her had had reference only to Lady Eliza's frequently voiced insinuations that he had married Nuala for her fortune? She remembered now that he had cut her short before she had succeeded in telling him the whole of what Lady Eliza had said to her, that, in fact, she had done no more than utter the barest hint that that lady had made her the recipient of confidences concerning him before he had curtly informed her that those confidences had been based on fact.

She cast the letter down upon a table, pressing both hands to her burning cheeks.

"Oh, what a *fool* I have been!" she cried. "Of course that is it! It *must* be! He thought I was speaking of Lady Eliza's hints that he had run off with Nuala only because she was an heiress; there was not a word he spoke that indicated anything other than that! If only I had been plainer—!"

She picked the letter up again and began to pace the room in wretched agitation, trying to think what she must do. Write to him—yes!—and tell him that she would not accept The Place, but how would that help to clear up the worse matter of the misunderstanding between them? Even if she were able to make it plain to him that she had been labouring under a misapprehension on the day of their last meeting, it was more than probable that he would persist in his belief that he had no right to ask her to marry him. She would never be able, she thought despairingly, to convince him by a mere letter that she did not care a fig for the accident of his birth, or for his having been human enough to succumb to the temptation of her cousin's beauty, fortune, and importunity. And the end of it would be that he would go to America and she would never set eyes on him again.

18 She was still turning the matter over hopelessly in her mind when she was disturbed by the sound of carriage wheels in the street, and a few moments later Finch announced the arrival of Sir Manning Hartily and ushered that gentleman into the room. Sir Manning looked gratified to find her alone, and, after complimenting her on being in high good looks, began at once, with a complete insensitivity to her obvious agitation, on a speech of formal gallantry, which she saw to her dismay was very likely to end in an offer for her hand.

"You must not believe, my dear Miss Power," he said, inclining himself toward her in his chair with an alarming creak of corsets, "that the assiduity of my attentions to your worthy mama and Lady Mercer has been due to my pleasure in their company alone. No, indeed! I have had an eye," he proclaimed, allowing himself a ponderously roguish smile, "on—if I may so express myself—younger game. In other words, my dear—your own fair person! From the moment that I was first privileged, at Stokings, to gaze upon the perfection of face and form embodied in your—"

"Oh, do stop!" Georgina broke in, forgetting her manners completely under the stress of this new vexation. Sir Manning rolled his eyes at her in astonishment, and she attempted to cover over her lapse by saying hurriedly, "I am very sorry to seem rude, but indeed, *indeed,* I am in no mood to listen to pretty speeches this morning, Sir Manning! I have had"—she glanced down at the letter, which she still held crumpled in her hand—"some very distressing news—"

"No, by God, have you?" Sir Manning exclaimed, staring. "From Ireland, perhaps—is it? Your cousins? But I ran into Jerry Barnwall only last evening—never said a word of anything amiss there to me."

He checked, looking uneasily at Georgina, on whose face a startled and quite radiant expression had suddenly appeared.

"Cousin Jeremy!" she gasped. "Of course! Why didn't *I* think of that! It is the very thing!" She sprang to her feet. "Sir Manning, will you do me a very great favour?" she demanded.

Sir Manning stared harder. "Happy to, of course!" he stammered. "Anything in my power! But I must say I don't quite understand—"

"It is a very long and very complicated story," Georgina assured him recklessly, "and I have no time to go into it at present. You know, I presume, where my cousin Barnwall is putting up? The Pelican, I believe you said yesterday? Will you drive me there—at once, please? That is, as soon as I have had time to run upstairs and put on my bonnet and gloves?"

Sir Manning, who was by this time completely at sea, assured her once more that he would be happy to serve her, but added that it seemed deuced queer to him that she couldn't wait until her mother or Lady Mercer returned to accompany her to the Pelican.

"Not quite the thing for a young female to go calling alone on gentlemen in hotels," he reminded her. "Cousin or no cousin. Lady Mercer wouldn't like it."

"Of course she wouldn't," Georgina agreed cordially. "Which is exactly why I know that I can rely on you, dear Sir Manning, not to breathe a word to her about it. But we really must hurry, or I shan't be back by the time she and Mama return. Will you excuse me, only for a moment? I presume you have kept your curricle waiting?"

Without pausing for a reply she dashed out the door, returning a few minutes later to find Sir Manning standing in the middle of the room with a bemused expression on his face.

"Don't understand this at all!" he proclaimed. "Dashed peculiar business! What do you want with Barnwall? And why should your cousins have written to you instead of to him?"

"I expect they were not sure of his direction in Bath," Georgina said, improvising rapidly. "Dear Sir Manning, I *cannot* explain the matter to you, but I am assured that I can trust you! Can I not?"

She gave him a coaxing glance, which had the effect of melting his opposition to the point that he followed her to the front door, where he received his hat, gloves, and cane from Finch with the air of a man who had not yet succeeded in deciding whether to be flattered or alarmed. Finch, for his own part, betrayed some slight surprise at seeing Miss Georgina leaving the house alone with Sir Manning—a circumstance which reminded Georgina that he might well mention the matter to Lady Mercer if the latter did not find her granddaughter at home when she returned. It also occurred to her that, even if she were fortunate enough to arrive back in Great Pulteney Street before her grandmother and her mother, she could not be sure of escaping the observation of one of her grandmother's bosom-bows while riding about the town in an open carriage with Sir Manning, so that she must certainly concoct some explanation to satisfy her as to the reason for her action.

At the present moment, however, she was far too involved in pulling together the threads of the scheme that had flashed into her mind when Sir

Manning had mentioned Mr. Barnwall to have room for anything else in her head. She had only a few minutes, she was well aware, in which to manufacture a story that would induce Mr. Barnwall to take the extraordinary step of escorting her to Ireland without the knowledge of either her mother or Lady Mercer, and, completely occupied with this task, she cast out answers quite at random to Sir Manning's attempts at conversation.

Not until Sir Manning's match-greys were drawing up before the Pelican, in fact, did she realise that she had given absent-minded assent to his inquiry as to whether it was her young cousin Brandon who had met with some mischance.

"Well, if that is so," he objected, "I still can't make out why you are in such a deuced rush to see Barnwall. Nothing *he* can do about it, is there? And he's on the point of leaving for Ireland, at any rate."

"Yes, I know that. I *can't* explain, Sir Manning, because—because, you see, there are family matters involved which I can't properly discuss with you— No! You mustn't go inside with me!" she added hastily, as he seemed inclined to entrust the horses to an ostler and descend from the curricle. "If you will only be so good as to wait for me here for a quarter of an hour—"

She jumped down from the curricle without staying for his expostulations and hurried inside, where she sent up her visiting-card to Mr. Barnwall in the fervent hope that that gentleman would not be found to be already gone out. Luck was with her, however, and in a very short time she was being ushered into a parlour on the first floor, where she found Mr. Barnwall regarding her card with a rather distrustful expression on his plump face. He was wearing an elegant, much-befrogged brocade dressing-gown, for which he apologised, adding immediately, as he looked at the card in his hand, "Thought there must be some mistake. You didn't come here alone?"

"Yes, I did," she said. "I—I was obliged to! I mean to say— Sir Manning Hartily drove me here in his curricle, but he has no idea why I wished to see you, and I am quite sure that if he had he would never have brought me!"

The uneasiness which her arrival at the Pelican had aroused in Mr. Barnwall did not appear to be allayed by this cryptic confession, but he recollected himself sufficiently to set a chair for her and to sit down himself.

"He wouldn't, eh?" he asked then, regarding her fixedly out of his round blue eyes. "I expect you'd best let me have the whole story, my dear. What is it? Come to cuffs with the old griffin?—your grandmother, I mean, Lady Mercer. Daunting sort of woman, but I can't for the life of me see how running off to tell *me* about it can save your groats."

Georgina reached into her reticule for her handkerchief, and was relieved to find that the tears necessary for the scene she would have to enact were quite ready to flow after the agitations she had suffered that morning.

"Oh, indeed, sir, you must believe that if there were anyone else to whom I could turn I would do so!" she said feelingly. "But there is no one! Grandmama has *quite* made up her mind that I am to marry Sir Manning, and Mama will have nothing to say against it—"

"Manning? Manning Hartily?" Mr. Barnwall looked thunderstruck. "Nonsense!" he said decisively. "Old enough to be your father! Matter of fact, he's older than I am. And hasn't a feather to fly with, into the bargain. Your grandmother must be dicked in the nob if she's even considering such a thing."

"Yes, that is what *I* think," Georgina agreed fervently. "But he has *quite* taken her in, you see—and Mama too. They will not *hear* of my marrying Brandon!"

Mr. Barnwall, who up to this time had displayed the somewhat uncomfortable mien of a man being dragged against his will into a matter that is not at all his concern, suddenly lost his air of reluctance and sat up straighter.

"Brandon, eh?" he said. "Then Bella wasn't talking moonshine when she said it might come to a match between the two of you!" He looked at Georgina with a more benevolent air. "Do you *wish* to marry Brandon, my dear?" he inquired.

"Oh, yes!" she sighed, with a feeling of inward shock at her own mendacity. "You see, we had quite come to an agreement with each other on that head when I was in Ireland, only Grandmama would not hear of it, and packed me off home to Bath instead. And now she wishes me to marry Sir Manning, and I am so *very* unhappy!"

Mr. Barnwall was looking thoughtful. "Well, you needn't marry Manning if you don't like the idea, you know, my dear," he advised her, in a fatherly tone. "I daresay, if you stick to your guns, your grandmama will grow tired of urging you, sooner or later."

"Oh, no, I am quite certain that she will not!" Georgina assured him tragically. "And even if she were to do so, there is *still* Mr. Hession."

"Mr. Hession?" Mr. Barnwall looked blank for a moment. "Oh! You mean Sir Landers' young chub? What the deuce has *he* to say to anything?"

Georgina cast her eyes down in maidenly confusion. "He—wishes to marry me, too," she confessed. "And Grandmama says that the title is a very respectable one, and the estate as well, while poor Brandon will have nothing at all but Craythorne—"

"I see. I see."

Mr. Barnwall rose and took a turn or two about the room. It was obvious to Georgina, regarding him from under lowered lashes, that he was considering the advantages that must accrue to an impecunious gentleman from having his nephew marry a young lady of considerable expectations. She felt a strong qualm of guilt about deceiving him so grossly, but resolutely put it aside, feeling that the time was now ripe to come forward with the proposal that was the reason for her visit.

"If you would only take me with you to Ireland when you return there—" she suggested, cautiously. "I am sure, if Mama and Grandmama were to see how much in earnest I am about not marrying Sir Manning—"

Mr. Barnwall's first response to the feeler she had cast out was not encouraging.

"Help you to run off?" he ejaculated. "No, no! You are a naughty puss to think of such a thing! Deuce take it, my dear, reason—persuasion—always carry the day in the end!"

Georgina cast her eyes down at her hands, which she had folded tightly in her lap. "I fear you do not know my grandmama, sir," she said sadly. "When she takes a scheme into her head, *nothing* will move her from it—and I am quite dependant upon her, you know."

Mr. Barnwall took another turn about the room. "Yes, yes, I see!" he said. "Dashed awkward situation for you, of course—but still I can't think what you hope to gain by running off to Ireland. You ain't of age, are you? Couldn't marry Brandon at all events without the old lady's consent."

"No, I couldn't," Georgina admitted. "But I am quite persuaded that if Grandmama is brought to see how *unalterably* opposed I am to marrying anyone but Brandon, she must come round. Only how I am to accomplish this merely by reason I cannot see! She quite bears me down, and there is no one to take my part. But if I were to go to Ireland she *must* realise that I am truly in earnest—and besides," she added ingeniously, "she is in the greatest dread of scandal, you know. So I daresay, if I *were* to succeed in running off, she would make the best of it and allow me to marry Brandon, rather than being obliged to come and fetch me back, and have everyone know of what I had done."

She paused, fixing her blue eyes rather anxiously on her cousin's face. Mr. Barnwall was frowning, but he had been struck, she could see, by her arguments. Certainly it stood entirely within the bounds of probability that a young girl, left alone to face the pressures of her family, might eventually find herself obliged to succumb to them. Mr. Barnwall also—though Georgina could not know this—was thinking of the tearful recriminations and frequent applications to him for aid which he would be forced to endure from his sister if she were to discover that Brandon had missed his chance at landing a fortune merely because of his uncle's timidity.

He sat down abruptly, slapping his hand against his thigh. "Tell you what," he said, "I'll do it! Curst rum business if a pretty gal like you is to be forced into Manning Hartily's arms! Nothing to say against Manning—devilish obliging fellow—but *not* the husband for you, my dear. Troubled with gout, you know. Wouldn't do for you at all."

Georgina could scarcely restrain herself from jumping up and throwing her arms about his neck. She controlled herself, however, and managed to express her gratitude in somewhat less exuberant terms. Mr. Barnwall, who found himself rather enjoying playing St. George to Sir Manning's dragon, with Georgina's blue eyes rewarding him for his labours by bestowing the sweetest of glances on him, was inclined to prolong the moment, but her more practical mind had flown quickly to the arrangements still to be made, and she brought him back at once to more mundane considerations. The possibility of adding to the propriety of her flight by taking her abigail with her was quickly raised and as soon abandoned, for, though she believed she might rely on that damsel's loyalty, she was not at all certain of her discretion, and any premature betrayal of her scheme to Lady Mercer must, she was well aware, result in its instantly being interdicted. Mr. Barnwall, whose own notions of propriety were not of the strictest, and whose straitened circumstances made the idea of any additional financial burden unwelcome, readily agreed to this, possibly considering that the reprehensibility of his action in abetting her granddaughter to run off from her home would scarcely be alleviated in Lady Mercer's eyes by his bringing along the young lady's maid.

"But we must really decide on our plans quickly, you know," Georgina reminded him, unwilling to dwell on a subject that she was aware might raise scruples in her cousin's breast, "for Mama and Grandmama may return at any moment, and there is Sir Manning waiting outside—"

Mr. Barnwall, who had not previously considered the oddity of a gentleman's having been obliging enough to escort his inamorata to visit a second gentleman who was to assist her to run away from him, interrupted her here to inquire with interest how she had managed to accomplish this feat.

"Oh, I told him the most shocking story!" she acknowledged. "He thinks that Cousin Bella has written me bad news from Ireland on a very *delicate* family matter!"

Mr. Barnwall laughed indulgently. "Well, well," he said, "I suppose we must grant that a little deception is warranted in a good cause."

Georgina, endeavouring to quell a blush, agreed, and hastily turned the conversation once more to the arrangements to be made for her departure. It was her idea that Mr. Barnwall should await her in a hired post-chaise at the corner of the street before sun-up the next morning. It would be some hours after that, in the normal course of events, before her absence would be discovered, and, when it was, she believed that the household would be thrown into such turmoil that it would be at least several more before anything would be done, or even decided upon.

"That," she said, "should give us a clear enough start so that we shan't be overtaken before we are safe on board the packet for Ireland." She considered. "If I write a note now, will you have one of the servants here deliver it to Great Pulteney Street no earlier than three o'clock tomorrow afternoon? I don't wish to worry poor Mama more than is absolutely necessary, you see, but I dare not leave a note in my room at home for fear it may be found, by some mischance, before we have had time to get well away."

He agreed to this plan, and she accordingly sat down and dashed off a hasty missive to her mother, in which she assured her that she was perfectly safe, and on her way to Craythorne under Mr. Barnwall's escort. She said nothing at all about what she intended to do when she reached there, merely informing Mrs. Power that she was excessively sorry to cause her so much worry, but that she could not bring herself to accept either Sir Manning's or Mr. Hession's suit.

Having sealed her letter with a wafer, she left it in Mr. Barnwall's keeping and took her leave to rejoin Sir Manning. She found him waiting impatiently, an uneasy expression clouding his brow.

"Not at all the thing, this business, you know, my dear Miss Power!" he said reprovingly, as she mounted up beside him. "No matter how urgent it was for you to see Barnwall, should have waited! Sent him a message!

Would have been glad to pop round to Great Pulteney Street, if I know Jerry. Very obliging sort of fellow!"

"Exactly what he remarked of you," Georgina said approvingly. "And I am sure he was quite right, Sir Manning, for I cannot find words to express how very grateful I am to you for your kindness to me this morning! I do not know what I should have done without you."

She had been racking her brains to discover an excuse for asking him not to speak of their little excursion to her mother or to Lady Mercer, but to her relief he solved the matter for her himself by remarking a little doubtfully, as they left the Pelican behind, "By the bye, no need to mention to Lady Mercer that I drove you here this morning, Miss Power—that is, if some tabby on the high gab don't get to her with the tale. A devil of a high stickler, your grandmother, you know. Wouldn't do to cast her into high fidgets over nothing."

"Well, I do think it might be better if I were merely to tell her that you had called, and had taken me for a short drive when you saw I was not quite in spirits this morning," Georgina agreed. "There is no need to trouble her over the affair, for I find, on talking with my cousin Barnwall, that the matter is not at all as bad as I had believed, so that there is no need for her to concern herself in the least."

She was glad, as she uttered this exceedingly vague explanation of her activities that morning, that Sir Manning's understanding was far from being acute, for no man of sense, she thought, would have accepted such a Banbury story. Sir Manning, however, appeared much more preoccupied with the possible repercussions that might occur if Lady Mercer discovered he had been unwise enough to abet her granddaughter in visiting a gentleman alone at a hotel, and fell in at once, with an air of considerable relief, with her mildly deceptive scheme.

Mildly deceptive, she thought, she might call that portion of her morning's work, but what words, she asked herself in dismay, as she untied her bonnet-strings in her own bedchamber after Sir Manning had set her down in Great Pulteney Street, was she to use to describe the rest of her behaviour? She had perpetrated a shocking hoax on her unsuspecting cousin; she had involved Brandon, who, as she well knew, had not the slightest wish to marry her, in a romance which was likely to prove highly embarrassing to him, if nothing more; and she had devised a scheme for running off from her home for the sole purpose of meeting a man of whom her relations strongly disapproved and who, as far as she knew, had no desire whatever to meet her. And she had done all this without an instant's hesitation, as if such reprehensible conduct were second nature to her. When she sat down to think calmly of what she had done, she was so horrified that she could find relief only in a hearty burst of tears.

A few minutes' reflection, however, and a reperusal of Brandon's letter, had the effect of convincing her that, blameworthy as her actions had been, there had actually been no other course open to her if she wished to forestall Shannon's plan of giving over The Place to her and going to America. Lady Mercer, she knew, would never consent to her returning to Ireland, and she could not go alone—for financial reasons, if for no other. She had very little money, certainly not nearly enough for such a journey, and if she had confided to Mr. Barnwall the real reason for her wishing to go to Kerry, she was quite sure that he would not have agreed to take her.

Having come to this somewhat comforting point in her mental arguments, she made up her mind to put the topic of her distressing lack of principle out of her head, and to bend her thoughts instead to the more immediate problem of how she was to succeed in smuggling herself and a proper supply of luggage for the journey out of the house in the small hours of the following morning.

The first of these matters presented few difficulties. Both Lady Mercer and Mrs. Power were sound sleepers and late risers, and she had had sufficient forethought to appoint an hour for her rendezvous with Mr. Barnwall early enough that none of the servants would be stirring.

The problem of her luggage, however, was a more vexing one. It would be impossible for her to have a portmanteau brought to her bedchamber, or even for her to fetch one there herself, without its being observed, and she was at last obliged to content herself with the plan of packing a pair of bandboxes with the bare essentials she would require, after the rest of the household should have retired for the night. Of course she would find herself horridly at a stand as to her wardrobe when she arrived in Ireland, but as she had not the slightest idea what she would do when she reached there, or how long she would remain, she decided to trust to luck and to Mrs. Quinlevan to see to it that she might appear at least respectably attired during her stay.

With these decisions arrived at, she had now nothing further to do but to concoct a version of her morning's excursion with Sir Manning that would be suitable for Lady Mercer's ears, and to await with what composure she could the arrival of the hour when she would begin her journey.

19 At first light on the following morning she crept down the stairs, carrying her bandboxes, let herself out the front door, and walked rapidly down the street to the appointed rendezvous. She had a horrid moment of doubt, when she reached the corner and saw no waiting chaise, that Mr. Barnwall had reconsidered his pledge to her; but the instant appearance of the vehicle she had been hoping to see allayed her fears, and in a few moments she had the satisfaction of being handed up into it by her cousin, and of leaving Great Pulteney Street safely behind her.

She had been in the chaise for only a very few minutes, however, when she began to realise that she was not yet out of the woods. Mr. Barnwall, having had almost four-and-twenty hours in which to consider the rashness of assisting a young female to run away from her lawful guardians, was in a nervous mood, and spent the better part of the first hour of the journey in an earnest endeavour to induce his companion to reconsider her decision.

"Thing to be done," he put it to her, "is for Brandon to come over *here*, not t'other way about. Two of you, hand in hand, make a push to change the old lady's mind. Much better that way, I assure you. Chances are the two of you together could bring her about. Devilish engaging young chub, Brandon, you know. Shouldn't wonder in the least if the old Tartar were to take to him amazingly."

He went on in this way for quite some time, in spite of Georgina's obstinate objections, and when he finally gathered that she was not to be moved in her determination lapsed into discontented mutterings. She began to fear that the journey might turn out to be a far from agreeable one—a foreboding that was strengthened when the skies shortly afterward clouded over and a steady rain began to fall. Mr. Barnwall, sitting back in his own corner of the chaise, relapsed into a sulky silence, and Georgina now had the leisure she had hitherto lacked to consider what course she had best pursue when she arrived at Craythorne.

Her one purpose in making the journey, of course, was to obtain an interview with Shannon, but she could scarcely imagine that she would have the hardihood to confess this to Mrs. Quinlevan. It was equally impossible, though, for her to conceive of carrying on with her cousins the deception by which she had lured Mr. Barnwall into taking her to Ireland. Rack her brains as she might over the matter, she could not but come to the dismaying conclusion that, once she had arrived at Craythorne, she would be in a situation so embarrassing that she might well wish she had never set out on this journey.

Even her full conviction of this fact, however, was not sufficient to make her agree to Mr. Barnwall's obvious desire to return her to her grandmother's house before her flight from it had been discovered. A telling mental vision of Shannon, penniless and thousands of miles removed from her in America, made her grit her teeth and determine to go on with her scheme. Her resolution supported her through Mr. Barnwall's sulks, through the dismal weather, through posting-houses that seemed to be in a conspiracy to render their journey inconvenient and disagreeable, through a miserably rough crossing, during the course of which both she and Mr. Barnwall became intolerably sick, and through the final discomfort of being obliged to put up for the night, on the road to Kerry, in what Mr. Barnwall scathingly characterised as a hedge-tavern, owing to the accident of a broken perch on the chaise which he had hired to take them to Craythorne.

Added to the inconvenience of this final stroke of the malignant fate that had pursued her was her fear that the comfortable start she had had on any pursuit that might have been begun behind her had been so greatly diminished by these delays that she could no longer be certain that she would not be overtaken before she had reached her goal. This anxiety cast her into a fit of the dismals such as all the discomforts of the journey had been unable to produce, and as a result she quarreled so roundly with Mr. Barnwall, who was also in a snappish mood, during the final miles of the journey that they were scarcely on speaking terms when the chaise at last drew up before the door at Craythorne.

It was by that time late in the day, since the problem of having repairs made to the chaise in an out-of-the-way spot had obliged them to make a very late start. Georgina, mounting the steps to the door beside Mr. Barnwall, found that her apprehension over the scene before her had risen to such a pitch that her knees were trembling under her. Her fears were not at all allayed when Murtaugh, the butler whose services had replaced, but scarcely improved upon, those of the unlamented Higgins, opened the front door in response to Mr. Barnwall's vigorous summons, and gazed upon the pair of them with such palpable astonishment that Mr. Barnwall was moved to say peevishly, "Well, don't stand there gaping, man! We've had a deuced bad trip, and I want my dinner! Where's your mistress?"

Murtaugh closed his mouth, but opened it again to stutter, as Georgina and Mr. Barnwall walked past him into the hall, "G-gone out, sir! Dining at Mott House. Excuse me, sir! Was she expecting you? And—*and* the young lady, sir?"

"No, she wasn't," Mr. Barnwall said. "Exactly like that woman to be out when she's wanted! And I daresay there's not a curst thing fit to eat in the house on the head of it; I'll do better to go straight on to my own place and see what Mrs. Banting can do for me. A nice dish of ham and eggs, if nothing more! Here, you!" he addressed a bemused footman, who had appeared at the back of the hall and was regarding the visitors out of a stolid country face. "Fetch in Miss Power's luggage, and tell the post-boy I shall want him to take me on to my own house."

The footman, receiving a corroborative nod from Murtaugh, hastened to carry out this order. At the same moment the door of the yellow morning-room opened and Brandon appeared, one finger marking his place in the book he held in his hand and an abstracted frown upon his face.

"What's this infernal racket, Murtaugh?" he demanded. "Who's doing all the shouting?" His eyes fell upon Georgina and his uncle and flew wide. "Uncle Jerry! And Georgie! What the *devil*—?"

"Well, you needn't look at us as if we'd fallen from the moon," Mr. Barnwall said crossly. "The pair of you have cost me the deuce of a worry, I can tell you, but I warn you, now that I've brought the gal here, I wash my hands of the whole affair." He satisfied himself that Murtaugh was engaged in superintending the bringing in of Georgina's luggage, and said in a somewhat lower voice to Brandon, with a glance of marked disfavour in Georgina's direction, "Curst obstinate piece, if you want my opinion! Glad *I'm* not the one has to marry her. Lead you a dog's life, my boy! Take my advice and think twice before you do it!"

"Before I do what?" Brandon asked, looking puzzledly from his uncle to Georgina, who seemed to be trying to signal him, with a slight, agitated motion of one hand, to let the matter rest.

Mr. Barnwall put up his heavy brows over his baby-blue eyes. "Now *don't* try to gammon me that you haven't a notion what I'm talking about," he said, with asperity. "*I* know what kind of rig the two of you are running."

"Do you?" Brandon asked. "Well, that's more than *I* do! What the devil is this all about, Georgie? Did you travel here in my uncle's company?"

"Dragooned me into it," Mr. Barnwall corroborated gloomily, as Georgina merely stood looking at her cousin in imploring embarrassment. "Said that fellow Hartily would be sure to have her if I wouldn't stand buff. And no budging her, either, once she'd made up her mind. Wild horses wouldn't have done it! I'll tell you what, my boy, nobody would like better than me to see you snugly settled, but when it comes to leg-shackling yourself for life to an obstinate female—well, I wouldn't do it, and that's a fact! The money ain't worth it; a man can always contrive in another direction."

He broke off, eyeing his nephew with misgiving, for Brandon's face had suddenly become alarmingly red. He appeared to be doing his utmost to restrain some violent emotion, but his efforts were of no avail, and the next moment he had broken into a shout of helpless laughter.

"Oh, Georgie! You *Trojan!*" he cried, wiping his streaming eyes with his handkerchief when he could speak again. "You *didn't* gammon him into bringing you over here by pitching him a Banbury story about wanting to marry *me!*"

The answer must have been clear to him without Georgina's uttering a word: the guilty colour that had overspread her face told its own tale. Mr. Barnwall as well—though his mental processes were not noted for their rapidity—had begun to grasp the fact that something was sadly amiss in the Romeo-and-Juliet tale in which he had been induced to play a part, and stared belligerently from his nephew to Georgina and back again.

"What's this? What's this?" he demanded. "Do you mean to tell me she *don't* want to marry you, after all?"

"Brandon, *do* be quiet!" Georgina begged him, herself torn between a reprehensible desire to giggle and a lowering conviction of her own complete depravity. "I'll explain everything to you later. But now you must see that Cousin Jeremy is fagged to death and wants his dinner—"

She broke off as a new voice introduced itself into the controversy. It was Murtaugh, standing beside the young footman who had borne her two wholly inadequate bandboxes into the hall.

"Begging your pardon, miss," he said deprecatingly, "but there appears to be a slight misunderstanding on the subject of your luggage. The post-boy persists in stating that you have brought no more than these—these—"

"He is quite right," Georgina said hastily, not daring to catch Brandon's eye. "I—I was obliged to leave very—very unexpectedly, you see!"

"Yes, I'll warrant you were!" Brandon said, showing a marked tendency to give way to mirth again. He said to Murtaugh, "Have them taken up to the Blue Bedchamber, Murtaugh, and you'd best warn Mrs. Hopkins that Miss Power is come. And tell her as well that my uncle is here, and that both of our guests would appreciate sustenance at the earliest possible moment—"

"No, no! Not for me!" Mr. Barnwall said, raising a restraining hand. "I'm on my way! You may tell Bella I'll drive over to call on her tomorrow." He added severely, to Brandon, "I don't know what sort of wheedle you and your cousin are trying to cut, my boy, and, what's more, I don't want to know! It will be bellows to mend with me as it is, when Lady Mercer finds out my part in this affair. I'll give you one word of advice, and then I'm off. If you *ain't* going to marry this young woman, pack her back home by the very next boat. That is," he concluded, again bestowing a glance of concentrated disfavour on Georgina, "if she'll oblige you by going—which I very much doubt!"

He turned toward the door, leaving Georgina to stammer her belated thanks for his assistance behind him. Brandon laughed again, and took her arm.

"Come along," he said. "I want to hear the whole story of this adventure. Murtaugh, tell Mrs. Hopkins my cousin and I will be in the morning-room; she may have a tray brought to Miss Power there. Are you hungry?" he asked Georgina, as he led her into the room and assisted her to remove her bonnet and pelisse.

"Famished!" she confessed. "But, oh, Brandon, I am so overset that I don't think I shall be able to eat a morsel! What an odious wretch you were to laugh at me! And so slow to take my meaning! You *might* have pretended, only for this evening, at any rate, that you really did want to marry me! We could have made up some story later—a falling-out, or some such thing—instead of which you landed me in a dreadful hobble!"

"I should think you had landed yourself in it," Brandon said unrepentantly, still frankly enjoying the situation. "How was *I* to guess what brummish tricks you were up to? Good God, did you *have* to involve such a bobbing-block as my uncle in this? And what have you been doing to him, to make him regard you with such loathing?"

"Well, I could not help it!" Georgina said, sitting down and putting up her chin defiantly. "He wanted me to go back to Grandmama and Mama as soon as he had had time to turn the whole matter over in his mind, and of course I would not do it. I couldn't possibly have done, for how else was I to manage to get over here?" She looked at him a trifle resentfully. "It's all very well for you to ask why I needed to involve Cousin Jeremy," she said, "but you will admit that *you* were of no help to me, merely throwing it out to me that I ought to come here. How in heaven's name did you suppose I was to manage it, with my own pockets to let and

Grandmama and Mama both certain to oppose any such scheme if I had even dared to broach it to them?"

"They don't know where you are, then?" Brandon inquired. "Good Lord, what a kick-up there must have been when they discovered you were gone!" Mirth overcame him again, and he lay back in his chair and laughed until he cried. "I c-can't help it!" he gasped at last, as he saw Georgina regarding him in high dudgeon. "It's too m-much—the picture of you and Uncle Jerry p-posting away together in secret like a p-pair of lovesick—"

"Turtledoves," Georgina finished it for him obligingly, her own lips curving into a smile in spite of herself. "Only we weren't," she confided. "He was as cross as crabs all the way. I *did* think he might become reconciled to the idea once we were fairly on our way, but he didn't—and then the weather was dreadful, and the chaise broke down—"

"Don't!" said Brandon, threatening to relapse once more. "Dash it, we had better be serious for a while, Georgie. We shall have to concoct some sort of story before Mama comes home to account for your coming here, and we haven't much time."

"Well, I do not see how we are to say anything other than that I came to marry you, because that is what Cousin Jeremy will tell her," Georgina said doubtfully. "I shall tell her too, of course, about Sir Manning's wanting to marry me—"

Brandon grinned again. "Not seriously! You're bamming me!"

"No, indeed I am not! And Grandmama is *quite* persuaded that I ought to accept his offer, for she likes him much better than she does Peter Hession. So I shall tell Cousin Bella that all I could think of was to come over here and marry *you* instead—only now that I have arrived I have changed my mind—" She broke off suddenly and started out of her chair. "Oh!" she exclaimed. "I must be a perfect mooning to sit here talking of such things, when there is no doubt that Grandmama has already sent someone posthaste after me to fetch me back to Bath! Brandon, I *must* see Shannon at once! Will you drive me to The Place?"

"Now?" Brandon asked. "I should think not! Besides, he ain't there."

"Not—?" She stared at him, her eyes wide with fright. "He hasn't gone to America?"

"No, no! Nothing of the sort. Not that I expect Rothe will be able to hold him here much longer—but he's only gone to Kenmare just now, he and Rothe. They ain't expected back until late, so there's no use your getting into high fidgets about going there tonight." He looked at her curiously as she reluctantly sat down again. "What are you going to say to him when you do see him?" he asked bluntly. "I expect you still feel the same way about him that you did when you left here?"

She nodded, colour suffusing her cheeks. He saw that she was looking at him imploringly, and shook his head.

"No, you needn't expect me to tell you how *he* feels," he said. "You know he wouldn't confide in me—and from what Rothe says, he's buttoned up against him as well." A more sober expression appeared on his face. "I know I've seemed to be taking this as a great jest, Georgie," he said, "but to tell you the truth, it's nothing of the sort. Shannon is determined on this crazy start of his, and to my mind it won't answer at all. Oh, I know it might suit you to be independently wealthy, but, dash it, Lady Mercer will leave you very well to pass, whereas Shannon would be without a feather to fly with."

"There is no need to argue with me on *that* score," Georgina said decisively. "I have no intention of allowing him to give up The Place to me."

"Yes, but how will you stop him? It's no use your saying that you can solve the whole affair by marrying him, because ten to one he's got it in his head that he ain't going to ruin your prospects and create another scandal by offering for you. That is, if he even wants to do so—though I'm dashed if I see why he'd go about to do a crackbrained piece of work like giving over The Place to you unless he was nutty upon you. Rothe says there is *something* the matter with him—says he never saw him so resty as he is these days."

They were interrupted at this point by the entrance of Nora Quill, who came in bearing a tray on which a pot of tea, a mutton pie, and a dish of fruit held prominent places. As she was highly disposed to linger in the room with the stated purpose of expressing her pleasure at Georgina's unexpected return to Craythorne, and the unstated one of satisfying her curiosity as to the reason for it, the two cousins found, when she had finally been prevailed on to leave them, that they had very little time remaining before Mrs. Quinlevan might be expected to return from Mott House, and put their heads together in earnest as to their future course of action.

It was decided between them that Brandon would drive Georgina over to The Place on the following morning, on the pretext of taking her for a jaunt about the countryside. Shannon, he assured her, was likely to be found at home at that time, for he had disclosed to Brandon that he was expecting a visit from a Cork attorney that morning.

"To draw up the papers turning The Place over to you, I should think," he remarked, "though of course he didn't tell *me* so. At any rate, he won't be out and about the estate, as he usually is. It won't look so odd, your going over there, if *I* go with you—and then I'll sheer off, if you like, and leave you to have it out with him alone." He looked at her rather curiously. "*I* should think it 'ud be deuced awkward for you, bearding him in his den like that," he said frankly. "No other girl I can call to mind who'd do such a thing. But I expect you didn't come all this way to turn craven now."

"No, I didn't!" Georgina said, wishing her heart would not mount so uncomfortably into her throat every time she thought of that unnerving interview before her. "I *must* go! How else can I stop him from giving me The Place?"

"*Or* give him a chance to say whether he wishes to offer for you or not," Brandon said cheerfully. "You'll be in a deuce of a hobble if he don't, won't you? Your grandmother will be mad as fire about your running off like this. But then I expect she will be in just as great a pelter if you wish to marry Shannon. Lord! I wouldn't be in your shoes, in either case!"

"Well, you are not in my shoes, and you are not being very helpful, either, talking of such things," Georgina said, with some asperity. She had been recruiting her spirits with tea and mutton pie, and, while these did nothing to untangle the apparently inextricable confusion in which her affairs stood, they at least made her feel somewhat more fit to face the difficulties that lay before her. "The thing is," she said, "we must decide at once exactly what I am to say to Cousin Bella when she comes in. I have been thinking it over, and I believe it will not do at all to tell her that shocking rapper about my coming over here to marry you. She has been too kind to me; I cannot deceive her so grossly! I shall simply say that I ran away to escape being forced into marrying Sir Manning Hartily." She looked ruefully at her cousin. "Oh, dear! I feel such a complete wretch!" she said. "Grandmama is sure to give her a dreadful rakedown if she does not send me directly back to Bath, and I am persuaded that she is far too kind-hearted to do that!"

She was quite correct in her estimation of her cousin's probable behaviour. Mrs. Quinlevan, arriving home shortly afterward from an evening spent in the atmosphere of pleasurable anticipation, with romantic overtones, produced by the recent betrothal of Miss Betsy Mott to Mr. Robert Darlington, was exactly in the proper frame of mind to appreciate the difficulties in which her young cousin found herself in being forced into a loveless marriage with a man old enough, as she declared, to be her father.

"It is the most shocking thing I ever heard of," she exclaimed, when she had got over her first amazement at finding Georgina once more at Craythorne, and had been given the expurgated account of the reasons for her flight from Bath on which she and Brandon had decided. "Indeed, I am quite surprised that your grandmama should do such a thing, my love, for she is a woman of strong good sense, and must know that such matches *never* answer. I recall poor Caroline Mullingar, who could never bear to be called by that odious name, which she disliked before she had so much as laid eyes on the man—she swooned dead away in the church just as she was called upon to pronounce her vows, and not six months after the ceremony ran off with a half-pay officer. Not that *you*, I am sure, would ever do such a ramshackle thing as that, my love!"

She rambled on for some time in this fashion, happily losing sight of the difficulties of her own situation when Lady Mercer and her daughter should demand an accounting from her, and gazing fondly at the picture the two young people made sitting together on the sofa, until Georgina was obliged to believe that she had herself conceived the very idea she had so scrupulously omitted to put into her head—that her young cousin had come to *this* house for refuge because she had marriage with Brandon in her mind.

Mrs. Quinlevan put an end to the conversation at last by saying that she was sure Georgina was fagged to death and would like to go upstairs to her bedchamber—a suggestion with which Georgina very thankfully fell in. She was, indeed, grateful to be allowed to retire early, but she had little anticipation of enjoying a restful night, and in the event she was not mistaken. The clock had chimed midnight before she at last fell into a restless sleep, and long prior to the first cockcrow in the morning she was lying full awake again, nervously awaiting the hour when she and Brandon would set out for The Place.

20 They had a fine summer morning for the excursion, but the drive was accomplished in almost total silence, Georgina apparently being completely occupied with the task of plaiting and unplaiting the handkerchief she held in her hands, and Brandon falling prey to a very young man's natural embarrassment at finding himself in the position of interfering in a much-admired older friend's affairs.

But as he and Georgina did not allow themselves to voice their misgivings to each other, the gig proceeded steadily onward and at a still early hour bowled up the sweep to the door of The Place. A stable-boy, coming around at the sound of carriage wheels on the drive and going to the horse's head, looked on without surprise as Brandon dismounted from the driver's seat, but stared with some astonishment when he saw him hand a young lady down. The same startled expression appeared on the face of the sturdy individual who opened the front door to the youthful pair.

"Good morning, Sturgess," Brandon said, trying to carry the situation off and managing only to look as uncomfortable as he felt. "Is Mr. Shannon in?"

"Yes, sir, he is," Sturgess said, looking doubtfully at Georgina, whose efforts to appear unself-conscious were, she knew, quite as unsuccessful as Brandon's. "But—is he expecting you, sir? I rather fancy he is engaged. I shall have to inquire—"

"You needn't. I'm not," said a voice that made Georgina's heart turn over and then begin to beat most uncomfortably fast. She looked up and saw Shannon, who had apparently just emerged from the estate-room, regarding her with a quite unfathomable expression on his face. For a single joyous moment it had seemed to her that there had been glad, incredulous welcome in those grey eyes—but the moment had passed at once, and the expression she saw now seemed to be compounded of indifference and a rather sardonic coolness. "What brings you here at this hour, Brandon?" Shannon went on, dismissing Sturgess with a curt nod and ushering his visitors into the book-room. "And you, Miss Power? I was not aware that you had returned to Ireland."

"Yes, I arrived last evening," she said, in a voice which, in spite of her efforts at composure, was most lamentably tremorous. "I—had to see you."

"To see *me*?"

She received the full force of a glance of harsh surprise, and, quailing visibly, turned to Brandon for support. He came to her rescue manfully, if somewhat confusedly, saying, "Yes, sir. You see, I had written to her—well, deuce take it, I felt I had to!—about your intending to make over The Place to her—"

This time it was Brandon who received that direct, harsh glance, and he, too, fell into instant discomposure.

"Well, I *know* I had no right to interfere, of course—" he began, defensively.

"You are quite correct! You had none," Shannon said grimly. "In fact, it was a piece of damned unconscionable meddling on your part, my lad!"

"*I* do not think so!" Georgina said, instantly rallying her own forces against this attack on her cousin and finding, to her relief, that quarrelling with Shannon restored her to her natural spirits much more rapidly than civility had done. "After all," she continued, "the matter concerns me quite as much as it does you, and it appears to me that I had a perfect right to know of it." She glanced around for a chair. "Are you not going to ask us to sit down?" she inquired. "Or do you mean to keep us standing here the whole while?"

A reluctant grin forced itself on Shannon's face. "No, you little gypsy, I do not," he said, "though you would be properly served if I did!" He added, as Georgina and Brandon sat down side by side on the sofa, "What is it that you wish to say to me? If it has anything to do with The Place you may save your breath, for my mind is made up on that point."

"Is it?" Georgina asked, looking speculatively at the determined lines of his face and deciding that an indirect attack might be the better policy. "Well, as a matter of fact," she said, "perhaps that is not what I came to speak to you about, after all." She saw Brandon, beside her, give a start of surprise, but she went on quite serenely, "The truth of the matter is that I came to apologise to you."

Shannon's brows snapped together. "To apologise? To *me*? For what?"

"For misjudging you so dreadfully the last time we met. But, really, it was quite your own fault, you know, for cutting me off before I had had time to tell you what it was that Lady Eliza had said of you."

Brandon, turning slightly pale as he gathered what subject it was that his unpredictable cousin now meant to introduce into the conversation, at this point rose abruptly and muttered something rather inarticulate about going to see if he could find Major Rothe.

"You won't find him. He's gone fishing," Shannon said. His brows drew together again. "What is the matter with you, Brandon? Sit down!"

"No—really—not my affair!" Brandon managed to say. "I never believed it from the start, sir! Told my cousin so!"

"Believed what?" Shannon demanded. "Either you've gone as mad as Bedlam, Brandon, or I have! And what has Lady Eliza to say to this?"

"She—made some dashed ugly insinuations to my cousin," Brandon said, in a placative voice. He frowned down meaningfully at Georgina. "No need to repeat them, Georgie!"

"Oh yes, there is every need!" Georgina said. "Otherwise Mr. Shannon will go on believing that I was so shocked by the idea that he had married my cousin Nuala without being head-over-ears in love with her that I was quite overcome!" She turned to Shannon. "It is not at all so," she said kindly. "I know I have had very little experience in the world, but I *am* aware that gentlemen, even of the first respectability, frequently marry ladies for whom they do not care a great deal, merely to possess themselves of a handsome fortune. In fact, I am quite assured that that is Sir Manning Hartily's chief reason for offering for *me,* and Grandmama, who is the soul of propriety, is extremely anxious for me to accept him—"

This time she had the satisfaction of seeing a positive explosion of wrath appear on the strong-featured face before her.

"Manning Hartily! You are not serious! That bag-pudding offer for you!"

"But indeed he has," Georgina assured him. "What is more, nothing would please both Grandmama and Mama more than for me to become Lady Hartily."

Shannon, who had recovered himself by this time, said sardonically, "Coming it a little too strong, my girl! No one in his right mind can seriously contemplate such a marriage."

"Oh, but they can!" she retorted. "In fact, that is one of the reasons that I ran away—"

"Ran away!" Shannon sprang up and stood looking at her in unmixed disapproval. "Good God! Do you mean to tell me your grandmother does not know where you are—that you travelled here alone—?"

"Oh, no! I came with Cousin Jeremy," she reassured him. "And Grandmama knows where I am *now*—or, at least, she knows I have gone to Craythorne. I left a note for her, you see."

Shannon, who had taken up his position before the fireplace, driving his hands into his breeches pockets as if rejecting a pressing impulse to shake her as she deserved to be shaken, received this statement with something less than satisfaction and demanded, "And all this for the sake of apologising to *me?* In what way did you misjudge me so grossly, Miss Power, that you felt it necessary to take such an extraordinary step?"

She wrinkled her brow in distaste. "I wish you will not call me 'Miss Power' in that odious way," she said. "You *know* I do not like it. And it is quite unnecessary to remind yourself any longer about Nuala, because she is dead, and as you did not kill her, there is really nothing for you to tease yourself about."

"As I did not—!" She looked into his thunderstruck countenance as he uttered the words. "Of course I did not kill her!" he ejaculated. "But what —who—?" His eyes narrowed suddenly. "Eliza Malladon!" he exclaimed. "So that is what it was! And, my God, you believed—you actually believed—!"

"What else was I to do, when you assured me yourself that it was true?" she pointed out, reasonably.

"But I had no idea—! By the Lord, if Malladon doesn't wring that harpy's neck, I shall do it myself one of these days! Is this story going around the neighbourhood, then?"

"Oh, no, I shouldn't think so," Georgina said placidly. "I am quite sure now that she only told it to me because she believed you were becoming far too interested in me—though I daresay," she observed, with a well-paraded innocence, "she was quite mistaken about that, too?"

He did not answer her. She saw his lips twitch slightly and, somewhat encouraged, was about to go on when she was interrupted by the appearance of Sturgess in the doorway. He wore a rather shaken air, which became quite explicable to all three persons in the room when he announced woodenly, "Lady Mercer!"

Brandon was the first to recover himself. "Good God!" he exclaimed, and made a dash for the open window, only to be restrained by Shannon's iron grip on his arm.

"Oh, no, you don't, my lad!" Shannon said grimly. "You came here to play chaperon and you shall do it!" He went on, to Sturgess, "Show Lady Mercer in"—a quite unnecessary command, as it developed, for the next instant Lady Mercer herself, in an olive-brown pelisse and flat-crowned bonnet, both of which still bore the dust of the roads, appeared in the doorway. Her eyes fastened themselves at once on Georgina, and an outraged exclamation overbore the curt civilities with which Shannon was welcoming her to his house.

"So, you wicked girl! You are indeed here!" She plumped herself down on the sofa from which Georgina had risen in dismay. "I am *quite* overcome! Quite overset! You must forgive me, Mr. Shannon—if you *are*, as I presume, Mr. Shannon— If I do not wait for an invitation to be seated! The shock of finding my granddaughter *here*—!"

"Quite understandable, ma'am," Shannon said dryly. "May I offer you some refreshment—a glass of sherry, perhaps?"

"Nothing," declared Lady Mercer with a shudder, sitting bolt upright on the sofa, "would induce me to swallow a mouthful of refreshment in this house, sir! If I may represent to you the infamy of your conduct in luring a delicately bred young female to leave the protection of her home—"

"But he didn't *lure* me, Grandmama!" Georgina protested, her blue eyes kindling as her dismay passed into anger at this unfounded accusation. "In fact, he had not the least notion that I meant to come here! Had you, Shannon?"

"I had not," Shannon agreed. "I am afraid, though, that my word will carry very little weight in this matter with Lady Mercer."

"You are quite right, sir! It will not!" she snapped. "I flatter myself that my granddaughter—as faulty as her education may have been—would not have flouted the proprieties in this shameless manner, and refused two highly advantageous offers of marriage as well, if she had not been encouraged to do so by—if I may put the matter without roundaboutation—an experienced libertine."

"No, really, Lady Mercer!" Brandon protested, finding his tongue in his indignation at this attack on his friend. "There you are fair and far out, you know! Mark had nothing to do with the matter. It was I who wrote the letter to Georgie that made her come here."

Lady Mercer favoured him with a comprehensive glance, which seemed to take in and record for uncompromising judgment every item of his appearance, from the Belcher handkerchief he wore in place of a neckcloth to the lack of a proper polish on his boots.

"You, I presume," she stated, "are young Quinlevan. In what way you are involved in this most distressing affair I do not care to learn. I have already had a most disagreeable interview with your mama on the subject, and, from the lack of principle she herself has shown in receiving and countenancing my granddaughter, I can only say that I shall not be surprised to find you involved to any extent in these proceedings."

Georgina looked perturbed. "Oh, dear!" she exclaimed. "I do hope you have not upset Cousin Bella, Grandmama! Indeed, she is not in the least to blame, for what else could she do when I appeared on her doorstep but take me in? Is she *very* much disturbed?"

"I left her," Lady Mercer said austerely, "indulging in a fit of the vapours in the drawing-room. I may say that if *I*, who have at my age endured the discomforts of a lengthy journey, am able to retain *my* spirits and composure under the agitations I have had to bear, it might not be too much to expect that Arabella Quinlevan should do the same. That, however, is neither here nor there. I have your cousin's landaulet waiting outside the door, Georgina. You will oblige me by stepping outside and waiting for me in it while I exchange a few words with Mr. Shannon."

Georgina cast a despairing glance at Shannon, saw that he was regarding her grandmother with a quite impassive expression on his face, and said, "No, Grandmama! Indeed, I cannot leave here yet! I came to Ireland because I had something of particular importance to discuss with Mr. Shannon—"

"I can well imagine *that!*" Lady Mercer said, her lips curving in a thin, contemptuous smile. "However, I fancy *he* will be something less than eager to discuss this important matter with *you* when I inform him that he can no longer hope to gain any pecuniary advantage from it. In point of fact, I intend to alter my will in favour of your mama, who at least has a proper sense of what is due to her name and breeding." She concluded majestically, with a full appreciation of the bombshell she was dropping on the company, "*She* is soon to become the wife of Sir Manning Hartily!"

If she had hoped that this disclosure would have a discomposing effect upon Shannon, she was doomed to disappointment. He received the news with the utmost equanimity. It was Georgina who ejaculated faintly, "*Mama!* But he wants to marry *me!*"

Lady Mercer turned a quelling gaze on her. "I find such a statement *quite* lacking in delicacy, my dear Georgina," she said. "I am sure that Sir Manning has always distinguished *both* of you by his attentions—and how you can imagine, at any rate, that a gentleman of his impeccable manners would care to ally himself with a young female who has had the shocking effrontery to run away from her home in the company of a gentleman— even though distantly connected with her—is entirely beyond my comprehension. I may tell you as well that Lady Hession and young Mr. Hession had the misfortune to arrive on my doorstep just as your mama and I were perusing the note which you left behind you. It was naturally impossible to conceal our distress from them, and Lady Hession, whom I consider to be a woman of excellent principles, at once gave it as her opinion that a young woman who had compromised herself as recklessly as you have done could no longer hope to contract a marriage with any gentleman of birth or fortune. Mr. Peter Hession seemed somewhat less thoroughly convinced of this fact, but I make no doubt that his mama will soon succeed in bringing him to a proper realisation of the justness of her observations."

Brandon, who had been listening to this speech with an increasingly wrathful expression on his face, at this point appeared to be incapable of keeping silent any longer, and burst out angrily, "Well, by Jupiter, it *ain't* so, ma'am! I mean about no gentleman's being willing to offer for Georgie! I'll do it myself if she'll have me! No wish to be rude to a lady of your years, but, dash it, she can't go back and live under *your* roof now, if that's the way you think of her!"

Georgina, quite startled, and blushing at this totally unexpected offer, looked rather confusedly at her cousin, but she was spared the necessity of making him any reply by Shannon's calm voice, addressing him.

"No need to go to such lengths of sacrifice, you young cawker!" he said. "I fancy Miss Power will not lack for offers, in spite of anything her grandmother may believe to the contrary." He glanced at that lady with an expression almost of lazy amusement on his face. "What would you say, ma'am," he inquired, "of the matrimonial prospects of a young lady who is able to call herself the mistress of this estate? Would not such a fortune cause even so strict a female as Lady Hession to have second thoughts about discouraging her son's pursuit of her?"

Lady Mercer looked at him, dumbfounded. "Mistress of *this* estate!" she ejaculated. "But how is that possible? This property, I understand, sir, belongs to *you!*"

"At the present moment, you are correct," Shannon said coolly. "Tomorrow the matter will be altered, however. It is my intention to give it over at that time to Miss Power. Then, ma'am, you may spite her to the top of your bent and she may feel herself quite independent of you. I realise that she is not of age, and so must be subject for some time still to her guardians' wishes, but her fortune will be in the hands of trustees who are entirely beyond either your reach or her mother's."

Georgina could remain silent no longer. She jumped to her feet and said with all the emphasis she could command, "I won't accept it! Do you understand me, Shannon? I *won't!* If you can give it over to me, I am sure it is just as possible for me to give it back to you—and I shall do it! You may go to America or anywhere you please—"

She checked, regarding him suspiciously. There was a glint in those grey eyes that she was quite sure did not betoken submission to her wishes, yet there seemed no hint of obstinacy in them, either.

"Very well," he said, equably. "If that is how you feel, there appears to be only one solution to the problem, for it seems to me that we cannot spend the rest of our lives enriching the legal profession by passing this estate back and forth between us. If you were to agree to marry me, however, I believe the difficulty might be overcome."

Georgina choked. "What an abominable way to make me an offer!" she said indignantly. "Is *that* your only reason for doing it?"

"Oh, no!" he said immediately. "I have several others. One is the dislike I have of seeing you obliged to return to live under either your grandmother's roof or Sir Manning Hartily's. I have been used to consider that you could not possibly do worse with your life than to marry me, but I see now that I was sadly mistaken, for you would no doubt run away with the first plausible scoundrel who offered for you, merely for the sake of escaping from either of those ménages. And I flatter myself that I have one advantage, at least, over any man of that sort."

"And that is—?" Georgina asked shyly.

But before he could reply, or Lady Mercer give vent to the emotions which this new turn of events had aroused in *her* breast, the conversation was once more interrupted by Sturgess.

"Mrs. Quinlevan—Mr. Barnwall!" he announced.

21 The lady and the gentleman in question entered the room hard on the heels of this announcement, for apparently, as had Lady Mercer, they considered the urgency of their errand to be such as to preclude any attention to conventional niceties of conduct. Mrs. Quinlevan, in fact, with her bonnet on quite askew and a pelerine hastily draped over her half-dress of lilac cambric, appeared to be in a state of such agitation that she could scarcely speak, and it was Mr. Barnwall who said to Shannon, surveying the group before him with an appearance of the greatest uneasiness, "Must offer you a thousand pardons, sir! Uncalled-for intrusion—unseasonable hour—but, dash it all, you know what females are! Insisted I drive her here instantly—nothing else to be done—threatening strong hysterics—"

"There's no need to put yourself about," Shannon said, taking pity on him and interrupting this somewhat incoherent apology. "You are perfectly welcome, I assure you." He turned to Mrs. Quinlevan. "Will you sit down, ma'am? Perhaps a glass of wine—"

"No! No, I thank you, I will *not* sit down!" Mrs. Quinlevan said, her bosom swelling with an animosity which seemed, however, to be directed at Lady Mercer rather than at her host. "Not in the same room with That Woman!" She stretched out one hand—in which, unfortunately for the dramatic effect, she was clutching her vinaigrette—in Lady Mercer's direction, and ejaculated with the greatest indignation, "How dare you—how *dare* you, madam, take advantage of my indisposition to order out *my* carriage and *my* horses to bring you to this house! If you had had a spark of humanity, you would have remained to look after me when you saw how greatly your quite unfounded accusations had affected me—yes, unfounded, I say!—for I had no more idea that that poor child intended to fly to me for protection than—than—"

"A babe unborn," Mr. Barnwall supplied helpfully. He, too, turned to Lady Mercer. "She's quite right, you know, ma'am," he assured her. "Perfectly innocent, my sister. If anyone is to blame, I'm your man. But deuce take it, if you've been behaving to the girl as you have done to Bella, I can't say I wonder at her rubbing off! Devilish uncivil sort of thing to do—leaving a lady in strong hysterics, while you order out her carriage to come jauntering over here!"

"If I had known, sir," Lady Mercer said, favouring him with a freezing glance, "that your sister would allow herself to be cast into such a taking over a few home truths plainly put to her, I should of course have remained. However, as she seems to be recovered now, and as it was quite imperative for me to extricate my granddaughter *at once* from the compromising situation in which I was persuaded she had placed herself, I cannot regret my decision. My one miscalculation, it seems," she concluded, with bitter emphasis, "was in dismissing the post-chaise in which I arrived at Craythorne, in the belief that hospitality and assistance would be offered me there."

Georgina, who had been a distressed spectator to this acrimonious dispute, now moved toward Mrs. Quinlevan, crying warmly to Lady Mercer, "But you are mistaken, ma'am; indeed, my cousin does not look at all recovered." She put her arm around Mrs. Quinlevan. "Dear Cousin Bella, let me make you comfortable in this chair," she urged. "And perhaps a glass of wine, as Mr. Shannon has suggested—"

She glanced at Shannon. He moved at once to the bell-rope, and ordered Sturgess—who appeared on this summons with a promptitude suggesting that he had not removed to any great distance from the interesting scene going forward in the book-room—to fetch a bottle of sherry.

Georgina, meanwhile, had prevailed on Mrs. Quinlevan to sit down, but, as the chair in which she found herself seated was directly opposite the sofa on which Lady Mercer sat, hostilities between the two ladies were continued in an exchange of highly unfriendly glances. Mr. Barnwall, who had also accepted his host's invitation to be seated, broke the pregnant silence that had fallen by saying puzzledly, "Thing is, I don't know at all why we've come here in the first place. Couldn't make head or tail of what Bella was trying to get at as we were driving over here. *She* says the gal don't want to marry Brandon. Well, I can understand that. Rather thought from the start she was cutting a sham of some sort; sure of it when we arrived at Craythorne yesterday and my young nevvy didn't seem to know what the deuce I was talking about when I mentioned the idea to him. But what has Shannon to do with the affair?"

"Mr. Shannon, sir," Lady Mercer informed him icily, "has had the brazen effrontery to offer marriage to my granddaughter in this room, under my very eyes—which I can scarcely say surprised me, in view of the fact that she has flung herself at his head by coming to him here with a complete disregard for all propriety!"

At this point Georgina, her eyes kindling dangerously, cut in to say, "Oh, no, Grandmama, how can you say you were not surprised, when you were so perfectly certain that, once you had informed him that you intend to cut me off without a penny, he would have no further interest in me?"

She would have gone on, but Shannon, effectually silencing her by a firm hand laid on her shoulder, said coolly, "It seems to me that we have had quite enough of this brangling. Lady Mercer, you are right; I have indeed made an offer for your granddaughter's hand. I shall of course apply to her mother for her consent. If it is necessary for me to obtain yours as well, I shall hope to receive it, but I must tell you that, in any event, unless your granddaughter herself does not desire it, our marriage will eventually take place. You may, I believe, save yourself a good deal of unnecessary trouble if you do not require us to wait until she has attained her majority, for, from my own rather limited experience with her character, I have been led to believe that it is one of remarkable firmness—not to say tiresome pertinacity—"

"Wretch!" Georgina interjected, blushing.

"No, indeed!" Mr. Barnwall said earnestly. "Couldn't have put it more neatly myself, sir! Devilish obstinate gal; no doing a thing with her once she has taken an idea in her head!" He turned to Lady Mercer. "Not my affair, ma'am, of course," he advised her, "but if I were you I wouldn't throw a rub in the way. Look at the trouble she's cost you already, having to jaunter all this way after her when I daresay you would much prefer to be sitting snug at your own fireside. Point is, though, she's a fine-looking gal, ten to one, with no fortune and the devil's own obstinacy, you won't find another fellow willing to become a tenant-for-life who'd be able to settle her as handsomely. A fine property this, you know. First in the neighbourhood, even though there ain't a title to go with it."

The arrival of Sturgess with the sherry caused a temporary suspension of the conversation. When he had left the room again Mrs. Quinlevan, somewhat fortified by the excellent wine, showed an alarming tendency to resume her altercation with Lady Mercer, stating with some belligerence that even though, as she gathered, that lady intended to cast her granddaughter on the world without a fortune, she herself would not see the girl sacrificed to marry merely for the sake of an establishment, but would give her a home at Craythorne and do her possible to bring about a suitable marriage for her.

"But you do not understand, Mama!" Brandon said impatiently. "There is not the slightest need for Georgie to marry anyone she don't like. Shannon is prepared to hand over The Place to her tomorrow, if she will only agree to receive it from him. But I think she had much better marry him, myself. Then Mark will be able to stay here, too—"

His mother interrupted him, her eyes widening in disbelief. "Hand over The Place to her! Oh, no, what are you saying, Brandon? That cannot be! No one could be so generous!"

"Generous! Besotted!" Lady Mercer said, rising abruptly and gathering her pelisse about her with the air of a woman who has finally reached the end of her patience. "No one but a madman would do such a thing! *I* shall wash *my* hands of the whole affair. You, sir"—she looked bitterly at Shannon—"will live, I expect, to regret this day!"

"Oh, I think not," Shannon said, the glint of amusement still in his eyes. "Whether the property is my wife's or my own, I believe I shall contrive to keep her tolerably in hand. But I daresay it will be a great deal more comfortable for *you*, ma'am, when you no longer need to worry yourself over her getting into such scrapes as you have just been attempting to extricate her from." He perceived that Lady Mercer, who apparently had been about to follow her last speech to him with a majestic exit from the room and his house, had been brought to a stand by the sudden realisation that she had now no means of transportation from it, and inquired civilly, "May I order out a carriage to take you—er—wherever it is that you wish to go, ma'am?"

"I thank you—no!" Lady Mercer snapped, regarding him with loathing. She turned to Mr. Barnwall. "If *you* would consent, sir, to drive me to the nearest respectable inn in whatever conveyance you used to bring your sister to this house, I should be highly obliged to you," she said. "Mrs. Quinlevan may then make use of her own carriage—a matter which seems of such *paramount* importance to her—"

Mrs. Quinlevan began ruffling up again. "I am sure," she said stiffly, "you might have taken the carriage and welcome, ma'am, except for the manner of it—" She caught Shannon's unencouraging eye and said hastily, "Oh, very well! It does not signify, I am sure! After all, there has no harm been done—and I daresay everything will turn out very well in the end, for it will not do at all for Brandon to think of marrying his cousin if she is to have no fortune—which she will *not* have, of course, if you intend to behave so shabbily toward her, ma'am. And if she *is* to have The Place, I expect Mr. Shannon would much rather marry her himself than not, which seems only fair, and I give you warning, Lady Mercer, that if *you* will not give her a proper wedding, she will be married from Craythorne in the *first* style—which will give me great pleasure, I am sure, if only to spite that *odious* Lady Hession, who was so certain that *her* Peter could cut *my* Brandon out with dear Georgina."

She was still rambling on in this vein when Shannon, having seen Lady Mercer and Mr. Barnwall off in that gentleman's phaeton, ushered her firmly outside to her waiting carriage.

"You are not at all so bad as you have been painted, I daresay," she said, smiling confidentially at him as they parted, "for Major Rothe has already brought Sir Humphrey Mott, in whose judgment I have the *greatest* confidence, to believe so. And I am sure I shall be so very happy to have dear Georgina settled near me that it will not matter a button to me *who* her husband is!"

Her host was still smiling over this last remark as he re-entered the book-room, where he found Brandon and Georgina in animated discussion.

"*She* wants to stay here. *I* say she shall come back to Craythorne with me at once!" Brandon said, frowning. "Ain't I right, sir? If my mother weren't so jingle-brained, she'd have taken her with her—but though *she* hasn't sense enough to see to it that people ain't set in any more of a bustle about the two of you than they already will be when the news that you are to be married gets about, *I* have!"

"You are quite right," Shannon said. "I fancy if you were to go around to the stables now and tell Hanger you wish to have your gig, your cousin will be ready to leave by the time you reach the front door." Georgina began to protest, but Brandon only grinned and limped out of the room, and Shannon then effectually put an end to any further remonstrances on her part by taking her quite ruthlessly into his arms and kissing her in a manner that left her breathless.

"Oh!" she said, burying her face against his coat as he released her. "I am sure I should not say this, but I believe I have been wanting you to do that ever since the first day you walked into this room!" She raised her eyes to his. "Am I very shameless to say such a thing? You have not even told me that you love me, you know!"

"The fact that I do," Shannon assured her, kissing her once more in a manner that left her with no reasonable doubts as to his feelings, "is the advantage I spoke of, which I have over any other of the unsuitable husbands you might choose if I were to allow you to go back to your grandmother's house."

She made some slight demur, however, at his expressing himself in this oversimplified way, and remarked thoughtfully that Sir Manning had made a very pretty speech about "perfection of face and form" when *he* had been on the point of making her an offer.

"But you did not, I collect, wish to accept Sir Manning's offer," he reminded her.

She shook her head. "No, for I could not possibly have fallen in love with *him!*" she said, finding occupation for herself in twisting one of the buttons of his coat. "Still, it would be nice to be *quite* certain that you did not offer for me merely because, once you had determined you must give The Place over to me, you found, on consideration, that you really could not give it up."

His arms tightened about her. "Is that what you think?"

"N-no! But—why *do* you wish to marry me?" she asked naïvely. "You said I was tiresome—you've often told me that—"

She saw his face twist slightly. "Nay, I'm no hand at speeches!" he said, in a rough voice she had never heard before. "I knew you were *my girl* when I first laid eyes on you—only I had no right, I never had the right, to tell you so. Well, I've taken it now, let the world say what it may, and I'll not let you go again, no matter what a stir it makes!"

She looked into his face, a little awed and wholly satisfied by what she saw there. Even the sound of Brandon's footsteps in the hall scarcely brought her to herself, and she was still standing in the circle of Shannon's arms when her cousin came into the room.

"Oh!" he said, regarding the two of them with some disapproval. "I thought you might have got through with all that by this time. Are you ready to leave, Georgie?"

"She is not," Shannon said, releasing her, "but leave she certainly shall. No, my little love," he said, with mock severity, as she would have uttered a remonstrance, "you are going to become a pattern of propriety from this day out. *I* do not mind being ostracised by society, but I shall mind it very much if my wife is, and so—for the time being, at least—we shall contrive to be a model couple. Go back to Craythorne with Brandon, and when I have returned from Bath, where I shall see the future Lady Hartily and request her permission to pay my addresses to you, I shall lose no time in calling upon you there."

"It sounds very respectable and unsatisfactory," Georgina said, with a sigh. "I had much rather you did not go—at least just yet."

"Well, of course he must go!" Brandon said, with asperity. "Don't be such a gudgeon, Georgie!" He looked at Shannon, sudden doubt in his eyes. "You're *quite* sure you want to go on with this, sir?"

"Quite sure."

"Well, I can't think why! You'll have a deuced amount of trouble with her, you know!"

"No doubt," Shannon said. "But I believe I shall be able to fortify myself to endure it. If you will wait only a moment in the hall outside, Brandon—I find I am in need of a slight additional degree of fortification before I allow your cousin to leave."

"A slight additional— Oh!" Brandon grinned. "Oh, very well, sir! I daresay a minute or two more won't signify."

He left the room. As the door closed behind him Georgina said approvingly, "That was very clever of you!"

"I thought so," Shannon admitted. "And now, my love, shall we endeavour to convince me that you are really *not* going to be too much trouble for me to cope with during the long and—I have no doubt—turbulent years of our married life?"

"Oh, yes!" Georgina agreed, with a satisfied sigh, allowing herself very willingly to be taken into his arms.

Clare Darcy

Lydia

or Love in Town

WALKER AND COMPANY
New York

To C.L.D

1

Cupitt, opening the front door at Great Hayland on a warm May morning, suffered a shock at sight of the gentleman standing before him—a shock so severe, in fact, that the magisterial calm cultivated over fifty years of service came near to deserting him entirely.

"My lord!" he gasped. "Oh, dear! Oh, my gracious! Why, we never expected—Your lordship never wrote—"

At first glance, there would have appeared to be little in the figure before him to cast even an elderly butler into such affliction. The Fourth Viscount Northover, who until some seven months previous had rejoiced in no more impressive title than that of Captain of Dragoon Guards, was a young man still, not quite thirty-four, and one, moreover, whom Cupitt had found totally disinclined to stand upon his new dignity on the brief visits he had earlier made to Great Hayland. He had a trim, powerful figure, considerably above medium height, a face which, although of too swarthy and aquiline a cast to be called handsome, had a certain appearance of careless distinction, and satirical dark eyes set beneath brows as black as his hair, which he wore in the severe style known as the Stanhope crop.

He greeted Cupitt in his usual offhand manner, cocked a quizzical eyebrow at the butler's failure to budge from his panic-stricken position in the doorway, and uttered an equable enquiry as to whether there were some particular reason why he might not enter his own house.

"No, my lord! Certainly not!" Cupitt stammered, stepping back and allowing the Viscount to walk inside. "It was only the shock—the surprise of seeing you so unexpectedly—"

The Viscount, who had had experience in many quarters of the world with the universal look of a Guilty Conscience lurking behind the dignified façade of an upright servant, cast a speculative and somewhat amused glance about him as he stepped through the doorway, but saw nothing that might immediately account for Cupitt's odd behaviour.

It was true that a critical eye might have found much to cavil at in the appearance of the hall, where the furniture stood gloomily swathed in holland covers, and tarnished gilt, faded brocade, and peeling paint gave evidence of a shocking state of neglect. Lord Northover, however, was not shocked. He was well aware that his great-uncle, the Third Viscount, had been far too clutchfisted to spend a groat on keeping up an estate where he had never resided and which he had valued purely from the point of view of the income that it had brought to him. And he himself, having every intention of disposing of this Berkshire property which had come into the family barely thirty years before, and which lay in a quite different part of the country from his principal seat, had not troubled himself over the restoration of the house, but had been content to leave it as it had been in his great-uncle's day, under the care of a pair of elderly servants.

He was aware, therefore, that it was not the state of the house that was responsible for Cupitt's present perturbation. Neither, he guessed, was it possible that petty pilfering had set that guilty look on the butler's ruddy face, for the Third Viscount Northover, he knew, had been totally disinclined to hire servants capable of making off with even the smallest part of his substance.

The matter intrigued him only for a moment, however, and he would have dismissed it from his mind entirely as he handed his curly-brimmed beaver and York tan gloves to Cupitt, assuring him meanwhile that he had stopped off only to have a look in at the place on his way to London, had not Cupitt himself brought it into the open.

"My lord, if you please—" said Cupitt, in an agitated voice. "If you will but allow me to explain—"

"Yes?" Northover paused. "What is it, Cupitt?"

But Cupitt seemed to find it less than easy to come so directly to the point.

"You must believe, my lord," he said almost tearfully, "that I would never in the world have done it if I had had the least expectation of your lordship's arrival—or that your lordship was even in this part of the country—"

"Done what?" demanded Northover. "Cut line, Cupitt! What the devil have you been up to?"

Thus adjured, Cupitt made a desperate attempt and gathered his resolution. "My lord," he plunged into his confession, a look of the deepest mortification upon his face, "I regret to be obliged to inform you that you will find a—a young female in the library!"

The Viscount's black brows went up slightly. "Really, Cupitt?" he said gravely. "At your age? You astonish me! And what has Mrs. Cupitt to say to this?"

The colour surged back into Cupitt's face. "My lord!" he said, affronted. "You quite mistake the matter! I should not dream of engaging in such—such—" He saw the gleam of a smile lurking in Northover's ordinarily rather cynical eyes and drew himself up, on his dignity again. "Your lordship may find the matter a subject for amusement," he went on, rather stiffly. "I assure you that it is not so to me. The fact is that I have been induced by—by past attachment to commit an act which I must anticipate you will take the most serious view of. I cannot think how I—But there it is!" he said, despair overcoming him once more. "In short, my lord, there are persons unknown to you staying in this house!"

The Viscount, who was beginning to find the matter increasingly interesting, maintained a creditable calm in the face of this disclosure. "Indeed?" he said. "I hope you won't consider it uncivil of me to enquire who they may be?"

"No, my lord." Cupitt resigned himself, sighed heavily, and said, "Mrs. Leyland, Miss Leyland, and Mr. Leyland—and Mrs. Leyland's maid, Miss Winch. From America, my lord."

"From America? Have you ever *been* to America, Cupitt?"

"No, my lord."

"Then how—?"

"Mrs. Leyland, my lord," Cupitt explained unhappily, "is the former Miss Tresselt."

The Viscount considered this statement. "I gather," he remarked presently, "that that fact is expected to explain the matter to me, but I confess I am still in the dark. No doubt it is lamentably dull-witted of me—"

"The Tresselts, my lord," Cupitt said, in the same hopeless tone, "are— were the former owners of this estate. I daresay you may not recall, but this house was in their family from the time it was built, in the reign of Queen Anne, until some thirty years ago, when Mr. Gerald Tresselt was obliged, owing to financial reverses, to see it pass into your great-uncle's hands. You may not recall, either, that I began my service here as a lad some fifty years ago, when the Tresselts were still in possession."

"I see! Or do I?" Northover again considered. "Deuce take it, Cupitt, I can well imagine your former Miss Tresselt's wishing to *see* the place, but —staying here, with her entire family, it appears?"

Cupitt nodded gloomily. "Yes, my lord. Her grandson and grand-daughter, at any rate. Not too plump in the pocket, I fear, if I may so express myself. They are on their way to London from Bristol, and—and I believe Mrs. Leyland fancied it a good idea, for purposes of both senti-ment·and economy—"

The Viscount could control his risibilities no longer, and gave vent to a shout of laughter. "In short, she bullied you into taking her in here!" he said. "My poor Cupitt, what a termagant she must be! Assuredly, I must meet her! In the library, you said?"

"No, my lord. It is *Miss* Leyland who is in the library," Cupitt said, looking doubtful at this totally unexpected reaction to his news. "Mrs. Leyland and the young gentleman, I believe, have gone for a stroll about the grounds."

"Then I shall have to postpone the pleasure and settle for *Miss* Leyland for the moment," Northover said, and strode off purposefully in the direction of the library.

Cupitt, left alone, trotted off apprehensively to the housekeeper's room to seek counsel of his wife, a round, ruddy woman, cut in the same mould as himself, whom he found engaged in a comfortable chat with Miss Winch. The dire news he had to impart to them, however, swiftly put an end to this conversation. Mrs. Cupitt fell back in her chair with a hollow exclamation that she was sure she felt one of her spasms coming on, while Miss Winch attempted instant succour with the aid of a vinaigrette fetched from her capacious reticule, at the same time adjuring her old acquaintance not to be so henwitted as to go off on her now.

"This is no time for the vapours, Martha Cupitt!" she said tartly. "We are in the suds, and must keep our wits about us. Drat the man! What possessed him to turn up when he was least wanted! What sort of creature is he, Mr. Cupitt? Cutting up stiff over the business—is he, now?"

"No, no." Cupitt sank down helplessly into the nearest chair, turning a bewildered face on Miss Winch's homely one. "As a matter of fact, he—he laughed when I told him!"

"Laughed?" Miss Winch shook her head, between amazement and disapproval. "Not queer in his attic, is he?"

"Lord Northover! Oh, no—no, indeed!" Cupitt said, shocked. "He appears to have an excellent understanding—though I am not, of course, well acquainted with him. He never visited here in the old lord's day, you see."

"He didn't? Why didn't he?" enquired Miss Winch, whose discourse was nothing if not direct. "He was the heir—wasn't he?"

"The heir? Oh, dear me, no!" Cupitt said. "That would have been Mr. Matthew Brome, the old lord's son. I knew *him* very well. But he was killed in a carriage accident only two months before the old lord died, and his son with him, so that it was Captain Christopher Brome, his lordship's great-nephew, who inherited. I knew *him* only by reputation," he concluded heavily.

"Well?" said Miss Winch. "And what sort of reputation has he?" Mrs.

Cupitt groaned, and Miss Winch transferred her gaze to her. "Bad, is it?" she demanded.

Mrs. Cupitt nodded, with tragic emphasis. "You wouldn't credit the stories they tell, Amelia!"

"Women?"

Mrs. Cupitt, looking somewhat shocked at this frankness, managed a prim little nod. "The *first* one," she confided—"well, he wasn't twenty yet, they say, and her a married woman!—so *that* was when they sent him off to the Army. But from all accounts he was no better there—got himself into every sort of scrape and scandal, till I've heard it said the old lord swore he wouldn't so much as have him in the house."

"Now, Martha!" Cupitt said uneasily. "That's only gossip, you know. You'd best hold your tongue."

"Gossip, is it?" Mrs. Cupitt kindled at the aspersion. "And didn't Sarah McNish hear with her own ears Lady Sealsfield say she hoped Sir Peter wouldn't call on him if he came into the neighbourhood, for she wouldn't have *her* daughters exposed to the conversation of such a man?"

"Lady Sealsfield," said Cupitt, with unexpected spirit, "is a platter-faced old harridan. And I noticed Sir Peter *did* call when his lordship was here last—ay, and invited him up to the Manor as well, and pestering the soul out of him to tell him about Waterloo and the Peninsula—"

Miss Winch, who had listened to this interchange with increasing impatience, interrupted at this point to remark, "Ay, that's all very well, but it has nothing to say to the pickle we are in *now*. What are we to do, Mr. Cupitt? Had I best go and try to catch Madam and Mr. Bayard before they come into the house? And much good *that* would do!" she answered her own question. "Eh, the fat's in the fire now, and no mistake! I warned Madam how it would be, but when once she takes a notion into her head—!"

"She was always a—a very persuasive lady," poor Cupitt said, his head in his hands. "I can remember when she was no more than sixteen and not even out, she coaxed me into carrying letters to young Sir Harry Brinley at Crossflats—I very nearly got the sack over *that!* Ay, she had every spark in the neighbourhood at her beck and call—and to think that, in the end, she threw herself away on no better than a Brigade-Major in a Line Regiment, and went off to America to live among the savages—"

"Savages!" Miss Winch interrupted him, bridling. "I'll have you know, Mr. Cupitt, that Madam lived in as great a house as this one ever was, with all the furniture and carpets brought from France, and so many servants underfoot that you tumbled over them! Major Leyland did very well for himself in America, I can tell you, and was considered one of the first gentlemen in Louisiana when he died. It was only afterwards that we fell on hard times, for Madam's son, Mr. Henry, cared for nothing but his horses and his books, and let it all slip away from him, so that when he died there was nothing left but a nasty, damp plantation off in the midst of nowhere. And Madam is quite as bad as he was," she added darkly, "for she's no more sense than a baby when it comes to managing, and spent every penny she could lay her hands on in New Orleans, tricking herself and Miss Lydia out in the latest fashions, before they ever stepped on the boat to come over here. And now she must give way to one of her starts and stop off here to see the old place—and only look what's come of it! You'll be lucky if you and Martha don't lose your places on the head of this day's work, Mr. Cupitt!"

Cupitt was inclined to agree. He said dismally that he had best be getting back to his post, in case he might be needed there—to say nothing of the fact, he added, that it hardly seemed right to leave Miss Leyland in the library alone with a man of Lord Northover's reputation.

But, somewhat to his surprise, Miss Winch merely shrugged up her shoulders at this expression of anxiety. Miss Lydia, she said, was well able to take care of herself—a remark which drew a shocked protest from Mrs. Cupitt.

"Oh, no! How can you say so, Amelia? Didn't you tell us yourself, she has been living for four years completely retired in the country? And she can't be more than twenty—"

"True," Miss Winch agreed, imperturbably. "But that don't make a ha'porth of difference, Martha, my dear. She has the sense for the whole family—what there is of it to go round, that is—and as for her looking out for your precious Lord Northover, he'd best look out for *her*, instead!" A slight, unaccustomed smile briefly lit her wintry face. "Ay, let him look out for *her*," she repeated. "She can handle him, or any other man alive, I dare swear, but as for his handling *her*—that's another kettle of fish entirely. For she's neither to lead nor to drive, as the saying goes, and what he will make of her I'm blessed if I know!"

2

The master of the house, at that precise moment, might have been somewhat inclined to agree with these words.

Opening the library door, on parting with Cupitt, he had found himself facing, not the dowdy, bashful young provincial he had expected, but a young lady with a decided air of fashion, dressed in a thin chemise gown of apricot muslin with short, puffed sleeves, which his experienced eye immediately recognised as being in the latest French mode. She was seated at the top of a pair of library steps with a book in her hand, looking perfectly at home, and, glancing up as he strolled into the room, addressed him at once in a rich alto voice.

"Well, I call *this* pretty cool!" she said.

The Viscount, finding himself the object of a direct and somewhat accusing gaze, paused and gave her back a look of considerable amusement.

"I beg your pardon?" he said.

"I should think you might!" Miss Leyland remarked, rising from her perch and descending from it to show him at full length a tall, slender, elegant figure, perfectly in accord with an almost classically cut face which was redeemed from the coldness usually associated with this type of beauty by the ripe colour of the lips and the riot of black curls modishly confined by an apricot ribbon above it. "Walking into a man's house as if you owned it!" she continued, with some severity. "I wonder where you can have learned your manners, sir!"

The Viscount was privately wondering where she had learned *hers*, for, though he had been acquainted with most of the audacious beauties of the past dozen Seasons, he could not recall one who would have greeted him with exactly this combination of nonchalance and candour.

"Shocking, isn't it?" he agreed, preserving a grave face. "The point is, though, that I am—er—particularly well acquainted with the owner."

"That," Miss Leyland observed forthrightly, "is *not* an excuse. I suggest that you leave at once and return when Lord Northover is in residence."

She appeared to believe that he would follow her advice, for she moved to a chair and sat down in it with her book, looking up rather speculatively after a moment, as she saw that he had not moved, to remark to him, "I daresay you would not particularly care for me to send for someone to *escort* you out?"

"Frankly, I don't think you would find anyone who could," he retorted. "At any rate, I have an idea that I have quite as much right as you to be in this house. If Northover is not in residence, what are *you* doing here?"

"That is none of your affair," she said largely.

"It might be, if I happened to be Northover."

"But you are not—" She broke off, her eyes narrowing suddenly as she regarded him. "Oh!" she said. "You *are* Northover! Let me tell you that I regard *that* as completely unfair!"

"Not at all," he said, the smile he had been endeavouring to repress appearing upon his lips. "It was you who began it, you know, by accusing me of the most abominable rag-manners. In mere self-defence, I could not lower myself further in your opinion by being ill-bred enough to contradict your assumption."

She regarded him darkly. "Slippery, as well!" she pronounced. "*And* extravagant. How could you have expected me to imagine that you were Northover when you came strolling in here in that dapper-dog rig? From the looks of your house, you ought to be in rags. But I daresay that is *some* people's idea of economy—to let their house go to rack while they spend their last penny on a well-tailored coat!"

"I am glad," Northover returned, glancing down at his sleeve, "that my coat, at least, meets with your approval, Miss Leyland."

"Well, actually, it does," she conceded. "I wish you will be good enough to give your tailor's name and direction to my brother when he comes in, for he swears that no Frenchman can make a well-fitting coat, and, after seeing you, I am inclined to believe it."

"You and your brother have been travelling in France, Miss Leyland?"

"Oh, no!"

"But your gown—?"

"New Orleans," she explained, looking with a critically approving gaze at the narrow silk braid with which the high waist and hem of the apricot gown were decorated. "Of course, direct from Paris—*not*," she confessed, "that I can afford it any more than you can afford that coat." She regarded him speculatively once more. "I daresay you are wondering what we are doing here," she observed. "You have been talking to Cupitt, of course, since you know my name. What did he tell you?"

"Only that your—grandmother, is it?—had formerly lived in this house before going to America, and that he had been induced to allow her and her party to spend the night here—or were you perhaps planning on a longer stay?" he broke off to enquire politely.

"Well, we *should* have liked to stop over until tomorrow," she acknowledged, not at all disconcerted by this thrust. "But I expect that is out of the question now, since *you* have arrived in this totally disgruntling way. You really should have given poor Cupitt notice, you know! How was he to imagine that you would behave so unceremoniously as to turn up here without the least warning? It is not at all the thing to do in your position— is it?"

Northover, who was beginning to enjoy the conversation, said that he supposed it was not, but explained that, having been used to occupy his exalted position for less than a year, he was no doubt somewhat remiss in fulfilling all the obligations owing to his rank.

"You don't mind if I sit down?" he added, moving towards a chair. "Unless, of course, that too would not suit your notions of propriety—?"

"Well, it is *your* house, so I suppose you may do as you like," she conceded handsomely. "Would you like me to ring for some refreshment?"

"If you please," he said, maintaining his gravity with even more of an effort.

But the quiver of a telltale muscle at the corner of his mouth as she rose to pull the bell-rope beside the mantel gave him away to her observant eyes, and a sudden ripple of laughter rose to her own lips.

"Abominable—isn't it?" she agreed. "To be playing the hostess in *your* house! But, you see, I am feeling very lady-of-the-manorish today. Grandmama's family have lived here since the beginning of time, and she has told me so much about it that I believe I could walk through it blindfolded. It is all exactly as she described it—though I must say I never expected to find it in such bad loaf. However," she added kindly, "I daresay you are as hungry as a churchmouse, in spite of your title, and have no funds to set things in better order."

The Viscount, whose inheritance had included, in addition to Great Hayland, one of the most extensive properties in Derbyshire, did not see fit to enlighten Miss Leyland concerning her misapprehension, but devoted himself instead to interrogating Cupitt, who appeared in the doorway at that moment, as to the refreshments it might be possible for the house to provide.

These, it developed, were neither numerous nor elaborate, but Cupitt was able to inform him that a tolerable sherry and some Queen-cakes baked that morning by Mrs. Cupitt would be forthcoming. He appeared quite nonplussed by the sight of his master seated in amicable conversation with Miss Leyland, and confided in amazement to Mrs. Cupitt and Miss Winch, when he repaired to the kitchen for the Queen-cakes, that the young lady had seemed quite as unperturbed as his lordship by the very awkward situation in which she found herself.

Upon this, Miss Winch unfolded her rather forbidding lips in a slight smile. "Lord bless you, Mr. Cupitt, if you think a little thing like *this* is enough to overset Miss Lydia," she said tolerantly, "it's plain to see you don't know her yet!"

Cupitt, rather dazed, admitted that he did not, and wondered, as he departed with his laden tray, if all American young ladies were as unreserved as Miss Leyland, or whether it was only this particular one who was so unconcerned with the conventions.

He found her, on his re-entry into the library, regaling Lord Northover with an account of her former life in America.

"We are land-poor, you see," she remarked, as Cupitt set the tray down upon a heavy oak table. "I expect poor Papa had the worst judgement, when it came to business, of any man in the world, for he *would* buy Belmaison, which is nothing but a dismal swamp, fit only for snakes and mosquitoes. Of course no one was so bird-witted as to offer to take it off our hands when he died, so there we were set down for four long years, with no hope of escape, until my Great-aunt Letty, Grandmama's sister, was so obliging as to die here in England and leave her her jewels. Of course we have no idea as yet how much they will bring, but at least we have got to England on our expectations, where Grandmama says there is not the least doubt that I shall soon be able to make an advantageous marriage that will set us all up famously."

Unfortunately for Cupitt, he was obliged at this point to leave the room, so that he heard no more of Miss Leyland's past history or future plans; but Lord Northover, privileged to continue the conversation, was moved to interrupt here to enquire why this laudable plan could not have been carried out on Miss Leyland's home grounds.

"I have been in America myself, you see," he explained, "and it appears to me that you might find gentlemen there who are quite as wealthy and susceptible as any in this country."

"Oh, yes!" she agreed. "It was Grandmama's idea that we come to England—not merely because it will be more convenient in taking up her inheritance, but also because she has been longing for years to settle here once more. She *cannot* like America, you see. Even when Papa was alive, and we were still well enough off to visit New Orleans for several months each year, she disliked it, and if she could have persuaded him to return here, I am sure she would have done so."

"I see. And her plan now is that it is you who are to repair the family fortunes?"

"Yes, for Bayard—my brother—is exactly like Papa, with not the least notion of how to go on. Grandmama thinks he would do very well in the Army, however, if someone were so obliging as to buy his commission in a cavalry regiment."

"The obliging 'someone,' of course, being your future husband?"

"Well, it certainly seems as if he might—don't you think so?" she enquired. "If one were tremendously rich, it would be a mere bagatelle!" She added, "Of course, there is Sir Basil Rowthorn, Great-aunt Letty's husband—"

"What—the Nabob? Are you connected with him? He is as rich as Croesus, by all accounts."

"Yes, but he has never seemed in the least inclined to do anything for us. However, that *may* have been merely because he did not know us. Now that we shall be able to go to London and meet him, it may put our relationship on quite a different footing."

The Viscount, regarding with a connoisseur's eye the slender, elegant figure and enchanting face of the young lady before him, agreed that it might, and enquired whether, in that case, the need for an immediate search for a wealthy husband might diminish.

"Well, I suppose so," she said, considering the matter. "But I don't *think* it is particularly likely that Sir Basil will actually do anything for us. My great-aunt was his second wife, you see, and he has a great-nephew and a great-niece on his first wife's side as well, who I should imagine have been turning him up sweet for years. So I expect, in the end, it will have to be the husband." She looked at him with a suddenly interested expression upon her face. "I daresay that *you*, being a peer, are well acquainted in *ton* circles," she said, "so if you have any advice for me, I should be very glad to hear it. Of course, Grandmama was a famous belle in her day, but that was years ago, and I expect things have changed a great deal since then and *her* ideas will be considered quite gothic."

"Not if yours bear any relation to them," Northover assured her, a gleam in his dark eyes.

She surveyed him, arrested. "Oh!" she said. "Do you think I am *fast*? To be sitting here talking to you alone, I mean?"

"Let us say—unconventional," Northover emended it. "And—if you care for my opinion—delightful. I abominate missish females."

She shrugged her shoulders, her composure not at all disturbed by the frankness of the compliment. "That is all very well," she said candidly, "but I shall get nothing by pleasing *you*, you know."

Northover gave a crack of sardonic laughter. "You are in the right on that point, my dear," he said. "I am not a marrying man."

"Well, it cannot signify to me if you are or are not, since you are not rich," she said decidedly. "Grandmama has warned me not to be taken in by a title alone, for she says there are peers who have not a feather to fly with, and it seems, from the look of this house, that you must certainly be one of them. But I daresay there are dozens of others who are quite affluent?"

"Oh, dozens!" he agreed. "But if I were you, Miss Leyland, I shouldn't set my cap at men who were quite above my touch. A girl without a fortune can hardly hope for one of the greatest prizes on the Marriage Mart, you know. If you will heed a word of the advice you sought from me, you will not look for rank and title along with the fortune you are so frank in saying you must have."

Her chin went up slightly. "In other words," she said, "you don't think I could do it—marry *both* wealth and title, that is. What a very poor opinion you must have formed of me, my lord!"

"Not of you—of my own sort," he said cynically. "You will find plenty of us to dangle after a pretty face, but few to offer marriage, except where there are family and fortune to make up the balance."

"Well, of course, one will get nowhere if one is poor-spirited enough to give up before one has even made the attempt!" she said. She broke off to add, at the sound of footsteps in the hall, "but here are Grandmama and Bayard now. You *will* be civil to them—will you not? Grandmama—Bayard—" she addressed the newcomers as they stepped into the room, "this is Lord Northover. He has dropped in from nowhere and intends to send us packing at once—that is, unless one of you is clever enough to talk him out of the idea!"

3 The two persons at whom this rather startling statement was flung stopped short upon the threshold, regarding the Viscount out of what appeared to him to be identical pairs of very dark blue eyes.

There, however, the similarity ended, for one pair belonged to an aquiline-featured, rather startlingly raven-haired lady of some sixty years, attired in a modish bronze-green walking-dress and carrying a Chinese sunshade, and the other to a tall young gentleman in a slate-blue coat, who bore a striking resemblance to Miss Leyland. Northover, rising, greeted both with an imperturbability quite unimpaired by Miss Leyland's blunt charge, and invited them to be seated and partake of the refreshments that Cupitt had provided.

"Miss Leyland has been telling me something of the circumstances that have brought you here, ma'am," he went on, addressing himself to the lady. "An unexpected pleasure, I assure you! I only regret that it is not in my power to offer you more adequate hospitality."

Mrs. Leyland, accepting his invitation to be seated with aplomb, regarded him with approving eyes.

"How very kind of you!" she said graciously. "But then I knew how it must be, once you were acquainted with the circumstances! Poor Cupitt was cast into such a taking when we arrived, but I assured him he was making a piece of work over nothing, for no one—*no one!*—could be so marblehearted as to dispute the propriety of my wishing to revisit the scenes of my girlhood." She regarded the Viscount interestedly as he handed her a glass of sherry. "I knew your father—no, I daresay it must have been your grandfather," she said. "A most disagreeable man, as I remember him."

Northover laughed. "I imagine it is my great-uncle to whom you are referring, ma'am, and I entirely agree with you," he said.

He poured a glass of wine for young Mr. Leyland, who seemed to find the sudden appearance of the owner of the house no more disturbing than did his grandmother, and only smiled at him lazily as he sat down and stretched his long legs comfortably before him. He was a tall young man, almost a head taller than his sister, whose senior he might have been by a year or two, and he had the same air of unself-conscious assurance that Miss Leyland herself possessed, without, however, her vivacity of manner. Northover, observing the brief glances that occasionally passed between the two, realised that in their case the usual bond between brother and sister had been reinforced to such an extent—probably, he thought, by those four years of isolation on a remote Louisiana plantation—that each knew almost without the necessity for words what the other was thinking.

He guessed Miss Leyland to be the leader of the pair—which explained her feeling that it was she who must manage to provide for her brother, rather than the more usual alternative of the latter's undertaking to look after her. Looking after Miss Leyland, in fact, the Viscount decided, would be an exercise in futility, for it was apparent that she was a young lady of great resourcefulness. It was, he reflected, the very devil that the circumstance of her being a guest under his roof precluded his initiating what he was sure would be one of the most interesting flirtations it had been his privilege to indulge in over a dozen years.

That it might have required some address on his part to inaugurate such a flirtation he was well aware, for Miss Leyland, he thought, showed no sign of considering him as anything but a somewhat troublesome and probably—since she had applied to him for advice—respectably avuncular figure.

In this latter notion, however, he was not entirely correct. Miss Leyland, critically surveying the bronzed countenance on which years of campaigning and not infrequent bouts of dissipation had carved somewhat harsher lines than his actual years might have accounted for, had indeed dismissed him as being beyond the age to take her interest; but she was far from considering him in an avuncular light. As a matter of fact, the thought had immediately entered her mind that her host—except for the fact that he seemed to possess rather too much levity of disposition to take himself seriously in the role—might have stood very well as a model for the Byronic heroes who had enlivened her solitude and Bayard's at Belmaison. His penetrating dark eyes and indefinably reckless air, she considered, gave him very much a "corsairish" appearance, and the elegance of the cut of his olive-green coat and fawn-coloured buckskins could not conceal the powerful muscles that rippled beneath them.

As he had guessed, however, she was far from feeling an inclination to carry on a flirtation with him, and was more disposed merely to make use of him in learning more of the world of fashion which she desired to enter. Her brother, on the other hand, discovering in the course of the conversation that the Viscount had been a soldier for more than a dozen years, and had been engaged in most of the Duke of Wellington's campaigns, immediately lost his air of tolerant detachment and began to ply him with eager questions. Had he been at Salamanca? At Waterloo? Had he ever seen Napoleon himself? What was the Duke like? Was it true that he was the greater commander of the two?

Northover, who had been accustomed for years to this sort of catechism flung at him by ardent young subalterns, handled it with the ease of long practice, winning the approval of Mrs. Leyland by refusing to pronounce Napoleon either a monster or a hero.

"Quite a vulgar little man, by all I have been able to learn," she gave it as her opinion, "with a habit of setting up his brothers and sisters as pinchbeck royalty that I cannot but consider as excessively bad *ton*." She glanced about the room in which she sat, where the windows looked out upon an unkempt lawn and the gilt grillés enclosing the bookshelves showed the tarnish of long neglect, and said, with a disapproving shake of her head, "I hope I shall not find such sad changes in London as I have done here; but indeed it appears to me, from what I have seen since setting foot in England, that that dreadful war has had quite a *devastating* effect upon Society. When I remember this house as it used to be—!" She fixed Northover with an eye quite as accusing as her granddaughter's had been and observed, "I cannot but think that persons who take advantage of the difficulties in which distinguished families may find themselves to purchase their estates have an obligation at least to keep them in respectable repair!"

"Oh, what does it signify, Grandmama?" Bayard said impatiently. "Besides, Lord Northover has told you that he has been serving abroad until only recently, so how should he have known how things were going on here?"

"He knows now," said Mrs. Leyland, with awful incontrovertibility, which, however, quite failed to quell the Viscount. He remarked instead, with a wicked glance at Lydia, that Miss Leyland had already informed him of her plans for entering the no doubt sadly decayed but still exclusive world of London Society, and enquired whether Mrs. Leyland had connexions at present living in England who could be of service to her to that end.

"Oh, as to *that*," replied Mrs. Leyland, with undiminished assurance, "I daresay I shall be able to find out *someone* who is willing to sponsor us. I was acquainted with *hundreds* of people when I was a girl here, and there are always cousins, you know. It is so much in their interest not to have a set of relations on the town who are quite outside of Society that they are usually only too happy to put one in the way of entering into fashionable circles. Would you happen to know, for example, my dear sir, if Lady

Fowlie is still alive? We quite loathed each other when we were girls, but, after all, she *is* my first cousin and married to a baronet, which is exactly the rank for her to fret excessively at the idea of having relations setting themselves up in London whom no one feels obliged to receive!"

"I am afraid," said Northover, reflecting with some amusement that it was easy to see whence Miss Leyland's peculiar notions of propriety derived, "that I can give you no information on that head, ma'am. I am unfortunately not acquainted with the lady."

"Well, it is of no consequence." Mrs. Leyland shrugged, dismissing Lady Fowlie without regret. "There are the Whitefords, as well, who are connected with my mother's family—and then there is Lucinda Pettingill, who is only a very distant connexion, but was my bosom-bow when we were girls. She married Sir Henry Aimer after I went to America—"

The look of amusement deepened on Northover's face. "Good God, are you acquainted with Lady Aimer?" he asked. "Now *there*, ma'am, is someone who can be of real service to you, if you can but induce her to take you up. She knows everyone, and goes everywhere—but I should warn you that she has no great reputation for amiability."

"Oh no, I expect she has not," Mrs. Leyland said tranquilly. "She had always a waspish tongue. I shall certainly look her up."

"Berkeley Square," Northover said helpfully, advising her further, with a gleam of unholy amusement in his eyes, "You might find it useful to request her to furnish you as well with an introduction to her daughter, Lady Gilmour. She entertains widely and, as she has a marriageable daughter of her own, may be able to be of more assistance than Lady Aimer in bringing Miss Leyland into company with a somewhat younger set, more suitable for her purposes."

Miss Leyland, who had not failed to observe the glint in his lordship's eyes and the slight emphasis he had placed upon his last words, regarded him suspiciously.

"Are you hoaxing us, Northover?" she demanded. "I don't like the look in your eye!"

"Not in the least. You will have everything to gain from Lady Gilmour's taking you up. She married within the past twelvemonth a gentleman of the first rank, after having been left a widow a few years before, and has every intention, I believe, of making a great stir in Society with her new consequence. Under her aegis you may meet all the most eligible peers in London and take your pick among 'em."

"I do not consider, my lord," Mrs. Leyland remarked, an expression of some hauteur upon her face, "that it is quite proper for you to speak in such terms to my granddaughter—as if she were on the catch for a husband, to use the vulgar phrase. Naturally she will wish to be introduced to the company of eligible gentlemen—"

She was interrupted at this point by Miss Leyland, who said to her frankly, "Oh, it is of no use your trying to wrap it up in clean linen, Grandmama. I have already told him what our situation is, and that I *must* have a rich husband."

"A confidence which I am highly honoured to have received," said Northover, with a slight bow, "but may I advise you further, Miss Leyland, not to be so devastatingly truthful with *every* gentleman you meet? We are an abominably sensitive lot, you know, and are apt to shy away from the bargain if we are allowed to see that it is only our purses, and not ourselves, that are in demand."

"Well, of course," Mrs. Leyland put in, superbly, "my granddaughter will not marry *any* gentleman for whom she does not feel the proper regard. But it is *quite* as easy for a girl to fall in love with a gentleman of rank and wealth as with a nobody! I am sure if I had known as much at *her* age as I know now, I should have been a marchioness. But my mama was a very unworldly woman, who gave me no proper advice at all, and as a result I ran off with a mere Brigade-Major—something that I am *determined* shall never happen to Lydia."

Northover, with a commendable command of his countenance, agreed that such a contingency was indeed to be avoided at all costs, and Mrs. Leyland then relented in her disapproval sufficiently to spend an agreeable quarter hour in conversation with him concerning the present state of those now elderly members of the *ton* whom she remembered from her girlhood. At the end of this period his lordship arose to take his leave, saying that he must speak with Cupitt before he departed.

As his instructions to that anxious functionary contained no hint of censure over his having so far overstepped his authority as to allow the Leylands to remain overnight at Great Hayland, Cupitt was cast into such a fervour of relief and gratitude that he nobly offered to have the entire party out of the house before another hour had gone by; but this drew an entirely negative response from the Viscount. Mrs. Leyland and her young relations, he said, were to remain as his guests for as long as it suited them, and the Cupitts were to show them every attention in their power. This statement so much staggered Cupitt that he returned to Mrs. Cupitt and Miss Winch, after seeing his lordship off, with the freely expressed opinion that either his master was the easiest touch he had ever known or the Leylands a party of magicians.

Miss Winch smiled slightly, showing no surprise at the Viscount's unaccountable complaisance.

"Well, I told you how it would be," she said. "Between Madam and Miss Lydia, I wouldn't lay a groat on the chances of any man, lord or no, holding out against them. But you needn't fret yourself, Mr. Cupitt, for we won't be stopping here long, I'll be bound. Madam has other fish to fry, and if I know her, we'll be off to London in the morning. And then," she concluded, with a certain martial air of scenting future triumphs as yet unsuspected by the less knowing, "*then*, Mr. Cupitt, mark my words —*then* you'll begin to see action!"

4

It developed that Miss Winch's prediction was correct in at least one respect: the following morning found the Leylands on their way to London.

On arriving there, Mrs. Leyland instructed the chaise to set them down at Grillon's Hotel, where she proceeded to direct her grandson to engage a set of excellent rooms. The appearance of the party, travelling in the first style and displaying the latest mode in their attire, procured them a degree of attention at this exclusive hostelry which must have been sadly abated had it become known that barely enough remained in their common purse to pay the post-charges.

"Not that it signifies, of course," Mrs. Leyland remarked, surveying with equanimity the small heap of coins that now represented her total fortune. "Tomorrow morning we shall call upon Sir Basil's man of business, Mr. Peeke, and I have no doubt that he will be obliging enough to advance us any trifling sums we may have need of before I am put in possession of the money that can be realised from the sale of poor Letty's jewels."

Her granddaughter and grandson were too well used to living under a system of economy in which the morrow's necessities were no part of the present day's cares to evince any opposition to this plan. In point of fact, they were able, the next morning, fully to approve their grandmother's project to have the hackney-coach that was to convey them to Mr. Peeke's office first drive them about the town so that they might have a glimpse of the sights of London. Mrs. Leyland was eager to set eyes once more on the scenes that had been so familiar to her forty years earlier, and her granddaughter and grandson were equally interested in seeing the streets and edifices of which they had heard and read so much.

The excursion, however, was not an unmitigated success. Mrs. Leyland, though in transports to find herself driving by the fashionable shops in Bond Street once more, yet lamented the passing of old landmarks; and Lydia and Bayard, whose knowledge of town life had been drawn from their visits to New Orleans, missed the colour and softness of the American South in this bustling, noisy metropolis. Lydia, indeed, her ears assailed by the ceaseless rumble of traffic on the cobblestones, and assaulted by the raucous cries of vendors of coals, rat-traps, silver-sand, and doormats, gave it as her opinion that Londoners must all have been deafened long since, which accounted for their addressing one another in such piercing voices.

But to this Mrs. Leyland would not agree.

"No, no," she said decidedly. "It is *your* accent that is deficient, my love. If I have told you and Bayard once, I have told you a hundred times that it will not do for you to drawl your words here as Louisianans do."

Lydia, who was looking thoughtfully at a modish hat of satin-straw, trimmed with puffs of ribbon, in a milliner's window, said encouragingly, "Nonsense, Grandmama! Lord Northover said he found my accent charming."

"I daresay he would," Mrs. Leyland remarked with asperity. "Winch has told me that, according to the Cupitts, he has a shocking reputation, and no doubt is perfectly used to insinuating himself into the good graces of unwary young females by fulsome and *quite* insincere compliments."

Lydia turned her head, opening her eyes wide. "Is *that* what he was doing?" she enquired innocently. "Good gracious, and I had not the least notion—"

Bayard grinned. "Coming it a little too strong, Lyddy!" he said. "Is that the tone you mean to try on the London beaux? I don't advise it; it don't suit you in the least."

"No, I don't think it does," she agreed, considering the matter with a critical air. "All the same, Northover *did* advise me to try for a little more *maidenly reserve*."

Her brother's eye caught hers; she broke into a gurgle, and Bayard into a shout, of laughter. Mrs. Leyland looked at Lydia disapprovingly.

"Yes, it is all very well for you to laugh, but on *that* point Lord Northover was *quite* correct," she said. "I can't think where you have learned such unbecomingly frank manners, my love! Not from *me*, certainly—and your poor papa, whatever his faults may have been, had the most polished of addresses. But I daresay it comes of his having allowed you to read any book you fancied out of his library—some of which I am sure were not at *all* suitable for a young girl's eyes."

"*And* of his having carried her to New Orleans so often, and allowed her to flirt outrageously with every man who came in company with her before she had ever put her hair up," Bayard said cheerfully. "You'd best give it up, Grandmama. Lyddy cut her eye-teeth on men's hearts; she knows exactly how to handle them. Do you remember that Russian baron who wanted to marry her when she was fifteen? Said she was *La Reine des Coeurs*, in the most execrable French imaginable—"

"Abominable! *The Queen of Hearts!* A chit of her age!" Mrs. Leyland said. "Your papa found it very amusing, but I am sure I did not! The man must have been all of forty!"

"Yes, but very plump in the pocket, Papa always said," Bayard remarked. "I'll tell you what, Lyddy—*I* think you would better have remained at home and set up your search for a husband in New Orleans. Scores of plump purses there, you know, and you might choose your nationality—Spanish, French, German—"

"Do *not* be talking so, you wicked boy!" Mrs. Leyland chided him. "You encourage her unbecoming language by your own! I vow I have never seen such exasperating children—but so it has always been, since you were in shortcoats! Your poor mama was used to say that it was always double mischief with the two of you, for one never misbehaved but he pulled the other into it as well. But here we are, I daresay!" she ended these reminiscences suddenly, as the hackney stopped before a row of respectable-looking buildings in the City. "Come now, the pair of you! *Do* try for a little conduct!"

She allowed herself to be assisted from the carriage by Bayard, and waited with an air of unruffled calm while he attempted to persuade the driver, in the most good-humoured of tones, that the sum of money still remaining in his possession was sufficient to defray the expense of the rather extended journey they had just made in his vehicle. The driver, however, was adamant in requiring the full amount he had originally demanded, and Mrs. Leyland was finally moved to summon one of Mr. Peeke's junior clerks, who had been peering interestedly from a window at the altercation going forward outside, and dispatch him to his employer with an imperious request that he pay the charges due. The clerk, who was rather dubious of accepting this commission, soon reappeared with the necessary sum and an altered air of great civility, and invited the Leylands to step inside, where Mr. Peeke, he said, would be glad to see them at once.

Mr. Peeke, in fact—a small, neat gentleman of some fifty-odd years—had himself by this time hurried out to usher them personally upstairs to his office, assuring them meanwhile of his eagerness to be of service to them. When he had seen them comfortably seated in his private room, he sat down himself behind his desk and, placing the tips of his fingers together, made a civil enquiry concerning their journey.

"Very tedious," Mrs. Leyland dismissed the topic summarily. "Perhaps you will be so good, Mr. Peeke, as to come to the point at once, for we have a great deal to do if we are to establish ourselves properly in town before the Season is far under way, and have no time to waste upon details. If you will merely inform me to what amount my sister's bequest will come, and when I may receive possession of it—"

Mr. Peeke blinked, but made a quick recovery and said that, regretfully, he could not answer the first part of her question categorically, as the amount must depend on what the jewels would bring, in the event she wished to sell them.

"Of course I wish to sell them!" Mrs. Leyland said, staring at him. "My good man, if I did not, I should not have a feather to fly with! Now do *not*," she begged, as she saw him pick up a sheaf of papers from his desk, "go into niggling details, but merely tell me if I shall be able to realise enough to hire a house in a fashionable neighbourhood for the Season and maintain myself and my grandchildren there in good style. That is *all* I am interested in, for I am sure that, if Sir Basil Rowthorn entrusts you with *his* affairs, you are perfectly capable of seeing to everything else yourself."

Mr. Peeke appeared somewhat overwhelmed by this tribute to his competence, but almost immediately displayed his acuity as an observer of human nature by taking Mrs. Leyland at her word and assuring her that Lady Rowthorn's bequest was sufficient to allow her to follow, within reason, the programme she had just outlined.

"You must understand, of course," he added, "that the bequest does not extend to any jewels that might be considered as family heirlooms, but includes only those personal tokens of his regard which Sir Basil—"

He was interrupted by an expressive exclamation from Mrs. Leyland. "*Family* heirlooms! My good man, there *is* no family; are you not aware of that? If Sir Basil knows who his grandfather was, it is as much as he can tell you. He is the veriest mushroom, and if his father had not had the good fortune to find himself in India at a providential moment, with diamonds apparently dropping out of the trees into his lap, I daresay he would count himself happy to find employment as your clerk." She appeared struck by a new idea at that moment, and added, "Though I expect he would be considered somewhat superannuated for such a post *now*. Good heavens, he must be all of eighty by this time, for he was years older than poor Letty when he married her."

Mr. Peeke agreed that Sir Basil was indeed hard upon his eightieth birthday. He spoke somewhat absently, however; he was looking thoughtfully at Lydia and Bayard, and appeared to be turning some new notion over in his mind. Before Mrs. Leyland could speak again he had addressed her abruptly.

"My dear Mrs. Leyland, may I speak frankly to you?"

She eyed him a trifle warily. "Upon what subject? You are *not* going to tell me, I hope, that there is some obstacle in the way of my receiving this inheritance?"

"Not in the least. It has merely occurred to me—" Mr. Peeke suddenly threw caution to the winds and said, lowering his voice conspiratorily, "My dear ma'am, you must be aware that this bequest from Lady Rowthorn is a mere bagatelle compared to what might come—not to yourself, of course, but to your grandson, if Sir Basil were to make him his heir! Sir Basil is, as you have remarked, superannuated, and in failing health, and, as there are no nearer relations—"

He paused, a prim smile unexpectedly appearing upon his face as he observed the arrested expression in Mrs. Leyland's eyes.

"Go on!" she commanded. "No nearer relations—except, as I understand, for a great-nephew and a great-niece of his *first* wife's. Are you trying to tell me that *they* have been such jingle-brains as not to have already put themselves in Sir Basil's good graces to the extent that he intends to leave his fortune to *them?*"

The smile widened on Mr. Peeke's face. "They have *attempted* to do so —oh yes, I should be deceiving you, ma'am, if I did not admit *that!*" he said. "But whether they have succeeded is another matter. Indeed, as Sir Basil's man of business—in the strictest confidence, of course—I can assure you that the thing is still hanging fire. He is not, if I may say so, greatly taken with either young Mr. Pentony or his sister, and as for Lady Pentony, their mother—an estimable lady, but of a somewhat talkative and lachrymose disposition—I believe he has expressed himself in such uncomplimentary terms concerning her that she no longer dares to call upon him."

"Indeed!" said Mrs. Leyland, favouring him again with her penetrating stare. "And what is *your* interest in this, Mr. Peeke? Why should *you* care a button whether it is these Pentonys who inherit from Sir Basil or my grandson?"

Mr. Peeke coughed genteelly. "My dear ma'am," he confessed, "I will tell you frankly that the notion of doing so never entered my head until you were so good, a few moments ago, as to indicate that you were willing to honour me with your confidence by placing your affairs entirely in my hands. You will not have given the matter your consideration, of course, but if you will do so now, you must realise that it is extremely profitable to me to have the management of such an extensive property as Sir Basil Rowthorn's. Now if it were to fall to Mr. Pentony upon his demise, I am most certain that it would immediately be taken out of my hands."

"I see! Whereas, if my grandson were to inherit—"

"Exactly." Mr. Peeke regarded the tips of his fingers, which he had once more joined together, with demureness. "May I suggest," he said, "that we might be of—er—mutual assistance to each other, my dear ma'am? I have very little influence, I will confess, over the decision Sir Basil will make in regard to the disposal of his fortune, but I have gleaned a certain knowledge of his character over the years, and may be able to advise you as to the—er—tactics that might be most successful in obtaining his good will."

"I never heard of such impudence!" Mrs. Leyland declared with some hauteur, but then continued briskly, without giving Mr. Peeke time in which to frame an apology, "However, beggars can't be choosers. Bayard, my dear—I daresay you would be very happy to have Mr. Peeke manage your affairs, would you not?"

Lydia, anticipating her brother's rather lazily amused nod of assent, burst into an irrepressible ripple of laughter. "Grandmama, you are too absurd!" she said. "Sir Basil does not know us—nor, it would appear, from the way he has completely ignored the letter you wrote him announcing that we were coming to England, does he wish to know us."

"Ah," Mr. Peeke put in eagerly, "but you must not be deterred by *that*, Miss Leyland! Sir Basil—if I may so express myself—is somewhat eccentric in his habits. In point of fact, he receives no one these days but a certain—er—set of his intimates—and very odd creatures they are, to be sure!" he added, permitting himself a slight titter. "He has taken quite a disgust of Society, you see, which I understand is the result of his having failed many years ago to attain the entrée into its more exalted circles to which he felt he was entitled by his wealth and his marriage to a young lady—your sister, ma'am," he said, bowing to Mrs. Leyland—"of excellent family. This did not come to pass, however—owing to some extent, I believe, to Lady Rowthorn's preferring the country and refusing to exert herself in the world of Society."

"Good heavens! What a ninny!" Mrs. Leyland said, with marked disapproval. "What a vexing thing it is that Letty should not have had *my* opportunities and I hers! But I still do not see, my good man, what all this has to say to my grandson's chances of inheriting Sir Basil's fortune."

Mr. Peeke's prim smile appeared once more. "Let me put it to you in this way, ma'am," he said. "Sir Basil has, I believe, suffered a second disappointment in the fact that neither Mr. nor Miss Pentony—though both are well-looking, genteelly educated young persons—has had a marked success in that world of the *ton* to which he himself aspired in his younger days. You may be aware that the family of his first wife, with whom they are connected, was quite undistinguished, and that the greatest honour achieved by their father was a knighthood, bestowed upon him when he was an official of the city of Nottingham. I do not say," he acknowledged, "that Mr. and Miss Pentony have not attained the entrée into a more elevated stratum of Society than *that* on the strength of their somewhat dubious expectations from Sir Basil, but Sir Basil chooses to sneer at the fact that they do not move in the first circles—"

He paused, seeing that Miss Leyland was observing him with an appreciative gleam in her eyes.

"Why, Mr. Peeke," she accused him, "what a totally Machiavellian plot you are hatching! You think that if *we*—my brother and I—can succeed in making a great splash in Society, poor Sir Basil will be so completely overcome—"

"I believe he would be highly gratified, Miss Leyland," Mr. Peeke said, twinkling at her in unexpected responsiveness. "Dear me, you are a very acute young lady, I see! I have no doubt that, in spite of your lack of fortune, you will succeed in making a very good thing of your—if I may say so!—undeniable beauty and excellent background in London this Season, to the extent that it must come to Sir Basil's ears. Perhaps even an engagement to a gentleman of rank—"

"Disgraceful!" said Lydia severely, adding pensively, "I daresay it would require a great deal of money to carry out such a scheme—perhaps more than Great-aunt Letty's bequest would come to?"

Mr. Peeke bowed gallantly. "You must allow me to be your banker, Miss Leyland," he said. "Upon—speculation, shall we say? I am sure, if your brother should be named in Sir Basil's will, I should have no difficulty in obtaining repayment."

"And if he is not, you will be gapped!" Lydia said frankly. "However, that is your affair, and if you are *quite* determined to behave in such an utterly unscrupulous way toward poor Mr. and Miss Pentony—"

"Lydia, do give over!" Mrs. Leyland said reprovingly. "There is nothing in the least unbecoming in Mr. Peeke's kind offer to assist you to make yourself agreeable to your great-uncle! Perhaps we should call upon him this very morning—"

"I rather think—if you will permit me—not," Mr. Peeke said firmly. "Sir Basil is at present recovering from a severe attack of the gout, which has left his temper—never, I may say, an even one—quite exacerbated. I cannot believe that your visit would be welcomed under such circumstances; indeed, I am of the opinion that you would do better to wait to bring yourselves to his notice until you have made an entrée into Society."

As none of the Leylands was in the least eager to make Sir Basil's acquaintance, this suggestion was agreed to without demur, and a conversation of greater interest to them was then entered into on the subject of the house and servants which they would require for the Season. Here Mr. Peeke promptly showed his mettle, for he declared that, if Mrs. Leyland would but leave the arrangements in his hands, he would engage to have them settled within the week in an elegantly furnished house in an excellent neighbourhood, with a capable staff—complete from housekeeper to footman—to go with it.

"Green Street, I believe," he said, considering the matter. "Yes, yes, by the greatest stroke of fortune I shall be able to settle you there, for Lady Woodforde and her daughter, whom I have the honour of numbering among my clients, have been obliged to go into the country for several months for reasons of health. Then you will wish, of course, to set up your carriage—a barouche, I think, for landaulets have gone sadly out of fashion. And a hack, no doubt, for Mr. Leyland—"

Bayard, however, interrupted here to say that that was a matter which he would prefer to take into his own hands, for he was eager to look in at Tattersall's himself and inspect some of the sweet-going bargains he had seen advertised in the columns of the *Morning Post*. Mr. Peeke made no objection to this, and in a short time, agreement having been reached on all points, the Leylands took their leave—having first been provided, owing to Mrs. Leyland's remembrance of their impoverished state, with an advance against her inheritance which would enable her to cope with present necessities.

5

On a bright morning in early June, several days after this interview had taken place, a sporting curricle drawn by four perfectly matched greys halted before my Lord Gilmour's town-house in St. James's Square and Lord Northover, who followed the currently fashionable practice of driving with a diminutive Tiger perched up behind in place of an adult groom, tossed the reins to the undersized but intelligent-looking stripling who filled this post and strode up the steps to the door. He was admitted into the hall by a magnificent butler, who, having received the Viscount's hat and gloves, which he immediately, with an air of ineffable hauteur, consigned into the care of a powdered and liveried footman, unbent sufficiently to inform their owner that her ladyship was expecting him, and thereupon conducted him up the crimson-carpeted stairway to a small saloon, all yellow satin and gilded mirrors. A lady who had been standing before a pair of windows overlooking the square quickly came forward to greet him.

"Kit! I made sure it was you!" she exclaimed. "I peeped from behind the blinds like a schoolgirl! Where *did* you find those splendid greys? Ned will be green with envy!"

Northover, taking both Lady Gilmour's outstretched hands in his own, gave them a friendly clasp, dropped a kiss lightly upon her cheek, and surveyed the splendour about him with frank dislike.

"Good God, it's like living in a jewel-box!" he said. "Did Ned know you were doing this? I think not!" He sat down beside her, at her invitation, on a sofa resting on crocodile legs inlaid with silver. "As for the greys, they're Laycock's breakdowns—eight hundred pounds, and dog-cheap at the price, but tell Ned he shan't have them from me for twice the sum. How *is* Ned, by the bye? I haven't seen him since Brussels."

"Nor have you seen me—though I gather you don't care about *that*, from that very *coolish* greeting!" the lady said, her brows lifting slightly. She was past the age—as she was well aware—at which a pout might have appeared attractive, but if she had been a dozen years younger there could have been no doubt that she would have made use of one.

This was not to say that she could not still vie with her daughter—an acknowledged beauty, whom she was bringing out that Season—at almost all points. Sir Thomas Lawrence had begged to paint them together, declaring that each made a perfect foil for the other—Lady Gilmour tall, slender, and fair, with a dazzling complexion and hair which, with some assistance to nature, was still the colour of a new-minted guinea; Miss

Beaudoin delicate and dark, with a clear olive colouring and great liquid brown eyes. But Lady Gilmour, though scarcely noted for prudence in any other respect, was very wise when it came to her own looks, and as a result it was her ladyship's portrait alone that hung over the mantelpiece in the Crimson Saloon, untroubled by odious comparisons with a younger beauty.

The same careful consideration had caused her to choose this morning a half-dress of deep gold, veiled by a tunic of amber muslin, which made the room in which she sat appear as if it had been designed for the express purpose of providing a background for her beauty. Northover, eyeing her appreciatively, said, "Was I coolish? I'd say I was overcome!"

"Fiddle!"

"Perhaps. But you seem to forget, my dear, that Ned's a friend of mine —and a deuced good friend, if it comes to that!"

"Does that matter? I thought all was fair in—"

Northover laughed. "Don't come the Bath miss on me, Trix! Finish your quotation! In love and war? What very odd ideas you females have of men, to be sure! Of course it was fair while you were married to Beaudoin. He was old enough to be your father, and as ramshackle an old court-card as ever I came across into the bargain, and if he had any notion, when he got himself riveted to you, that either of you was about to set up as a pattern-saint, it escaped my notice! But Ned's a different case. I told you when you married him that you were making your choice, my dear."

"I had no choice!" Lady Gilmour said, rather pettishly. "You never offered to marry me!"

Northover grinned. "And you wouldn't have accepted me if I had—not before my great-uncle and both my cousins were so obliging as to stick their spoons in the wall and leave me heir to a title and property as good as Ned's. Now don't pitch me any Banbury tales, love; you know it's the truth as well as I do. You were determined to make a good match this time!"

"And why shouldn't I have been?" Lady Gilmour demanded. "After years of odious pinching and scraping, trying to keep up an appearance, at least, that we weren't always outrunning the bailiff—" She waved her hand to indicate the room. "So you needn't wonder at this! I told Ned when I married him that I was bored to death with being poor, and had every intention of making a stir in Society."

"Well, he's rich enough to stand the nonsense, and he's such an easy-going fellow that I daresay he won't mind," Northover said, a satirical look on his dark face. "You may think yourself very well off that I didn't marry you, Trix, for the first thing I'd do, if I had, would be to pitch all this"—he glanced around at the overornamented room—"out the window."

"It is in the very *latest* fashion!" Lady Gilmour defended herself indignantly, and then, catching the look in his eyes, relaxed and said, "Oh, very well! You are roasting me, as usual, you provoking creature! Now *don't* let us come to cuffs with each other, but tell me instead what you have been doing since you left the Army, and all the latest crim. con. stories—"

"Why you should couple *those* two items has me in a puzzle," the Viscount said, with a great assumption of virtue. "Besides, I've been far too busy to get into mischief. Taking up the reins from my great-uncle's hands has worn me down more than following the Duke all through Portugal and Spain ever did."

She surveyed him skeptically. "I must say you don't *look* worn to a thread," she said. "Are you too exhausted to show your face at my dress-party tomorrow evening? I'd have sent you a card, but I had no notion that you were coming to town until I met you yesterday in Bond Street. You *might* have let me know!"

"Of course I'll come," he said, ignoring her last words. "Whom am I to meet? Have you snabbled the Regent, or at least a Royal Duke or two?"

"Oh, I expect York will look in," she conceded, without a great deal of enthusiasm. "But I shall not mind in the least if he does not, for I have been obliged by Mama to invite a set of distant connexions from America whom I should be mortified to death to introduce to him! You *know* how unpresentable provincials are! But it seems that Mama and Mrs. Leyland were bosom-pieces when they were girls, and so she is determined to do what she can to bring her and her granddaughter into fashion."

The Viscount, who had crossed one leg, clad in the tightly fitting biscuit pantaloons that were the approved townwear for gentlemen of the *ton*, over the other, examined the tip of a gleaming Hessian boot and enquired in an innocent voice, "Have you met them as yet—your provincials?"

"No, for, as kind Providence would have it, they were out when Mama insisted on dragging me to call upon them." Struck by something in the tone of his question, she asked, "Why? Have *you* met them?"

"Oh, yes!"

"But where? Mama says they are but just come to town, and have been nowhere as yet—"

She was interrupted by the opening of the door and the entrance of a young lady wearing a pretty China-blue walking-dress and a chip-hat tied under her chin with blue ribbons. She was accompanied by a much older lady, of a square, stout figure, with her quivering dewlaps and magnificent dark eyes rather startlingly complemented by a splendid full-poke bonnet of puce silk, trimmed with drapings of thread-net.

"Mama, see whom I found on the doorstep as I came in," the younger lady began gaily, and then, observing the Viscount, broke off to exclaim in some confusion, "Oh—Captain Brome—I mean—Lord Northover, of course! I did not see you! I beg your pardon!"

Northover rose, and stood looking approvingly at the lovely little face before him.

"Well, Minna!" he said, taking the small gloved hand which she shyly offered him. "So you've managed to grow into a young lady while my back was turned! Lady Aimer—"

He moved from her to the older lady, who stared him up and down frankly before she gave him her hand.

"You look like a town dandy, Northover!" she said. "That rig don't become you half so well as your regimentals. Well, and I daresay you are finding it a dead bore, eh?—being a respectable member of the *ton*, instead of careering all over Europe and America raising riot and rumpus, like the hell-born babe you are?"

Northover laughed. "Now I know why I am so fond of you, Lady Aimer," he said, kissing her hand with an air of great gallantry. "You always have such flattering things to say of me."

"I don't flatter, and you wouldn't like me any the better for it if I did," her ladyship said bluntly, as she plumped herself down in a winged armchair. "And I'll open my budget to you even further, Northover, now that I've begun—I don't want you running tame in this house, dangling after Beatrix and causing trouble between her and Gilmour. This isn't Brussels or Madrid, and she isn't Beaudoin's widow, or even Beaudoin's wife, any longer."

Lady Gilmour gave a tinkling little laugh. "Dear Mama, *must* you be quite so outspoken before Minna?" she said. "At any rate, I assure you it is perfectly unnecessary! Kit has the greatest sense of his obligation to his friendship with Ned; he has only now been telling me so! I do not believe he would even have called here today if I had not met him in Bond Street yesterday and pressed him to do so."

Lady Aimer's hard eyes surveyed Northover in a not unfriendly manner. "Well, that doesn't surprise me overmuch," she said. "You may be a loose-screw, Northover, but you're not a scoundrel. The thing of it is, I've had such a time of it putting this girl of mine into a position where I don't need to lie awake nights worrying because she's in the briars from one cause or another that I don't intend to have my peace cut up again by you or any other man! We made a great mistake with Beaudoin; I'd be the first to admit that—though, lord! how was I to know he'd turn out to be such a hedgebird, with his name and fortune? But we've made no mistake with Gilmour, and there'll be no havey-cavey business to set his back up, if I have anything to say about it!"

Lady Gilmour, shrugging resignedly at her mother's blunt speaking—a trait for which that lady was famous—gave up the attempt to silence her and said to her daughter, "Minna dear, had you not better run upstairs? You need not stand upon ceremony with Lord Northover, and Phipson is waiting to help you to try on your gown for tomorrow evening, now that that odious Celeste has at last had it sent round."

Miss Beaudoin docilely rose and, murmuring her excuses, left the room, upon which Lady Aimer said downrightly to her daughter, "Upon my word, Beatrix, you are a positive dragon when it comes to that girl! She is not in the schoolroom any longer, you know. It will do her no harm to hear a little plain talk. You can't keep her wrapped in cotton-wool forever!"

Lady Gilmour gave a rather angry little laugh. "Oh, dear Mama, allow me to know my own business when it comes to Minna!" she said. "*You* may not credit it, but there are still men who prefer to marry innocence and simplicity—yes, and men of the first rank and consequence, let me tell you! Lord Harlbury, for one, seems not in the least repelled by the idea of a bride who knows no more of the world than Minna does, and you will grant that he is a far greater catch than I snared at her age, for all my having been so much more up to snuff than she is!"

"Yes—*if* she catches him!" Lady Aimer retorted witheringly. "I shouldn't be too sure of landing *that* fish if I was you, my girl, for, in the first place, it's not what Harlbury likes or don't like that will settle the business in the end, but what his mama likes! A handsomer piece of nature than that boy I never clapped eyes on—I'll give you that; he's a very Adonis! But if he makes a move that his mother hasn't first given him permission to make, I wasn't by when he did it."

"Nonsense!" Lady Gilmour said, looking none too well pleased by this unflattering estimate of Lord Harlbury's character. "Merely because he is the soul of amiability and consideration—*both* of them attributes that should make him an excellent husband—"

Lady Aimer gave a crack of laughter. "To say nothing of his having a round forty thousand a year and an earldom; don't forget *that!*" she said. "No, no, Trix—you'd best set your sights a *leetle* lower, my dear. Not but what Minna isn't as pretty a girl as you'll see on display at Almack's this Season, but her fortune is nothing at all unless Gilmour takes a fancy to do something for her. And you haven't so many years in your dish yet that he can't expect to get children of his own by you, so it's not likely he'll come down handsome for her at *their* expense!"

Northover, who had been listening imperturbably to the dispute, enquired at this point if he ought to be acquainted with this paragon.

"Oh, I shouldn't think so; he is half a dozen years, at least, younger than you," Lady Gilmour said, "and has never been much on the town. I believe he is addicted to country pursuits and to—to scientific farming—"

"I fancy he has been pointed out to me in the Park," Northover said gravely. "A young genius—is he?"

"*I* should not say his understanding was more than moderate," Lady Aimer said. "But that is neither here nor there, for I cannot think that Beatrix's scheme has any great chance of success." She gave another bark of laughter and said, "If you are so fond of matchmaking, my dear, I wish you will set your mind to finding a husband for your poor little cousin from America, Erminia Leyland's girl. Lord! I thought I should drop when Erminia told me she wishes me to obtain vouchers for Almack's for her, since she has her heart fixed on her marrying into the *ton!* She's a well-looking girl, according to Erminia—though I haven't seen her myself to decide upon that—but as poor as a church-mouse, and you know what deplorable figures these provincials cut—no ease of manner, no air of fashion, and dressed as if they'd bought made-up clothes in Cranbourne Alley!"

"Kit says he has met them," Lady Gilmour said, "and I wish you will not call them *cousins*, Mama! You have told me yourself that there is only the slightest of connexions."

Lady Aimer ignored this, turning to the Viscount. "Ay, I recollect now —old Northover owned Great Hayland, did he not? Erminia spoke of having stopped to have a look at it. Lord! it is forty years since I've set eyes on it, but it was used to be a mad, gay place when I was a girl, with Erminia and Letty and Gerald to set the pace—What did you make of her?" she broke off to ask abruptly.

"Of Mrs. Leyland?"

"Of the girl."

Northover considered. "Why, she is—quite unusual, ma'am," he assured her, after a moment.

"Humph!" said Lady Aimer. "A dowdy, I expect?"

"I should not call her so."

"Well, I will give Erminia credit for being rigged out in prime style herself," Lady Aimer granted, "but even *she* can't make a silk purse out of a sow's ear, and I daresay the girl hasn't the least notion of how to go on in a ball-room, or even of how to behave properly when she is in company."

"Yet you foist her upon *me!*" Lady Gilmour said tragically.

"Well, she has to learn somewhere—doesn't she?" her mother demanded practically. "And with Erminia to teach her she'll come along fast, if she isn't a ninny. *Is* she a ninny?" she asked Northover.

The Viscount's eyes glinted. "I believe I shall leave you to make up your own mind on that point, ma'am," he said.

"As bad as that—is it? Well, I should have known it!" her ladyship said philosophically. "We must set our sights on some respectable widower who is hanging out for a healthy young wife to mother his brood, or a half-pay officer, Trix. And even *that* may be above her touch, if she turns out to be a Homely Joan or one of those May-poles they seem to breed in America!"

6

Lord Northover, arriving early in St. James's Square on the following evening with the express purpose of being present at Miss Lydia Leyland's entry into Society, was privileged to behold the faces of both Lady Gilmour and her mama when that young lady swam into their ken. Miss Leyland wore for the occasion an Indian mull muslin gown far removed from any suspicion of provincial dowdiness; her dark hair, cropped and curled in front and twisted up behind into a high Grecian knot, was dressed in the latest mode; and the diaphanous gown and the length of silver net which draped her shoulders *à la Ariane* did nothing to conceal the elegant lines of her figure and the gracefulness of her carriage as she mounted the grand staircase between her grandmother and her brother and sustained an introduction to Lord and Lady Gilmour.

The Viscount noted that Lord Gilmour, though not, as he himself expressed it in his bluff, good-humoured way, much in the petticoat-line, gave her a most appreciative glance, while Lady Gilmour, her eyes narrowing slightly at this new beauty suddenly appearing upon the London scene, had difficulty in concealing her incredulity on learning that *this* was the "poor little cousin" who must consider herself fortunate to find a worthy middle-aged widower content to take her as housekeeper and spouse.

A fan rapped sharply on Northover's arm. He looked down to see Lady Aimer's pugnacious face thrust up at him.

"You are a humbug, Northover!" she said.

"A humbug, Lady Aimer?"

"You know very well what I mean, you rogue! That girl. You said she was—unusual."

"Is she not?"

"Unusual! A diamond of the first water! Look at Trix; she's as blue as megrim! Lord, she never could endure to see a woman handsomer than she was herself! And, to make it worse, the chit's as self-possessed as if she'd been reared at Chatsworth or Woburn, instead of in a swamp full of savages and mosquitoes! The boy's a well-looking lad, too," she added, looking with approval at young Bayard Leyland, impeccable in blue dress-coat and satin knee-breeches, as he bowed over Lady Gilmour's hand. "Resembles her, don't he? The two of 'em together make a handsome picture."

That she was not the only person who thought so was evident from the shyly admiring expression upon Miss Beaudoin's face as she, in turn, was introduced to her cousins from America. Miss Beaudoin, herself demurely lovely in a white sarsnet gown, its tiny puffsleeves trimmed with seed pearls, was too much accustomed to being cast into the shade by her mama to be envious of the advent of a new beauty who might be expected to steal more than one of her own admirers from her; and, as a matter of fact, she had spared only a cursory glance and one of her gentle smiles for her new rival. Her gaze was riveted, instead, upon Bayard. Really, Northover thought, amused, the cub *did* make a romantic picture, with his dark hair brushed *au coup de vent* in careless locks over his forehead, his handsome face with its air of composed detachment, and his intense dark-blue eyes. And not sixpence to scratch himself with! If Minna were to cast sheep's eyes in that direction, she would be in for a pretty rating from her mama, he thought ironically.

He was the recipient of a friendly nod from Mrs. Leyland, resplendent in garnet satin and a Spartan diadem, and of a dazzling smile from Miss Leyland as they passed on into the ball-room, but Bayard halted for a more extended greeting.

"I say," he remarked reverently, his eyes upon Miss Beaudoin, "what a *devilish* pretty girl, sir! Is she—is she much sought after?"

"Moderately so, I believe," Northover replied. "She is indeed a little beauty—but her fortune is nonexistent, which makes a great many eligible gentlemen quite impervious to her charms."

"What a set of gudgeons!" Bayard said scornfully. "As if that signified!"

"It may not signify to you, but I assure you that it does to Lady Gilmour," Northover said dryly. "*That* bird is above your touch, halfling. Her mama is looking out for a plumper purse than yours."

Bayard reddened slightly. "You are very good to warn me, sir," he said, with a stiffness quite at variance with the usual lazy good-humour of his manner, and moved away, to be seized upon at once by Lady Aimer, who was apparently bent upon making herself known without delay to her young relation.

Northover strolled on into the ball-room, where he found, not at all to his surprise, that Miss Leyland's hand had already been claimed for the set of country dances that was forming. He watched her as she went down the dance, observing with approval that she performed her part in it with all the aplomb of a young lady to whom the glitter of a fashionable ball-room, with its high, pilastered walls, silk-hung windows, and hundreds of candles in gleaming chandeliers, was the merest commonplace. Her partner, he saw, was Sir Carsbie Chant, a well-known figure in *ton* circles, for not only was he the possessor of an enormous fortune, but he aspired, in spite of having reached middle life, to the leadership of the most extravagant wing of the dandy-set. His narrow shoulders were broadened by an absurd amount of buckram padding set into a wasp-waisted, bottle-green coat of Nugee's cut; his thin legs were encased in exquisite black satin knee-breeches and striped silk stockings; and his sallow, self-important countenance was propped above a towering neckcloth tied in the style known as the *Sentimentale*.

But, in spite of the singularity of his appearance, Miss Leyland, Northover conceded, had made a notable first conquest. Sir Carsbie was an intimate of the Regent's and an accepted connoisseur of female beauty, and it was certain that the cachet of his approval, so immediately bestowed upon Miss Leyland, would inspire other gentlemen to seek the honour of leading her out for subsequent dances.

Meanwhile, Lord Gilmour, presently released from the necessity of greeting his arriving guests, came to seek out Northover and drag him off to exchange Army reminiscences over iced champagne, and it was some little time before the two returned to the ball-room. When they arrived there a quadrille was in progress, and Northover, propping his shoulders against the wall beside a sofa on which a pair of dowagers sat gossiping, listened with amusement to the astonished comments of one of these ladies on the facility with which Miss Leyland, now partnered with a young baronet, performed even the most difficult of the steps.

"Where she can have learned them, I cannot conceive," she remarked, "for I have been assured that she has only just arrived from America, where she lived *quite* out of society. I am sure my Louisa has spent *hours* with her dancing-master without obtaining sufficient proficiency in the *grande ronde* and the *pas de zéphyr* to feel herself capable of standing up for the quadrille with any gentleman who is a master of those steps." She added in a lowered voice, behind her fan, "However, I must say that I should *never* allow Louisa to appear in such a gown as Miss Leyland is wearing. Entirely too *French*, my dear, if you wish my opinion, and I am quite certain, too, that she must have dampened her petticoat to make it cling so—a custom of which I thoroughly disapprove!"

"And I," virtuously agreed her friend. "I hear that Lady Aimer intends to ask one of the Patronesses of Almack's to procure vouchers to the Assembly Rooms for the girl, and poor Lady Sefton is so good-natured that I daresay she may allow herself to be imposed upon to do so. But she is not here tonight, I believe, and, although I have seen both Lady Jersey and the Countess Lieven, I doubt if even Lady Aimer will be bold enough to ask either of *them* to sponsor a girl from the backwoods of America!"

"At any rate," said the first lady, with some satisfaction, "since Miss Leyland has not yet been approved by the Patronesses, she cannot dance the waltz at a London ball—which means, my dear, that she must resign herself to being a wallflower at least for this next while, for no gentleman will be foolish enough to ask her to stand up with him!"

"If, indeed, she has any idea of how to perform the steps!" the second lady tittered—and then broke off, apparently stunned by the sight of what was occurring before her on the ball-room floor.

Northover himself muttered, "Oh, the devil!"—and took a step forward, but it was too late. Miss Leyland, finding herself relinquished, partnerless, into her grandmother's hands as the musicians struck up the opening measures of a waltz, had glanced around, seen her brother standing nearby, and beckoned to him; the next moment the two had swept off together to the center of the floor, the lady's draperies flowing seductively about her, her partner's arm lightly encircling her waist, the two moving together with such effortless precision and grace that the shocked murmur which has arisen at sight of what Northover was sure was an unconscious audacity was quickly augmented by an even more audible murmur of admiration.

It was, in fact, quite evident to anyone looking on that not only were brother and sister superbly matched partners, but that they must have waltzed together so frequently that each was responsive to the slightest movement the other made. As if by mutual agreement, they introduced several graceful variations in the basic steps of the dance, and these were so smoothly and exquisitely performed that the couples around them involuntarily halted to watch, so that in the space of a few minutes the Leylands were almost alone upon the floor. Northover felt a tug on his sleeve, and looked down at Lady Aimer's despairing face.

"Can't you *do* something?" she demanded of him. "I've spoken to Gilmour; all I can get from *him* is, 'Dashed fine, by Jupiter!' And Lady Jersey looking on, and the Countess Lieven! I could *flay* myself for not having warned Erminia that the girl must on no account waltz in public until she has been approved by the Patronesses of Almack's!" She glanced with some asperity across the ball-room at Lady Gilmour, who, although standing in conversation with several gentlemen, was quite evidently missing nothing of what was going forward on the floor. "I vow, Beatrix is actually enjoying this!" she said tartly. "How she can be such a widgeon as not to realise that it cannot add to *our* consequence to have the girl ruin herself—"

"Oh, I doubt if it will come to that!" Northover said, with a slight smile. "To tell you the truth, I am enjoying it, too!" She gave an angry exclamation and he said soothingly, "Never mind, ma'am. I'll engage to give Miss Leyland the opportunity to right herself—and, if my impression of her is to be trusted, she is quite capable of doing so, with only a hint to set her in the right direction."

Lady Aimer, still fuming, looked skeptical, and, after a sharp admonition to him not to make the chit any more conspicuous by paying attentions to her himself, went off to find Mrs. Leyland and apprise her of the solecism she had allowed her granddaughter to commit. Northover, left alone, went back to his appreciative contemplation of the two young Leylands' performance, but as the music wound to a close he took care to change his position so that, when the final notes sounded, he was standing near enough to them that a half dozen rapid steps brought him to their side.

"Now, children," he said amiably, as the two, who appeared somewhat surprised to find themselves almost alone upon the floor, turned identically questioning eyes upon him, "you are to listen most carefully to what I say! You are in disgrace, Miss Leyland, because you have presumed to break one of the canons of London Society—no young lady is to dance the waltz until the Patronesses of Almack's have set the seal of their approval upon her doing so. I shall now introduce you to two of those ladies—Lady Jersey and the Russian ambassador's wife, Countess Lieven—both of whom have been observing you as you flouted their authority. Therefore, if you do not wish your first appearance in Society to be your last, you will manage somehow to propitiate their wrath—"

He paused, looking sternly down into Lydia's face, where an expression of startled incomprehension had been replaced, as he spoke, by a look of pure amused mischief.

"I mean what I say, you abominable little gypsy!" he said severely. "*Will* you be serious!"

She tucked her hand into his arm. "Oh, you may trust me!" she said confidentially. "What shall it be? Tears and remorse? Shall I beat my breast and promise amendment of my ways? I warn you, that is definitely *not* one of my better acts."

Bayard grinned at Northover's exasperated face. "Never mind, sir! She'll contrive to rub through," he said cheerfully. "She's *not* such a goosecap as she sounds, you know."

"Well, you *said* I was to be propitiating!" Lydia said, in an injured tone, and then, as they approached the group in which Lady Jersey and the Countess stood, composed her countenance swiftly into an expression of enchantingly rueful contrition. Northover made the introductions, which were acknowledged by the two ladies with the most arctic of bows. But they had no time in which to make clear their opinion of what they evidently considered Northover's outrageous audacity in bringing Miss Leyland up to them before that young lady herself had rallied to his support.

Fixing the most beguiling of smiles upon Lady Jersey, she said in a rush, in her rich alto voice, "Oh dear, and I had *so* looked forward to meeting you! Dear ma'am, have I quite sunk myself beneath reproach? If I had had the least idea I was running counter to your wishes, I should have stabbed myself with the nearest convenient implement—I daresay there *are* fruit knives in the supper-room?—before I permitted my brother to lead me out on to the floor."

Lady Jersey, who had herself a very volatile sense of humour, could not prevent herself from laughing, though she said nothing, but merely glanced with slightly lifted brows at the Countess Lieven. That lady, who was accounted, along with Mrs. Drummond Burrell, as among the haughtiest of the Patronesses, appeared unmoved by Miss Leyland's appeal, which, her manner seemed to indicate, while it might be accepted by such a light-minded madcap as Sally Jersey, did nothing to lessen the impression in *her* mind that Miss Leyland was a hoydenish provincial, whose lack of *savoir faire* she would do nothing to countenance.

Her expression changed markedly, however, when Lydia, as if in comprehension of her attitude, turned to address her prettily in fluent French, with an impeccable accent, begging her forgiveness in far more formal terms than she had used with Lady Jersey, and assuring her that the thought of disregarding her authority had been farthest from her mind. She then, Northover observed with rising admiration, unblushingly enlisted the aid of her brother in softening the hearts of the two offended ladies, and, as Bayard seemed perfectly capable of continuing the conversation his sister had begun with the Countess in the same effortless and idiomatic French, and of addressing Lady Jersey in terms of rather shy but admiring gallantry that could not but please her, coming from a handsome young man of excellent address, Northover judged that the time was ripe to put an end to Lydia's rôle in the proceedings. He therefore bore her off, to Lady Jersey's parting shot, "You had best find her a *respectable* partner instead of dancing with her yourself, Northover! You are an unprincipled wretch, and will only set more tongues to wagging if you stand up with her!"

"What an excellent piece of advice, Sally! I shall!" Northover assured her. He glanced rapidly about the room as he strolled off with Lydia, remarking, "Respectable *and* fashionable he shall certainly be, my dear. And mind that you charm him so thoroughly that he looks to be enjoying himself—Ah! Harlbury! The very man!" he broke off, observing with satisfaction a magnificently tall, classically handsome young giant who was just entering the room. "Come along, my girl!"

"*That* splendid young man? I should rather think so!" Lydia said, matching her steps to his with alacrity. "Who *is* he?"

"He will be Lady Gilmour's son-in-law one day, if he comes up to scratch," Northover said briefly. "However, that is neither here nor there. I should warn you, though, that for the next half hour you are going to be devotedly interested in scientific farming."

"I *am*? Oh! I see! You mean Harlbury is!"

"I do." The Viscount, purposefully approaching Lord Harlbury, greeted him warmly. "Allow me, sir," he said cordially, "to present this young lady to you as a very desirable partner. Miss Leyland—Lord Harlbury."

Lord Harlbury, appearing considerably startled, looked from the Viscount to Miss Leyland, but good breeding came to his aid and he politely expressed his appreciation of the pleasure of meeting the young lady. She held out her hand; he took it.

"I fancy they are about to begin. You had best take your places," Northover said, shepherding them ruthlessly across the floor to where the set was forming.

Having seen them installed in the ranks of the dancers, he promptly departed, leaving Lord Harlbury to gaze after him with a rather dazed air.

"I daresay it is very remiss of me, but I can't quite place—" he began.

"Lord Northover," Lydia explained helpfully.

"Oh! Northover. Still, I don't quite recall meeting—"

"I have the same difficulty," Lydia said sympathetically. "I practically *never* can recall names, which causes me to make some of the most totally *anachronous* blunders. I daresay it will turn out to be a bond between us."

Lord Harlbury did not appear to find this statement of much consolation at the moment, but he was not so perplexed that he did not presently realise that—however oddly he had come by her—his partner was an excessively pretty girl, and he set himself to the task of making himself agreeable to her. This he did in a manner which struck Lydia as being—in view of his rank and appearance—somewhat overdiffident. His observations to her were all of the most formal nature, and were delivered with a certain air of uneasiness, as if, while enjoying himself, he had a guilty sensation of behaving not quite as he ought.

Since he had not arrived in the ball-room in time to view her error in dancing the waltz, nor could he have had the opportunity of hearing it discussed by others, Lydia was at a loss to account for this attitude on his part, until she observed that it appeared to become more marked whenever he found himself facing a certain middle-aged lady in a impressive purple turban, who had placed herself on a routchair drawn up directly in view of the dancers. Her frowning regard, Lydia noted, was fixed unwaveringly upon Lord Harlbury, while he, on the other hand, appeared to make every effort to avoid hers.

"Who *is* that lady?" she enquired at last, with a candid curiosity that would have won her Northover's severest censure.

"That lady?" Lord Harlbury glanced down at her, somewhat startled.

"In the purple turban," Lydia said perseveringly. "She is looking at you very oddly. Do you know her?"

"*Know* her?"

"You really *should* try to lose this habit of repeating everything one says to you," Lydia advised him, somewhat severely. "It does nothing to advance a conversation. I have asked you an extremely simple question, and it *does* seem to me—though perhaps I may be mistaken, for you did appear unable to make up your mind just now whether you knew Lord Northover or not—that you *should* be able to answer it."

"Of course I am able to answer it! She is my mother!" said Harlbury, stung, it seemed, by the extreme frankness of this speech.

"Your mother! Well, she certainly appears to disapprove of your dancing with me!"

"I fancy she expected—that is, she told me Lady Gilmour expected—" his lordship said guiltily. "What I mean to say is, I fancy they *both* expected I should stand up first with Miss Beaudoin."

"With Miss Beaudoin? Oh! You mean Lady Gilmour's daughter. Well, you may stand up with her for the next set," Lydia said magnanimously, "though I *do* wish you will ask me again for the one after *that*, for I can see that it is doing an immense deal to restore my credit to be seen dancing with you, after the horrible crime I have just committed. I expect I had best tell you about that myself, for some utterly corrosive female is sure to do so the very instant you escape from me."

She thereupon confided to her bewildered partner—after first extracting from him a solemn promise to stand up with her for the next set but one— a highly coloured account of the waltzing incident and her subsequent interview with Lady Jersey and the Countess Lieven—"which I *do* think I handled rather beautifully," she said, "for I simply pushed Bayard into the breach, and no woman past thirty can ever *remain* angry with him. He has poise, you see, but at the same time he *looks* shy, which has a totally blighting effect upon them. You might study him; you are somewhat in the same style yourself, you know, though I don't believe you *really* have poise and it's all a bit too stiff, the way *you* do it." She added kindly, seeing the harassed look again appearing in Lord Harlbury's eyes, "Bayard is my brother, and you *haven't* met him."

What response he might have made to this information was never to be known, for Lydia, suddenly recollecting Northover's admonition, immediately turned the conversation into other channels, informing his lordship with some abruptness that she understood him to be an authority on scientific farming, in which, above all other subjects, she was passionately interested. Lord Harlbury, who, in spite of having shown to considerable disadvantage under the series of shocks to which he had just been subjected, was not dull of understanding, looked somewhat skeptical upon hearing this; but, as it was difficult even for the most acute of observers to discover exactly how much of Miss Leyland's conversation was meant to be taken seriously, she eventually succeeded in persuading him that she was in earnest. As a result, she was treated to the spectacle of his lordship in a fluently conversational mood. Such phrases as "cross-breeding" and "rotation of crops" assailed the ears of those standing beside them in the set, and when the conversation was perforce interrupted by the exigencies of the dance, it was once more resumed when his lordship and Miss Leyland came together again.

Northover, watching them from across the room, was discovering that he was finding this ball quite as amusing as any during which he himself had been engaged in the liveliest of flirtations when his appreciative observation of Miss Leyland's skill in drawing her partner out was interrupted by Lady Gilmour's coming up to him and addressing him, not in the kindliest of tones.

"Kit, you wretch! What in the world did you mean by it, flinging that girl at Harlbury's head? It was quite understood that he was to stand up first with Minna this evening."

"Was it? Good God, how maladroit of me!" said the Viscount, with a not very convincing air of compunction.

"And don't try to flummery me! You are not in the least sorry," Lady Gilmour said, laughing in spite of herself. "But I *should* like to know why you felt yourself obliged to help her out of that bumblebath she had fallen into."

"I rather thought you'd be grateful," Northover said virtuously. "After all, she's *your* relation."

"Fiddle! I shan't care in the least if she finds herself in the briars! She appears to me to have the most abominable lack of delicacy—"

She was not permitted to go on, for at this the Viscount broke into a shout of laughter. "From *you*, Trix!" he said, when he was able to speak again.

She tapped her ivory-brisé fan vexedly against the gloved palm of her free hand. "Oh, very well! But I am not a miss in her first Season, you will remember!" She looked at him with sudden sharpness. "Tell me—are *you épris* there, Kit?" she asked.

"Of course I am!" retorted the Viscount. "What do you take me for? I haven't seen anything as amusing in half a dozen years. I am on tenterhooks to see what next she will do!"

She shrugged, almost angered, it seemed, by this flippant reply. "What a cold devil you are!" she said, after a moment. "Do you know—though I admit I should be abominably jealous!—I should almost be glad to see you caught at last. I believe you look upon us as creatures in a raree show, set up merely for your entertainment."

"Well, you will concede, at any rate, that it was a master-hand that set this one up tonight," he said, not at all perturbed, it seemed, by this thrust. "By the bye, did young Bayard succeed in propitiating the two offended goddesses? I saw you talking to Sally Jersey just now."

"Oh, you know very well that Sally is not disposed to banish anyone from Almack's who promises to be amusing!" Lady Gilmour said discontentedly. "But I declare I am in an even worse humour with that troublesome boy than I am with his sister. Would you believe that this is the third dance for which Minna has stood up with him? I don't know what has come over her, for she is usually the most biddable girl in the world, and she knows she is not to stand up with anyone—except Harlbury should ask her—more than twice in an evening."

Northover, raising his quizzing-glass to observe Miss Beaudoin and Mr. Leyland more closely, let it drop in an moment and said succinctly, "Romeo and Juliet."

"What!"

"Come, come, Trix, you are not so poorly educated as that!" he said reprovingly. "They met at a ball, fell in love at first sight—"

"Don't you *dare* say such a thing! Why, he hasn't a penny to bless himself with!" Lady Gilmour looked angrily at her daughter. "She *can't* be such a little fool!"

"Care to lay odds on it?"

"No, I do not! And if she *is* idiotish enough to believe she has conceived a *tendre* for him, that will very soon be put a stop to!"

Northover laughed. "No, no, Trix—don't go to playing Lady Capulet!" he said. "I promise you it won't serve—not if they really *have* fallen top-over-tail in love."

"Love! What do you know of love?" her ladyship said tartly. "I wish you will stop talking such nonsense! People do not fall in love at first sight, and even if they do, it does not signify, for I will *not* have Minna marrying a pauper!"

"He is, you know," Northover remarked conversationally, "a great-nephew of old Rowthorn's, who has, I believe, no closer relations."

"Yes, except for another great-nephew who has been on close terms with him for years!" Lady Gilmour said scathingly. "Thank you, I know all about that situation from Mama. There is not the least hope that young Leyland will come in for so much as a shilling from *that* source."

"Ah, but then Miss Leyland's husband may be expected to do something handsome for him," Northover reminded her gravely, though with a telltale muscle twitching at the corner of his mouth.

Lady Gilmour stared at him in astonishment. "Her husband? But she has not got a husband!"

"She will have, Trix—she will have! What would you say to Harlbury, for example? There is still the Leyland plantation in America, I believe; should not that challenge the imagination of a wealthy young peer with a burning interest in scientific farming?"

"Kit, you are abominable! You *know* I intend Harlbury for Minna. Good God, I am on the very verge of bringing Lady Harlbury round, and if you make mischief now, I'll—I'll—"

"Scratch my eyes out? Oh no, you won't," Northover grinned. "If you must come to cuffs with someone, let me recommend Miss Leyland. But I warn you," he added, as he strolled away, "that I consider you will be engaging a formidable opponent. No holds barred, and the devil take the hindmost! I am not acquainted with the motto upon the Leyland escutcheon, but I should think that would be as suitable as any!"

7

Lydia, sipping chocolate in her bedchamber in Green Street at an advanced hour the following morning, was indeed inclined to feel a certain satisfaction with the results of her debut in London Society. She had stood up twice with Lord Harlbury and twice with Sir Carsbie Chant, who had paid her several pretty compliments and engaged himself to drive her in the Park in his phaeton the following afternoon. She had been presented to the Regent's brother, the Duke of York, who had looked in late in the evening and bestowed several minutes of jovial conversation upon her. And even the contretemps with the august Patronesses of Almack's had had its compensations, for it had ended, after all, in her being pardoned by both ladies for her lapse, and it had certainly brought her to the notice of every gentleman in the room.

When she came downstairs a little later, she found her grandmother and her brother in equally good spirits. Mrs. Leyland, who had spent much of the evening in the card-room, playing whist with some happily encountered acquaintances from earlier days, had had an amazing run of luck which had sent her home with her reticule bulging with her winnings, and, beyond a brief tiff with Lady Aimer, who had accused her of being far too casual in her chaperonage of her granddaughter, she had found nothing in the evening's events to lessen her enjoyment in her first reappearance in London Society.

As for Bayard, he was *aux anges* over Miss Beaudoin's kindness in standing up with him no fewer than three times in the course of the evening, and was engaged in wearying his sister and his grandmother for the dozenth time with a recital of that young lady's manifold perfections when Sidwell, the excellent butler engaged by Mr. Peeke, entered the room to announce the arrival of Lord Northover.

Lydia, who had been the recipient the evening before of some chance-given information concerning that gentleman which made her feel strongly that she had a crow to pluck with him, at once desired him to be shown upstairs, and greeted him, as he entered the room, with her customary lack of ceremony.

"Northover, you have deceived me!" she said accusingly. "I have never been so disappointed in anyone in my life!"

Mrs. Leyland looked startled. "Deceived you, my love!" she said. "Lord Northover? Nonsense! I am sure he has never offered you the least—the least discourtesy!"

"Not if you think it courteous to encourage me to believe an outrageous faradiddle, he hasn't!" Lydia said darkly.

Northover grinned. "What 'outrageous faradiddle,' Miss Leyland?" he enquired.

"That you were as poor as a church-mouse! I have it on excellent authority that you are not only very well to pass, but even disgustingly rich!"

"Well, I certainly do not recollect making any statement to you at all about my financial condition," the Viscount said, calmly seating himself. "You ought not to jump to conclusions, Lydia *mia*. It is one of your chief —and, if I may say so—most endearing faults."

"I am *not* your Lydia, *nor* one of your Spanish flirts," Lydia stated categorically. "And if you think *that* is an excuse, it is a very poor sort of one! However," she added handsomely, "I will admit I am in your debt for having extricated me from the scrape I fell into last night, so I have every intention of forgiving you this time."

"Thank you!" said the Viscount, bowing. "Am I to gather that your reason for resenting the delusion into which I permitted you to fall was that you might otherwise have added me to your list of matrimonial prospects?"

"Pray do not flatter yourself, my lord!" Lydia said, with proper primness. "At any rate, you have already told me that you are not a marrying man, so I should merely have been wasting my time if I had spared any of it in attempting to entrap you—which I can assure you I have never had the least intention of doing."

"Lydia! My *dear!*" said Mrs. Leyland, shocked. "One must never make use of such a term in describing one's intentions toward eligible gentlemen, even in jest! Of course you will not attempt to *entrap* anyone!"

"Not even Harlbury?" Northover said wickedly. "My dear ma'am, surely one may make an exception there! I believe Miss Leyland, at least, already agrees with me on that point. What was he saying to you to make you hang so raptly on his words last evening, Lydia? Somehow it puzzles me to picture such a magnificently sober young gentleman paying pretty compliments!"

A gurgle of laughter, immediately repressed, escaped Lydia.

"If you must know," she said loftily, "we were discussing crop rotation and—and crossbreeding." Bayard and Northover burst into simultaneous shouts of laughter. "I daresay it may amuse *you*," she continued, with unimpaired dignity, "but let me tell you that Lord Harlbury considers my

understanding quite capable of grasping the intricacies of such subjects."
Bayard gazed at her, awed. "Lyddy, he didn't *say* that to you?"
"Yes, he did," Lydia averred. "What is more, you odious wretches, he meant it! He is a very *worthy* young man—and the most *beautiful* creature I have ever set eyes on—*and* an earl—*and* fabulously rich—"
"Take care, Lydia!" Northover warned. "Harlbury will do very well for you to flirt with, and enhance your consequence in the Marriage Mart, but you had best not allow yourself to be carried away. If his mama and Miss Beaudoin's have anything to say to it, there will be an interesting announcement concerning the pair of them appearing in the *Gazette* before the cat can lick her ear."

Lydia's chin went up. "And what, pray, has Miss Beaudoin to offer that I have not?" she demanded. "*She* has no fortune."

"No," Northover retorted, "but she has something which Lady Harlbury considers more valuable, and which I don't think even *you* have sufficient brass to lay claim to for yourself—a biddable disposition."

Lydia appeared about to utter a spirited rejoinder, but she was interrupted by Bayard, whose face had grown suddenly paler at Northover's pronouncement concerning Miss Beaudoin and Lord Harlbury.

"You must be mistaken, sir!" he jerked out abruptly. "About—about Miss Beaudoin, that is! She—does not love him."

"No?" Northover cynically raised his brows. "And what has that to say to anything?"

"A great deal, I should imagine!" Bayard said doggedly. "Good God, sir, you cannot mean that her relations would force her into a marriage with Lord Harlbury against her inclination!"

"I did not say that," Northover returned, speaking somewhat more gently as he saw the intense earnestness and anxiety with which Bayard was regarding him. "On the other hand, it is quite possible that Miss Beaudoin herself will have no wish to reject such an advantageous offer merely because she has as yet formed no great attachment for Harlbury."

"I don't believe it!" Bayard said. He jumped up and walked to the window, where he stood looking out, evidently unwilling to allow the others to see how strongly disturbed he was. "She has too much delicacy of mind —too great a sensibility—"

Northover shrugged, and Lydia, who had been watching her brother with unusual thoughtfulness, rose and crossed the room swiftly to lay her hand upon his shoulder.

"Never mind, Bayard," she said. "It is nothing but tittle-tattle, at any rate, and I do not believe Harlbury has at all made up his mind to offer for her. He certainly gave no appearance to *me* last night of being a man in love."

"No," the Viscount agreed, amusement lighting his eyes again as he remembered Lord Harlbury's astonishment on being presented with an obviously willing partner by a gentleman quite unknown to him, "I daresay he did not—not with you bursting upon him like a comet! He must be a man of iron nerves even to have been able to carry on a sensible conversation with you under the circumstances. Tell me, Lydia, how did you manage to put together such a bag of tricks as you dazzled the company with last evening? Flawless French, a talent for waltzing that cast every other young lady in the shade—"

"Oh," Lydia said, shrugging, "New Orleans swarms with *émigrés*, you know, and Mademoiselle de Levaillant, who was my governess when I was small, was very willing to continue living with us at Belmaison even after Papa died, until she died herself—poor thing!—last year. And as to the waltzing—pray, what else was there for Bayard and me to do, when we were not riding or reading? We were used to waltz for hours, with Mademoiselle playing *Ach du lieber Augustin* on an impossibly out-of-tune old pianoforte with broken strings."

As she spoke, she still appeared to be giving most of her attention to Bayard, who had not sat down again, but was walking restlessly about the room, paying little heed to the conversation. He was brought back to a consciousness of his surroundings abruptly, however, when Northover signified his intention of taking his leave, announcing that he had stopped in only for the purpose of learning if Bayard wished to accompany him to Gentleman Jackson's famous Boxing Saloon in Bond Street. Bayard's face at once lighted up, and Miss Beaudoin was for the moment forgotten.

"Oh, by Jupiter, that is very kind of you, sir!" he said. "Of course I should like it above anything!"

"For my part," Mrs. Leyland said disapprovingly, "I consider boxing an excessively vulgar form of amusement, and can only regret that gentlemen of the first rank should see fit to indulge in it. What astonishes me even more is that many of them are said to frequent the company of professional pugilists in such places as—Cribb's Parlour, I believe it is called?—where they imbibe a highly intoxicating beverage known as Blue Ruin."

Northover's lips twitched. "Just so, ma'am," he said gravely, shaking his head. "Now in *your* day, I daresay, such shocking practices were quite unknown."

"Well, no—they were not," Mrs. Leyland confessed unexpectedly. She added composedly, "In point of fact, I daresay your grandfathers were far wilder sparks than you young men are today. But that still does not signify that I approve of your introducing my grandson into low company."

"Low company!" Lydia laughed. "Good God, Grandmama, even I have learned by this time that *Gentleman* Jackson's clientele is as select as his name. Bayard will rub shoulders with quite as many peers in his Saloon, I daresay, as he will at Almack's, if Lady Aimer succeeds in procuring vouchers for us."

She added a few words of obviously sincere gratitude to Northover, which somewhat surprised him, and caused him to realise that Miss Lydia Leyland, in spite of her volatility, was genuinely attached to her brother, and prepared to look kindly upon anyone who exerted himself in his behalf.

However, the brief period of good feeling between them was quickly brought to a close when Miss Leyland, reminded by his doing so again, took exception to the Viscount's making so free with her name as to call her Lydia, and, upon his choosing to laugh at this assumption of propriety, favoured him with such a pungent reproof that all thought that she was about to behave, for once, like any other young lady of quality was removed from his mind.

The Viscount had scarcely taken his leave, bearing Bayard off with him, when the butler announced the arrival of Lady Pentony, Mr. Pentony, and Miss Pentony. Lydia and Mrs. Leyland had time only to exchange glances of surprise before the visitors were ushered in. These were a somewhat faded middle-aged lady, attired in a garnet-coloured walking-dress lavishly trimmed with silk floss, a tall, fair-haired young man who, without being handsome, made an agreeable appearance, and an excessively pretty young girl with melting blue eyes.

Mrs. Leyland had risen to greet the visitors, but her words of welcome were forestalled by Lady Pentony, who in a failing voice begged forgiveness for presuming upon the slight connexion between them—"which I am persuaded you will scarcely consider a connexion at all, based as it is only upon Sir Basil's having married first my dear aunt and then your sister, Mrs. Leyland. But, as I said to Michael only this morning—*do* allow me to present my son Michael—Mrs. Leyland—Miss Leyland, is it not?—and this is my little daughter Eveline—as I was saying, Mrs. Leyland, I should not feel I had done my duty, imperfect as the state of my health is —for dear Dr. Chessick has warned me that any overexertion may cause the most serious damage to my constitution—if I had not made the effort to welcome you to London—"

Lydia, perceiving that Lady Pentony was one of those women whose inability to bring a sentence to a conclusion makes conversation with them a matter of choosing one's opening and dashing in, interposed here to beg the visitors to be seated and, leaving her grandmother to cope with Lady Pentony, herself inaugurated a conversation with the younger members of the party. Miss Pentony seemed very shy, and at first could scarcely be prevailed upon to say a word, but Mr. Michael Pentony, who had very easy manners, followed Lydia's lead in carrying on a civil conversation concerned chiefly with commonplaces until, in answer to an enquiry from him, she remarked that she liked London very much.

"But not more, evidently, than it likes you, Miss Leyland," he said then, with a smile which for some reason made her realise not only how even and white his teeth were, but also how pale were the blue eyes beneath his sandy brows, and how narrow and shrewd the face above his impeccably arranged neckcloth. "Even we—who live rather retired from Society—have already learned of your triumph last night at Lady Gilmour's ball."

"My triumph? Dear me, what an imposing word!" Lydia said coolly, her fine eyes narrowing slightly as she surveyed Mr. Pentony's smiling face. "I should not dream of using it myself! I wonder who can have been so extremely kind as to have exaggerated my small success to you so out of reason, Mr. Pentony?"

"Why, I cannot say that," he replied, with an archness that did nothing to recommend him to her. "It might expose him to your censure, even ridicule, and he has already—poor fellow!—become your slave."

Lydia saw that this speech caused Miss Pentony to colour up and look somewhat self-conscious, and had little difficulty in gathering that the news of what had occurred at Lady Gilmour's ball had actually probably been relayed to Lady Pentony by one of those elderly females whose pedigrees procured them the entrée into fashionable houses, and whose lack of means impelled them to repay invitations from socially aspiring hostesses by relaying to them tit-bits of the gossip they had gleaned in more exalted circles.

"Indeed!" she said, with an assumption of guileless pleasure. "Well, that makes it all quite plain then, for there is only *one* gentleman to whom your description can apply. I shall certainly make a point of it to tax him with running about gossiping to you in the most unwarranted manner of my poor little success!"

Mr. Pentony looked somewhat disconcerted. "No, no!" he said quickly. "I am sure you cannot know—No doubt you are thinking of the wrong person!"

"Oh, I do not think so!" Lydia said, favouring him with a brilliant smile, and then, satisfied that he would think twice before he engaged to impose upon her again with such an obvious fiction, turned her attention to Miss Pentony.

A persevering effort succeeded in drawing a sufficient amount of conversation from that damsel to inform Lydia that she was cast in quite a different mould than her brother. *He* appeared to be keenly determined to put himself forward in the fashionable world, and evidently possessed a degree of intelligence sufficient to guarantee him some success in this, while *her* nature seemed to be one of rather insipid sweetness. Her brother, Lydia saw, held her somewhat in contempt and, when he perceived that Lydia was determined to draw her into the conversation, abandoned his own part in it to devote himself instead to Mrs. Leyland.

His attempts to ingratiate himself with her were far more successful than they had been with Lydia, for on the visitors' departure Mrs. Leyland pronounced him to be a delightful young man, and added that, upon her mentioning that she had a great desire to see Richmond Park again, he had very kindly offered to drive her there—together with Lydia and Bayard, if they cared to join the party—on the Monday of the following week.

"Of course I engaged that you would be very happy to go, my love," Mrs. Leyland said to Lydia, "and I daresay we may count upon Bayard as well. Mr. Pentony will bring his sister with him, he says, but *not* his mother, as her health does not permit her to indulge in excursions of such length. For which, my dear, I cannot but be grateful, for a more disagreeable conversationalist I have never met! Chatter, chatter, chatter—and all in that die-away tone, as if she were preparing to expire before your very eyes! It is no wonder to me that Sir Basil cannot endure her! However, young Mr. Pentony is quite a different matter, and it does not in the least surprise me that Sir Basil intends to make him his heir."

Lydia frowned. "Did *he* tell you that?" she demanded.

"Oh dear, no!" Mrs. Leyland said. "But I gathered, from what Lady Pentony let fall—"

"I am quite sure that what she 'let fall' was perfectly calculated to make you believe a great deal that has not an iota of foundation in fact!" Lydia said. "She is not such a widgeon as she appears, I think—and if she did not decide of her own accord to come here to discourage us from any attempt to make Sir Basil's acquaintance by giving us to understand that he has already decided to make Michael Pentony his heir, I am sure her son took care to put the idea into her head. Scheming is something quite in his line, I should imagine!"

Mrs. Leyland looked startled and not best pleased. "My dear, you are too severe!" she said. "I will admit that it is the most vexatious thing in the world that Sir Basil's fortune will go the Pentonys instead of to us, but it is to be expected, after all—"

"Only if we are poor-spirited enough to allow it to happen," Lydia said resolutely, "and that I do *not* intend to be! Only think how Bayard's position would change, Grandmama, if it were known that *he* was to be Sir Basil's heir! He has not the slightest hope of marrying Miss Beaudoin otherwise, I am sure."

"Marry? Miss Beaudoin?" Mrs. Leyland said faintly. "Dear child, what in the world are you talking of? He has only just met the girl!"

"Oh yes, I know that! But I know Bayard as well, and I am certain that this is no ordinary affair with him." She knit her brows thoughtfully. "I shall write to Mr. Peeke today and enquire of him about the state of Sir Basil's health," she declared. "If it is at all improved, I believe we should call upon him at once."

Mrs. Leyland shrugged. "Very well, my dear—but I fear it will be of no manner of use. I have never met the man myself, for Letty did not marry him until after I had left England, but from everything I have heard of him he is excessively set in his ways, and it scarcely seems likely that, after all these years, he will turn against young Mr. Pentony if he has indeed settled it in his mind that he is to inherit his fortune."

"According to Mr. Peeke, he has not at all settled it so," Lydia retorted. "And if he has the least discernment, there will be no question in his mind, once he has seen Bayard, which of the two to favour." She jumped up and implanted a hasty kiss upon the top of her grandmother's head. "At any rate, we must certainly make a push to bring him to realise what a lamb Bayard is," she said. "Dear Grandmama, I shall *just* have time to scribble a note to Mr. Peeke, and then we must positively order out the barouche and go for a shopping excursion in Bond Street. I have exactly the bonnet in mind to wear when we call upon Sir Basil—blue, I think, with just a touch of demureness but decidedly *à la mode*. And one of those dispiriting little shawls with fringe on it, that make one look *quite* fragile and helpless—"

"Baggage!" said Mrs. Leyland.

"Not at all!" said Miss Leyland. "I have the best of intentions: I only wish to help Bayard with my great-uncle. And Mr. Michael Pentony shall most definitely learn that *he* is not the only person who can scheme!"

8 Whatever Lydia's ideas might be concerning the attire suitable to be worn by a young lady paying a first call upon an elderly relation, there was certainly nothing either demure or dispiriting about the costume she donned for her drive in the Park with Sir Carsbie Chant the following afternoon. She wore an extremely dashing promenade dress of coral craped muslin, with gathered sleeves and a high arched collar, which drew an immediate look of approval from her brother when he returned to Green Street shortly before five o'clock to find her just coming down the stairs. When he learned what the engagement was for which she had so adorned herself, however, his air of approbation vanished.

"Good God, you aren't going for a drive with *that* man-milliner!" he exclaimed, with a brotherly lack of tact.

"Oh, but I am!" Lydia retorted. "What is more, I shall enjoy every minute of it, for I have been assured on the highest authority that that absurd creature is one of the chief arbiters of London fashion and fabulously sought after! I shall be the envy of every young lady—*and* her mama—who claps eyes on me in his company."

Bayard shrugged derisively. "Well, I hope you may be, for I can think of nothing else that will make up to you for having to spend an hour with such a dead bore as he is!" he said. "He's a popinjay, you know."

She gave an appreciative gurgle of laughter.

"Oh, the Prince of Popinjays," she agreed cordially. "But beggars can't be choosers, you know, and in spite of Great-aunt Letty's bequest I fancy we are very close to fitting that description—even though Grandmama *has* taken it into her head, after her run of luck at Lady Gilmour's party, that she is about to make all our fortunes at the card-table." She added, "If you really *do* wish to do something to make my day a little brighter, you will instantly decide to ride in the Park yourself this afternoon, and manage to bring me someone to talk to who has more to offer in the way of conversation than tales of his own self-consequence. All the world will be there at this hour, you know. Perhaps you may even see Miss Beaudoin."

The arrival of Sir Carsbie put an end to their conversation at that moment, but Lydia was scarcely surprised some half hour later, as she sat bowling sedately along in the Park in Sir Carsbie's yellow-winged phaeton, to find her brother cantering toward them on the raking bay mare he had purchased at Tattersall's a few days before. He was about to spur the mare forward to come up with them, she saw, when his attention was evidently attracted by some object of far greater interest to him. Turning her head, she beheld an elegant barouche a short distance behind her, in which Miss Beaudoin, Lord Harlbury, and the latter's mother were seated. Lydia at once exclaimed, somewhat startling her escort, "Oh, Sir Carsbie, do pull up your horses for a moment! Here is someone I must speak to!"

She was already signalling for Harlbury's attention, and had the satisfaction of seeing that gentleman give an order to his coachman that brought the two carriages to a halt just abreast of each other. True, the expression upon his face did not indicate any overwhelming delight at this unexpected meeting, but rather the sort of wariness with which a man approaches an object he believes may possibly be capable of some disconcerting action directed against his dignity. Lydia read it very accurately, as the hint of laughter in her eyes betrayed, but she kept her countenance commendably and merely said, with a dazzling smile directed towards her hapless victim, "Oh, my lord, I am so very glad to have had the good fortune to meet you today! You *did* promise—did you not?—that you would bring me the pamphlet on crossbreeding that we were discussing the other evening? I shall be at home all the morning tomorrow expecting you! Have you met my brother Bayard? Lord Harlbury—"

Bayard, who had moved his mare forward at the words, reached down his hand to take his lordship's civilly extended one; but his eyes, Lydia saw, had gone swiftly to meet Miss Beaudoin's. Nor did it escape her attention that that damsel's lovely little face had coloured up rosily beneath the enchanting Lavinia chip hat that crowned her dark locks, or that the eyes she turned to meet Bayard's wore an expression so worshipful that it must have drawn the notice of anyone not entirely absorbed in his own emotions.

Fortunately, that description exactly suited everyone else in the group. Sir Carsbie, as usual, was wholly occupied with the effect his dress and equipage were making upon the company; Lord Harlbury was mustering up his resolution to present Miss Leyland and her brother to his obviously unreceptive parent; and the parent herself, having received the friendliest of smiles from Lydia, was preparing a frigid rebuff for her.

Unfortunately for her intentions, the guns of her opening attack—the merest inclination of her bonneted head as her son pronounced Miss Leyland's name—were immediately spiked by that young lady's remarking sunnily to Lord Harlbury, "Indeed, I need no introduction to your mother, my lord! Your very striking resemblance to her must inform every-one what the relationship between you is."

As it had long been a sore point with Lady Harlbury that her son—an Adonis by any standard—was universally held to resemble his late father, and to owe nothing of his good looks to her, the delicacy of this compli-ment was as gratifying to her as it was astonishing. She cast a somewhat suspicious glance at Lydia, but, finding nothing in that accomplished young lady's countenance to suggest that she was *cutting a wheedle*, de-cided to accept her words at their face value and therefore inclined her head a second time, in a rather more gracious manner.

"As to that, Miss Leyland," she conceded majestically, "I believe he *may* be said to have my nose."

"Not a doubt of it!" said Lydia, regarding without a blink her ladyship's decidedly pug nose, which bore not the slightest resemblance to the classi-cal feature adorning her son's face. "Dear Lady Harlbury, I quite *knew*, the moment I saw how greatly you resembled your son, that I should find in you a sympathetic spirit! *You*, I am persuaded, must share his attach-ment to country life—which to one like myself, reared in rural surround-ings and quite lost in the bustle of a great, noisy town like London, must be of all things most refreshing!"

Lady Harlbury, who, in spite of her pompous manners, was no fool, cast a second rather sharply suspicious glance at Lydia. "You do not care for London, Miss Leyland?" she enquired. "It surprises me to hear that. *I* should have said that you were enjoying yourself excessively at Lady Gil-mour's ball the other evening."

"Oh, do you really think so?" Lydia asked cordially. "I am very glad to hear you say so, for it was excessively kind of Lady Gilmour to invite us, and I would not for the world have appeared ungrateful! But I have been used for so long, you see, to living quite retired in the country that I doubt if I shall ever come to care for town life as other young females are said to do."

She flicked a brief glance across the barouche to see that Bayard, who had contrived to bring his mare around into an advantageous position for a conversation with Miss Beaudoin, was in earnest colloquy with her, and hastened to continue the conversation, drawing first Lord Harlbury and then Sir Carsbie into it so that no notice should be taken by the other oc-cupants of the barouche of the fact that Miss Beaudoin and Bayard were pointedly occupied otherwise.

It was Sir Carsbie, in fact, who first discovered that a tête-à-tête was going on under their noses. He gave a waspish titter that drew Lady Harlbury's attention to the situation as well, and her formidable disapproval immediately fell upon the two guilty participants. She sent Bayard an annihilating glance, put an end to Lydia's persevering chatter with the curtest of adieux, and ordered the coachman to drive on by the simple expedient of prodding the tip of her parasol into the small of his back.

Lydia, blinking as the barouche swept past, looked up at Bayard, a gleam of laughter in her eyes.

"*Definitely* unloving," she pronounced. "Do you have the feeling that we were both *de trop,* Bayard my own?"

But Bayard, who seemed in no mood for frivolous conversation, only gave her a brief, rather forced smile and cantered off, leaving her to Sir Carsbie's quizzing.

"You are well acquainted with Lord Harlbury, Miss Leyland?" Sir Carsbie enquired, not, it appeared, best pleased by this supposition.

"Oh dear, no! I met him for the first time only the other night," Lydia replied, composedly unfurling a very fashionable sunshade and raising it above her head.

"Indeed?" said Sir Carsbie, with rather peevish archness. "I gathered, from the freedom of your tone with him—the manner in which you requested him to call—"

"Shall we say '*commanded* him to call'?" Lydia said, on a ripple of laughter. "Dear Sir Carsbie, I believe you are jealous! Shall I command *you* to call upon me—even though I met you, too, for the first time only the other night?"

"I shall be delighted," Sir Carsbie said, unbending a trifle at her flirtatious tone, and glancing about him to make certain that the world was aware he was dallying fashionably with the attractive young lady seated beside him. "Shall I bring you a bouquet as well, Miss Leyland?"

"Oh, by all means! I wish you will do everything in your power to bring me into fashion, Sir Carsbie, and I am sure that if you do so I shall soon achieve my ambition to become the rage of London. *Your* approval, I am told, is all that is necessary for that."

Sir Carsbie, with somewhat half-hearted modesty, attempted to deny this, but, upon Lydia's desiring him not to talk flummery to her, admitted that his taking her up might be the only thing wanted to make her a success in the *haut ton.*

"I may say that even the Prince Regent relies greatly upon my judgement in such matters," he observed, with natural pride. "'Carsbie,' he has frequently said to me, 'would you call Miss Blank a Beauty or would you not?'—depending upon me, you see, to make those nice distinctions in regard to eyes, nose, teeth, complexion, figure, et cetera, that are so important in such matters."

Lydia, who had rather the feeling of being a prime bit of horseflesh paraded for sale as Sir Carsbie's eyes patently surveyed her own qualifications in each regard while he spoke, bit her lip but, deciding that being brought into fashion demanded its sacrifices, managed to return a light answer. However, her face, as she entered the front door of the house in Green Street a half hour later, bore an expression of such distaste that Bayard, who had apparently come in only a few moments before and was still in the hall, making some enquiry of Sidwell, cocked a questioning eyebrow at her.

"Why, what is it, Lyddy?"

"Oh—nothing at all!" She shrugged, and walked across the hall rapidly to take his arm. "Come with me a moment; I want to talk to you," she said, drawing him toward the small morning-parlour at the back of the house.

He followed her, and she closed the door behind them.

"What is it?" he asked again.

She looked at him, seeing an expression on his face which she—who thought she had been acquainted with all his moods—had never observed there before. He looked resolute, unhappy, and a little desperate, and before she could reply to his question he forestalled her by saying quickly, "No—wait! There is something I must tell you first. I—talked with Miss Beaudoin today—"

"Are you in love with her, Bayard?" Lydia asked directly, as he halted, apparently undecided how to continue.

He threw her a grateful glance. "Yes!" he said. "I thought you must have guessed. How could any man not be—? Is she not an angel? But, Lyddy, it is true, what Northover said! She is being pressed to marry Harlbury; he has not spoken to her yet, but she is sure that everything now hangs only upon her consent."

In spite of herself, Lydia's lips curved in a smile. "You managed to get all that from her this afternoon with the Dowager seated just beside her?" she said. "Good God, I had not realised you could be so adroit!"

Bayard shrugged, but did not respond to the playfulness in her voice.

"Of course it was impossible for her to talk freely," he said, "but a word —a glance—I should have been an idiot if I had not been able to gather the whole situation from what she let fall!" He took a hasty, restless turn about the room. "But it must not be—it *shall* not be, if anything *I* can do can prevent it!" he said, with subdued energy. "If only I were not so new in the country—if I had had time to settle myself in some way, so that I might support a wife!"

Lydia, who had seated herself quietly in a chair beside the table, looked at him keenly and gravely, as serious now as he was himself.

"So it has come to that already!" she said. "I thought as much! But, do you know, it seems quite incredible to me, Bayard—like something one finds in books, but never in real life. Can you really have fallen so much in love with her already—and she with you?"

"Yes!" Bayard said. "That is—of course I can't speak for her, but I believe—I hope—" He sat down suddenly in a chair near hers, sinking his head in his hands. "But, oh God! it is of no use to talk of it!" he said miserably. "I have no fortune, no prospects; Lady Gilmour will never consent to her marrying me! I am a scoundrel even to think of such a thing until I have the means to support her respectably—and how I am to come by them I have not the least idea!"

"Perhaps if you could purchase your commission in a good cavalry regiment—"

He raised his head, giving a shaky little laugh. "Even with that, do you seriously think an offer from me would weigh against one from Harlbury, in Lady Gilmour's eyes? And I have no prospects of being able to do even that."

"Sir Basil—?" Lydia said tentatively. "After all, you do not *know* that he will not make you his heir."

"God, that *is* a forlorn hope!"

"Perhaps." Lydia put up her chin. "We shall see. I did not tell you, I believe, that I sent round a note to Mr. Peeke yesterday, and he says we may call upon Sir Basil on Monday morning." He shook his head unhopefully, and she went on, trying for a lighter note, "At any rate, it may be that we shall do very well without him. Have you forgotten why we came to London? If *I*, instead of Miss Beaudoin, should be fortunate enough to receive an offer from Lord Harlbury—"

Bayard looked up quickly. "You? You do not tell me that *you* have fallen in love with *him?*" he asked incredulously.

"Heavens, no! I seriously doubt that I know what the term means—not as *you* would use it, at any rate. As you well know, I have not had a *tendre* for a man since I was nine years old and tumbled head-over-ears in love with the Esterlys' coachman—and *that* was only his elegant livery, for the moment I saw him out of it, all my affection for him vanished." She had the satisfaction of seeing a faint smile appear on her brother's face and went on, with a gaiety which even she, however, felt was rather forced, "At any rate, Harlbury is certainly all that is amiable—and rich, handsome, and an earl as well—and if I can draw him off from your Minna, why should I not do so, and even marry him if I like? And then he shall do something very handsome for you, and you may marry Minna after all, and we shall all four be as happy as grigs—"

Bayard looked at her searchingly, his face rather pale. "Lyddy, that is horrible!" he said quickly. "Why should I have *my* happiness at the expense of yours?"

"At the expense of mine? Why, what a high flight, my dear! Why should I *not* be happy, married to a rich, amiable, titled Adonis?"

"If you do not love him—"

"Fiddle! I shall love him well enough for all practical purposes. I am not at all like you, you know, in spite of Grandmama's insisting that the two of us were cut from the same cloth; and if I have reached the age of twenty without once tumbling seriously into love, it does not seem likely that I shall ever do so." She could not prevent a somewhat wistful note from creeping into her voice as she spoke the words, but she threw off the mood in a moment and continued more brightly, "At any rate, don't fall into the mopes, I beg you! I promise you, we shall come about! If Miss Beaudoin has as great a fondness for you as you have for her, Harlbury will never succeed in bringing her to the point of accepting an offer from him, for he is *not* an impetuous lover, I am sure. On the contrary, I daresay he will have to be prodded into matrimony."

Bayard could not help smiling at the mischievous look with which she pronounced these last words, and, as she rose, got up too, slipped his arm about her, and gave her a brotherly hug.

"I expect I should forbid you to meddle in the affair at all, for you are sure to land yourself in the suds, one way or another," he said ruefully. "But, to tell you the truth, I am too much in need of help from any quarter to do that. But you *will* promise me, Lyddy, that you won't do something completely bird-witted only to save my groats?"

"I shall be the soul of discretion," Lydia said virtuously. "Am I not always?"

"No! And, by the bye, what was it *you* wanted to speak to *me* about? I had almost forgotten, in worrying you over *my* affairs."

She laughed. "We had the same thing in mind—as we so often do! My own affairs are prospering splendidly, thank you—Harlbury has promised to call, and the Prince of Popinjays needed no prodding whatever to invite me to drive out with him to see the flowers in the Botanical Gardens."

"Lyddy! You are *not* to encourage *that* countercoxcomb! I draw the line there!"

She gave his hand a pat, slipping from under his arm and running into the hall before he could restrain her.

"Can you not fancy me as the Popinjay Princess?" she called back provocatively over her shoulder—almost colliding as she did so with Winch, who, halting her, enquired in minatory tones whether or not she intended to come upstairs and sit still long enough to allow her to do her hair before dinner.

9 Monday morning found the Leyland barouche arriving in Russell Square, where Sir Basil Rowthorn had his town-house, at an hour which Mr. Peeke had signified would be convenient for a call upon his client. The Square, which had been built on the former site of Bedford House since Mrs. Leyland's departure for America, was unhesitatingly characterised by that lady as fit only for the Cits and mushrooms who dwelt in its massive brick edifices, but Bayard and Lydia, unacquainted with the nicer points of London geography, felt that it was all very fine.

Nor were they disappointed with the interior of Sir Basil's house, when the front door was opened to them by a very proper butler: everything, from carpets to chandeliers, seemed in the richest style. They had little time to look about them, however, for, as it appeared that they were expected (that would be Mr. Peeke, Lydia thought appreciatively), they were ushered upstairs at once to a large saloon where, in a corner beside one of the tall windows overlooking the square, an elderly gentleman sat with a gouty leg propped upon a footstool.

It was a warm, bright June morning, but there was a fire in the grate and a shawl about Sir Basil's shoulders. At first glance, Lydia would have taken him for a much younger man than the eighty years with which Mr. Peeke and her grandmother had endowed him, for the rim of hair encircling his almost bald head was still black, and there was an expression of active malevolence on his rather pinched features which age might have been expected to soften. He looked the three callers up and down without a word of greeting, and then motioned them to be seated as cavalierly as if they had been menials whom he was about to interview for some minor post in his household.

This was too much for Mrs. Leyland. She threw back her head, regarding him with a majestic stare, and said bluntly, "My dear sir, if you do not intend to be civil, we are wasting our time. Lydia—Bayard—come, my dears, we shall not stay. I had had the intention," she added acidly, to Sir Basil, "of offering you condolences on the demise of my poor sister, but I see now that it is Letty to whom condolences should have been offered, while she was yet alive—"

"You're Erminia, I suppose," Sir Basil said, opening his lips at last and interrupting her without ceremony. "You don't favour her, but that girl does." He pointed the handsome gold-headed stick that stood beside his chair in Lydia's direction and said to her, "Come over here and let me have a look at you. What's your name?"

"Lydia, sir," said Lydia, casting an irrepressibly mirthful glance at her grandmother, but at once composing her countenance and walking across the room to stand demurely before Sir Basil's chair.

His sharp eyes looked her up and down, the result of his scrutiny being a sardonic, "Humph!" He added, "You're a flighty baggage, I make no doubt. Letty to the life! Well, what d'ye want of me—eh?"

"Dear Uncle Basil," Lydia said, looking him straight in the face, "if I told you it was merely to make your acquaintance, you would not believe me—would you? After all, it would be too totally eccentric of us not to be in the least interested in your fortune!"

Sir Basil, taken unawares by this devastating frankness, emitted another—"Humph!"—this one in a somewhat startled tone. He made a quick recover, however, and remarked grudgingly that at least he was glad to see she was not one to use roundaboutation.

"Not," he added, "that that'll do you any good when it's a matter of loosening *my* purse-strings. I'm not such a maw-worm as to be taken in by a pretty face and wheedling manners."

"No, I should rather think you are not," Lydia agreed, continuing to survey him with an interested air. "You are not at all as I imagined you— but then I daresay that is for the best, for I do not feel in the least in the mood to play the Dutiful Niece today, in spite of this bonnet, which I purchased *particularly* for the purpose."

"Your bonnet? What's a bonnet to say to anything?" Sir Basil demanded, looking irritated and somewhat bewildered. "You *are* like Letty; there was never any sense to be made of her talk, either."

However, he relented sufficiently to invite the party to sit down, and, ringing a hand-bell that stood on the table beside him, to order the butler who responded to its summons to bring some refreshment for them. He then turned his attention to Bayard, enquiring ungraciously if he was another such skitterbrain as his sister.

Bayard gave him his lazy, good-humoured smile. "As to that, sir," he said, "I should consider it an honour to be bracketed with Lydia, but I fear I am not in her class."

"No, I should think not," Sir Basil said, regarding him keenly. "You don't look to want sense, but *she's* the needle-witted one of the pair of you, if I'm any judge of the matter. Nothing like that simpering, milk-and-water Pentony chit."

"Oh, as to that," Lydia remarked composedly, "I should think Mr. Michael Pentony's wits were quite sharp enough for all *that* family!"

He swung round to her. "You've met 'em, then—have you?" he asked. "How did that come about?"

"Why, they called upon us the other day," Lydia said, "for the purpose, I should imagine, of discovering how much of a threat we should be to their hopes of inheriting your fortune, sir—though, according to Lady Pentony," she added pensively, "you have already quite made up your mind that her son is to be your heir."

"That woman!" said Sir Basil, in tones of strong loathing. "If I thought Michael was fool enough to let *her* get her hands on any of my money, he'd never see a groat of it. But he's a neat article, Michael," he added, with satisfaction—"as shrewd as he can hold together. It's not likely anybody will be able to cozen *him* out of anything, once he has it in his grasp."

"Dear me!" Lydia said. "That *does* rather sound as if we were wasting our time here, doesn't it?"

"Nothing of the sort! Don't run to conclusions!" Sir Basil snapped. "I don't say, if I wanted a man to manage my affairs, I might not engage Michael to do it. The point is, that ain't what I want. Damme, I've never been beaten on any suit but one: I've got a knighthood; I've got enough brass to buy and sell half the fine gentlemen in the kingdom; I even married one of their daughters—but I never was taken to their bosom, so to speak." He gave a sudden, quite unexpected crack of laughter. "Well, I ain't done yet, by a long chalk!" he said. "Pentony-Rowthorn or Leyland-Rowthorn—it's all one to me, but I've a fancy to see Rowthorns in the *haut ton,* or whatever they call it these days, and, by Jupiter, I shall do it yet!"

Mrs. Leyland stared at him. "Do you mean to tell me," she demanded, "that you will make the bequest of your fortune contingent upon your heir's adding your name to his own?"

"Yes, I do," he said promptly. "What's amiss with that? Done all the time, ain't it?"

Mrs. Leyland acknowledged that it was, but seemed inclined to make objections. Lydia, however, gave her no opportunity to utter them.

"Why, of course!" she said cordially. "What a splendid idea! But I must say that in that case you have no choice in the matter: you *must* decide upon Bayard, for no one can imagine that Michael Pentony is capable of establishing himself in the first circles."

"And what do *you* know about that, miss," Sir Basil interrupted her sarcastically, "when you've only just arrived from America? *You* hadn't the wit, it seems, not to make yourself the talk of the town at a *ton* party t'other night—"

"That is quite true," Lydia said, with aplomb, "but I doubt that it was a party to which Mr. Pentony could have received an invitation. I know it is excessively vulgar to boast of such things, but did your informant tell you as well, dear sir, that Sir Carsbie Chant has twice driven me out in his phaeton this past week, that we have received invitations to Lady Forward's Venetian breakfast and Lady Micall's cotillion-ball, and that Lord Northover will be kind enough to put Bayard's name up for membership at White's?"

Sir Basil surveyed her with an interested frown, failing to observe that the last portion of her statement had drawn a start of surprise from Bayard.

"No, he didn't," Sir Basil acknowledged.

"What is more," continued Lydia superbly, "Lady Aimer has every expectation of being able to procure vouchers for me for Almack's, where I doubt very much that I shall meet either Mr. or Miss Pentony—"

The arrival of the butler with a tray of refreshments interrupted the conversation at this point. Lydia noted that these provisions were laid on with a lavish hand, and that the silver tray upon which they were borne was of a baronial size and opulence: evidently Sir Basil's eccentricities did not prevent him from maintaining a style of living quite in keeping with the first circles to which he aspired.

He did not press them to stay, however, once the cakes and sherry had been consumed, nor did he invite them to return for a second visit when they rose to take their departure.

"I shall keep myself informed as to how you go on without the need to hear from any of you," he said bluntly. "And if I want to see you, I'll send for you."

"Thank you!" said Mrs. Leyland, witheringly. "If we should happen to be at leisure, we shall certainly come! Lydia—Bayard—"

She swept them out of the room with her, giving it as her opinion, as soon as the front door had closed behind them, that her brother-in-law was certainly mad, and that, at any rate, there was not the least use in their placing any dependance upon his leaving a penny to them.

But to this Lydia would not agree.

"He was quite taken with us, *I* believe," she said optimistically, bringing a smile to Bayard's face as he informed her that it was not generally considered the most suitable way to put yourself into a wealthy relation's good graces to confess candidly that you were interested only in his fortune.

"Well, he must be a perfect cabbagehead if he believes that is not the Pentonys' chief object as well," Lydia said, "and, whatever else he is, he is not *that*. I am rather sorry for him, poor lamb, for I daresay it is horridly uncomfortable to be in the gout, to say nothing of having suffered such a *disgruntling* disappointment as to have been snubbed by the *ton*, when he so much wishes to become one of its ornaments. I wonder if it would satisfy him if I named my first-born for him when I marry? *Rowthorn Chant* —or *Rowthorn*—what is Harlbury's family name? Do you know?"

"I haven't the least idea," Bayard said, "and if you are thinking of having a first-born by Sir Carsbie Chant, I warn you that you will have me to deal with! I refuse to stand uncle to any of *his* brats."

This made Lydia laugh, and Mrs. Leyland frown at such unbecoming language, and the subject of Sir Basil and his foibles was thereupon dropped.

Upon returning to Green Street, they learned that Lady Aimer had called in their absence, and, finding them out, had left a note apprising them that Lady Sefton had agreed to grant the much-desired vouchers for Almack's. Lydia, delighted, at once claimed Bayard's escort to the Assembly Rooms for the very next subscription ball, and was beginning to plan her toilette in detail when Bayard, recalled by the incident to a remembrance of his sister's somewhat vainglorious vaunting of future triumphs to Sir Basil, interrupted to say, "Well, your luck has been in this time, Lyddy; I'll grant you that. But what the deuce were you thinking of when you told Sir Basil that Northover intended to put me up for membership at White's? He has said nothing at all to me of any such intention, and I certainly shan't ask it of him."

"Well, you need not ask him," Lydia said placidly. "I shall do so myself."

Bayard frowned slightly. "I wish you will not," he said. "He has already shown us civility quite beyond anything we deserve from him, and—and it will not do, you know, for you to put yourself under any particular obligation to him."

Lydia turned to stare at him. "And why not, pray?" she enquired. "Surely *you* are not going to warn me, as Lady Aimer did, of his shocking reputation! I assure you, he has no designs upon me."

"Much *you* know about it!" Bayard retorted, galled by her assumption of superior knowledge. "I don't wish to say anything to his discredit, for he's been devilish kind to me, but—but a man of his cut don't put himself out for a chit like you out of the pure goodness of his heart, you know! Oh, I daresay he's not such a rake-shame as to try to give you a slip on the shoulder now, but if you want my opinion, he'll do his possible to see you riveted to some clothhead like Chant, and then hope to enter into a little game *à trois* that will admirably suit his convenience."

"Bayard!" interrupted Mrs. Leyland, who had been a scandalised auditor of this conversation. "You will immediately cease using such improper language to your sister! If you have reason to believe that Lord Northover is guilty of designs upon her virtue, *I* am the person to whom you should confide such thoughts."

Lydia laughed. "Good heavens, I don't know which of you is the more absurd!" she said. "Northover, I daresay, hasn't an idea in the world beyond amusing himself by seeing how far we can rise in the fashionable world with nothing but our wits to aid us—" She broke off, finding that, for some unaccountable reason, this explanation of his lordship's behaviour was no more satisfactory to her than it appeared to be to Bayard, and went on after a moment, rather shortly, "At any hand, I am not in the least afraid of anything he may do. And if he is amusing himself at our expense, that is all the more reason why he should pay for his entertainment. I shall certainly ask him to put your name up at White's when next I see him, and if he will not do so I shall ask Harlbury—"

"Harlbury!" said Bayard, aghast. "Lyddy, you wouldn't! Good God, I have only just met him!"

"I am considering," said Lydia, a somewhat martial light in her eye, "making him your brother-in-law, so that need not signify. And I am sure *his* principles are far too high to allow *him* to wink at any such arrangement as you have described as being in Lord Northover's mind."

Upon which scathing statement she swept out of the room, leaving Mrs. Leyland and Bayard to gaze at each other in speechless dismay behind her.

The Pentonys arrived in Green Street not long afterward, at the hour appointed for the Richmond Park excursion, in a smart barouche which Lydia—in spite of the derogatory terms in which she had referred to their pretensions of fashion before Sir Basil—privately acknowledged she need feel no qualms about stepping into. Bayard, who had been persuaded to join the party, elected to ride beside the barouche on his bay mare, and, as his good manners led him to direct his conversation chiefly to Miss Pentony, while Mr. Pentony devoted himself to satisfying Mrs. Leyland's curiosity concerning the many alterations that had taken place in the countryside during the years of her absence in America, the drive passed in a generally agreeable manner.

Even Lydia, who was not disposed to be prejudiced in the Pentonys' favour, was obliged to admit that Eveline was a very pretty girl, and that Mr. Michael Pentony's conversation showed that he was deficient neither in understanding nor in address. Her grandmother, she saw, was even quite in the way to making him a favourite, in spite of the peculiar situation in which he and Bayard stood in regard to Sir Basil, for he had exactly that deferential manner and ready consideration for her comfort which an elderly lady must find irresistible in a young man.

It was a fine day, and when they had arrived at Richmond it was discovered that many other parties had been before them in driving out to admire the celebrated view of the Thames from the top of the hill and to enjoy a stroll upon the grass. As the Leylands had so small an acquaintance in London, it was not surprising that they met no one they knew, but Mr. Pentony, in addition to pointing out to them such well-known members of the *ton* as Lord Petersham and Lady Cowper—neither of whom, Lydia noted, did he venture to approach—came across a quietly but fashionably dressed middle-aged lady strolling in company with a younger and more dashing-looking couple, and halted to make her known to the Leylands as a friend of Lady Pentony's, a Mrs. Collingworth. She was persuaded to leave her own party and join theirs for a time, and Mr. Pentony, giving one arm to her and the other to Mrs. Leyland, walked on between the two older ladies, leaving Bayard to squire Miss Pentony and Lydia.

A quarter of an hour later, when the two groups came together again and Mrs. Collingworth made her adieux and returned to her own friends, Lydia learned that her grandmother had been sufficiently taken with her new acquaintance to agree to make one of a card-party she was giving at her house in Curzon Street the following evening. For herself, she would have been little inclined to seek further intimacy with anyone in the Pentonys' circle, but she could not direct her grandmother's conduct, and was obliged to attend with what complaisance she could to Mrs. Leyland's encomiums on the lady. She was, in fact, glad to escape from them when

Mr. Pentony, having seen Mrs. Leyland comfortably installed upon a green bench with Miss Pentony, offered her his arm so that they might continue their exploration of the park.

But in five minutes she would, if offered her choice, eagerly have returned to them, for Mr. Pentony, finding himself tête-à-tête with her, at once began attempting to ingratiate himself with her by the most persistent means in his power. She was the target of compliments, flattery, even hints of incipient devotion, delivered to the accompaniment of subtle pressures of the hand which she had unwarily allowed to be drawn beneath his arm—all this with the addition of a series of speaking glances, the meaning of which she could not fail to understand.

His conduct, in short, was such as would have driven most young females into pleasurable confusion; but Lydia was not an ordinary young female, and she was neither pleased nor confused.

"I don't believe you can have the least notion," she said composedly, after having allowed him to run on in this manner for a few minutes, "how very disagreeable it is, when one wants nothing but the support of a gentleman's arm in walking over uneven ground in absurdly thin sandals, to find oneself involved in an utterly *redundant* flirtation with him. Because if you had, I *do* rather feel that you would give over. You *must* be able to see that I am not at all in the mood."

Mr. Pentony looked considerably taken aback for a moment at this remarkably frank statement. But he made a quick recover and, smiling with a somewhat forced air, murmured something about his feelings no doubt causing him to act in too precipitate a manner.

"Your feelings!" Lydia said reproachfully. "Oh, come now, Mr. Pentony! I am *not* a moonling, you know!"

"No—certainly you are not!" Mr. Pentony said, his eyes narrowing slightly as he turned his head to look into her face. "Though why you should think it beyond the bounds of reason to imagine that a remarkably handsome young woman like yourself should attract admirers—"

"Oh, I do not think *that* is beyond the bounds of reason in the least," Lydia conceded promptly. "But in your case I am *not* a remarkably handsome young woman—or, at least, that is not all I am. I am that *malevolent* Lydia Leyland, who has turned up when she was least wanted to cast a rub in the way of your inheriting a fortune."

Mr. Pentony, though evidently unprepared for this direct attack, demonstrated his native shrewdness by accepting it at its face value and casting aside any further pretence that he was not as cognizant of the situation between them as was Miss Leyland herself. He gave her a slight smile and remarked calmly, "Well, I should not put it in that way, but, if you like, I will admit that the news of your and your brother's arrival in England—before I had become acquainted with you—*did* appear to give me some little cause for apprehension."

"And it does not do so now? Well, I should not be *too* certain of that, if I were you, for it is just possible that Sir Basil may not think quite so poorly of us as you appear to do!"

"I? Not in the least!" Mr. Pentony denied. He seemed quite at his ease, in spite of the rapid reversal of form into which he had been forced, and regarded her with what appeared to her to be the faintly smug air of a man who holds all the trump cards in his own hand. "I am aware, Miss Leyland, that you might be a very formidable opponent. I am also aware— as I believe you are not—that you might be an equally formidable ally."

He paused on the words, observing the suddenly arrested expression upon her face. Of course! she was thinking, castigating herself mentally for not having seen before this moment the glaringly obvious reason for his attentions to her. It would certainly be much to his advantage, in his efforts to bring Sir Basil to make him his heir, if he were to contract an alliance with some highly eligible damsel of the *haut ton*—but, failing that extremely unlikely event, what could do more to forward his claims, and at the same time cut the ground from under Bayard's feet, than marriage with Miss Lydia Leyland? *A neat article*, Sir Basil had called him, and certainly, thought Lydia, the phrase appeared to be justified.

She decided in the same instant, however, not to make things easier for Mr. Pentony by allowing him to see that she understood the meaning of his words, and merely parried them with an innocent—"Well, I do not at all know what that signifies. I only know that if Sir Basil *should* chance to take a liking to Bayard or me, it would go very much against the pluck with you."

"You know very well that he *has* taken a liking to you," Mr. Pentony said, as if he were uttering the merest commonplace—but the words brought her eyes to his face with a jerk.

"He has taken—?" she repeated. "Then you know already that we saw him this morning—?"

"Yes. I do know," Mr. Pentony said baldly. He looked down at her, the slight, self-assured smile again upon his narrow face. "Pray, Miss Leyland," he said softly, "credit me with the ability to be quite as formidable an opponent as you are, if you should choose to cross swords with me. Sir

Basil's fortune—as I am certain you know—is not a merely genteel one; it is truly a golden prize. Is it likely then, do you think, that I shall allow anyone to chouse me out of it because of my own negligence in not keeping careful account of everything that concerns it? You saw Sir Basil this morning; you charmed him into complaisance by your audacity, though your brother did little to aid you and your grandmother was a positive hindrance to you—"

Lydia interrupted him indignantly. "You must have bribed the servants, of course, since you know so much so quickly!"

He smiled again. "That will be difficult to prove—will it not?" he said lightly—"since it can hardly be expected that any of them will admit to such a charge, even if it is true. And I should not advise you," he said, as he observed the contempt flashing in her eyes, "to turn your brother and your grandmother against me by repeating such suspicions to them, Miss Leyland. It may make for awkwardness in the future, you see, if you should decide, after all, that you had rather be my ally than my opponent."

It was perhaps unfortunate for Mr. Pentony that he was not better acquainted with Miss Lydia Leyland. If he had been, he would have realised that, in dealing with her, the use of threats—no matter how politely veiled—was even less advisable than the use of cajolery. She made no comment now, but merely advised Mr. Pentony of her wish to return to the others, and when they did so no one would have gathered, from the serene expression upon her face, that she had anything more on her mind than enjoyment of the outing.

Mr. Pentony, driving back to town, might even have congratulated himself upon the success of his little *éclaircissement* with her; but if he did, it was no more than she desired him to do. It was always best, she had decided, to put one's enemy off his guard.

10 On the following Wednesday evening the Leyland barouche set Mrs. Leyland, her granddaughter, and her grandson down at Almack's Assembly Rooms well before eleven, after which hour the august Patronesses had decreed that no one should be admitted within its doors. Lydia, when they had been greeted by the Master of Ceremonies and had passed on into the ballroom, was somewhat surprised to find that the rooms, though elegant and spacious, were by no means magnificent, for she had heard so much of the awesome importance to a young female of admission to the club—known as the Matrimonial Mart among the irreverent—that she might have been pardoned for expecting something quite out of the common way.

The toilettes of the ladies, however, and the throng of fashionably tailored gentlemen surveying through supercilious quizzing-glasses the array of hopeful young beauties marshalled for their notice, quite equalled her anticipations; and she was glad that she herself had chosen to appear to her best advantage in a gown of primrose gauze, to which long white gloves, sandals of Denmark satin, and Italian filigree ear-drops added the final modish touches.

The first person to approach them as they entered the ball-room was Sir Carsbie Chant, who at once begged the honour of leading Lydia into the set of country dances that was just forming. She accepted the invitation, casting a droll glance at Bayard as she walked off with her exquisitely attired gallant that prompted the latter to enquire curiously as to its meaning. However, since she had already discovered that he had not the least sense of humour, she carefully refrained from giving him the slightest hint that it was he who had aroused her amusement, and led him instead into a discussion of the merits of a gentleman's coat, selected at random from the array before her. This was a subject that happily engaged his attention during the entire set, as he expatiated upon the rival merits of Nugee, Weston, and Stultz in cutting a coat and pointed out to her various examples of the art of each.

Her attention was thus left free to move about the ball-room, for Sir Carsbie required no more of an auditor than an occasional comment admiring his wide knowledge of his subject. She picked out Lord Harlbury at once, dancing with Miss Beaudoin—much to the satisfaction, it appeared, of Lady Gilmour, who had sacrificed her own enjoyment of the evening so far as to sit chatting with Lady Harlbury instead of standing up with one of her own many admirers. Lady Jersey, stunningly attired in blue silk and diamonds, also took her eye. And there was Northover presently, strolling in to chat with Lord Gilmour and a gentleman attired in the brilliant regimentals of the Dragoon Guards. His gaze raked her appreciatively and, as her eyes met his, he bowed slightly and smiled. She had the feeling that he had looked in at Almack's, which she knew was considered an excessively dull place by men of his stamp, only to appraise her success, or lack of it—a thought which at once put her upon her mettle.

Fortunately, she had no lack of partners. Such a remarkably pretty girl, new upon the London scene and already with the reputation of being very much out of the common way, could not fail to attract admirers, and for a time she was content to flaunt each new conquest under Northover's eyes —until it presently occurred to her, rather uncomfortably, that the quality of these admirers left something to be desired. Middle-aged dandies like Sir Carsbie Chant, who had been on the town for so long that matchmaking mamas had all but given up hope of their being caught in Parson's mousetrap, rackety young men interested only in an à suivie flirtation with the latest beauty—these were hardly the stuff of which brilliant marriages were made. She caught Northover's ironical eyes upon her as she went down the set with one of these latter, while he stood idly chatting with Lady Gilmour, and an ireful sparkle, boding no good for the Viscount when he did deign to approach her, appeared in her eyes.

She had reason to be grateful to him a few minutes later, however, when the musicians struck up a waltz. No gentleman, it appeared, rackety or not, was daring enough to invite her to stand up with him for that dance in this place, after what had occurred at Lady Gilmour's ball. She was left to sit fanning herself, like the other wallflowers, with what she hoped was an air of indifference, at the side of the room—until suddenly, hopefully, she saw Northover go up to Lady Jersey and say something to her. The next moment the two came across the room toward her.

"You are not dancing, Miss Leyland," Lady Jersey said, a sparkle of mischief in her eyes. "It is a pity to deprive us of so much talent and skill." Lydia had the grace to blush, and Lady Jersey continued, "Northover assures me that he is bold enough to stand up with you; perhaps you will favour him—?"

The Viscount's hand had already taken hers; he was drawing her to her feet, and the next instant his arm was lightly encircling her waist and he was guiding her out into the center of the floor.

"Poor Lydia!" she heard his mocking voice. "What a faint-hearted set of cavaliers you have, to be sure! Believe me, I have no wish to imperil your chances by making you the object of *my* gallantry, but it *did* appear to me that you were in need of someone to break the ice—even someone as ramshackle as myself."

"Don't crow!" she said, regaining her composure beneath this rather blighting speech and regarding him with some asperity. "I should have done very well without you, Northover. I should have contrived *something.*"

"Yes, I daresay you would have done," he agreed. "But tell me—how do you go on, Lydia *mia?* It is almost a week now since I have seen you, and I am disappointed to say that no tales of your activities have reached my ears—by which I gather that, for once in your life, you have been behaving with perfect propriety." She cast him a speaking glance and he laughed, continuing, "No new conquests to report? No proposals of marriage from eligible young men?"

"I have," she said with dignity, "received a—a *nibble* in that direction." He grinned. "Only a nibble? What, is he too timid to speak out?"

"No, he is not in the least timid—only cautious. It is Mr. Michael Pentony, Sir Basil Rowthorn's great-nephew," she confided, "and I rather *think* he believes it would be a brilliant stroke of policy to marry me, as he says Sir Basil has taken a fancy to me, and—well, you can see for yourself how it would favour his chances to inherit if he were to marry into the rival camp."

Northover digested this. "He didn't, I hope," he remarked after a moment, "make you a present of all this information? He must be a skip-brain, if he did!"

"Well, he did," she said. "And he is not a skip-brain in the least; in fact, I think it is far more probable that he is one of the tightish clever sort. But I daresay he saw, after I told him that I was not in the mood for a flirtation with him, that it would be as well for him to put his cards upon the table."

"And did that take the trick for him?"

She glanced up at him, continuing to respond effortlessly to each of his movements as he whirled her expertly around the floor.

"If you mean, will I marry him—of course not!" she said. "I have never met a man I more *totally* disliked!"

"Ah, but if he is to inherit old Rowthorn's fortune—! I thought you had decided that *that* was to be the criterion; and, after all, if it is a fortune you are after, you cannot afford to be too nice in your ideas, you know!"

She gave him a withering glance. "Is it quite natural for you to be such a complete adder, or do you have to try for it?" she enquired. "Besides, I shan't need to marry him to inherit Sir Basil's fortune—I mean, for Bayard to—well, you *know* what I mean! The only thing that seems to be quite devastatingly important to Sir Basil is that we have a great success in Society—which puts me in mind of something I wanted to ask you to do. Will you put Bayard up for membership at White's?"

"At White's? No, I will not," his lordship said promptly.

"You won't!" Lydia's brows drew together in a frown. "*Well!* I had not imagined you would be such a—such a—"

"You may spare the epithets, my dear; they'll gain you nothing," Northover said, with composure. "If you are so remarkably foolish as to wish me to introduce your young cub of a brother into circles that are quite above his touch, and that will be certain to lead him into extravagances that he can ill afford, I am not such a gudgeon as to gratify you."

Lydia did not appear mollified by this explanation. "I think it is *dastardly* of you," she said darkly—"especially since I have already told Sir Basil that you would do so!"

"That was *your* error, my dear. You may plume yourself on your conquests as much as you like, but don't make the mistake of taking them *too* much for granted."

"I don't consider *you* one of my conquests. If you care to know the truth, I practically abominate you—especially when you take that utterly *superior* tone with me!"

"Do I sound superior? That's *my* mistake," he said cheerfully. "What it is meant to be, my love, is merely the tone of one conscienceless adventurer recognising another—or should I say adventuress?"

"I am *not* an adventuress!" she said hotly. "If you had a family quite dependant upon you, you would understand that it is necessary for *me*, at least, to be prudent! There is Grandmama, for instance, who has suddenly taken what *she* thinks is the nacky notion that she is about to make all our fortunes at the card-table, and Bayard, who has fallen in love with the most unsuitable girl—"

"Yes, I want to talk to you about that," Northover said, abruptly becoming more serious as the music wound to a close. "I'll call in Green Street tomorrow—What is it?" he broke off to ask, as her fingers tightened in his and he felt her figure stiffen under his hand.

"Harlbury!" she exclaimed urgently. "Over there! *Could* you contrive it that we shall be just beside him when the music ends?"

"But why—?" he began, amused.

"Never mind! Just *do* it—pray!"

He obligingly turned their circling steps in the desired direction, bring-ing her up with a swirl of draperies immediately before Lord Harlbury, who had just entered the room from the refreshment saloon. His lordship found himself confronted by a vision in primrose gauze, who smiled at him guilelessly and exclaimed, "Lord Harlbury! Oh, how glad I am to see you again!" A shadow suddenly overspread the radiant face; the vision hesitated and then faltered, looking quite crushed, "Oh! I beg your par-don! I should not have said that! You—you haven't even called in Green Street, as you promised; I daresay I have been *much* too forward—"

"Not at all! Not in the least!" Harlbury denied, casting a harassed glance at Northover, an appreciative auditor of the scene. "I am delighted —that is, I should have been delighted to call—only I was unavoidably—"

"Oh, I *quite* understand!" Lydia said mournfully. "I daresay you had no intention of asking me to stand up with you this evening, either—so if Lord Northover will be good enough to take me back to my grand-mother—"

"No, no! Of course I should be honoured!" Harlbury stammered. "Pray allow me, Miss Leyland—"

Northover, with a wickedly quizzing glance at Lydia, made his excuses and strolled off, leaving Lydia to allow herself to be led into the set by Lord Harlbury. Having succeeded admirably in her intention to put him into such a position that he could not fail to dance with her, she was in a mood to be generous, and kindly drew his lordship out of the state of con-fusion in which she had placed him by leading him on to expatiate upon his favourite subject. Lord Harlbury, already inclined to be bewitched by the bewildering Miss Leyland, was at the end of a quarter hour thor-oughly convinced that he had never had a more delightfully attentive auditor, and became so totally engrossed in the pleasure of the dance and of his conversation with his partner that he quite failed to observe that his mama was sitting at the side of the room with an expression as dark as a thundercloud upon her face.

It was Lydia, in fact, who drew his attention to this.

"Your mama," she said pensively, "does not like me a great deal, I fear."

"Does not like—?" His lordship's eyes, following hers, flew across the room to his mother's martially erect figure. "Oh no, you are quite out there, Miss Leyland!" he said, uncomfortably. "Her manner is sometimes not quite—quite *complaisant,* but it means nothing at all, I assure you!"

"Truly? Oh, I am so very glad to have you tell me so," Lydia said, looking up meltingly into his eyes, "for I have a great favour to ask of you, and I was *so* afraid that your mama would say that you must on no account gratify me by doing it!"

"My mother say—?" Harlbury stiffened. "I do not take your meaning, Miss Leyland! Pray, what can my mother have to say to any request that you make of me?"

They were separated at that moment by the movement of the dance, and Lydia found herself sighing almost exasperatedly as she went down the set: really, this handsome young giant was such easy game that it scarcely seemed sporting to lure him into the trap. She much preferred dealing with Northover, who could be counted on to hold his own with her and even to take the trick if it suited him to do so, or with Michael Pentony, who, no matter how greatly she disliked him, was at least an opponent well worthy of her steel.

However, when she came together with Harlbury again there was no hint of these reflections in the appealing smile she gave him, or in the rather hesitant tones of her voice as she said to him, "Yes, but—but it is a very *large* favour, my lord, and I am sure she would think it quite dreadful of me even to broach it to you! Indeed, I should never dare to do so if I were not so certain that I can *utterly* depend upon your understanding and good nature."

The expression upon his lordship's face, as she paused, appeared to indicate that he found this preamble slightly alarming, but he stood his ground and gallantly assured her that she might certainly rely upon him for both.

"Oh!" said Lydia, quite overcome. "I *knew* I could do so! There is something—some sympathy between us—that made me quite sure—You see, I have felt it from the first moment I saw you!"

Lord Harlbury, who was obviously beginning to be aware of the fact that he was getting into very deep waters indeed, replied quite untruthfully, but with an air of conscious bravado implying, *In for a penny, in for a pound,* that he had felt something of the same nature himself.

"Have you, indeed! Oh, my lord!" Miss Leyland, an excellent actress, found that she was being carried quite away by her enthusiasm for her rôle, and managed such a lifelike portrayal of a young lady cast into the most agreeable confusion that Lord Harlbury felt impelled to press her hand reassuringly. This action appeared to give her courage to continue, and she went on bashfully, "But I must not presume, my lord! Your very kindness is reason enough for me not to place you in a situation in which you would feel obliged to—"

"Not at all!" said Harlbury, encouragingly. "Whatever it is, Miss Leyland, I pledge you my word that I shall do my utmost—"

"Oh, in that case—since you are so *very* kind—" Lydia lifted adoring deep-blue eyes to his. "*Would* you put my brother Bayard up for membership at White's?" she breathed.

Harlbury gazed down at her, looking blank. Whatever he had expected, it had certainly not been this, and for a moment he was too taken aback to utter a word. When he did recover his voice, it was to stammer, "Your—brother? Oh, of course! Quite! I met him the other day—didn't I?"

Lydia glanced down, overcome once more. "Oh, I *knew* I ought not to ask it of you! Are you *very* much vexed with me? Indeed you must not do it if it will inconvenience you in the slightest—"

"No, no!" Harlbury interrupted hastily. "You must not blame yourself, Miss Leyland! I am happy to be of service to you—"

"You *are!*" Lydia gave him an ecstatic glance. "Oh, I *do* think you must be the kindest person in the world! Do you know, I asked Lord Northover and he positively *refused* me?"

Harlbury looked grave. "Well, I should not make such a request of a man like Northover if I were in your place, Miss Leyland," he said. "I have nothing to say against him—good God, I hardly know him!—but gossip, you understand—"

"*I* never listen to gossip," Miss Leyland said virtuously, "and I am surprised to learn that *you* do, my lord. Lord Northover," she went on, giving a lofty stare to that gentleman, whom she observed to be propped against the opposite wall, observing her with an appearance of the greatest enjoyment, "is a very good sort of man in his way, I believe—though not in the least obliging when it does not suit him to be."

Having unburdened herself of this remark, which she only regretted had not been able to reach the Viscount's ears, she returned to her former sweetly complaisant tone, thanked her partner effusively for his kindness, and proceeded to enjoy the remainder of the dance—much to the ire of Lady Harlbury, who was obliged to sit for another quarter hour watching her son smiling down in besotted admiration at Miss Leyland, while Miss Beaudoin danced with Bayard.

It may be said that it had not escaped Lydia's observation, either, that, while she had snared Harlbury as a partner, Bayard had succeeded in persuading Minna Beaudoin to stand up with him. Lydia was aware, in fact,

that he had led no other young lady on to the floor during the course of
the evening, for each time her eyes had sought him out she had found
him standing in the same position at the side of the room, his eyes steadily
following Miss Beaudoin as she passed from one partner to another. Such
behaviour, she knew, could not go unnoticed; she had indeed surprised
more than one angry glance cast in his direction by Lady Gilmour, and, as
she passed into the refreshment saloon on the arm of a debonair young
baronet, Lady Aimer waylaid her for a moment to say to her bluntly, "I
wish you will speak to your brother, Lydia. He is making a great cake of
himself, standing there all the evening following my granddaughter with
his eyes like one of those nonsensical heroes in that fellow Byron's poems.
I have spoken to your grandmother, but she is in the card-room, so immersed in her game that I doubt she would attend if the ceiling dropped
upon her!"

Lydia smiled, and promised to let fall a word in Bayard's ear if the opportunity should present itself. She spoke carelessly, but she was actually
even more anxious than Lady Aimer, and quite vexed with Bayard for
having allowed his emotions to betray him into making himself conspicuous. Nothing, she knew, was to be gained by his making it plain to all
Miss Beaudoin's connexions that he was in desperate earnest in his attentions towards her; the next thing, she thought, would be that his Minna
would be forbidden to have any dealings with him whatever.

She was pondering this thorny matter as she sat in the refreshment saloon, waiting for her young baronet to return with a glass of lemonade for
her, when she became aware that someone had slipped into the seat beside
her. She turned; it was Miss Beaudoin.

"Oh, Miss Leyland," that young lady said, placing her hand upon her
arm and speaking in a rather tremulous voice, "please, may I speak to you
for a moment? Bayard—Mr. Leyland—said you would help us if you could
—and—and, indeed, I must talk to *someone* who is—who will—"

"Well, of course you may talk to me as much as you like!" Lydia said
bracingly, hoping that the obviously almost overwrought girl beside her
would not begin to cry under the gaze of the entire assembly. She was reassured, however, on looking into the delicately lovely little face, to see
that, although the cheeks were burningly flushed, the dark eyes were
quite steady and bright. She continued, "But this is hardly the place, is it?
Perhaps we might arrange—"

"Oh, yes!" Minna interrupted gratefully. "That is just what I was about
to beg you to do! But I dare not ask you to call upon me, or go to visit you

myself, for Mama would be sure to learn of it, and then everything would be in an even worse state than it is in now!"

"Then we must meet elsewhere—by accident, as it were," Lydia said promptly. "Do you often ride or walk in the Park?"

"Oh, yes!" Minna regarded her with respectful admiration. "Bayard said you were very resourceful; that will be the very thing! Mama will not think it at all odd if I go for a walk in the Park with Berky—she is my old governess, and will not breathe a word to anyone about my meeting you if I ask her not to."

Lydia, seeing her swain bearing down on her with cakes and lemonade, quickly concluded the matter by arranging to meet Miss Beaudoin at the Stanhope Gate at eight the following morning, an hour early enough to preclude the likelihood of their meeting's being observed by any of Lady Gilmour's friends, and Minna thereupon slipped away. Lydia saw her a few minutes later being supplied with a glass of orgeat by Lord Harlbury, and toyed for a moment with the idea of removing that earnest young peer from her side by a manoeuvre that would benefit both her own and Minna's cause.

She rejected it, however. An expert angler, she was aware, must allow his fish room to play at the end of his line or risk having his catch escape him, and she quite saw that, if she desired to bring Harlbury into her net at last, she must not be too precipitate in her pursuit.

She therefore allowed the remainder of the evening to pass without doing more than remarking wistfully, during a set of quadrilles in which they both found themselves, that she was still hopeful of receiving from his hands the interesting pamphlet he had described to her on the occasion of their first meeting—an observation which elicited a promise from him to call with it on the very next day, and which sent her home in a mood of modest satisfaction over the results of her evening's work.

11   Lydia had learned enough of London ways not to go unaccompanied to her meeting with Miss Beaudoin on the following morning, and she accordingly enlisted the services of Miss Winch—services which were at first rather grudgingly granted, until that estimable female learned that the excursion was in the interests of Bayard's future happiness. Whatever stringent comments Miss Winch might feel herself called upon occasionally to make on the subject of the shortcomings of the young Leylands, she would have allowed herself to be boiled in oil in order to secure the well-being of either —a sacrifice compared with which that of a June morning walk in good weather, no matter at how unreasonably early an hour, must certainly appear quite insignificant.

She therefore contented herself with the utterance of a severe admonition to Lydia not to allow herself to be up to any of her usual harebrained schemes, since it was Master Bayard's happiness that lay in the balance, and, upon their arriving at the appointed rendezvous, took it upon herself to fall behind her young mistress with the meek elderly lady who had accompanied Miss Beaudoin, leaving the two younger ladies to carry on their conversation in privacy.

Miss Beaudoin's first words, as soon as this had been accomplished, were not calculated to inspire Lydia with the conviction that this meeting was destined to serve any very useful purpose.

"Oh, Miss Leyland, what *am* I to do?" she said, in a distraught voice. "I have been thinking and thinking, and I have not the least idea!"

"Well, I shan't have, either, unless you tell me what this is all about," Lydia said prosaically. "What exactly is it that you feel you ought to do, or want to do?"

"Why, to marry Bayard—Mr. Leyland—of course!" Minna said, her innocent dark eyes opening wide. "Has he not told you?"

"He *has* let fall a few hints in that direction," Lydia acknowledged, "but I hadn't realised there was such pressing haste—"

"Well, there is!" Minna swallowed a sob. "I am sure Lord Harlbury means to offer for me soon—indeed, from something Mama let fall to Grandmama, I believe he may do so in a very few days—and if he does, I shall be in a dreadful case! I have tried to tell Mama that I cannot care for him, but she says that is only missish scruples on my part, and that I must realise she knows what is b-best for me."

Lydia bit back an impulse to inform her that Lady Gilmour was probably right; certainly, she told herself ruefully, no parent could be expected to believe that her daughter's happiness would be more secure if she were to marry a penniless young man like Bayard Leyland than it would be if she married Harlbury, the personification of any mother's fondest dreams. However, as she was not Miss Beaudoin's mama, but Bayard's sister, it did not suit her to take this view of the situation, and she accordingly said encouragingly to Miss Beaudoin, "Well, that need not signify, if you remain resolute. No one, not even your mama, can force you to marry Harlbury against your wishes—and, at any rate, he may not offer for you, after all."

"But what is to prevent him?" Minna cried. "That is"—she faltered and blushed—"I do not at all mean that he feels an unalterable preference for me, but Mama says *his* mama has quite decided that we shall suit, and—and I believe you cannot know Lady Harlbury well, Miss Leyland, but she is the horridest creature, always ordering poor Shafto about and forever having her own way with him—"

"Shafto!" Lydia interrupted, thunderstruck. "Good God, is *that* his Christian name?"

Miss Beaudoin looked at her wonderingly. "Yes, it is," she said. "Doesn't it please you?"

"No, it does not!" Lydia said, with revulsion. "However, I daresay he has another—perhaps several others—and I shall be able to use one of them." She added kindly, as she saw the wonderment deepen on Miss Beaudoin's face, "I am considering marrying Harlbury myself, you see."

"Marrying—Lord Harlbury—you?" Miss Beaudoin said faintly. "But I don't understand! Has he asked *you*—?"

"Oh, no!" Lydia said sunnily. "I shouldn't think the idea has ever crossed his mind. But it is not at all out of the question, you know. Practically anything can be accomplished if one seriously sets one's mind to it."

Miss Beaudoin gazed at her with an expression of distinctly awed admiration upon her face. "Perhaps it is for *you*," she said. "*I* should never dare—" She broke off, lifting her chin with an air of resolution. "Only I *will* dare anything for Bayard's sake," she corrected herself. "Anything, so that we shall not be parted!"

Lydia accepted this romantic speech without visible gratification; her brow was wrinkled in thought as she began to wrestle with more practical aspects of the situation than those involving valiant self-sacrifice and eternal devotion.

"Do you suppose Lord Gilmour would be prepared to assist you in any way?" she enquired presently. "He seems a very good-humoured sort of man, and I daresay he is fond of you."

"Oh yes, he is," Minna agreed, but not very hopefully. "He is the kindest person imaginable, only—only I fear he will never do anything that Mama dislikes, and she is quite dreadfully set against my having anything at all to do with Bayard, you see. She is *determined* that I shall marry Lord Harlbury!"

"Well, if *you* are determined that you will not, there is really nothing that she can do about that," Lydia reminded her. "But as to gaining her consent to your marrying Bayard—that is another matter altogether, and I confess I do not at this present see exactly how we are to bring it about. He really has not a feather to fly with, you know!"

"He has—he has been telling me about the plantation in America," Minna faltered. "Could not we live there, perhaps?"

"Well, I daresay you *could,* and that you would not starve, for *we* never did; but I should not condemn my worst enemy to be buried there as we were these four years past," Lydia said frankly. "And Bayard is *not* the person to take the place in hand and make a success of it in its present state, though I daresay he might do well enough if there were money to put into it. But if you believe there is no hope of Lord Gilmour's doing something handsome for you—"

Minna shook her head. "Not if I wish to marry Bayard," she said unhappily. "Mama would *never* permit it, I am sure."

Lydia shrugged. "Well, then, we must contrive to do without him," she said. Seeing the downcast expression upon Minna's face, she said more encouragingly, "Never mind! We shall come about, I am sure. *I* shall manage to draw Harlbury off, at any rate—and in the meanwhile, if you are wise, you will say not a word about Bayard to your mama, and will show him in company only the same civility you would show to any other young man—"

She broke off suddenly. They had reached the promenade beside the carriage-way and had been walking slowly along it, paying little heed to the occasional early-morning rider cantering past; but now Lydia abruptly became aware that a good-looking hack had been reined in, snorting, just beside them and that a gentleman was jumping down from it.

"Northover!" she said, in considerable disapproval. "What are *you* doing here?"

"I might ask the same question of *you!*" he retorted, twitching the bridle over his horse's head and fixing a sardonic glance upon the two young pedestrians that sent the guilty colour flooding at once into Minna's cheeks.

Lydia, however, merely said superbly, "As you see, I was having a morning stroll, and was fortunate enough to meet Miss Beaudoin, who had come out for the same purpose." She added darkly, *"If* it is any of your affair—"

They were joined at that moment by Miss Winch and Miss Berker, who, seeing their charges accosted by a gentleman of dubious reputation, instantly came hurrying up to add the respectability of their chaperonage to the gathering. For Miss Beaudoin, at least, their arrival came in the light of rescue; she seized thankfully upon her old governess's arm, stammered a frightened word of leave-taking to Lydia, and scurried off like a frightened mouse.

Lydia gave Northover a severe glance. "I wonder what you can have done to her," she said, "that the mere sight of you casts her into such a taking!"

"Oh, no! Don't try laying that in *my* dish!" Northover said. She turned away, shrugging her shoulders, but he stopped her by the simple expedient of reaching out his free hand and seizing her arm. "No, you are not going yet," he said coolly. "I told you last evening that I wished to talk to you, and this little episode strongly confirms me in that notion. Walk on with me a little way; this will save me a call in Green Street."

Lydia, indignantly detaching her arm from his grasp, appeared for a moment as if she would have denied this very peremptory request, but something in the look on the Viscount's face made her think better of it, and she said grudgingly, "Oh, very well! You may wait for me here, Winch; I shan't be more than a pair of minutes."

Miss Winch, folding her arms tightly across her meagre breast, stood looking the picture of disapproval, but unfortunately neither Northover nor Lydia paid her the least heed. She had her mind set to rest, however, as to the Viscount's having any improper intentions towards her young mistress by his remarking to Lydia, before the pair of them were out of hearing, "I wish you will tell me what sort of mischief you have been up to this morning with that wretched girl. Have you been addlebrained enough to encourage her in that remarkably silly attachment she believes she has formed for your brother?"

"It is *not* silly!" Lydia said. "They are truly in love, and if I can assist them, I shall—whatever *you* may think of it."

"What *I* think of it is of no importance," he said, a trifle grimly. "But what her relations think is another matter, and I can assure you that your young brother has not the least chance of winning their approval of his marrying Miss Beaudoin. If you had the slightest degree of sense you would realise that, and exert any influence you have with him towards warning him away from an attachment that can lead to nothing but distress on both sides."

Lydia paused, looking at him scornfully. "Well, of course, I should expect a man of *your* stamp to take such a view!" she said. "I daresay you have never in your life been in love—I believe that emotion is considered quite unnecessary in the sort of connexions you usually form?"

Northover grinned, showing his teeth, between exasperation and amusement. "You little vixen! What do you know about 'the connexions I usually form'?"

She shrugged. "I know quite as much as I wish to; I am *not* so green as you think me, you know!" She added, goaded by the deepening amusement on his face, "And it is enough to make me feel it necessary to hope, at any rate, that you will not run off at once to your *dear* Lady Gilmour with the tale that you met Miss Beaudoin here in the Park in my company this morning—"

The expression of amusement vanished suddenly from Northover's face; he seized her arm once more, this time so roughly that she gave a gasp of mingled pain and surprise, and swung her around so that she was face to face with him. "Now you *have* gone your length, Lydia!" he said in a harsh voice. "Permit me to tell you, my girl, that your manners are those of a hoyden, and that it would afford me the greatest satisfaction to give you the thorough shaking you richly deserve!"

"Let me go!" said Lydia, in an unsteady voice. Her cheeks were burning, and her heart had begun to beat so hard that she felt he must surely hear it in the sudden silence between them.

Then a stout gentleman trotted by on a rat-tailed grey and Northover released her arm abruptly, quieting his own horse, which had curvetted restively at the approach of the other.

She said then, much annoyed to find that her voice was still shaking oddly, "I am not going to stay here another instant for you to speak s-so *insultingly* to me! You are a *beast*, Northover, and I am quite sure now that I really do abominate you! And if you do anything to hurt Bayard, I give you fair warning that I shall *strangle* you!"

Her lack of composure seemed to restore his own to the Viscount; he laughed and said, "Well, at any rate, you are welcome to try! But you are mistaken about which one of us is likely to do harm to your brother, my dear! The course *you* are taking is more certain to land him in the basket than anything I should be able to contrive—even if I wished to do him an injury, which I don't." He added, in a more serious tone, "Good God, Lydia, you are not such a wet-goose that you cannot realise that you will be doing those two children no favour by encouraging them in an attachment that must come to nothing in the end! It had far better be broken off now, at this early stage, before it is too late—"

"It is too late now," Lydia said. She was still mortified and furious over her momentary loss of command over herself, and spoke curtly, without meeting the Viscount's eyes. "And it is quite false to say that it must come to nothing, for any number of things may occur that will alter the situation."

"Such as your own marriage?" Northover asked, his voice suddenly mocking her unpleasantly. "Which is it to be, Lydia? Chant or Harlbury? I hear they are laying wagers at White's that you will be able to bring Carsbie up to scratch, for he seems uncommonly taken with you, and has reached an age at which he may be thinking seriously of settling down. Yes, on consideration, I believe it would be wiser for you to concentrate on him. Harlbury may be the more attractive game, but then the chances that you will be able to land him are so very much more remote—"

"A beast, and an adder, and completely *loathsome,* besides," Lydia said, regarding him with glowering disfavour. "And if I wish to marry Harlbury, I *will* marry him—in spite of your thinking I could not bring it off!" She added dangerously, "If you say one more uncivil word to me, Northover, I shall hit you—so you had best stand out of my way! I wish you a very good morning, sir!"

She swept him a magnificent curtsey and marched back to Miss Winch, who received her with the air of one snatching a cherished charge from the jaws of perdition. The Viscount, however, merely laughed, gathered his reins, and, swinging himself into the saddle, cantered off.

"Oh!" said Lydia, staring after him with narrowed eyes. "He is the most despicable, odious—! Winch, we must go home at once! Lord Harlbury intends to call this morning, and if I do not utterly *stun* him with the most becoming gown I own and the highest kick of fashion in coiffures, you may call me the greatest mooncalf of your acquaintance! Laying wagers at White's, indeed! And I daresay my Lord Northover foremost among them! Well, I will show him if I must settle for Sir Carsbie Chant! I'll show him, if I must go to perdition to do it!"

12 Lydia's determination to appear at her most fashionable best that morning, coupled with the rage into which her meeting with Northover had flung her, resulted in her being in such magnificent looks when Lord Harlbury dutifully presented himself in Green Street a little later that day that he quite forgot the purpose for which he had come, and it was not until Lydia had reminded him of it that he collected himself sufficiently to present to her the pamphlet which he bore under his arm.

As luck would have it, both Mrs. Leyland and Bayard were gone out, so that she received his lordship alone. This quite suited Lydia's purpose, and, after she had exclaimed in suitable gratitude over his kindness in coming in person to deliver the pamphlet, and had permitted Sidwell to fetch some refreshment for her noble guest, she came rapidly to the point that she had determined to make with his lordship.

"There is a matter," she said to him pensively—"since your lordship has been so kind as to honour me with your—may I say friendship?—that I feel I *must* open with you, difficult as it is for me to speak on such a delicate subject to a gentleman. It concerns," she went on, as she saw Harlbury looking at her in some astonishment, not unmixed with alarm, at this portentous preamble, "it concerns Miss Beaudoin."

"Miss Beaudoin?"

The introduction of the name appeared to do nothing to enlighten his lordship's mystification. He looked questioningly at Lydia, who—having cast herself for the moment in the role of the devoted confidante—went on with an appearance of self-sacrificial fortitude, "Naturally, *nothing* could induce me to betray the confidence which she has reposed in me by speaking of this matter to anyone other than *you,* my lord. The point is that we are dealing here with a matter of such delicacy—You will not be offended if I speak *quite* openly to you?"

"No, no! Not in the least!" his lordship assured her, looking as if he wished very much that she would do just that and put him out of his suspense.

Lydia nodded. "So kind! So understanding!" she murmured, giving him such a soulfully admiring glance from under dipping lashes that his lordship understandably felt his pulses beating a good deal more rapidly than they normally did. "I must tell you," Lydia continued, "that Miss Beaudoin, in the natural distress she feels in her situation, greatly feared to approach you on the matter, greatly feared that you would not understand—"

Harlbury, who was making a desperate attempt to rally his mental forces sufficiently to comprehend what there was in Miss Beaudoin's situation to cast her into distress of any kind, made an inarticulate sound designed to indicate that he was prepared to be understanding on any suit— an action which encouraged Lydia to continue.

"You see," she said, casting down her eyes and speaking gently but firmly, as if in the performance of a painful duty, "she is under the apprehension—the mistaken apprehension, I must fervently hope—that you are—in short, that you are about to request permission to pay your addresses to her, my lord!"

Lord Harlbury, on receiving thus baldly this totally unexpected piece of information, looked for a moment as if he had suddenly swallowed a red-hot poker, and to compose himself found it necessary to rise precipitately and take a hasty turn about the room. Lydia's eyes flew up to watch him, but when he turned to her again they were once more cast modestly downward to the carpet.

"I am dreadfully afraid that I have wounded you," she said, in obvious self-reproach.

"Not at all! Not in the least!" Harlbury hastily denied. "That is to say— well, I *had* thought—that is to say, my mother thought—"

"Exactly!" Lydia said sadly, raising her eyes to his face. "Your mother is, as I understand, eager for the match; Lady Gilmour is no less anxious to see it concluded—but the feelings of the two unhappy people most closely involved have—alas!—been consulted by neither. But I have told Miss Beaudoin—I have *assured* her that a man as generous as you are, my lord, once he is acquainted with the fact that the young lady concerned in the matter is unalterably opposed to it, will act in such a manner that she no longer need fear being forced into a repugnant marriage—"

She broke off, seeing from the stunned expression upon his lordship's face that he had quite enough to cope with for the moment. He sank, in fact, once more into a chair beside her with the air of a man who has suddenly found the solid ground beneath his feet rocking as precariously as the deck of a ship in a storm.

"But I d-don't understand!" he stammered, brushing his carefully arranged dark locks from his brow into a picturesque disorder that made him look even more romantically handsome than before, the effect being spoiled only by the rather piteously uncomprehending stare in his eyes. "I was given to believe—that is, she never showed the least—the least *reluctance!*"

Lydia shook her head. "Ah," she said feelingly, "you little know the restraints by which a properly brought up young female is bound! *Could*

Miss Beaudoin, in the face of her mother's insistence upon her compliance, have behaved towards you publicly in a repulsive manner? You will not yourself say, I believe, that she has *encouraged* you?"

"No," Harlbury admitted. "But she—But I—Good God, this is a dreadful situation!" he exclaimed, jumping up again and striding about the room. It was a rather small room, as the drawing-rooms in the Green Street house did not run to noble dimensions, and Lydia was in some apprehension lest some of the expensively hired bric-a-brac it contained fall victim to the emotions of the very large young man so impetuously traversing it. Much to her relief, he came to a halt presently before her. "I was to have offered for her this very evening!" he said, in an agitated voice. "Everything had been arranged—and now—this! My dear ma'am, what in heaven's name am I to do?"

"Well, in the first place, I should not worry about it, if I was you," Lydia said kindly. "Sit down here"—she patted the sofa beside her—"and we shall put our heads together and think what course you had best follow. I daresay we shall be able to hit upon the very thing—but *do* stop looking so *stricken!*" she added, lapsing into severity as Harlbury sat down obediently beside her. "You *won't* try to tell me that you are in love with the girl?"

"In love? No! But I—" Harlbury appeared to recollect himself suddenly, and said somewhat stiffly, "Naturally, I was prepared to entertain that regard for Miss Beaudoin that is proper to the married state! She is a very amiable young lady, and there is nothing in either her person or her manners to disgust—"

Lydia said irrepressibly, "Oh, if *that* is all you require in a wife, I am sure we shall be able to suit you admirably, half a dozen times over, before the Season is out!" But then, recalling the part she was playing, she once more assumed her pensive air, and said softly, "I am so happy to learn that your feelings are not engaged! Indeed, you do not know what a relief it is to me, for I would not for the world be the unfortunate instrument of causing you pain!"

Lord Harlbury, finding himself confronted, at this staggering crisis in his affairs, by a pair of blue eyes as meltingly sympathetic as any it had ever been his fortune to encounter, discovered with some surprise that his situation was not nearly so black as it had appeared a few moments before, and went so far as to give Lydia a slight, reassuring smile.

"*You* give me pain, Miss Leyland!" he said. "No—I can only honour you for your frankness in laying the matter before me—at a considerable cost, I am persuaded, to your own delicacy of feeling." His brow wrinkled once more. "But I must confess that I am at a loss as to what course I had best pursue now. If Miss Beaudoin's aversion to the match is indeed insuperable—"

Lydia sighed. "Alas, I fear it is!" she said. "Her affections—I should not betray this to you if it were not absolutely necessary, you understand!—her affections are engaged Elsewhere."

"Ah! Indeed!" Harlbury digested this news gloomily.

"It is an attachment," Lydia went on, "which—though the young man is of unexceptionable birth and character—does not, for reasons of fortune, meet with Lady Gilmour's approval. She is quite unwilling to accept it as a reason for breaking off her daughter's projected match with you, my lord —which is why the initiative in doing so *must* come from you."

"Yes, but—dash it, Miss Leyland!" his lordship said, running a harassed hand once more through his dark locks, "I can't just walk smash up to my mother—that is, to Lady Gilmour—and say that I've changed my mind!"

"Certainly not!" Lydia agreed cordially. "They would think that very odd indeed, and I don't doubt that your mother—that is, Lady Gilmour— would be quite unimpressed by such a reason. But if you were to tell them that *you* had formed another attachment—an unalterable one—and had already committed yourself so far as to disclose it to the young lady in question—"

Harlbury stared at her. "Yes, but I *haven't* formed another attachment!" he protested.

Lydia returned his gaze with some impatience. "I know that! It needn't be a *real* attachment," she said. "Merely, if you could persuade some other young lady to allow you to *pretend* an attachment between you until the matter of your marrying Miss Beaudoin has gone off—"

Harlbury shook his head, looking serious. "Oh no, I couldn't do that, Miss Leyland!" he said. "It wouldn't be fair to the young lady."

"Fiddle! If she were your friend, she would think nothing of obliging you in such a matter. I am very sure that *I* should not!"

"You wouldn't?" Harlbury looked at her doubtfully, but with an expression of dawning hope on his face. "You mean *you* wouldn't mind if I were to tell my mother—that is, Lady Gilmour—that an attachment had grown up between us, and that I felt myself bound—because of certain declarations I had made to you—"

"Exactly! Now you are going on beautifully!" Lydia said approvingly. "What could she—they—say, under such circumstances? You have not yet committed yourself as far as Miss Beaudoin is concerned, but in *this* matter, having gone so far, they could not expect you, in honour, to draw back." She went on, warming to her subject, "And then, of course, when the whole matter of your offering for Miss Beaudoin has been laid to rest, you may discover that you have mistaken your feelings, after all, and *I* shall pretend to discover the same, and so you will have escaped from your predicament without the slightest inconvenience to anyone—for we shall have broken off, of course, before any formal announcement is made. Now is not that an excellent scheme?"

Lord Harlbury, who was looking a trifle dazed, said that he supposed it might be, but he added almost immediately, with an air of revulsion, "But it will not do, Miss Leyland! Eternally grateful as I must be to you for so nobly offering to come to my assistance, it will not do! *Your* reputation, *your* peace of mind—"

Lydia curbed an exasperated shrug, and managed a meekly noble expression once more.

"Indeed, my lord, you refine too much upon the matter," she said. "What can such a small sacrifice upon my part signify, if it is to be the means of sparing you and Miss Beaudoin a lifetime of regret? I assure you, I should think the less of you if you declined to make use of my assistance in such a case. Oh, I am well aware that your principles are too high to allow of your accepting it for merely selfish reasons—but there is Miss Beaudoin to be considered. Can you, my lord—because you are too proud to accept my help—condemn *her* to misery?"

"No—no—indeed not!" his lordship said disjointedly. "But have I the right—?"

"The right *and* the duty," Lydia said firmly, and then, losing patience at last, went on in a far more normal voice, "Good heavens, Harlbury, don't put yourself into such a taking! A pretty hobble you will be in if you don't do it, for you know as well as I do that your mama will never be put off without your giving her some totally *momentous* reason for your crying off at this point in the proceedings!"

His lordship was obliged to agree to this view of the situation, and after a quarter hour more of conversation finally took himself off, his resolution apparently screwed to the point of bearding his mother forthwith and informing her of the alteration in his matrimonial plans. Lydia saw him go and then sat down with a sigh of exhaustion to formulate her own plans for the future—plans which must involve, as she was well aware, the inescapable necessity of a confrontation with Lady Harlbury, who would certainly lose no time in calling upon the young lady who had the effrontery of designing to become her daughter-in-law without her approval and even without her knowledge.

13 Lydia thought it prudent to acquaint Bayard, when he came in presently, with the turn affairs had taken that day in regard to Harlbury's courtship of Miss Beaudoin; but if she had expected him to be grateful to her for her interference, she soon discovered her mistake.

"*You* marry Harlbury!" he exclaimed, drawing his brows together in a startled frown. "Good God, I thought you were merely jesting when you spoke of that the other day! What can you have been thinking of, to have put the notion into his head? Of all the hey-go-mad tricks—!"

"Handsomely over the bricks, my dear," Lydia said composedly. "There is no need for you to fly into a pelter *yet,* you know! Harlbury has not asked me to marry him, nor have I said that I would. All we have agreed upon is to *pretend* to an understanding, so that he may have a reason to give his mama for not offering for Miss Beaudoin."

"Yes, but I know you, Lyddy!" Bayard said, his face the picture of misgiving. "That may be *his* notion of what he has let himself in for, but if *you* have made up your mind that he is to marry you, he will have no more to say about it than a lamb on its way to the butcher."

A slight flush appeared on Lydia's face. "Now you are talking like Northover," she said. "To hear the pair of you, I am an odious, scheming wretch—"

"Gammon!" Bayard cut her off, throwing an arm about her shoulders and giving her a brotherly hug. "What you are is a heedless madcap, who will fight like a tigress for anyone she takes under her protection. But it isn't your place to protect *me,* love. I shall have to make my own way— though God knows I don't see at present how I am to do it! But I still can't have you entering into an engagement with Harlbury on *my* account!"

"Perhaps it is not all upon *your* account," Lydia said, putting up her chin. "Perhaps I have a fancy to be a countess. And, at any rate, there is nothing that either you or I can do about it now, for Harlbury is already gone to tell his mother. If he has not grown hen-hearted at the awful prospect before him and hedged off," she concluded, with a gurgle of laughter. "He is in the liveliest dread of her, you know—which is absurd, for there is nothing she can do to him if he will only make up his mind to face her down."

She cut the conversation short to run upstairs and communicate the news of her "engagement" to her grandmother, who had also returned to the house after what Lydia assumed to be a round of calls. To her surprise, however, she found Mrs. Leyland stalking about her dressing-room with the air of an offended Juno. At sight of Lydia she said, "Ha!" in a highly dramatic voice, and invited her to guess where she had been.

"I haven't the least notion," Lydia confessed, seating herself in a bergère armchair. "But, wherever it was, something has obviously sent you flying up into the boughs. What on earth has happened?"

"Oh, that wretched little man has nettled me into such a flame that I can scarcely endure to speak of it!" Mrs. Leyland said. "Merely because I told him I had lost a trifling sum at cards and must have the money to pay it!"

Lydia's face altered. "Oh, dear!" she sighed. "I gather you mean Mr. Peeke? But, Grandmama, how could you bear to apply to him when he has been so very generous in advancing you such sums already? Could you not have contrived, if it is indeed a trifling amount—?" She halted, observing the guiltily austere expression with which Mrs. Leyland appeared to be discouraging any further enquiry into the subject. "Grandmama!" she said forebodingly. "How much *did* you lose?"

Mrs. Leyland tossed her head. "Well, well, that is none of your affair, my dear child!" she said airily. "It is merely a temporary embarrassment, for I shall soon be able to recoup my losses."

"How *much?*" Lydia insisted.

Mrs. Leyland gave a pettish shrug. "Well, if you *must* know—two thousand pounds," she said. "But there is no need for you to look so dismayed, for I am quite sure that the next time I sit down to play—"

"Two—thousand—pounds!" Lydia found her voice at last and repeated the figure in appalled tones. "Good God, Grandmama, where could you have lost such a sum? Are Great-aunt Letty's jewels worth so much?"

"I am sure I have not the least idea," Mrs. Leyland said superbly. "At any rate, it does not signify, for, as my dear brother Gerald was used to say, one's luck must always turn if one has but the resolution to continue playing."

"Your dear brother Gerald," Lydia reminded her, a trifle tartly, "lost Great Hayland, I have always understood, by following his own advice in that respect. Oh dear, Grandmama, how *could* you have been so very imprudent? And you have not told me yet where you have lost such a sum. Certainly not at Almack's, for I have heard that the play there is very tame."

"And so it is," Mrs. Leyland said feelingly, "for I was sat down to whist the whole time you and Bayard were enjoying yourselves in the ball-room last evening, and rose from the table not twenty pounds the better for it in the end."

"Then where—?"

"Oh, at Mrs. Collingworth's house," Mrs. Leyland said. "But it was only through the most vexatious run of ill luck that I lost so much—the sort of thing that will not occur twice in a dozen years. I am certain that when I play there again this evening, the cards will fall in quite another fashion for me."

Lydia stared at her. "When you play there again—!" she repeated. "Grandmama, no! Surely you will not be so gooseish as to go there a second time! Besides, how can you?—for you know you have no money."

"My dear child," Mrs. Leyland said impatiently, "what can that signify? Naturally they will accept my vouchers. They must be quite aware, you know, that I shall settle them just as soon as ever my luck turns."

"But if it does not turn? Grandmama dear, surely you must be able to see what a dreadful situation we shall be in if you cannot pay! We shall be done up—forced to retire from Society—even from England—"

"Nonsense! Now you are running on like that tiresome Peeke, who read me such a scold that I was finally obliged to leave his office without obtaining the least thing I had gone there for! Of course I shall come about; it only needs a little time." She added, casting a somewhat indignant glance at Lydia's stunned face, "I do not at all see why you should get up on your high ropes over the matter. It is entirely for your sake, and Bayard's, that I play at all. Heaven knows I am not desirous of winning a fortune upon my own account!"

Lydia shook her head, a smile irresistibly curving her lips, in spite of herself, at the picture her grandmother had drawn of herself labouring virtuously and unselfishly at the card-table for the sake of her two young relations.

"Yes, but, Grandmama, I assure you that we shall get on a great deal better if you do not go to such lengths to help us," she said perseveringly. "Heavens, are things not in enough of a coil already without our adding debt to the matter! I expect I should tell you, by the bye, that Harlbury has been here today, and has now gone off to inform his mama that, as he has conceived a *tendre* for me and has made certain declarations to me, he is unable to offer for Miss Beaudoin—"

She was interrupted by her grandmother, who exclaimed, in ecstatic astonishment, "Harlbury! Lydia, you have never succeeded in bringing him to the point so quickly! Oh, my dearest girl, why did you not tell me so at once, without talking all this miff-maff about a paltry two thousand pounds?"

"No, no!" Lydia said, laughing. "Pray do not be jumping to conclusions, ma'am! At the present moment Harlbury's interest in me is merely a pretext I have offered him, to allow him to draw back from paying his addresses to Miss Beaudoin. It is to remain the greatest secret; indeed, I should not have mentioned it even to you if I were not persuaded that we must soon receive a visit from Lady Harlbury—in which case it might be awkward if you knew nothing of the matter. But there is *nothing* concluded; you must understand that! Indeed, I have promised Harlbury that he will be perfectly free of any obligation to me as soon as he feels it safe to tell his mama that he does not wish to marry me, after all." She explained patiently, as she saw the stupefaction with which her grandmother was regarding her, "I only made up the scheme in order to help Bayard, love. If I had not stepped into the picture and persuaded Harlbury that he must not offer for a girl who is desperately in love with someone else—and then given him an excuse to present to his mama for not doing so—it would never have entered his mind to tell Lady Harlbury that he was enamoured of me."

"Lydia!" Mrs. Leyland interrupted at this point, apparently unable to contain her feelings any longer. "You *cannot* mean to tell me that, when you have succeeded in bringing him this far, you are going to let him go! That would be *too* much to bear! Even you, I am persuaded, could not be so—so *wasteful* as to do a thing like that! Why, he has forty thousand pounds a year!"

Lydia laughed. "I don't care if he has a hundred thousand," she said. "I have no fancy to trick him into marrying me." She added mischievously, "Oh, I do not say that if, on closer acquaintance, he finds me irresistible, I might not—perhaps!—be brought to find him so as well—"

Mrs. Leyland moaned. "Good heavens, you unnatural girl, what has that to say to anything! Forty thousand a year, and an earldom—and you talk of whistling him down the wind! Why, if you were to marry him, it would be the end of all our difficulties forever! What would a mere two thousand pounds signify in such a case!"

The mention of the debt her grandmother had incurred brought Lydia's thoughts back with a disagreeable start to that pressing matter.

"Well, it signifies a great deal now," she said, frowning over a new idea that had suddenly occurred to her. "Grandmama," she asked abruptly, "what sort of house is this Mrs. Collingworth's, that play so deep goes on there? Mr. Pentony said she was a friend of his mother's, but surely Lady Pentony is by no means able to move in circles where such sums can change hands in a single evening."

"Oh, what does *that* matter?" Mrs. Leyland said impatiently, her mind still upon higher things. "I daresay one need not move in quite the same circles as *all* one's friends do. Mrs. Collingworth's house is excessively elegant, I can assure you, and one meets persons of the highest *ton* there."

"Yes, I was afraid of that," Lydia said, with misgiving. "And they have all come with one purpose—have they not? Play!" Mrs. Leyland made a gesture of outraged denial, but Lydia, her eyes narrowing slightly, continued slowly, "And it was Michael Pentony who introduced you to that woman! A polite gaming-house—oh yes, I can see it all now! *That* would take the trick very nicely for him—to see us rolled-up, obliged to leave town—"

"What *are* you talking of, my love?" Mrs. Leyland exclaimed, in the highest dudgeon. "A gaming-house! It is nothing of the sort! Merely a private party where the play ran a trifle deep."

"And you plan to return there tonight? Grandmama, you must not!" Lydia said earnestly. "Believe me, it will not do! Heaven knows how we are to pay the two thousand pounds you have already lost, but if any more is added to it, we shall certainly all go home by way of beggar's bush!"

Nothing she could say, however, had the least effect in altering her grandmother's resolution to endeavour to recoup her losses that evening. Mrs. Leyland would only say bitterly that if Lydia was so unpardonably foolish as not to make a push to bring Harlbury to a public announcement of their betrothal, she herself was not bird-witted enough to cast aside the only means by which they might hope to escape from the predicament in which they found themselves.

Lydia was at last reduced to going downstairs again to seek Bayard's aid in persuading her recalcitrant grandparent; but here too she met with a check, for she was informed by Sidwell that he had already gone out, having an engagement, it appeared, to dine with friends at the Daffy Club.

She was therefore left to her own resources, which turned out to be quite inadequate, for Mrs. Leyland was as convinced of the rightness of her own reasoning as was Lydia of hers, and was even more obstinate in adhering to the course she had chosen to pursue. The matter ended in their dining together very uncomfortably and then parting on somewhat inimical terms, Mrs. Leyland to go on to Mrs. Collingworth's house in

Curzon Street and Lydia to sit down alone in the front drawing-room to
consider what steps she might take next.

The idea of enlisting Mr. Peeke's aid was the first that came to mind,
but it was soon discarded; her grandmother's description of the scene that
had already taken place between them gave her little grounds for hoping
that any arguments he might make would prevail with her. Lady Aimer?
She and Mrs. Leyland—both outspoken and highly opinionated—had all
but come to cuffs several times already over much lesser matters, and it
was doubtful that interference on her part now would lead to anything
more helpful than another quarrel.

All Lydia could hope for—and, suspecting that Michael Pentony was
behind the scenes in the matter, she could place little reliance upon her
hope's being realised—was that her grandmother might really fall into the
luck she was so convinced must come her way, and thus manage to extricate herself from her difficulties. Having come to this conclusion, she
then allowed her thoughts to revert to her own affairs, which appeared to
her to be also in pressing need of examination, for it was certainly to be
expected that she might even that evening receive a call from Lady Harlbury, apprised by this time of her son's change in intentions and hot to do
battle with the interfering Miss Leyland.

14

As it developed, however, Lady Harlbury did not appear in Green Street that evening. Neither did she call there on the following morning, and it was gradually borne in upon Lydia that that lady, far from choosing to cross swords with her, had no intention of dignifying the information her son had presented to her by according Miss Leyland any notice whatever.

To say that Lydia accepted this turn of events with meek complaisance would be to do her a singular injustice. She found her temper rising steadily as the hours progressed, and was almost on the point of taking the bull by the horns and setting out herself to pay a call upon Lady Harlbury when the horrid thought crossed her mind that perhaps that formidable lady knew nothing of the interesting situation in which she and Lydia stood vis-à-vis Lord Harlbury, for the simple reason that Lord Harlbury had not informed her of it.

This was a new and dismaying thought. If his lordship's courage had failed him at the last moment and he had been craven enough, after all, to carry out his intention of offering for Miss Beaudoin, Bayard's hopes must be forever dashed, unless Minna herself had had sufficient resolution to give Harlbury a refusal. Lydia was on tenterhooks to know what had happened, and only the remembrance that she and Bayard and her grandmother were engaged to accompany Lady Aimer to the theatre on the following Monday evening, and that they must surely learn from her if her granddaughter had become betrothed to Harlbury, prevented her from embarking upon some scheme of her own to find out what had occurred in the matter.

Meanwhile, she had other cares, for she found her grandmother, on the morning following her second visit to Curzon Street, in a much subdued humour, scarcely suggesting that she had met with the good fortune there that she had confidently expected. She refused, however, to satisfy Lydia's curiosity on the subject, and only as she came downstairs on the evening they were to accompany Lady Aimer to the theatre, attired in stately purple and ostrich plumes, did she finally confide to her in tragic accents that there seemed nothing for it now but for her to have recourse to Mr. King.

"To *whom?*" Lydia enquired, startled.

"To Mr. King, my dear. I am told that he has an establishment in Clarges Street where one may borrow money—"

"A moneylender? Grandmama, you couldn't—you mustn't!" Lydia felt her heart sink down into the pretty white kid slippers that completed her own diaphanous toilette of sea-green sarsnet. "You *know* how poor Papa was ruined by them! Surely there must be some other way!"

They had no opportunity to discuss the matter, however, for they were interrupted at this point by the arrival of Lady Aimer, who had come to call for them in her barouche. One glance at that redoubtable dame's keen-eyed survey of her as she went to meet her was sufficient to convince Lydia that she had been wronging Harlbury by her doubts, and she was made doubly certain of the matter when Lady Aimer said to her bluntly, "Well, miss, fine doings you have been up to, it seems! So Minna is not to have Harlbury, after all! But I should not be too certain of bringing him up to scratch, my girl, even if you have succeeded in marring that match. Louisa Harlbury is as mad as fire over the affair, and if that boy has the rumgumption to stand out against her, it's more than *I* know of him. Hasn't made you an offer yet—has he?"

"Dear ma'am," Lydia said with a demure look, her spirits rising as she realised the success her strategy had obtained, "it is certainly not to *me* that you should apply for such an announcement. I am sure that Lord Harlbury will say everything that is proper."

Lady Aimer gave her sudden bark of laughter. She was more than ordinarily magnificent that evening in a gown of pomona-green satin, with a turban of green silk shot with orange crowning her square, pugnacious face.

"Well," she said philosophically, "you don't lack for wit, at any hand, and if my granddaughter is not to land Harlbury, I had as lief you got him as anyone else, if only to see Louisa made to look nohow for once in her life. But you had best be prepared for battle, my dear. She will be at Drury Lane herself tonight, and, unless I very much miss my guess, you will find yourself in for a thundering set-down from her."

"I daresay I shall," said Lydia, looking not in the least alarmed by the prospect; and, seeing that Bayard had now come downstairs to join them, she drew a delicate Indian shawl about her shoulders and prepared to follow Lady Aimer out to the barouche.

The theatre was full that evening, Mr. Kean being the attraction. Lydia, when the party had settled themselves in their box, allowed her eyes to range casually over the boxes opposite, and was rewarded presently by the sight of Lady Harlbury entering one of them, followed by her son and a group of several other persons. As Lady Aimer's box was almost directly opposite, the members of the two parties could not fail to observe one another, and bows were exchanged—Lady Harlbury's perforce including Miss Leyland. Lydia observed that Harlbury himself, though he appeared embarrassed by the encounter, greeted them with the greatest civility. A few moments later she perceived him in earnest conversation with his mother, and that she herself was the subject of it she could not doubt, from the glances cast in her direction by both.

The rising of the curtain, however, put an end to any further interchange. It cannot be said that Lydia, in spite of the fact that this was her first opportunity of seeing Kean, of whose histrionic powers she had heard so much, attended very carefully to what was going forward on the stage. She was fully occupied in trying to formulate some plan of action for the evening, but could hit upon none that satisfied her. Everything, it seemed, must depend upon Harlbury. She could not very well throw herself at his head in public, and, unless he chose to acknowledge the situation between them, she must accept with what grace she could Lady Harlbury's triumph in publicly displaying the fact that she still had her son in a string.

The curtain came down.

"Well? What d'you think of him?" Lady Aimer's voice demanded beside her.

"Him? Oh—you mean Mr. Kean!" Lydia said. She was observing the opposite box, where Harlbury, after a brief colloquy with his mother, had risen and made his way out. "He is very fine."

"Ay, that is what they all say, but for my part, I had as lief he did not go into such high flights, my dear. It is enough to frighten children, the way he goes on. Lord! you never saw such a to-do as there was in the theatre when he first took the part of Sir Giles Overreach. There were several ladies had to be removed in strong hysterics, and they say Lord Byron had a convulsive fit."

Lydia, quite unable to keep her mind on the overpowering impression Mr. Kean had made in his celebrated revival of Massinger's *A New Way to Pay Old Debts,* gave an absent reply, but then, suddenly recollecting herself, put on for Lady Harlbury's benefit a performance of a young lady enjoying herself to the utmost that rivalled anything the great actor had attempted upon the stage.

She was interrupted by a knock upon the door of the box; the next moment Harlbury himself stood before her. He looked rather red and, after exchanging greetings with the other members of the party, said to her with somewhat uneasy abruptness, "I wonder if you will do my mother the favour of waiting upon her in the box, Miss Leyland. It would be very good of you."

"Yes, of course," said Lydia, rising and accepting sedately the tribute of the surprised and meaningful glances exchanged by her grandmother and Lady Aimer. "I shall be delighted." And she sailed off on Lord Harlbury's arm.

In the corridor her manner changed. "Well?" she said to him conspiratorially. "How did it go? You have told her, of course?—about us, I mean."

Harlbury nodded nervously. "Yes. Oh, yes—I did!" he said, looking pale at the very remembrance of the scene.

Lydia gave his arm an encouraging pat. "Well, it was not so *very* dreadful—was it?" she said. "After all, she could not eat you—and, really, it is quite absurd, you know, that she should have anything to say about whether you choose to offer for a girl or not. It is certainly not *her* affair!"

Lord Harlbury looked as if he were far from being convinced of this, but he had no opportunity to put the thought into words, for Lydia went on at once to enquire whether it had been his notion or his mother's to ask her to visit their box.

He immediately looked, if possible, even graver than before. "Hers," he said. "And I cannot imagine why—for I fear I cannot believe, my dear Miss Leyland, that she wishes to distinguish you publicly by her attention. In point of fact," he said scrupulously, "she has already told me that if I were to marry you she would not receive you."

"Well, as you are not going to marry me, that does not signify—does it?" Lydia said lightly.

He returned no reply. They were by this time approaching the door of the box, and as they entered Lydia composed her features into a smile holding the balance nicely between ease and deference, which she was quite aware would infuriate Lady Harlbury by showing her refusal to be intimidated by the ordeal of meeting her under such circumstances. In tight situations it was Miss Leyland's maxim to attack; nothing, she felt, could be gained by allowing the enemy to take the initiative.

She saw by the tightening of Lady Harlbury's lips as she beheld her presenting herself thus charmingly beside her son that she had succeeded in her purpose. It had been Lady Harlbury's intention, when she had first observed Miss Leyland across the theatre, to ignore her presence there; but this decision had soon given way to a resolution to take advantage of the opportunity afforded by their meeting to put Miss Leyland firmly in her place. She would not deign to call in Green Street, thus acknowledging that she considered her son's infatuation with Miss Leyland a serious threat to her peace. But, since the minx was delivered by fate into her hands this evening, she felt that she might properly make use of the occasion to let her see how little good it would do her to think she might be able to form an alliance with a family so very much above her touch.

The battle lines were thus clearly drawn—a fact of which both ladies were well aware as Lord Harlbury, caught in the unhappy position of being in both lines of fire, placed a chair for Lydia. Fortunately for the combatants, Lady Harlbury had had the forethought to clear the box of its other occupants before her opponent's arrival, and the field was therefore ready for open warfare. This was at once begun by Lady Harlbury, who made a polite enquiry as to when Miss Leyland was returning to America.

"Returning to America?" Lydia opened her eyes with an assumption of naïve surprise. "My dear ma'am, I cannot conceive what you mean! How could I think of being parted by so many thousands of miles from Shafto—*now!*"

She gave Harlbury, who had taken up an uneasy station behind her chair, the flutter of an upward glance, and had the satisfaction of seeing Lady Harlbury's lips thin grimly.

"Indeed!" said Lady Harlbury. "Am I to gather, Miss Leyland, that you consider the remarkably unsuitable influence which you seem suddenly to have acquired over my son to be of a permanent nature? Let me assure you that nothing can be farther from the truth! A gentleman in Harlbury's position may indeed indulge in attachments for persons below his own station in life, but I am persuaded that *my* son has received an education of such a nature that the thought of perpetuating such an attachment in marriage is as abhorrent to him as it is to me."

"Mama—please!" said Lord Harlbury, in an agony of embarrassment. "You do Miss Leyland the greatest injustice!"

Lydia put her hand on his sleeve in a gesture which she was quite aware must cause Lady Harlbury to wish to strangle her out of hand.

"Do not distress yourself, my lord," she said gently, but with her eyes now expressing genuine indignation. "It is not to me that Lady Harlbury does the greatest injustice; it is to you. Permit me to say, ma'am, that your reading of your son's intentions toward me does far more discredit to yourself than any he might bring upon his family by seeking to connect himself with me in marriage. I am persuaded that—"

She was interrupted by the sound of a knock falling upon the door of the box; the next moment it opened, and Lydia was astounded to see Mr. Michael Pentony walk in. She had not been aware that he was in the theatre that evening, and what he was thinking of, to enter the Harlbury box so unceremoniously, she could not imagine, for she did not believe him even to be acquainted with either Lord Harlbury or his mother.

It soon developed that she was correct in this assumption.

"Hullo, coz!" he greeted her, speaking in a broad, rather common tone which she had never heard him use before and at the same time bestowing an offhand nod upon Harlbury. "Saw you from the pit—hobnobbing with all the smarts tonight, ain't you?—and thought I'd come round and do the polite. Well?" he gazed at her expectantly. "Ain't you going to introduce me?"

Lydia, forced into a corner, said from between gritted teeth, "Lady Harlbury—Lord Harlbury—Mr. Pentony." She saw immediately what game Mr. Pentony was up to; he had, no doubt, with his usual enterprise, managed to get hold of the rumours concerning herself and Harlbury that would certainly be flying about London, and, having seen her in the Harlbury box, had taken instant advantage of his opportunity to throw a rub in the way of the match.

He was nodding to Lady Harlbury now with a cheerful air quite at variance with his usual careful manner as he remarked to her familiarly, "Fine gal, my cousin Lydia—don't you agree, ma'am? Not quite up to snuff yet, but give her a little more town-bronze and she'll beat 'em all to sticks, is what I say!"

"Thank you!" said Lydia, interrupting him scathingly. "I fear you do me too much honour, however, sir, in bestowing the title of 'cousin' upon me."

She cast a swift glance at Lady Harlbury, hoping that her obvious disgust at Mr. Pentony's ill-bred interruption would lead her to take the initiative which belonged to her of obliging him to retire from the box; but she saw at once that that hope was vain. No matter how angry Lady Harlbury might be at the intruder's rudeness, she had immediately realised the advantages it offered her in presenting Miss Leyland to her son in an unfavourable light, and was therefore determined to do nothing to relieve the situation.

Naturally Mr. Pentony was not behindhand in summing up this attitude of her ladyship's, and he accordingly went on in the same manner in which he had begun, now addressing himself to Harlbury.

"If you are Harlbury, I daresay you've been thinking of having a touch

at her yourself," he remarked confidentially; "at least, that's what the tattle-boxes are saying. But let me warn you that you've taken the wrong sow
by the ear if you think there's a fortune to pick up along with her when
old Rowthorn has his notice to quit. *I'm* to be the lucky man there, it
seems—I'm his great-nevvy, you understand. Not that it signifies, when a
gal is as pretty as Lyddy is. A regular dazzler, *I* call her—"

Lydia rose with decision. There was no hope of stopping his mouth,
short of removing him from the box, and she could see that—quite beyond
the effect his words might have on Lord Harlbury and his mother—they
were already attracting curious attention from the neighbouring boxes. Restraining the impulse to give Mr. Pentony a dagger-glance, she said to him
with noncommittal civility, "It is time for me to return to my friends, I
fear. If you will excuse me, Lady Harlbury—No, there is no need for you
to disturb yourself, my lord; Mr. Pentony will escort me."

She laid her hand upon the latter gentleman's arm, and he gave a broad
wink to Lord Harlbury and an exaggerated bow to the rigid Lady Harlbury.

"Your servant, sir—ma'am. Well, you see how it is: she can't wait to
have me to herself! Always a bit on the impatient side, our Lyddy—"

He had no opportunity to conclude this speech, for Lydia, nipping his
arm compellingly, obliged him to retire from the box.

Outside in the corridor she faced him with indignant contempt.

"You really are a despicable person, Mr. Pentony!" she said. "Is there
nothing to which you will not stoop to gain your ends?"

"No, I shouldn't think there was," he replied dispassionately, and in his
ordinary manner. "I warned you, Miss Leyland, that I was in earnest over
this matter. Do you remember? You should have guessed that it would not
suit me to read in the *Gazette* of your engagement to Lord Harlbury."

She began to walk on, too angry to remain any longer under his
shrewd, considering gaze. He followed her, and after a moment, to her astonishment and distaste, murmured in her ear, "You are magnificent
when you are angry! Do not credit me with playing that little scene entirely for monetary reasons, Miss Leyland. Perhaps it does not suit me *personally*, either, to see you married to Harlbury."

She rounded on him scornfully. "Pray spare me your gallantries, Mr.
Pentony!" she said. "You have already made it abundantly clear to me—do
you remember?—what your interest in me is inspired by."

"At one time," he said swiftly. "Believe me, I find my feelings altering more greatly each time I see you! You are—an exceedingly attractive young woman, Miss Leyland!"

She shrugged. "I might be more inclined to believe you," she said, "if you were not doing your best to ruin my family, Mr. Pentony. Oh, yes!" she went on, as she saw him about to utter some remonstrance. "You will not deny, I believe, that it was you who introduced my grandmother to Mrs. Collingworth. Nor need you try to tell me that it was quite by accident that she turned up at Richmond Park on the same day that you were engaged to drive Grandmama there."

She threw him a challenging glance as she concluded, and received in return a slight, composed smile.

"Why, what do you mean?" he enquired smoothly. "What harm can your grandmother have taken from a lady who, to the best of my knowledge, is of the first respectability?"

"Ladies *of the first respectability* do not, I believe, ordinarily keep discreet gaming-houses where unsuspecting people are fleeced of large sums of money!" Lydia retorted. "Don't, I beg you, play the innocent with me! If you are prepared to risk your hopes of attaining a respectable position in Society to gain your purpose—as you plainly showed by your performance in Lady Harlbury's box just now—it can surely be nothing to you merely to play the go-between in a matter of that sort. You ran no risk there!"

They had reached the door of Lady Aimer's box by this time; she was about to enter, without a word of adieu to him, when he put his hand on her arm to forestall her. She cast a glance at the attendant, who stood waiting to open the door for her, and, composing her angry countenance with an effort, said in a low tone, "I have nothing further to say to you, sir."

"But I have something to say to you." He drew her a little away, out of hearing of the attendant. His narrow face, she saw, had a slight, intent smile upon it as he said to her softly, "Come, come, Miss Leyland—would you be making such a bad bargain, after all, if you came to terms with me? Harlbury may be infatuated with you, but it is common knowledge that he will never venture to marry where his mother disapproves. And as for other chances that you may believe will offer—try them and see how many men you find who are willing to take a penniless young woman to wife." She made an indignant movement, as if to turn away from him, but he checked her once more. "One moment!" he said. "You must realise that you have very little time in which to indulge in indecision on this point, Miss Leyland. Of course, if you were to place me in the position of being able to go to Sir Basil and inform him that you have agreed to become my wife, I should be happy to settle the debts that your grandmother appears so imprudently to have incurred. On the other hand, if you do *not* give me the right to make that announcement to Sir Basil, I fear I shall regretfully be obliged to inform him of the insecure foundation on which Mrs. Leyland's hopes of establishing herself and her family in Society presently rest—"

"Yes!" said Lydia, who had listened to quite enough to send her temper soaring once more. "I can well imagine that you will lose no time in running to Sir Basil to tell your tale, Mr. Pentony! But do not underestimate *me*, I beg you! I have not shot my bolt as yet—as certain as you are that you have brought me under your thumb!"

She thereupon moved forward determinedly to the door of the box, which she entered so impetuously that her grandmother looked at her in astonished disapproval. Lady Aimer, noting her flushed, indignant countenance, said shrewdly, "No need to ask you how you and Louisa Harlbury dealt together, my dear! Well, I warned you what you might expect!" She levelled her glass at the opposite box. "Lord! Harlbury looks regularly blue-devilled!" she said. "A pretty scold she is reading him, I'll warrant you!"

Lydia, who for once in her life was too angry and exasperated to return a light answer, made no reply. She was wondering, as the curtain rose, how she could possibly sort out the dreadful tangle into which her own affairs and those of her family seemed to have got themselves. It was a problem, it seemed to her at the present moment, that would require all her best efforts to solve.

15 It did not take Lydia long on the following morning to come to the conclusion that, if she were to succeed in extricating her grandmother from the difficulties that had caused that much-harassed lady to propose again, at the breakfast-table, to seek relief at the hands of a moneylender, she required the counsel of some older and wiser head than her own. It was useless to expect Bayard to take the matter in hand; she had, in fact, advised her grandmother against even acquainting him with the results of her imprudent visits to Curzon Street. Introduced into the exclusive and highly expensive gaming-rooms of White's Club through the promised good offices of Lord Harlbury, he was already elated at having been lucky enough to come off with a modest success in play that was quite above his touch; and Lydia could only shudder at the idea of his taking it into his head that his grandmother's lack of good fortune at the gaming-tables could best be retrieved by his plunging still more heavily there.

Advice, however, she considered, she must have, and, as she sat frowning alone over her second cup of coffee in the breakfast-parlour, it suddenly occurred to her that she might do worse than to enlist Northover's aid.

It was the matter of a few minutes to jump up and run to the escritoire in the back drawing-room to scribble a few lines to him requesting him to call in Green Street as soon as convenient, and to dispatch the note by the hand of the footman, who was rapidly instructed as to those establishments, customarily frequented by gentlemen of the Viscount's sporting proclivities, where he might most probably run his lordship to earth if he did not find him at home. Of course, she told herself severely, as she sat down to await the results of this venture, she had not at all forgotten that she was very much at outs with Northover, and had parted from him in the greatest dudgeon on the occasion of their last meeting in the Park. But that did not mean that it was necessary for her to refuse to enlist his aid when she needed it.

It did occur to her, though, that his lordship might take a less magnanimous view of the situation, and it was therefore with some relief, an hour or so later, that she heard the sound of carriage wheels outside the door and saw—as she peeped through the blinds of the front drawing-room—Northover's athletic form springing down from his curricle.

She hastily sat down and picked up at random a volume of sermons, which he found her interestedly perusing when he was shown into the room a few minutes later. The title immediately took his eye, and he burst out laughing before he was well within the door.

"No, no, Lydia *mia!*" he said, coming across the room and taking the book out of her hands. "If you wish to persuade me that you have not been sitting here waiting on tenterhooks for my arrival, you will have to think of something more plausible than that!" He tossed the book upon the table and drew up a chair so that he could look directly into her darkling face. "You must be in the deuce of a pucker to have to send your fellow out scouring the town for me."

"I suppose he found you in Jackson's Boxing Saloon?" Lydia said loftily, not deigning to dignify the Viscount's undiplomatically direct remark with an equally direct reply.

"As a matter of fact, it was at Manton's Shooting Gallery. I was trying out a new piece there." The Viscount's penetrating dark eyes searched her face. "Cut line, Lydia!" he commanded. "You didn't drag me here only to rake me down. What have you been up to this time?"

"*I?* Nothing at all!" Lydia said, with dignity. "It is Grandmama—"

"Your grandmother?" Northover's black brows went up and he grinned again. "Come now—"

"It's true!" Lydia said, with some asperity. "She has got herself into the most *afflictive* hobble, and it will ruin us all if I cannot manage somehow to bring her about. Are you by any chance acquainted with a Mrs. Collingworth who lives in Curzon Street?"

The brows went up again, and the Viscount gave a long, low whistle. "So that's the game, is it? Yes, I know her. You don't mean to say that your grandmother has let herself be drawn into *that* net?"

"Yes, she has," Lydia replied, her anxiety rising as she saw the suddenly more sober expression upon the Viscount's face. "What is more, she lost two thousand pounds the first night she went there, and heaven knows how much more on the second—and we can't afford to pay such a sum, Northover; truly we can't! I am at my wit's end as to what to do, for she is talking now of borrowing from a moneylender, and I know from what happened to my own father how disastrous such a course can be!"

"Yes, by God!" Northover said, frowning. "If she once gets into the hands of the cents-per-cent, she'll never be clear of them. But how came she to fall into the Collingworth's clutches? Surely you haven't been moving in *that* set?"

"No, of course not; in fact, I don't even know what set you are speaking of. We met her quite by accident in Richmond Park—or at least it

seemed so at the time, but Mr. Michael Pentony, who introduced us to
her there, has all but admitted that *he* arranged the meeting. Naturally,
his purpose is obvious: if Grandmama is involved in a scandal over her
gaming debts, it must certainly ruin any chance Bayard may have of
inheriting Sir Basil's fortune."

She had been speaking impetuously, too full of her problem to note
anything unusual in the Viscount's manner; but it occurred to her suddenly, as she looked into his face, that it wore a rather odd expression. As
a matter of fact, she now recollected, it was the same harsh and constrained look she had seen upon it fleetingly as he had walked into the
room, before he had burst into laughter at the prim tableau of her sitting
there deep in a volume of sermons.

He only said to her, however, in a level, offhand voice, "That would
certainly seem to be a valid assumption. But why come to me with the
problem? Why not enlist Harlbury's aid?"

"Harlbury's?" She stared at him.

He gave a short laugh. "I see," he said. "You are not sure that he, too,
might not sheer off at the hint of a scandal. Hardly the height of devotion,
one would say! However, when one is angling for rank and fortune, perhaps a commodity worth so little in pounds, shillings, and pence as devotion can be dispensed with."

"I don't know what you are talking of!" she said indignantly, and then,
in a blank voice, as the meaning of his words broke over her, "Oh! You
mean—you think Harlbury and I—?"

He said dryly, "As the news is by this time spread over half the town,
you can scarcely believe it has not reached my ears as well. Pray forgive
me for being so remiss as not to have offered you my felicitations—or perhaps, in your case, it would be more correct to say 'congratulations.'"

Her cheeks flew scarlet at his tone. "Oh! You are the most *abominable*—!
I knew I should never have sent for you!"

"Then why did you? No, no—you needn't answer that. Friendship—it *is*
friendship that we are presumed to feel for each other, isn't it, my dear?—
can be appealed to so much more safely than—er—love—"

Lydia jumped up. "If this is your idea of *friendship*," she said fulminatingly, "to come here and insult me, when I am in the briars and merely
want your advice, it is not mine! And if you don't care to give it to me,
you can go away! I—I shall manage somehow!"

He gave a rather jeering little laugh. "What, and jeopardise such a
promising arrangement as you have come to with Harlbury? No, no—I am

not so hard-hearted as *that!* What is it that you really want me to do, Lydia? Lend you the money? Very well; you have only to find out from your grandmother the sum you require and I'll write you a cheque on Drummond's. No doubt, once you are married to Harlbury, you will find the means to repay me."

"When I am—? I am not going to marry Harlbury! How can you be such a—such a *gudgeon!*" Lydia, incensed, took a rapid turn about the room and came up to stand before him with flashing eyes. "If I were, I should not need *your* help!"

Northover looked at her, the rather ugly, jeering look still there on his face. "Come, my girl, that cock won't fight," he said shortly. "I have it from Lady Gilmour herself that Harlbury's match with her daughter is off, and that his intentions toward you are known at least within his family."

"Yes, they are known there, but that is all—or, at any rate, it *should* be all!" Lydia said. "I am not betrothed to Harlbury; I only offered to allow him to tell his mama that he had an attachment for me so that he might have an excuse for not offering for Miss Beaudoin."

"And why didn't he wish to offer for Miss Beaudoin?" Northover enquired skeptically. "It appears to me that he was quite willing to do so before you thrust *your* finger into that pie. But I will give you credit for being up to every move on the board, my love. If *this* was the ruse you used to bring him into your net—"

"Oh!" Lydia choked. "How *can* you be so hateful! I did it to help Bayard!"

"Very pretty! So, out of the purest altruism, you have scotched Harlbury's match with Minna Beaudoin. It will never have occurred to you, of course, that, having brought him so far, it will no doubt be a simple matter for you to bring him a little farther, into the bonds of matrimony. A fitting end for him, I should think; after all, his mother has kept him in leading-strings all his life, and he will merely see them transferred now from her hands to his wife's." He grinned suddenly, not very pleasantly. "No, don't look at me as if you'd like to murder me, Lydia *mia,*" he said. "Have you forgotten? There is still a favour you want me to do for you. It would be too bad if all these beautiful plans of yours were to go astray merely for the lack of a few thousand pounds at the crucial moment."

Lydia said, from between gritted teeth, "I would not take a penny from you, Northover, if it was to save myself from—from the gallows! I wish you will go away! I have nothing more to say to you!"

"Gammon!" he said coolly. "You are angry now, but when you have had time to think it over you will realise that the use of four or five thousand pounds at a critical moment is well worth having a few disagreeable home truths put to you."

It was this inauspicious moment that Sidwell chose for his entrance with the news that Lord Harlbury had called to see Miss Leyland.

For a moment neither of the participants in the rather spirited scene that had just been taking place appeared to comprehend this statement: then Northover gave a crack of laughter and Lydia, flushing and biting her lip, ordered Sidwell curtly to show his lordship upstairs. Sidwell departed, and Northover, turning to follow him, said mockingly, "Send me word of the sum you must have, Lydia. No, there is no cause for you to get up upon your high ropes; I have been a needy rascal myself in my day, and am quite aware of the shifts one may be forced to in such a situation." He had moved to stand beside her, and now, reaching out a hand, flicked her cheek with a careless forefinger. "Don't despair, my sweet love," he said. "You will come about. I am not in the position to go into detail on the matter as yet, but I am strongly of the opinion that there is no need for you to worry as far as old Rowthorn's intentions toward your family are concerned. And if you succeed in inducing Harlbury to leg-shackle himself to you, that should certainly clinch the matter."

He did not stay to give her the opportunity to utter the startled questions that rose to her lips, but walked out of the room, encountering—as she was able to hear—Harlbury on the stairs. A brief greeting passed between them, and then, as Harlbury entered the room, she was forced to compose herself sufficiently to smile and extend her hand to him.

She saw at once that he was looking very serious, and as soon as he had seated himself he said to her, with an air of resolution, "Miss Leyland, I am come to ask if you and your brother and Mrs. Leyland will do me the honour to make a party for Vauxhall tomorrow evening. It will be a gala night, and I believe I may promise that you will enjoy it."

The manner in which he brought the words out suggested that they held a great deal more significance than a mere party of pleasure would imply. Lydia, who had sat down opposite him, wrenched her mind with difficulty from its wrathful contemplation of the scene with Northover and replied with somewhat absent civility, "I should be delighted, of course—and so, I believe, will Grandmama and Bayard." She then added, not entirely tactfully, "Does your mother know you have come here?"

A dark-red flush overspread his lordship's handsome face. "I cannot think," he said rather stiffly, "what my mother should have to say to it!" "Can't you?" Lydia said. "Then you must be a greater moonling than I would have believed possible!" She saw him staring at her, and realised the rather startling change in manner from the sweetly sympathetic tone she had used during their last conversation in this room that he was being required to digest; but she was too hot still from her encounter with Northover to alter her course. "You know very well," she went on frankly, "that she was as mad as Bedlam over the whole affair last night—and that outrageous scene Mr. Pentony put on for her benefit must have capped the climax. So if she knew you were coming here—"

"She didn't," Harlbury said, the flush still high upon his face. "But I fail to see what concern it is of hers if I escort you to Vauxhall tomorrow evening, Miss Leyland!"

Lydia, who was still wondering what Northover had meant by his cryptic parting remarks concerning Sir Basil, was roused sufficiently by this declaration to say with some appearance of approval, "Do you know, I believe you are coming on, Harlbury! That was very nicely said. Of course it is none of her affair, and the sooner you realise that, the better it will be for you." She conceded after a moment, "I daresay, though, that she read you a horrid scold last night, and that cannot have been very agreeable."

His lordship gloomily agreed that it had not been. He appeared to be in a far from happy mood, and showed distinct traces of the nervousness engendered within him by the knowledge that this visit to Green Street, if it were to come to Lady Harlbury's ears, would no doubt cause her to put him through exactly another such scene as he had been forced to participate in the night before. Lydia, who was scarcely in frame, considering her own difficulties, to humour him out of his depression, was relieved when another pair of morning callers arrived to interrupt their tête-à-tête, even though these callers turned out to be Lady Pentony and Miss Pentony.

Neither of these ladies betrayed the slightest knowledge of what had taken place at the theatre the evening before, but Lydia was very certain, after five minutes' conversation, that Lady Pentony, at least, knew all about it, and that the purpose of her call in Green Street was to discover what effect it had had upon Lydia's matrimonial prospects. The presence of Harlbury himself in the Leyland drawing-room could give her little comfort, Lydia considered with some gratification, and she was ungenerous enough to twist the knife further in Lady Pentony's bosom by behaving towards his lordship in the offhand manner of a young lady so certain of her conquest that she need make no attempt to call attention to it.

So she devoted her conversation amiably to Lady Pentony, leaving Harlbury to entertain Eveline—a task in which he appeared to succeed a good deal better than Lydia had hoped. This, however, was not entirely surprising, for Miss Pentony, in addition to being an exceptionally pretty girl, was obviously so much in awe of his lordship's rank and magnificent good looks that she attended to every word that fell from his lips with the worshipful interest she might have accorded the utterances of a god. Lydia observed in some amusement the manner in which Harlbury gradually blossomed under this unfeigned admiration; the poor fellow, she thought, must rarely have had such an experience. Courted and sought after as he was by the young ladies of his own circle, his grave, stiff manners could never have made him a favourite with them, and he was not so deficient in understanding that he could have failed to realise that no warmer sentiment than ambition lay behind the many lures cast out to him.

Miss Pentony, on the other hand, was casting out no lures at all. She was too dazzled by her good fortune at being allowed to sit beside the handsome young Earl of Harlbury, and even to converse with him, to think of doing more than drinking in the words he uttered and, when necessary, replying to them with a blushing phrase of respectful assent. When his lordship rose to make his adieux, saying politely that he hoped they should meet again, she said, "Oh, so do I!" in accents so nicely divided between a mournful realisation of the unlikelihood of this event and a shy, desperate hope that it might indeed come to pass that his lordship could not but have felt complimented. He said reassuringly that he was certain they would, and then, having reaffirmed his engagement to escort Lydia to Vauxhall on the following evening, took his departure, in a much more cheerful frame of mind, it seemed to her, than that in which he had arrived.

His exit was the signal for Lady Pentony to set to work, with half-hints and smiling innuendoes, to discover how matters really stood between Lydia and his lordship. It was perhaps fortunate for her that the entrance of Mrs. Leyland within a very few minutes put an end to Lydia's being required to cope with her manoeuvres singlehanded, as that young lady was on the point of giving vent to one of her singularly frank expressions of opinion when her grandmother providentially arrived on the scene.

Mrs. Leyland, who detested Lady Pentony, soon put her to rout; but the martial spirit evoked in her by this encounter faded into gloom at once on the visitors' departure, and only the news that Harlbury had called to invite them to Vauxhall stirred her into some slight cheerfulness again.

"But, there!" she said pessimistically, upon Lydia's immediately turning the subject and putting a question to her as to whether she had had any fresh ideas on how to deal with her financial difficulties, "I know how it will be! You will do nothing to fix his interest, and it will end with his mama's prevailing upon him to offer for the Beaudoin girl, after all. I vow, my love, it is *too* provoking of you, for it is not as if you had an inclination for any other gentleman! Do but think of the pin-money you might have, and the gowns, and the carriages, to say nothing of the position you would occupy in Society as the Countess of Harlbury! And then poor Bayard might be comfortable, too, for I daresay Lord Harlbury would be happy to purchase a commission for him in an excellent regiment."

"Nothing," said Lydia shortly, "will make Bayard comfortable except being able to marry Minna Beaudoin. Have you *looked* at him lately, Grandmama? He is quite miserable, I know, though he does his best to conceal it from us."

"Nonsense!" said Mrs. Leyland. "He will probably tumble in and out of love with half a dozen girls before he is ready to settle himself. And I have it from Lucinda Aimer herself that Miss Beaudoin's fortune is nothing at all, which makes it highly unsuitable that Bayard should fix his choice on her." She shook her head with a desponding air. "I do not know how it is," she said, "that you both *refuse* to take advantage of the opportunities I have provided you with by bringing you to London, at the greatest sacrifice of my own health and convenience! And the result—if I am able to escape a debtors' prison—will be that we shall be obliged to retire again to that *odious* plantation, where *you* will dwindle into an old maid and *I* into my grave!"

Lydia could not help being diverted by this highly coloured statement of the situation, and a gurgle of laughter escaped her. She was at once reproved for her levity and required with some severity to inform her afflicted grandparent what she found to amuse her in the bleak picture of their joint future that had just been drawn for her—a task which she declined to undertake, on the grounds that Mrs. Leyland's mood was such that she would be quite unable to find amusement in anything at the present moment.

"But we shall come about somehow, Grandmama, I promise you," Lydia said. "If the worst comes, I can always borrow the money from Northover to preserve you from the dire fate you are imagining for yourself—though I confess I had rather go to prison myself than be obliged to do so."

Mrs. Leyland stared at her. "From Northover! But—will he lend it to you? Why should he do such a thing?" A gleam of hope suddenly appeared upon her face. "Lydia! Tell me the truth!" she exclaimed. "Has *he* made you an offer? Oh, my love, that would be beyond anything great, for, though he has *not* the kind of reputation I should choose to see in your husband, he is splendidly rich, and I daresay quite amiable if one can bring oneself to overlook a certain sarcastic levity—"

Lydia, upon whose face a sudden flush had risen, got up quickly.

"Oh, Grandmama, do give over!" she said rather sharply. "Of course he has not made me an offer—nor has he the slightest intention of doing so! Indeed, I shall be surprised if he ever marries. Why should he, when he is so well entertained by his *chères-amies?*"

"*That* statement," said Mrs. Leyland, disapprovingly, "is not what I like to hear from your lips, Lydia! Not that I see what his having mistresses has to say to anything, for I am sure that *that* does not prevent a gentleman from wishing to set up his nursery when he reaches a certain age— particularly one in Northover's position—"

"Grandmama, if you do not stop, I shall scream!" Lydia threatened, her face still suffused with angry colour. "You may put Northover quite out of your mind as a matrimonial prospect for me, I assure you! Nothing is more unlikely than that he will make me an offer. He is so odiously rich that he can afford to tow us out of the River Tick for his own amusement and never count the cost—that is all!"

Mrs. Leyland, on whose face an expression of increasing foreboding had appeared during this speech, at this point could contain herself no longer.

"Good God, Lydia," she said, in a failing voice, "do not tell me that you have conceived a *tendre* for Northover, and *that* is why you are being so gooseish about Harlbury!"

"For Northover!" Lydia, who had been about to leave the room, swung around, stung on the raw, it seemed, by this accusation. "For—*Northover!*"

"Really, my dear, there is no need to fly into such a taking if it is not so," Mrs. Leyland said. "I am sure nobody could be happier than I should be to hear I am mistaken, but it *does* appear to me—"

"I," said Lydia, controlling herself with a great effort and speaking in a quite calm voice, "am going to leave this room. Carrying on a conversation with one's grandmother when she has obviously taken leave of her senses—"

"But it will be *you* who have taken leave of *your* senses if you have been foolish enough to fall in love with a man who has no intention of marrying you!" Mrs. Leyland pointed out, piteously. "Oh, my love, surely you would never be so lost to all propriety as to let him make *you* his mistress—for if he has indeed offered you the money to bring us out of our present difficulties, without having the intention of marrying you, you may depend upon it that that is what he has in mind! And *that* would quite ruin everything! It is not as if you were married and settled, you know; I should *never* be able to find a husband for you!"

She got no further, for at this point Lydia made good her threat and swept from the room.

It was quite beneath Miss Leyland's code of behaviour to give way to tears, as other young ladies might have done under the agitating influence of the facts that had suddenly been brought into the open by the frank speaking of the scene she had just taken part in; but it must be reported that she stood for a full quarter hour, with her eyes unnaturally bright and her lips ominously quivering, at the window of her bedchamber before she was calm enough to go on about the ordinary business of her day. To which it may be added that when she did emerge from her room she appeared unwontedly subdued, and even endured a scold from Winch on the subject of a rent in the sea-green sarsnet gown she had worn the evening before without attempting so much as a single saucy word in her own defence.

16

Lydia, who had not had the least intention, even before her disastrous conversation with her grandmother, of obeying Northover's injunction to let him know the extent of Mrs. Leyland's debts, sent no message to the Viscount on either that day or the next, and was therefore more than a little surprised, on the afternoon following his visit, to receive from him a brief missive, brought by hand, and containing a cheque in the amount of five thousand pounds made out to her grandmother.

It is not like you to be missish, Lydia, my love, with so much at stake, the accompanying careless scrawl ran. *If this doesn't cover the lot, let me know. Yours, etc. Northover.*

"What is it, my dear?" Mrs. Leyland, who was sitting with Lydia, forebodingly enquired, seeing her granddaughter's face alter and the colour rush up into her cheeks as she perused the note. "I hope it is not from Harlbury, saying that he must relinquish the Vauxhall scheme."

"From Harlbury? No! It is from Northover!" Lydia tossed the cheque across the table to her contemptuously. "You see at how high a rate he sets me!" she said. "I should be flattered, I daresay. And more if I desire it! There are no limits to his generosity, it seems!"

Mrs. Leyland, who had picked up the cheque, eyed it incredulously. "Five thousand pounds!" she gasped. "Oh, my love, it is a great deal more even than we require! Was there ever anything so providential!—for now I shall be able to settle that odious Celeste's bill as well, and you may have the jaconet muslin with the Russian bodice that so becomes you, after all—"

"Grandmama!" Lydia's startled voice cut into these delighted reflections. "What can you be thinking of? Of course we cannot accept it! I shall send it back to him at once!"

"Send it back—" Mrs. Leyland's voice faltered, and then strengthened into tones of outraged incredulity. "Send—it—back! My dear child, you must be all about in your head! Do you realise that I have been driven quite to desperation by our situation over these past days? First you say I am to have no dealings with Mr. King—and now you wish me to return this—this *honeyfall* to Northover!"

"But, Grandmama," Lydia protested, "*you* were the one who said that Northover could have only one idea in mind in offering me such a sum! Surely you cannot wish me to keep it!"

Mrs. Leyland looked at her with some hauteur. "Naturally *we* shall not *keep* it," she said. "We shall merely accept it as a loan. No doubt I shall be able to repay the entire sum within a very short time, for I am quite convinced that my luck must turn—"

"*No!*" Lydia said, snatching the cheque from her grandmother's fingers. "Grandmama, you *would* not be so imprudent as to sit down to play again, after what has happened—and with Northover's money! It would be infamous!"

"Infamous! To attempt to establish my granddaughter and grandson respectably in life?—for that is the *only* reason, you must know, that I indulge in cards at all—"

"Well, I will not have it!" Lydia said implacably, carrying the cheque over to the escritoire and sitting down there. "I shall send this back to him at once."

"Lydia!" intoned Mrs. Leyland dramatically. "Unnatural girl! You cannot do it! I implore you—to save us all from the Fleet—!"

"No!" said Lydia ruthlessly, already scribbling furiously upon a sheet of hot-pressed notepaper. "Don't put yourself into a taking, Grandmama! I shall marry Harlbury if it is necessary—or Sir Carsbie Chant—or even that odious Michael Pentony—*anything* rather than give Northover the right to think he has been able to—"

She broke off to reread with satisfaction what she had written. *My lord, I herewith return the cheque you have sent, and must beg that you will not call in Green Street again. It will be quite useless, as I do not aspire to the honour of the position you have designed for me. L.L.* She then folded the paper, enclosed the cheque within it, and, having sealed it with a wafer, rang the bell for the footman and directed him to carry it immediately to Lord Northover.

Having accomplished this, she fell into a very cheerful and lighthearted mood, if one were to judge by her conversation, and embarked upon a highly interested discussion as to whether she should wear green ribbons or white with the gown of jonquil sarsnet she had chosen for the Vauxhall party that evening. Only the arrival of a bouquet of yellow roses in an elegant holder, with the compliments of Lord Harlbury, prevented her grandmother from characterising her as the most unfeeling girl it had ever been her misfortune to become acquainted with, the posy having the effect of diverting her mind once more to the happy prospect that Lydia might yet exert herself to bring that unexceptionable young man to the point.

It was therefore a moderately cheerful party that set out for Vauxhall

Gardens that evening. Harlbury, who was apparently intent on doing everything in his power to make the project a success, had hired sculls to
carry them from Westminster to the water-gate of the famous gardens,
and Lydia, who had never visited Vauxhall before, was in transports—
slightly overdone, her somewhat amused brother considered, but obviously
quite satisfactory to Lord Harlbury—over the sight that greeted her eyes as
she was handed ashore. The gardens, which were lit by thousands of lan-
terns, glittering in brilliant colour about the giant kiosk where the orches-
tra played and hanging in graceful festoons to illuminate the long pillared
colonnades, had all the appearance, she assured Harlbury, with some lack
of originality, of a fairyland, and as they trod the leafy walks towards the
Rotunda where they were to attend a concert before partaking of supper,
she indulged in a constant flow of exclamations of wonderment that could
not but have been gratifying to his lordship.

He seemed, however, to be in a somewhat distrait mood that evening—a
circumstance that was presently explained by his confiding to Lydia, as
they were taking their places in the concert-hall, that his mother had also
decided to visit the gardens that evening in company with Lord and Lady
Gilmour.

"I told her, of course," he said, "that I should have invited her to join
our party if I had had the least notion she would have cared to do so. It
will look very odd, you know, for her to come with Lord and Lady Gilmour instead."

"Which is exactly what she desired, of course," Lydia said, quite unperturbed. "Well, if she wishes to parade her differences with you before the
world, that is her affair, and certainly need not concern you in the least."
She added, looking up and bestowing a brilliant smile upon a party making their way to seats in the row just before them, "But here they are
now. Dear Lady Gilmour, how do you do? And Lady Harlbury—what an
agreeable surprise!"

Both ladies returned exceedingly cool bows to this cordial greeting, but
Miss Beaudoin, following in her mother's wake, cast a glance upon the
group behind her—including, as it did, both young Mr. Leyland and Lord
Harlbury—which immediately sent a suffocating flush up to mantle her
clear olive skin. She stammered a word of greeting, her eyes seeking
Bayard's with such beseeching intensity that it must have required a man
far less in love than he was not to understand that she urgently wished for
an opportunity to speak to him alone that evening.

But it was impossible for him, with the concert about to begin, to do
more than acknowledge this mute message with a fervent glance. Both

parties then settled back in their chairs to find what enjoyment they could in the music, Lady Harlbury's rigidly erect pose suggesting, however, that she, at least, found it impossible to do anything of the sort in such close proximity to Miss Lydia Leyland.

If the truth were told, it is probable that few of the members of either party—with the exception of the pair of very fashionable young gentlemen who had come in Lady Gilmour's train—were able to concentrate sufficiently upon the music to know whether they were listening to a much-admired oratorio by Handel or to a street-singer's ballad bawled in their ears. Lydia spent the greater part of her time in endeavouring to contrive a scheme by which it might be possible to detach Miss Beaudoin from her mama and Lady Harlbury, so that she might have the interview with Bayard she evidently so much desired; but even her ingenuity boggled at the task, and she was obliged at last to give it up and to hope that chance might later be kind enough to present the lovers with the opportunity they craved.

When the first act ended, the Gilmour party, disdaining to view the spectacle of the Grand Cascade, in which a waterfall, with a mill, a bridge, and a succession of vehicles crossing the latter, was represented upon the stage with a lifelike similitude extending even to the sound of rushing waters and rumbling wheels, passed out of the Rotunda. With the exception of Lord Gilmour, who paused for a friendly word with Mrs. Leyland and Harlbury, no communication took place between the opposing parties, unless the term might be applied to the dagger-look Lydia received from Lady Harlbury as she passed by.

"I *do* think," Lydia said to Harlbury, looking thoughtfully at the pretty painted fan she carried, "that if I were you I should make arrangements to live apart from your mama, Harlbury. She could not drive you into such a panic if she were not able to see you whenever she wishes—"

"I am *not* in a panic!" his lordship said, in a low, indignant voice.

"Yes, you are, Harlbury," Lydia contradicted him, incurably frank. "I can scarcely blame you, for there is nothing horrider than being raked down by someone for every least thing one does; but if you saw her less frequently it would not signify so much. And it would be excellent practice for you to begin living without her, you know, for when you are married you must expect to do so."

"When I am married—!" His lordship cast a somewhat startled glance at her. "But I am not—"

"Of course you are not—just now," Lydia said, giving his arm a reassuring pat. "But you will wish to marry some day, and once we have quite put the idea to rest that you are to offer for Miss Beaudoin, we shall set about it to find a more suitable young lady for you."

Lord Harlbury appeared to be about to enter some protest to this scheme, but was silenced by the resumption of the entertainment. His handsome countenance, however, had taken on an even more harried look than that which it had worn at the start of the evening, and it was apparent that he looked forward with no great anticipation to the hours that must still elapse before he could decently bring his party away from the gardens.

But if one of the apprehensions he harboured was that Lydia meant to set about it immediately to implement her matrimonial plans for him, he need not have concerned himself. Miss Leyland, with Bayard and Minna on her mind, had other things to think of. And, as if that were not enough, she was greeted, when they left the Rotunda and repaired for supper to one of the boxes overlooking the principal grove, by the sight of Northover lounging in the box just opposite, chatting easily with Lady Gilmour.

A slight flush appeared upon Lydia's face; she shut her fan with a snap, and Bayard and Minna and all their tribulations, together with Harlbury and all of his, instantly flew out of her head.

Of course it was not lost upon Harlbury that, by the most vexatious of coincidences, he was for the second time that evening obliged to attempt to enjoy himself under the basilisk stare of his offended mama. But he pulled himself together with commendable fortitude and ordered an excellent supper for the party, which included the ham-shavings and rack punch for which Vauxhall was famous.

He had scarcely completed this task when Northover, having left the Gilmour box by the simple method of vaulting over the low barrier in front, instead of using the more conventional form of egress by the door at the back, strolled across and, after exchanging casual greetings with the company, enquired pointblank of Miss Leyland, "Just what the deuce did you think you were about, Lydia, to send that remarkably henwitted message to me?"

Lydia, in the act of swallowing a morsel of chicken, choked, and gave him a glance that fully expressed her indignation at the unfair advantage he was taking in bringing the matter up in a situation in which she could not speak openly. She controlled herself, however, and merely said loftily, "I do not care to discuss the matter, Lord Northover."

"You don't, don't you? Well, I do—and, what is more, I shall call in Green Street tomorrow to do exactly that."

"I have asked you *not* to—" Lydia began, fulminatingly.

"I am aware, my dear." His mocking dark eyes appreciatively surveyed her flushed face. "It was abominably ill-bred of you, but I shall overlook it. No," he added to Bayard, who had started up with an irate exclamation at this uncomplimentary speech, "never mind looking like bull-beef, half-ling. Your sister is quite capable of fighting her own battles; in fact, I should think it hardly sporting of you to deprive her of the privilege when it affords her so much harmless amusement."

With a nod to his stunned auditors, he walked off, leaving Mrs. Leyland, who recovered herself first, to say in a rather anguished voice to Lydia, "Indeed, he is the oddest man! But need you have been so very abrupt with him, my love? After all, he—"

"Abrupt!" exclaimed Bayard wrathfully. "I should rather hope she was! What the deuce does he mean by it, to speak to her so?"

"I do *not* wish to hear another word on the subject!" Lydia said ominously. She saw Lady Gilmour, who had been looking very ill-pleased at Northover's departure from her box, laughing now as he re-entered it, and tapping his arm with her fan while glancing in Lydia's direction. Her bosom swelled. "He is rude and—and unprincipled—and if he thinks I am another Lady Gilmour, I promise you that he shall very soon learn his mistake. Harlbury, where in the world are you going?" she broke off to enquire in surprise, as his lordship arose and evinced a sudden intention of leaving the box.

He turned a slightly flushed face upon her. "You are my guest, Miss Leyland," he said, "and if Lord Northover has insulted you—"

"For heaven's sake, Harlbury," she said severely, "do not be so absurd! Of course he has insulted me; he has been doing it since the first day I met him—but that does not mean that either you *or* Bayard need feel called upon to interfere! *I* shall deal with Lord Northover, and I promise you that he will be very sorry indeed before I have done that he has dared to cross swords with me."

Harlbury and Bayard exchanged glances, the former looking uncertain and rather puzzled; but a rueful grin gradually replaced the lowering expression upon Bayard's face.

"She's right, you know, Harlbury!" he said cheerfully. "We had as well both sit down. We should only make cakes of ourselves, trying to force a quarrel upon Northover because he and Lyddy have come to cuffs again."

"I should rather think so!" Lydia said, and added darkly, "Never believe I shall not get my own back with him! I have my methods!"

Lord Harlbury, resuming his chair, looked as if he could well believe this latter statement. But his rather bemused mental contemplation of the unorthodox Miss Leyland was interrupted almost at once by the appearance of a newly familiar face among the strollers passing by: Miss Eveline Pentony, wearing a pale-blue gown with a bodice cut in the Austrian style, which made her look rather more sweetly angelic than usual. She was on her brother's arm, and it was probable that Harlbury, seeing them together, for the first time made the startled connexion in his mind between the vulgar young gentleman who had invaded his mother's box at Drury Lane and the worshipping young lady he had met in Green Street the day before.

As for Lydia, one glance at the pair was sufficient to bring to *her* the exasperated remembrance that both Lady Pentony and Miss Pentony had heard Harlbury refer to his Vauxhall scheme the day before—a fact which was undoubtedly responsible for Mr. Michael Pentony's having determined to visit the gardens that evening himself.

It was impossible for her to pretend that she had not seen them, however, for Harlbury, starting up at once, had already greeted Miss Pentony. Mrs. Leyland was not behindhand in doing likewise, and Lydia was resigning herself to the prospect of a repetition upon Mr. Pentony's part of the scene he had played in Lady Harlbury's box when she saw his eyes fix themselves suddenly upon Harlbury's face. She turned her head, and observed in an instant what it was that had no doubt caught Mr. Pentony's attention.

Lord Harlbury was gazing upon Miss Pentony with the intent, earnest, self-revelatory expression which only a very sober and literal-minded young man could have been betrayed into allowing upon his countenance in a public place. What was more, he was inviting her—stammering a little over the words—to join his party, an invitation which naturally had to include Mr. Pentony as well. Miss Pentony, looking much as if the heavens had suddenly opened and deposited before her a magnificently handsome angel in a well-fitting blue coat and starched neckcloth, gave an immediate and dazzled assent, which she then recollected herself sufficiently to qualify by a shyly enquiring glance cast at her brother.

But even she, Lydia reflected resignedly, could not have been gooseish enough to anticipate opposition from *that* quarter; and the upshot of the matter was that in the space of a pair of minutes both Mr. and Miss Pentony had entered the booth and joined the party there.

If Lydia had expected Mr. Pentony to resume the boorish manner he had displayed in Lady Harlbury's box at Drury Lane, she was doing an injustice to that gentleman's powers of observation. It had taken him no more than thirty seconds to note that Lord Harlbury, far from being absorbed in Miss Leyland's charms, was showing a lively interest in his sister's; and it required very little longer for him to come to the surprising conclusion that Miss Pentony's milk-and-water disposition and total lack of pretension to anything in the nature of liveliness or wit were exactly what Lord Harlbury liked.

The idea that anything might come of this very odd—to her brother, at least—predilection was not one on which he laid much weight, particularly in view of his lordship's notorious lack of independence from the wishes of his mama. But Mr. Pentony was not the man to neglect a possible *coup* because it seemed a long chance, and he determined on the instant to do nothing that might jeopardise it in any way.

He therefore remained discreetly in the background, devoting his conversation chiefly to Mrs. Leyland, and sustaining with an appearance of perfect equanimity the cold shoulder that Lydia turned to him.

As for Lydia, the chief amusement she was able to obtain from the trying hour that followed was the sight of Lady Harlbury's burning curiosity as to the identity of the ethereally blonde young lady to whom her son was paying such marked attentions. As Miss Pentony was entirely unknown in the exalted circles in which Lady Harlbury herself, and the other members of Lady Gilmour's party, moved, this curiosity perforce remained unsatisfied until, the supper being concluded, the members of Lord Harlbury's party chose to leave their box to stroll through the grounds and watch the exhibition of fireworks that was about to take place.

This instantly decided Lady Harlbury that she, too, wished to watch the fireworks. The rest of the company rose to accompany her for civility's sake, with the result that the two parties came face to face with each other in the neutral territory between their boxes.

"Shafto," Lady Harlbury said, coming up immediately to the attack as she confronted her son, "I do not believe that I am acquainted with this young lady." And she favoured Miss Pentony with a comprehensive stare, from the crown of her fair head to the tips of her little kid slippers, that had that modest young lady instantly in a blush.

Lord Harlbury, looking startled but resolute, presented Miss Pentony to his mother.

"Pentony?" Lady Harlbury repeated, her brows on the rise. "Pentony? I seem to have heard the name—"

"I had the honour, my lady," Mr. Pentony, stepping forward, suavely remarked, "of making your acquaintance the other evening at Drury Lane. Miss Pentony is my sister."

A look of horror overspread Lady Harlbury's face. "*Your* sister!" she ejaculated. "*Your* sister! Good heavens!"

"I am afraid," Mr. Pentony said, himself having the grace to colour slightly, "that I must apologise for my behaviour upon that occasion, my lady. The truth is that I was labouring at the time under the double difficulty of a strong misapprehension and considerable emotional stress, which may have caused me to appear in a somewhat invidious light to you. I must beg, however, that—even if you feel it impossible to pardon *me*—you will not extend your disapprobation to my sister."

But Lady Harlbury, far from being mollified by this speech, appeared on the verge of suffering one of the spasms which—as her son had bitter reason to know—invariably attacked her iron constitution on the occasion of any shock caused to it by her offspring's behaving in a manner not entirely in accord with her own ideas. On the present occasion the attack was sufficiently violent for her to demand his arm upon the instant, and, though Lord Gilmour and the other gentlemen in the party immediately offered her any assistance that lay in their power, it was Harlbury alone whom she would allow to lead her to a seat and extract, under her directions, the hartshorn that she carried in her reticule.

Her indisposition naturally threw both parties into confusion. Lady Gilmour, hovering over her afflicted guest, forgot entirely for the moment the danger that lay in permitting Minna to remain unguarded in Bayard Leyland's company; Lydia, who, in spite of her dislike of Mr. Pentony, was kindhearted enough to pity his sister's embarrassment, was occupied in preventing that damsel from bursting into tears by addressing some bracing small talk to her; and Mrs. Leyland, who cared nothing for Lady Harlbury's dramatic indisposition, but who had not yet given up hope that Northover might be induced to return, on the strictly businesslike terms of a loan, the cheque that Lydia had so cavalierly flung back at him, was endeavouring to take advantage of the brouhaha around her to drop a word to this effect in his lordship's ear.

It was the opportunity for which the two lovers had been waiting. Miss Beaudoin saw her mama's preoccupation; Bayard was not behindhand in noting that his inamorata was, for the moment, unguarded. An exchange of glances, a murmured word—and two figures detached themselves quietly from the now twinned parties and melted into the darkness of a leafy walk.

17

"I had to talk to you!" Minna said. They had reached the darkness of one of the secluded paths leading to the little temple at the end of the Long Walk and had halted there, feeling themselves at last safe from pursuit or observation. Huge trees rose above them, their branches motionless in the summer night air; the strains of distant music came softly to their ears. "The most dreadful thing has happened!" she said, swallowing the sob that threatened to choke her voice. "Mama has decided that we are not to go to Brighton at the end of the month, after all; she is taking me to Scarborough instead. I shall be miles and miles away from you—and, oh, Bayard! I fear that is not the worst! If you should' find the means to come to Scarborough, too, I am quite certain that she will take me even farther away, perhaps to Paris, for she is determined that, even if I am not to marry Lord Harlbury, I shall never marry you!"

All this grievous news came tumbling from Miss Beaudoin's lips in a mournful torrent, and the effect upon Bayard was to impel him irresistibly to take her in his arms and assure her, with the fervour of young lovers from time immemorial, that, come what might, they should not be parted; somehow they would find a way.

"Yes—but how?" said Minna despairingly, her head resting against his well-tailored blue coat. "We cannot marry—you have no money, and I am not of age—and, oh, I cannot bear it, to lose you forever!"

"Nor I to lose you," he said. "And we shan't, my darling! I shall contrive something—"

She raised her head, looking at him trustfully. "Oh, I knew you would do so!" she said. "I am too stupid to think of the least shift myself that will serve us, but *you* will do so—will you not, Bayard? Only we must act quickly or it will be too late. We are to leave on Friday, you see."

"On Friday!" Bayard looked appalled. "But—good God!—that is only two days from now! How can we possibly—?"

"Perhaps we could go to America," Minna suggested timidly. "I have—I have a little money put by from my quarter's allowance, and there are my pearls—"

Her hand rose to touch the single valuable strand that encircled her slender neck.

Bayard shook his head emphatically. "No, my God! I couldn't let you do that! Besides, it's not necessary; I'm not so purse-pinched as *that*, though I'm in no position to set up as a married man—you know that!"

Minna's dark eyes looked up at him tragically. "Not even in America?" she asked. "You have Belmaison still, and Lydia says we shouldn't starve there."

"No, no, we'd not starve, sweetheart—but how could I take you there, thousands of miles from your home, miles even from any other society than my own and that of a few ignorant servants?"

"I should not mind it, if *you* are there," Minna said forlornly. "But I—I daresay it would be different for you."

This assumption was sufficient to cause Bayard to fold her tightly in his arms again, and to declare fervently that *she* was the only thing necessary to *his* happiness—after which it somehow seemed to be settled between them that they were to spend the rest of their days in idyllic bliss at Belmaison, the only matter remaining to be settled being by what means they were to succeed in reaching this secluded Paradise, and to manage to be married on the way.

Meanwhile, Lydia had been the first of the party gathered around Lady Harlbury to realise that Bayard and Minna had disappeared. She herself would have been quite content to have them spend the remainder of the evening in each other's company, but only a few moments after she had made her own discovery of their absence she saw Lady Gilmour begin to look about her as well, and then speak a few hurried words to her husband. Lord Gilmour laughed, and returned a reply that caused Lady Gilmour to say in a voice of sufficient asperity to reach Lydia's ears, "I don't consider that amusing, Ned! Do you wish the child to ruin herself? Do go off and find her, for I cannot leave Lady Harlbury as yet!"

Lord Gilmour shrugged good-humouredly and moved off down the path. It occurred to Lydia that Lady Gilmour herself would doubtless join in the search before many minutes had passed, and that the guilty couple would be in for an uncomfortable scene if they were discovered by her ladyship alone in each other's company; and with her usual resolution she made up her mind to join the two culprits herself, if possible, before Lady Gilmour succeeded in coming up with them.

She had, of course, no idea in which direction they had gone, and, as she was entirely unfamiliar with Vauxhall, she could do no more than wander at random along the paths, hoping that chance would sooner or later bring her to the pair she sought. She soon discovered, however, that Vauxhall on a gala night was scarcely the most comfortable place in the world for a young lady unencumbered by an escort, for a number of town bucks, attracted by the sight of a remarkably pretty young woman straying alone down dimly lit paths, had approached her with overtures of gallantry before she had been five minutes absent from her party. The most importunate of these, a young blade whose gigantically high neckcloth and striped green-and-gold waistcoat proclaimed his aspirations to dandyism, had, after following her the length of the path she trod, actually had the audacity to come up beside her and seize her arm when, to her relief, she suddenly caught sight of Sir Carsbie Chant standing in a group at the end of the path.

He saw her at the same moment and, grasping her predicament, came at once to her rescue. True, the impressiveness of his action was somewhat impaired by the slurring remarks cast upon his appearance by the encroaching buck, who addressed him as "old spindle-shanks," and enquired derisively how many pounds of buckram wadding were required in his coat to give him more of a figure than a starving clerk. But some indignant flourishing of the gold-headed cane Sir Carsbie carried, together with the interloper's knowledge that his opponent's friends stood nearby, ready to aid him if it should come to blows between them, eventually decided the matter in Sir Carsbie's favour.

"Puppy! City mushroom!" Sir Carsbie ejaculated as he watched the intruder make off, and he dusted his coat-sleeve with an exquisite cambric handkerchief, as if he felt himself contaminated by having merely stood in near proximity to such a person. "My dear Miss Leyland, how very fortunate that I chanced to be by! You have become separated from your party, I apprehend? Allow me the honour, pray, of escorting you back to them."

"Oh yes, that would be very kind of you!" Lydia said immediately, suppressing a tiny gurgle of laughter at her rescuer's air of self-congratulatory heroics. "Indeed, I did not think I should encounter such difficulties merely by walking alone for a few minutes in a place as fashionable as this!"

Sir Carsbie, who was feeling quite puffed up with his own bravery in putting the annoying buck to rout, assured her that a young lady of such ravishing appearance must always be prepared, in any surroundings, to find admiration overleaping the bounds of civility. He then enquired, a trifle jealously, in whose party she had come to Vauxhall that evening.

"In Lord Harlbury's," she replied. "But I do not wish to return to it quite yet, if you please. I left it, you see, on purpose to try to find Miss Beaudoin, who has become separated from *her* party, so if you would be so very kind as to help me to look for her—"

Sir Carsbie obviously considered it a trifle odd that the search for one unchaperoned young lady should have been placed in the hands of a second; but he was more than willing to stroll with Lydia through Vauxhall Gardens, and therefore made no demur to this plan. In point of fact, as he stole surreptitious glances at her exquisite profile and perfectly proportioned figure, it occurred to him forcefully that he might do worse than to benefit from his present opportunity by pressing upon her the suit which he was just about determining to make for her hand. The news concerning an imminent engagement between her and Lord Harlbury had recently reached his ears, and, though he had pooh-poohed the idea of such a match at his clubs, it had been more than a little disagreeable to him to feel that he was generally considered to have been cut out by his lordship.

It was unlike Sir Carsbie, who had reached his middle years, when it was possible for him to contemplate such a step as marriage with entirely dispassionate consideration, to permit himself to be rushed into precipitate action; but he could not but feel that, to a young lady, this was the very kind of romantic setting and occasion that must appeal, and he therefore somewhat unwisely allowed himself to be hurried into taking advantage of it.

Thus it came about that Lydia, walking alone rather absently beside him, her mind occupied with quite other matters than her companion's intentions towards her, was suddenly startled to find herself seized about the waist and Sir Carsbie's voice murmuring fervidly into her ear, "I can no longer contain my ardor! Miss Leyland—Lydia—you must allow me to express my feelings toward you!"

With this, he attempted to implant a kiss upon her lips, but Lydia, wresting herself free of his grasp, succeeded in receiving it only as a glancing salute upon her cheek. She gave a gasp, half of indignation, half of amusement, and said in a reproving tone, "*Dear* Sir Carsbie—not in this place, I beg you! Someone may come upon us at any moment!"

"Do you think I care for that?" Sir Carsbie, who had dined at White's with a party of friends, by whom he had been encouraged to imbibe rather freely of the excellent wine procurable there, was a trifle pot-valiant as well, and, once excited to action, was not to be so easily fobbed off. "My dear—*dearest* girl, you must know that you have bowled me out at last—yes, damme, though I am sure the town has said these fifteen years that Carsbie Chant was far too downy ever to become a tenant-for-life!"

This was accompanied by another attempt to implant a kiss upon

Lydia's lips—again, owing to that young lady's artful manoeuvring, an unsuccessful one.

"For heaven's sake, Sir Carsbie," she said, with slight severity, "do give over behaving in this totally *unnecessary* manner!"

"But I am proposing marriage to you, Miss Leyland!"

"Marriage!" Lydia for the first time looked a trifle startled.

"Yes! Marriage, Miss Leyland!" Sir Carsbie reiterated magniloquently, himself as impressed, apparently, by the immense condescension of this statement as he obviously expected her to be. "The fact that you have no fortune," he continued, "that your position in life is such that you could not anticipate that a gentleman holding my position in Society would consider an alliance with you, weighs nothing with me, I assure you! I consider that you will admirably fill that position in the *haut ton* to which marriage with me will raise you."

"But I do not *wish* to marry you, Sir Carsbie!" Lydia said, with more truth than civility—and, having said it, found herself genuinely surprised at the sound of such an immediate negative issuing from her lips, since it had been only that day that she had declared her complete willingness to wed Sir Carsbie or any other gentleman who would relieve her of the necessity of accepting Northover's largesse.

But if her utterance of this statement was surprising to her, to Sir Carsbie it was perfectly staggering.

"Not wish to marry me!" he ejaculated incredulously. "Not wish—! Nonsense, my dear Miss Leyland! You are distraught—you do not know what you say—and this is not, after all, surprising, since you can have had no notion of such an offer's being about to be made to you."

"No, no, of course I had not," Lydia said soothingly, recovering her own poise as Sir Carsbie appeared on the verge of losing his. "But, dear Sir Carsbie, honoured as I must be by your offer, it is definitely my opinion that we should not suit. Besides," she added, candour getting the better of good intentions once more, "I do not think you would *really* care for being married, after all—having children, I mean, and giving up all your flirts to become a settled sort of man—"

The reference to his amorous conquests somewhat mollified Sir Carsbie; the mention of the production of children offended his sense of the delicacy suitable in a young female upon such an occasion; but by far the chief emotion engendered in his breast by Lydia's speech was a dark suspicion that, in rejecting such an advantageous offer, she must have another even more advantageous in mind.

He tittered suddenly, and said, "Oh, if you are thinking of Harlbury, my dear, you had best put the thought quite out of your head. He will never marry without his mother's approval, and I assure you she has been running about the town these three days telling everyone who will listen to her the most dreadful stories about you—that you have low connexions, and that you positively *entrapped* poor Harlbury by the most shameless manoeuvres. To be sure, she does not go *quite* so far as Lady Gilmour, who has termed you, it has been reported to me, a scheming wench—"

Lydia unexpectedly bestowed a dazzling smile upon him. "How very kind of you to tell me this, Sir Carsbie!" she said cordially. "And how much kinder, even, of you to make an offer for a young lady of such a shocking reputation! I wonder that you could bring yourself to do it!"

"Ah—well—er—" Sir Carsbie looked somewhat taken aback. "Of course *I* didn't believe a word of it," he hastily disclaimed. "Very respectable families, the Leylands—the Tresselts—though they have fallen on bad times—"

"Thank you!" Lydia said. "But *not* on such bad times, I assure you, as to oblige me to marry where I feel no inclination." She added briskly, "And now *do* let us get on with our search for Miss Beaudoin, for I fear we have wasted our time far too long already."

"Wasted—our—time!" This description of the tendering of an offer of marriage from himself to Miss Leyland was too much for Sir Carsbie. He stiffened visibly, drew himself up, and uttered a—"Well!"—of such explosive hauteur that it brought Lydia, who had already taken a step or two along the path, around to gaze at him enquiringly. "Perhaps you do not realise, Miss Leyland," he continued waspishly, "that it is not likely you will soon again find a gentleman of fortune and high position who is willing to overlook certain deplorable facts concerning your situation in life and—if I may say so—a somewhat unseemly levity in your conduct as well—"

"But you are *not* overlooking them, Sir Carsbie," Lydia said reasonably. "Indeed, I cannot conceive why you should wish to marry me at all, since they appear so offensive to you, and I am quite sure that when you have had time to think the whole matter over, you will be very glad indeed that I did not accept you. You *are* a trifle foxed, you know," she added, looking at him critically. "Perhaps, after all, you had better remain here and I shall go on looking for Miss Beaudoin alone, for I certainly cannot be stopping every half minute to engage in an argument with you."

The expression on Sir Carsbie's face had by this time become indicative

CLARE DARCY 547

of such outraged indignation that even Lydia realised that she had said quite enough, and deemed it prudent to slip away without any further discussion. She was obliged to stifle a ripple of laughter as she did so, for the picture of Sir Carsbie standing in all his offended dignity in the middle of the path, with the first of the evening's rockets rising in a great burst of whizzing light behind him, as if in apt symbolism of his mental state, appealed irresistibly to her risibilities.

Not, she told herself ruefully, that she was likely to find it so amusing, when she returned to Green Street and all her problems there, to think that she had whistled Sir Carsbie and the undeniable advantages of an alliance with him down the wind.

But she had no time in which to consider her lack of prudent conduct further, for around the next turn in the path she came upon a pair of familiar figures—Northover and Lady Gilmour, standing together in conversation beside one of the fountains that dotted the gardens. Its graceful cascades, with the falling drops glittering in the light of the coloured lamps above it, made a charming background for Lady Gilmour's diaphanous, spangled gown, but Lydia did not find the tableau before her at all charming. Her eyes narrowed slightly, and she would undoubtedly have gone on, with only the briefest of acknowledgements of the couple's presence, if Lady Gilmour had not halted her by enquiring if she had seen Minna.

"No," said Lydia shortly, looking at Northover so disapprovingly that his lordship grinned and said virtuously, "Don't pull that Friday-face at me, Lydia! *I* didn't slip off to a rendezvous, as you did; *I* came merely to find Miss Beaudoin."

"A rendezvous!" Lydia repeated indignantly. "It was no such thing!"

"It's no use your trying to bamboozle *me*," Northover said cheerfully. "I saw you."

"You *saw* me? *You?* And you—you merely stood there and allowed that abominable little creature to maul me about!"

"I most certainly did," the Viscount admitted shamelessly, his black eyes wickedly alight, "and then retreated in good order. Somehow I scarcely thought you would thank me for interrupting what was obviously a proposal of marriage."

Lady Gilmour, who had been attending with some impatience to this interchange, at this point interrupted sharply. "A proposal of marriage!" she exclaimed. "What—was it Harlbury?"

Lydia, framing a spirited rejoinder to Northover's last speech, checked as she found herself confronted by a pair of icy blue eyes in Lady Gilmour's delicately flushed and very handsome face. Turning her attention to that lady instead, she remarked, with very little attempt to moderate the baldness of the statement by a civil tone, that she did not believe *that* to be an affair that concerned her ladyship.

Lady Gilmour's fan closed with a snap. "My dear Miss Leyland," she said, with a somewhat excessive sweetness, "you will permit me to differ with you. It may do very well in the wilds of America for a female to pursue a *parti* who is all but affianced to another young lady with the same ardour that gentlemen use on the hunting-field; perhaps that is the way in which such matters are arranged there. I am thankful to say I know nothing of that. But—"

She got no further, for Lydia, with a ruthless sweetness that rivalled her own, broke in to remark, "Is that indeed so, ma'am? Then it only goes to show one how mistaken gossip may be, for I am sure if I have heard once since I came to London I have heard a dozen times that my Lord Gilmour was quite on the verge of offering for Lord Aubry's youngest daughter when she was *cut out* by your ladyship."

Northover's shoulders shook slightly—a sight which did nothing to cause the flush on Lady Gilmour's face to abate. Her fan was flirted open again; she said rapidly, "Your manners, Miss Leyland, are deplorable. Let me warn you that your position in Society is not such as to allow you to indulge in such insolence without losing the precarious foothold which you now hold there—and which, I might remind you, you owe entirely to my mother's condescension in taking you up!"

"Oh, yes!" Lydia agreed cordially. "Lady Aimer has been everything that is kind! But do you not think that such a *scheming wench* as I am—I believe that that was the term your ladyship has applied to me?—is sufficiently clever to make her way even without Lady Aimer's kind offices? I have, you see, the advantage of having a respectable reputation, in spite of my *deplorable manners*, so that at least *one* handicap your ladyship was obliged to surmount in your own rise to affluence is quite lacking in my case!"

What response Lady Gilmour might have made to this last truly outrageous speech was not to be known, for Lydia, with a slight curtsey directed impartially at her and Northover, was gone the next moment along the path.

Lady Gilmour, stiff with rage, rounded on the Viscount. "*Oh!*" she exclaimed. "Was there ever a more impertinent, odious—!" Her blue eyes shot fire that rivalled the showering sparks of a rocket descending the summer night skies above them. "And you—!" she ejaculated. "You can *laugh*—!"

"No, no, Trix!" Northover bit his lip, attempting to speak soothingly, but the situation was too much for his gravity; he gave one gasp and broke into a shout of laughter. "Oh, lord, Trix, I warned you not to cross swords with her!" he said, when he could speak again. "Don't come to dagger-drawing with *me!* Didn't I tell you how it would be?"

18

But Lydia, returning home to Green Street later that evening, was little in the mood to congratulate herself on the successful outcome of her encounter with Lady Gilmour. Harlbury's obvious interest in Miss Pentony, her own refusal of Sir Carsbie, and above everything, the strained, desperate look in Bayard's eyes that she had noted when he had at last returned to the company with Miss Beaudoin to face the icy censure of that young lady's mama—all these combined to cause her to feel that events were fast hastening to a climax, and that something must be done at once to avoid catastrophe.

As if this were not enough, Mrs. Leyland, to whose dressing-room she repaired before retiring to her own chamber that night, was found to be equally on the fidget over her own affairs, and capped the sum of her granddaughter's woes by announcing her intention of going early on the morrow to see Mr. King, it being her firm conviction that, since Lydia had refused Northover's assistance, her only hope now lay in borrowing from a moneylender.

Lydia was notoriously an excellent sleeper, even when her own affairs were not in good train; but it could not be said that she enjoyed peaceful slumbers that night. She tossed and turned, while Northover's sardonic smile, Bayard's haggard face, and Sir Carsbie's eyes starting, affronted, at her, chased one another through her mind; and when she fell asleep at last it was to dream of being cast out from Polite Society, like Eve from the Garden of Eden, by Lady Gilmour in the guise of an avenging angel.

She awoke with only one clear idea in her head—that she must do something, and do it at once. Winch, whom she encountered in the upstairs hall as she was going down to breakfast, informed her that her grandmother was already gone out, and she thought, with a sinking of the heart, that this early excursion could have only one meaning—that Mrs. Leyland was in truth making good her threat to visit Clarges Street and Mr. King.

She went into the breakfast-parlour, sipped a cup of coffee, and nibbled half-heartedly on a piece of toast. It was while she was engaged in this occupation that she suddenly started up, exclaiming—"Sir Basil!"—in a tone that considerably startled Sidwell, who was just entering the room to enquire if there was anything more she desired.

"I beg your pardon, miss?" he said, in some disapproval.

"Never mind!" Lydia turned a slightly absent but highly determined face upon him. "Tell me, Sidwell—did my grandmother take the barouche when she went out this morning?"

"No, miss, she did not." Sidwell, who was far from considering the erratic Leylands among the more desirable parties by whom he had been employed, put on his primmest face. "She desired me to fetch a hackney-carriage for her, instead."

Lydia had become acquainted, during her sojourn in London, with the convention which wisely decreed that a lady visiting a gentleman's lodgings should engage one of these anonymous vehicles rather than risk her own carriage's being seen and recognised on such an adventure, and she had a moment's diverting curiosity as to whether Sidwell suspected her grandmother of slipping away to an assignation. But her own affairs were too pressing to allow her to pursue it.

"Good!" she said. "Then will you have the barouche brought round as soon as possible, Sidwell? You may tell my grandmother, if she returns before I do, that I have gone to call upon Sir Basil Rowthorn in Russell Square."

She ran upstairs immediately to change the simple morning-dress she was wearing for a modish promenade gown of primrose craped muslin with sleeves *à la mamelouk,* and to tie a very fetching Italian straw bonnet over her dark curls. Thus attired, she ran down the stairs again to find the barouche waiting at the front door, and, mounting into it at once, ordered the coachman to drive to Russell Square.

It was a sultry morning, threatening rain, but Lydia had no thoughts to spare for the weather; she was fully occupied in considering what she would say to Sir Basil. It had seemed an inspiration of high order, in the breakfast-parlour in Green Street, to approach her great-uncle frankly with her difficulties and to request his aid before Mr. Michael Pentony should have presented the matter to him in the worst possible light; but by the time she descended from the barouche in Russell Square it had somehow become much less clear to her that she had done the right thing, and she was almost hoping that Sir Basil's butler, when he opened the door to her, would inform her that his master could not, or would not, receive her.

The butler, however—a different man, she noted, from the one who had admitted her on her previous visit—though he looked at her a trifle doubtfully, did nothing of the sort, but invited her instead to wait in a small saloon opening off the hall while he acquainted Sir Basil with her arrival. Lydia, too preoccupied with the importance of her errand to wait quietly, walked up and down the room, inspecting its elegant appointments with-

out the slightest notion of what she was doing, until the butler returned to
tell her that Sir Basil would see her. She then followed him up the stairs
to the apartment in which she had been received on her first visit to Russell Square, where she found Sir Basil, as on that occasion, seated in a
chair beside the long windows with a rug drawn over his knees. He was
not alone this time, however, for a very small, red-faced man with a very
large head, wearing a shabby, old-fashioned, full-skirted coat and the knee-
breeches that had been popular in the last century, was in the act of bowing himself out of the room. He gave Lydia a frank, scrutinising glance,
which appeared satisfactory to him, for on concluding it he laid his finger
alongside his nose, winked broadly at Sir Basil, and said in a hoarse aside
to him, "Ay, guv'nor, she'll do! Knocks 'em all into horsenails! Lay your
blunt on *her*, and you'll have backed the right filly this time!"

He then favoured Lydia with a bobbing bow, advised her not to try to
cut any wheedles with the guv'nor, since he still knew one point more
than the devil, and departed, leaving Lydia staring at Sir Basil in considerable astonishment.

"Well, well—sit down, sit down!" Sir Basil said testily. "Have you never
seen a dwarf before?"

"Not in a drawing-room," Lydia replied truthfully, recalling Mr.
Peeke's ambiguous reference to the odd circle of friends Sir Basil enjoyed.

"Well, you've seen one now," Sir Basil said, summarily dismissing the
subject and going on at once to more important matters. "Now then, what
do you want—eh? I thought I'd told you and that brother of yours I'd let
you know if I cared to see either one of you in this house."

Lydia, who had seated herself in the chair drawn up before him in the
window, perversely found her spirits reviving under this Turkish treatment.

"You have a very good memory, sir," she said composedly, "for that is
exactly what you did say. However, as it happens—"

"Of course I have a good memory! Why shouldn't I have a good memory? I ain't in my dotage yet!" Sir Basil interrupted, wrathfully. "Don't
put on airs to be interesting with *me*, miss! I asked you what you wanted,
and you can give me a plain answer, without any skimble-skamble roundaboutation, or you can take yourself off, and that's all there is about it!"

"Oh, very well," said Lydia, unperturbed. "I *had* thought we might
have enjoyed an agreeable quarter hour of conversation first, but if that
seems *totally* redundant to you, I shall come to the point at once." She
drew a breath. "I want four thousand pounds—that is, not *personally*, but
for Grandmama—and I want you to decide at once that you will make

your will to divide your fortune between Bayard and Mr. Pentony. Well, you *must* do so one day," she went on hastily, seeing the choleric colour rising in Sir Basil's face—"that is, decide to make your will, I mean—and it had as well be now, for I daresay it would make all the difference to that *odious* Lady Gilmour if she knew Bayard was to inherit at least half your fortune, and then he may marry Miss Beaudoin, after all—"

She halted, observing that Sir Basil was by this time looking quite alarmingly red.

"Are you well, sir?" she enquired solicitously, after a moment.

"Well! How should I be well," Sir Basil demanded, in almost apoplectic ire, "when a slip of a minx sits there telling me what I must and must not do? Have you run mad, girl?"

"No, I do not *think* so," Lydia said cautiously. "But I am so put about that I daresay I am behaving a little strangely. It *did* seem to me, though, that it would be much the better plan to come directly to you with the matter, rather than allowing you to learn of it from Mr. Pentony."

Sir Basil's brows shot up. "Pentony?" he barked. "What's Michael to do with it?"

"Well, nothing at all, actually—though he *did* introduce Grandmama to Mrs. Collingworth, and it was at her house that Grandmama lost four thousand pounds at play. But you *must* know that he is very desirous of inheriting your fortune, and will do everything in his power to accomplish that—"

"Including," Sir Basil interpolated grimly, "bribing my servants!"

Lydia halted, looking at him in surprise. "Oh! Do you know about *that?*" she enquired.

A tiny, almost inward smile appeared upon Sir Basil's face, erasing not a jot of its grimness.

"Ay, I know it!" he said. "I told you, I ain't in my dotage yet! Damned rascally set of fellows, the servants you come by these days, ready to sell you to the devil if he'll but take the trouble to grease their fists—but they don't pull the wool over *my* eyes!" He nodded with an appearance of some satisfaction, and after a moment went on, in the same vindictive tone, "And so Michael was behind that, too—your grandmother getting into the hands of those sharps! Well, that's one more point against him, but it don't make a ha'porth of odds now, for he queered his game with me the day I found him going behind my back with my own servants. Damme, that brother of yours may be a soft 'un, but he's a gentleman, at any rate—not a curst sneaksby!"

Lydia stared at him, her brain reeling a little under the import of the words he had just uttered.

"But—but—do you mean," she managed to say at last, "that you have decided *not* to make Mr. Pentony your heir?"

"Why should I make him my heir?" Sir Basil demanded irascibly. "He's a—a twiddle-poop! Coming around here all these years, turning me up sweet like a damned simpering macaroni-merchant! *He* knew I knew what he was about, for he ain't bacon-brained, but what he didn't know was that he might have carried the business off if he hadn't tried to run sly with me as well. Well, he caught cold at that! Coggins is right—I still know a point or two more than the devil!"

Lydia, who could scarcely believe the good fortune that seemed to be tumbling into her—or, at least, Bayard's—lap, said in a rather stunned voice, "But, dear Uncle Basil, do you mean, then, that you will leave your fortune to *Bayard?*"

"Yes, I do," snapped Sir Basil. "Or, at any rate, I shall if he don't put me off it by giving me reason to think as ill of him as I do of Michael, for you'd have to say I had windmills in my head if I was fool enough to cut Michael out for another good-for-nothing Jack Straw as bad as he is. But if your young brother don't queer himself by running off to Gretna with some silly chit, or getting caught fuzzing the cards, or doing any of the other ramshackle things a man can ruin his chances by in the *ton,* I'll have him in here next week and make things all right and tight, as soon as I've settled with Northover about Great Hayland."

"Great Hayland!" Lydia exclaimed, neglecting, in her astonishment at this new matter introduced at the conclusion of her great-uncle's speech, to assure him that it was totally unlikely that Bayard would commit any of the social solecisms against which he had so strongly inveighed. "Good gracious, do you mean—?"

"Well, naturally!" Sir Basil said, with some acerbity. "It's the family seat—ain't it? Letty was forever after me to buy it back for her, but while old Northover was alive I wouldn't touch it, for the old snudge held out for twice what it was worth. This present man, though, wants nothing better than to be rid of it, and he's agreed to a fair price—"

"So *that* was what he meant!" Lydia exclaimed, recalling Northover's cryptic words to her implying that there was no need for her to despair over Sir Basil's intentions towards her family. Her indignation kindled suddenly. "Well, he *might* have told me," she said, "instead of allowing me to believe—"

She halted abruptly, seeing that Sir Basil was looking at her keenly.

"What's this?" he demanded. "Did Northover tell you of the business, then?"

"No, he did not," Lydia said resentfully, "though he *knew* what straits I was in."

"Humph! Didn't think he would," Sir Basil said, with satisfaction. "Asked him to keep it close till it was settled. Not that I had any reason to expect he'd let it out to you. Didn't know he was that particular a friend of yours."

"He isn't," Lydia said, with dignity. "In fact, I *practically* loathe him."

"Not much use in that," said Sir Basil unfeelingly. "*He* won't care what a chit like you thinks of him. You ain't in his line, by all *I've* heard of him." He added abruptly, "You've caught Harlbury on your hook, though, I hear. Has he made you an offer?"

"No!" said Lydia unequivocally.

"Well, you'll have better luck, I don't doubt, when it comes out what I mean to do for you," said Sir Basil, with his usual lack of civility. "Yes, yes, throw a good dowry into the balance and you'll go off like a shot, for you're a fetching piece, for all your damned queer manners. But what about that brother of yours—eh?" he went on. "You were saying *he* had it in mind to get himself riveted. Who is the gal? Is she a lady? Or is she the sort of high-flyer a young ramstam's as like as not to dangle after, and come to perdition on the head of it?"

Lydia said, rallying to do her best for Bayard, "By no means, sir! Miss Beaudoin moves in the first circles of Society. She is the daughter, by her first marriage, of the Viscountess Gilmour, and is making her come-out this Season. She and Bayard are very much in love indeed, but I must tell you that Lady Gilmour has set herself strongly against the match. It is not, I believe, that she has objections to Bayard personally, but his lack of fortune—"

"Well, she sounds like a sensible woman," Sir Basil said coolly, "so it's Lombard Street to a China orange she'll change her tune in a hurry when she learns what I have in mind to do for young Leyland. *Leyland-Rowthorn*, I should say, for the name goes with the bargain, you know!" He rubbed his hands together gleefully. "Ay, we'll have the notice in the *Gazette* and the *Morning Post*," he said, "and the wedding at St. George's in Hanover Square—everything in the first style! And I mean to bring Great Hayland up to what it was in your great-aunt's day—"

Lydia could only sit nodding in stunned assent as Sir Basil unfolded his plans for Bayard's future, her one wish being that Bayard himself were with her to hear them as well. She was on tenterhooks to return to Green

Street so that she might acquaint him with his good fortune, and made not the slightest objection when Sir Basil, abruptly winding his peroration to a close, informed her baldly that he had had quite enough of her company and that she might go.

"You'll be hearing from Peeke," he said as she rose, trying to gather the proper words in which to thank him. "No need for you to come around here again, interfering in matters that are none of your concern! Told you more than I intended already, and I daresay it's too much to expect you to keep it to yourself!"

"Well, sir," Lydia said, with proper meekness, "you can scarcely expect me not to tell Bayard—though I shall *endeavour* not to, if you really wish it."

"You had better tell him, instead, to take care to conduct himself like a gentleman, or he'll find he's whistled *his* chances for a fortune down the wind," Sir Basil said testily. "As for that grandmother of yours—I expect I shall have to tow her off Point Non-Plus, since it was Michael who lured her into the business. But she needn't think I'll do it without ringing a peal over her! I cured Letty of gaming, and I daresay I shall be able to do the same for her, for I won't have her playing wily beguiled with *my* brass after I've gone to roost! And now go away, go away!" he concluded, violently ringing the hand-bell that stood on the table beside him. "I've no more time to spare for you this morning! Beal! Beal! Where is the fellow?"

The butler arrived almost immediately, and in another moment Lydia found herself being ushered out of the room and down the stairs to the door.

The return journey to Green Street was accomplished perfectly prosaically in the Leyland barouche, but if Lydia had found this vehicle suddenly transformed into a golden coach, and herself set down in it in company with a beaming fairy godmother, the circumstance would scarcely have appeared strange to her. Her brief interview with Sir Basil had indeed wrought such a total change in her family's prospects that she believed no further transformations, however magical, would have had the power to astonish her. All her anxieties had been laid to rest: she need no longer fear Mr. Pentony's disclosure of her grandmother's debts to Sir Basil, or the dire consequences of those debts' remaining unpaid, and that Lady Gilmour would soon be brought to abandon her opposition to her daughter's marriage to Bayard, if he were to become heir to one of the largest fortunes in the kingdom, she had not the slightest doubt.

When the barouche arrived in Green Street she descended from it quickly and entered the house, enquiring of Sidwell, the moment she was inside the door, where her brother might be found.

"Mr. Leyland is not in the house, miss," the butler informed her.

"Not—?" Something in Sidwell's face, which bore an expression nicely balanced between the desire to impart some portentous piece of news and the feeling that it was beneath his dignity to concern himself with the eccentric starts of his employers, caught Lydia's attention. "Has he gone out, then?"

"Yes, miss."

"Did he say where?"

"No, miss." The desire to communicate conquered Sidwell's severe reserve; he went on, with a carefully wooden countenance, "He *was*, however, carrying a cloak-bag, so that I can only assume he was contemplating an overnight stay."

He paused, observing with some satisfaction the effect that his words had had upon Miss Leyland. She was gazing at him with obvious astonishment, not unmixed with apprehension. But, seeing his eyes fixed upon her, she managed to control her countenance and said, with a fair attempt at sang-froid, "Oh, yes—I believe he did mention something about going out of town. Has my grandmother returned yet, Sidwell?"

"No, miss, she has not," said Sidwell, looking disappointed at Lydia's quick recover, which promised nothing to gratify his curiosity.

She nodded dismissal to him and mounted the stairs with the calm air of a young lady who had no other thought in mind but to retire to her own chamber to remove her hat and gloves. But once upstairs she called immediately for Winch and, when that austere handmaiden appeared, enquired of her in considerable agitation if she knew when Bayard had left the house and where he had gone.

"*That* I don't know, miss," Winch replied, folding her arms with the resigned air of one whose patience was about to be tried yet again by the vagaries of the young master's behaviour, "for I have been out of the house myself, on an errand for Madam. But he was here when I left an hour ago, if that's of any help to you." She looked forebodingly into Lydia's flushed countenance and enquired, "What is it now?"

"I don't *know*," Lydia said, "but Sidwell told me he went out carrying a cloak-bag."

Her troubled blue eyes met Winch's grey ones, and a mutual suspicion, communicating itself between them, was given voice by Winch.

"Merciful heavens, Miss Lydia," she said hollowly, "he's gone and run off with that Miss Beaudoin!"

Lydia winced. From the moment she had first heard from Sidwell of Bayard's having gone out carrying a cloak-bag, that horrid idea had been haunting her own mind, but, with her conviction of what such a scandalous action on his part would do to jeopardise what only half an hour before had appeared the certainty of his becoming Sir Basil's heir, she had not dared to acknowledge it.

She said hastily to Winch, "No, no, you must be mistaken! There is some other explanation, I am sure! He has received an invitation from one of his friends to go into the country, and has merely forgotten to mention it."

Winch shook her head, unconvinced. "I knew how it would be!" she said, with the gloomy satisfaction of a prophetess whose dire foretellings have at last been proved correct. "Ever since Madam took this notion into her head to come to London, I knew no good would come of it! He's gone off to Gretna Green with Miss Beaudoin, as sure as check, Miss Lydia, for when a young man's as deep in love as he is he'll never give a thought to consequences."

"Nonsense!" said Lydia, with a certainty she was far from feeling. "I am sure he would never do anything so improper, nor would Miss Beaudoin. She has been *very* carefully brought up, you know!"

"So was Madam, but that didn't stop *her* from running off with the Major," Winch said incontrovertibly. "You wait till *your* time comes, Miss Lydia, and you'll know how it is when you're to be parted forever from the creetur you adore."

"Oh, *do* give over talking such fustian, Winch!" Lydia said crossly. She pressed one hand to her forehead, as if she could somehow succeed in this way in quieting the turmoil of anxiety behind it. "He must have left *some* word if he has indeed gone off on such a journey, for he would know he could never be absent for so many days without our scouring the country to find him!"

She broke off abruptly, remembering the habit she and Bayard had long had of scribbling notes and leaving them in the other's room when obliged to go off somewhere in the other's absence. Parting from Winch without ceremony, she went swiftly down the hall and entered her own bedchamber. A quick glance around it showed her the object she was seeking—a sealed and folded sheet of notepaper laid upon her dressing-table. She pounced upon it and tore it open.

Lyddy, love, the firm black letters covering the page read, *this is a despicable thing to do to you and Grandmama, but you must see, when I tell you all, that there is no other way. Lady G.'s intention was to take Minna to Scarborough tomorrow, and, if I succeeded in following her there, to Paris. So my dear, brave girl has consented to go with me to America, where we shall contrive to be married and then go to live at Belmaison. I never thought, Lyddy, that we two should part in such a way, without so much as a word of farewell between us, but there is no help for it, my dear, for I know you too well to think you would not try to stop me if you knew what I was about.*

But when you read this I shall be on my way to Bristol with Minna, and it will be too late for you to throw a rub in our way. This news, of course, is strictly for your eyes alone. Lady G., I apprehend, will believe us gone to Gretna when Minna is missed, and I do not think you will be so unkind either to me or to Minna as to disabuse her mind of this idea until it may reasonably be expected that we have taken ship for America.

One last word, Lyddy, my own. Don't marry Harlbury. You do not love him, and I should not like to think of your missing forever what Minna and I have. Believe me, it is well worth waiting for. B.

By the time she had come to the conclusion of this letter, Lydia's face was as white as the paper on which it was written. She found herself, for the moment, quite unable to put together two coherent thoughts: the one dire realisation drumming desperately through her head was that, by this single rash act, Bayard was irrevocably throwing away all hope of inheriting Sir Basil's fortune. The scandal that such an elopement must give rise to would prevent his ever being able to take that place in Society to which Sir Basil vicariously aspired, and it was not to be expected that that irascible gentleman, once it reached his ears, would adhere to his plan of making him his heir.

And the most damnable part of the whole affair was that it was only by an hour, or even less, that Bayard had missed his good fortune. No doubt, Lydia thought, he and Minna were even now seated in a post-chaise rattling along a road not a dozen miles from London, and she was ready to scream with frustration at the realisation that, were she able now to converse with him only for five minutes, he would certainly agree to abandon the projected elopement and allow his and Minna's affairs to follow the socially accepted course of a conventional marriage, with parental approval, in the full light of public knowledge.

Standing with the note crumpled in her hand, her mind grappling hopelessly with the problem of how she might succeed in recalling Bayard from his mad venture, she did not hear Winch approach the door behind her, and it was only when that long-suffering handmaiden spoke her name that she whirled about.

"Yes? What is it, Winch?"

"Lord Harlbury," Winch said succinctly, her eyes upon the paper in Lydia's hand. "He's below, and wishful to see you, Sidwell says. Is that from Mr. Bayard, Miss Lydia?"

"Yes—no!" Lydia placed the note hastily in a drawer of her dressing-table and looked distractedly at Winch. "I cannot see Lord Harlbury now!" she said. "Tell him—"

She halted, struck by a sudden thought. Harlbury, she knew—though he had no desire to ape either the fashions or the morals of the Corinthian set—had one thing in common with those dashing blades: he was a first-rate whip, who took justifiable pride in the beautiful team of matched chestnuts he was accustomed to drive. Lydia, still under the influence of that sudden inspiration, flew to the window, which overlooked the street, and peered down. As she had hoped, she was rewarded by the sight of his lordship's lightly sprung curricle standing before the house, with a groom at the heads of his team of glossy chestnuts.

"Oh, famous!" she exclaimed.

She turned back impetuously into the room, snatched up the gloves she had thrown upon her dressing-table, hastily retied her bonnet-strings before the mirror, and moved quickly towards the door, only to find that aperture blocked by Winch's angular figure.

"And what," enquired Miss Winch, ominously folding her arms, "do you think you are up to now, Miss Lydia?"

"Oh, Winch, do stand aside!" Lydia said, almost dancing with impatience. "I am going after Bayard, of course!"

"After Mr. Bayard! And how do you know where he may be? And you'll not be starting a journey in that dress, with never so much as a nightgown put up in a portmanteau, and with no one to escort you—Miss Lydia!"

Winch's voice rose as Lydia determinedly thrust her aside and emerged into the hall, but Lydia was already flying down the stairs.

"Never mind, Winch! I shall have Lord Harlbury to escort me!" she called back; and thereupon vanished from sight into the drawing-room below.

19 Lord Harlbury, finding himself confronted by a very flushed and eager young lady, already attired for the outdoors and demanding to know if he would instantly drive her out of town in pursuit of her brother, had for a moment the startled conviction that Miss Lydia Leyland had finally taken leave of her senses. No less distressing reason, he felt, could account for such very odd behaviour, and he was wondering in some alarm how he might get Sidwell into the room and, through him, acquaint Mrs. Leyland or some female servant with the necessity of her coming immediately to assist the young lady, when Lydia observed the distraught expression upon his face and gave vent to a rueful chuckle.

"Oh, dear! I daresay you think I have run quite mad!" she said. "But indeed I have not; it is only that there is such desperate need for haste that I cannot spare the time to tell you properly what I am about! But will you not at least humour me sufficiently to take me for a drive in your curricle in the direction I wish to go, while I tell you exactly what I have in mind? And then, if you do not wish to oblige me by going further, you may bring me back here—only I do not think that you will. *Nobody* could be so hard-hearted as *that!*"

His lordship looked down indecisively into Lydia's pleading face. He was a chivalrous young man, and it would go sorely against the pluck with him, he felt, to deny such an urgent request from so charming a young lady—but at the same time he was a sensible man as well, and he was damned, he told himself firmly, if he was going to embroil himself in such a harebrained business as this promised to be.

He was about to open his mouth to utter a kind but decisive negative when Lydia, on whom the growing look of resolution upon his face had not been lost, abruptly abandoned her cajoling air and took command.

"Harlbury," she said with perfect civility, but with an ominous ring of determination in her voice, "I warn you that you had best not say *No* to me! If you do, I shall drive those chestnuts of yours myself—oh, yes! I am quite capable of handling a team!—for I *must* come up with Bayard before he has utterly ruined his entire future. Now—you may come with me or not, as you choose, but *I* am going after Bayard!"

With these words she turned and walked towards the door. Harlbury, who by this time knew enough of Miss Leyland to realise that she was perfectly capable of carrying out her threat, had no choice but to follow her, and emerged, remonstrating, into the street behind her, greatly to the interest of Sidwell and his own groom.

"For heaven's sake, Miss Leyland," he urged her in a low voice, desperately trying to keep up the appearance that he was conducting a perfectly normal conversation with her, "do let us return to the house and discuss the matter there! We cannot do so in the street!"

"No!" said Lydia obdurately. She stood beside the curricle, her eyes running rapidly and approvingly over the chestnuts. "There is no time, my lord. Every minute we waste here lessens our chances of overtaking him in time. Now—do you intend to drive, or shall I take the ribbons myself?"

Harlbury cast an anguished glance at his gaping groom and closed his eyes for a moment, as if in prayer.

"Very well," he capitulated, handing her up into the curricle and mounting beside her. He took the reins from his groom and said to him, with a praiseworthy attempt at achieving a casual tone, "I shan't need you, Hemlow. You may walk back to Harlbury House."

"Very good, sir."

The man touched his hat and stepped back from the curricle as his master gave the horses the office to start. As the curricle rolled off down the street, Lydia said, "Bayard has set out for Bristol, so that is the road that we must take. I daresay you will know the way?" She added approvingly, "That was very clever of you to dismiss your groom. The fewer people who are aware of the matter the better it will be, for you know how easily gossip spreads."

"My dear Miss Leyland," Harlbury said, in a voice that, for him, was unwontedly stern, "the reason I have dismissed my groom is so that we may discuss this matter in privacy before I set you down again at your own door. Surely you cannot believe that I am going to drive with you to Bristol in an open carriage, without a chaperon, and without our having informed anyone of our intention! I have not been able to gather exactly why your brother has gone off to Bristol, but certainly, if it is essential that someone pursue him, *you* are not the proper person to whom the matter should be entrusted!"

Lydia sighed. "Oh, dear!" she said. "I daresay I shall have to tell you the whole story. But you must solemnly swear, Harlbury, before I do, that you will not divulge it to *anyone!*"

"I see no reason," his lordship said austerely, "why you should believe I would violate any confidence you may choose to entrust to me, Miss Leyland."

"*That,*" Lydia pointed out to him, "is *not* solemnly swearing, Harlbury."

"Yes, but, my dear Miss—"

"Oh, *do* stop saying, 'My dear Miss Leyland!'" Lydia said. "You *know*, you are as cross as crabs with me, and would like nothing better than to tell me to go to the devil!"

"No, indeed!" Harlbury said, shocked.

"Then why won't you swear?"

His lordship gave up. "Very well, I swear it," he said resignedly. "But we shall *not* go to Bristol!"

"Well, not the *whole* way, certainly," Lydia agreed, mollified, "for I should not think that will be at all necessary. I am quite sure, you see, that Bayard has no money to spare, and so has hired only a pair of horses. And he cannot have had more than an hour's start of us, and perhaps not nearly so much as that, so that it is entirely likely, if you spring your horses, that we shall be able to come up with him before he has got anywhere near to Bristol."

"And why," enquired his lordship, "is it so imperative for you to bring him back, Miss Leyland?"

"Because he is eloping with Miss Beaudoin—Oh! *Do* look what you are about!" she broke off to say severely, as Harlbury started so violently at this announcement that he jobbed at his leaders' sensitive mouths. "What a cow-handed thing to do!"

"I beg your pardon!" his lordship said stiffly. "But to hear such a shocking piece of news—! How is it possible! Miss Beaudoin! I should not have thought it of her!"

"Well, she is in love with him, you see," Lydia explained, "and Lady Gilmour is planning to take her to Scarborough tomorrow, and then to Paris, if necessary, to separate her from Bayard. So of course they were driven to do something desperate—only I have been to call upon Sir Basil Rowthorn this morning, and have discovered that it is his intention to make Bayard his heir, so that there is no need for them to elope, after all. In fact, if they succeed in doing so it will spoil everything, for all depends upon Bayard's being accepted in the first circles of Society—which he *never* will be, of course, if he does anything so ramshackle as running off to America with Miss Beaudoin."

She paused for breath, and Harlbury, who was looking rather dazed, said, "Good God, if this is true—"

"Of course it is true!" Lydia said indignantly. "Why should I lie to you about it? And that is why I *must* stop Bayard before he has got clean away —and if you can think of any other way to do so than what I am doing at this moment, I shall be very much obliged to you if you will tell me of it!"

But to this request his lordship had no answer. It was perfectly clear, as Lydia had said, that if the runaways were to be overtaken before they had irretrievably committed themselves to their reckless scheme, the utmost haste was necessary. Even if they were not able to engage passage immediately on a vessel leaving for America—and Harlbury had no way of knowing that a stroke of good fortune might not allow them to do just that—it was obvious that, once they had reached Bristol, they might easily manage to evade pursuit in that populous port until their joint disappearance had become one of the scandalous *on-dits* of the town and it was too late to salvage the reputation of either.

The situation therefore presented his lordship with a truly dreadful dilemma. The reputations of two young ladies, it seemed, lay in his hands, and it appeared impossible that, whatever decision he now made, both could emerge scatheless. If he acceded to Lydia's request that he pursue the fleeing couple, he was exposing her to the censure of her acquaintance, should any of them come to learn of this most unorthodox journey. On the other hand, if he refused it, Miss Beaudoin would most certainly be ruined.

A very short period of earnest cogitation was sufficient to convince his lordship that the latter alternative presented by far the darker consequence. If he were able to come up quickly with the young couple, he told himself, they might all return to London together that same day with reasonable propriety, whereas, if he turned back now, there could be no hope of rescuing Miss Beaudoin from the consequences of her romantic folly.

With great misgiving, therefore, he informed Lydia that he would do his best to overtake the fleeing pair—a statement which caused her to remark handsomely that she had never really doubted that he would stand buff.

Now that agreement had been reached on the course to be followed, Harlbury lost no time in directing his curricle out of town by way of Knightsbridge and Hammersmith, and was soon able to let his team out on the open road. Lydia, whose spirits had risen quite to their accustomed buoyancy as soon as she was assured that there was now a reasonable hope that they might overtake Bayard and Miss Beaudoin within the next several hours, at first occupied herself with questioning Harlbury as to the roads and towns that lay before them, with which she was but imperfectly acquainted, having passed this way only once, on her journey from Bristol to London on first arriving in England. But she soon realised that if she conversed with her companion it must be to the detriment of his handling of his team, and accordingly fell accommodatingly silent. She was able to see, at any rate, that his lordship was now quite as anxious as she was to come up quickly with the eloping pair, and she determined to leave in his hands the necessary enquiries at turnpikes and posting-houses along the way.

Harlbury did not halt to change horses at Hounslow, declaring that his chestnuts were good for two stages, but at the Crown Inn at Slough, where he turned in to have a fresh team put-to, they came upon definite news of the runaways. An ostler, his memory jogged by a handsome *douceur* slipped into his hand, clearly recollected that a chaise-and-pair containing a young gentleman and a young lady had come through not half an hour before, and the description he gave of the pair left no doubt in Lydia's mind that they had indeed been Bayard and Miss Beaudoin. Moreover, the ostler informed them, the young gentleman had been in something of a fret, one of his horses having pulled up dead lame a few miles before Slough, and the chaise consequently having been obliged to come halting into the Crown at a snail's pace.

Lydia could scarcely wait until they were back on the road again to express her jubilation.

"Could anything be more fortunate!" she exclaimed. "We are certain now to come up with them at least not long after they pass through Reading. And then we may all return quite comfortably to London, with no one the wiser for what has occurred except Lady Gilmour. And perhaps even she need not know, if Minna was prudent enough to make some excuse to her that would account for her being gone from home the whole day, so that she and Bayard might be farther on their road before any alarm was raised."

Harlbury, whose wishes in this regard most emphatically coincided with Lydia's, said that he earnestly hoped she might prove to be correct in this assumption. He was beginning, however, to be concerned on another account. The sultriness of the weather was increasing as the afternoon advanced, and ahead of them the western sky was darkening ominously. It was probable, he thought, that they might be driving into a storm, and, though this was a matter of little concern to him personally, the thought of driving a young lady, attired in a thin dress and a modish straw bonnet, through a pelting rain in an open carriage was not one which he could face with equanimity.

He held his peace, however, hoping that his forecast of the weather might prove incorrect, until, as they were approaching the outskirts of Reading, a rumble of thunder and the pattering down upon their heads of a few widely spaced drops of rain alarmed him in earnest. He turned to Lydia.

"I fear," he observed, "that we are in for a storm, Miss Leyland."

Lydia cocked an eye aloft at the sky. "I daresay you are right," she agreed, with composure. "Must we change horses here? I do not like to take the time, now that we must be so close upon them, but it appears to me that this team is flagging, and it may save time in the long run if we have a fresh one put-to here."

Harlbury glanced over at her, a trifle nonplussed. "Yes, but—my dear Miss Leyland," he said, "you will not like to be driven through a storm in an open carriage!"

"Pooh!" said Lydia. "As if I should care for that when Bayard's whole future is at stake!"

Harlbury shook his head disapprovingly. "I have been thinking," he said, "that it would be best for me to leave you at the George here in Reading while I go on alone. If it should come on to rain hard—"

Lydia gave him an astonished glance. "Leave me behind!" she said. "You must be all about in your head, Harlbury! What does a wetting signify in such a case? I daresay you have a rug that I can throw over me—"

She was interrupted by a crash of thunder and a sudden quickening of the rain, which began to pelt down now in good earnest. They were by this time just entering Reading on the London Road, and as they progressed farther, along New Street, the traffic thickened, obliging Harlbury to give all his attention to his team. He was still determined, in spite of Lydia's objections, not to continue on in the storm, which gave every promise of becoming a severe one; but, as events transpired, the decision was very shortly taken out of both his and Lydia's hands.

For as he was threading his way skilfully between an overburdened wagon and a gig being driven by a dashing-looking young man in a sporting neckcloth, a sudden brilliant display of lightning, followed by a terrific thunderclap, caused the bay mare drawing the gig to rear up between the shafts in terror, overturning the gig directly in the path of the curricle. There was a moment of complete pandemonium, full of plunging horses, startled curses, and colliding vehicles; then, as Lydia clung to the madly rocking curricle, it went over abruptly with a splintering shock and she was flung out into the road.

When she came to herself she was lying on a sofa in what appeared to be an inn parlour, inhaling the pungent odour of the burnt feathers that were being waved under her nose by a very stout female in a mobcap. Dazedly, as her eyes blinked open, she saw Harlbury distractedly pacing the room, his coat darkened with damp and his wet hair clinging in disordered dark locks to his brow. He was insisting that a surgeon be fetched at once, to which the stout female responded soothingly that he need not put himself into a fret, for his lady wife was coming round very nicely now.

"She is not my—" Harlbury began, still in that half-distracted voice; and then, suddenly observing Lydia's now sapient and rather quelling gaze fixed upon him, he swallowed visibly, stopped short, and said hastily, "Yes, yes, I see that she is recovering. My dear Mi—" Lydia's minatory eye again halted him, and he continued awkwardly, "My dear *Lydia*, how do you feel? Are you in pain? Only lie still, pray; I shall have a surgeon called to you at once."

"Nonsense!" said Lydia, endeavouring to raise herself from the cushions against which she was reclining, but sinking back upon them immediately, overcome by a wave of giddiness. "I shall be all right in a *very* few minutes," she said firmly, but with tightly shut eyes, as she strove to steady her swimming senses.

"You may have broken something!" Harlbury said anxiously. "And you have certainly sustained a dreadful shock! Good God, when I saw you lying there on the paving-stones, I made certain that you were dead!"

Lydia opened her eyes cautiously, found that the walls of the room had become reassuringly steady after the disconcerting waltz they had been performing a few moments before, and said, "Pray do not go off into any high flights! Do you think I have never been overturned before?" She managed a little laugh. "Don't look so frightened! I am quite sure that nothing is broken. What is more to the point—is your curricle damaged?"

"Yes," said Harlbury. "But *that* is quite unimportant—"

"Unimportant!" Lydia shot up again from her recumbent position, but was once more obliged to own herself vanquished and lie back against the cushions. She went on, again with tightly shut eyes, "It is *not* unimportant; it is the most important thing of all! You must hire some other vehicle at once. I am sure to be better in a few minutes, and then we can be on our way again."

But to this scheme Mrs. Yarden, the landlady—for such, it appeared, the stout female was—added a negative as shocked and decided as his lordship's. It would be madness, she averred, for Madam to think of resuming her journey that day. Betty would have the best bedchamber ready for her in a trice, and when she had taken off her wet clothes and laid herself down on the bed there with a handkerchief soaked with lavender water on her forehead, and had swallowed a few drops of laudanum to compose her nerves, she might later on fancy a little Cressy soup and a bit of the chicken that was roasting in the kitchen at that very moment.

"And then in the morning, *after* you've had a good night's sleep, you may be fit to go on again," she said severely. "But jauntering about the country after a nasty accident like that is something *I* wouldn't wish to have it on *my* conscience to let you do, and I'll be bound your husband feels the same!"

Harlbury, meeting her expectant gaze, said hastily that he quite agreed with her, and, waiting for no further authorisation, she thereupon bustled out of the room to hasten the preparation of the best bedchamber, leaving Harlbury to confront Lydia with a harassed frown upon his face.

"Good God, what a dreadful situation, Miss Leyland!" he said, running a hand distractedly through his already dishevelled locks. "I cannot think what had best be done! You *must* remain here—but since that woman obviously believes that you are—that is, that I am—in short, that we are married—"

An irrepressible gurgle of laughter escaped Lydia. "Oh dear, Harlbury, *don't* look so dismal!" she begged. "It does not matter what she believes, for I have no intention of remaining here."

"That," said his lordship, with unwonted asperity, "is nonsense! You are scarcely able to lift your head from the pillow; you are undoubtedly suffering from severe bruises, if no worse injury has occurred; and it is raining torrents outside! If you believe that, under such circumstances, I shall *allow* you to go on, you are quite beside the bridge, I assure you! I should be worthy of being clapped into Bedlam if I permitted such a thing!"

Lydia lay blinking at him in some surprise. "Well, you *are* coming along, Harlbury!" she said approvingly. "I have never heard you speak in *this* vein before! If you will only use that tone to your mama, I should not at all wonder if your difficulties with her would come to an end." She raised herself as she spoke to a sitting position and cautiously lowered her feet to the floor. "But I *must* go on, nonetheless," she said. "You must see that, Harlbury! Under ordinary circumstances it might be different—but these are not ordinary circumstances."

She passed her hand in a rather dazed fashion over her forehead, looking so pale as she did so that Harlbury was constrained to move forward quickly and support her in his arms, lowering her gently to the cushions once more.

"There! You see!" he exclaimed anxiously. "You are not fit to go on!"

It was at that precise instant that the parlour door opened and Mrs. Leyland, her dress soaked with rain and her fashionably plumed bonnet drooping horribly over one eye, surged into the room, closely followed by Lord Northover.

20 In order to account for the sudden appearance of the Viscount and Mrs. Leyland in Reading at this point, it is necessary to turn to Green Street in the period immediately following Lydia's departure from it in Harlbury's curricle.

Scarcely half an hour had passed after the curricle had disappeared from before the front door when Mrs. Leyland, in a hackney-carriage, arrived there and, entering the house, was met by Winch, who confronted her with a face of doom and urgently requested the favour of a few minutes' conversation with her.

"Why, whatever is the matter?" Mrs. Leyland demanded, drawing off her gloves as she stepped into the small saloon just off the hall. "You look as if you had seen a ghost!"

"Oh, it's far worse than that, Madam!" Winch said, tearfully. "Oh, Madam, that we should live to see this day! There's Mr. Bayard run off with Miss Beaudoin, and Miss Lydia gone after him in Lord Harlbury's curricle, for all the world like she was a brass-faced lightskirt instead of a young lady of quality!"

Mrs. Leyland gazed at her elderly handmaiden with an expression of amazement, not unmixed with strong disapproval, upon her face.

"Winch," she pronounced awfully, after a moment's consideration, "you are drunk!"

Winch gasped. "Drunk! No, you daren't say such a thing of me, Madam—not for your life! As if you ever knew me to do such a thing, in all the years I've been in your service!" Her indignation at this unfounded accusation was so strong that for a moment she appeared likely to be drawn off from her original topic, but she mastered herself with an effort and, taking a folded sheet of paper from her pocket, thrust it upon her mistress. "If you don't choose to believe my word, Madam," she said, with dignity, "perhaps *this* will give you reason to think otherwise. I have not read it myself, being as I extracted it unbeknownst to her from a drawer of Miss Lydia's dressing-table, but if I'm not sadly out it's from Mr. Bayard, telling her all he intends to do."

Mrs. Leyland, her brows still drawn together in a frown, received the letter and, unfolding it, rapidly perused its single page. As she did so, Winch saw a look of horror appear upon her face, and nodded her own head in a Cassandra-like gesture of grim satisfaction.

"Ay, now you've seen for yourself how it is, Madam!" she said. "And Miss Lydia no sooner reads that letter, and hears me say Lord Harlbury is waiting to see her downstairs, than she flies out of the room with no more of a word to me than that she's going after Mr. Bayard, and the next I know she's mounting up into his lordship's curricle, and him looking as queer as Dick's hat-band, Sidwell says, and trying his best to get her to change her mind. *Which,* you know, Madam, he might have saved his breath doing, when Miss Lydia once takes a notion into her head! And then in the twinkling of a bed-post the two of them were driving off together down the street, *without* his groom, too, for at the last minute his lordship gave orders he was to stay behind."

"But she *cannot* have set off for Bristol with Lord Harlbury in such a fashion!" Mrs. Leyland, finding her voice, said faintly. "Bayard and Miss Beaudoin—and now Lydia—No, no I cannot believe it! She would not do such a dreadful thing!"

She was about to collapse into a chair when a sardonic voice behind her interrupted her grimly.

"Oh yes, she would, ma'am!" said the voice.

Mrs. Leyland, uttering a suppressed shriek, turned around to see Northover regarding her from the doorway. As she stared at him, she was alarmed to observe such an oddly baleful gleam in his dark eyes that her hand flew instinctively to her breast.

"My lord!" she exclaimed, summoning all her dignity to her aid. "What, may I ask, are *you* doing here?"

"I beg your pardon for the interruption, ma'am," Northover said, coolly advancing upon her and taking from her nerveless hand Bayard's letter, which he rapidly proceeded to peruse, "but I only this moment arrived to pay a call upon Lydia, and, as this door was open when I entered the house, I could not avoid overhearing something of what was being said inside. Young fool!"

These latter words, apparently, were his comment upon Bayard's letter, which he proceeded to drop upon a table. Mrs. Leyland again rallied her forces.

"Sir," she said in a quelling voice, "if it is your intention to reveal to anyone outside this room what you have learned in this clandestine way, give me leave to tell you that you are no gentleman!"

This was sufficient to bring a smile to Northover's face, but the grim look remained in his eyes.

"You may make yourself easy, ma'am," he said. "Not only will I not reveal what I have heard here, but I will make it my business to see that no one else learns of this double folly. I gather that Lydia has set out with

Harlbury in his curricle in pursuit of the love-birds? How long ago was this?"

"I have no idea," Mrs. Leyland said distractedly; but here Winch came to her aid with the information that little more than half an hour had passed since the curricle had driven away from the house.

"Good!" said Northover. "Was Harlbury driving those chestnuts of his?"

Winch nodded.

"Well, he has a bang-up set-out of blood and bone there," Northover said, "but I expect I can contrive to come up with him! The point is, though, ma'am," he went on, to Mrs. Leyland, "that I shall want your company. *My* presence can do little to add propriety to this harebrained escapade, but *yours* will make all right, so I fear I must ask you to accompany me."

"To—accompany you!" Mrs. Leyland stared at him. "To—to what place, my lord?"

"To Bristol, if it is necessary!" Northover replied impatiently. "But I scarcely think we shall need to go so far if you will come with me immediately."

"But—but—" Mrs. Leyland appeared to be having difficulty in collecting her thoughts. She looked at the Viscount in some bewilderment, enquiring, "But have you a post-chaise outside, my lord?"

"A post-chaise!" Northover gave a bark of laughter. "No! We should not have the least chance of overtaking them in a chaise. We shall go in my curricle, ma'am."

"In your curricle! To Bristol! Why, it will be a matter of a hundred miles or more! And without luggage!" Mrs. Leyland looked despairingly at Winch. "He is *quite* mad! Do show him out, Winch, and let me sit down quietly and think what I must do—"

"If you sit down here quietly, ma'am," Northover said bluntly, "you will see your grandson an outcast from Society and your granddaughter ruined—or, what is as bad, a partner in a contrived marriage that will be regretted by both. *You* are the only one who can prevent that from happening—so, damn it, you are coming with me, and there's an end to it!"

Mrs. Leyland, who had experienced long years of matrimony with a military gentleman who, in moments of stress, had been wont to use the same kind of unequivocal language to enforce his commands, recognised the voice of authority. She had just time to snatch up her gloves from the table where she had laid them before she found herself being ushered firmly and inexorably from the room. A moan escaped her as she emerged from the house and saw the exceedingly sporting vehicle in which she was to be transported upon her journey, but she uttered no further protest, and allowed herself to be handed up into it by his lordship with nothing more than an anguished backward glance at Winch and Sidwell, standing goggling on the doorstep.

The next moment the Viscount had mounted beside her and, gathering his whip and reins, given his team the office to start. His diminutive Tiger swung himself up behind, and off went the trio in a clatter of hooves and a rattle of wheels on the paving-stones.

Not for many, many years had it been Mrs. Leyland's fortune to be driven at such breakneck speed as she was called upon to endure for the ensuing hours. Of conversation between her and his lordship there was very little, for Northover's attention was fully concentrated upon his team, but she did startle him once, when they had progressed some dozen miles beyond the town, by enquiring abruptly, and with some asperity, "A *contrived* marriage! Pray, what did you mean by such a remark, my lord? How could Lord Harlbury possibly have *contrived* this most unseemly journey, since he had no means of knowing that the opportunity for it would arise?"

"Not Harlbury. Lydia," Northover said succinctly. He cast a brief glance at his companion, who he saw was ruffling up at this imputation. "Oh, very well," he conceded. "Perhaps I am mistaken. But you can scarcely blame me, ma'am, for believing that not even your remarkably impetuous granddaughter could go haring off into an adventure of this sort without realising that she was very likely to come out of it with a husband! Harlbury may be hag-ridden by that mother of his, but he is a man of honour, and Lydia must know very well that he will marry her, in spite of Lady Harlbury, if he feels that he has compromised her."

"Oh! Do you think so?" Mrs. Leyland asked, brightening momentarily; but dejection quickly overcame her once more. "Well, well, but I doubt that it will come about," she said. "She is the most vexatious girl, and it is very likely that, even if Harlbury *does* offer for her, she will be selfish enough to refuse him, without a *thought* for the hardships she will be inflicting upon Bayard and me by such an action."

She broke off, conscious of Northover's keen eyes upon her.

"Is that your opinion, ma'am?" he asked abruptly.

"Well—no," she conceded, giving the matter some thought. "That is—if we do not overtake Bayard and he really *does* succeed in carrying Miss

Beaudoin off to America, I daresay even Lydia cannot be so utterly without feeling as not to do her possible for her family by accepting Harlbury,
if he should offer for her."

"I daresay not," Northover agreed dryly, the grim look again settling
about his mouth.

No more was said upon the subject, and their journey progressed
thenceforth with very little more in the way of conversation between the
travellers than Mrs. Leyland's lamentations over the discomforts of being
driven at such high speed in an open carriage.

When they arrived at Reading, however, not a quarter hour after Harlbury's curricle had reached the same point, they were greeted by the new
discomfort of the thundershower that had caused the accident to his lordship's vehicle. Here the complaints of Northover's unwilling companion
rose to such a pitch that even the Viscount could no longer remain proof
against them. She would not, Mrs. Leyland declared, in accents of doom
that might have done credit to a Siddons, wish him to be obliged to carry
through the remainder of his days the remorse occasioned by having
obliged an elderly lady of weak constitution to drive unprotected through a
rainstorm, thereby bringing down upon her the inflammation of the lungs
that was sure to carry her off before her time.

Whether the Viscount would actually have given way before these
tragical representations was never to be known, however, for at this point
they came upon Harlbury's curricle lying overturned in the road, while
various zealous persons still attempted to clear the way of the entangled
horses, the gig, and the wagon that had all been involved in the accident.

The Viscount, having brought his own horses to a halt, entrusted them
to the care of his Tiger and, jumping down, made a few rapid enquiries of
the assembled throng. These immediately elicited the information that a
young lady who had been a passenger in the curricle had suffered some serious (perhaps even fatal, one onlooker helpfully added) injury in the accident, and had forthwith been carried by her male companion into an
inn nearby. The inn having been pointed out to him, the Viscount
quickly returned to his curricle, his face now so set and drawn that Mrs.
Leyland felt the shock of the news he had to communicate to her before
he had so much as uttered a word; he then proceeded to escort that
lamenting lady with all possible speed to the inn to which it was said the
injured young lady had been borne.

Thus it came about that Mrs. Leyland and the Viscount, after a few
hasty enquiries of the chambermaid who was the first person they encoun-

tered upon entering the front door of the inn, were directed by this damsel to the private parlour where Lydia was at that precise moment being assisted to lie back upon the cushions of her sofa by a solicitous Harlbury. The tableau presented by the handsome and interestingly dishevelled peer and the afflicted young lady was doubtless an exceedingly romantic one; but, in spite of the relief both Mrs. Leyland and the Viscount felt on finding that Lydia was neither lifeless nor severely injured, it appeared to awaken no correspondingly soft emotions in the breasts of either. Mrs. Leyland's first words, in fact, were, "Unfeeling girl! You will yet bring my grey hairs down to the grave!" (This was a slight hyperbole, her locks being, either by art or by nature, of the same raven hue they had possessed in her youth.)

She thereupon tottered to the nearest chair, while Northover, with a very unfriendly glint in his eyes, which were fixed upon Lydia, said to her in sardonic tones, "I should have guessed, I daresay, that any accident you were involved in would only serve to further your ends. I gather that we may felicitate you and Harlbury, then?"

Lydia had fallen back against the cushions in the liveliest surprise at sight of her grandmother and Northover entering the room—an action somewhat facilitated by Harlbury's relinquishing his hold upon her as rapidly as if she had suddenly turned into something in the nature of red-hot metal. At the Viscount's words, however, she started up again, exclaiming with considerable vehemence, "No, you may not! I don't know what you may be doing here, Northover, or how you got here, but if you intend to behave in this tiresome way I wish you will go away again! You have no more sympathy than a—a goat!"

"I have a great deal of sympathy—but it is for Harlbury, not for you, my girl!" Northover said unfeelingly.

He turned his eyes upon that harassed young man, whose fingers were tugging at his once beautifully arranged neckcloth as if that much-abused article of clothing were still in a state to interfere with his breathing.

"Sir—ma'am!" he stammered, turning from Northover to Mrs. Leyland. "I assure you that it is my intention—I am aware that my presence in this place with Miss Leyland may be construed as highly compromising to the young lady—"

"Oh, for heaven's sake!" interrupted Mrs. Leyland piteously. "Do not stand there talking to no purpose, Harlbury, but ring the bell for some refreshment for me! Lydia, you are a wicked, wicked girl, and your brother, as I have always said, is twice as bad, but if he chooses to run off with a penniless bride to Belmaison I wash my hands of him, for not another step will I take after him!"

"Not another step! Oh, but you must, Grandmama!" Lydia exclaimed, raising herself again from the cushions in a new access of energy that set her senses swimming once more. She shut her eyes, endeavouring to command herself, and said, urgently passing her hand over her forehead, "You don't understand, love! If you let Bayard go off with Miss Beaudoin now, the consequences will be far worse than you imagine! I called upon Sir Basil this morning, and he told me positively that he means to make Bayard his heir, but that his intention depends entirely upon Bayard's conducting himself in such a way that he will be able to hold a respectable position in Society. You *must* know, then, what will happen if he creates a scandal by this elopement! It will ruin all his chances forever!"

She let her hand fall as Harlbury, looking half-distracted with worry and embarrassment, again obliged her to lie back on the sofa, while her grandmother stared at her with an almost ludicrously stricken expression upon her face.

"Merciful—heavens!" that good lady ejaculated at last, with every evidence of being about to be overcome by a fit of strong hysterics. "Do you mean—*can* you mean that Sir Basil—?"

"Yes, yes!" Lydia assured her. "It was that that made me so desperate to overtake Bayard. But then we had that horrid accident, and now I cannot prevail upon Harlbury to let me go on! But all that is of no consequence, since you are here. Dear ma'am, you *must* go on at once, and not waste any more time in talking to me. How did you get here? Surely you did not overtake us in a chaise?"

"No, no," Mrs. Leyland said feebly. "Lord Northover drove me—in his curricle."

Lydia looked at Northover. "Well, then, you must go on with her," she said to him decisively. She saw the ambiguous, somewhat sarcastic expression upon his face and added, in imploring vexation, "Northover, even *you* cannot be so totally malignant as to refuse now! You *must* see how much depends upon it!"

Northover looked unimpressed. "And leave you here alone with Harlbury?" he said. "I think not!"

"Oh, what does that signify!" Lydia said impatiently, and was about to go on when Harlbury himself interrupted seriously, "As to that, my lord, I can only say that you may consider Miss Leyland and myself from this moment as a betrothed couple, for I have every intention, after this unfortunate episode, of making her my wife—"

"Of making me *what!*" Lydia gasped, bouncing off the cushions again, her pale cheeks suddenly flying scarlet.

Northover spoke briefly. "Never mind!" he said. "I'll deal with this." His dark eyes raked Harlbury; there was a slight and not entirely pleasant smile on his lips. "So, my lad," he said, "you intend to offer Miss Leyland the *amende honorable,* do you? Very *galant* of you, to be sure, but has it never occurred to you that you have been led down the garden path—?"

He got no farther, for Lydia at once repeated, her eyes blazing, "Led down the garden path! Northover, what do you mean? Do you believe that *I—?*"

"I don't believe it. I know it!" Northover retorted, giving her no more opportunity to finish her speech than she had given him to finish his. "Why else should you have sought out Harlbury, of all men, to escort you upon this charming little excursion *à deux?*"

"I *didn't* seek him out! He h-happened to come to the house just as I—" It might have been fury that caused Lydia's voice to stammer and break; certainly the Viscount believed this to be true, and he was cutting into her angry words in a tone quite as intemperate as her own when, to his blank astonishment and that of everyone else in the room, his antagonist suddenly burst into tears. "You are a b-beast!" she sobbed. "If you th-think I would do such an utterly l-loathsome thing as that—"

"My love!" Mrs. Leyland, startled at the rare sight of her granddaughter in tears, rose to comfort her, as Harlbury stepped nobly into the breach.

"My lord," he said, looking rather pale, but speaking determinedly, "I must tell you that I find your insinuations offensive in the extreme! I consider that Miss Leyland's conduct in this affair has been unexceptionable throughout, and if you persist in speaking of her in such—I can only say, such *insulting* terms, I shall feel myself obliged, as Miss Leyland's affianced husband, to call you to account."

Northover, who sustained this warning with complete equanimity and even with an appearance of some amusement, merely said softly, "You are a gudgeon, Harlbury!"—a remark which caused Lydia, who was being offered succour by her grandmother in the shape of the vinaigrette she had extracted from her reticule, to say to him in tones of strong loathing, her eyes flashing through her tears, "He is *not* a gudgeon! And I wish he *will* shoot you! I would do it myself if I were a man! Grandmama, I don't want that! I am perfectly all right!"

This last statement she proceeded to demonstrate by crying even harder than before—a mode of behaviour which caused Mrs. Leyland to declare in helpless tones that she feared she must really be suffering from some more severe injury than they had at first believed, and that a surgeon had best be called to her.

"Exactly my own feeling, ma'am," Harlbury said earnestly, and was starting towards the door when he was interrupted by the reappearance of the landlady, who stood gazing in some astonishment at the scene before her.

"Well, I'm sure I never—!" she exclaimed, looking to Harlbury for some explanation. "Who had the impudence to show *these* people into your private parlour, sir? No wonder your lady wife—"

"I am *not* his lady wife!" Lydia said through her teeth, thrusting the vinaigrette aside and regarding the startled landlady with an expression so stormy that that worthy dame instinctively retreated towards the door. "I shall never marry *anyone*—and—and"—she bit her lip, struggling with the sobs that threatened to overcome her again—"and what is more, I wish to be left *alone*! Totally *alone!*"

"My dear—" Harlbury began anxiously.

"I am *not* your dear! And there is *nothing* the matter with me—except people with m-minds like vipers' and no feelings whatever, who won't lift a f-finger to stop other people from ruining their whole lives—"

Northover flung up a hand. "Very well!" he said. "That will do, Lydia! The picture is clear." There was an odd gleam in his eyes and a suppressed, taut excitement in his manner that might have given Lydia to think if she had been in a calmer state of mind. He went on, "As the one sensible thing you have said since I entered this room is that your brother had best be brought back to London before he has completely ruined his chances of inheriting old Rowthorn's fortune, I propose to do just that. On that head, at least, you may make yourself easy, for, if I know Minna, she won't be in the least agreeable to travelling in a storm. With luck, we shall find the two of them at an inn not far along the road, waiting for the weather to clear." He crossed the room in three long strides and, with one hand on her arm, assisted—or, rather, compelled—Mrs. Leyland to arise from her seat on the sofa beside Lydia. "With your permission, ma'am," he said, "we'll be on our way."

"On our way!" Mrs. Leyland stared at him, dumbfounded. "Sir, you cannot be serious! Leave my granddaughter in such a situation—!"

"You have already heard her say that it is her wish to be left alone,"

Northover said coolly, "and, as a matter of fact, I think that is an excellent idea. A period of calm reflection should do her a great deal of good." "But it is still raining!" Mrs. Leyland said piteously. "And in an open carriage—!"

"No doubt the landlady will be happy to accommodate you with a cloak and an umbrella," Northover said ruthlessly. "Come, ma'am, you will not deny your grandson a fortune merely because of a wetting! Harlbury"—he turned to his lordship, who was looking on rather dazedly at what was occurring—"I should advise you—strongly advise you!—to await our return in the coffee-room. In Miss Leyland's present agitated state, I fear that any further discussion of her affairs cannot be beneficial to her. I trust I make myself clear?"

Harlbury, who had been about to protest this rather high-handed arrangement, read at that moment an expression in the Viscount's glinting dark eyes which caused him to suffer an emotion that could readily have been identified by a number of Northover's former subalterns who had suddenly been confronted by the iron behind their superior's ordinarily easy-going manner. He said rather hastily, to salvage his dignity, "Perhaps you are right. Miss Leyland will wish to rest—"

"Oh, go away—do!" Miss Leyland said cordially. "Go away! Go away, all of you!"

She had stopped crying, and, after looking vainly for a handkerchief with which to dry her wet cheeks, was reduced to accepting—with a dagger-glance—the one thrust upon her by Northover.

"There, Lydia *mia!*" he said soothingly. "Dry your eyes and compose your temper, and when I return we'll sort this all out."

"There is nothing to sort out! And I *never* wish to see you again!" Miss Leyland flung at him; but her words fell disregarded.

Northover, shepherding Mrs. Leyland and Harlbury before him, was already out of the room, leaving the landlady, with the bobbing of a quick, scared curtsey, to whisk herself out behind him.

21　It was growing dusk, and candlelight was glowing warmly from the windows of the inn, when a post-chaise-and-four turned into the yard and a gentleman, quickly alighting from it, strode—after bestowing a word upon his postboys—hastily across the courtyard and in at the front door. Encountering the landlady in the hall, he accosted her without ceremony.

"I understand," he said, "that a young lady who was injured this afternoon when her carriage overturned was brought here by her companion. Can you inform me, ma'am, whether she is still in this house?"

Mrs. Yarden, somewhat startled at having this question flung at her at the very moment when she had been endeavouring for the dozenth time to puzzle out the reason for the very odd behaviour of the young couple she was harbouring beneath her roof—one of them closeted upstairs in a private parlour, the other lounging gloomily in the coffee-room, consuming far more French brandy than was good for him—cast a harassed glance at this new element in the picture. She saw a tall, fair young man, obviously a member of the Quality, upon whose face was an expression of the keenest impatience. It seemed that the gentleman was in the greatest anxiety to come up with her young guest.

She said doubtfully, "Why, yes, sir, she *is* here—but I misdoubt she'd be wishful to see company."

"Is she badly injured, then?"

"Oh no, sir, not at all! It was only the shock, as you might say. I'm sure she was feeling quite recovered when I looked in on her half an hour ago."

"And the gentleman with her?"

Mrs. Yarden shook her head disapprovingly. "No, sir, there's nothing the matter with *him*," she said, "except that he'll be as drunk as a wheelbarrow before the cat can lick her ear if he don't leave off calling for more of my best brandy! He's in the coffee-room; I'm sure you can see *him* if you like."

This suggestion, however, appeared to find little favour with the newcomer. He was looking very thoughtful and not at all ill pleased, and for a moment seemed quite oblivious of Mrs. Yarden's presence, his pale-blue eyes wearing a considering look, as if he were rapidly formulating some plan in his mind.

After a few moments he said abruptly, "I must see the young lady. Will you direct me to her?"

Mrs. Yarden's honest face creased in a perplexed frown. "Why, to tell you the truth, sir," she said, "she is laid down upon the sofa, resting, and may not wish for visitors. Unless it might be a relation—"

"But, you see, I *am* a relation!" the gentleman said, a sterner look appearing upon his face. "In point of fact, I am her husband! And now, ma'am, if you will be good enough to show me to my wife's apartment—"

"Well, surely to goodness!" Mrs. Yarden breathed, the truth of the matter suddenly breaking upon her like a thunderbolt. "And she was running away from you with that young villain in the coffee-room! Why, I never in all my born days—! Such a nice young man as he looks, too, without rumgumption enough to say 'Boh!' to a goose!"

"Yes, yes!" said the gentleman, even more impatiently. "But my wife—?"

"Upstairs, sir, in my very best parlour," Mrs. Yarden said, glancing down at the handsome *douceur* that was being pressed into her hand. "But you won't go to be hard upon her, now, will you?—for I'm sure she's that sorry already that she ran off, and I can give you my word as a Christian woman that she's not been alone with the young gentleman for five minutes together as long as they've been in my house. He's been sulking down here in the coffee-room the whole time since the *other* gentleman and lady left—and why *they* didn't take her off with them I'm sure I don't know, if she *was* the young lady's grandmother, as she claimed to be—"

She had been leading the way up the narrow staircase as she spoke, but at this point the gentleman halted her with a sharply spoken, "Wait!" She turned her head in surprise, to find him regarding her frowningly.

"Yes, sir?"

"An elderly lady?" he enquired abruptly. "Dark, aquilined-featured? And escorted by a younger gentleman, also very dark?"

"Yes, sir. That's them to the life! Do you know them, sir?"

"I know them," the gentleman said. "Where are they now?"

"Oh, sir, truly, I couldn't tell you!" said the harassed landlady. "All I can say is that they went off again in the gentleman's curricle. There was a good deal of excitement, you see, what with the young lady crying and saying she wished to be left alone, and all of them at loggerheads, it seemed, like a bag full of cats—"

The gentleman, still frowning thoughtfully, appeared to abandon the hope of extracting any more information from her and bade her lead the way on up the stairs. He was still looking preoccupied when she halted before a closed door at the head of the staircase, but at this point shook off his abstraction and informed her that she might go.

"Yes, sir—but I—you—you won't go to offering violence to the young gentleman in my house?" she enquired, with renewed anxiety. "Being a female myself, I know the young lady is apt to lay all the blame upon *him*—but, to tell you the truth, he seemed to me as cast down to find himself in this case of pickles as she did, and I'm bound to say he's never made the least push to see her since the other lady and gentleman left, besides being clean raddled by this time with all the brandy he's drunk—"

The newcomer assured her that he had no intention of calling the young man to account within her house, his only concern being to remove his wife from the compromising situation in which she found herself; and, this point having been settled between them, Mrs. Yarden departed down the stairs, leaving the newcomer to rap upon the door she had indicated to him.

His knock was answered so immediately that it seemed obvious that Miss Leyland had been expecting it. That she had not been expecting to see *him*, however, was equally obvious from the look of total astonishment that crossed her face the instant her eyes fell upon him.

"Michael Pentony!" she exclaimed. "How in the world did *you* come here?"

"As it happens, by post-chaise, my dear Lydia," Mr. Pentony said composedly. "May I come in?"

He stepped past her, as he spoke, into the room, closing the door behind him. Lydia, still overcome by astonishment, demanded, "But how did you know I was here? It isn't *possible*—"

"On the contrary, it is quite possible," Mr. Pentony said, stripping off his gloves and laying down his curly-brimmed beaver with the air of a man who had every intention of remaining where he was for some time. "Fatiguing, yes—but perfectly possible, my dear. And a trifle expensive as well, I might add, for information is not to be come by gratis, you know."

Lydia, who had attended to this speech with growing indignation, which she felt quite capable now of expressing in her much improved state of strength and spirits, interrupted at this point to say rather ominously, "I daresay by *that* you mean that you have been bribing servants again! What did Sidwell tell you?—for I am sure you got nothing out of Winch!"

Mr. Pentony smiled his calm, narrow smile. "Really, you do me an injustice!" he said. "What could I do, on arriving in Green Street to find your household all in a turmoil—you and your grandmother apparently having gone out of town in the greatest haste, your brother absent too— but to attempt to learn if there was something I could do to assist you? And, as you see, I have spared no pains in this praiseworthy endeavour, which has involved really a tiresome number of enquiries at toll-gates and posting-houses, but which fortunately has at last been crowned with success."

"Oh! Would you say 'fortunately'?" Lydia, who had by this time overcome her first surprise and discomfiture, enquired with a sweetness that might have warned Mr. Pentony of danger. "I definitely would *not*—but then some people may *enjoy* jauntering about the countryside to no purpose."

"Ah, but I do not think it has been to no purpose," Mr. Pentony said. "May I sit down?"

"No!" said Lydia.

"But I think I shall," Mr. Pentony said, coolly suiting the action to the words, "and I should advise you to do likewise, my dear, for I have something to say to you that you would be well advised to attend to. And if," he added, as she stood looking furiously down at him, "you have any notion of calling upon Harlbury to assist you, let me inform you that he is at this present, in the landlady's words, as—er—drunk as a wheelbarrow on her best French brandy."

"*Harlbury!*" exclaimed Lydia, momentarily diverted. "I don't believe it!"

"Nevertheless, it is true," said Mr. Pentony. "I do not know what means you employed to embroil him in this business, but I can assure you that if you expected to use this affair to entrap him into matrimony, you have little chance of success. It must be quite as clear to you as it is to me, after observing him last night at Vauxhall, that he has not the smallest *tendre* for you, and, though I believe he must at present be suffering a considerable degree of remorse over the situation in which you have landed him, I do not believe it to be sufficient to cause him to lead you to the altar—especially since his mother would be so very greatly adverse to his taking such a step."

Lydia, seeing that her visitor had no idea of leaving, sat down in a chair opposite him and regarded him with marked contempt.

"I have not the smallest intention of marrying Lord Harlbury," she said. "And now, if you have anything more to say to me, Mr. Pentony, I wish that you will say it and go. I am *not* in the mood to be civil to you, you know!"

"Yes, I do know," Mr. Pentony said composedly, "but *that*, my dear, is an attitude I should advise you to amend. You are in no position to reject an offer of help from any quarter just now, with your brother having gone off in this most reprehensible way with Miss Beaudoin and your own reputation in the greatest danger of being compromised beyond repair. You had much better come to realise at once that you need me quite as much as I need you."

Lydia looked at him, her brows drawing together in a sudden frown. "As you need me?" she repeated. "Why should you—?"

"Come come," interrupted Mr. Pentony, with a slightly impatient shrug, "pray don't trouble to pretend that you don't understand me! You would not have been at such pains to prevent this elopement if you had not been persuaded that there is more at stake than the social blight that would be cast upon your brother and Miss Beaudoin by the manner of their marriage! I know, as a matter of fact, that you have been doing your best to promote the match; but the situation took a different turn—did it not?—when you learned that I had fallen from favour with Sir Basil and that there was now a chance that your brother might inherit a fortune!"

Lydia looked at him resignedly. "Is there anything that you *don't* know?" she enquired. "Really, you are the most utterly devious person! I imagine you must have a network of spies that would put the Bow Street Runners to shame!"

"Let us say, at any rate, that you would be obliged to get up very early in the morning indeed to best me on any suit," said Mr. Pentony, not at all discomposed by this thrust.

"Yes, but you are not *quite* so clever as you like to think," Lydia was goaded to retort, "or Sir Basil would not have found you out. He is furious with you—"

"He *was* furious," Mr. Pentony corrected her smoothly. He reached into his pocket and, drawing out a pretty enamelled snuff-box, refreshed himself unhurriedly with a pinch of its contents. "When he was informed, however, of how small the odds now are that Mr. Bayard Leyland will ever be able to take that place in the *haut ton* to which he—Sir Basil, that is—aspires for him—"

He broke off, satisfied that his shaft had found its mark. Lydia was looking perfectly white, and said after a moment, in a small, gritty voice, "Do you mean that you have already told him—?"

"My dear, only think a moment—would you have expected me to keep such a piece of news to myself? I am not *quite* so altruistic; as I have told you before, there is a fortune at stake, and I have no idea of seeing it slip out of my hands if I am able to prevent it."

He was watching her intently as he spoke; but if he had expected her to give way to despair he was disappointed. She did, indeed, jump up from her chair and walk away from him to the window, as if to conceal her agitation from him; but when she turned again her face, though still pale, wore a look of resolution.

"Well, it does not signify!" she said. "Northover and Grandmama are sure to have come up with Bayard by this time, and if he and Minna return to town in *their* company we shall be able to keep the tattle-boxes quiet, after all, and persuade Sir Basil that no harm has been done."

"Do you think so?" Mr. Pentony was engaged in dusting from his sleeve with his handkerchief a few grains of snuff that had fallen upon it, and gave his response in rather a negligent tone. "Dear me, what a trusting creature you are! To believe it would be in my power, that is, to restrain myself from letting fall to at least two or three of my mother's friends—ladies with such valuable connexions in the *ton,* and so anxious to be able to spread the newest *on-dit* amongst them—the diverting tale of this day's adventures—"

Lydia looked at him with frank loathing. "Yes, I might have known that you would do so!" she said. "Very well, then—you may succeed in ruining Bayard's chances with Sir Basil, I suppose! But if I were you, I should not be *quite* so certain of benefitting by it. Sir Basil has no liking for tale-pitchers, you know!"

Mr. Pentony raised his eyes to her face. "I am aware of that," he said, rising deliberately and bridging the few steps between them to possess himself of her hand. She snatched it away. "No, don't repulse me, Lydia," he said, taking it again and clasping it so tightly that she could not have withdrawn it without an undignified struggle. "Let us face facts. Alone, neither of us can be assured of winning the prize of Sir Basil's fortune, for your brother has scotched his chances forever by this scandal and I too am no longer in his good graces, owing—as you doubtless know!—to the curst tattling tongue of that butler of his. But together—if you were to marry me—"

"Well, I shall not marry you! I have told you that before!" Lydia said, again endeavouring to draw her hand from his.

This time he let her go, but she saw from the look on his face that this was far from the end of the matter.

"My dear—pray listen to me!" he said, in a slightly quickened voice. "What have you to gain by refusing me? I promise you, if I am able to go to Sir Basil and tell him that you will be my wife, I shall be able to bring him around. He has taken a liking to you, and his displeasure with me is not so deep-rooted that the knowledge that you have agreed to be my wife will not weigh the scales in my favour once more. And I can promise you that on my side, at least, it will not be a loveless marriage, and that I shall do my best to bring you to feel the same! You are—exceedingly attractive to me, Lydia!"

"Thank you very much, but *you* are not exceedingly attractive to me, Mr. Pentony, and I do not at all wish to marry you!" Lydia said rather distractedly, wondering what new trials to her composure this luckless day could bring. "And now will you *please* go away? I really have no more to say to you."

She had turned away, so that she did not observe the rather odd expression that came upon his face at these words, but it might have astonished her if she had. She had never seen him when caution and composure had not blended in his manner, and, if she had thought of the matter at all, would certainly have said that he was a man in whom emotion would never overcome calculation.

She was soon to learn how mistaken she had been. Apparently the events of the day, raising, as they had, both great anxieties and even greater hopes in Mr. Pentony's breast, had shaken his usual careful control, and the result was that she found herself the next instant enveloped in a greedy and importunate embrace, and heard his voice saying urgently in her ear, "Lydia! Only listen to me for a moment! You *must* marry me—"

"If you do not let me go this instant, I shall scream!" Lydia said, struggling furiously to free herself, but finding that coping with the determined advances of a well-muscled young man was quite a different matter from repulsing Sir Carsbie's dandified attempts to snatch a kiss. Her struggles had the effect only of causing Michael Pentony to tighten his embrace, as he said quickly in her ear, "No, no—it will not do, Lydia! You *must* have me; this has gone too far! I have told the landlady I am your husband, come to seek my runaway wife—"

"You have told her *what!*"

Even Mr. Pentony, involved as he was in the twin turmoils of passion and ambition, was momentarily shaken by the absolutely incredulous fury he saw at that moment in Miss Leyland's face, and only the fact that her voice had risen to a somewhat undignified squeak on the last word enabled him to retain his poise. He did not, therefore, relax the close embrace in which he still held her, and was hurriedly going further into his explanations of the reasons why it behooved her to receive his addresses with more complaisance—somewhat disjointed ones, it was true, for she had never ceased in her determined efforts to free herself—when the door suddenly opened behind him and a third actor burst upon the scene. Unfortunately for Mr. Pentony, he had his back to the door, so that the first intimation he had of this new turn of events was the feel of a heavy hand falling upon his shoulder, tearing him away from Lydia and swinging him violently around to face his attacker, but Lydia, facing the door, recognised her rescuer at once, and shrieked, "Northover!" at almost the same instant.

22 What happened next Lydia would have been put to it to describe, though, flung back by Pentony's abrupt release of her against a stout o table, she had an excellent view of the proceedings. Furniture went flying as Mr. Pentony, going down under a well-directed blow to the point of his jaw, crashed in his fall into a pair of chairs and a tall whatnot stand. Lydia, flying to rescue the lamp perilously tottering at the edge of the table, missed the next few moments, during which Mr. Pentony evidently succeeded in getting to his feet, for when she saw him next he was staggering across the room toward Northover with red fury in his eyes. There was a confused interval during which the two men, with Mr. Pentony doggedly clinging to Northover in a fierce attempt to wrestle him down, went careering about the room with sundry crashes and the sound of splintering furniture punctuating their progress—and then suddenly, to Lydia's amazed admiration, Mr. Pentony was hurled decisively to the floor in a manoeuvre too quick even for her to follow. In a moment he was up again, but only for an instant; a blow from Northover's left dropped him decisively this time and he lay prone, his head resting almost at Lydia's feet.

Northover came over quickly and took Lydia's hands in a hard grasp. "He hasn't hurt you?"

"No! Oh, no! But—thank you!" Lydia gasped. She looked down, awed, at Mr. Pentony's recumbent form. "Is he dead?"

"No—only stunned. Damned impudent dog! What the *devil* is he doing here, Lydia?"

"He—he found out somehow from Sidwell what had happened and—and managed to trace me here, I expect. But—oh dear, Northover, I am in the most dreadful coil! He has told the landlady I am his runaway wife—and, what is even worse, he says he has already told Sir Basil of Bayard's elopement with Minna! And now you have come back without them—!"

She got no further, for at that moment a shriek from the doorway brought her to a sudden halt. Her eyes and Northover's flew to the door, to light upon the petrified figure of Mrs. Yarden, her hands clasped to her plump, palpitating bosom as she surveyed the wreckage of her best parlour.

"Mercy upon us!" she gasped. "What's to do here? Jem! Jem!" She turned to a small boy of about ten who had come up behind her and was peeping around the corner of the door, trying to see what was going for-

inside the room. "Go and fetch the Constable as fast as you can
, " she implored, "and tell him there's a gentleman murdered in my
est parlour, and the furniture all broke to pieces—"

"Nonsense!" Northover cut in, coming across to the doorway in two
swift strides and collaring Jem—not a difficult matter, as Jem showed no
disposition to remove himself from the scene of these fascinating crimes,
and had remained rooted to the spot, goggling at Mr. Pentony's peaceful
form on the floor. "There is no need for the Constable; the gentleman and
I have merely had a slight disagreement. And as for the furniture—" The
Viscount cast a rapid glance about the room and, releasing Jem to draw
out his purse, thrust several gold coins into Mrs. Yarden's automatically
extended hand. "This will make all right, I believe," he said soothingly.
"And now, if you and Jem will leave us alone—"

"Miss Leyland!" a new voice suddenly broke into the conversation from
the doorway. Mrs. Yarden and Jem were thrust aside and Lord Harlbury,
looking extremely dishevelled but highly resolute, strode somewhat uncertainly into the room, where he halted and stood staring about him with an
uncomprehending gaze. His eyes lighting upon the Viscount, a guilty but
obstinate expression settled upon his face. "Know you don't like it—told
me to stay in the coffee-room," he said, "but—heard a noise—devilish sort
of commotion—came to see if—be of assistance to Miss Leyland—"

"Very commendable of you," Northover said approvingly. "But, as you
see, no assistance is required, Harlbury. I suggest that you return to the
coffee-room."

"No!" said Harlbury with unexpected spirit, speaking so loudly as to
make Mrs. Yarden jump. He added more mildly, "Been thinking it over.
Thinking for hours. Got it all clear now. Must marry Miss Leyland. Go
back to town tonight—uncle a bishop—special licence—no delay—"

"Harlbury, for heaven's sake, do stop talking fustian and go downstairs
as Northover bids you!" Lydia broke in indignantly. "There is nothing for
you to do here!"

But his lordship's eyes had by this time taken in Mr. Pentony upon the
floor and, quite disregarding Lydia's words, he said rather darkly to Northover, "That—that's Miss Pentony's brother. Friend of mine. Had a turn-up
with him?"

The Viscount acknowledged that he had, but again suggested the propriety of his lordship's leaving the matter to him. By this time, however,
both Lydia and Mrs. Yarden had recollected their duty, as females, to suc-

cour any gentleman stretched unconscious at their feet, and were bending together over Mr. Pentony, one lady loudly bidding Jem to run to her chamber and fetch the hartshorn, and the other wetting her handkerchief from the pitcher upon the table to apply it to his forehead.

Their attentions proved unnecessary, however, for Mr. Pentony, sitting up abruptly, and regarding the scene somewhat dazedly but quite sapiently out of one unmarked eye and another rapidly turning a horrid purple-red colour, uttered something that sounded remarkably like an oath. Lydia instantly rose from her knees beside him and resumed an expression of loathing, directed to his notice.

"Come, come, sir," Mrs. Yarden said soothingly, taking up the handkerchief that Lydia had dropped and dabbing professionally with it at the blood trickling from the corner of her patient's mouth, "you'll be feeling better in a moment now, I'll be bound. And if you'll be good enough to tell me if you'd like to charge either of these gentlemen before a magistrate, I'll see it done—for running off with other men's wives," she said, directing a quelling glance at Harlbury, "is what I can't abide, nor what business it is of the *other* gentleman's" (this to Northover's address) "if you choose to come to take back your lady wife, I can't imagine—"

"I am *not* his lady wife!" Lydia said violently, drawing a look from Mrs. Yarden's offended female sensibilities as much wounded as it was astonished.

"Not his, neither! Lawks, ma'am—*miss!*—but he said—"

"I don't care what he said! I am *not* his wife!"

"No," Harlbury corroborated her words, with a gloomy air. "Not *his* wife. Mine. Affianced, that is." He turned his harassed gaze upon Northover and repeated stubbornly, "Thought it all out. *Must* marry her. Good God, even my mother will see *that!*"

"I doubt it," Northover said equably. "But, at all events, this is hardly the time or the place to discuss your matrimonial plans."

Lord Harlbury, however, was paying him no heed; his eyes were fixed upon Lydia in a kind of detached and fascinated resignation.

"I shall probably murder her if I am obliged to live with her," he stated with unexpected clarity, after a moment. "*Not* a gudgeon. Can see that myself. But bound in honour—"

Northover, making a praiseworthy attempt to command his countenance, told his lordship that he doubted such a sacrifice would be required of him, and again directed him to take himself off downstairs.

But Harlbury stood his ground. "Not," he announced firmly, "until I now what's going on here!" He looked at Mr. Pentony, who had by this time, with Mrs. Yarden's help, managed to get to his feet and had collapsed into a chair beside the table, and enquired with some interest, "Is your sister here, too?"

"No, she is *not* here!" Lydia said, goaded quite beyond endurance. "*Do* go away, Harlbury! You are only making matters worse! And I am *not* going to marry you, so you may put that idea quite out of your head!"

"Not—?" His lordship looked at her hopefully.

"No! Under no circumstances!" Her eyes chanced to meet the Viscount's, and she saw the irrepressible quiver of a telltale muscle at the corner of his mouth. The colour flamed into her cheeks. "Northover, I warn you," she said, "I shall do you an injury if you laugh at me!"

"No, no, Lydia—not at you! At all of us!" said the Viscount, the gleam still in his dark eyes.

But he controlled himself sufficiently to guide Harlbury to the door, assuring him that supper and a pot of strong coffee were all that was necessary to set him on his legs again, and promising him that he need feel no further responsibility upon Miss Leyland's account. He followed this action with a firm representation to Mrs. Yarden and Jem that their presence was no longer required, and, in spite of Mrs. Yarden's protests against leaving a gentleman upon whom the Viscount had already wrought such horrid violence alone in the room with him, except for Lydia's dubious protection, she was inexorably swept outside and the door closed behind her.

"And now," said Northover, turning at once to Mr. Pentony with a somewhat grimmer expression upon his face, "we'll have this out to the finish, my buck." Mr. Pentony, turning a ghastly white under the purplish swellings that disfigured his countenance, cast a rather wild look at Lydia, as to the only person available who might shield him from further immediate mayhem committed upon his person—an action that drew an impatient shrug from the Viscount. "You must be a clothhead if you think I should attack a man in your state!" he said. "But I want an explanation from you, Pentony, and I intend to have one, so you had best make up your mind to give me the truth without any roundaboutation. How did you come here, and for what purpose?"

Mr. Pentony, mustering up what dignity he could under the handicap of a swelling eye, a cut lip, and what he was horribly convinced were several loose teeth, muttered a somewhat expurgated repetition of the explanation he had previously given Lydia—that, having discovered by a chance call in Green Street something of what had occurred there that morning, he had come in search of Miss Leyland to offer her any aid that lay in his power.

"Even," he added, with a somewhat vindictive look in that young lady's direction, "the protection of my name, my lord—which can scarcely be construed as a dishonourable offer!"

"On the contrary—a most honourable one," Northover said coolly, "if it had not been made in such a way as to place her under compulsion to accept it. Informing the landlady that she was already your wife, and then forcing your attentions upon Miss Leyland, scarcely go down with me as the actions of an honourable man." He saw Mr. Pentony open his mouth to utter a protest and added, with an impatient gesture, "No, don't try to justify yourself. You had much better cut line and tell me the truth, for I warn you that I have little time to waste upon you. You told Miss Leyland you had already informed Sir Basil Rowthorn that young Bayard has run off with Miss Beaudoin. Is that true?"

"Yes," muttered Mr. Pentony, with a glance, in spite of his injuries, of such malevolent triumph upon his face that Lydia could not forbear breaking in to say indignantly, "Of course it is true, for it is utterly what one might have expected of him! And now, if you please, he thinks that *I* will help him to chouse Bayard out of a fortune by marrying him. Well, I shan't! I daresay we shall all end in the Fleet, but I don't care: I had as soon marry a—a snake!"

The muscle quivered again at the corner of Northover's mouth, but he only said quite gravely, "I honour your principles, Lydia, but I scarcely think you need look forward to their dooming you to such a dismal future. You see, in the first place I do not believe that Mr. Pentony has yet seen Sir Basil."

"Not seen Sir Basil?" Lydia's eyes followed Northover's in swift incredulity to Mr. Pentony's face, but what she saw there made her exclaim suddenly, "Oh! I do believe you are right."

"I am quite sure that I am," the Viscount said dryly. "You were a widg eon to have swallowed *that* fling, my love. Is it likely, do you think, that your—er—ardent suitor here would have wasted his time in running to Sir Basil with what he could not yet dignify as anything more than a piece of steward's-room gossip, when every moment he delayed in setting out after you made it less likely that he would reach you in time to prevent Harlbury's becoming so entangled in the business as to feel that he must offer you marriage? *I* don't think it!"

"No—nor do I, now you put it to me so!" agreed Lydia, looking accusingly at Mr. Pentony. "So *that* was a lie, too! I might have known it! Only"—her voice faltered suddenly as she turned again to Northover, "even if he has not already done so, there is nothing to prevent him from telling Sir Basil *now*. Indeed, it must become known, since you were not able to find Bayard—"

"What makes you think I have not found him?" said the Viscount. "Or that I should have come back here if I had not? You need have no further worries on *that* score, Lydia. Your brother and Miss Beaudoin—well chaperoned, I may add, by your grandmother—are at this moment on their way to Great Hayland, where they have been so kind as to agree to pay me a visit—"

"On their way to Great Hayland!" Lydia looked utterly astounded. "But I don't understand—"

"Come, come!" said the Viscount reprovingly. "Surely you cannot have forgotten so soon that Great Hayland lies particularly convenient to the road from Bristol to London! I daresay they may even have reached it by this time, as it is a matter of only five miles or so to the south of here. And when you and I have joined them there, together with Lord and Lady Gilmour, to whom I have sent a most urgent invitation to be my guests as well, I have no doubt that we shall make up a very agreeable party—"

"Lord and Lady Gilmour!"

"Why, yes! I rather flatter myself that they will be on their way before first light tomorrow, so that the notice I am about to send to the *Morning Post* announcing their presence at Great Hayland—along with that of their daughter and your family—can scarcely be considered as premature. I fancy," he added, "that Sir Basil will be immensely pleased to read it there —for I understand that, even though he does not go into Society himself, he is addicted to perusing the columns devoted to the activities of the *ton* quite carefully each day."

"Oh!" gasped Lydia, gazing at him almost in awe. "You really have been frightfully *tortuous*, Northover! I should never have guessed it of you; it is *quite* as good as anything I might have contrived myself!"

"Thank you!" said Northover, overcome. "A notable tribute—but you must not be too generous, Lydia! I am quite sure *you* would not have compounded for anything so commonplace and respectable as a mere house-party if you had been given *my* opportunities." He turned his attention to Mr. Pentony once more, his face altering slightly, in a way that made that gentleman stir uncomfortably in his chair. "And now," he said, "since I shall take it upon myself to escort Miss Leyland to Great Hayland, may I suggest that I find your company quite unnecessary, Mr. Pentony? You will find the landlady eager to attend to your comfort, I have no doubt, if you wish to remain here for the night—which," he added, with a critical glance at Mr. Pentony's marred countenance, "I strongly advise you to do."

But Mr. Pentony, though he rose from his chair, made no immediate move to leave the room.

"Ay," he said, in a low, shaking voice that Lydia, with her customary flair for the dramatic, could only describe to herself as murderous, "you have contrived well, Northover—but you are bacon-brained if you think that I will keep silent about this day's work to old Rowthorn! I shall return to town at once—and when he hears of it—"

There was an odd gleam in the Viscount's dark eyes, but his pleasant drawl was, if anything, only the more marked as he said coolly, "No, no—it is you who have windmills in your head, Pentony, if you think you can carry *that* face to Rowthorn without his putting you through such a shrewd catechism on the head of it that *your* part in this business will not come out! He has a way of getting to the heart of a matter without ceremony, you know! And, at any rate," he added, "what makes you believe that he will care a rush for your tales? If you do not know him well enough by this time to realise that he is interested in results, not words, you have wasted the years you have spent in cultivating him. You may take my word for it that, while the world is treated to the sight of a young man of the highest expectations marrying a young lady of unimpeachable birth and breeding against a background of family approval, *ton* parties, and a fashionable wedding, he will have no fault to find with young Bayard."

The rather ghastly sneer upon Mr. Pentony's face became even more pronounced.

"And Miss Leyland?" he enquired. "Will she too find that her reputation is able to survive the test she has put it to today? I think not! When it becomes known that I found her here alone in this inn in Lord Harlbury's company—"

The odd light—almost phosphorescent, it seemed, to Lydia's fascinated gaze—leapt again in Northover's eyes, and this time there was something in the level composure of his voice that penetrated even Mr. Pentony's fury.

"As to that," said the Viscount very gently, "it may be as well for me to warn you that if I ever chance to hear of your having spoken of Miss Leyland in terms other than of respect, it will give me the greatest pleasure to call you to account for your words. It may enlighten you further, I believe, if I tell you that I intend to make Miss Leyland my wife."

If the Viscount had been in a mood to be amused at that moment, the astonished, even thunderstruck, expressions upon the two faces before him might have appealed irresistibly to his risibilities, never under stern control. But he was not in that mood, and neither pair of widened eyes directed now upon his face found the slightest trace there of anything to give them the idea that he was not entirely in earnest in what he said.

It was Mr. Pentony who recovered his voice first. He said, "Your wife! This is indeed news to me!"—with a profound chagrin that again the Viscount, in another mood, could not but have found comical.

Now, however, he merely remarked, "Yes, I rather fancy it is. All the same, I should advise you to believe me when I tell you that I should feel not the slightest compunction in putting a bullet through you if it were to come to my ears that you had been so indiscreet as to spread malicious gossip concerning Miss Leyland—and I must warn you that I am held to be an excellent shot. And now," he said again, this time in tones of marked impatience, "I am beginning to find you a dead bore, Pentony, and if you don't relieve us of your company at once I really think I shall be obliged to *encourage* you to leave."

Mr. Pentony, however, was in need of no more encouragement. With a crestfallen air that he tried in vain to conceal behind the tatters of his composure, he informed the Viscount that threats had no power to move him—adding hastily, however, as he saw that gentleman's hands double into a pair of purposeful fists, that he was no tattle-monger and his lordship need have no fear that any unwary gossip on his part would reveal the events of that day to the world.

This was more satisfactory, and Northover allowed him to depart in peace, observing cheerfully to Lydia as the door closed behind him that he would probably go and make himself agreeable to Harlbury—"for, though everything else has failed, he has still the hope, I daresay, that his sister's charms will bring him into Parson's mouse-trap with her one of these days," he said.

Lydia regarded him severely, but with a look of some shyness in her eyes—a very unusual look, which the Viscount had never seen there before.

"Yes, I expect you are right," she said, "but that is not to the point,

Northover! I wish you will tell me what can have possessed you to pitch him such an outrageous Banbury tale! Of course I am much obliged to you for trying to stop his tongue—as well as for finding Bayard, and all the rest," she added conscientiously, "but, since he is certain to find out the truth—"

"Ah, yes! The truth!" said the Viscount pensively, regarding her with very steady dark eyes in which, she felt, there was an odd, intent warmth. "And what if I have already told him the truth, Lydia *mia?*"

"That you—wish to—intend to—?" Lydia's heart began abruptly to beat unaccountably fast, and she turned away from him, saying hurriedly, "I wish you will not talk flummery to me, Northover! I am not in the mood. And now, if you don't mind—I am rather tired, and I should like to go on to join Grandmama and Bayard at once—"

"Yes, I know," Northover said. He moved closer and, before she knew what he was about, had both her hands firmly clasped in his own. "You have had a trying day, haven't you, my little love?" he said. "But if you can spare me another ten minutes of your conversation before we go—"

Lydia looked at the closed door behind him, and into her mind there stole the lowering thought that his lordship was about to take advantage of her present unchaperoned state to make an improper proposal to her. She managed to say in a rather suffocated voice, "No—please!"—and attempted to draw her hands away, but she discovered that, without an unbecoming struggle, this was quite impossible to accomplish. She also found it impossible, for some reason, to look up into his lordship's face.

After a moment she heard his voice asking abruptly, with what appeared to her a deceptive mildness, over her head, "Tell me, Lydia—why did you refuse Harlbury?"

The colour flew into her cheeks. She flung up her head, meeting his eyes.

"*That,*" she said, "is none of your affair!"—adding inconsistently, "If you *still* think I was abominable enough to lure him to take me off with him so that he would feel obliged to make me an offer—"

"I don't," Northover interrupted reassuringly. "But does it not seem a trifle odd to you, in view of what I have heard you say on the subject of matrimony, that you should be so very *determined* to have none of his suit?"

She gave him a darkling glance. "I know very well what I have said! But I am *not* a—a man-trap, Northover, whatever you may think!"

"Oh, no!" he agreed gravely. "I came to that conclusion myself last night at Vauxhall, when I heard you so cavalierly reject Sir Carsbie's very obliging offer—though I must admit that my faith in you suffered a slight set-back when I learned you had gone off with Harlbury—"

"Well, you *must* have known the reason I went off with him," said Lydia with asperity, again endeavouring vainly to draw her hands free of his firm grasp, "and that it had nothing to do with anyone's marriage except Bayard's. Which puts me in mind that you have not told me where you found him—"

"Oh, at an inn at Theale. I told you Minna would not travel in a storm."

"And you explained it all to him—about the inheritance, I mean?" Lydia enquired, a little anxiously. "Because he must have been very much surprised and—and put about to see you."

"He was," said Northover, grinning slightly. "In fact, your grandmother and I had quite a Cheltenham tragedy enacted for us, with Minna swooning away and your young brother ranting a great deal of fustian about thwarted lovers, before we could succeed in convincing him that not even Lady Gilmour's marble heart was likely to remain unsoftened before the affecting thought of her daughter's marrying a fortune to rival Golden Ball's. In fact, it is exactly my conviction that it will not, that makes me so certain that we shall see her and Ned at Great Hayland as fast as horses can bring them, once Trix has learned how the situation stands."

The mention of Lady Gilmour's name appeared to be an unfortunate one. Lydia, whose interest in her brother's affairs had caused her momentarily to forget that Northover still held her hands imprisoned in his, said, "Oh! I see!" in a determinedly cool voice, and then, more pettishly, as she again attempted to wrest her hands free, "*Do* let me go, Northover! What point is there in holding me here like this?"

"None at all," said the Viscount promptly, and thereupon swept her into his arms. "Shall I convince you that I am in earnest, Lydia *mia?*" his voice came in her ear as his lips brushed her hair—an oddly thickened voice, she noted, with a new, more urgent tone in it that she had never heard before.

Miss Leyland, firmly convinced by this time that she was experiencing in person the methods by which the Viscount had notoriously succeeded in making conquests of so many of her sex, found herself struggling against an ignoble desire to burst into tears. Perhaps, she thought, in not very logical confusion, it had been the offers made to her by Mr. Pentony and Lord Harlbury that had inspired him to use this particular manoeuvre to bring her into his net—but she was *not,* she told herself firmly, such a green girl as to be deceived by such lures! Spiritedly fending off North-over's attempts to turn his mouth from her hair to her lips, she managed to surprise him sufficiently by the violence of her resistance to free herself from his embrace, and, when he attempted to renew it, astonished both him and herself by dealing him a resounding slap, with the full force of her arm behind it.

"Now *that,*" said the Viscount, recovering himself first and speaking with a wounded air, "is unjust, my girl! The first and only honourable proposal of marriage I have ever made in my life, and to be received in such a fashion—!"

"If you do not stop making game of me, I shall do it again!" Lydia threatened, her voice breaking in spite of her furious efforts to control it. "I am *not* one of your lady-birds, Northover!"

The Viscount's brows rose in genuine surprise. "Good God, I should think not!" he said. "What can have put *that* idea into your head?"

Lydia swallowed a very hard lump in her throat. "You sent me f-five thousand pounds," she said. "And you s-said I could have m-more if I liked—"

"So that is it!" said the Viscount, taking her averted face in his hands and obliging her at least to turn it in his direction, although she refused to raise her eyes to his face. "A misunderstood gesture of the purest philanthropy if ever I saw one! Lydia, you absurd little vixen, will you *look* at me? I want to marry you, my girl!"

She glanced up at him suspiciously, quite unconvinced, and still on the edge of tears. "You are not a marrying man," she said accusingly, after a moment. "You told me so yourself, Northover. You know you did."

"I wasn't then. I am now," his lordship said, changing his ground in an entirely conscienceless manner.

"Oh!" said Lydia, shaken quite off her balance by these unfair tactics. She looked down again, appearing to become very much absorbed in contemplating one of the buttons on his lordship's waistcoat. "Well, I—I daresay a person *might* change his mind," she conceded presently, in a rather small voice.

"Especially," Northover said, "when he is given such irresistible temptation to do so. Oh yes," he went on, with a rueful smile, "it goes sorely against the pluck with me, Lydia *mia,* to be obliged to admit that I have met a woman I cannot live without, but, believe me, you have turned the trick!" His voice was suddenly serious again—that new, changed, vibrant voice. "I need you, by God I do!" he said, and the next instant—she did not quite know how—she was in his arms again, and his mouth came down on her parted lips almost fiercely, in a kiss that sent the blood racing through her body. "*Will* you marry me, you enchanting—exasperating—abominable little rogue?" he demanded, and then prevented her entirely from answering this urgent question by kissing her again so very roughly that she had an unaccountable sensation of being swept quite away from all safe past moorings on a flood of new and entirely uncharted emotions.

She came out of the darkness of his embrace to the sound of an insistent tapping upon the door.

"Kit!" she gasped, endeavouring to regain her lost poise. "Let me go! There is someone at the door!"

"Let there be," said his lordship, ruthlessly kissing her once more. "Will you marry me, Lydia?"

"Yes—oh, yes! But *do* let me go now! We *must* open the door or I shan't have a shred of reputation left!"

They were spared the trouble of doing so, however, by the door's being opened from the outside at that moment; Mrs. Yarden's round, anxious face peered into the aperture.

"Oh, madam—that is, miss—" she began, and then, catching sight of the Viscount, who still, most improperly, had his arm around Lydia's waist, exclaimed in scandalised astonishment, "Lawks a-mussy! Lunnon folks! And not married to this one, neither, I'll be bound!"

Lydia, casting a reproving look, somewhat marred by the fact that her eyes were brimful of laughter, at Northover, disengaged herself from his embrace and said soothingly, "No, but I am going to be, Mrs. Yarden. You may be the first to wish me happy, if you please!"

"Well, I'm sure I do, madam—*miss!*" said Mrs. Yarden, looking dubiously at the Viscount, whose attack upon Mr. Pentony, with its concomitant destructive effects upon the furnishings of her best parlour, apparently caused her to feel considerable doubt as to the future felicity of any young lady so unwise as to set up housekeeping with him. "Only it *does* seem odd, with *three* gentlemen to choose from, that—"

"That she's taken the worst bargain?" Northover finished it for her irrepressibly, as she broke off in some confusion at the path down which her unwary tongue was leading her. "Never mind; I have a fondness for her, you see, and if she conducts herself properly from this time out, I shall probably not feel obliged to break up the furniture more than once in a quarter. And now," he added, receiving with full appreciation the speaking look of reproof cast at him by his promised bride, "if you will be good enough to tell us why you have interrupted us—"

"Yes—to be sure, sir!" Mrs. Yarden collected her flustered thoughts. "It's about the post-chaise you said when you came in you was wishful to have at once—and ready at the door it is this minute—"

"Thank you!" said Northover. "We shall be down directly."

His tone did not encourage her to linger, and she was therefore obliged to curtsey herself out, with one last reluctant glance of curiosity at the very improper couple she was leaving behind her. Lydia turned laughing, self-conscious eyes upon Northover.

"Kit, we are abominable!" she said. "The poor woman! What on earth must she think of us?"

"On the whole," the Viscount said, considering, "I believe she thinks you a foolhardy young woman to undertake to share bed and board with a brute like me. But, on the other hand, I have Harlbury on *my* side, for he *did* say, you will recall, when he offered for you, that he was afraid he would be driven to murder if he were obliged to live with you."

Miss Leyland favoured him with a glance of great severity. "Yes, I *saw* the look in your eye when he said that," she accused him. "And you *are* a brute to laugh at me, for, after all, I only did what was necessary to bring Bayard back. How was I to know that Harlbury would be so nonsensical as to feel himself obliged to offer for me?"

"How indeed?" agreed Northover, his eyes alight. "It is only what any young woman of sense would have known. How happy I am that I have never been tempted to marry a young woman of sense!"

"But I *am*—" Lydia began indignantly; but her words were stopped very rudely indeed by the Viscount, who pulled her into his arms and kissed her with such ardour that it seemed, after a few moments, quite redundant to continue the argument.

"And now," he said presently, releasing her at last and gazing down at her with the regretful look of a man resolutely deciding to place duty above inclination, "we must really be off to Great Hayland, if my plan to lend respectability to this day's work is to succeed. I have even hired a post-chaise for you, you see, so that you will not be obliged to ride in an open carriage at this hour." He picked up the Italian straw confection that had begun the day so charmingly, but was now in a somewhat bedraggled condition, owing to the rough treatment it had sustained, and looked at it unfavourably. "Is this your bonnet? I cannot feel that Cupitt will approve of my bringing home a bride with such a dispirited creation upon her head," he was going on—but he was interrupted at that moment by a horrified exclamation from Lydia.

"Cupitt!" she ejaculated. "Good heavens, Kit, you *cannot* be bringing this houseful of people down on him and Mrs. Cupitt without warning! And not only *us*—I mean Bayard and Grandmama and me—but Lord and Lady Gilmour, as well! He will go mad, and I shall not blame him in the least!"

"Nor I," said Northover, looking at his love with his eyes again alight. "But it may be as well, after all, for him to accustom himself to such things if he intends to remain in my employ, for I have a decided presentiment that, once you are Lady Northover, he will be under the necessity of steeling himself to sustain even more disconcerting events. I know *I* am already endeavouring to do so myself."

"Wretch!" said Miss Leyland, blushing.

It was an appellation, however, which the Viscount scarcely seemed to resent, for his only response to it was to kiss her once more.